big NATE
NO WORRIES!

by LINCOLN PEIRCE

A special collection featuring comics from
Big Nate: Revenge of the Cream Puffs and
Big Nate: What's a Little Noogie Between Friends?

Andrews McMeel
PUBLISHING®

Big Nate is distributed internationally by Andrews McMeel Syndication.

Big Nate: No Worries! copyright © 2023 by United Feature Syndicate, Inc. This 2023 edition is a compilation of two previously published books: *Big Nate: Revenge of the Cream Puffs* © 2016 and *Big Nate: What's a Little Noogie Between Friends* © 2017. All rights reserved. Printed in China. No part of this book may be used or reproduced in any manner whatsoever without written permission except in the case of reprints in the context of reviews.

Andrews McMeel Publishing
a division of Andrews McMeel Universal
1130 Walnut Street, Kansas City, Missouri 64106

www.andrewsmcmeel.com

23 24 25 26 27 SDB 10 9 8 7 6 5 4 3 2 1

ISBN: 978-1-5248-8091-0

Made by:
RR Donnelley (Guangdong) Printing Solutions Company Ltd.
Address and location of manufacturer:
No. 2, Minzhu Road, Daning, Humen Town,
Dongguan City, Guangdong Province, China 523930
1st Printing – 2/27/2023

ATTENTION: SCHOOLS AND BUSINESSES
Andrews McMeel books are available at quantity discounts with bulk purchase for educational, business, or sales promotional use. For information, please e-mail the Andrews McMeel Publishing Special Sales Department:
sales@amuniversal.com.

big

NATE

REVENGE OF THE CREAM PUFFS

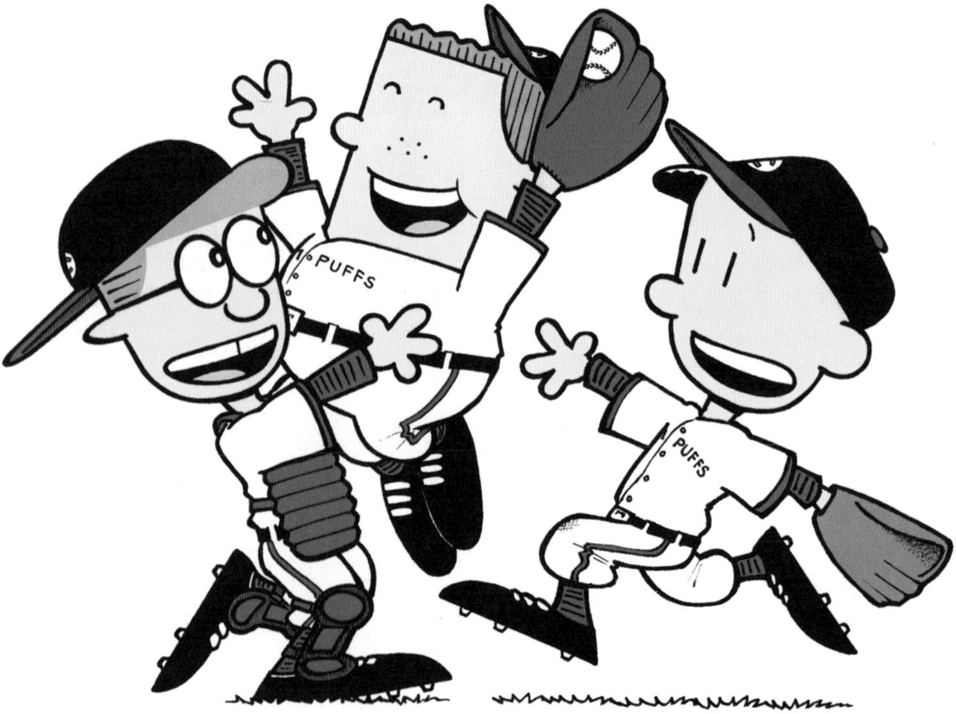
PUFFS
PUFFS

YOU HAVE FORTY MINUTES. AAAAAND... BEGIN.

OPTIMISM

FLIP!

SURPRISE

CONFUSION

DOUBT

DREAD

PANIC

FIVE MINUTES, PEOPLE.

TERROR

DESPERATION

WRITE WRITE

HAND 'EM IN.

LUNCH

I THINK I ACED IT!

SAME HERE!

5

WHERE IS EVERY-BODY?
YOU'RE THE ONLY ONE.
APPARENTLY THE REST OF THE SCHOOL HAS DECIDED NOT TO WASTE THE AFTERNOON IN DETENTION.
I'M NOT WASTING THE AFTERNOON, MRS. CZERWICKI! I'M SPENDING IT WITH YOU!
FLATTERER.
HOW'S ABOUT A GAME OF TABLE FOOTBALL?
Peirce

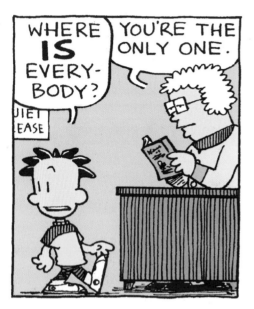

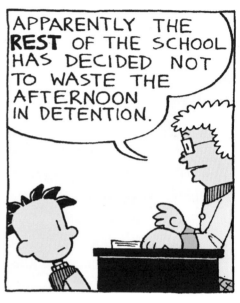

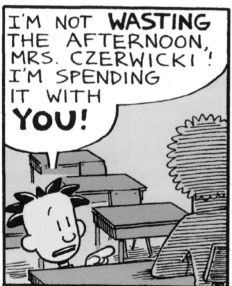

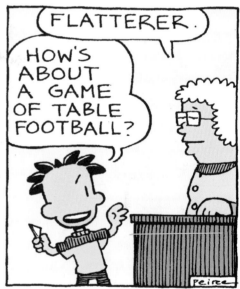

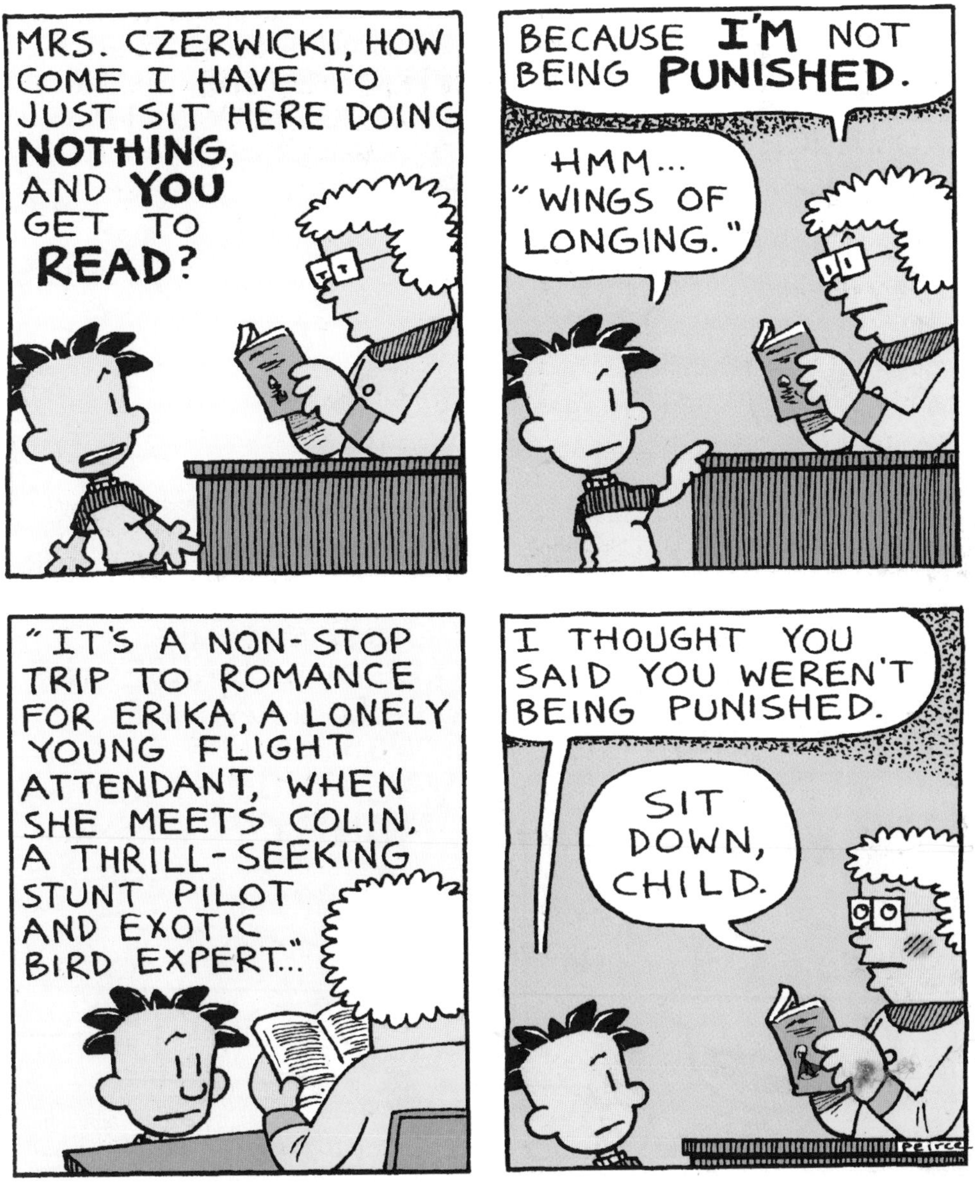
MRS. CZERWICKI, HOW COME I HAVE TO JUST SIT HERE DOING NOTHING, AND YOU GET TO READ?
BECAUSE I'M NOT BEING PUNISHED.
HMM... "WINGS OF LONGING."
"IT'S A NON-STOP TRIP TO ROMANCE FOR ERIKA, A LONELY YOUNG FLIGHT ATTENDANT, WHEN SHE MEETS COLIN, A THRILL-SEEKING STUNT PILOT AND EXOTIC BIRD EXPERT..."
I THOUGHT YOU SAID YOU WEREN'T BEING PUNISHED.
SIT DOWN, CHILD.
PEIRCE

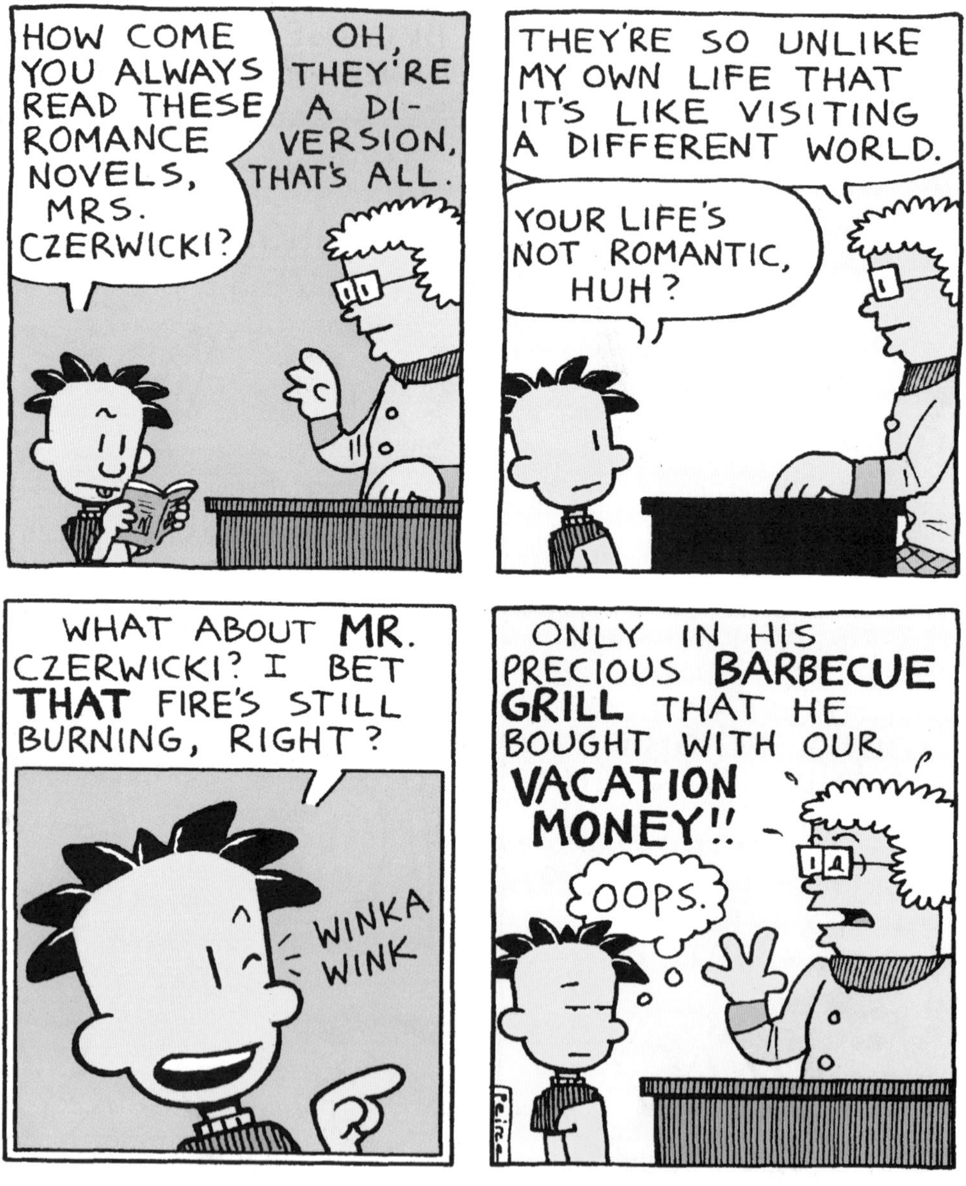
HOW COME YOU ALWAYS READ THESE ROMANCE NOVELS, MRS. CZERWICKI?
OH, THEY'RE A DIVERSION, THAT'S ALL.
THEY'RE SO UNLIKE MY OWN LIFE THAT IT'S LIKE VISITING A DIFFERENT WORLD.
YOUR LIFE'S NOT ROMANTIC, HUH?
WHAT ABOUT **MR.** CZERWICKI? I BET **THAT** FIRE'S STILL BURNING, RIGHT?
WINKA WINK
ONLY IN HIS PRECIOUS **BARBECUE GRILL** THAT HE BOUGHT WITH OUR **VACATION MONEY!!**
OOPS.
Peirce

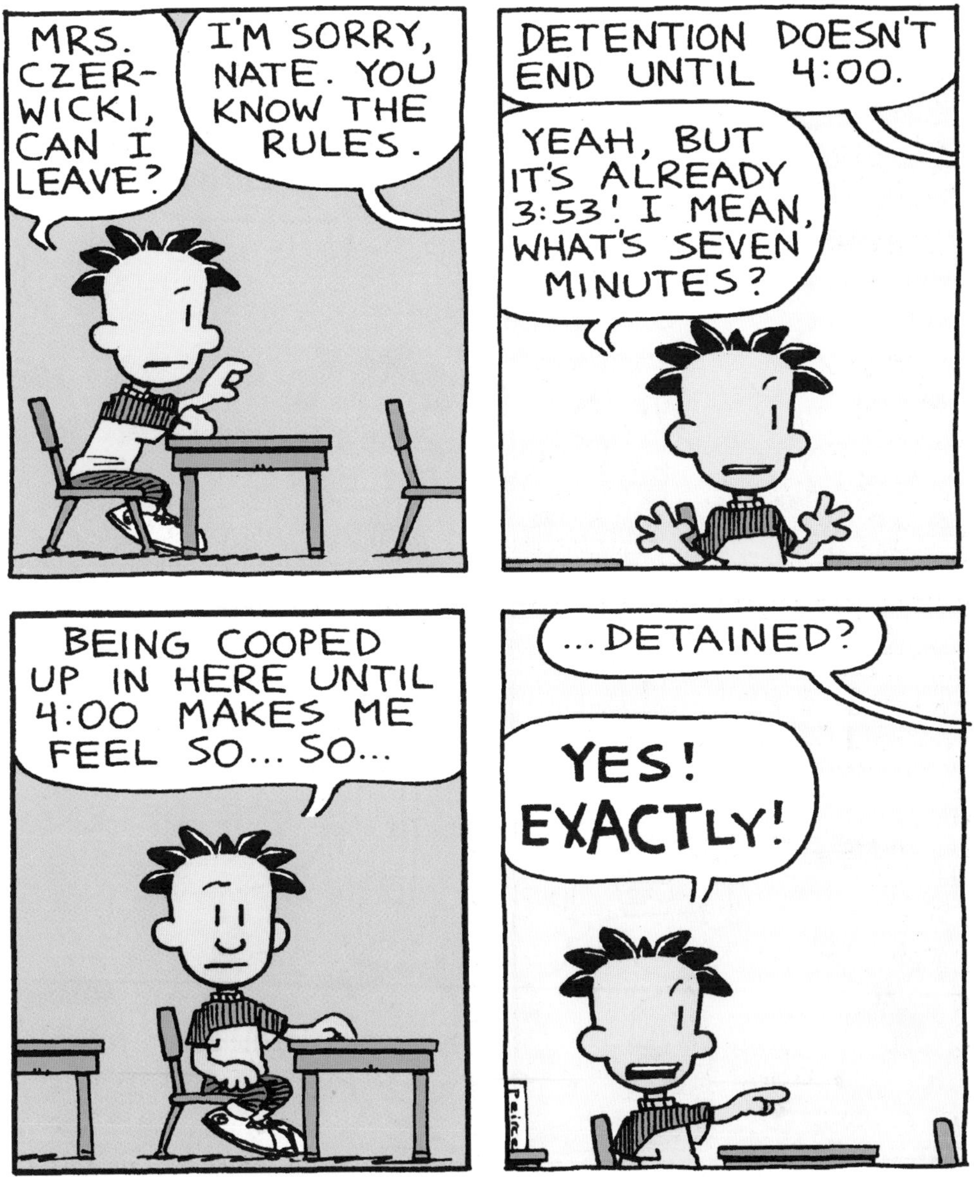
MRS. CZERWICKI, CAN I LEAVE?
I'M SORRY, NATE. YOU KNOW THE RULES.
DETENTION DOESN'T END UNTIL 4:00.
YEAH, BUT IT'S ALREADY 3:53! I MEAN, WHAT'S SEVEN MINUTES?
BEING COOPED UP IN HERE UNTIL 4:00 MAKES ME FEEL SO... SO...
...DETAINED?
YES! EXACTLY!

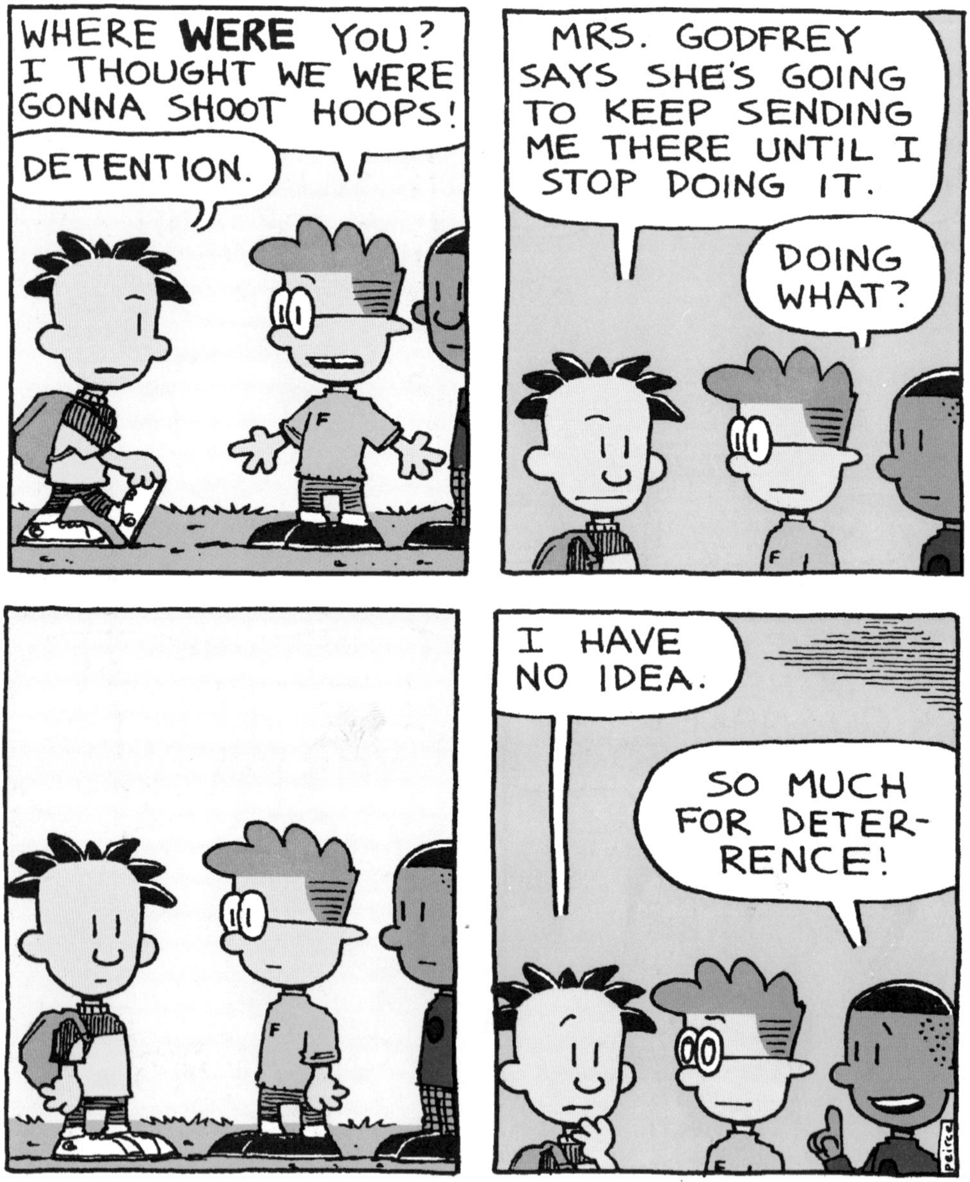
WHERE **WERE** YOU? I THOUGHT WE WERE GONNA SHOOT HOOPS!
DETENTION.
MRS. GODFREY SAYS SHE'S GOING TO KEEP SENDING ME THERE UNTIL I STOP DOING IT.
DOING WHAT?
I HAVE NO IDEA.
SO MUCH FOR DETER-RENCE!
peirce

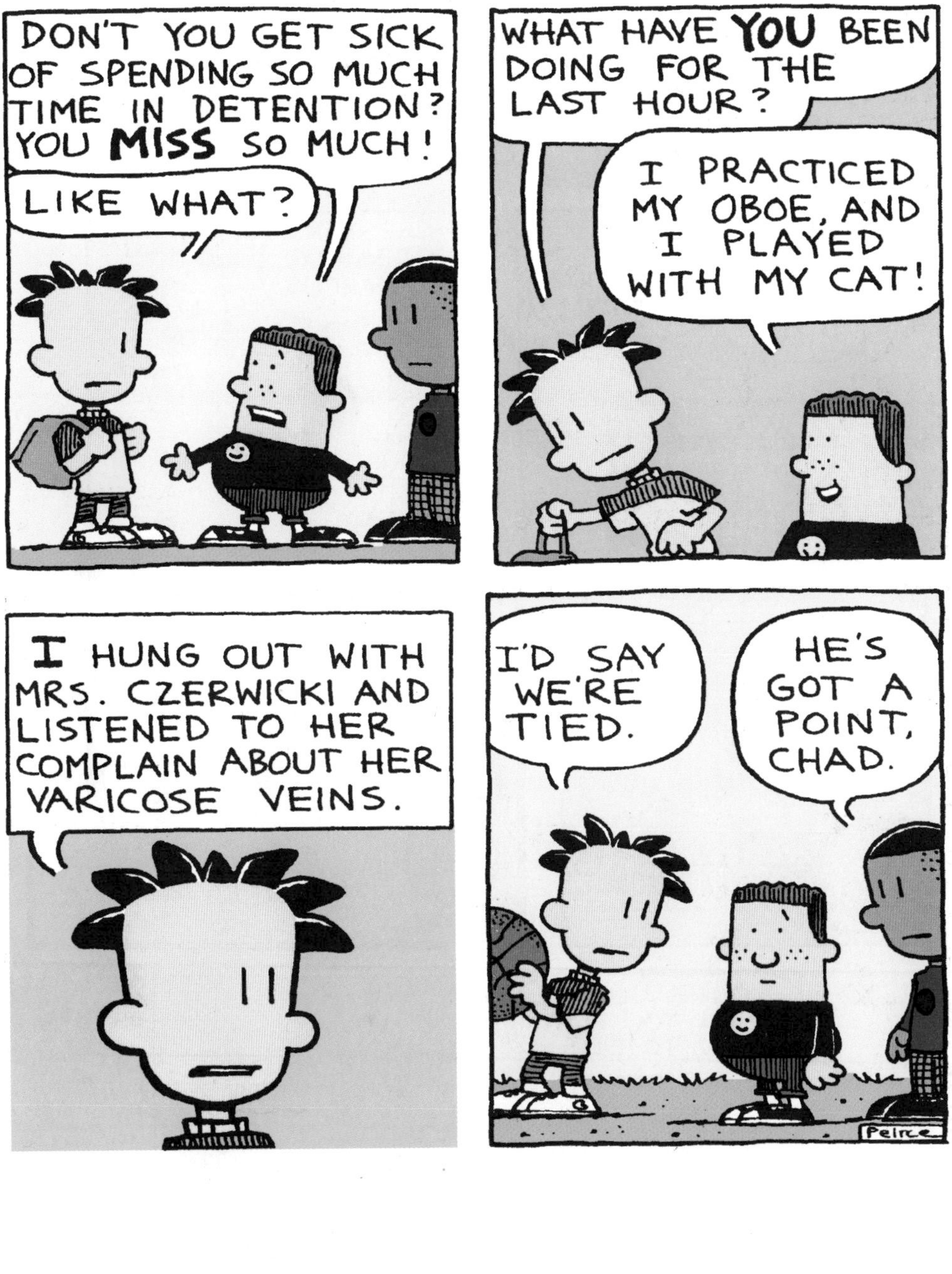
DON'T YOU GET SICK OF SPENDING SO MUCH TIME IN DETENTION? YOU MISS SO MUCH!
LIKE WHAT?
WHAT HAVE YOU BEEN DOING FOR THE LAST HOUR?
I PRACTICED MY OBOE, AND I PLAYED WITH MY CAT!
I HUNG OUT WITH MRS. CZERWICKI AND LISTENED TO HER COMPLAIN ABOUT HER VARICOSE VEINS.
I'D SAY WE'RE TIED.
HE'S GOT A POINT, CHAD.
Peirce

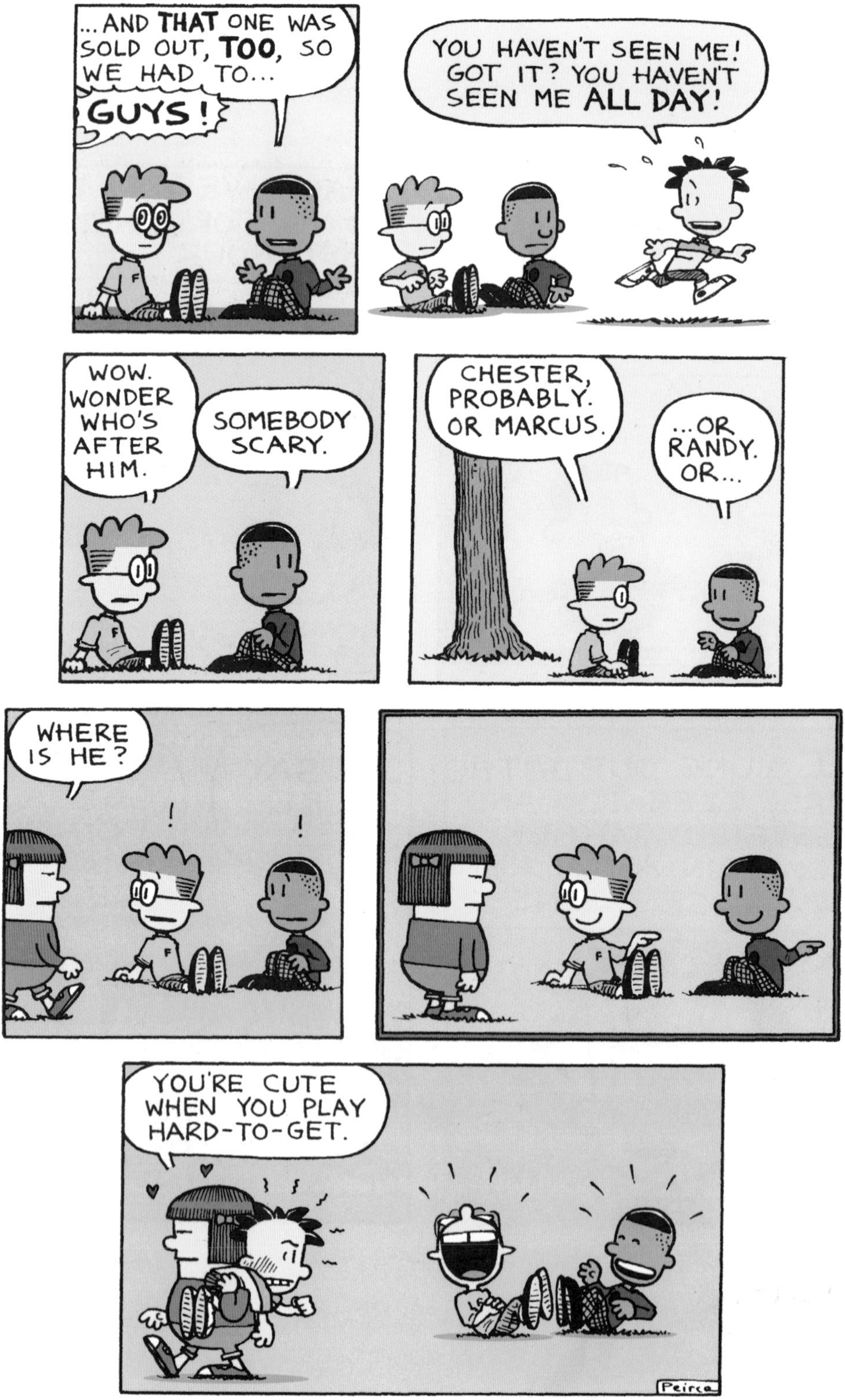
...AND THAT ONE WAS SOLD OUT, TOO, SO WE HAD TO...
GUYS!
YOU HAVEN'T SEEN ME! GOT IT? YOU HAVEN'T SEEN ME ALL DAY!
WOW. WONDER WHO'S AFTER HIM.
SOMEBODY SCARY.
CHESTER, PROBABLY. OR MARCUS.
...OR RANDY. OR...
WHERE IS HE?
!
!
YOU'RE CUTE WHEN YOU PLAY HARD-TO-GET.
Peirce

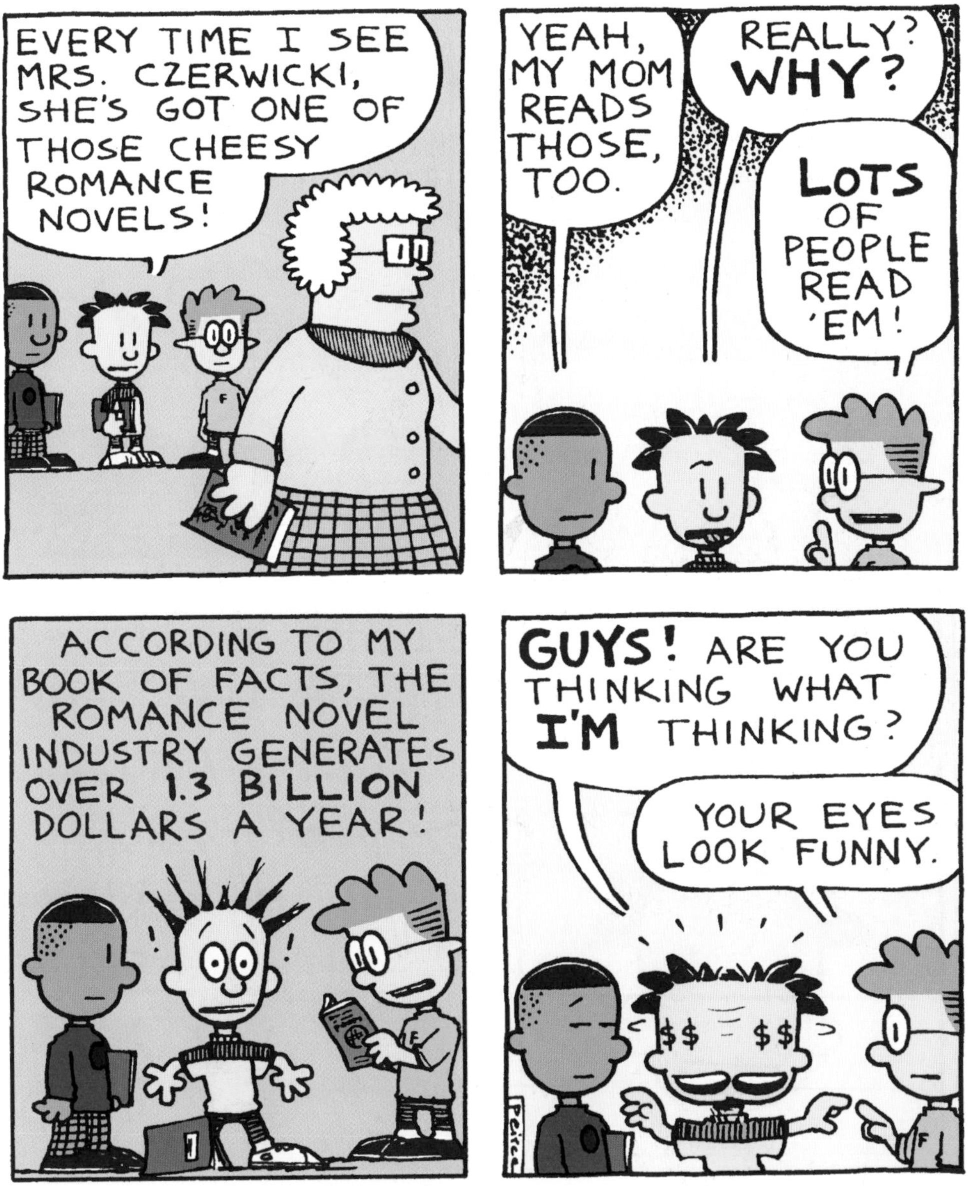
EVERY TIME I SEE MRS. CZERWICKI, SHE'S GOT ONE OF THOSE CHEESY ROMANCE NOVELS!
YEAH, MY MOM READS THOSE, TOO.
REALLY? WHY?
LOTS OF PEOPLE READ 'EM!
ACCORDING TO MY BOOK OF FACTS, THE ROMANCE NOVEL INDUSTRY GENERATES OVER 1.3 BILLION DOLLARS A YEAR!
GUYS! ARE YOU THINKING WHAT I'M THINKING?
YOUR EYES LOOK FUNNY.
Peirce

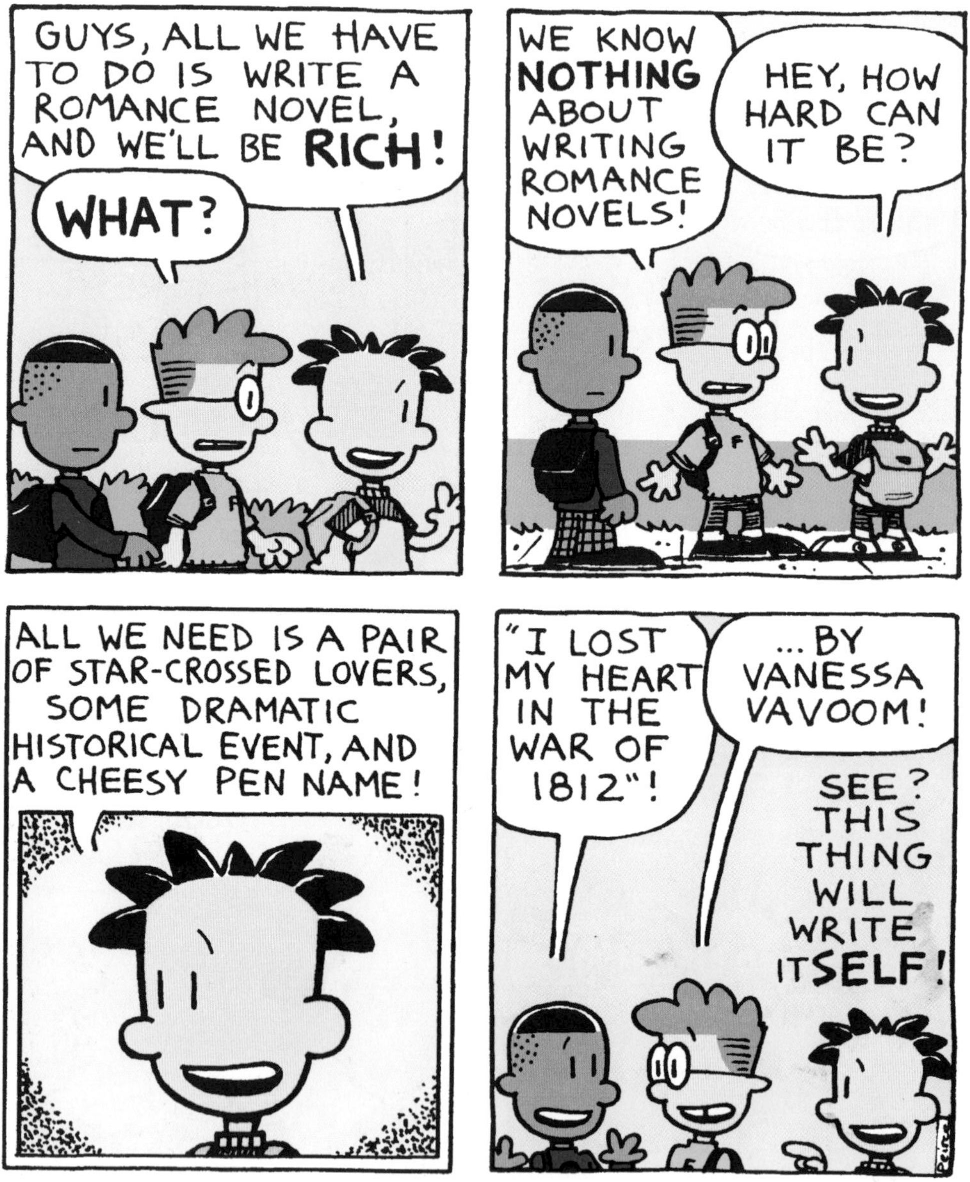
GUYS, ALL WE HAVE TO DO IS WRITE A ROMANCE NOVEL, AND WE'LL BE RICH!
WHAT?
WE KNOW NOTHING ABOUT WRITING ROMANCE NOVELS!
HEY, HOW HARD CAN IT BE?
ALL WE NEED IS A PAIR OF STAR-CROSSED LOVERS, SOME DRAMATIC HISTORICAL EVENT, AND A CHEESY PEN NAME!
"I LOST MY HEART IN THE WAR OF 1812"!
...BY VANESSA VAVOOM!
SEE? THIS THING WILL WRITE ITSELF!

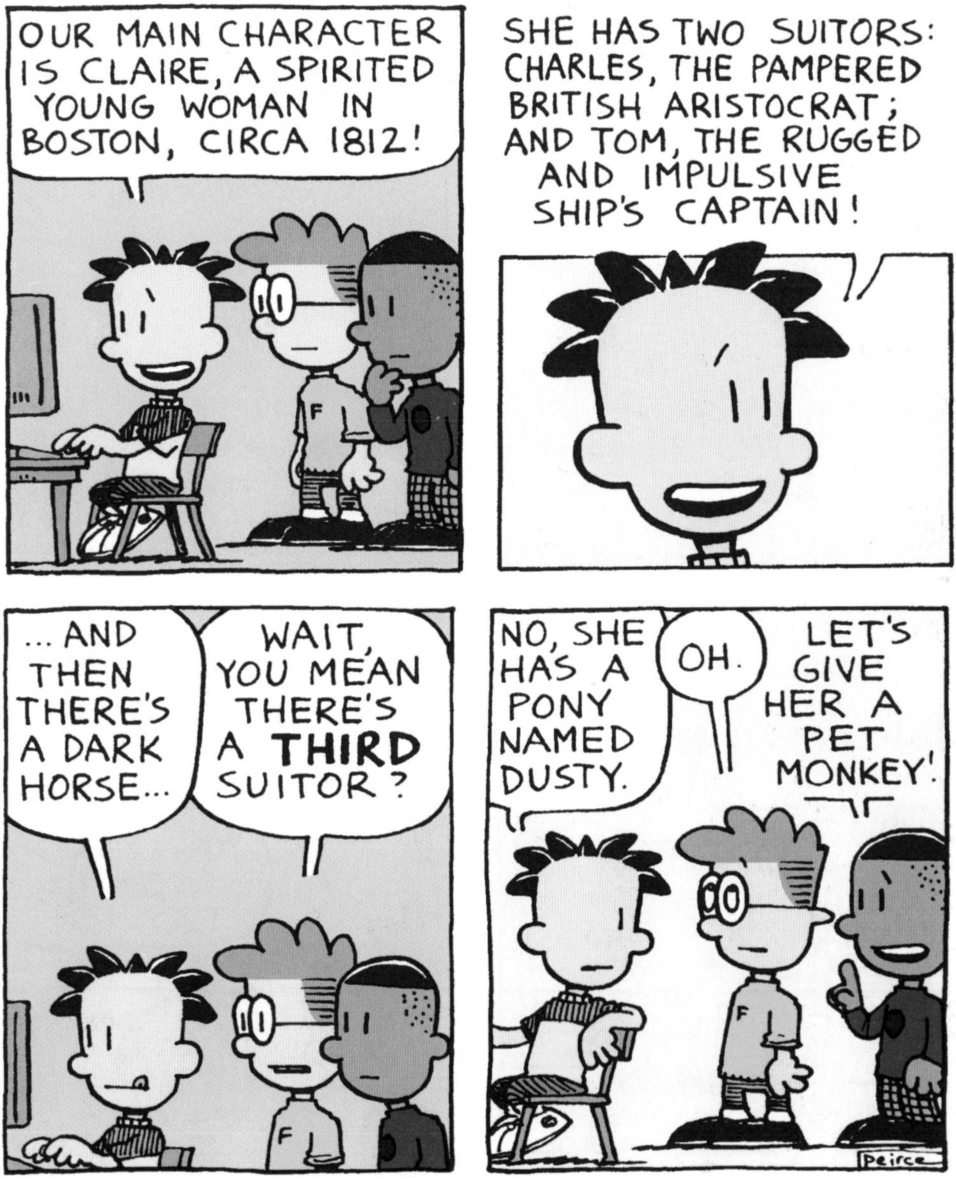
OUR MAIN CHARACTER IS CLAIRE, A SPIRITED YOUNG WOMAN IN BOSTON, CIRCA 1812!
SHE HAS TWO SUITORS: CHARLES, THE PAMPERED BRITISH ARISTOCRAT; AND TOM, THE RUGGED AND IMPULSIVE SHIP'S CAPTAIN!
... AND THEN THERE'S A DARK HORSE...
WAIT, YOU MEAN THERE'S A **THIRD** SUITOR?
NO, SHE HAS A PONY NAMED DUSTY.
OH.
LET'S GIVE HER A PET MONKEY!
Peirce

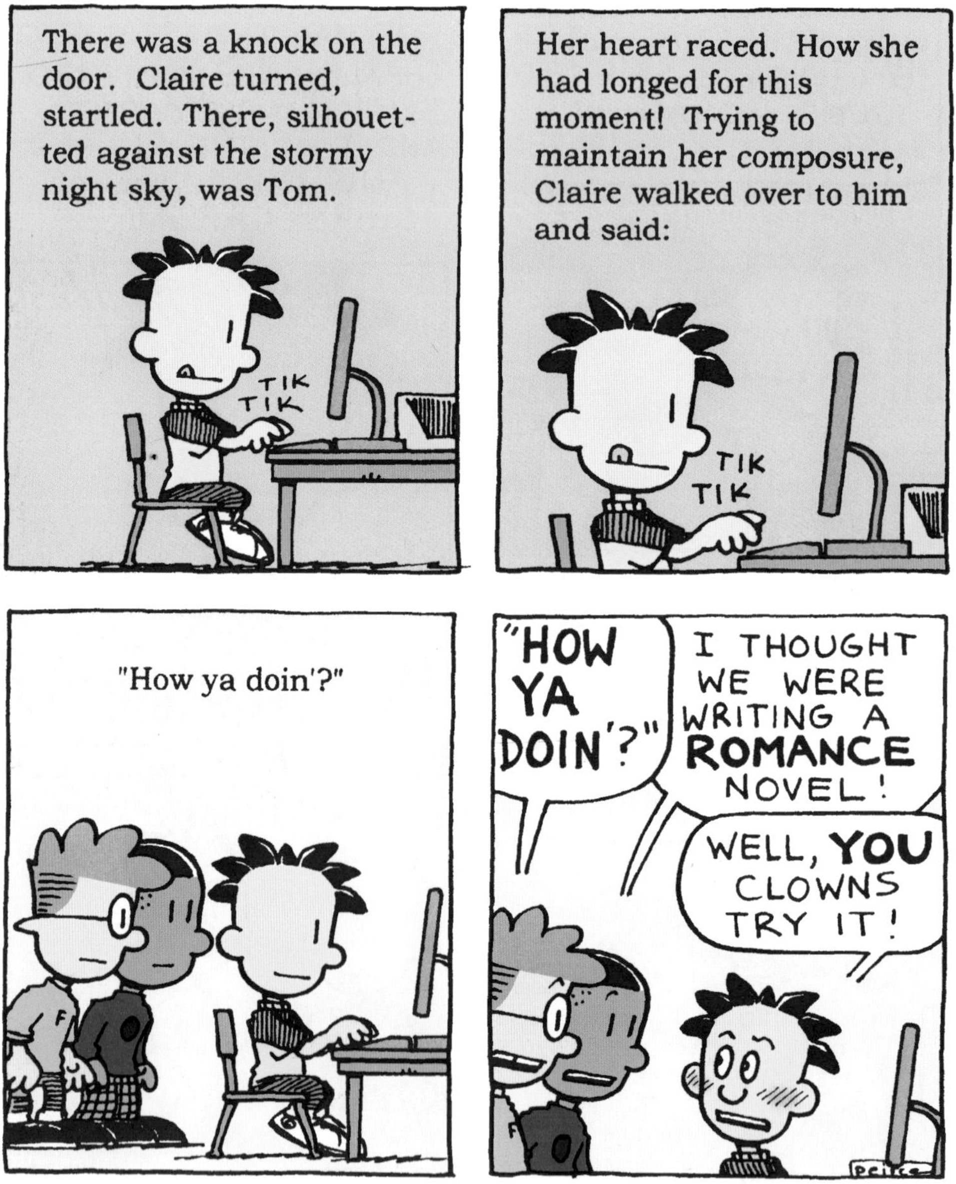
There was a knock on the door. Claire turned, startled. There, silhouetted against the stormy night sky, was Tom.
TIK TIK
Her heart raced. How she had longed for this moment! Trying to maintain her composure, Claire walked over to him and said:
TIK TIK
"How ya doin'?"
"HOW YA DOIN'?"
I THOUGHT WE WERE WRITING A **ROMANCE** NOVEL!
WELL, **YOU** CLOWNS TRY IT!

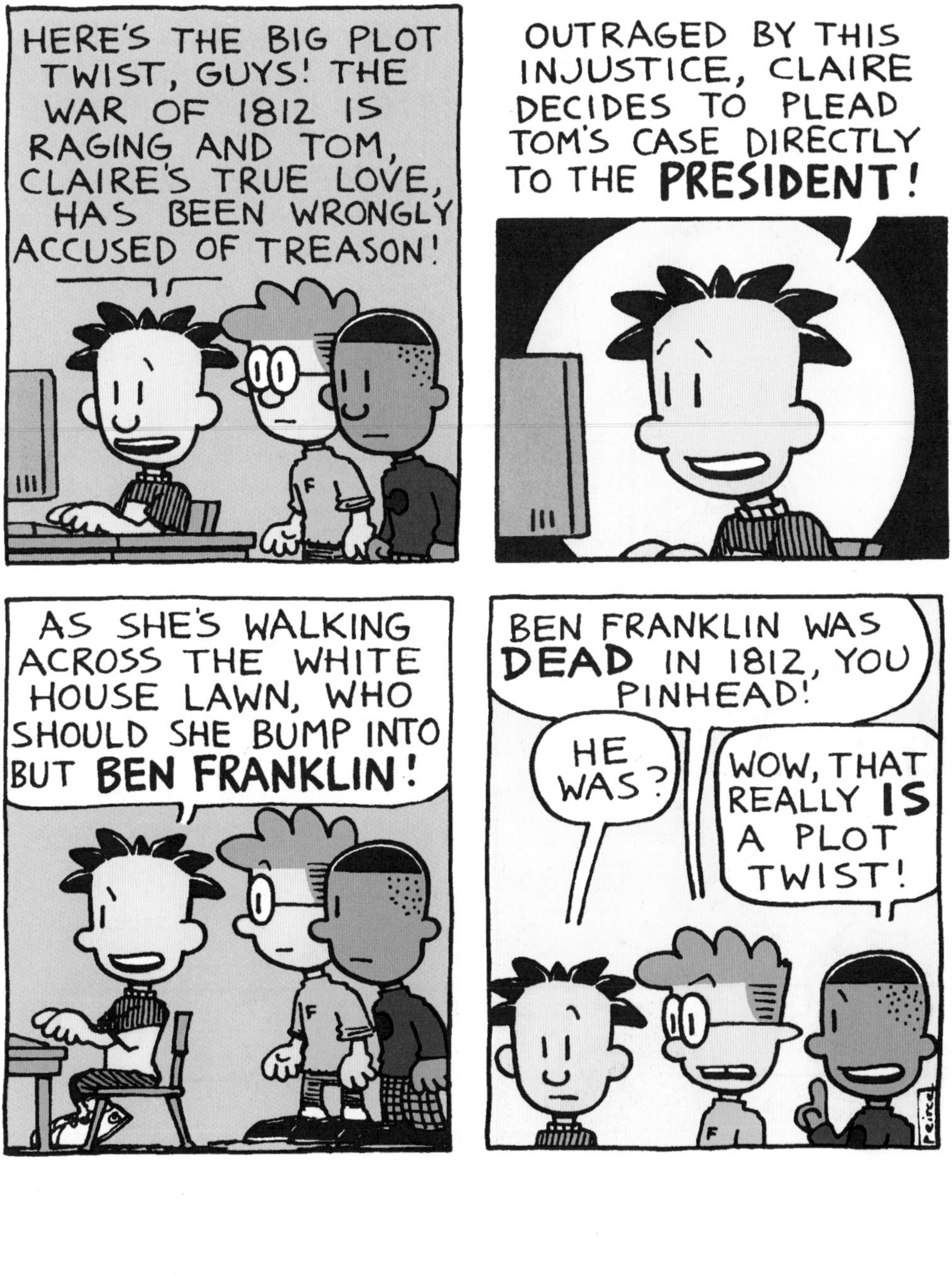
HERE'S THE BIG PLOT TWIST, GUYS! THE WAR OF 1812 IS RAGING AND TOM, CLAIRE'S TRUE LOVE, HAS BEEN WRONGLY ACCUSED OF TREASON!
OUTRAGED BY THIS INJUSTICE, CLAIRE DECIDES TO PLEAD TOM'S CASE DIRECTLY TO THE PRESIDENT!
AS SHE'S WALKING ACROSS THE WHITE HOUSE LAWN, WHO SHOULD SHE BUMP INTO BUT BEN FRANKLIN!
BEN FRANKLIN WAS DEAD IN 1812, YOU PINHEAD!
HE WAS?
WOW, THAT REALLY IS A PLOT TWIST!
Peirce

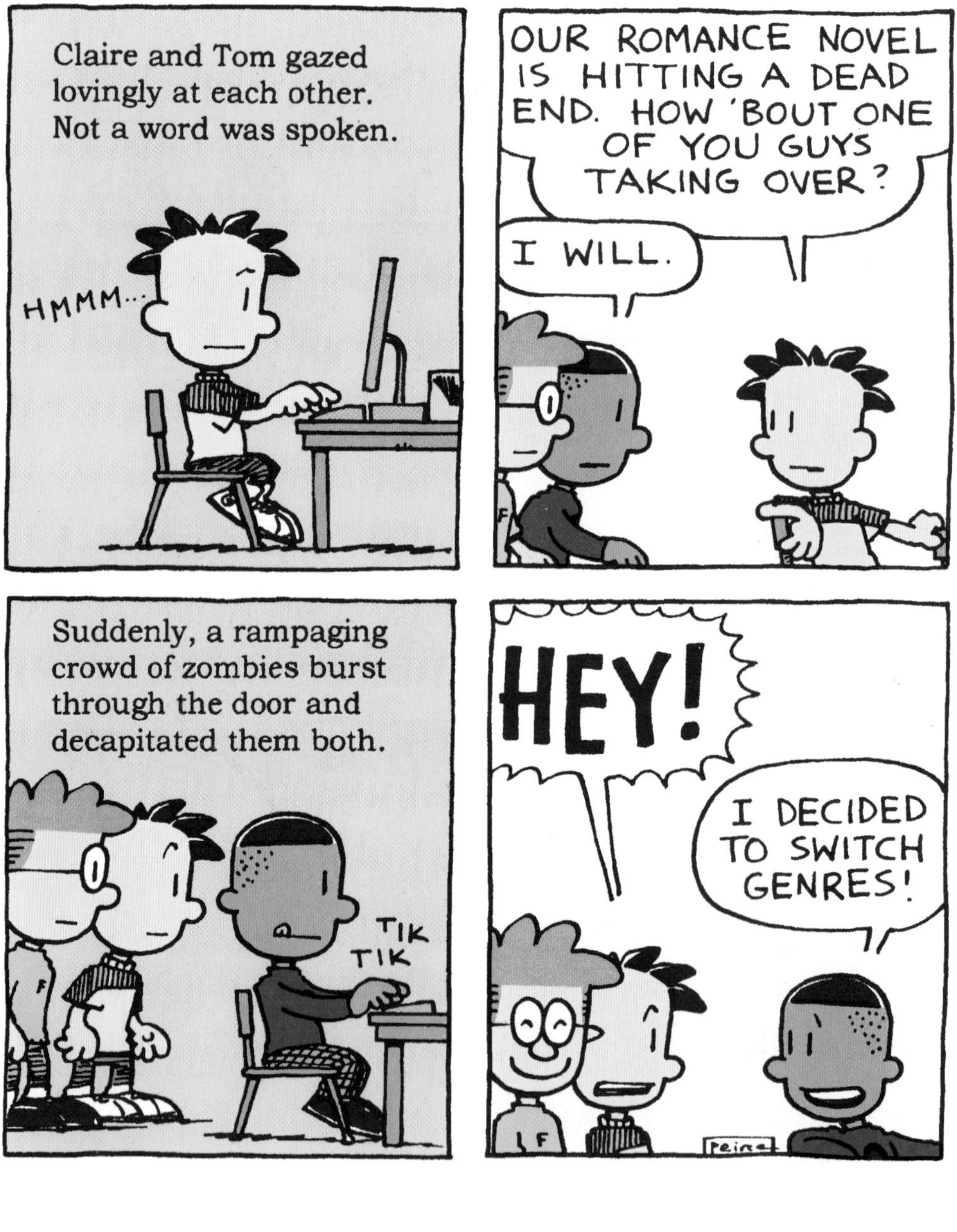
Claire and Tom gazed lovingly at each other. Not a word was spoken.
HMMM...
OUR ROMANCE NOVEL IS HITTING A DEAD END. HOW 'BOUT ONE OF YOU GUYS TAKING OVER?
I WILL.
Suddenly, a rampaging crowd of zombies burst through the door and decapitated them both.
TIK TIK
HEY!
I DECIDED TO SWITCH GENRES!

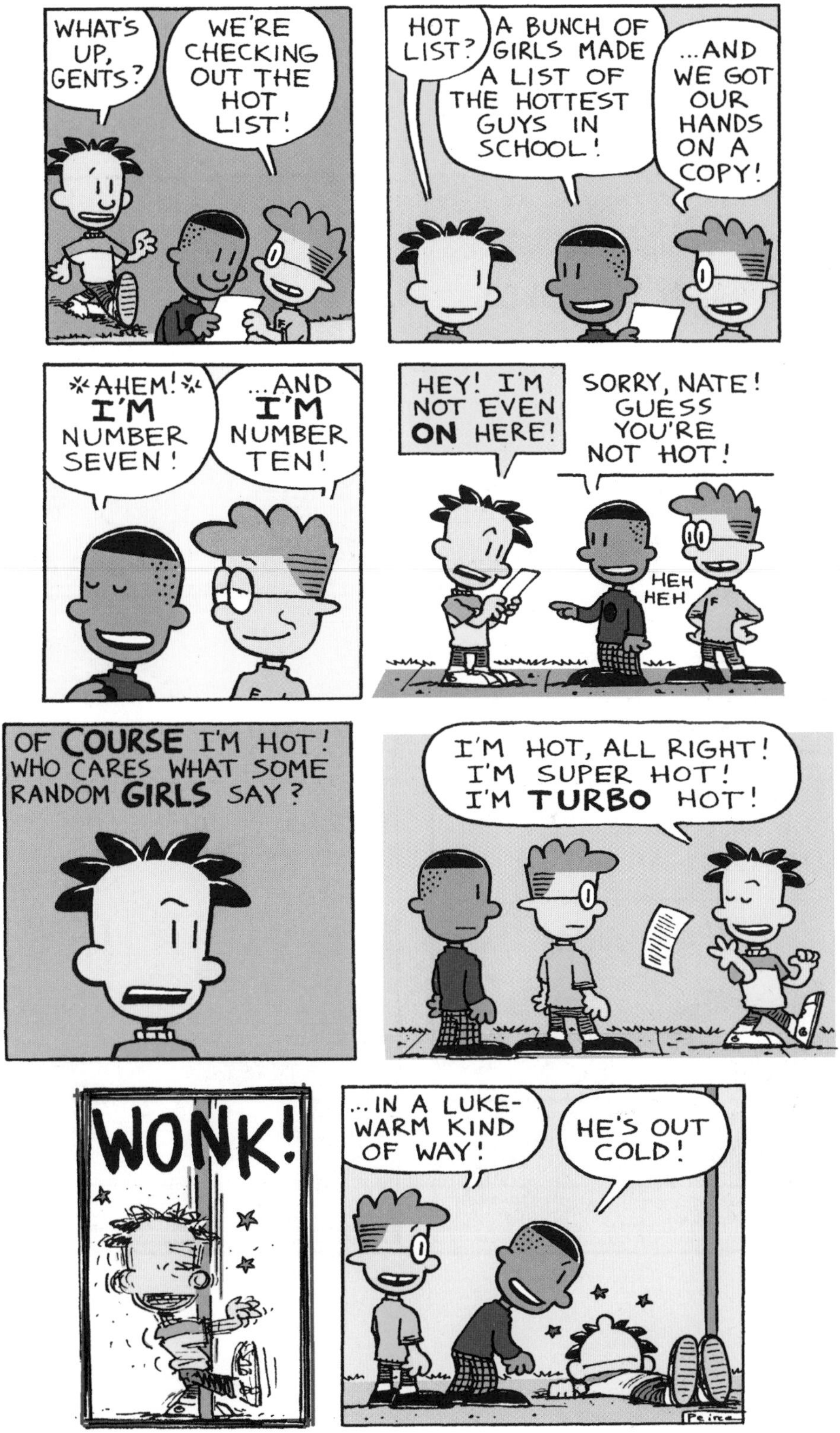

WHAT'S UP, GENTS?
WE'RE CHECKING OUT THE HOT LIST!
HOT LIST?
A BUNCH OF GIRLS MADE A LIST OF THE HOTTEST GUYS IN SCHOOL!
...AND WE GOT OUR HANDS ON A COPY!
AHEM! I'M NUMBER SEVEN!
...AND I'M NUMBER TEN!
HEY! I'M NOT EVEN ON HERE!
SORRY, NATE! GUESS YOU'RE NOT HOT!
HEH HEH
OF COURSE I'M HOT! WHO CARES WHAT SOME RANDOM GIRLS SAY?
I'M HOT, ALL RIGHT! I'M SUPER HOT! I'M TURBO HOT!
WONK!
...IN A LUKE-WARM KIND OF WAY!
HE'S OUT COLD!
Peirce

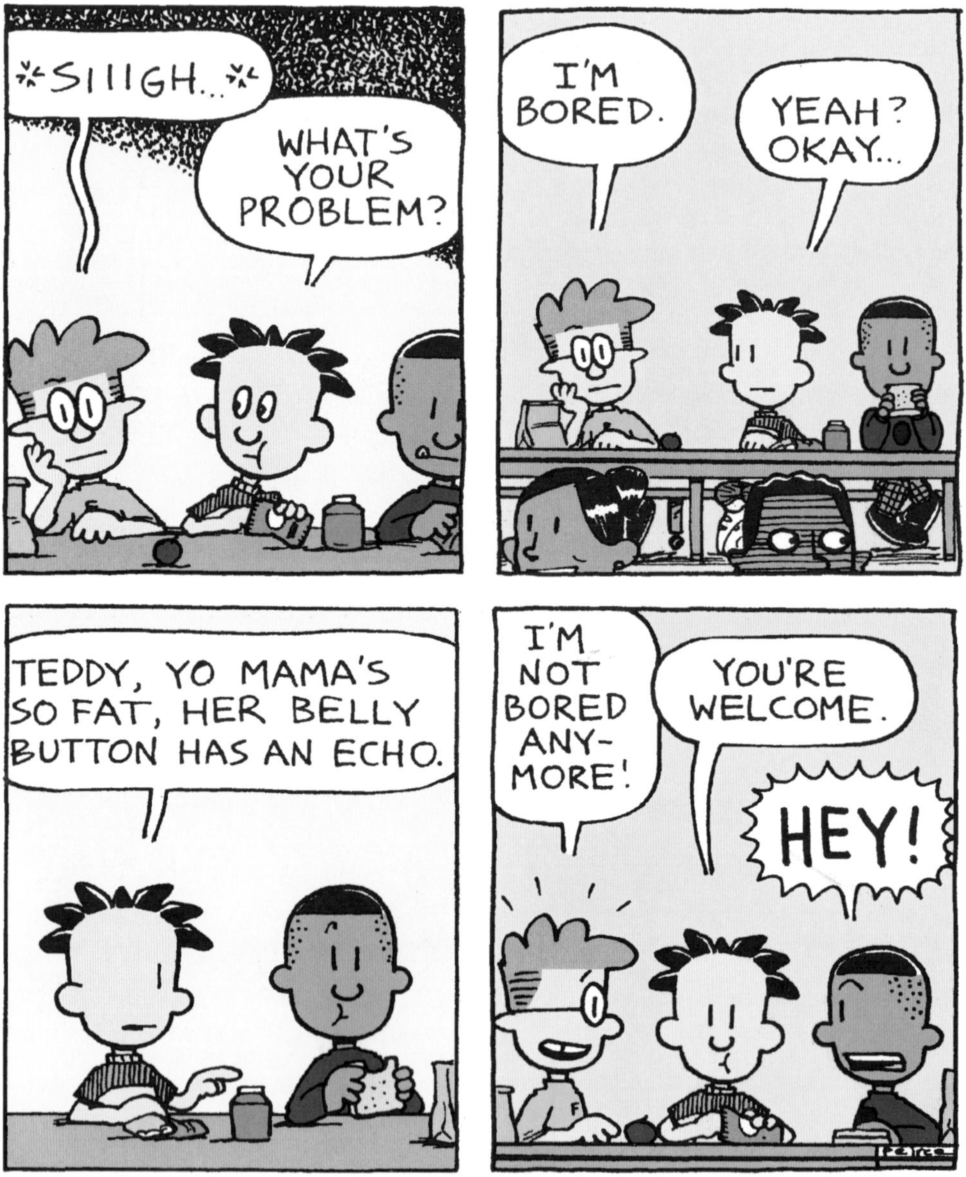
SIIIGH...
WHAT'S YOUR PROBLEM?
I'M BORED.
YEAH? OKAY...
TEDDY, YO MAMA'S SO FAT, HER BELLY BUTTON HAS AN ECHO.
I'M NOT BORED ANY-MORE!
YOU'RE WELCOME.
HEY!

WHAT'S THE BIG **IDEA**, NATE? HOW COME YOU YO MAMA'D ME FOR NO REASON?
BECAUSE FRANCIS SAID HE WAS BORED.
WELL, THEN, HIT **HIM** WITH A YO MAMA, NOT **ME**!
OH, COME ON, TEDDY...
FRANCIS WOULDN'T LAST **FIVE SECONDS** IN A YO MAMA SMACKDOWN! SHOW HIM, FRANCIS.
HUH? OH!...UM... YO MAMA'S SO UGLY, SHE... SHE... UH...
WELL, SHE'S JUST NOT VERY ATTRACT-IVE.
SEE?
YEAH. LET'S RUMBLE.

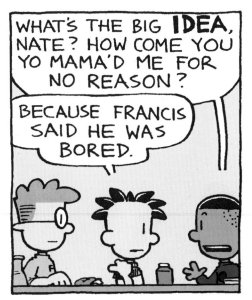

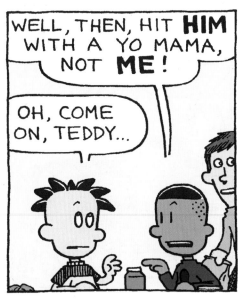

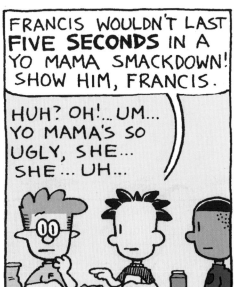

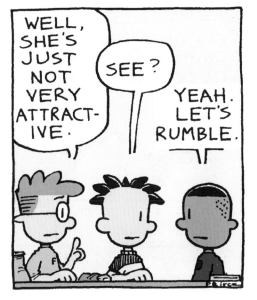

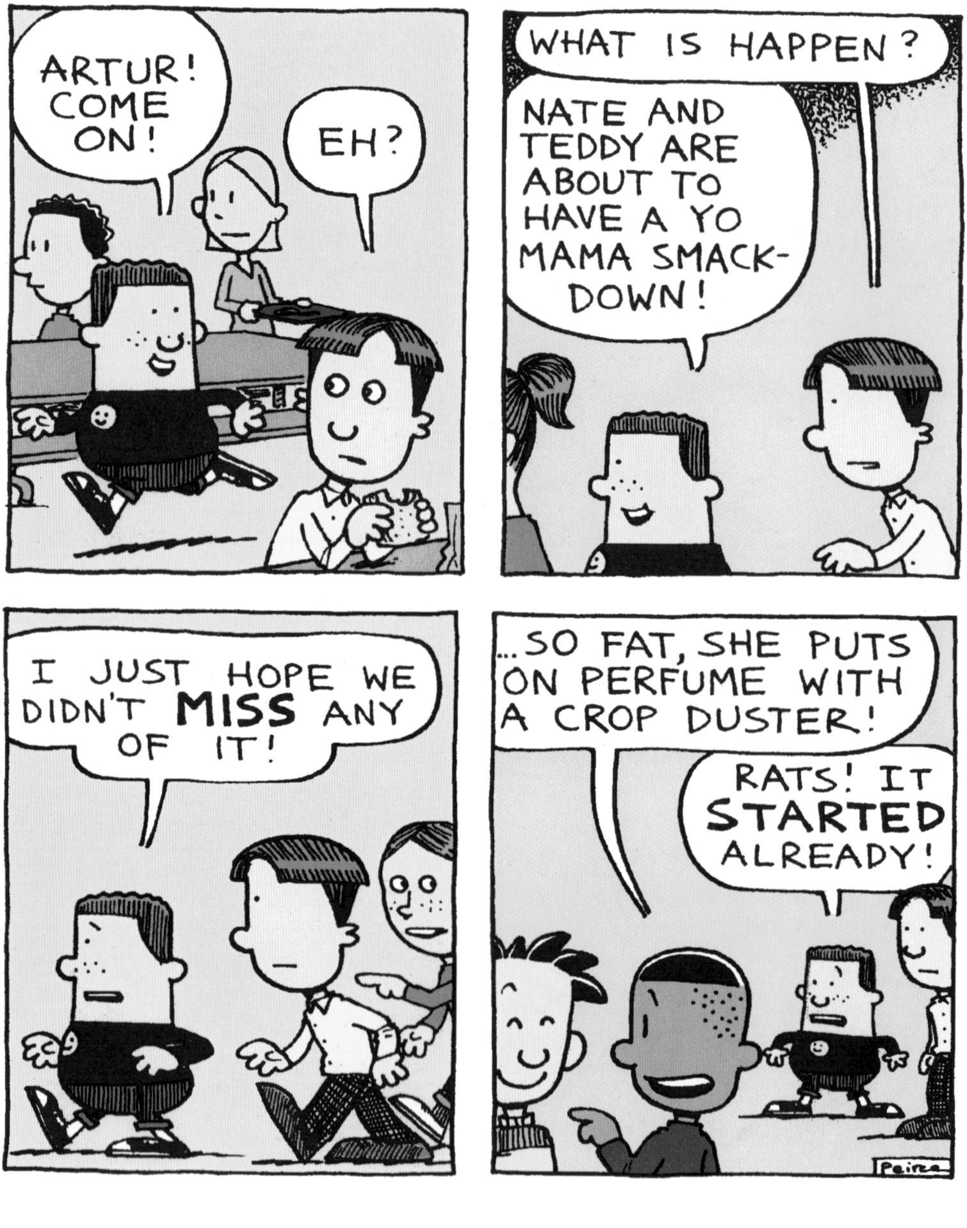
ARTUR! COME ON!
EH?
WHAT IS HAPPEN?
NATE AND TEDDY ARE ABOUT TO HAVE A YO MAMA SMACK-DOWN!
I JUST HOPE WE DIDN'T MISS ANY OF IT!
...SO FAT, SHE PUTS ON PERFUME WITH A CROP DUSTER!
RATS! IT STARTED ALREADY!
Peirce

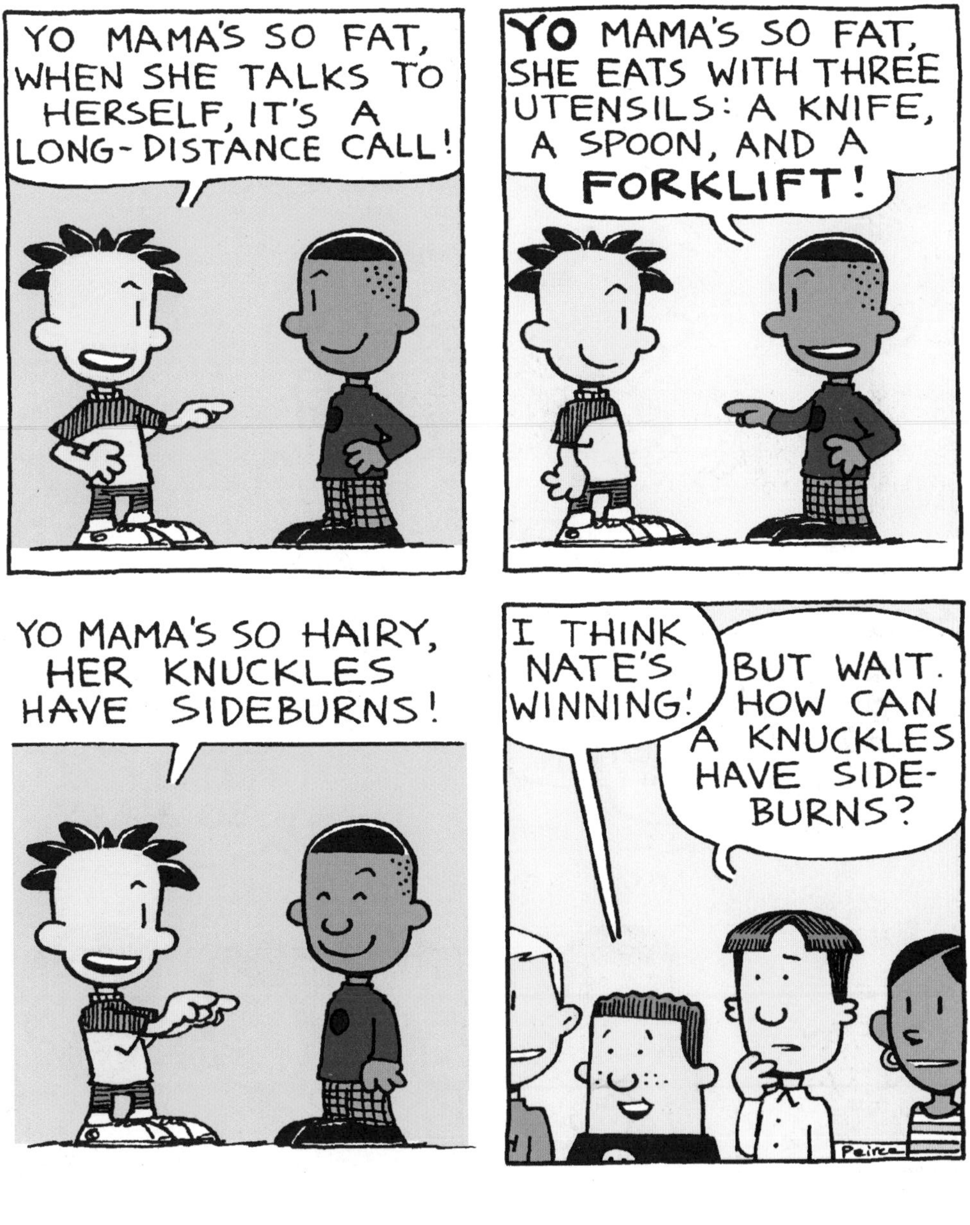
YO MAMA'S SO FAT, WHEN SHE TALKS TO HERSELF, IT'S A LONG-DISTANCE CALL!
YO MAMA'S SO FAT, SHE EATS WITH THREE UTENSILS: A KNIFE, A SPOON, AND A FORKLIFT!
YO MAMA'S SO HAIRY, HER KNUCKLES HAVE SIDEBURNS!
I THINK NATE'S WINNING!
BUT WAIT. HOW CAN A KNUCKLES HAVE SIDEBURNS?
Peirce

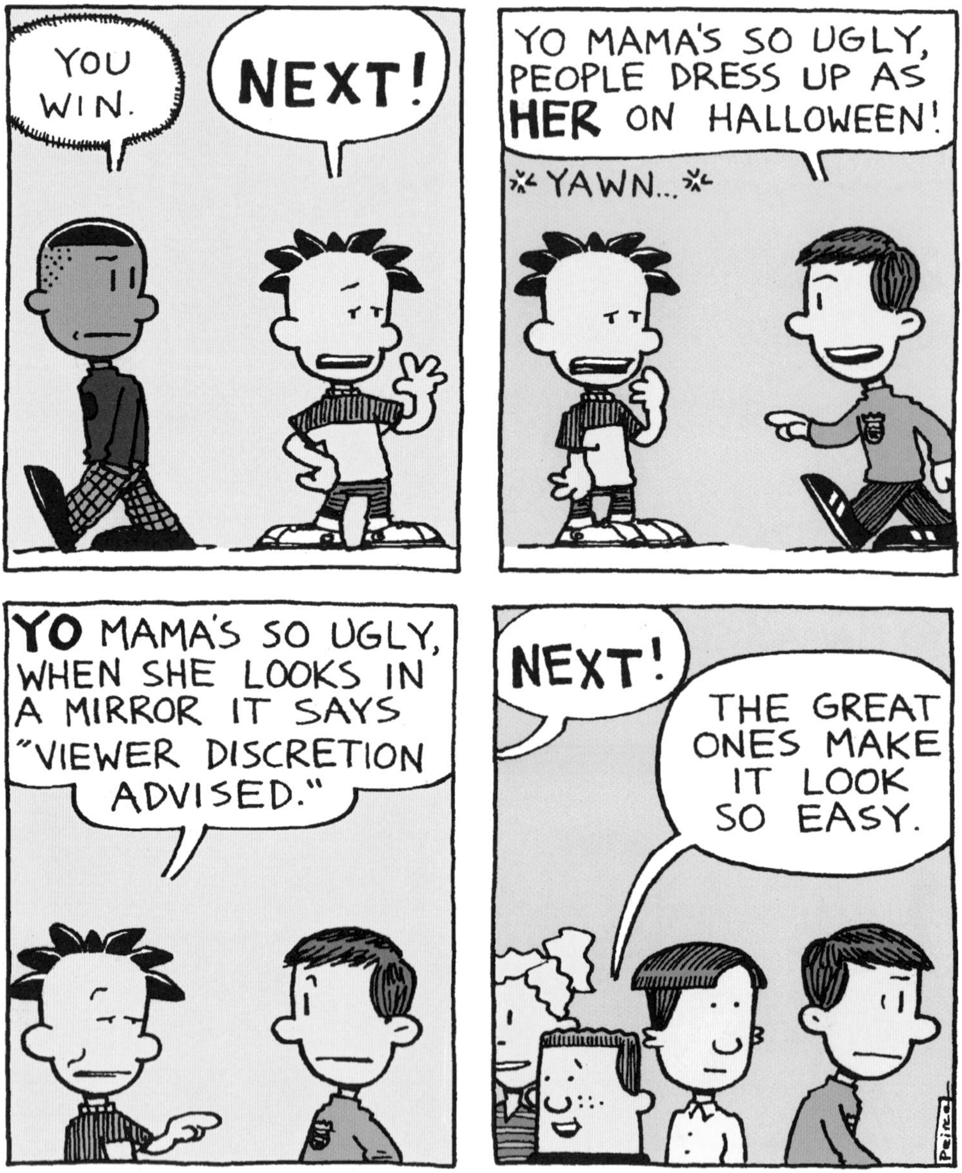

YOU WIN.
NEXT!
YO MAMA'S SO UGLY, PEOPLE DRESS UP AS HER ON HALLOWEEN!
YAWN...
YO MAMA'S SO UGLY, WHEN SHE LOOKS IN A MIRROR IT SAYS "VIEWER DISCRETION ADVISED."
NEXT!
THE GREAT ONES MAKE IT LOOK SO EASY.
Peirce

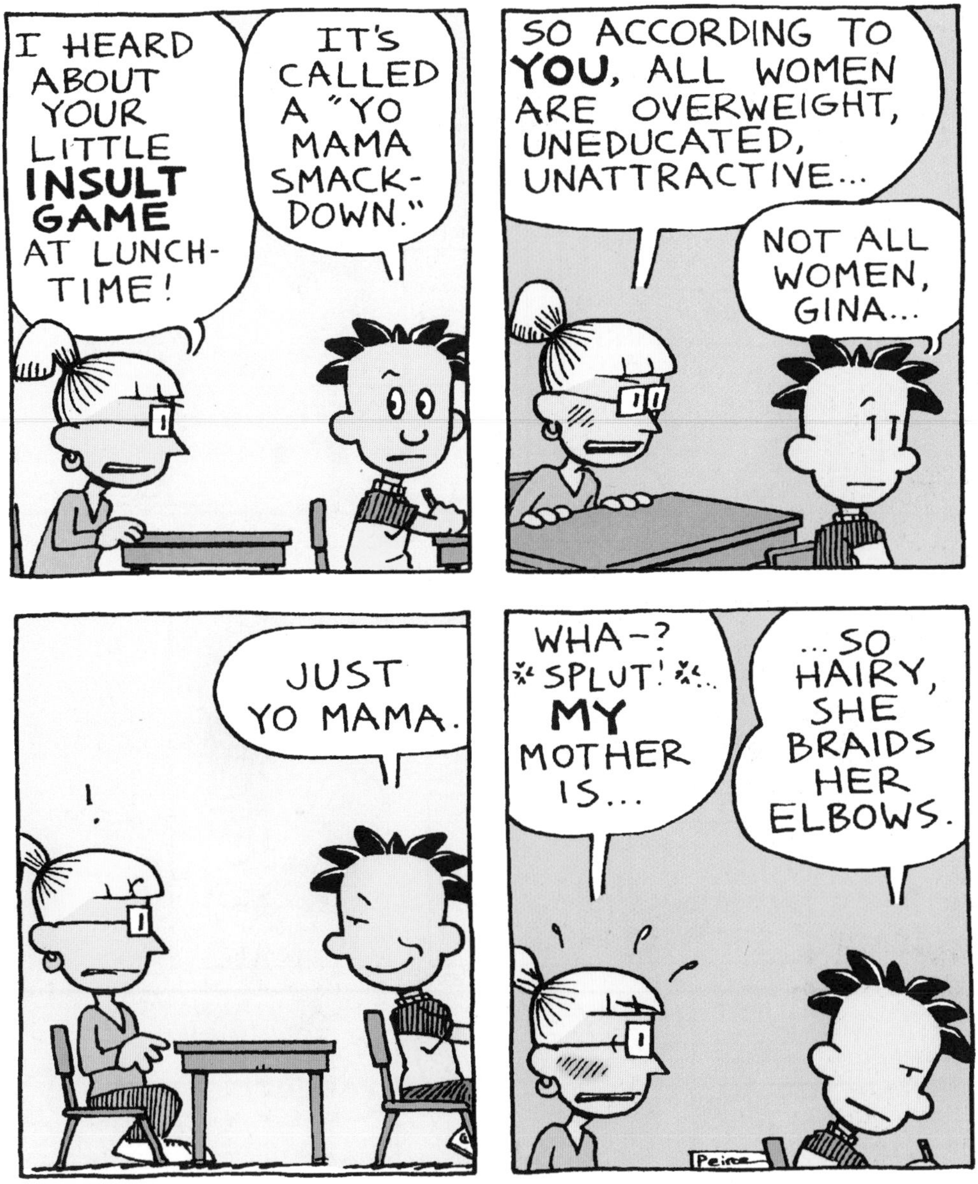
I HEARD ABOUT YOUR LITTLE **INSULT GAME** AT LUNCH-TIME!
IT'S CALLED A "YO MAMA SMACK-DOWN."
SO ACCORDING TO **YOU**, ALL WOMEN ARE OVERWEIGHT, UNEDUCATED, UNATTRACTIVE...
NOT ALL WOMEN, GINA...
JUST YO MAMA.
!
WHA-? SPLUT! **MY** MOTHER IS...
...SO HAIRY, SHE BRAIDS HER ELBOWS.
Peirce

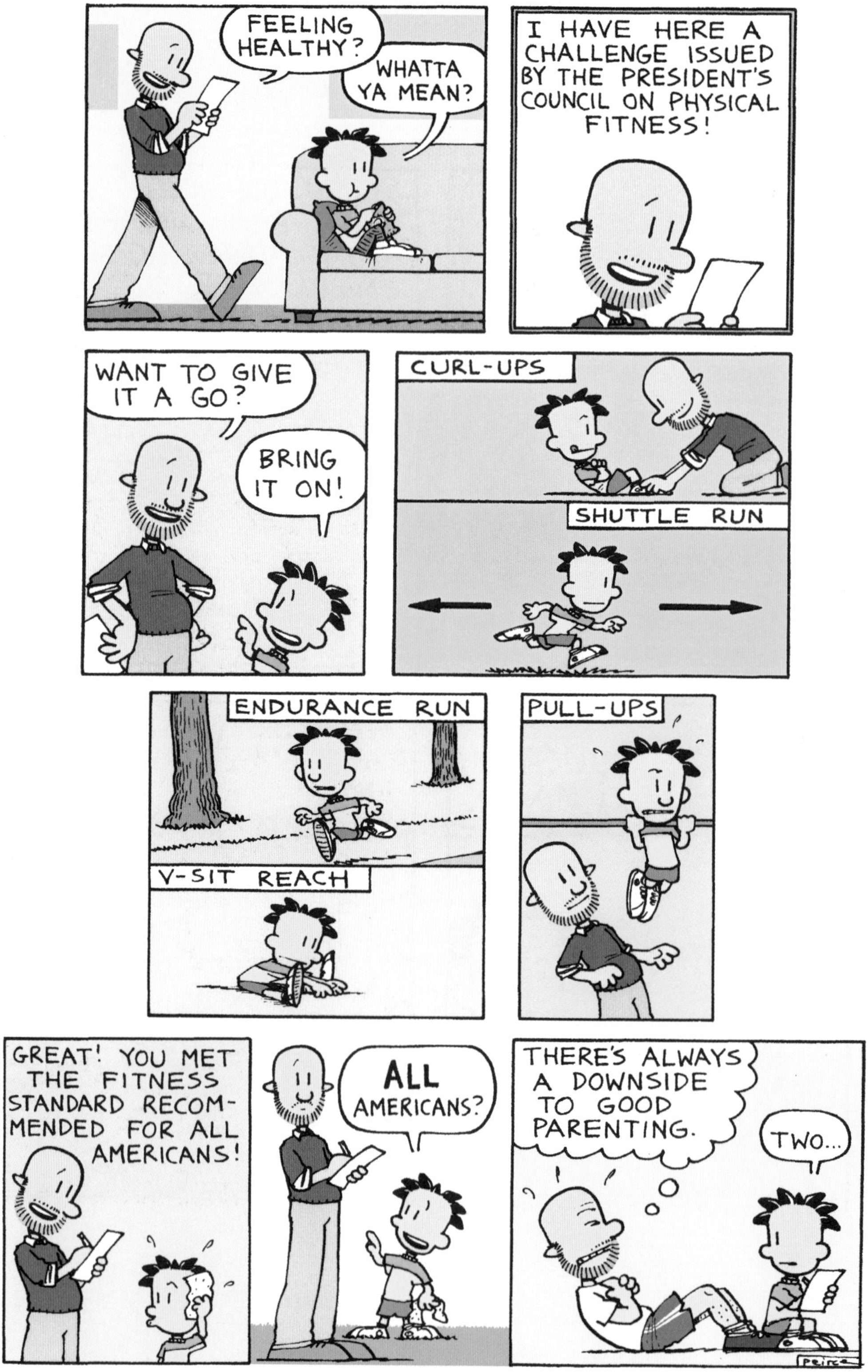
FEELING HEALTHY?
WHATTA YA MEAN?
I HAVE HERE A CHALLENGE ISSUED BY THE PRESIDENT'S COUNCIL ON PHYSICAL FITNESS!
WANT TO GIVE IT A GO?
BRING IT ON!
CURL-UPS
SHUTTLE RUN
ENDURANCE RUN
V-SIT REACH
PULL-UPS
GREAT! YOU MET THE FITNESS STANDARD RECOMMENDED FOR ALL AMERICANS!
ALL AMERICANS?
THERE'S ALWAYS A DOWNSIDE TO GOOD PARENTING.
TWO...

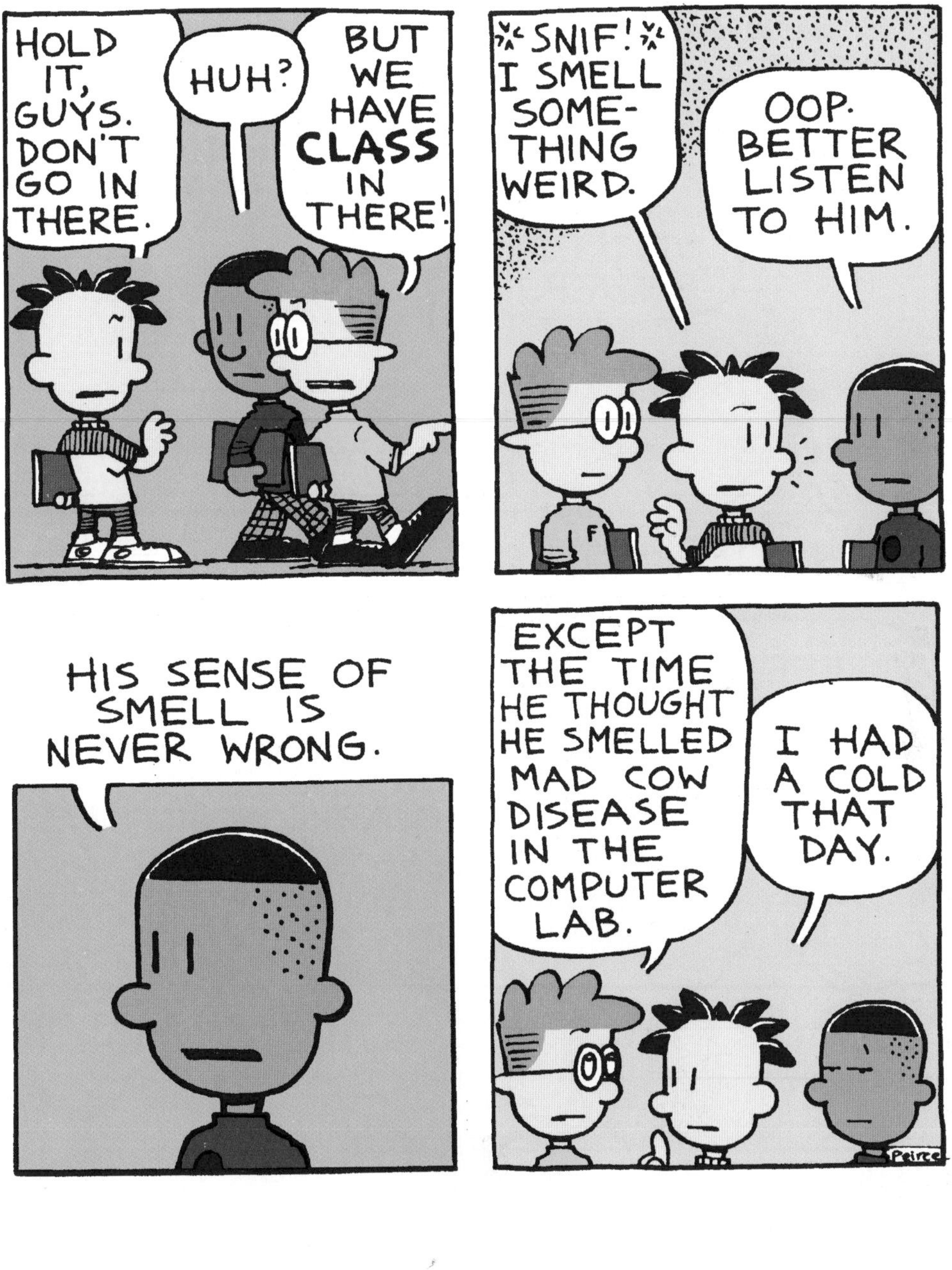
HOLD IT, GUYS. DON'T GO IN THERE.
HUH?
BUT WE HAVE **CLASS** IN THERE!
SNIF! I SMELL SOMETHING WEIRD.
OOP. BETTER LISTEN TO HIM.
HIS SENSE OF SMELL IS NEVER WRONG.
EXCEPT THE TIME HE THOUGHT HE SMELLED MAD COW DISEASE IN THE COMPUTER LAB.
I HAD A COLD THAT DAY.
Peirce

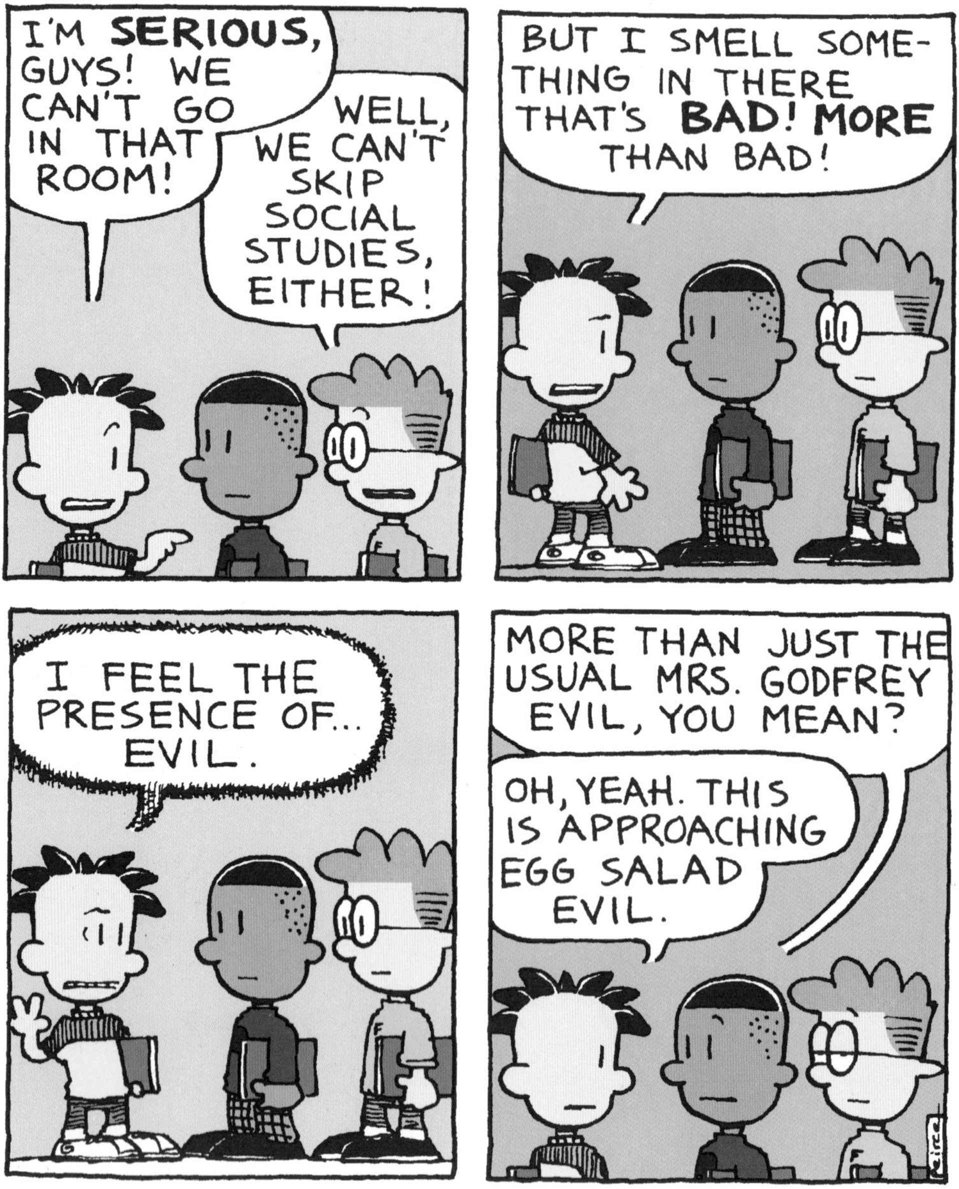
I'M **SERIOUS**, GUYS! WE CAN'T GO IN THAT ROOM!
WELL, WE CAN'T SKIP SOCIAL STUDIES, EITHER!
BUT I SMELL SOME-THING IN THERE THAT'S **BAD! MORE** THAN BAD!
I FEEL THE PRESENCE OF... EVIL.
MORE THAN JUST THE USUAL MRS. GODFREY EVIL, YOU MEAN?
OH, YEAH. THIS IS APPROACHING EGG SALAD EVIL.
Peirce

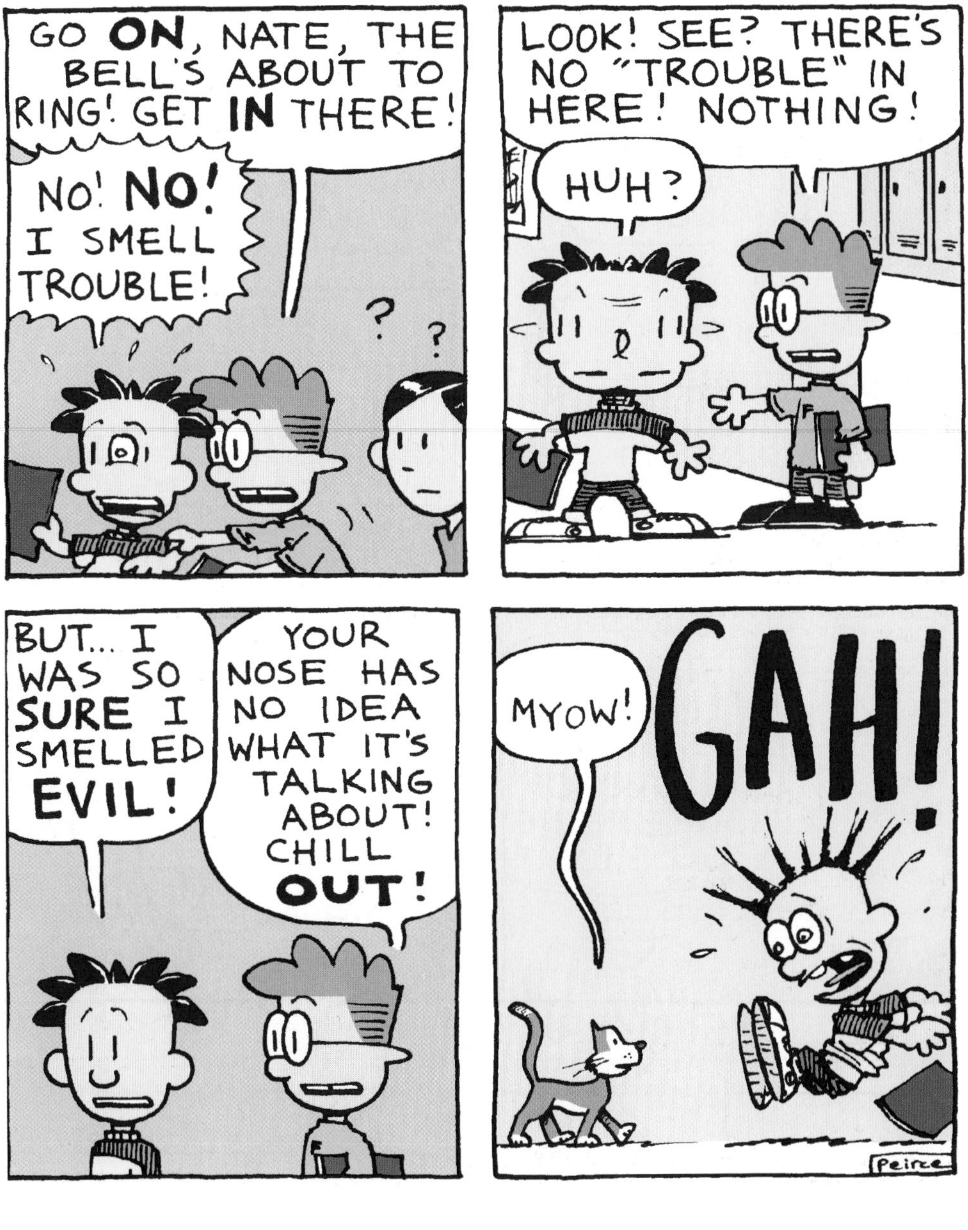
GO ON, NATE, THE BELL'S ABOUT TO RING! GET IN THERE!
NO! NO! I SMELL TROUBLE!
?
?
LOOK! SEE? THERE'S NO "TROUBLE" IN HERE! NOTHING!
HUH?
BUT... I WAS SO SURE I SMELLED EVIL!
YOUR NOSE HAS NO IDEA WHAT IT'S TALKING ABOUT! CHILL OUT!
MYOW!
GAH!
Peirce

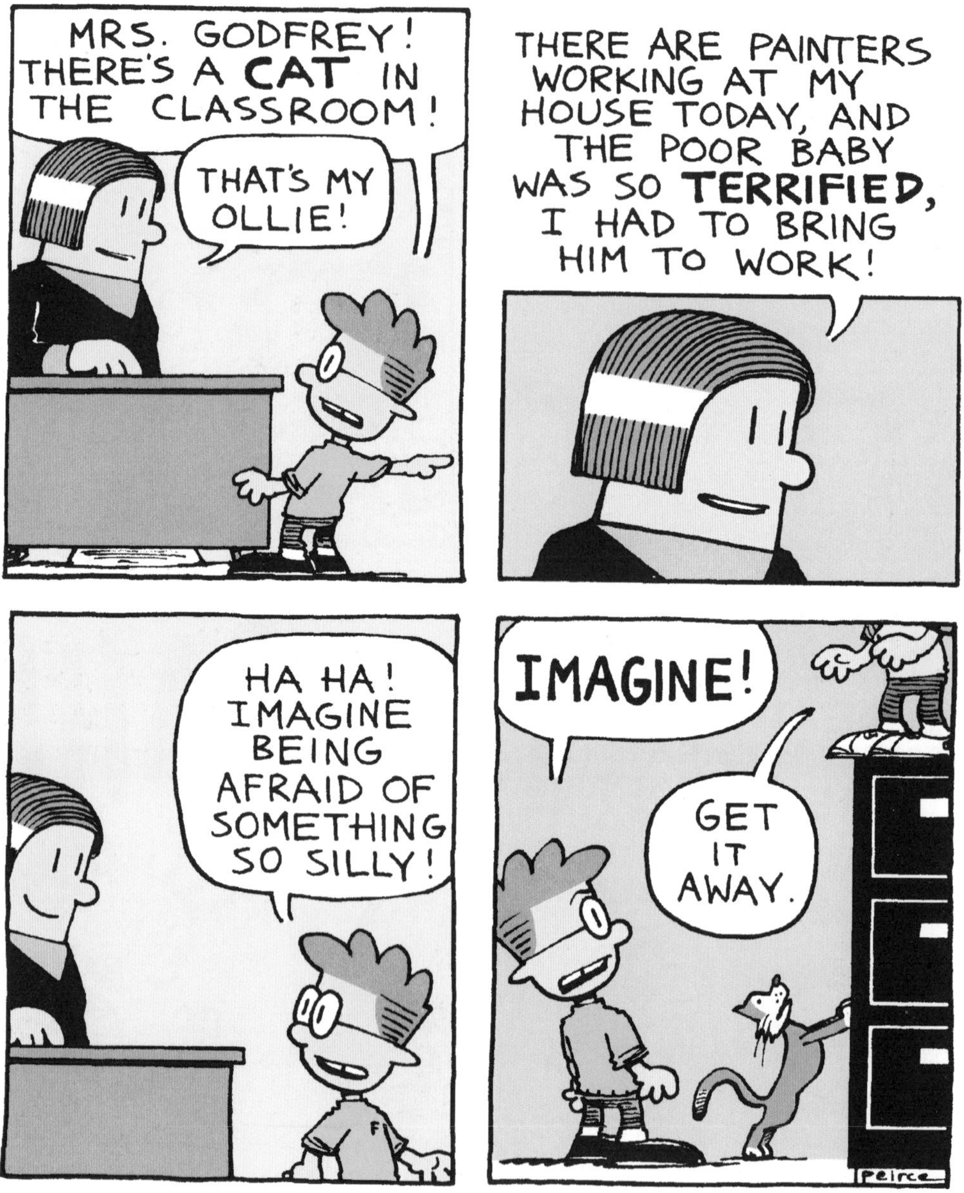
MRS. GODFREY! THERE'S A **CAT** IN THE CLASSROOM!
THAT'S MY OLLIE!
THERE ARE PAINTERS WORKING AT MY HOUSE TODAY, AND THE POOR BABY WAS SO **TERRIFIED**, I HAD TO BRING HIM TO WORK!
HA HA! IMAGINE BEING AFRAID OF SOMETHING SO SILLY!
IMAGINE!
GET IT AWAY.
peirce

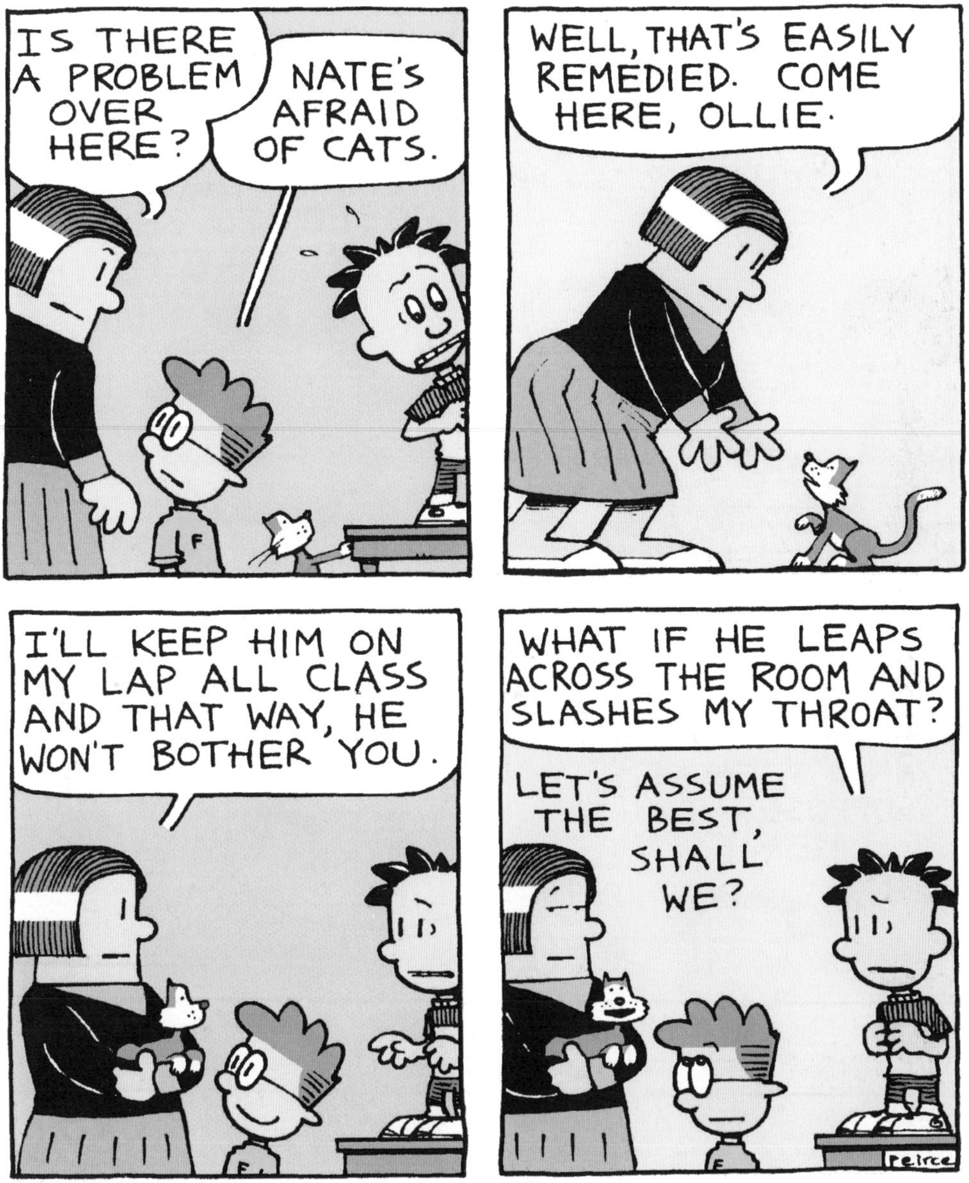
IS THERE A PROBLEM OVER HERE?
NATE'S AFRAID OF CATS.
WELL, THAT'S EASILY REMEDIED. COME HERE, OLLIE.
I'LL KEEP HIM ON MY LAP ALL CLASS AND THAT WAY, HE WON'T BOTHER YOU.
WHAT IF HE LEAPS ACROSS THE ROOM AND SLASHES MY THROAT?
LET'S ASSUME THE BEST, SHALL WE?
PEIRCE

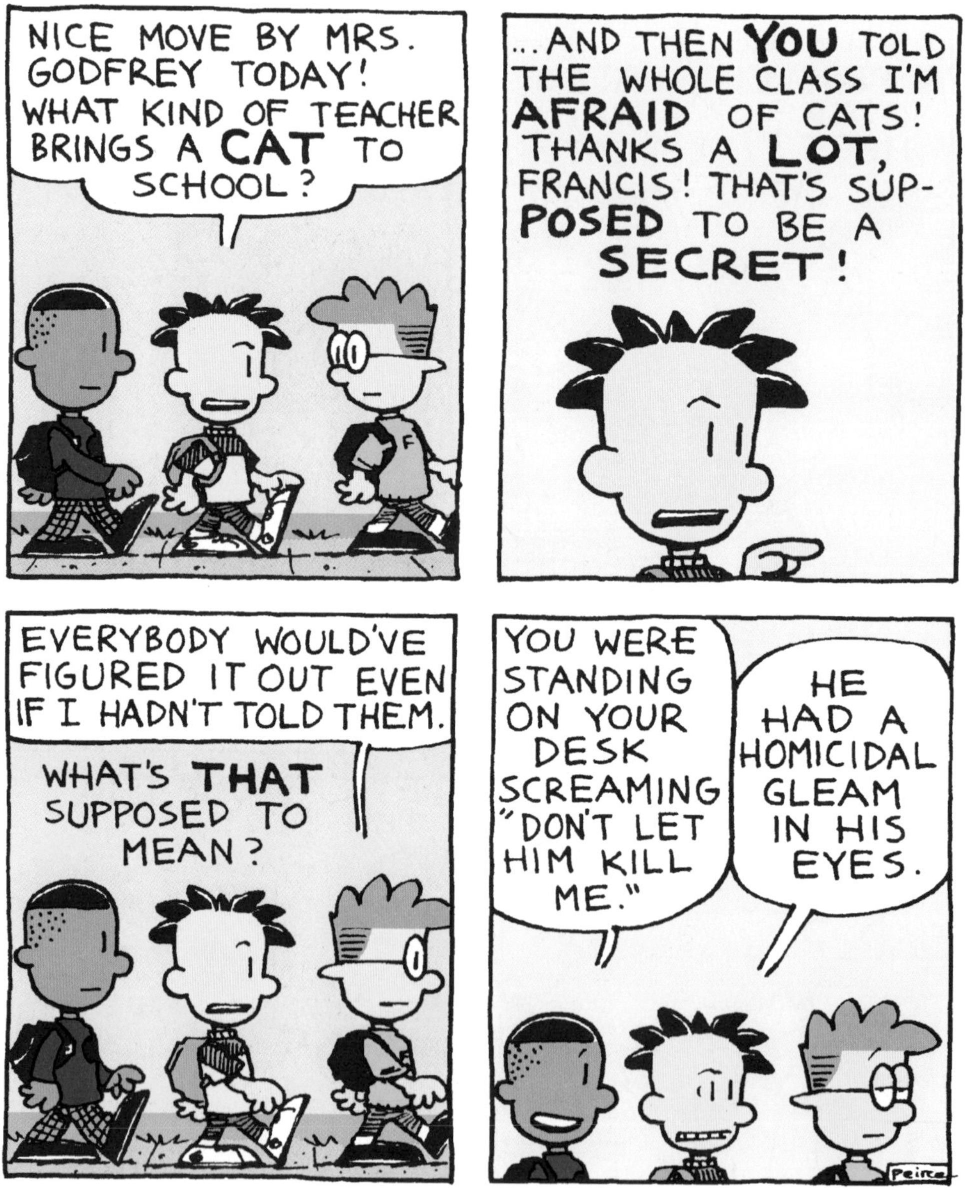
NICE MOVE BY MRS. GODFREY TODAY! WHAT KIND OF TEACHER BRINGS A **CAT** TO SCHOOL?
...AND THEN **YOU** TOLD THE WHOLE CLASS I'M **AFRAID** OF CATS! THANKS A **LOT**, FRANCIS! THAT'S SUP-**POSED** TO BE A **SECRET**!
EVERYBODY WOULD'VE FIGURED IT OUT EVEN IF I HADN'T TOLD THEM.
WHAT'S **THAT** SUPPOSED TO MEAN?
YOU WERE STANDING ON YOUR DESK SCREAMING "DON'T LET HIM KILL ME."
HE HAD A HOMICIDAL GLEAM IN HIS EYES.
Peirce

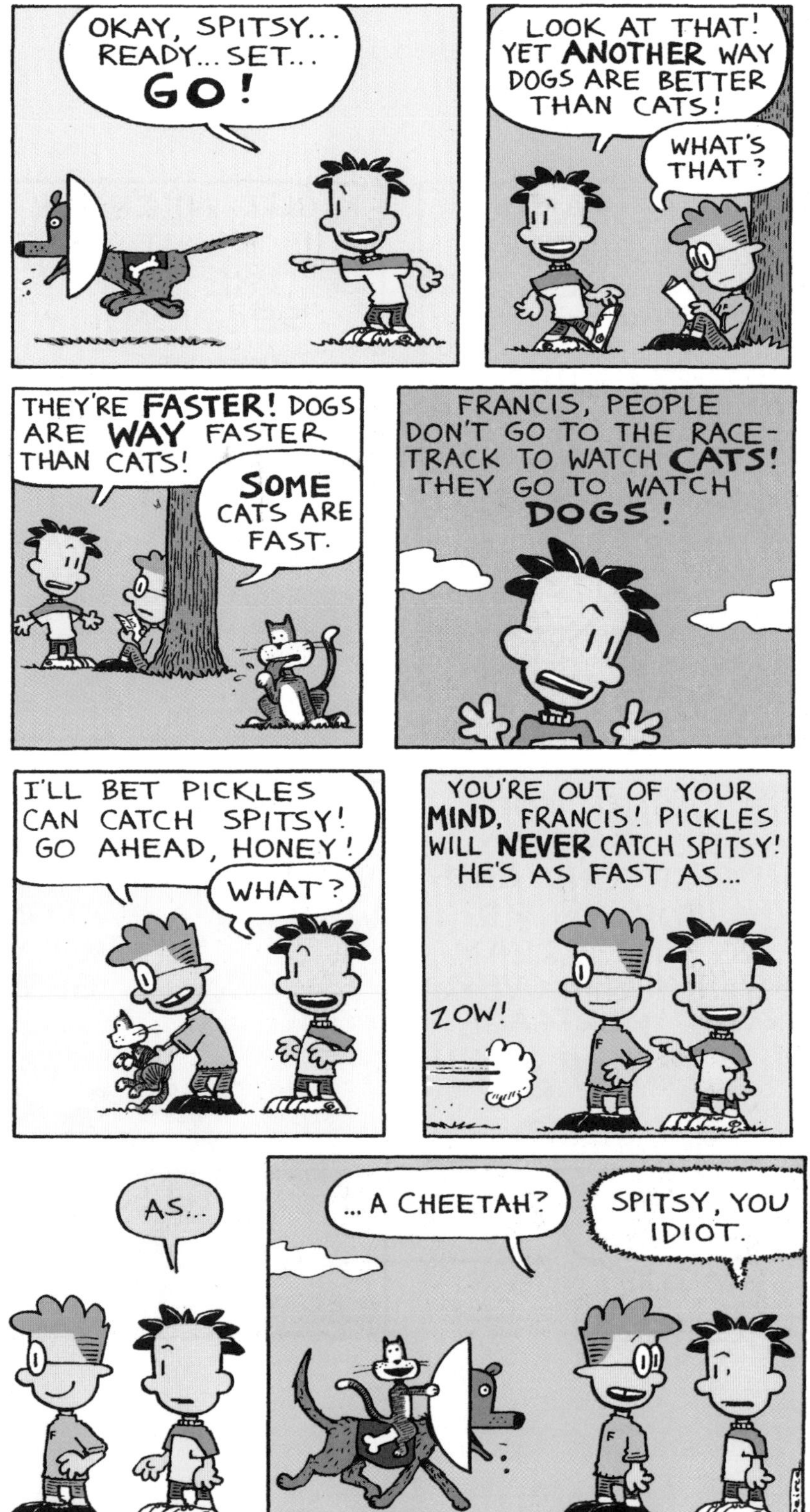
OKAY, SPITSY... READY... SET... GO!
LOOK AT THAT! YET ANOTHER WAY DOGS ARE BETTER THAN CATS!
WHAT'S THAT?
THEY'RE FASTER! DOGS ARE WAY FASTER THAN CATS!
SOME CATS ARE FAST.
FRANCIS, PEOPLE DON'T GO TO THE RACE-TRACK TO WATCH CATS! THEY GO TO WATCH DOGS!
I'LL BET PICKLES CAN CATCH SPITSY! GO AHEAD, HONEY!
WHAT?
YOU'RE OUT OF YOUR MIND, FRANCIS! PICKLES WILL NEVER CATCH SPITSY! HE'S AS FAST AS...
ZOW!
AS...
... A CHEETAH?
SPITSY, YOU IDIOT.

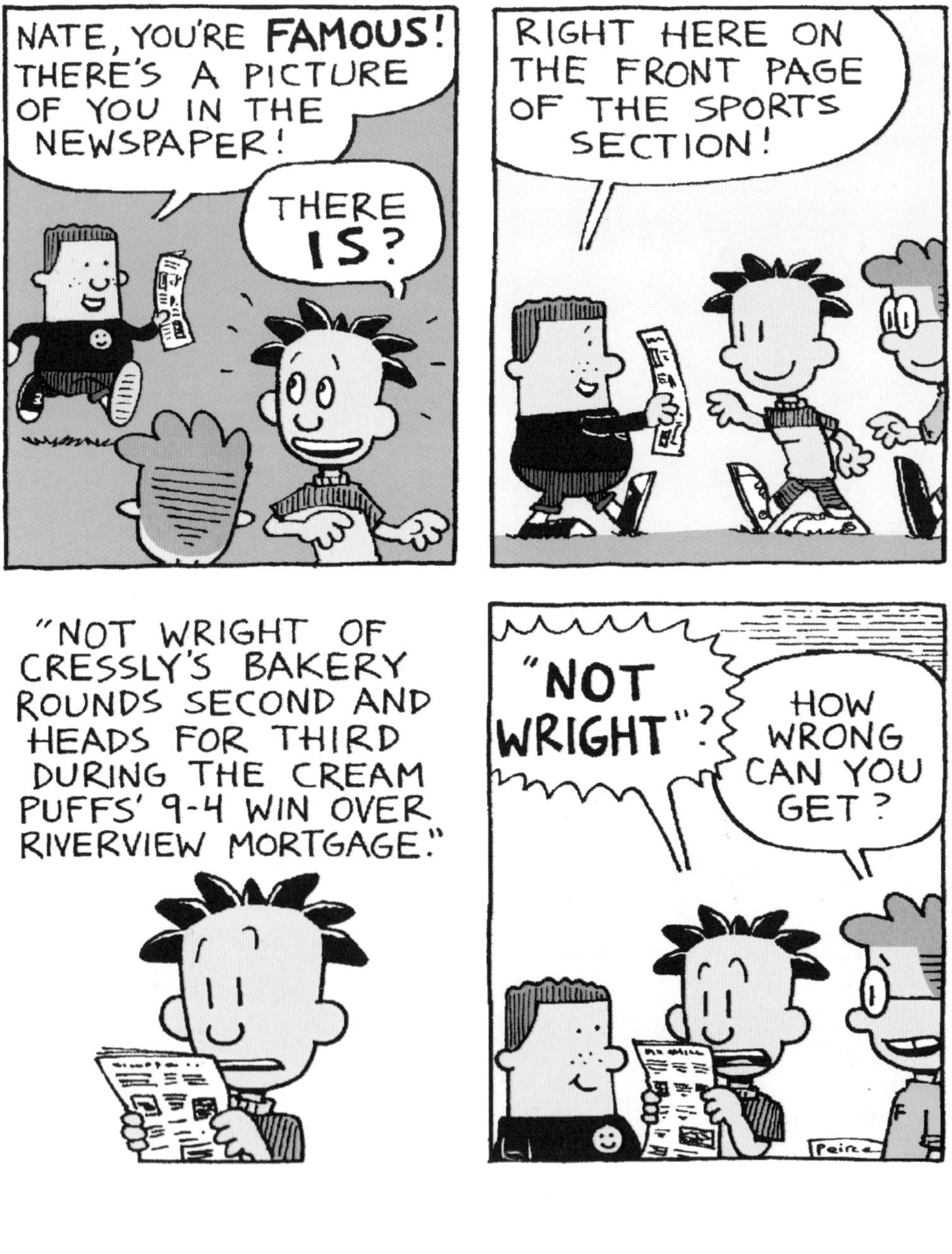
NATE, YOU'RE **FAMOUS**! THERE'S A PICTURE OF YOU IN THE NEWSPAPER!
THERE **IS**?
RIGHT HERE ON THE FRONT PAGE OF THE SPORTS SECTION!
"NOT WRIGHT OF CRESSLY'S BAKERY ROUNDS SECOND AND HEADS FOR THIRD DURING THE CREAM PUFFS' 9-4 WIN OVER RIVERVIEW MORTGAGE."
"**NOT WRIGHT**"?
HOW WRONG CAN YOU GET?

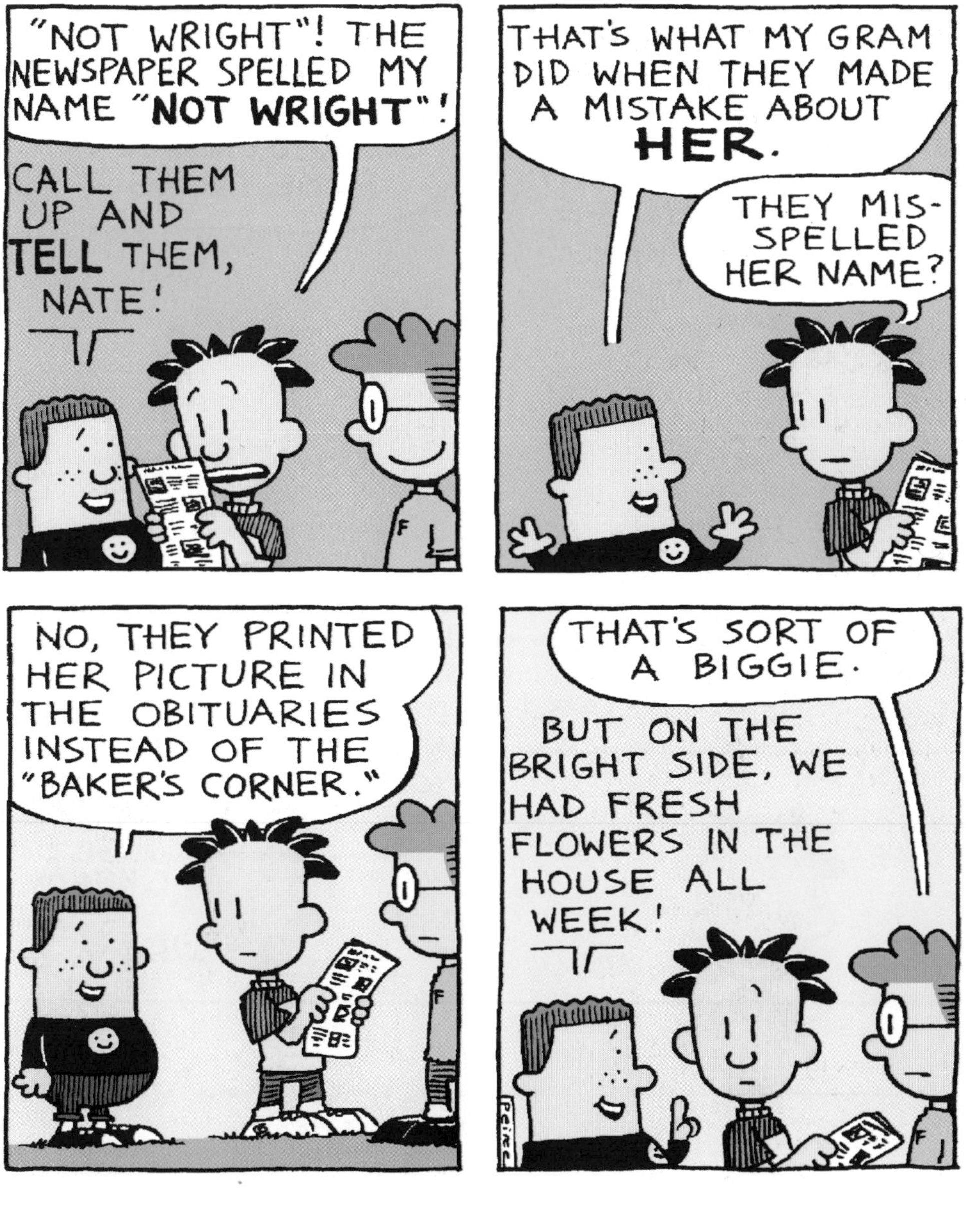
"NOT WRIGHT"! THE NEWSPAPER SPELLED MY NAME "**NOT WRIGHT**"!
CALL THEM UP AND **TELL** THEM, NATE!
THAT'S WHAT MY GRAM DID WHEN THEY MADE A MISTAKE ABOUT **HER**.
THEY MIS-SPELLED HER NAME?
NO, THEY PRINTED HER PICTURE IN THE OBITUARIES INSTEAD OF THE "BAKER'S CORNER."
THAT'S SORT OF A BIGGIE.
BUT ON THE BRIGHT SIDE, WE HAD FRESH FLOWERS IN THE HOUSE ALL WEEK!
PEIRCE

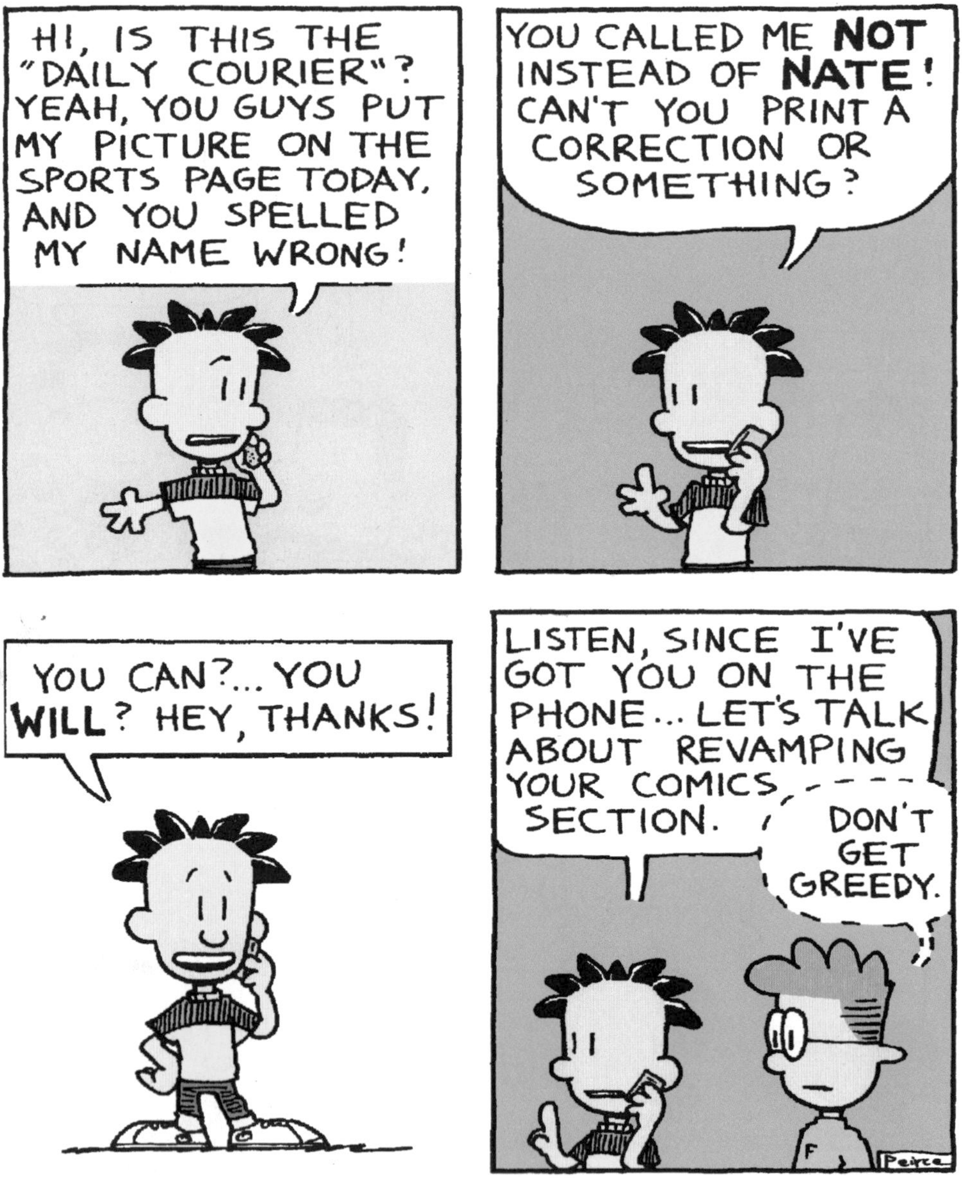
HI, IS THIS THE "DAILY COURIER"? YEAH, YOU GUYS PUT MY PICTURE ON THE SPORTS PAGE TODAY, AND YOU SPELLED MY NAME WRONG!
YOU CALLED ME **NOT** INSTEAD OF **NATE**! CAN'T YOU PRINT A CORRECTION OR SOMETHING?
YOU CAN?... YOU **WILL**? HEY, THANKS!
LISTEN, SINCE I'VE GOT YOU ON THE PHONE... LET'S TALK ABOUT REVAMPING YOUR COMICS SECTION.
DON'T GET GREEDY.
F
Peirce

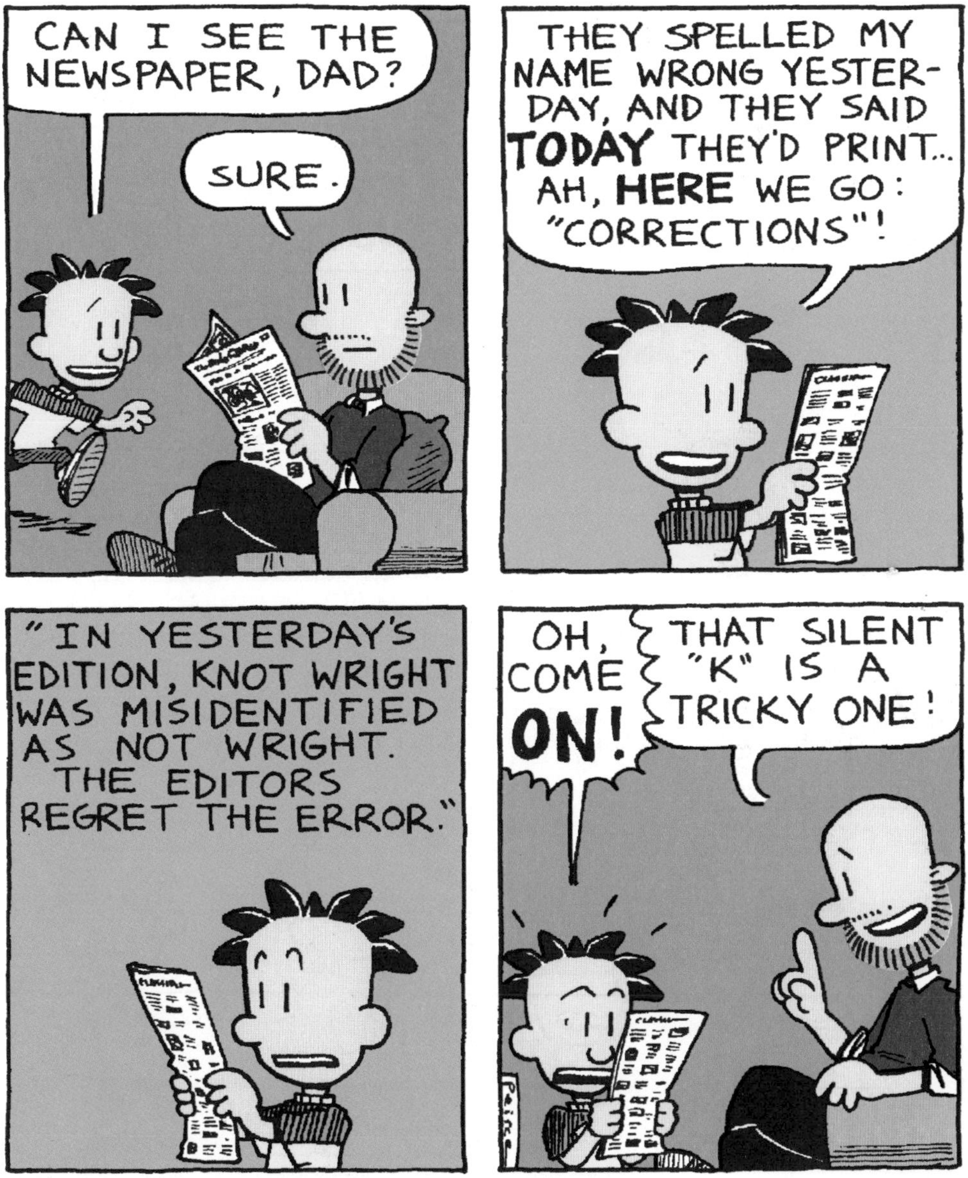
CAN I SEE THE NEWSPAPER, DAD?
SURE.
THEY SPELLED MY NAME WRONG YESTERDAY, AND THEY SAID **TODAY** THEY'D PRINT... AH, **HERE** WE GO: "CORRECTIONS"!
"IN YESTERDAY'S EDITION, KNOT WRIGHT WAS MISIDENTIFIED AS NOT WRIGHT. THE EDITORS REGRET THE ERROR."
OH, COME **ON!**
THAT SILENT "K" IS A TRICKY ONE!

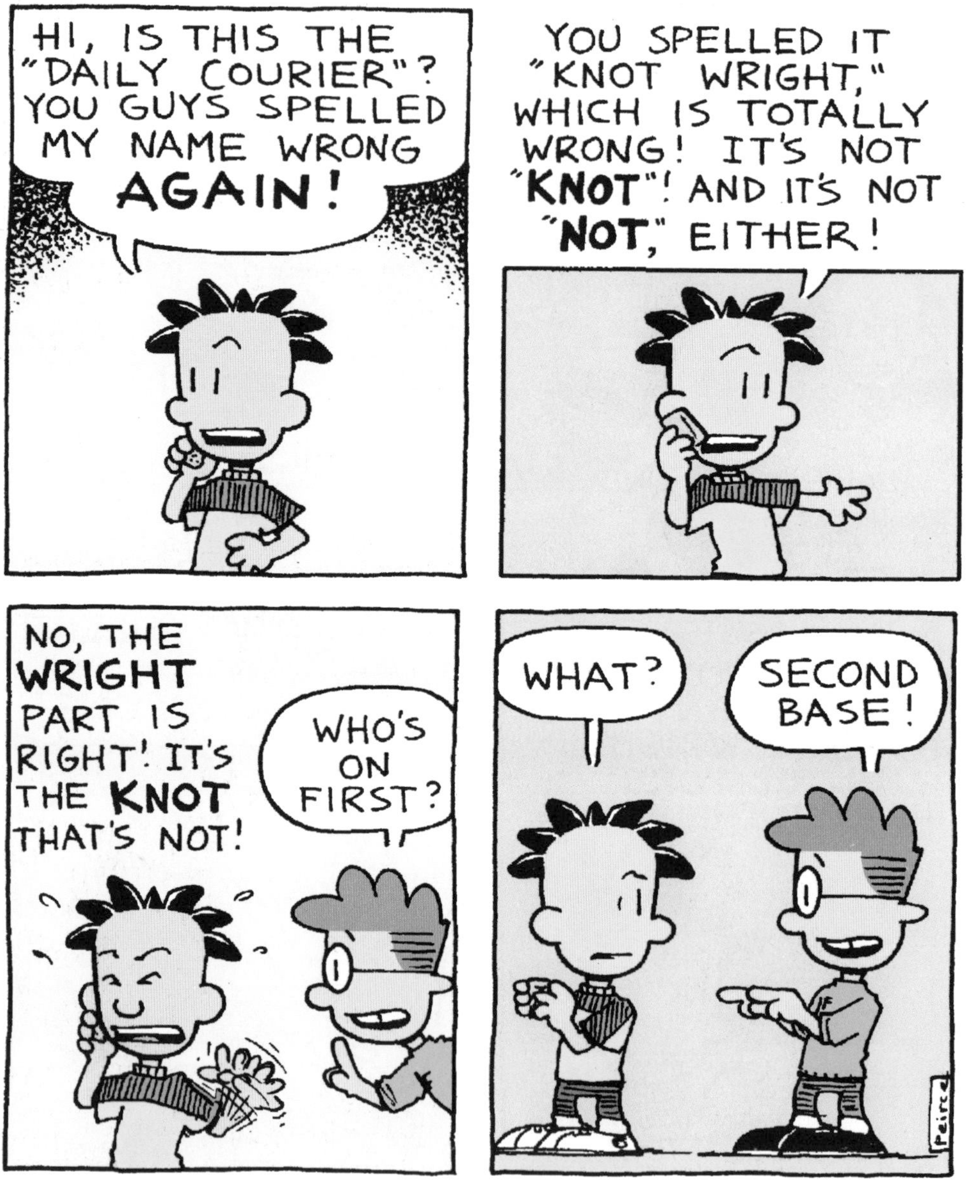
HI, IS THIS THE "DAILY COURIER"? YOU GUYS SPELLED MY NAME WRONG **AGAIN**!
YOU SPELLED IT "KNOT WRIGHT," WHICH IS TOTALLY WRONG! IT'S NOT "**KNOT**"! AND IT'S NOT "**NOT**," EITHER!
NO, THE **WRIGHT** PART IS RIGHT! IT'S THE **KNOT** THAT'S NOT!
WHO'S ON FIRST?
WHAT?
SECOND BASE!
Peirce

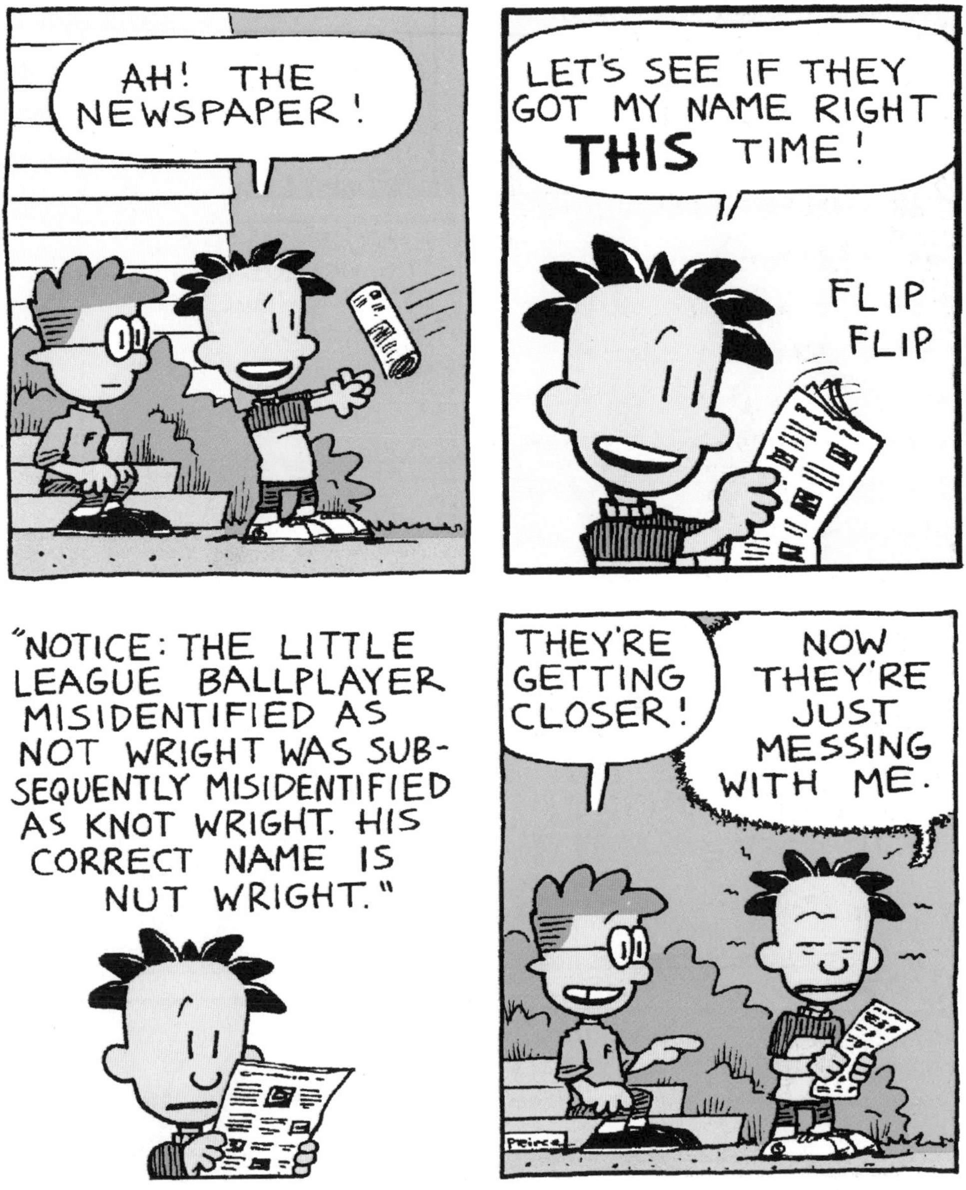
AH! THE NEWSPAPER!
LET'S SEE IF THEY GOT MY NAME RIGHT **THIS** TIME!
FLIP FLIP
"NOTICE: THE LITTLE LEAGUE BALLPLAYER MISIDENTIFIED AS NOT WRIGHT WAS SUBSEQUENTLY MISIDENTIFIED AS KNOT WRIGHT. HIS CORRECT NAME IS NUT WRIGHT."
THEY'RE GETTING CLOSER!
NOW THEY'RE JUST MESSING WITH ME.
PEIRCE

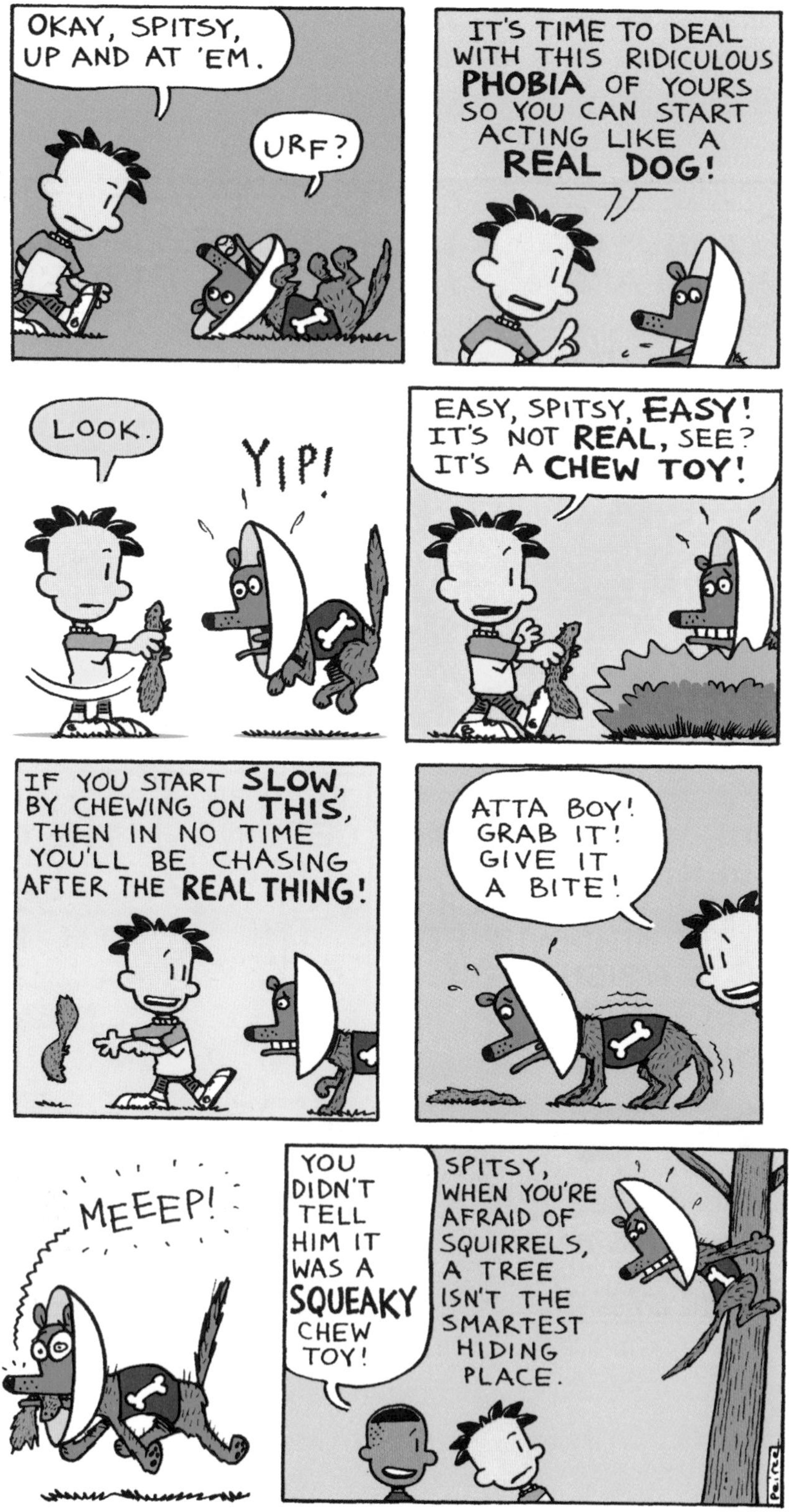
OKAY, SPITSY, UP AND AT 'EM.
URF?
IT'S TIME TO DEAL WITH THIS RIDICULOUS PHOBIA OF YOURS SO YOU CAN START ACTING LIKE A REAL DOG!
LOOK.
YIP!
EASY, SPITSY, EASY! IT'S NOT REAL, SEE? IT'S A CHEW TOY!
IF YOU START SLOW, BY CHEWING ON THIS, THEN IN NO TIME YOU'LL BE CHASING AFTER THE REAL THING!
ATTA BOY! GRAB IT! GIVE IT A BITE!
MEEEP!
YOU DIDN'T TELL HIM IT WAS A SQUEAKY CHEW TOY!
SPITSY, WHEN YOU'RE AFRAID OF SQUIRRELS, A TREE ISN'T THE SMARTEST HIDING PLACE.
PEIRCE

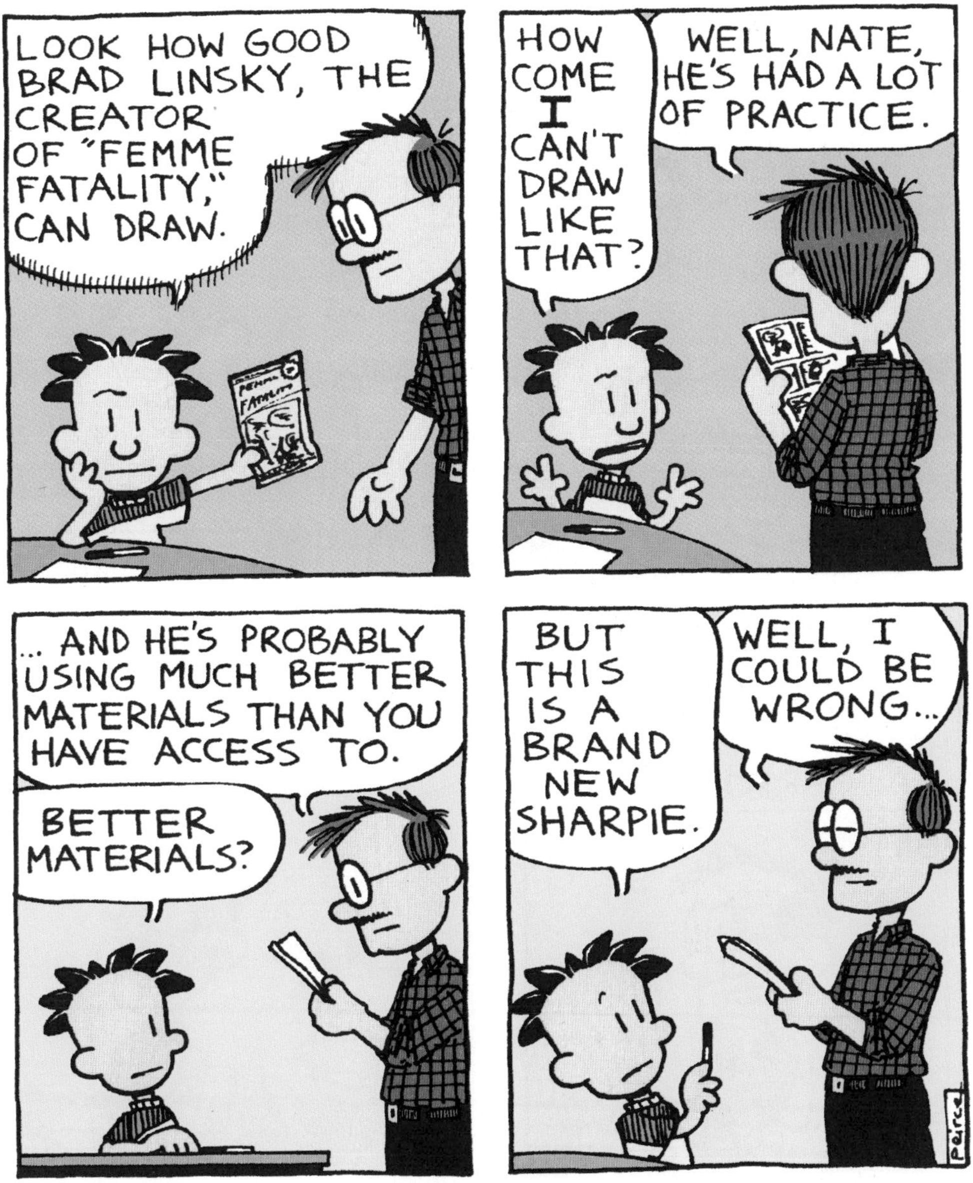
LOOK HOW GOOD BRAD LINSKY, THE CREATOR OF "FEMME FATALITY," CAN DRAW.
HOW COME I CAN'T DRAW LIKE THAT?
WELL, NATE, HE'S HAD A LOT OF PRACTICE.
... AND HE'S PROBABLY USING MUCH BETTER MATERIALS THAN YOU HAVE ACCESS TO.
BETTER MATERIALS?
BUT THIS IS A BRAND NEW SHARPIE.
WELL, I COULD BE WRONG...
PEIRCE

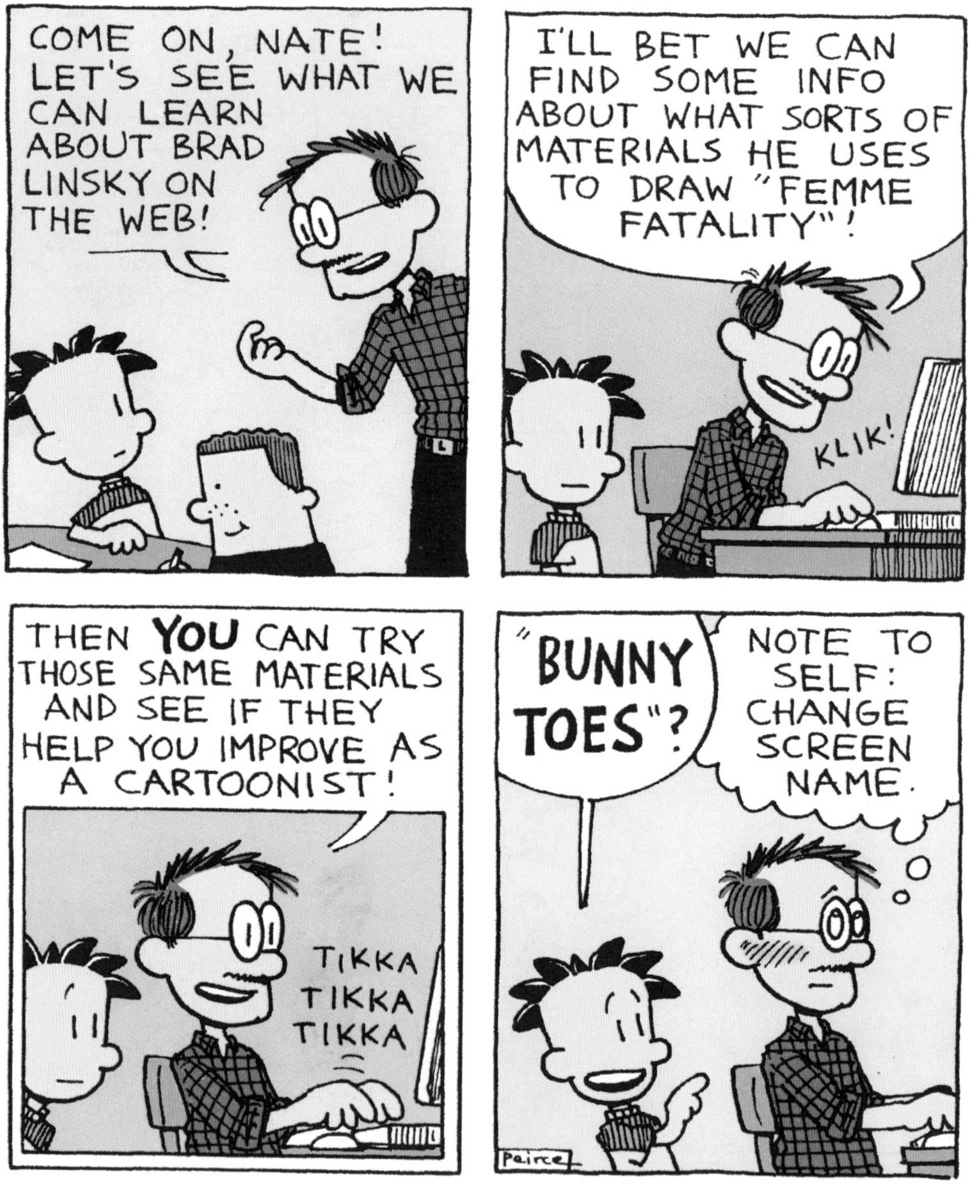
COME ON, NATE! LET'S SEE WHAT WE CAN LEARN ABOUT BRAD LINSKY ON THE WEB!
I'LL BET WE CAN FIND SOME INFO ABOUT WHAT SORTS OF MATERIALS HE USES TO DRAW "FEMME FATALITY"!
KLIK!
THEN YOU CAN TRY THOSE SAME MATERIALS AND SEE IF THEY HELP YOU IMPROVE AS A CARTOONIST!
TIKKA TIKKA TIKKA
"BUNNY TOES"?
NOTE TO SELF: CHANGE SCREEN NAME.
Peirce

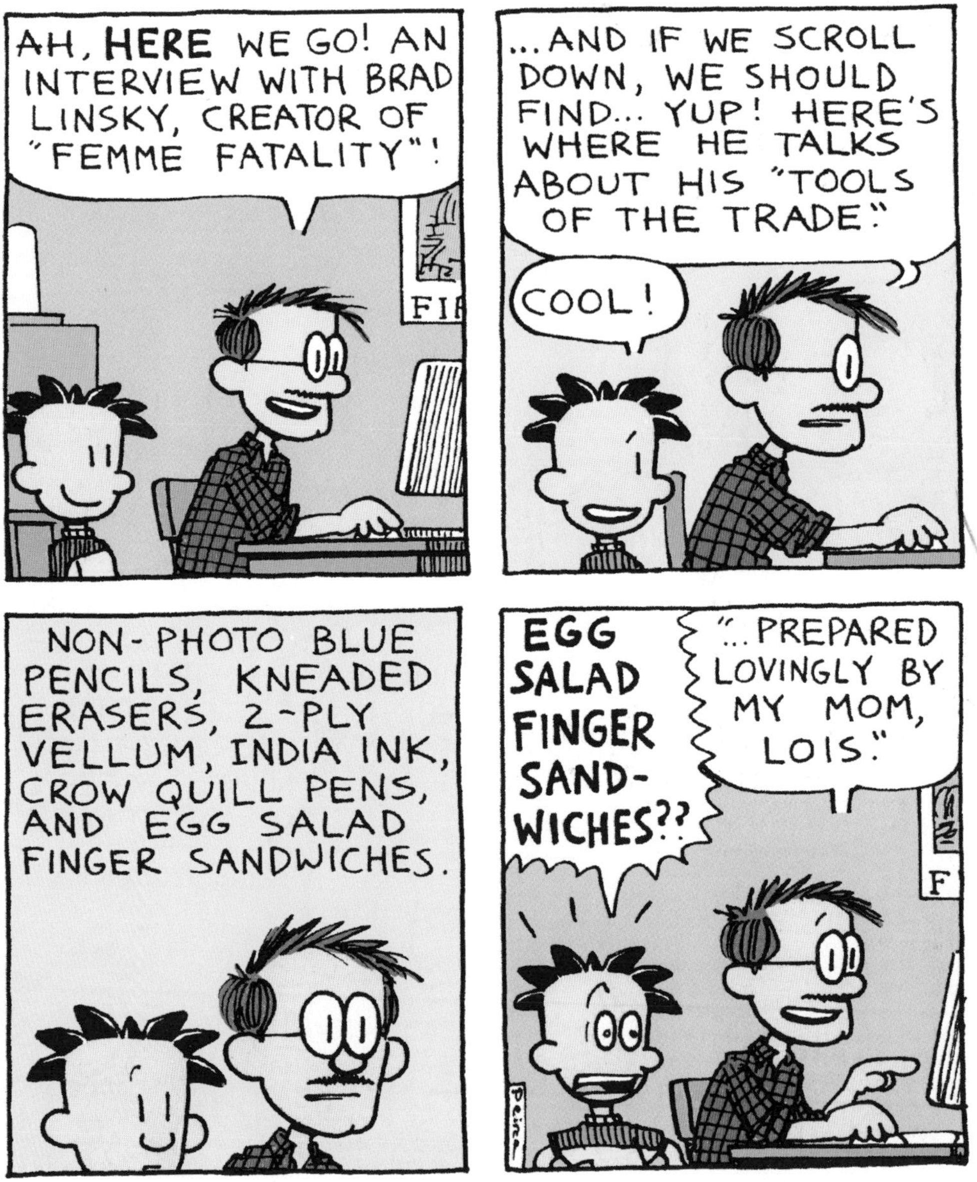
AH, HERE WE GO! AN INTERVIEW WITH BRAD LINSKY, CREATOR OF "FEMME FATALITY"!
...AND IF WE SCROLL DOWN, WE SHOULD FIND... YUP! HERE'S WHERE HE TALKS ABOUT HIS "TOOLS OF THE TRADE."
COOL!
NON-PHOTO BLUE PENCILS, KNEADED ERASERS, 2-PLY VELLUM, INDIA INK, CROW QUILL PENS, AND EGG SALAD FINGER SANDWICHES.
"...PREPARED LOVINGLY BY MY MOM, LOIS."
EGG SALAD FINGER SANDWICHES??

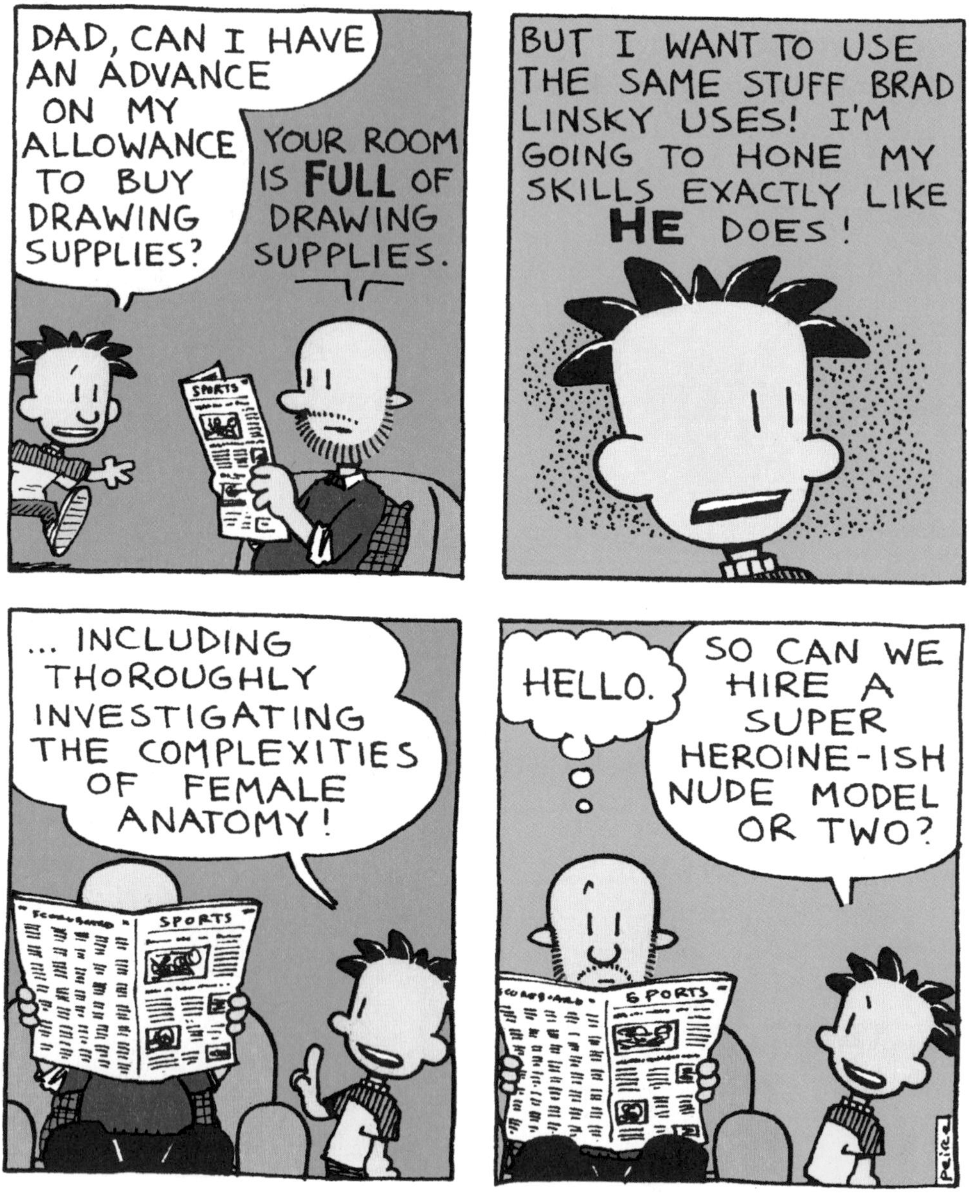
DAD, CAN I HAVE AN ADVANCE ON MY ALLOWANCE TO BUY DRAWING SUPPLIES?
YOUR ROOM IS **FULL** OF DRAWING SUPPLIES.
SPORTS
BUT I WANT TO USE THE SAME STUFF BRAD LINSKY USES! I'M GOING TO HONE MY SKILLS EXACTLY LIKE **HE** DOES!
... INCLUDING THOROUGHLY INVESTIGATING THE COMPLEXITIES OF FEMALE ANATOMY!
SPORTS
HELLO.
SO CAN WE HIRE A SUPER HEROINE-ISH NUDE MODEL OR TWO?
SPORTS
Peirce

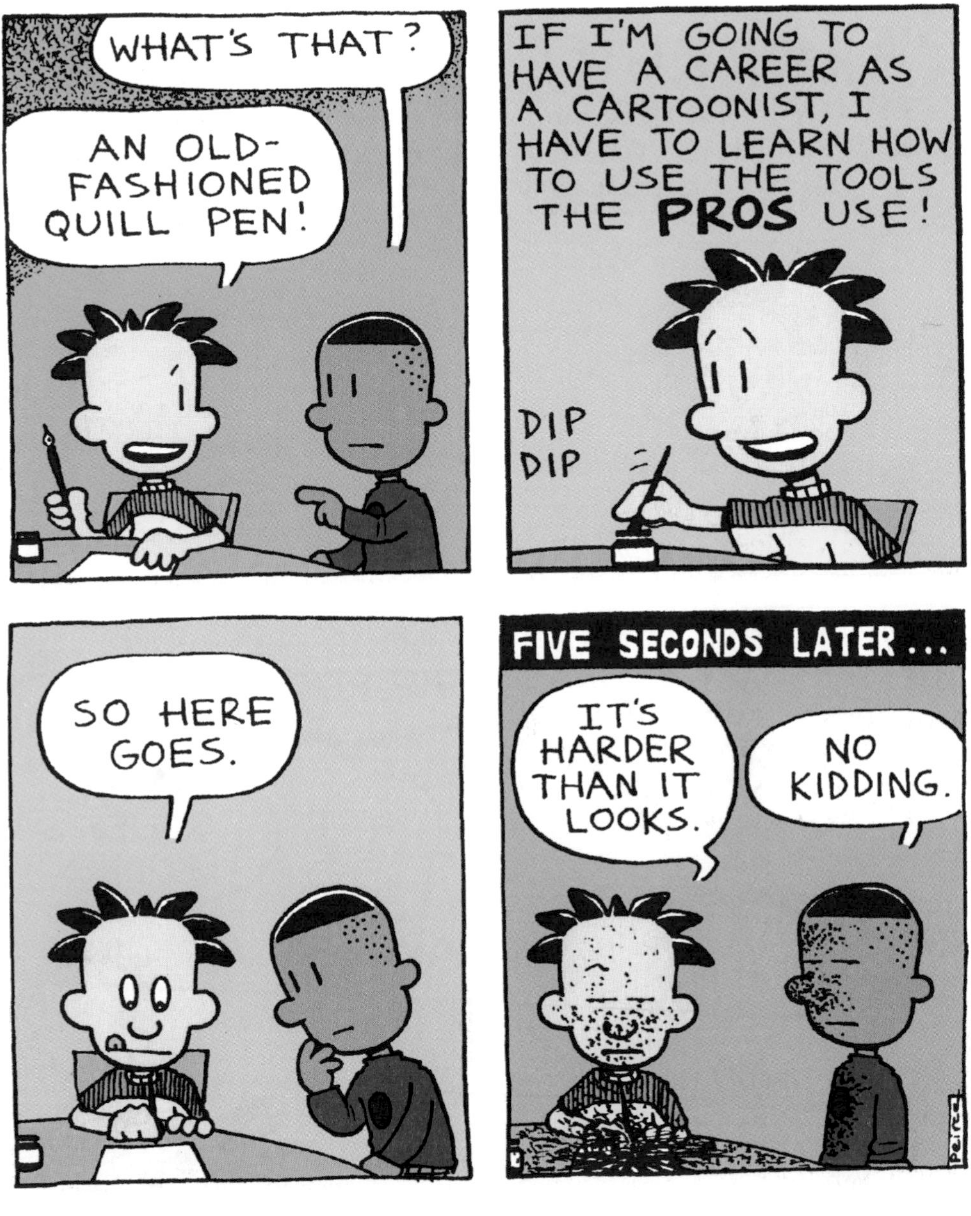
WHAT'S THAT?
AN OLD-FASHIONED QUILL PEN!
IF I'M GOING TO HAVE A CAREER AS A CARTOONIST, I HAVE TO LEARN HOW TO USE THE TOOLS THE PROS USE!
DIP DIP
SO HERE GOES.
FIVE SECONDS LATER...
IT'S HARDER THAN IT LOOKS.
NO KIDDING.
Peirce

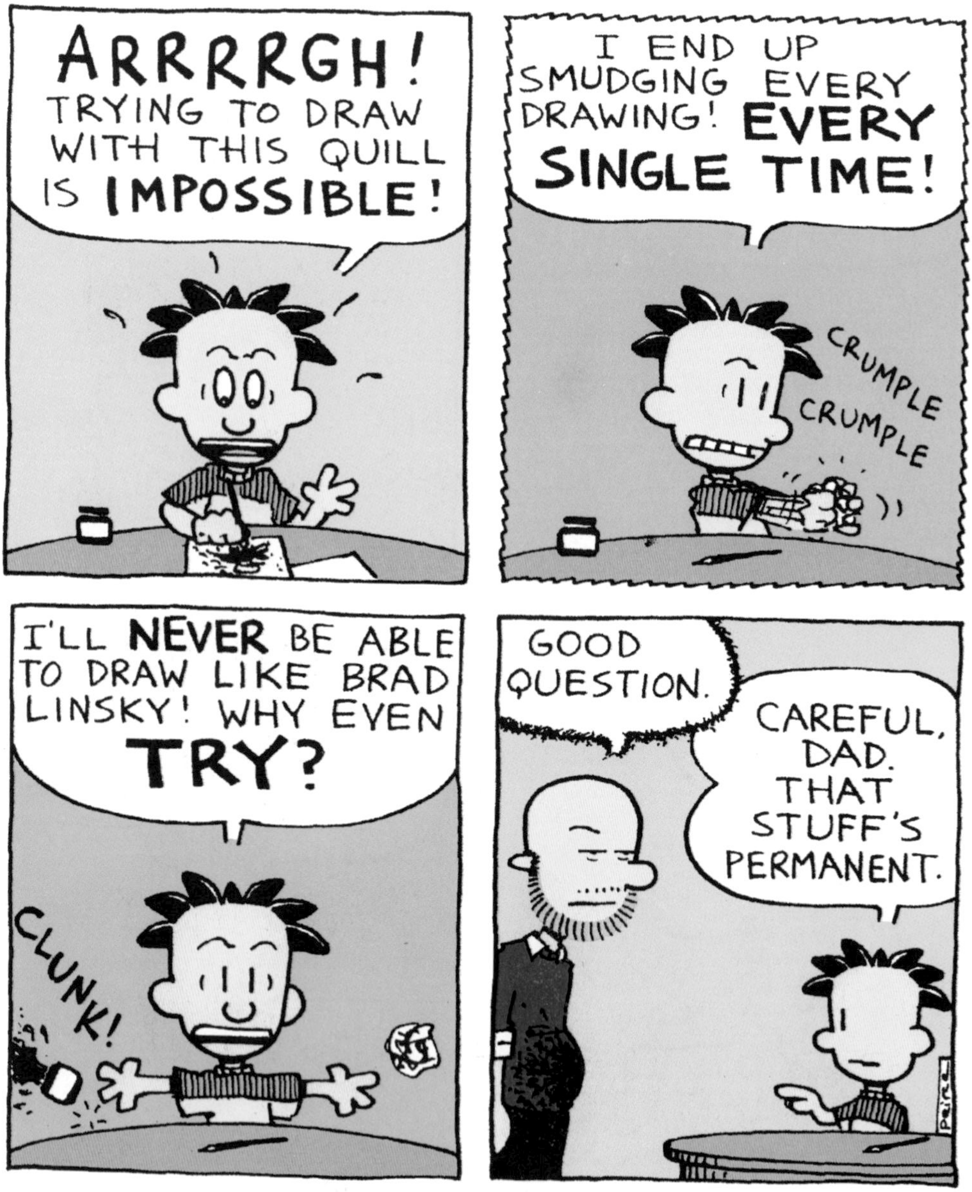
ARRRRGH! TRYING TO DRAW WITH THIS QUILL IS IMPOSSIBLE!
I END UP SMUDGING EVERY DRAWING! EVERY SINGLE TIME!
CRUMPLE CRUMPLE
I'LL NEVER BE ABLE TO DRAW LIKE BRAD LINSKY! WHY EVEN TRY?
CLUNK!
GOOD QUESTION.
CAREFUL, DAD. THAT STUFF'S PERMANENT.

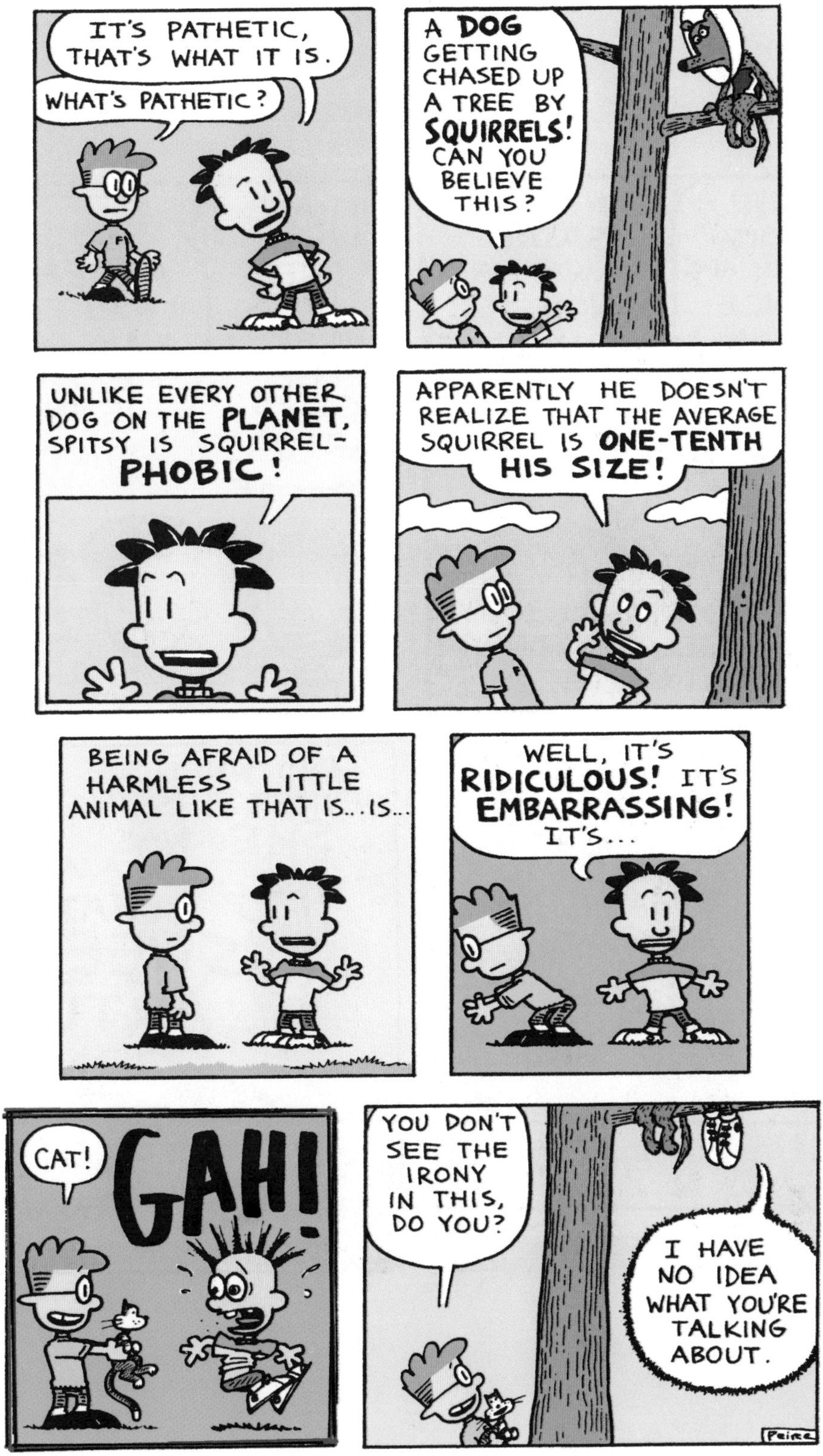
IT'S PATHETIC, THAT'S WHAT IT IS.
WHAT'S PATHETIC?
A DOG GETTING CHASED UP A TREE BY SQUIRRELS! CAN YOU BELIEVE THIS?
UNLIKE EVERY OTHER DOG ON THE PLANET, SPITSY IS SQUIRREL-PHOBIC!
APPARENTLY HE DOESN'T REALIZE THAT THE AVERAGE SQUIRREL IS ONE-TENTH HIS SIZE!
BEING AFRAID OF A HARMLESS LITTLE ANIMAL LIKE THAT IS...IS...
WELL, IT'S RIDICULOUS! IT'S EMBARRASSING! IT'S...
CAT!
GAH!
YOU DON'T SEE THE IRONY IN THIS, DO YOU?
I HAVE NO IDEA WHAT YOU'RE TALKING ABOUT.
Peirce

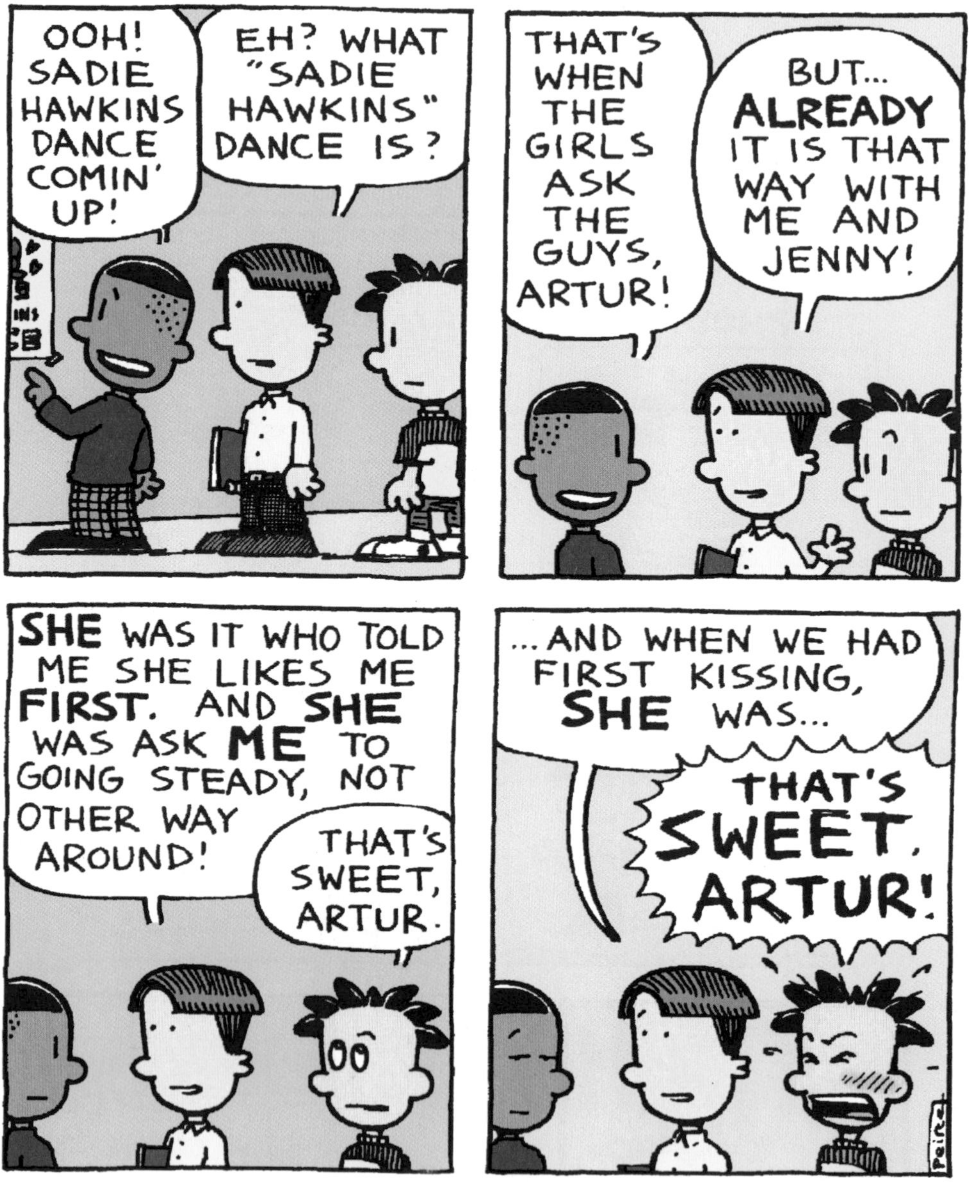
OOH! SADIE HAWKINS DANCE COMIN' UP!
EH? WHAT "SADIE HAWKINS" DANCE IS?
THAT'S WHEN THE GIRLS ASK THE GUYS, ARTUR!
BUT... ALREADY IT IS THAT WAY WITH ME AND JENNY!
SHE WAS IT WHO TOLD ME SHE LIKES ME FIRST. AND SHE WAS ASK ME TO GOING STEADY, NOT OTHER WAY AROUND!
THAT'S SWEET, ARTUR.
...AND WHEN WE HAD FIRST KISSING, SHE WAS...
THAT'S SWEET, ARTUR!
Peirce

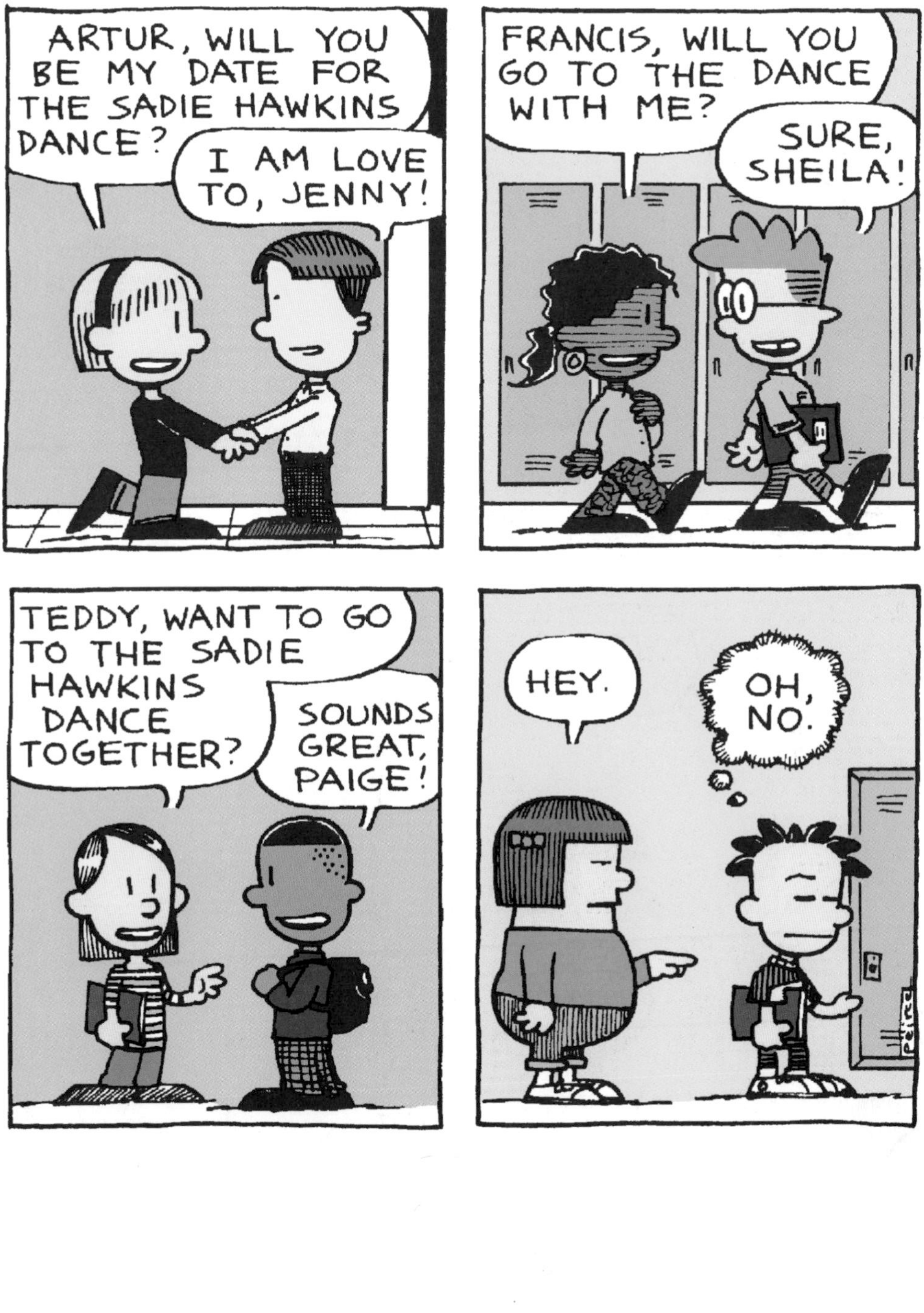
ARTUR, WILL YOU BE MY DATE FOR THE SADIE HAWKINS DANCE?
I AM LOVE TO, JENNY!
FRANCIS, WILL YOU GO TO THE DANCE WITH ME?
SURE, SHEILA!
TEDDY, WANT TO GO TO THE SADIE HAWKINS DANCE TOGETHER?
SOUNDS GREAT, PAIGE!
HEY.
OH, NO.

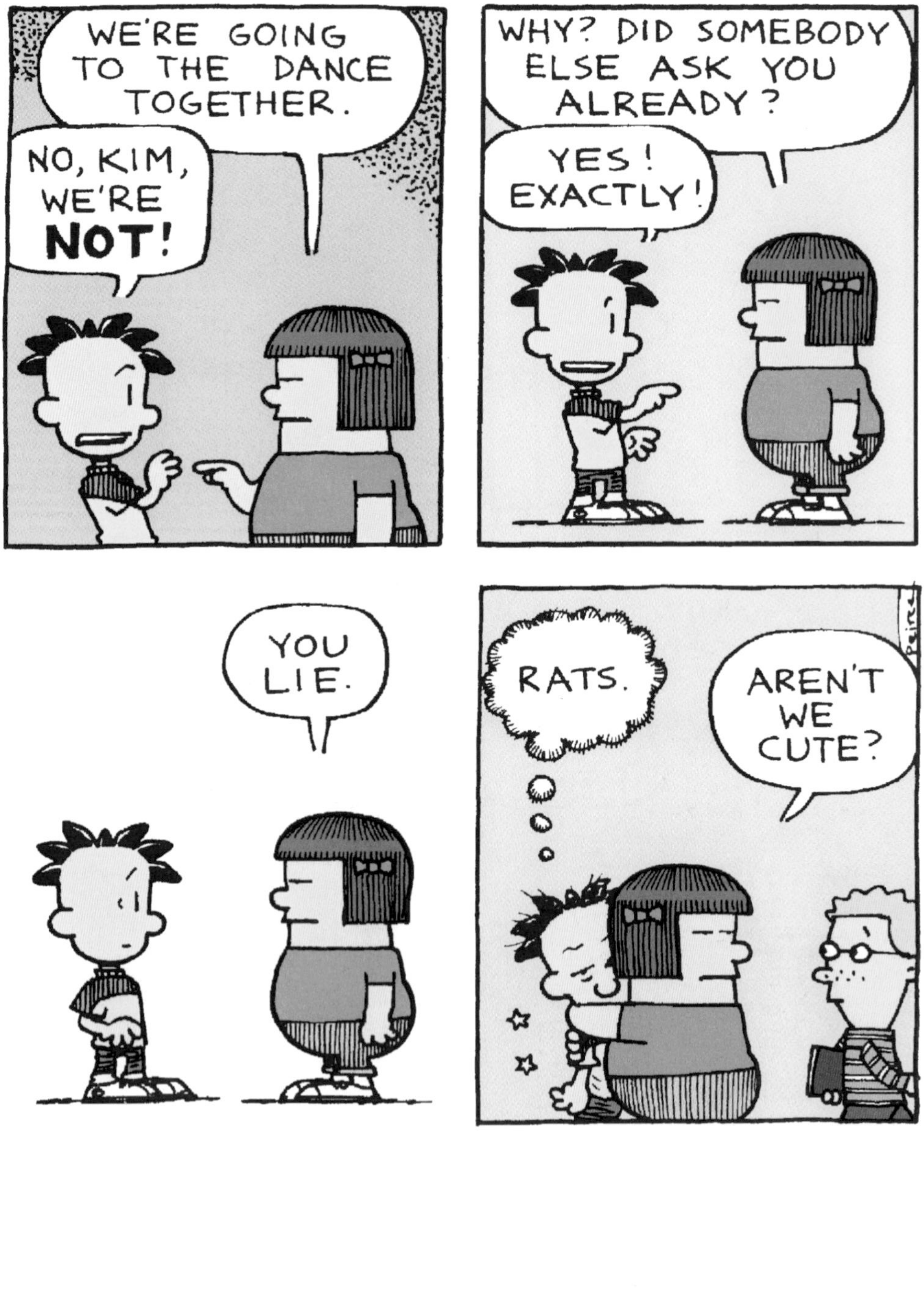

WE'RE GOING TO THE DANCE TOGETHER.
NO, KIM, WE'RE **NOT**!
WHY? DID SOMEBODY ELSE ASK YOU ALREADY?
YES! EXACTLY!
YOU LIE.
RATS.
AREN'T WE CUTE?

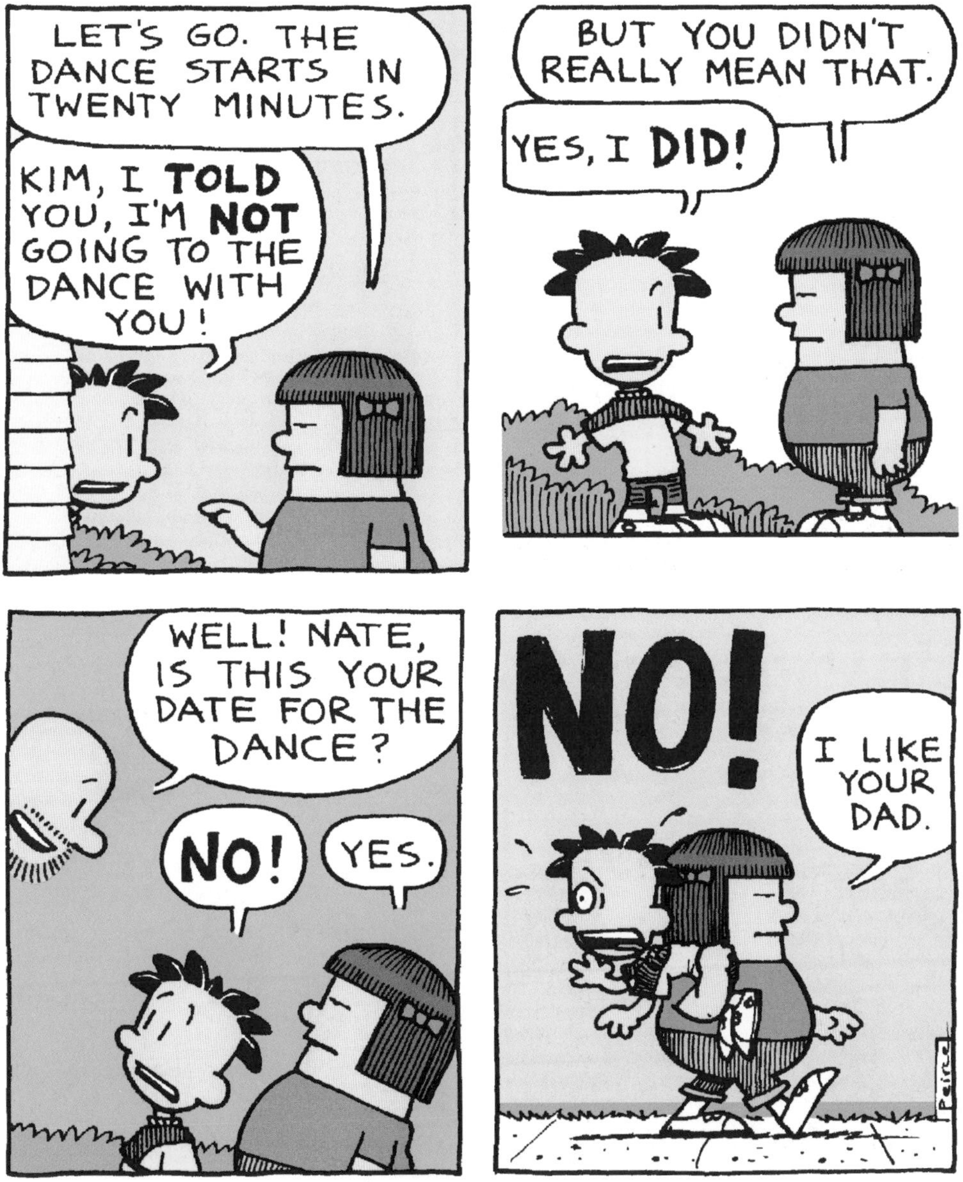
LET'S GO. THE DANCE STARTS IN TWENTY MINUTES.
KIM, I **TOLD** YOU, I'M **NOT** GOING TO THE DANCE WITH YOU!
BUT YOU DIDN'T REALLY MEAN THAT.
YES, I **DID**!
WELL! NATE, IS THIS YOUR DATE FOR THE DANCE?
NO!
YES.
NO!
I LIKE YOUR DAD.
Peirce

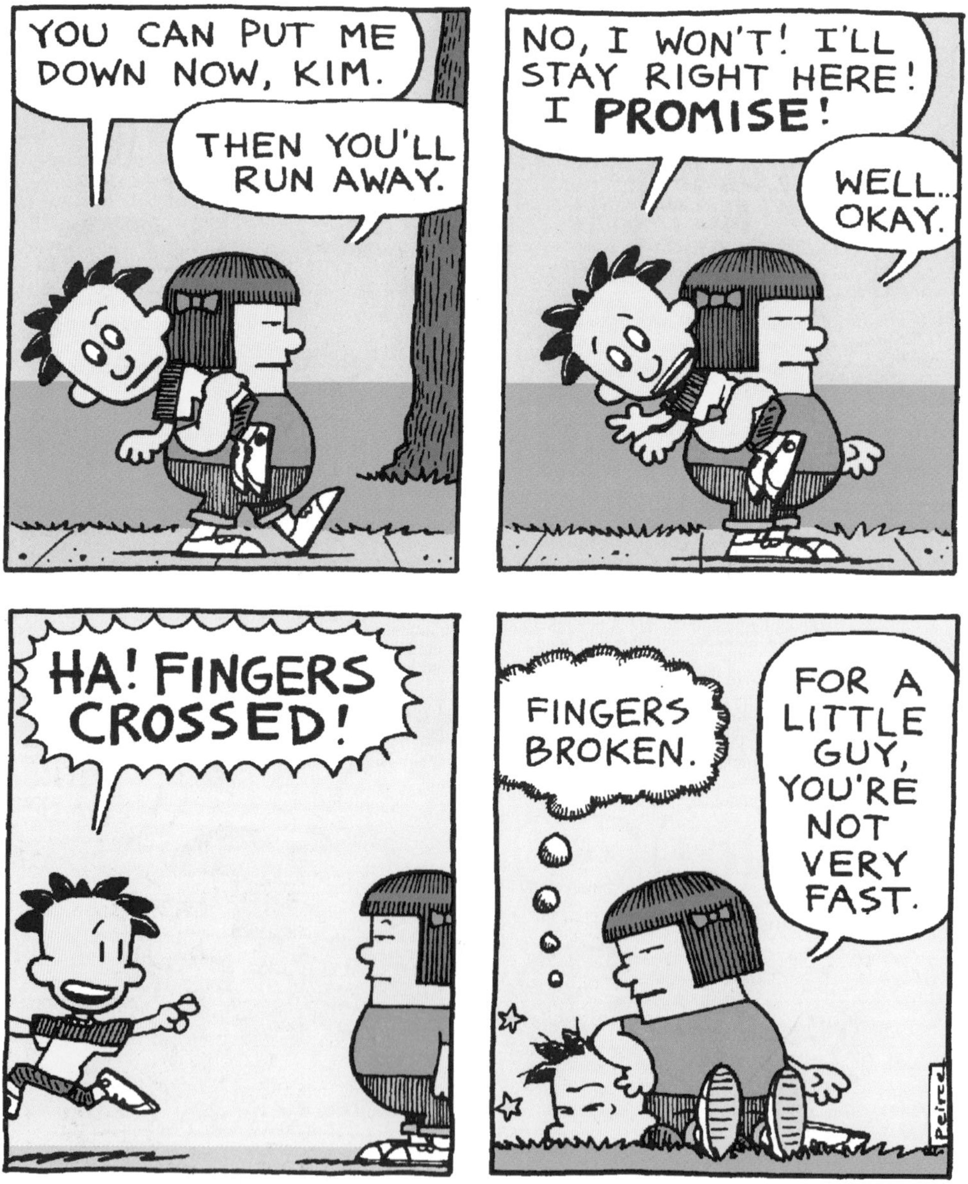
YOU CAN PUT ME DOWN NOW, KIM.
THEN YOU'LL RUN AWAY.
NO, I WON'T! I'LL STAY RIGHT HERE! I **PROMISE**!
WELL... OKAY.
HA! FINGERS CROSSED!
FINGERS BROKEN.
FOR A LITTLE GUY, YOU'RE NOT VERY FAST.
Peirce

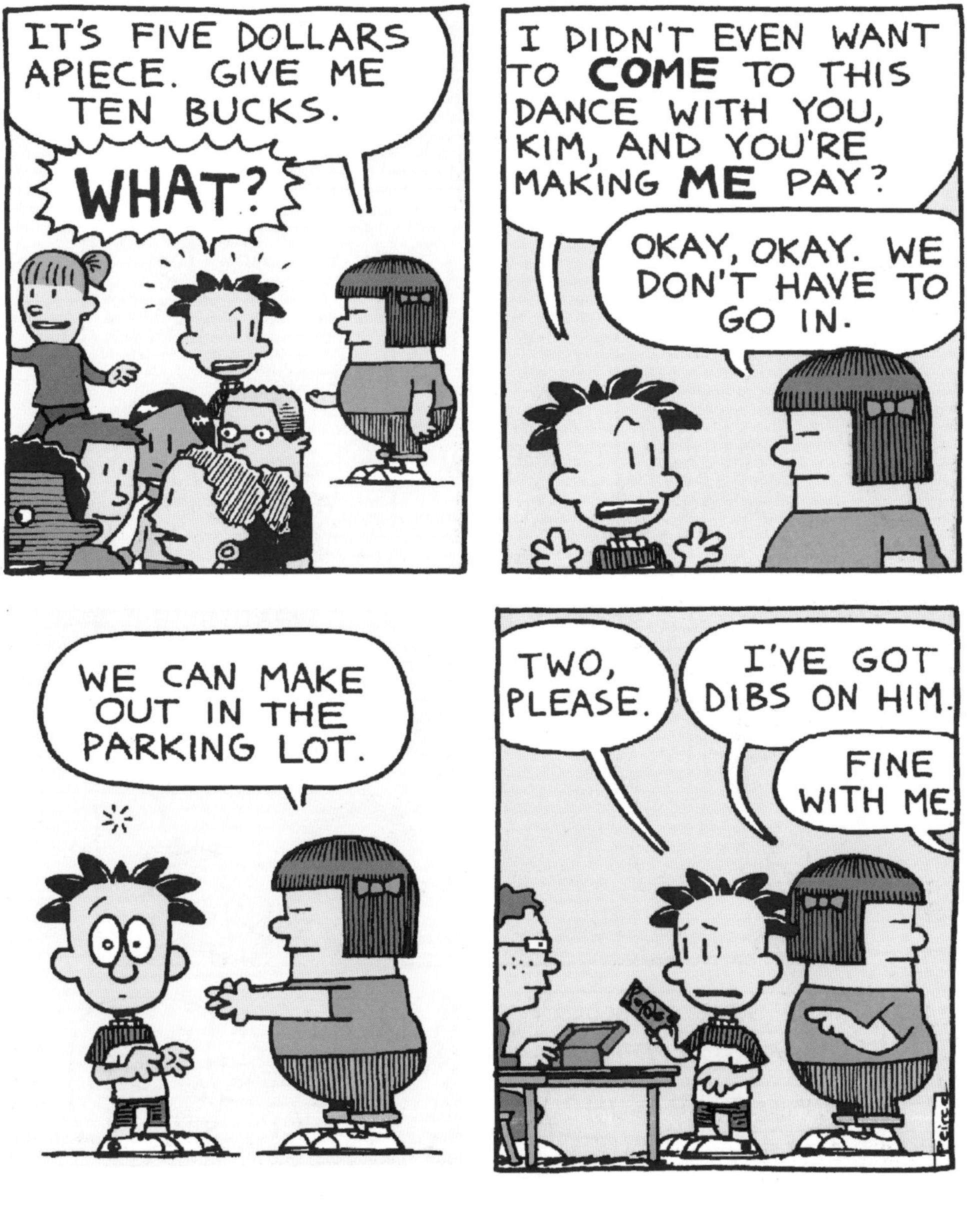
IT'S FIVE DOLLARS APIECE. GIVE ME TEN BUCKS.
WHAT?
I DIDN'T EVEN WANT TO **COME** TO THIS DANCE WITH YOU, KIM, AND YOU'RE MAKING **ME** PAY?
OKAY, OKAY. WE DON'T HAVE TO GO IN.
WE CAN MAKE OUT IN THE PARKING LOT.
TWO, PLEASE.
I'VE GOT DIBS ON HIM.
FINE WITH ME.
Peirce

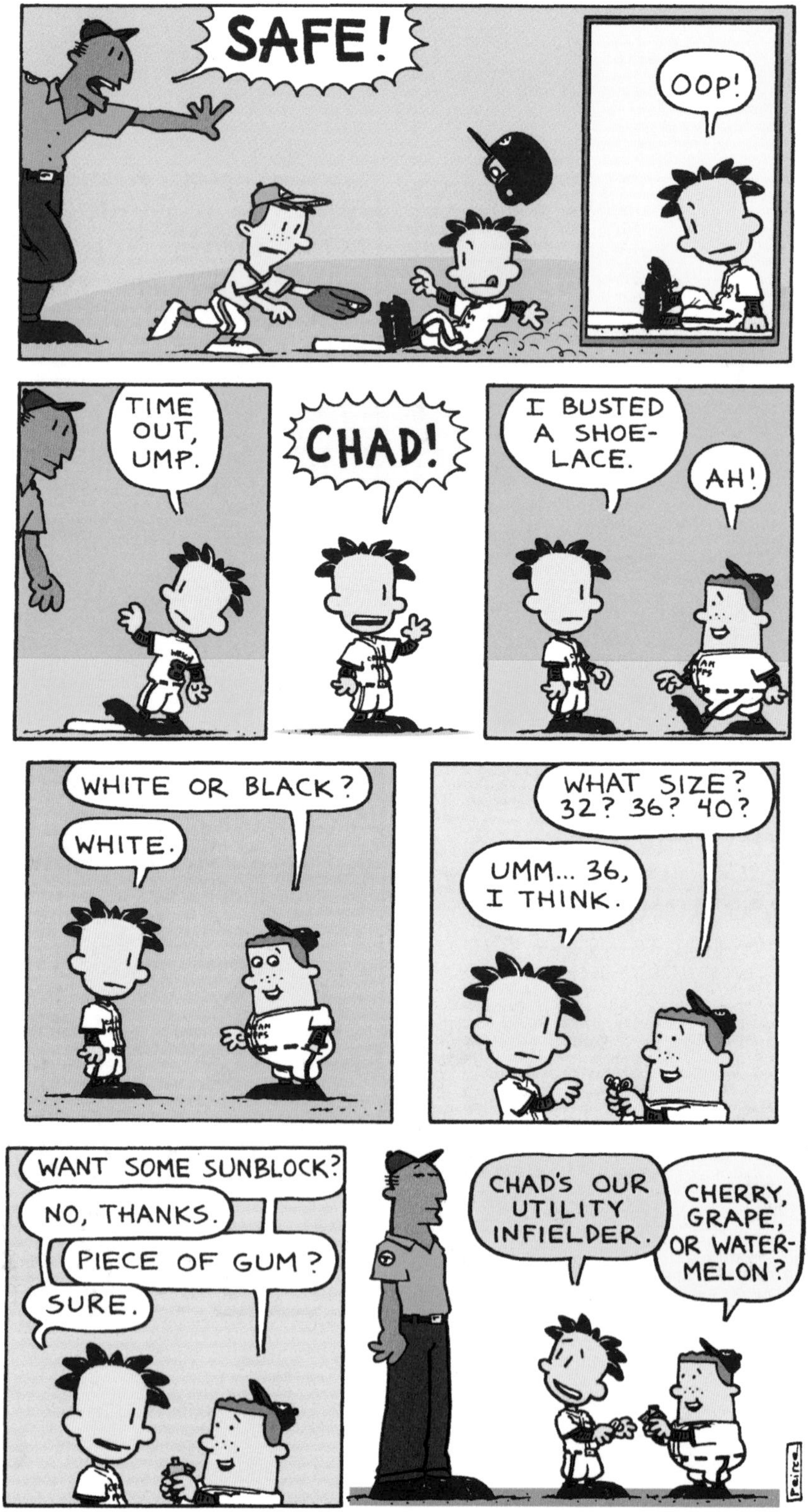
SAFE!
OOP!
TIME OUT, UMP.
CHAD!
I BUSTED A SHOE-LACE.
AH!
WHITE OR BLACK?
WHITE.
WHAT SIZE? 32? 36? 40?
UMM... 36, I THINK.
WANT SOME SUNBLOCK?
NO, THANKS.
PIECE OF GUM?
SURE.
CHAD'S OUR UTILITY INFIELDER.
CHERRY, GRAPE, OR WATER-MELON?
Peirce

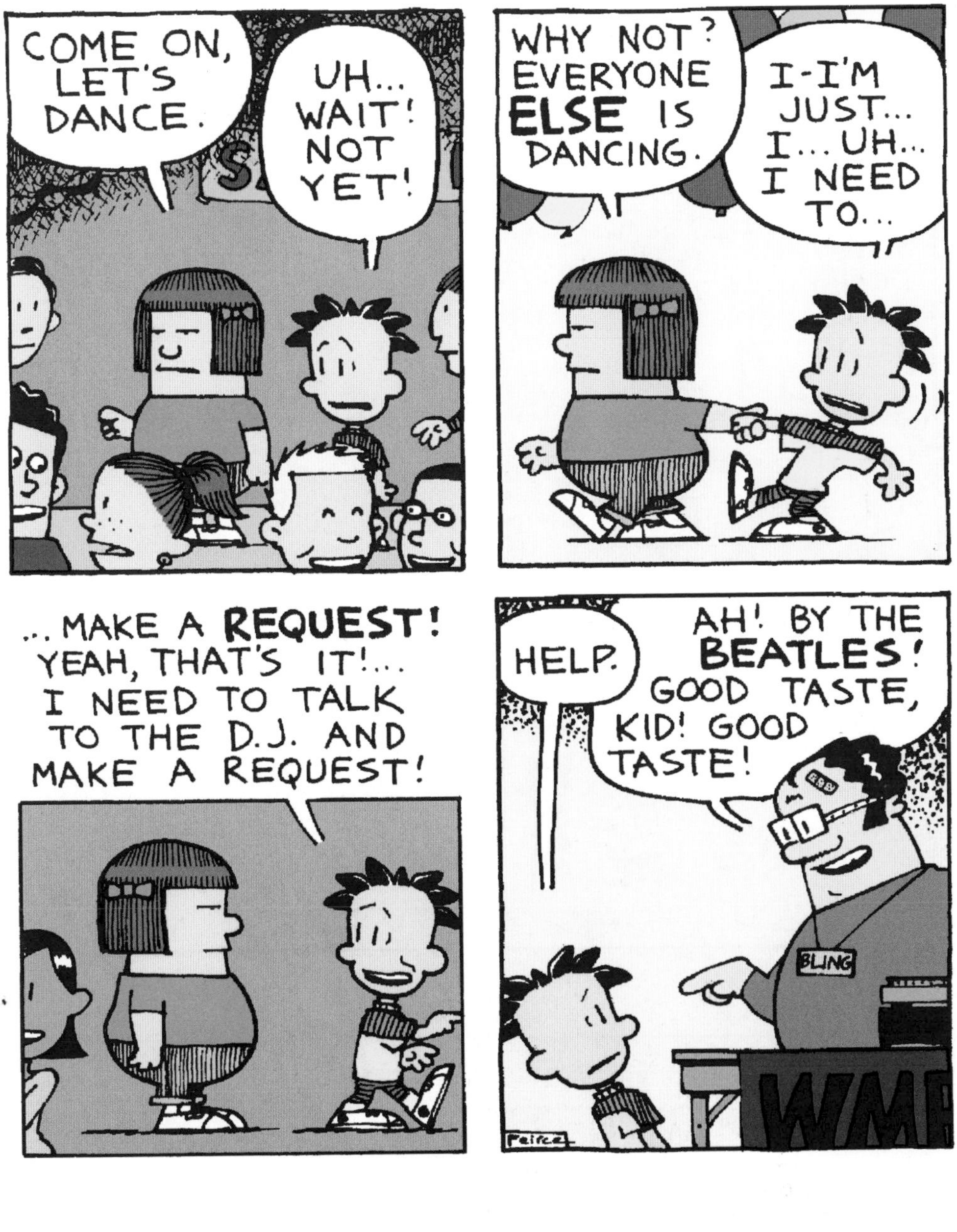
COME ON, LET'S DANCE.
UH... WAIT! NOT YET!
WHY NOT? EVERYONE ELSE IS DANCING.
I-I'M JUST... I... UH... I NEED TO...
... MAKE A REQUEST! YEAH, THAT'S IT!... I NEED TO TALK TO THE D.J. AND MAKE A REQUEST!
HELP.
AH! BY THE BEATLES! GOOD TASTE, KID! GOOD TASTE!
BLING

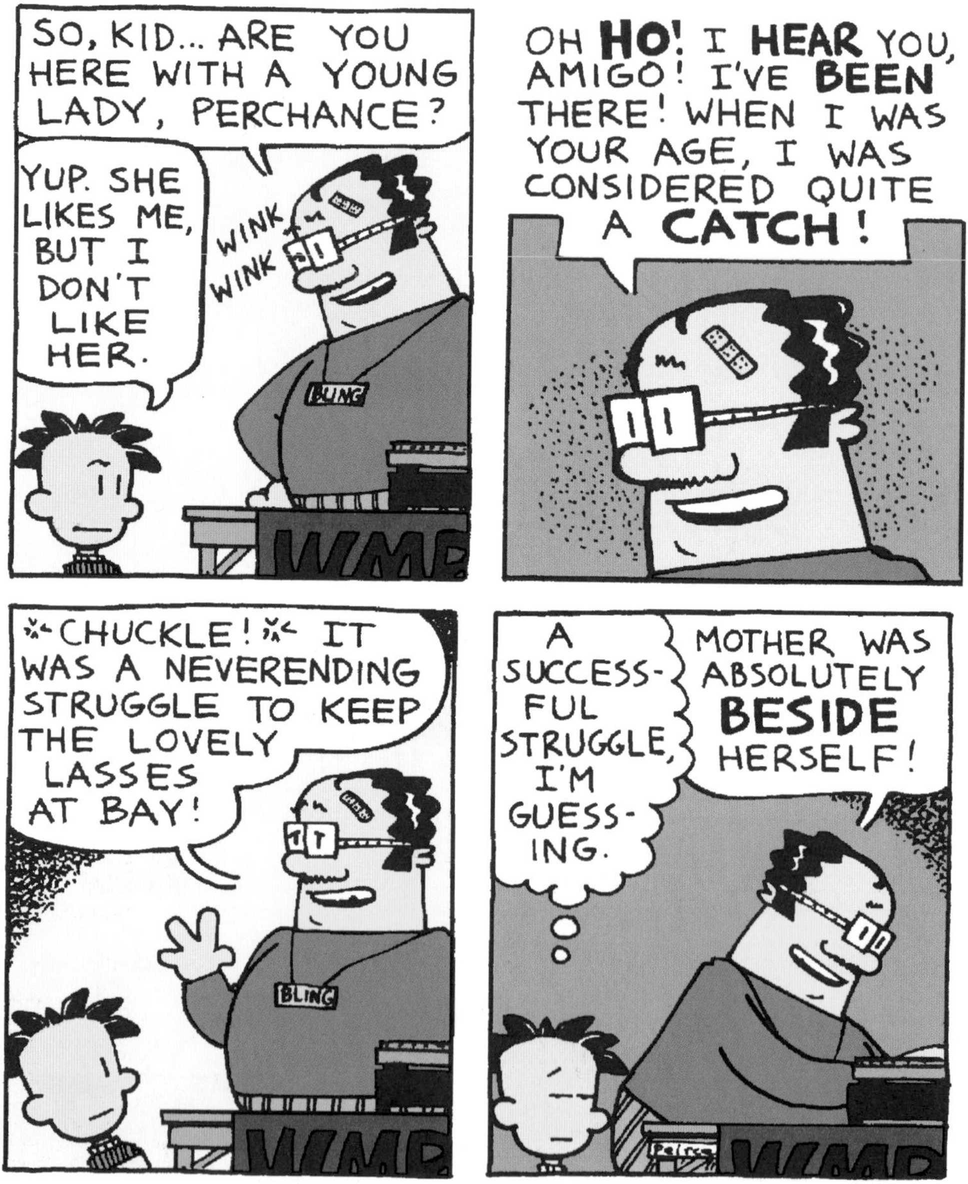
SO, KID... ARE YOU HERE WITH A YOUNG LADY, PERCHANCE?
YUP. SHE LIKES ME, BUT I DON'T LIKE HER.
WINK WINK
BLING
WIMP
OH HO! I HEAR YOU, AMIGO! I'VE BEEN THERE! WHEN I WAS YOUR AGE, I WAS CONSIDERED QUITE A CATCH!
CHUCKLE! IT WAS A NEVERENDING STRUGGLE TO KEEP THE LOVELY LASSES AT BAY!
BLING
WIMP
A SUCCESSFUL STRUGGLE, I'M GUESSING.
MOTHER WAS ABSOLUTELY BESIDE HERSELF!
Peirce
WIMP

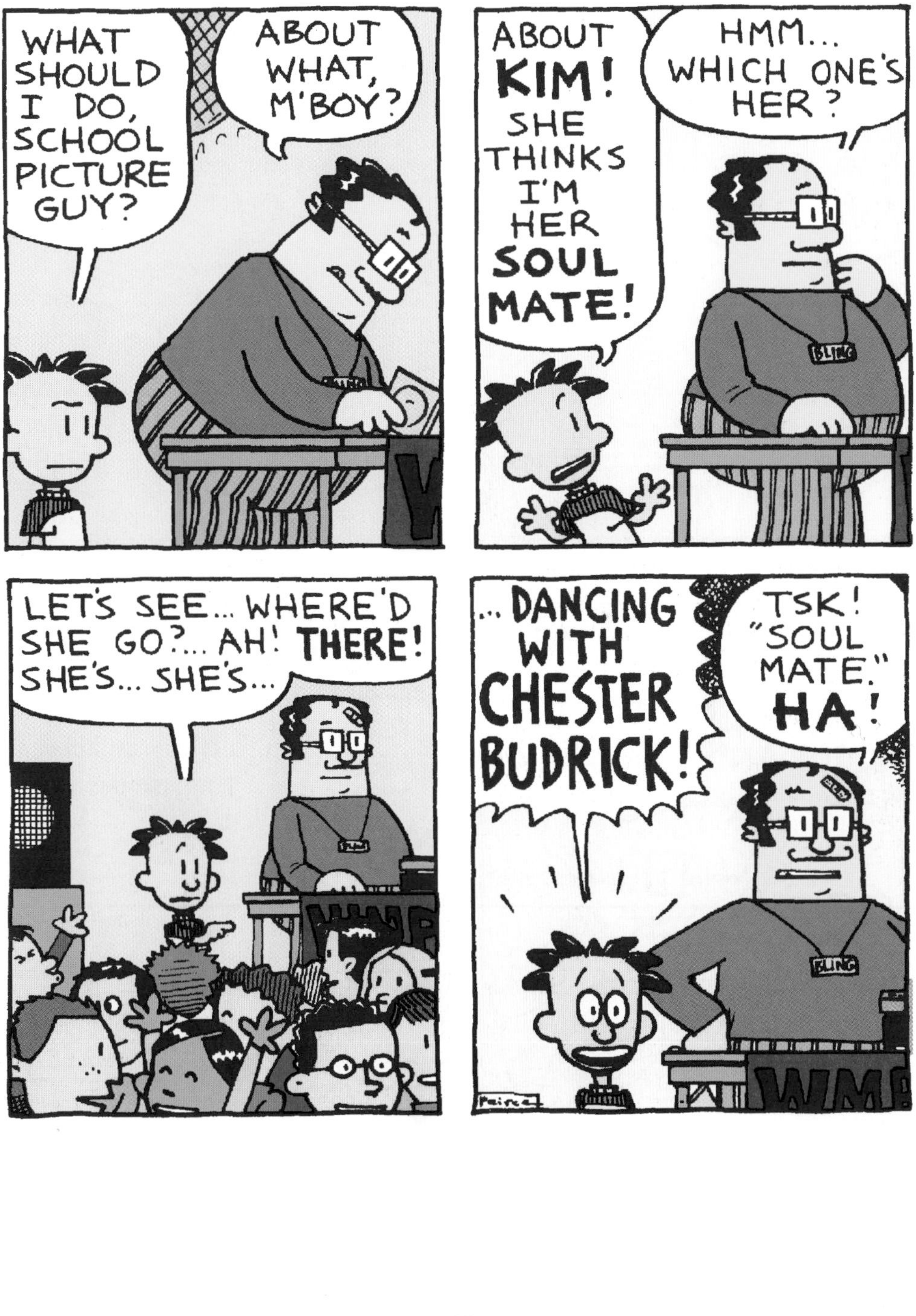
WHAT SHOULD I DO, SCHOOL PICTURE GUY?
ABOUT WHAT, M'BOY?
ABOUT KIM! SHE THINKS I'M HER SOUL MATE!
HMM... WHICH ONE'S HER?
LET'S SEE... WHERE'D SHE GO?... AH! THERE! SHE'S... SHE'S...
...DANCING WITH CHESTER BUDRICK!
TSK! "SOUL MATE." HA!
BLING
BLING
BLING
WIMP
WIMP
Peirce

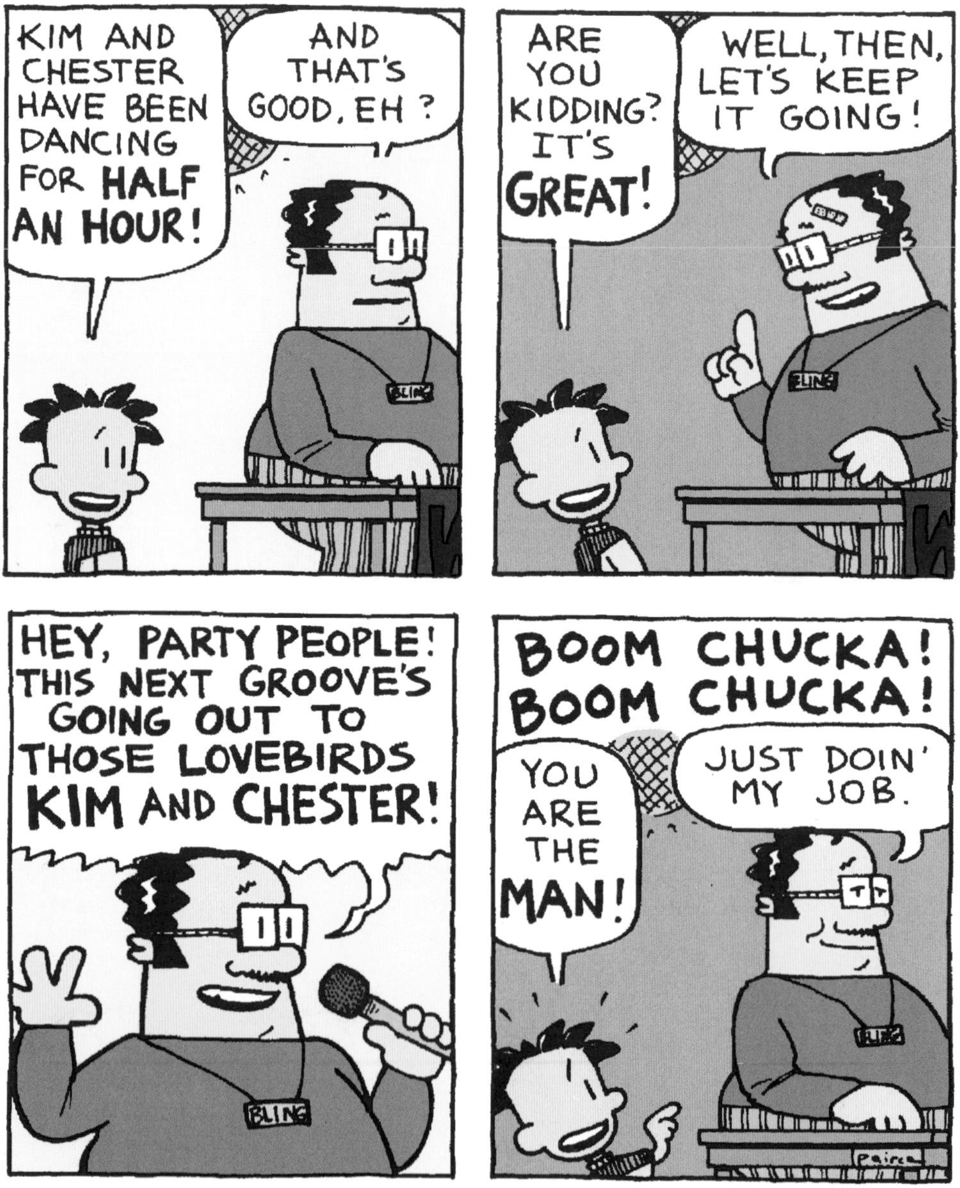
KIM AND CHESTER HAVE BEEN DANCING FOR HALF AN HOUR!
AND THAT'S GOOD, EH ?
BLING
ARE YOU KIDDING? IT'S GREAT!
WELL, THEN, LET'S KEEP IT GOING!
BLING
HEY, PARTY PEOPLE! THIS NEXT GROOVE'S GOING OUT TO THOSE LOVEBIRDS KIM AND CHESTER!
BLING
BOOM CHUCKA! BOOM CHUCKA!
YOU ARE THE MAN!
JUST DOIN' MY JOB.
BLING
Peirce

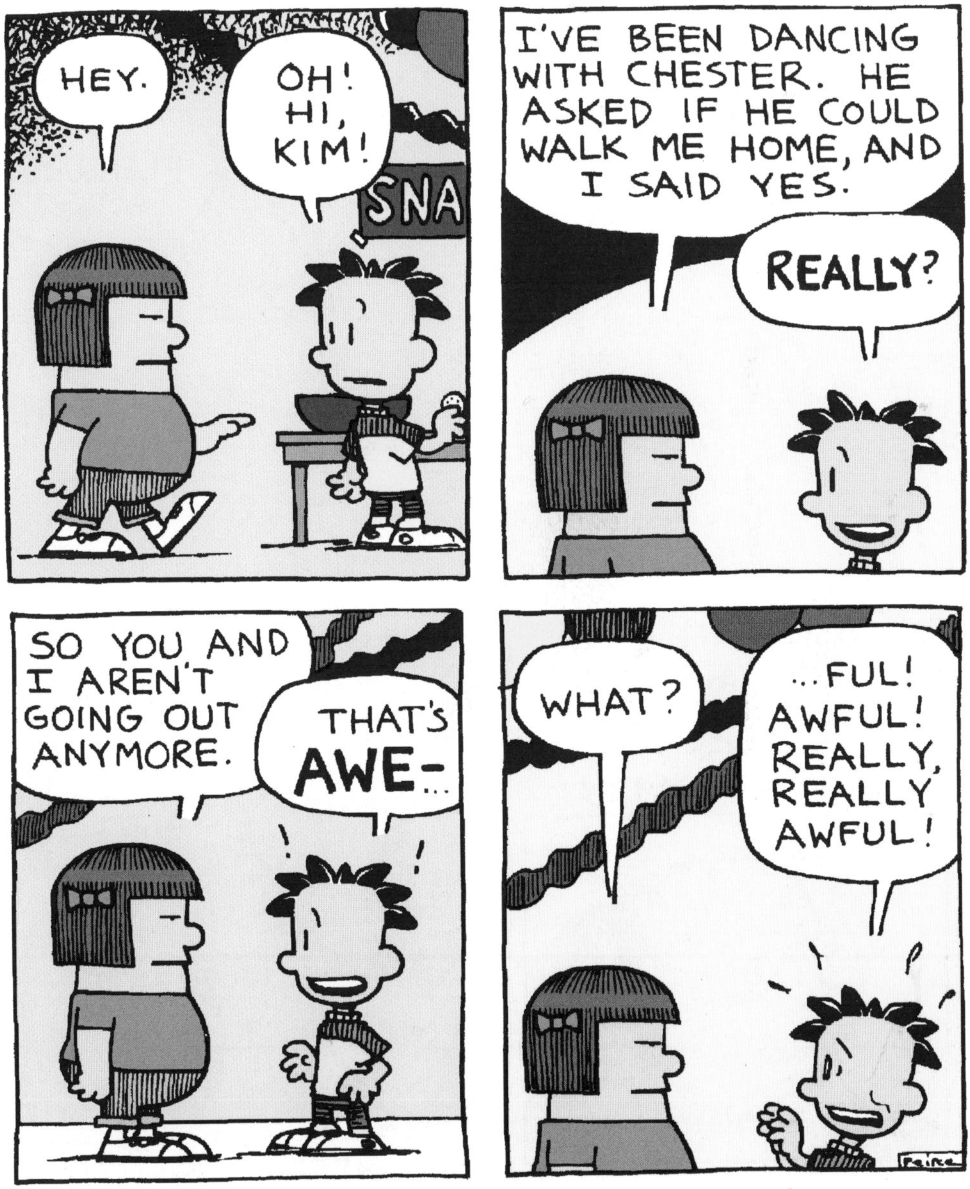
HEY.
OH! HI, KIM!
SNA
I'VE BEEN DANCING WITH CHESTER. HE ASKED IF HE COULD WALK ME HOME, AND I SAID YES.
REALLY?
SO YOU AND I AREN'T GOING OUT ANYMORE.
THAT'S AWE-...
WHAT?
...FUL! AWFUL! REALLY, REALLY AWFUL!

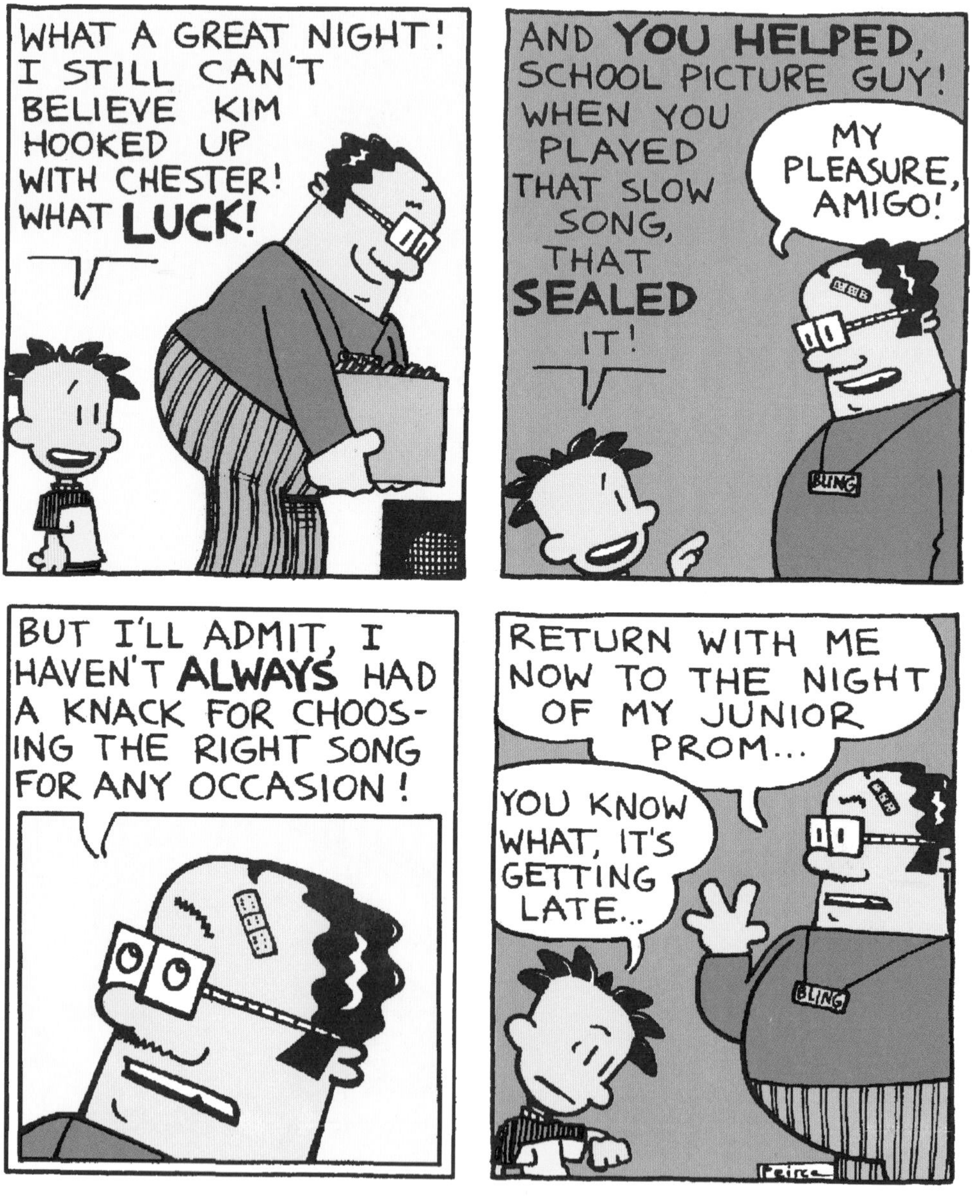
WHAT A GREAT NIGHT! I STILL CAN'T BELIEVE KIM HOOKED UP WITH CHESTER! WHAT LUCK!
AND YOU HELPED, SCHOOL PICTURE GUY! WHEN YOU PLAYED THAT SLOW SONG, THAT SEALED IT!
MY PLEASURE, AMIGO!
BLING
BUT I'LL ADMIT, I HAVEN'T ALWAYS HAD A KNACK FOR CHOOSING THE RIGHT SONG FOR ANY OCCASION!
RETURN WITH ME NOW TO THE NIGHT OF MY JUNIOR PROM...
YOU KNOW WHAT, IT'S GETTING LATE...
BLING
Peirce

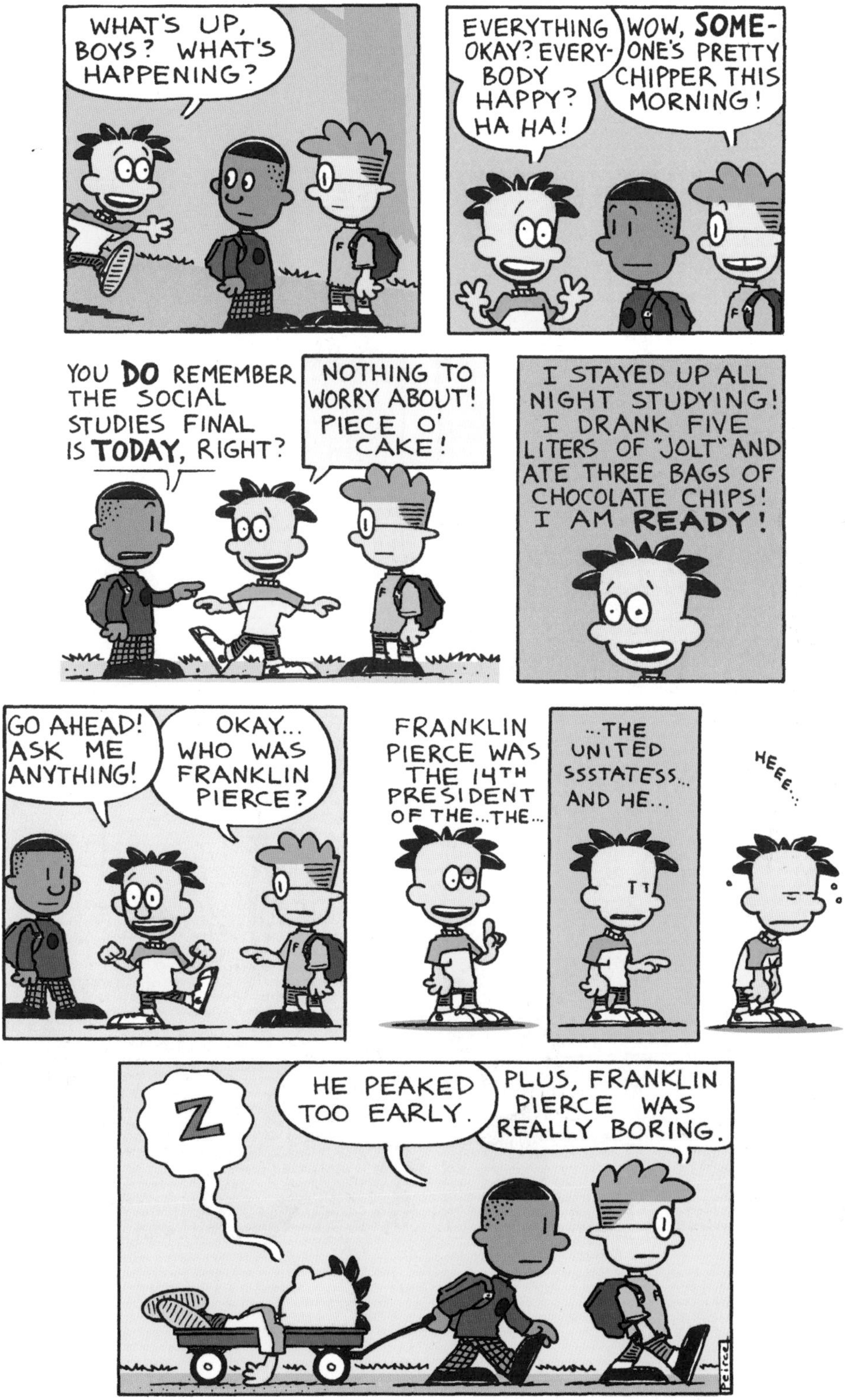
WHAT'S UP, BOYS? WHAT'S HAPPENING?
EVERYTHING OKAY? EVERY-BODY HAPPY? HA HA!
WOW, SOME-ONE'S PRETTY CHIPPER THIS MORNING!
YOU DO REMEMBER THE SOCIAL STUDIES FINAL IS TODAY, RIGHT?
NOTHING TO WORRY ABOUT! PIECE O' CAKE!
I STAYED UP ALL NIGHT STUDYING! I DRANK FIVE LITERS OF "JOLT" AND ATE THREE BAGS OF CHOCOLATE CHIPS! I AM READY!
GO AHEAD! ASK ME ANYTHING!
OKAY... WHO WAS FRANKLIN PIERCE?
FRANKLIN PIERCE WAS THE 14TH PRESIDENT OF THE...THE...
...THE UNITED SSSTATESS... AND HE...
HEEE...
Z
HE PEAKED TOO EARLY.
PLUS, FRANKLIN PIERCE WAS REALLY BORING.
Peirce

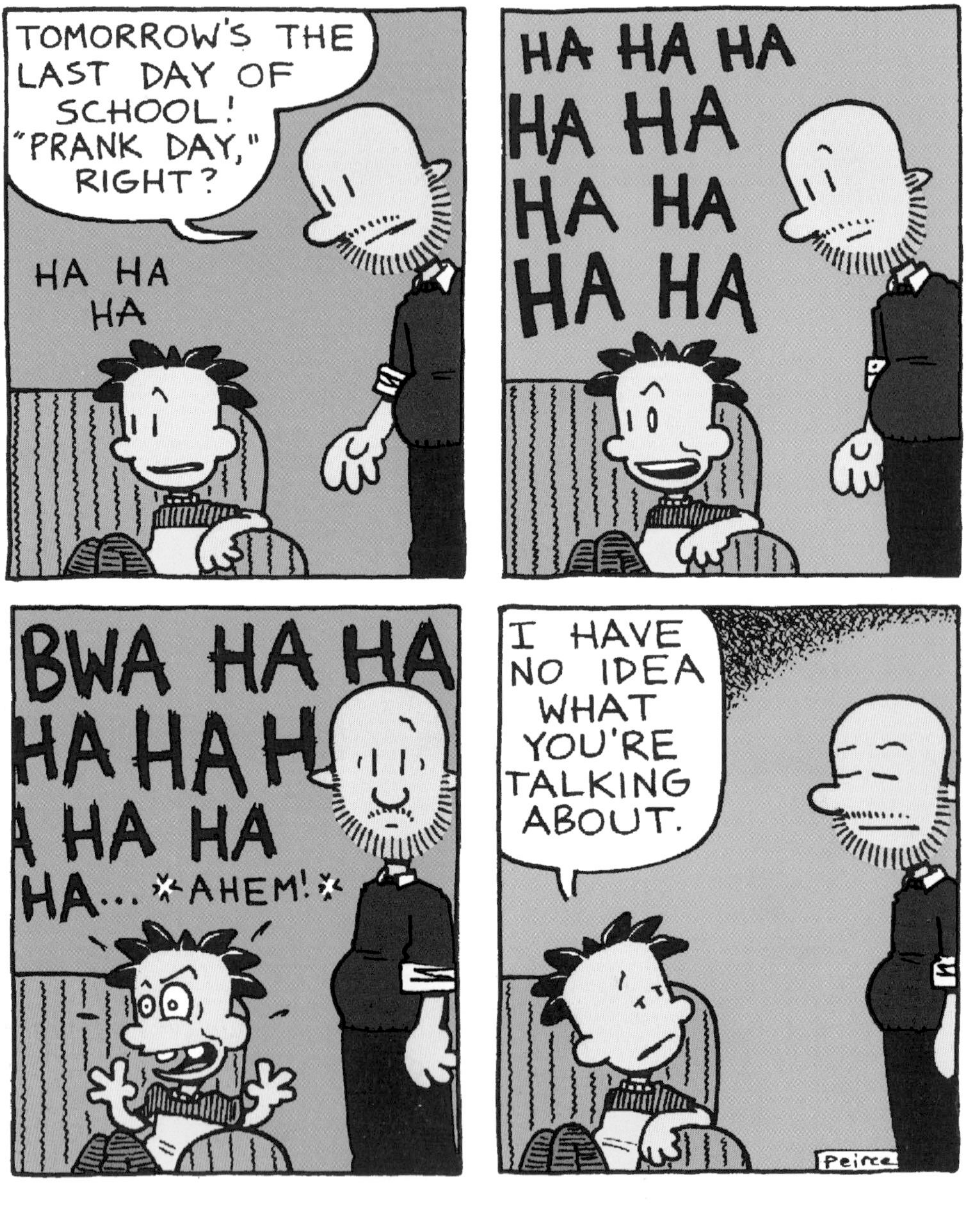
TOMORROW'S THE LAST DAY OF SCHOOL! "PRANK DAY," RIGHT?
HA HA HA
HA HA HA HA HA HA HA HA HA HA
BWA HA HA HA HA HA H A HA HA HA... *AHEM!*
I HAVE NO IDEA WHAT YOU'RE TALKING ABOUT.
Peirce

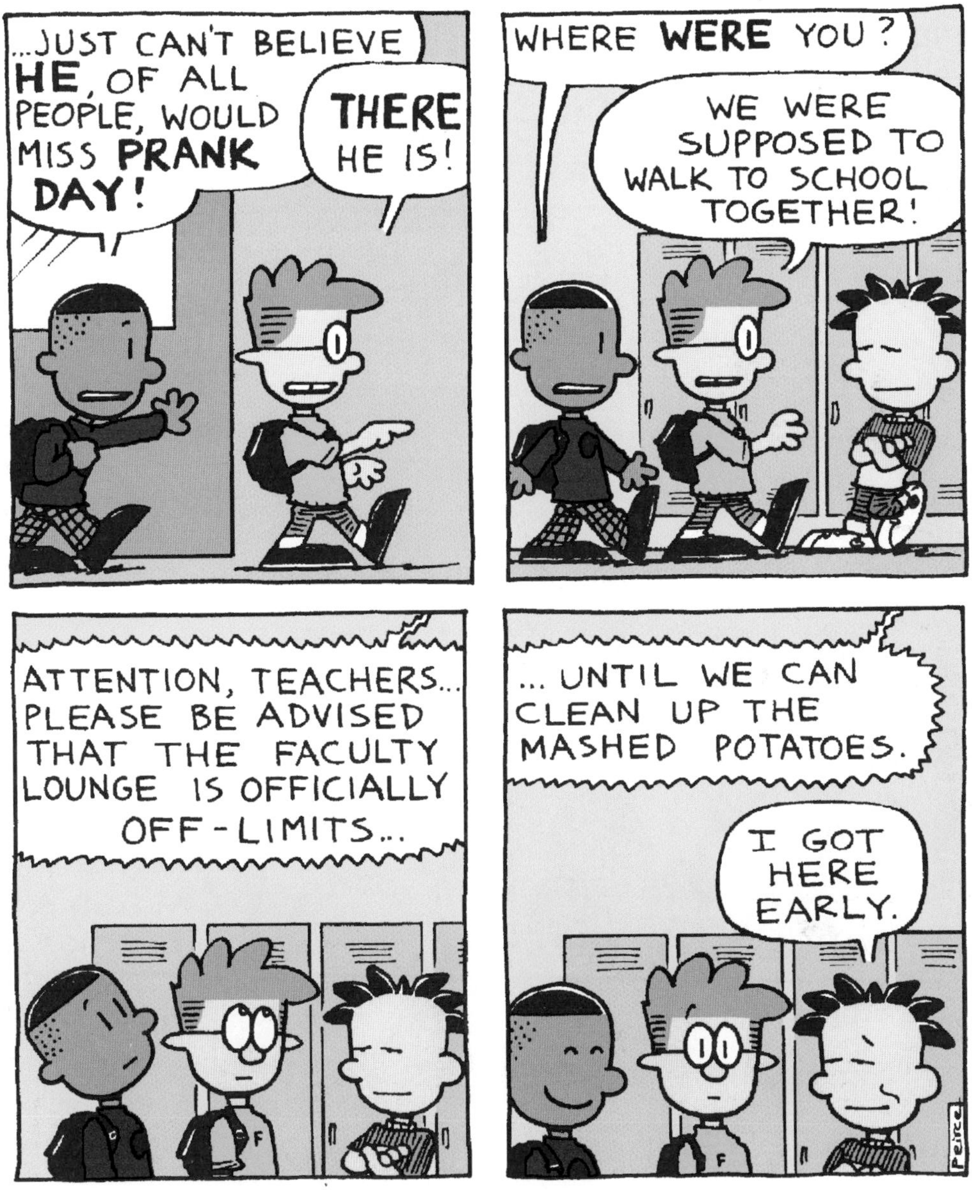
...JUST CAN'T BELIEVE **HE**, OF ALL PEOPLE, WOULD MISS **PRANK DAY**!
THERE HE IS!
WHERE **WERE** YOU?
WE WERE SUPPOSED TO WALK TO SCHOOL TOGETHER!
ATTENTION, TEACHERS... PLEASE BE ADVISED THAT THE FACULTY LOUNGE IS OFFICIALLY OFF-LIMITS...
... UNTIL WE CAN CLEAN UP THE MASHED POTATOES.
I GOT HERE EARLY.
Peirce

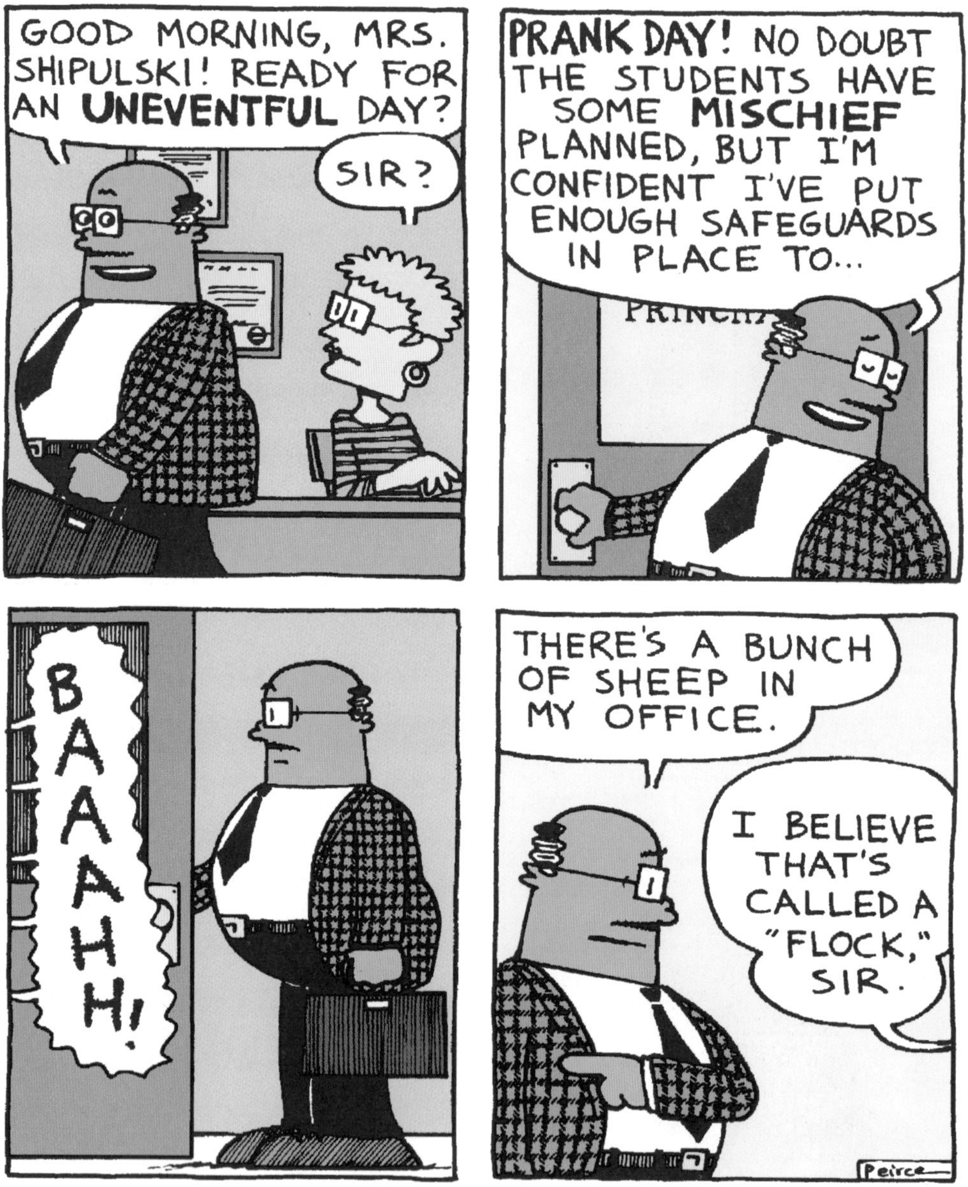
GOOD MORNING, MRS. SHIPULSKI! READY FOR AN **UNEVENTFUL** DAY?
SIR?
PRANK DAY! NO DOUBT THE STUDENTS HAVE SOME **MISCHIEF** PLANNED, BUT I'M CONFIDENT I'VE PUT ENOUGH SAFEGUARDS IN PLACE TO...
BAAAAHH!
THERE'S A BUNCH OF SHEEP IN MY OFFICE.
I BELIEVE THAT'S CALLED A "FLOCK," SIR.
Peirce

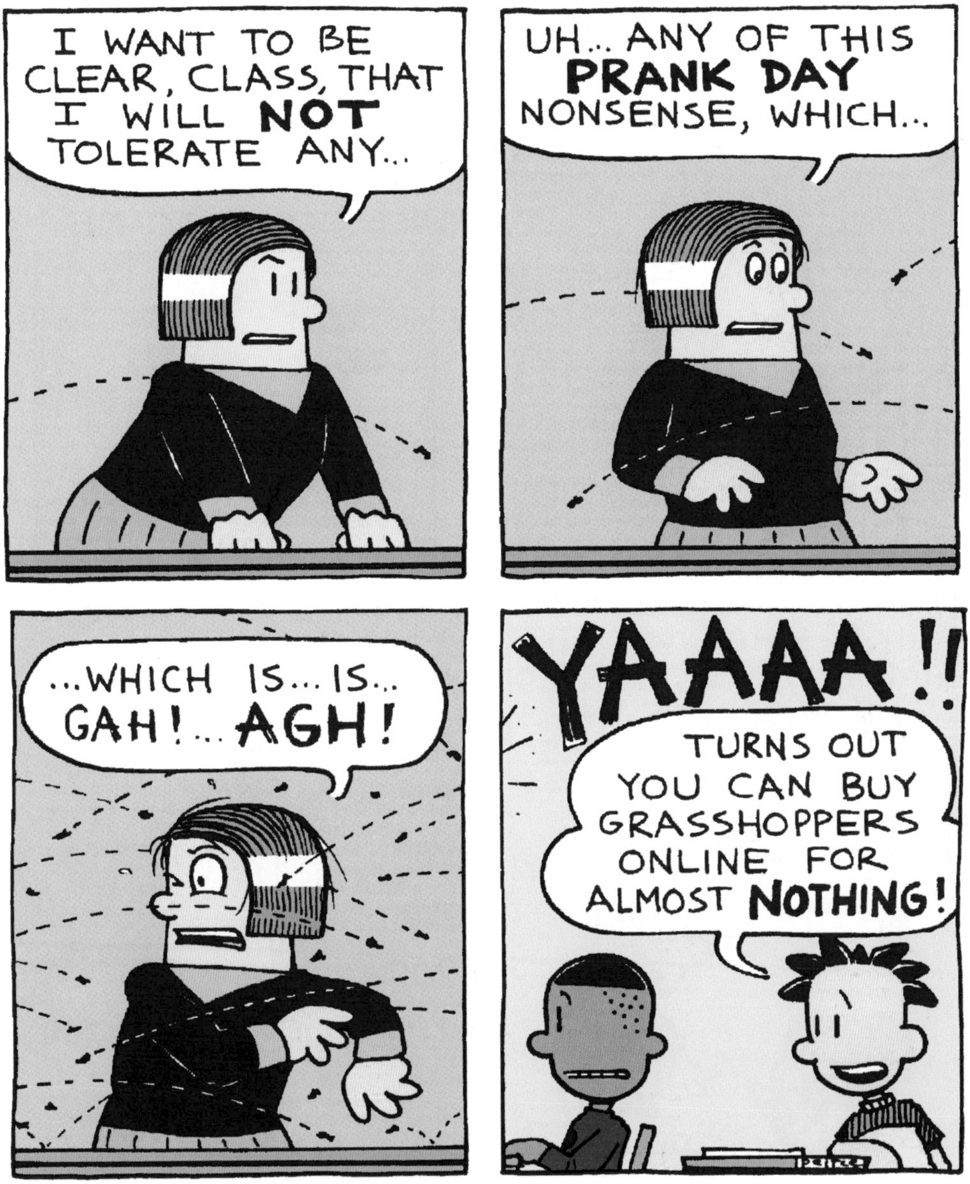
I WANT TO BE CLEAR, CLASS, THAT I WILL **NOT** TOLERATE ANY...
UH... ANY OF THIS **PRANK DAY** NONSENSE, WHICH...
...WHICH IS... IS... GAH!... **AGH!**
YAAAA!!
TURNS OUT YOU CAN BUY GRASSHOPPERS ONLINE FOR ALMOST **NOTHING**!

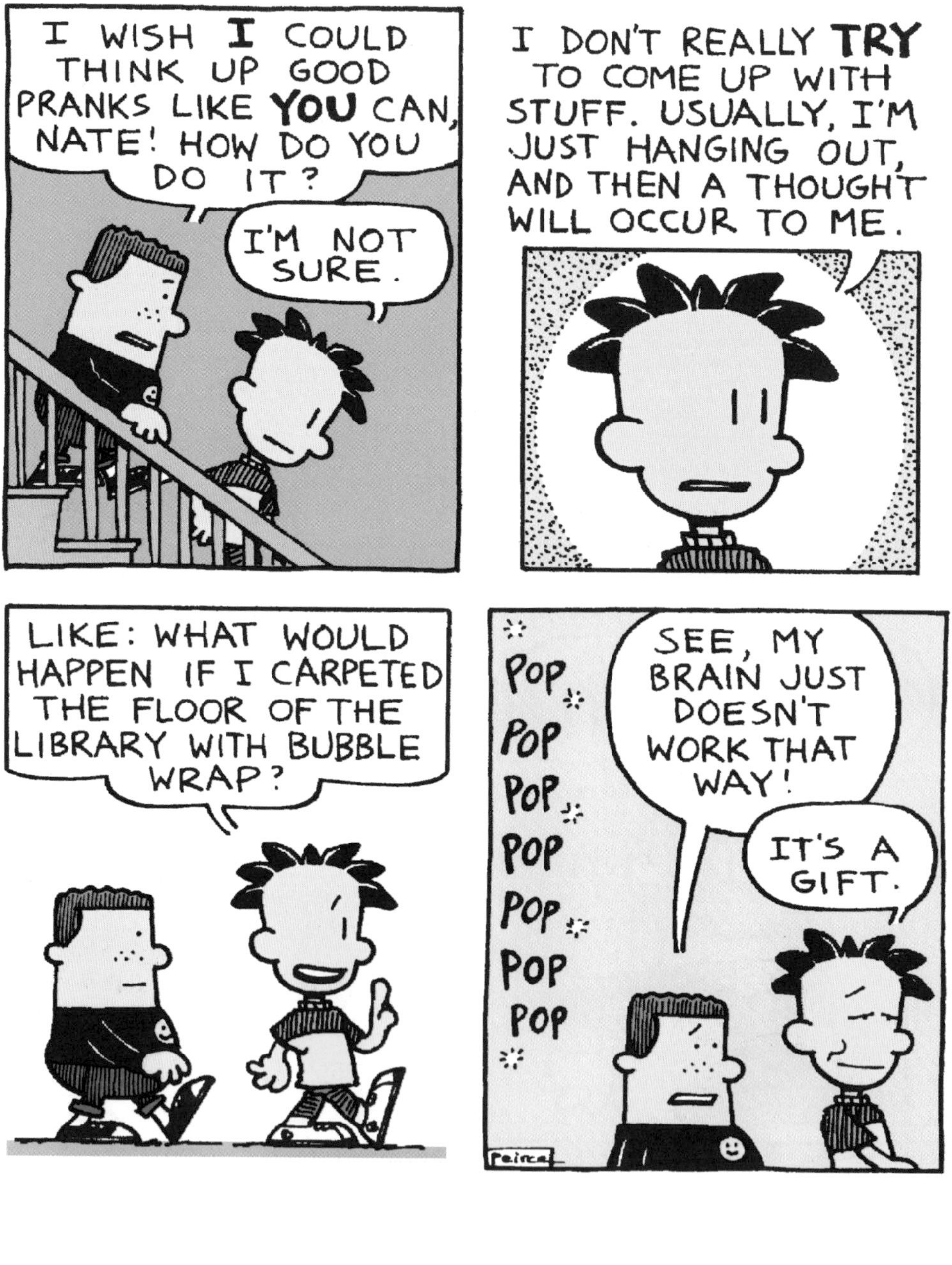
I WISH I COULD THINK UP GOOD PRANKS LIKE YOU CAN, NATE! HOW DO YOU DO IT?
I'M NOT SURE.
I DON'T REALLY TRY TO COME UP WITH STUFF. USUALLY, I'M JUST HANGING OUT, AND THEN A THOUGHT WILL OCCUR TO ME.
LIKE: WHAT WOULD HAPPEN IF I CARPETED THE FLOOR OF THE LIBRARY WITH BUBBLE WRAP?
POP
POP
POP
POP
POP
POP
POP
SEE, MY BRAIN JUST DOESN'T WORK THAT WAY!
IT'S A GIFT.
Peirce

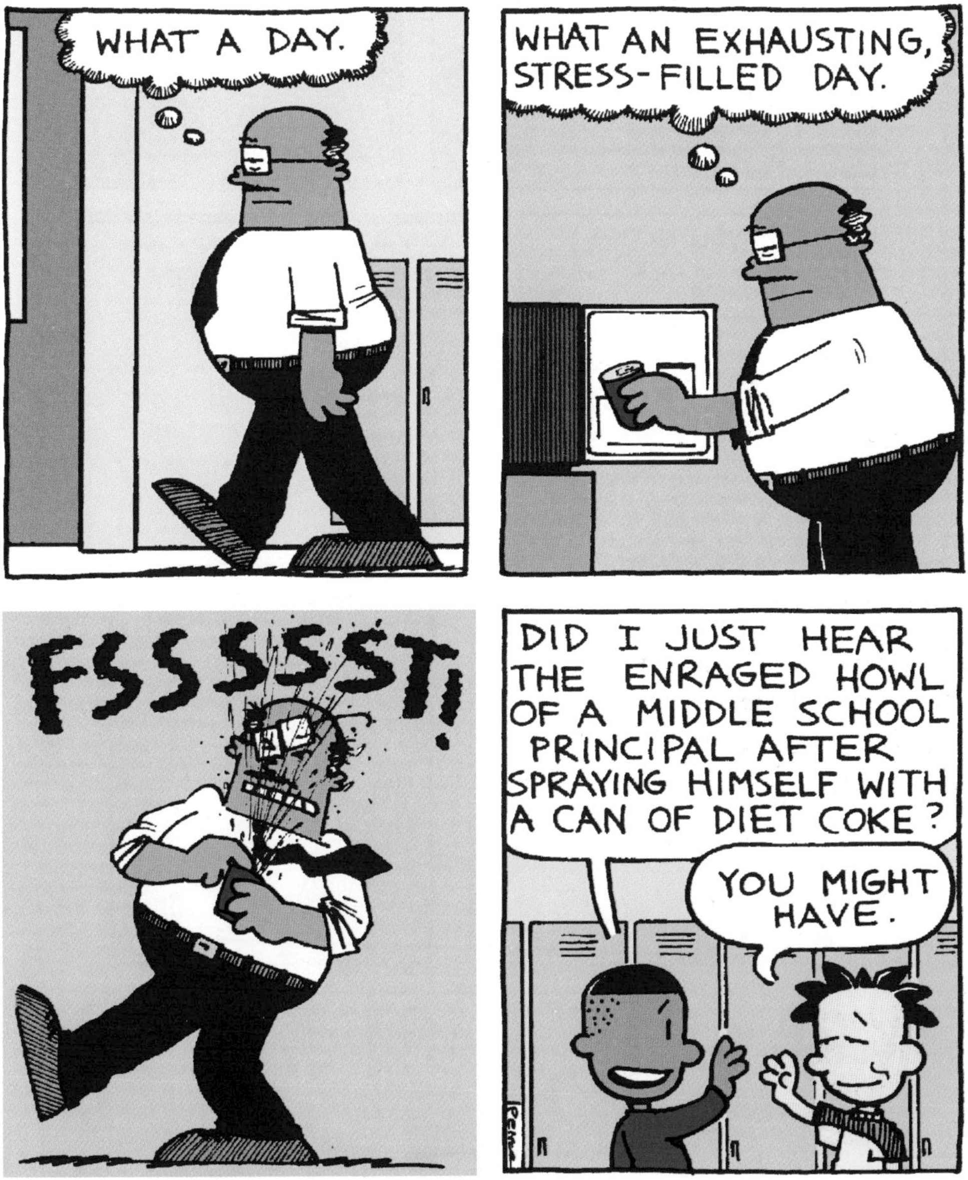
WHAT A DAY.
WHAT AN EXHAUSTING, STRESS-FILLED DAY.
FSSSSST!
DID I JUST HEAR THE ENRAGED HOWL OF A MIDDLE SCHOOL PRINCIPAL AFTER SPRAYING HIMSELF WITH A CAN OF DIET COKE?
YOU MIGHT HAVE.

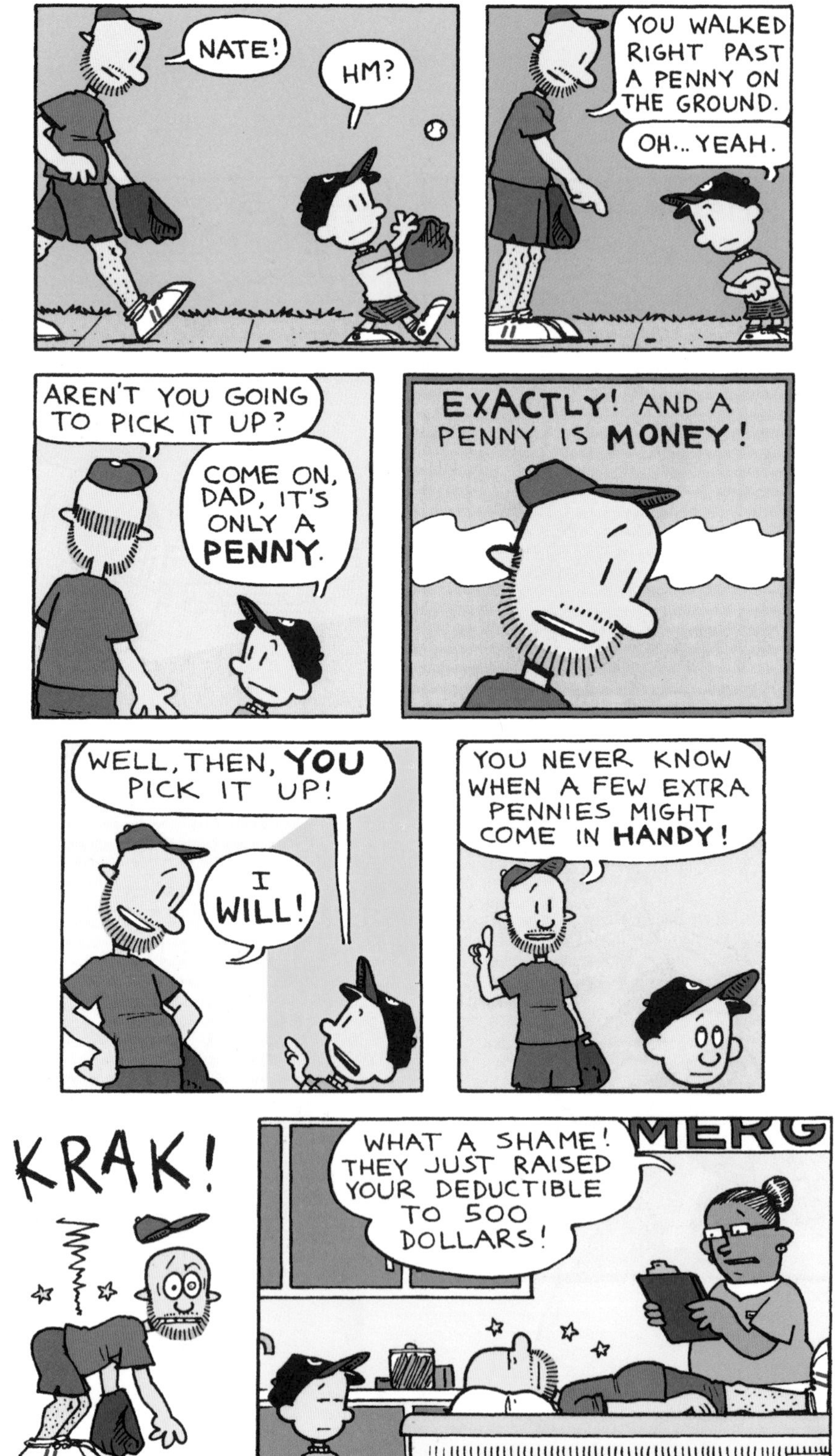
NATE!
HM?
YOU WALKED RIGHT PAST A PENNY ON THE GROUND.
OH... YEAH.
AREN'T YOU GOING TO PICK IT UP?
COME ON, DAD, IT'S ONLY A **PENNY**.
EXACTLY! AND A PENNY IS **MONEY**!
WELL, THEN, **YOU** PICK IT UP!
I **WILL**!
YOU NEVER KNOW WHEN A FEW EXTRA PENNIES MIGHT COME IN **HANDY**!
KRAK!
WHAT A SHAME! THEY JUST RAISED YOUR DEDUCTIBLE TO 500 DOLLARS!
MERG

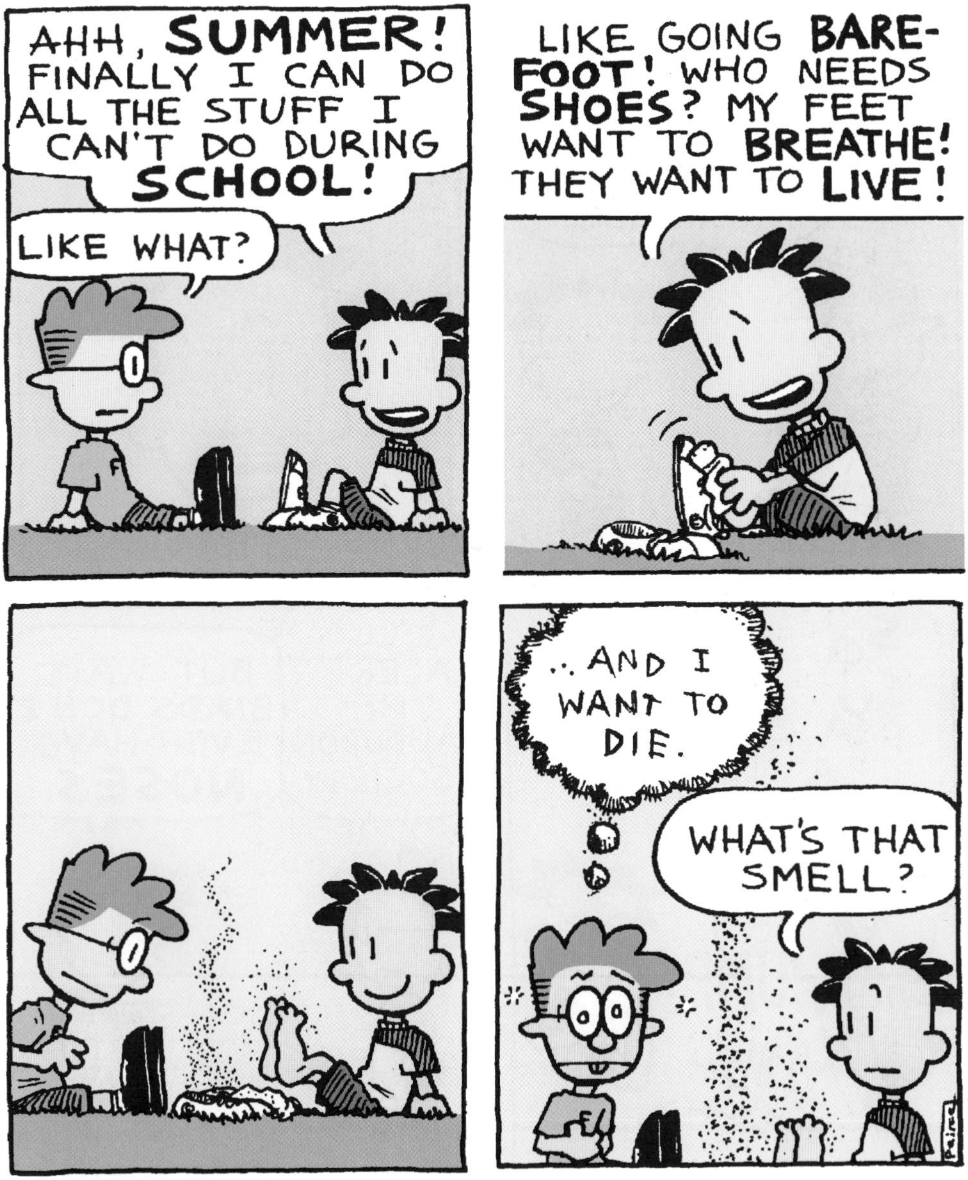

AHH, SUMMER! FINALLY I CAN DO ALL THE STUFF I CAN'T DO DURING SCHOOL!
LIKE WHAT?
LIKE GOING BARE-FOOT! WHO NEEDS SHOES? MY FEET WANT TO BREATHE! THEY WANT TO LIVE!
... AND I WANT TO DIE.
WHAT'S THAT SMELL?

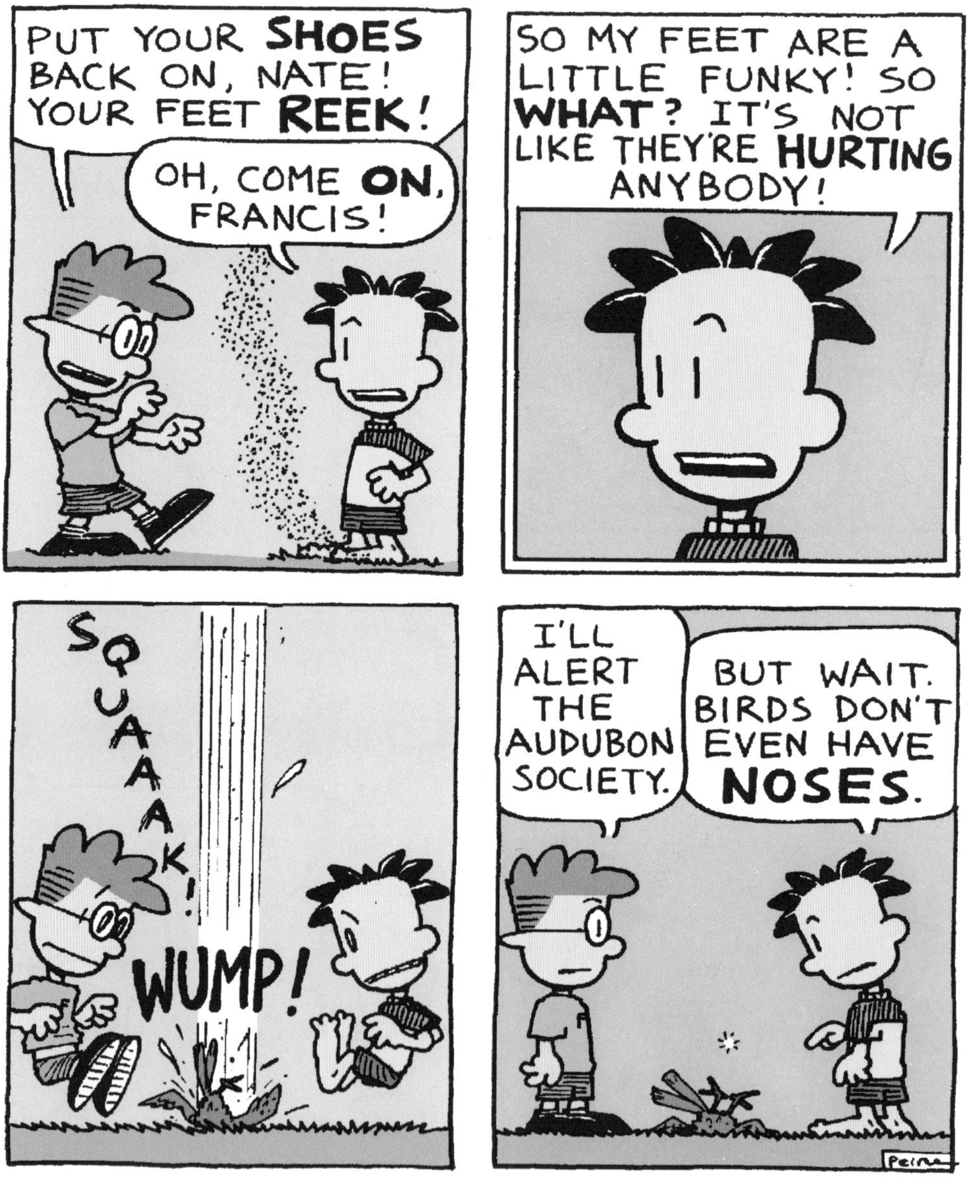
PUT YOUR SHOES BACK ON, NATE! YOUR FEET REEK!
OH, COME ON, FRANCIS!
SO MY FEET ARE A LITTLE FUNKY! SO WHAT? IT'S NOT LIKE THEY'RE HURTING ANYBODY!
SQUAAAAK!
WUMP!
I'LL ALERT THE AUDUBON SOCIETY.
BUT WAIT. BIRDS DON'T EVEN HAVE NOSES.

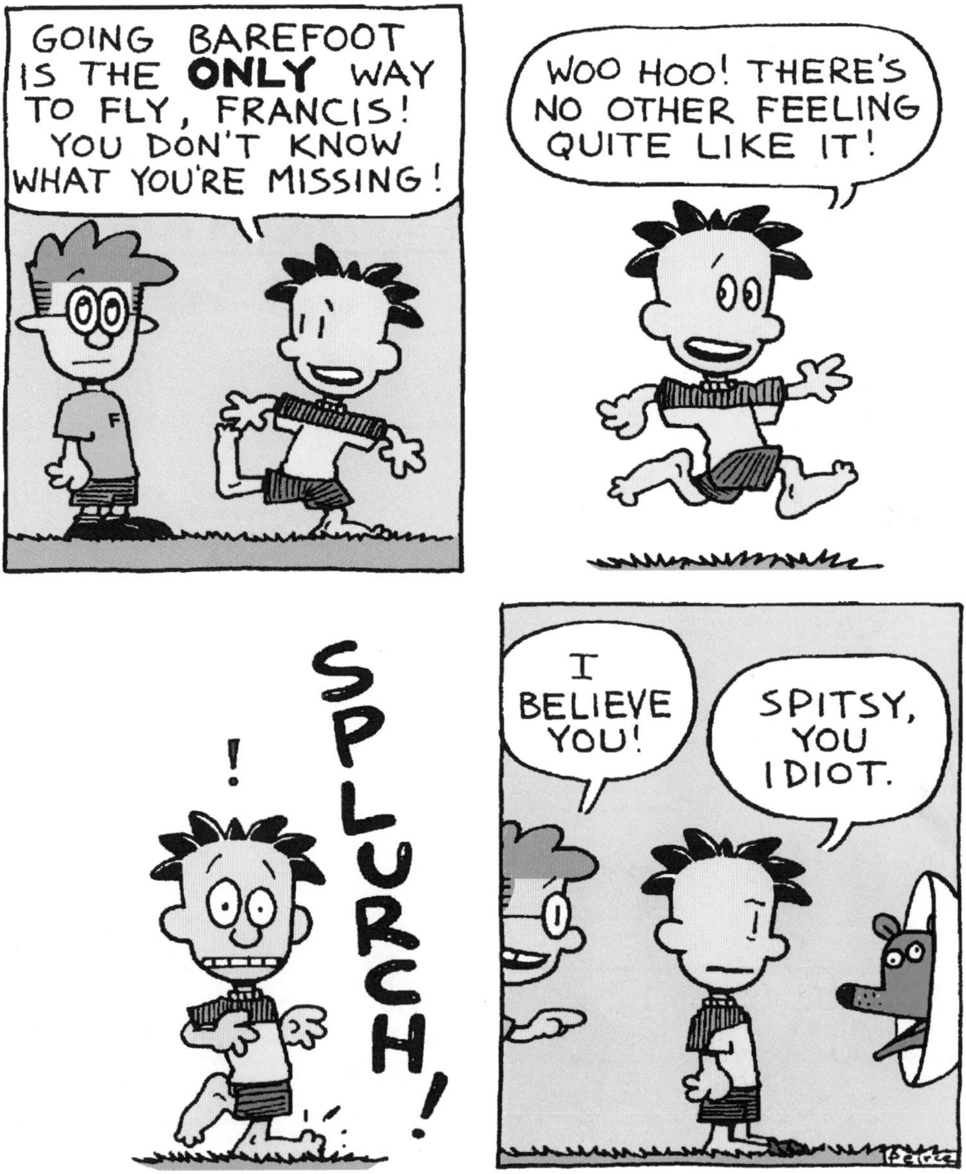
GOING BAREFOOT IS THE **ONLY** WAY TO FLY, FRANCIS! YOU DON'T KNOW WHAT YOU'RE MISSING!
F
WOO HOO! THERE'S NO OTHER FEELING QUITE LIKE IT!
!
SPLURCH!
I BELIEVE YOU!
SPITSY, YOU IDIOT.
Peirce

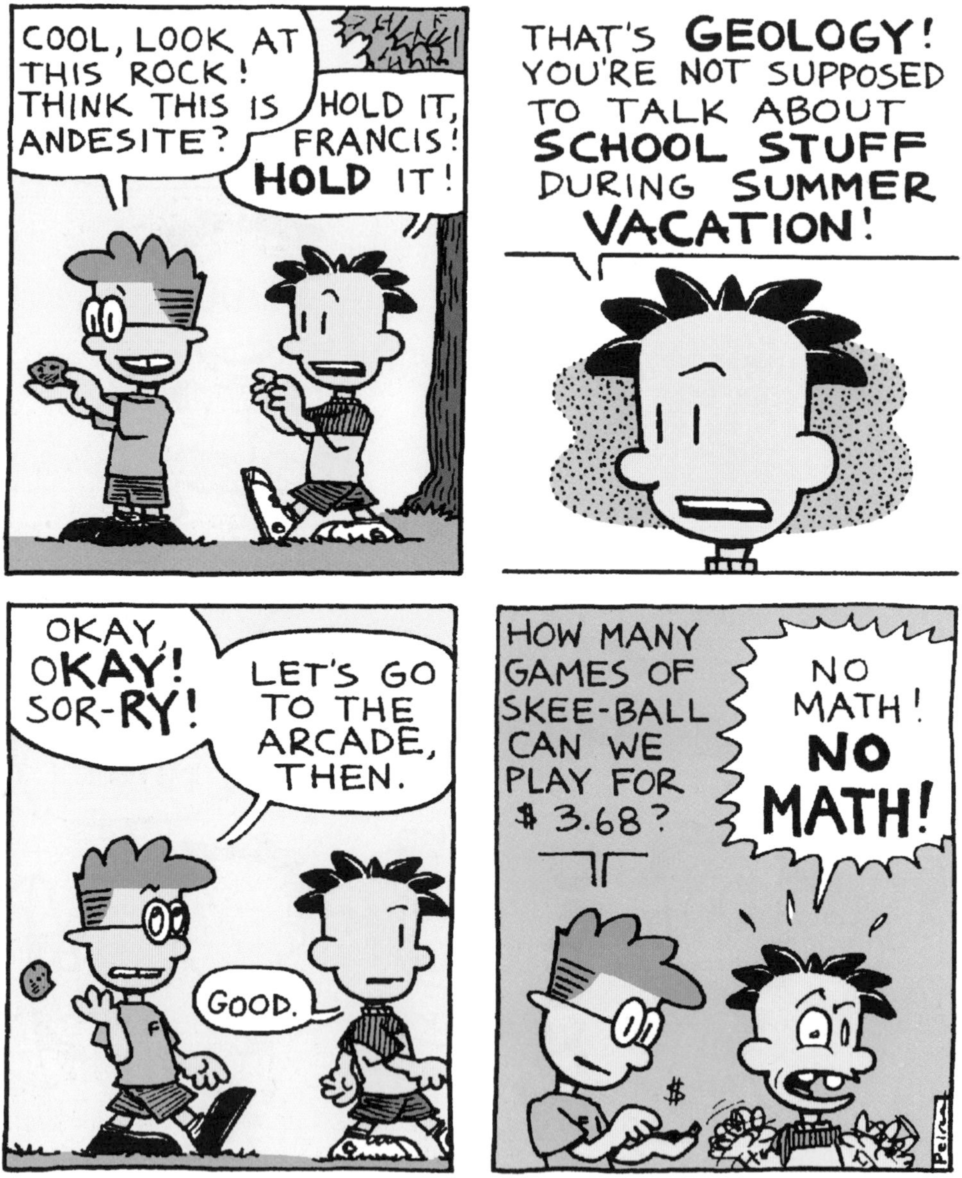
COOL, LOOK AT THIS ROCK! THINK THIS IS ANDESITE?
HOLD IT, FRANCIS! HOLD IT!
THAT'S GEOLOGY! YOU'RE NOT SUPPOSED TO TALK ABOUT SCHOOL STUFF DURING SUMMER VACATION!
OKAY, OKAY! SOR-RY!
LET'S GO TO THE ARCADE, THEN.
GOOD.
HOW MANY GAMES OF SKEE-BALL CAN WE PLAY FOR $ 3.68?
NO MATH! NO MATH!
Peirce

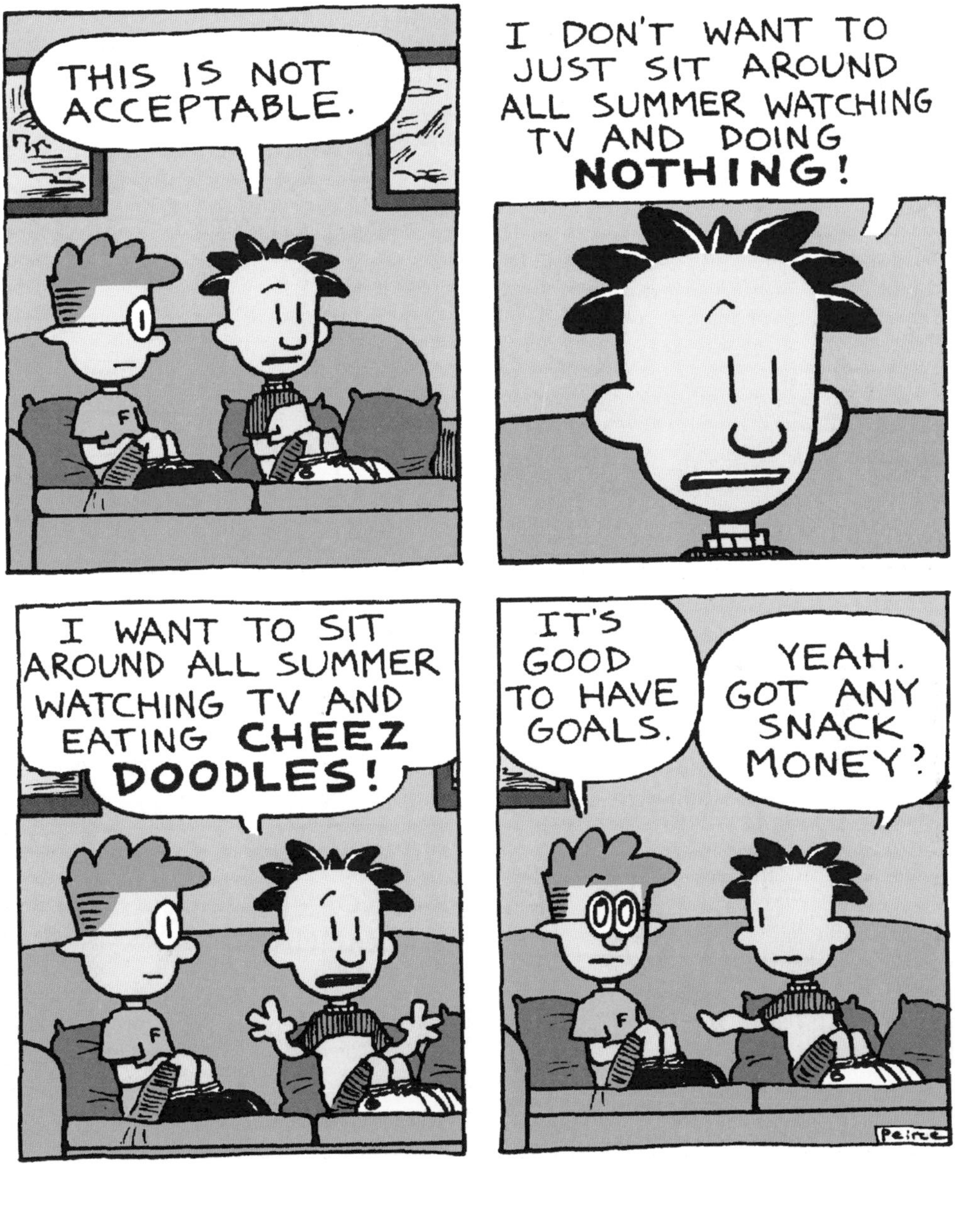
THIS IS NOT ACCEPTABLE.
I DON'T WANT TO JUST SIT AROUND ALL SUMMER WATCHING TV AND DOING **NOTHING!**
I WANT TO SIT AROUND ALL SUMMER WATCHING TV AND EATING **CHEEZ DOODLES!**
IT'S GOOD TO HAVE GOALS.
YEAH. GOT ANY SNACK MONEY?
Peirce

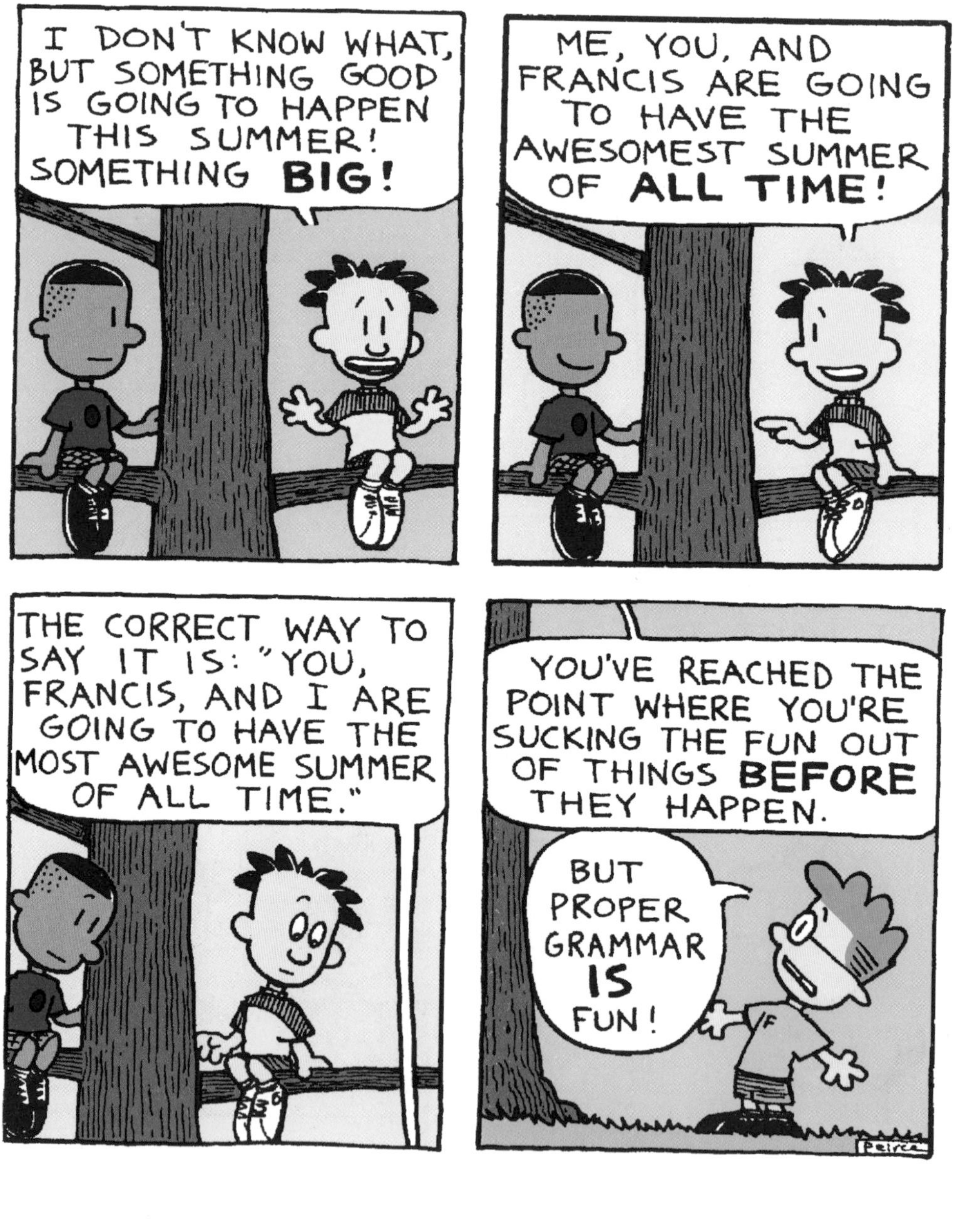
I DON'T KNOW WHAT, BUT SOMETHING GOOD IS GOING TO HAPPEN THIS SUMMER! SOMETHING **BIG**!
ME, YOU, AND FRANCIS ARE GOING TO HAVE THE AWESOMEST SUMMER OF **ALL TIME**!
THE CORRECT WAY TO SAY IT IS: "YOU, FRANCIS, AND I ARE GOING TO HAVE THE MOST AWESOME SUMMER OF ALL TIME."
YOU'VE REACHED THE POINT WHERE YOU'RE SUCKING THE FUN OUT OF THINGS **BEFORE** THEY HAPPEN.
BUT PROPER GRAMMAR **IS** FUN!
Peirce

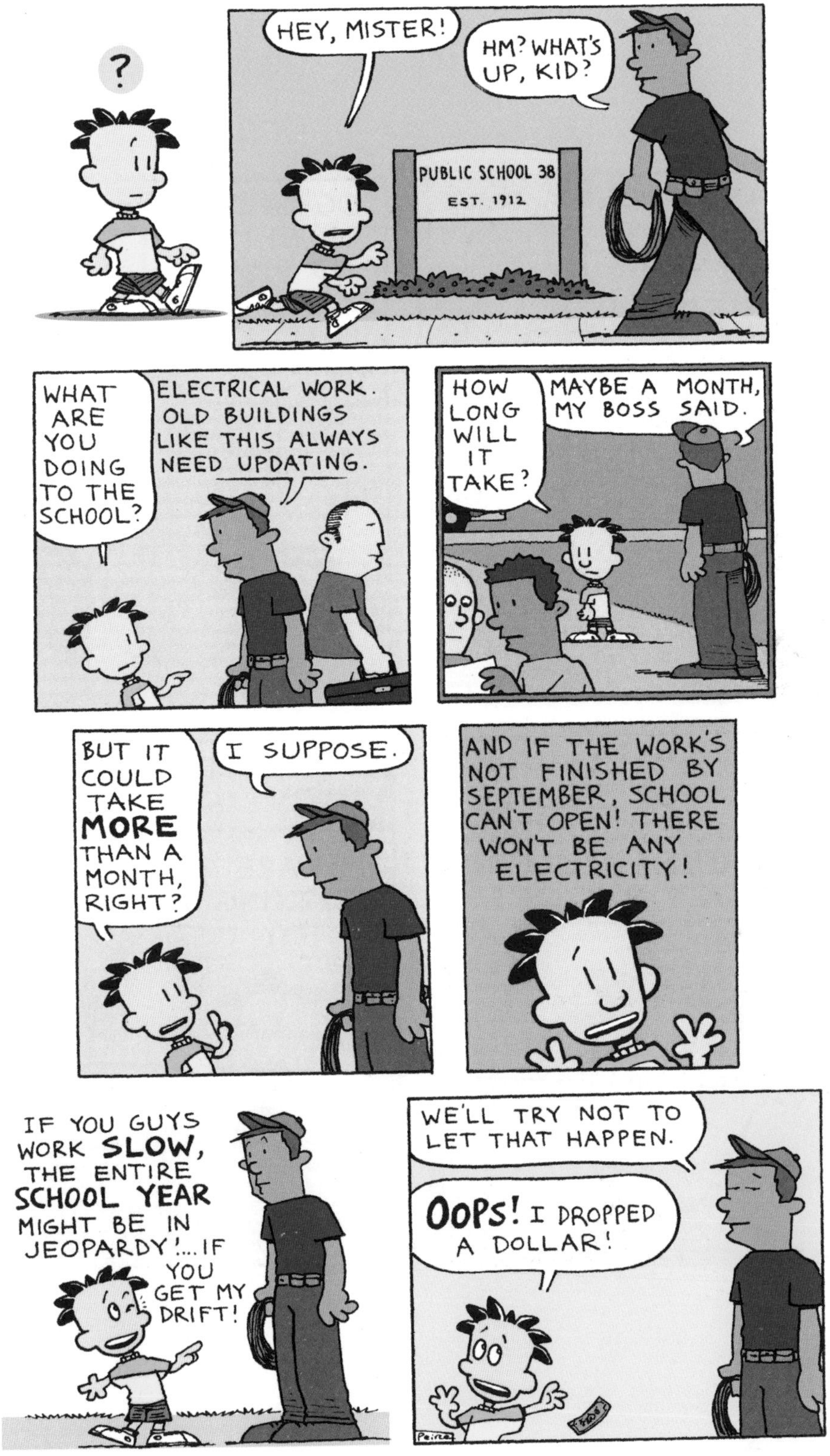
?
HEY, MISTER!
HM? WHAT'S UP, KID?
PUBLIC SCHOOL 38
EST. 1912
WHAT ARE YOU DOING TO THE SCHOOL?
ELECTRICAL WORK. OLD BUILDINGS LIKE THIS ALWAYS NEED UPDATING.
HOW LONG WILL IT TAKE?
MAYBE A MONTH, MY BOSS SAID.
BUT IT COULD TAKE MORE THAN A MONTH, RIGHT?
I SUPPOSE.
AND IF THE WORK'S NOT FINISHED BY SEPTEMBER, SCHOOL CAN'T OPEN! THERE WON'T BE ANY ELECTRICITY!
IF YOU GUYS WORK SLOW, THE ENTIRE SCHOOL YEAR MIGHT BE IN JEOPARDY!... IF YOU GET MY DRIFT!
WE'LL TRY NOT TO LET THAT HAPPEN.
OOPS! I DROPPED A DOLLAR!
Peirce

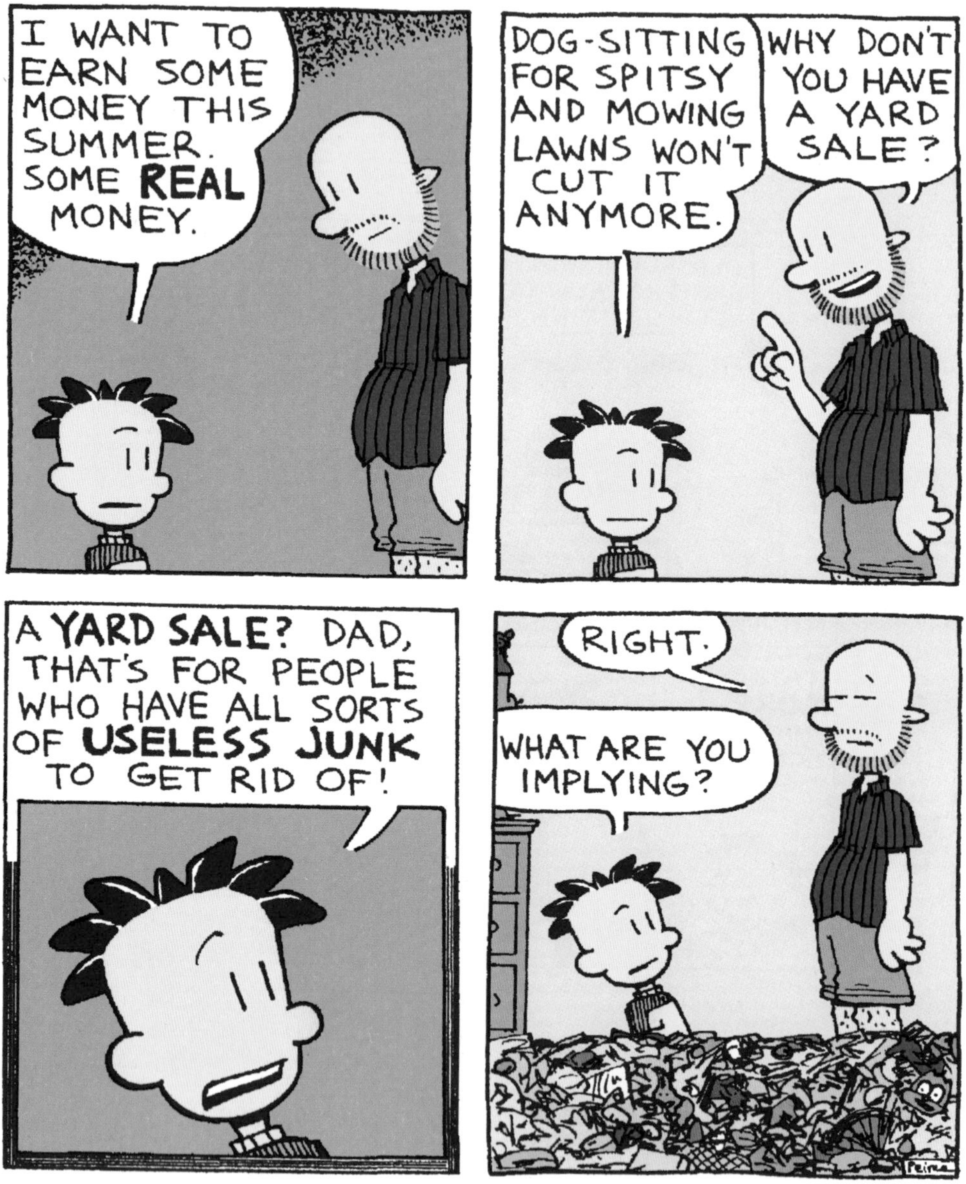
I WANT TO EARN SOME MONEY THIS SUMMER. SOME **REAL** MONEY.
DOG-SITTING FOR SPITSY AND MOWING LAWNS WON'T CUT IT ANYMORE.
WHY DON'T YOU HAVE A YARD SALE?
A **YARD SALE?** DAD, THAT'S FOR PEOPLE WHO HAVE ALL SORTS OF **USELESS JUNK** TO GET RID OF!
RIGHT.
WHAT ARE YOU IMPLYING?
Peirce

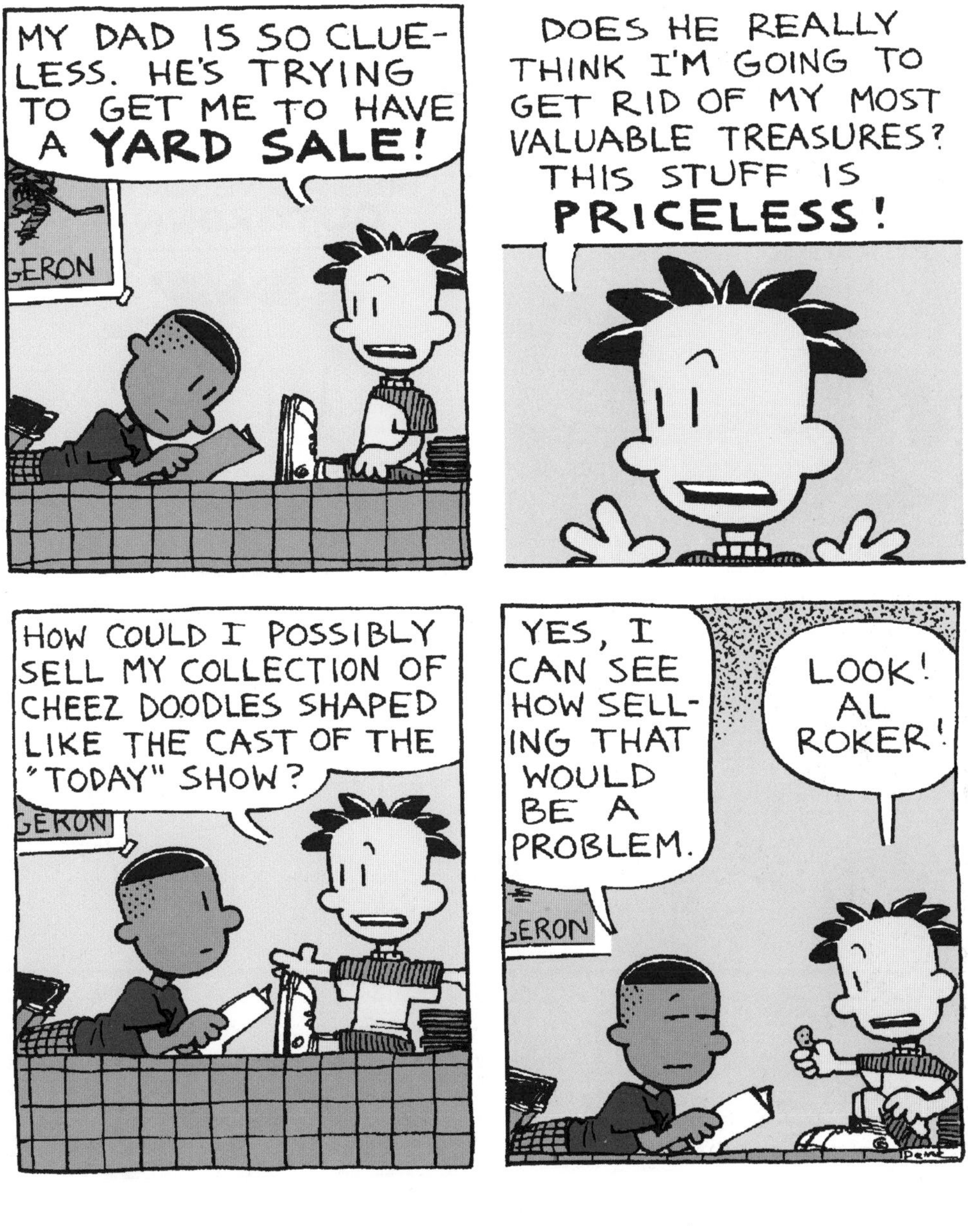
MY DAD IS SO CLUELESS. HE'S TRYING TO GET ME TO HAVE A **YARD SALE**!
GERON
DOES HE REALLY THINK I'M GOING TO GET RID OF MY MOST VALUABLE TREASURES? THIS STUFF IS **PRICELESS**!
HOW COULD I POSSIBLY SELL MY COLLECTION OF CHEEZ DOODLES SHAPED LIKE THE CAST OF THE "TODAY" SHOW?
GERON
YES, I CAN SEE HOW SELLING THAT WOULD BE A PROBLEM.
LOOK! AL ROKER!
GERON

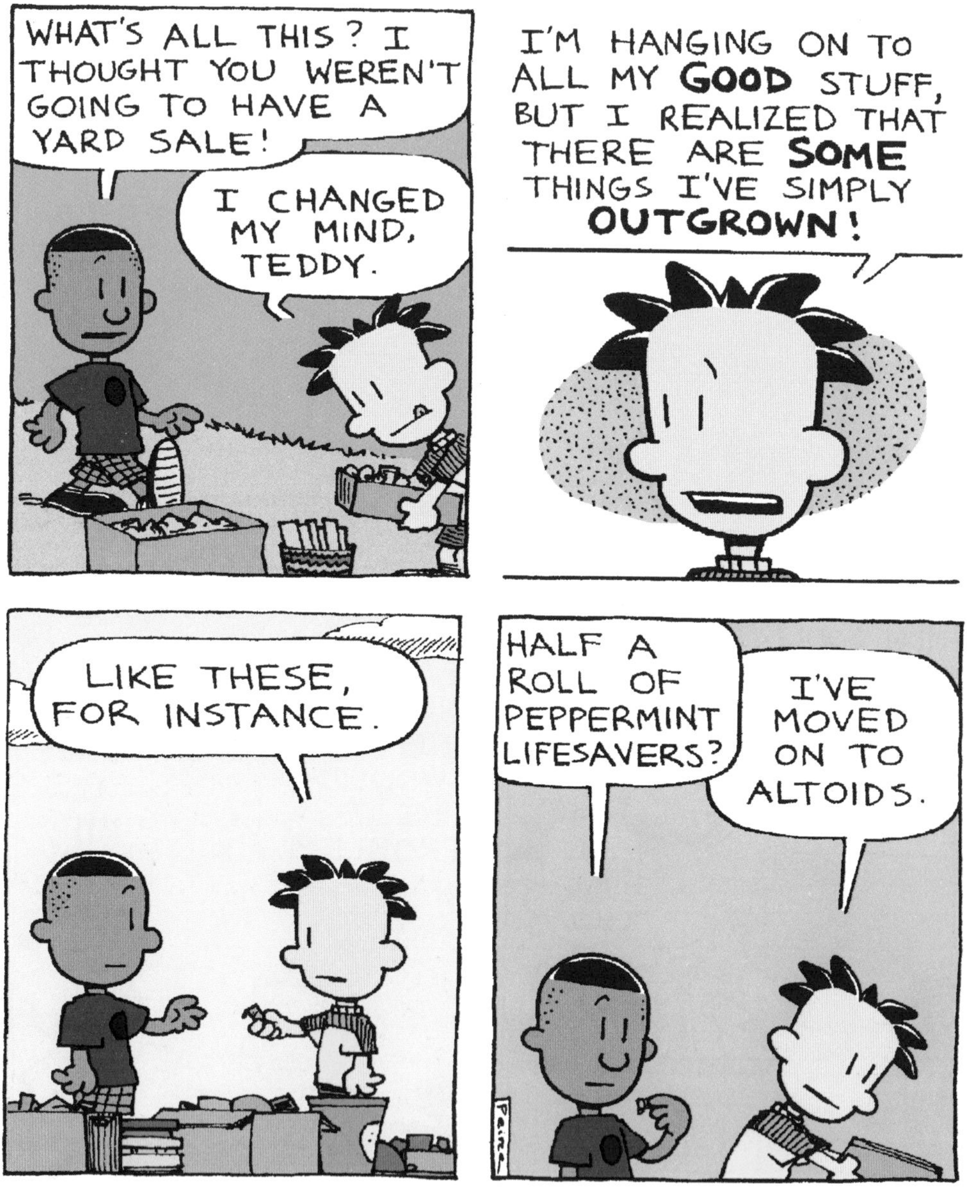
WHAT'S ALL THIS? I THOUGHT YOU WEREN'T GOING TO HAVE A YARD SALE!
I CHANGED MY MIND, TEDDY.
I'M HANGING ON TO ALL MY **GOOD** STUFF, BUT I REALIZED THAT THERE ARE **SOME** THINGS I'VE SIMPLY **OUTGROWN**!
LIKE THESE, FOR INSTANCE.
HALF A ROLL OF PEPPERMINT LIFESAVERS?
I'VE MOVED ON TO ALTOIDS.
Peirce

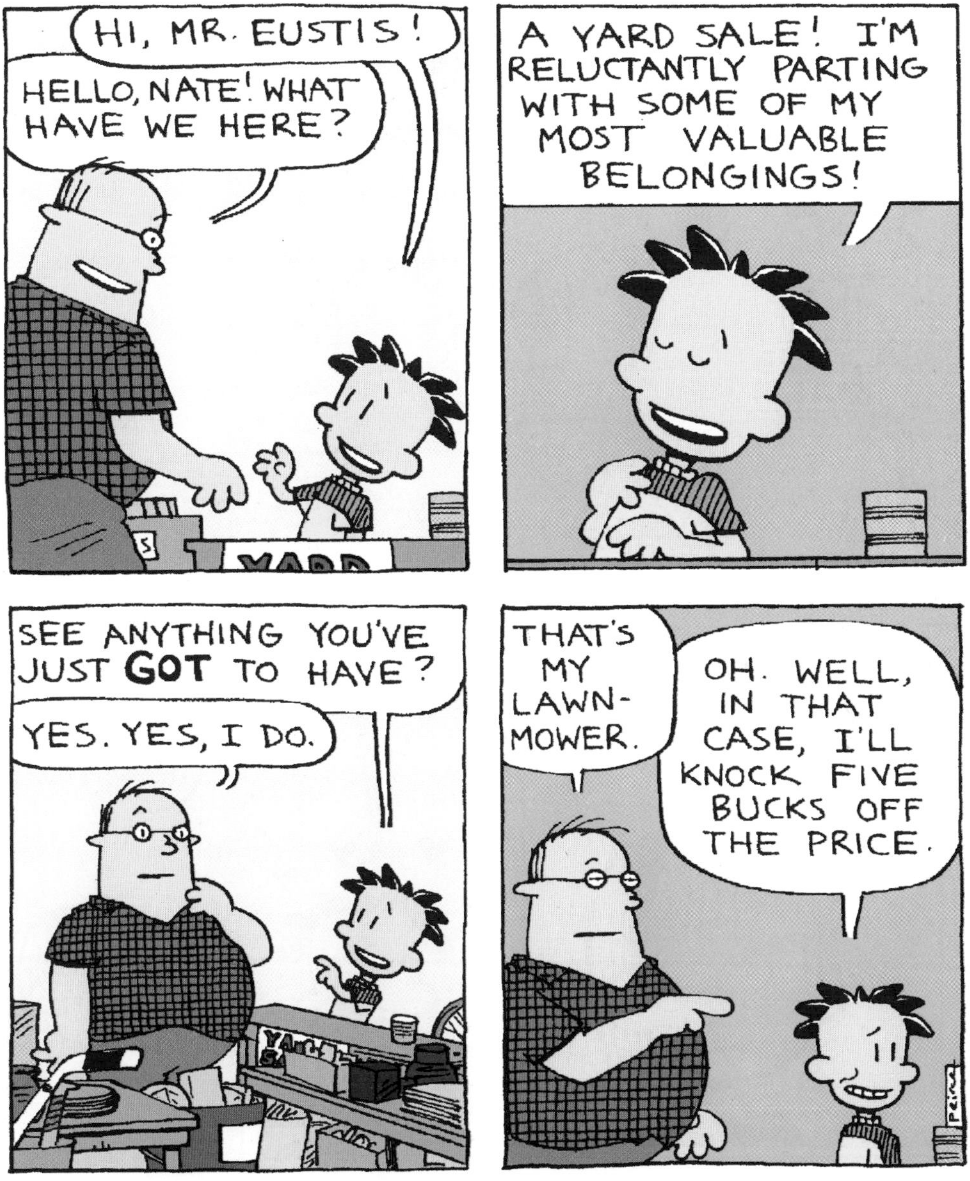
HI, MR. EUSTIS!
HELLO, NATE! WHAT HAVE WE HERE?
A YARD SALE! I'M RELUCTANTLY PARTING WITH SOME OF MY MOST VALUABLE BELONGINGS!
SEE ANYTHING YOU'VE JUST GOT TO HAVE?
YES. YES, I DO.
THAT'S MY LAWN-MOWER.
OH. WELL, IN THAT CASE, I'LL KNOCK FIVE BUCKS OFF THE PRICE.
PEIRCE

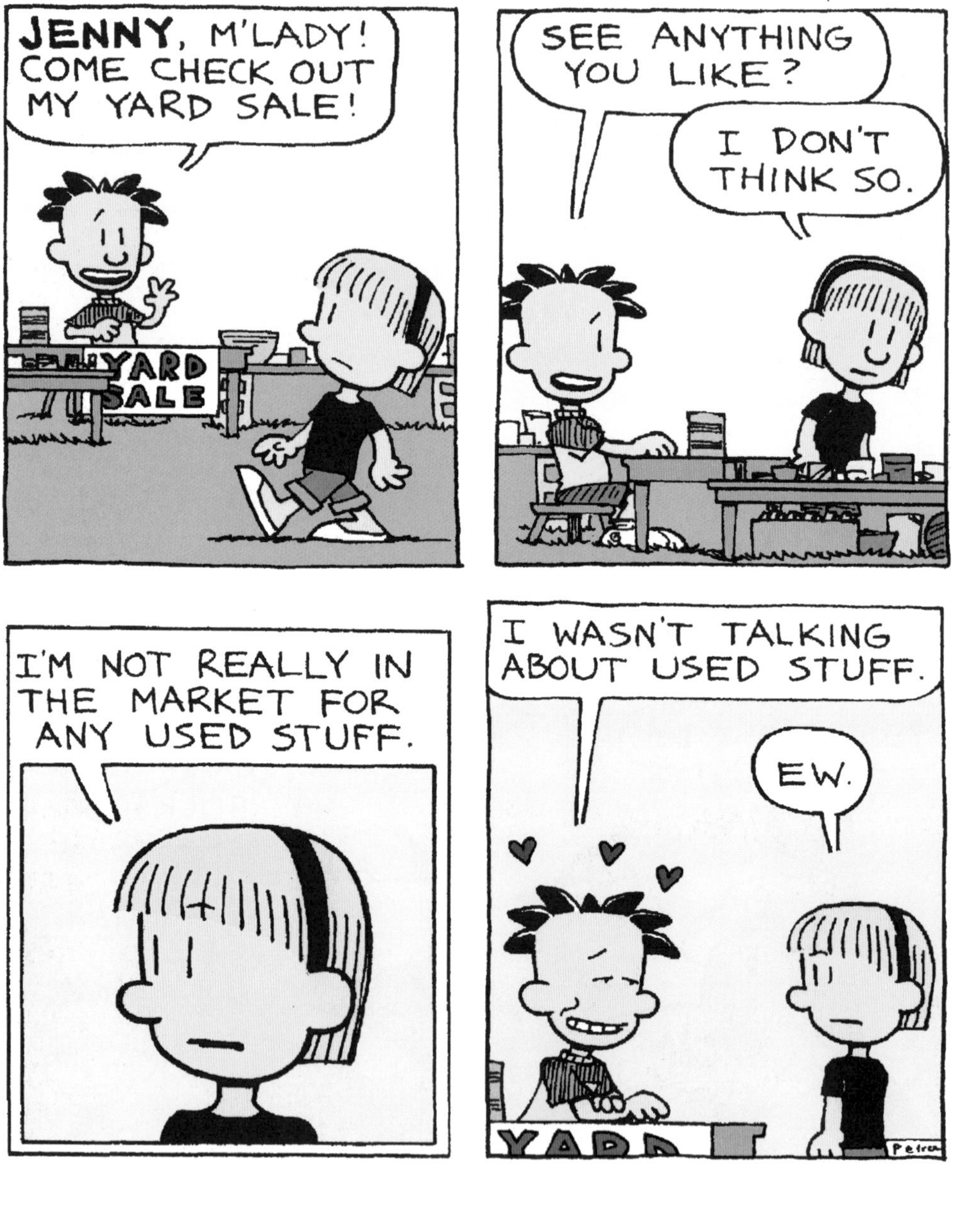
JENNY, M'LADY! COME CHECK OUT MY YARD SALE!
YARD SALE
SEE ANYTHING YOU LIKE?
I DON'T THINK SO.
I'M NOT REALLY IN THE MARKET FOR ANY USED STUFF.
I WASN'T TALKING ABOUT USED STUFF.
EW.
Peirce

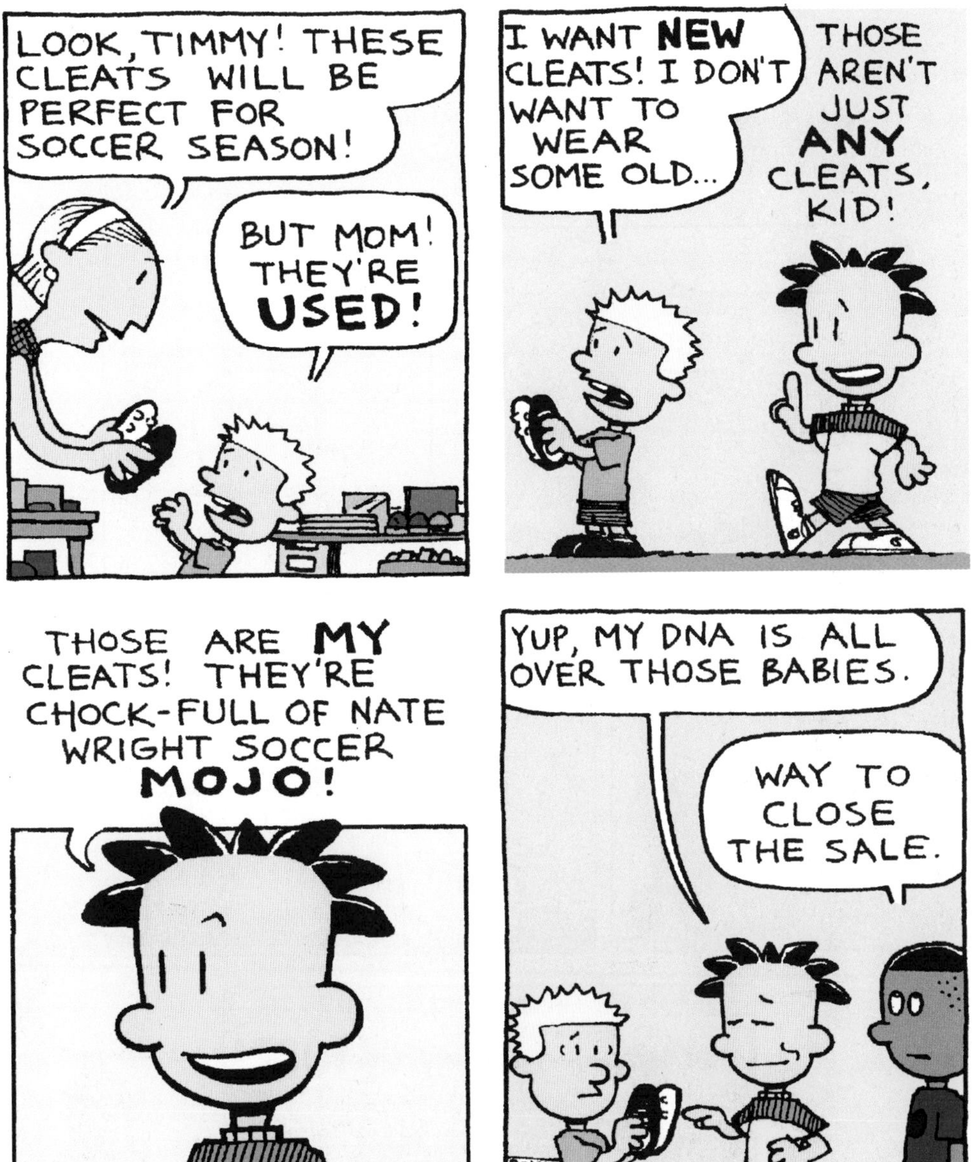

LOOK, TIMMY! THESE CLEATS WILL BE PERFECT FOR SOCCER SEASON!
BUT MOM! THEY'RE USED!
I WANT NEW CLEATS! I DON'T WANT TO WEAR SOME OLD...
THOSE AREN'T JUST ANY CLEATS, KID!
THOSE ARE MY CLEATS! THEY'RE CHOCK-FULL OF NATE WRIGHT SOCCER MOJO!
YUP, MY DNA IS ALL OVER THOSE BABIES.
WAY TO CLOSE THE SALE.

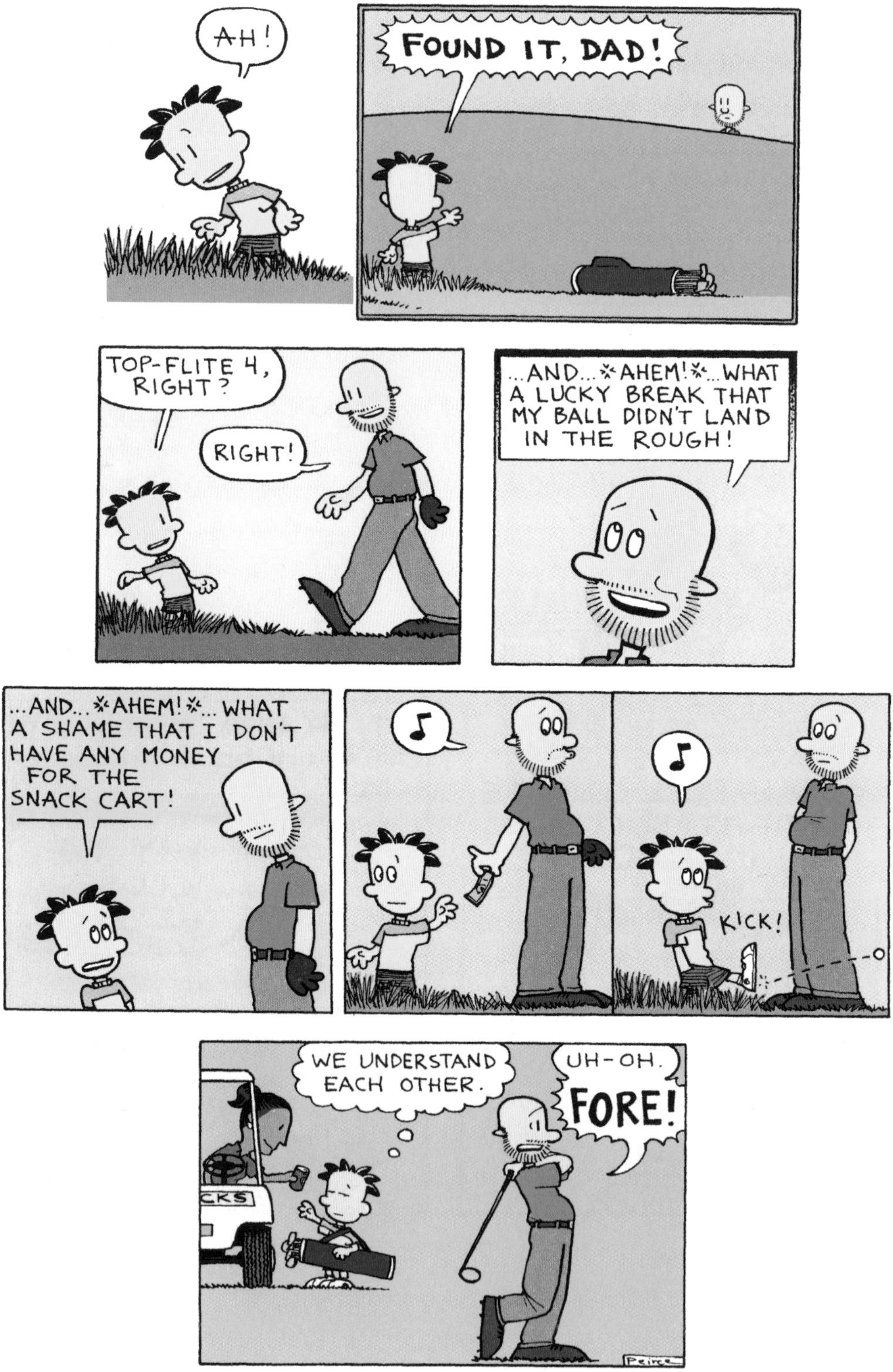
AH!
FOUND IT, DAD!
TOP-FLITE 4, RIGHT?
RIGHT!
...AND... AHEM! ...WHAT A LUCKY BREAK THAT MY BALL DIDN'T LAND IN THE ROUGH!
...AND... AHEM! ... WHAT A SHAME THAT I DON'T HAVE ANY MONEY FOR THE SNACK CART!
KICK!
WE UNDERSTAND EACH OTHER.
CKS
UH-OH.
FORE!
Peirce

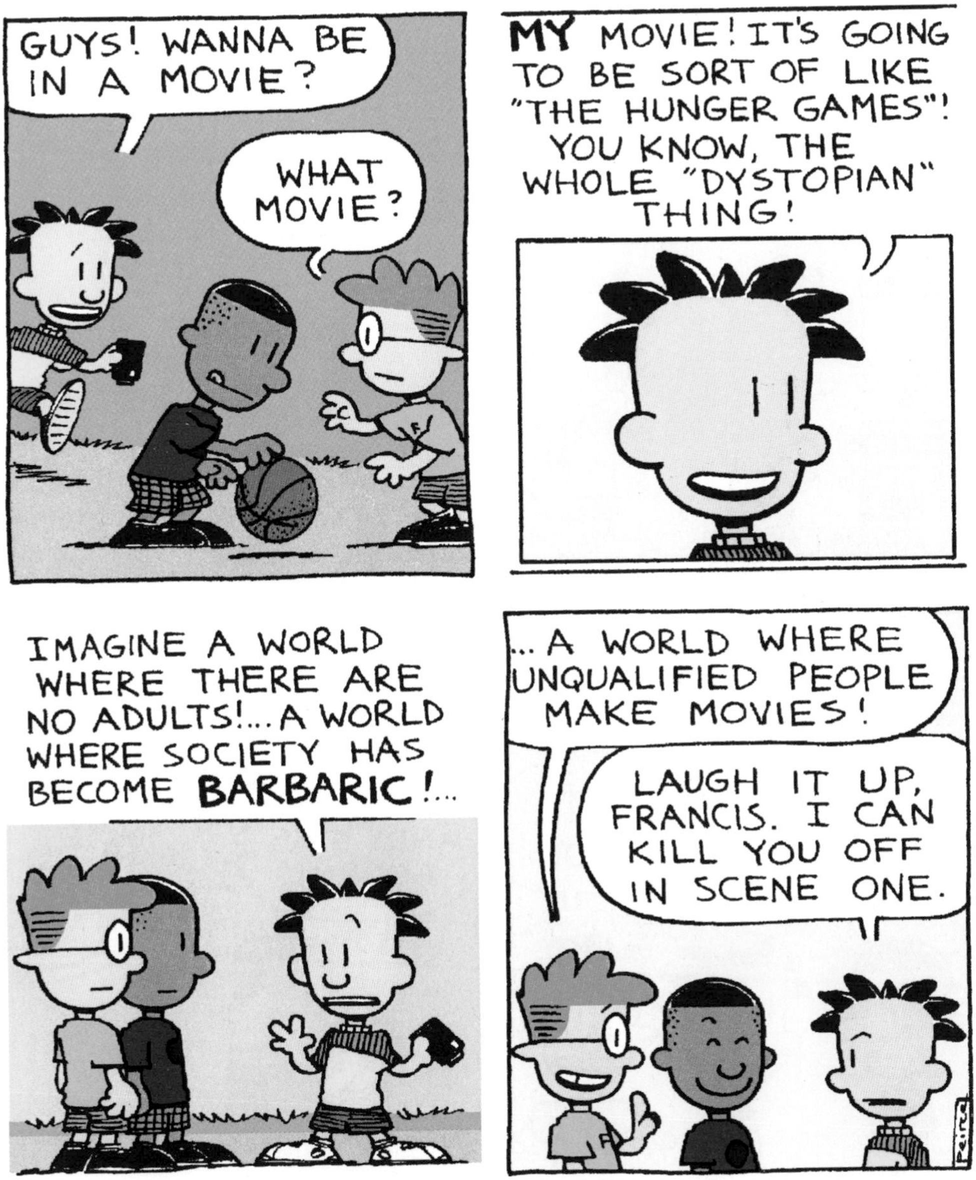
GUYS! WANNA BE IN A MOVIE?
WHAT MOVIE?
MY MOVIE! IT'S GOING TO BE SORT OF LIKE "THE HUNGER GAMES"! YOU KNOW, THE WHOLE "DYSTOPIAN" THING!
IMAGINE A WORLD WHERE THERE ARE NO ADULTS!... A WORLD WHERE SOCIETY HAS BECOME BARBARIC!...
... A WORLD WHERE UNQUALIFIED PEOPLE MAKE MOVIES!
LAUGH IT UP, FRANCIS. I CAN KILL YOU OFF IN SCENE ONE.
Peirce

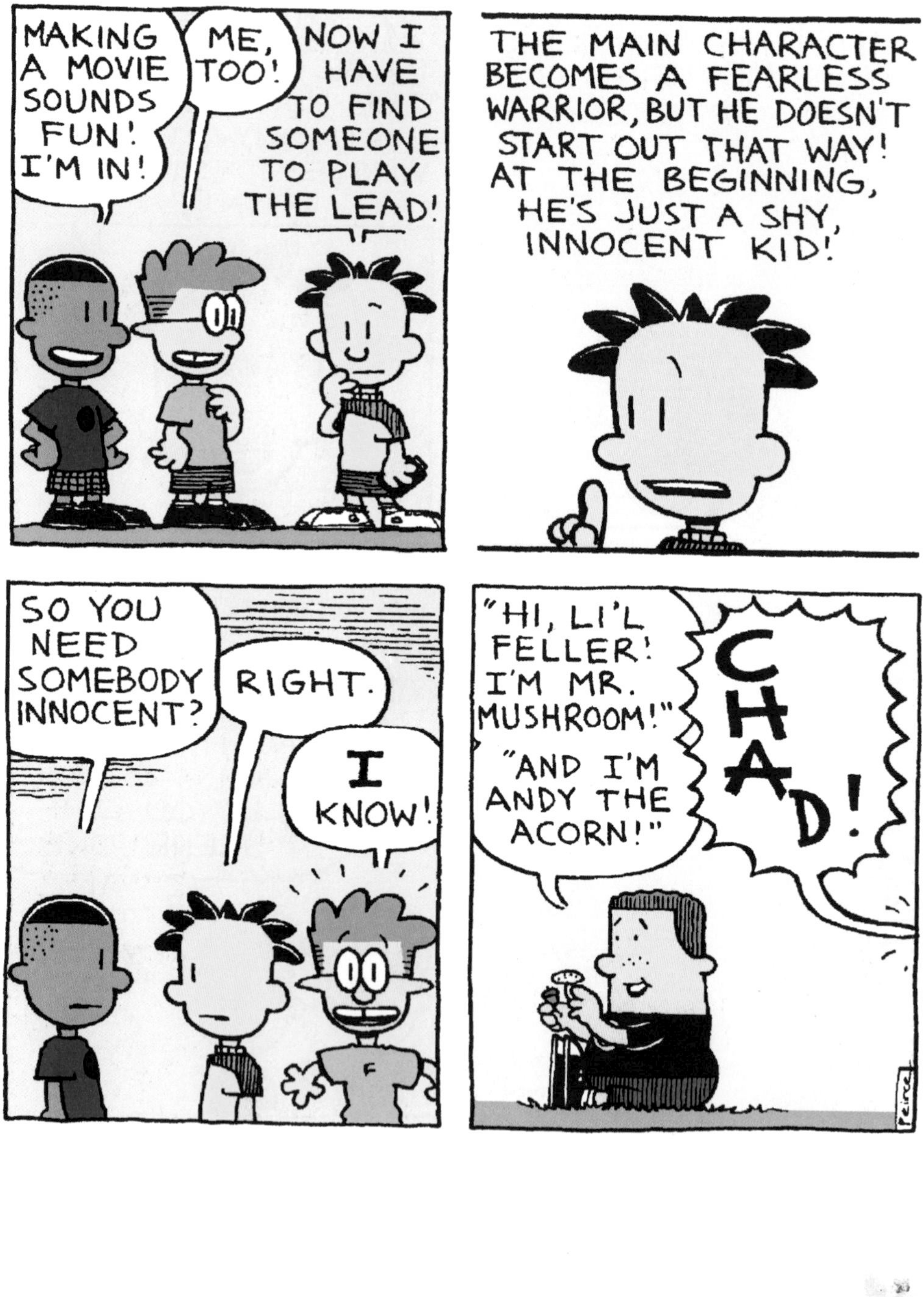
MAKING A MOVIE SOUNDS FUN! I'M IN!
ME, TOO!
NOW I HAVE TO FIND SOMEONE TO PLAY THE LEAD!
THE MAIN CHARACTER BECOMES A FEARLESS WARRIOR, BUT HE DOESN'T START OUT THAT WAY! AT THE BEGINNING, HE'S JUST A SHY, INNOCENT KID!
SO YOU NEED SOMEBODY INNOCENT?
RIGHT.
I KNOW!
"HI, LI'L FELLER! I'M MR. MUSHROOM!"
"AND I'M ANDY THE ACORN!"
CHAD!
Peirce

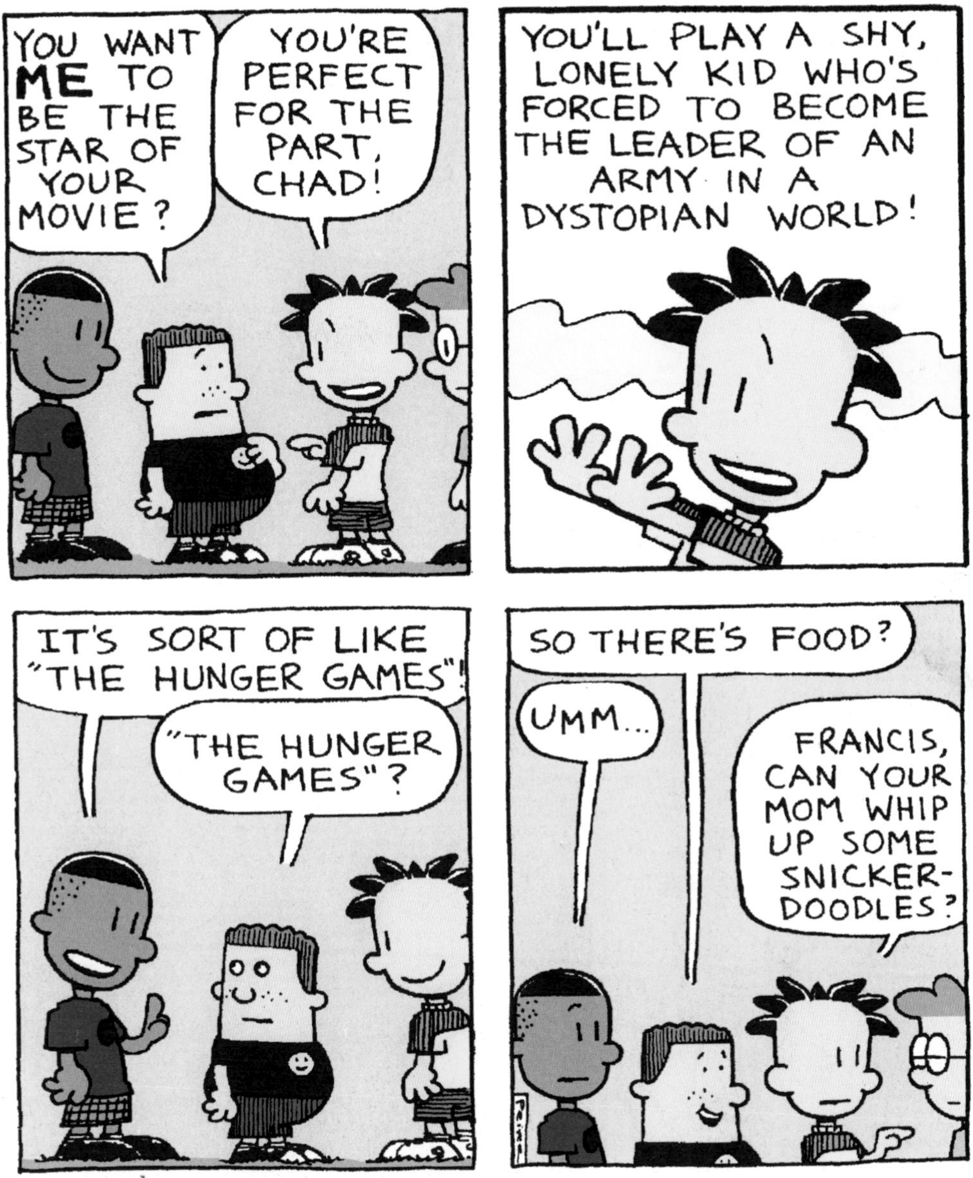
YOU WANT **ME** TO BE THE STAR OF YOUR MOVIE?
YOU'RE PERFECT FOR THE PART, CHAD!
YOU'LL PLAY A SHY, LONELY KID WHO'S FORCED TO BECOME THE LEADER OF AN ARMY IN A DYSTOPIAN WORLD!
IT'S SORT OF LIKE "THE HUNGER GAMES"!
"THE HUNGER GAMES"?
SO THERE'S FOOD?
UMM...
FRANCIS, CAN YOUR MOM WHIP UP SOME SNICKER-DOODLES?

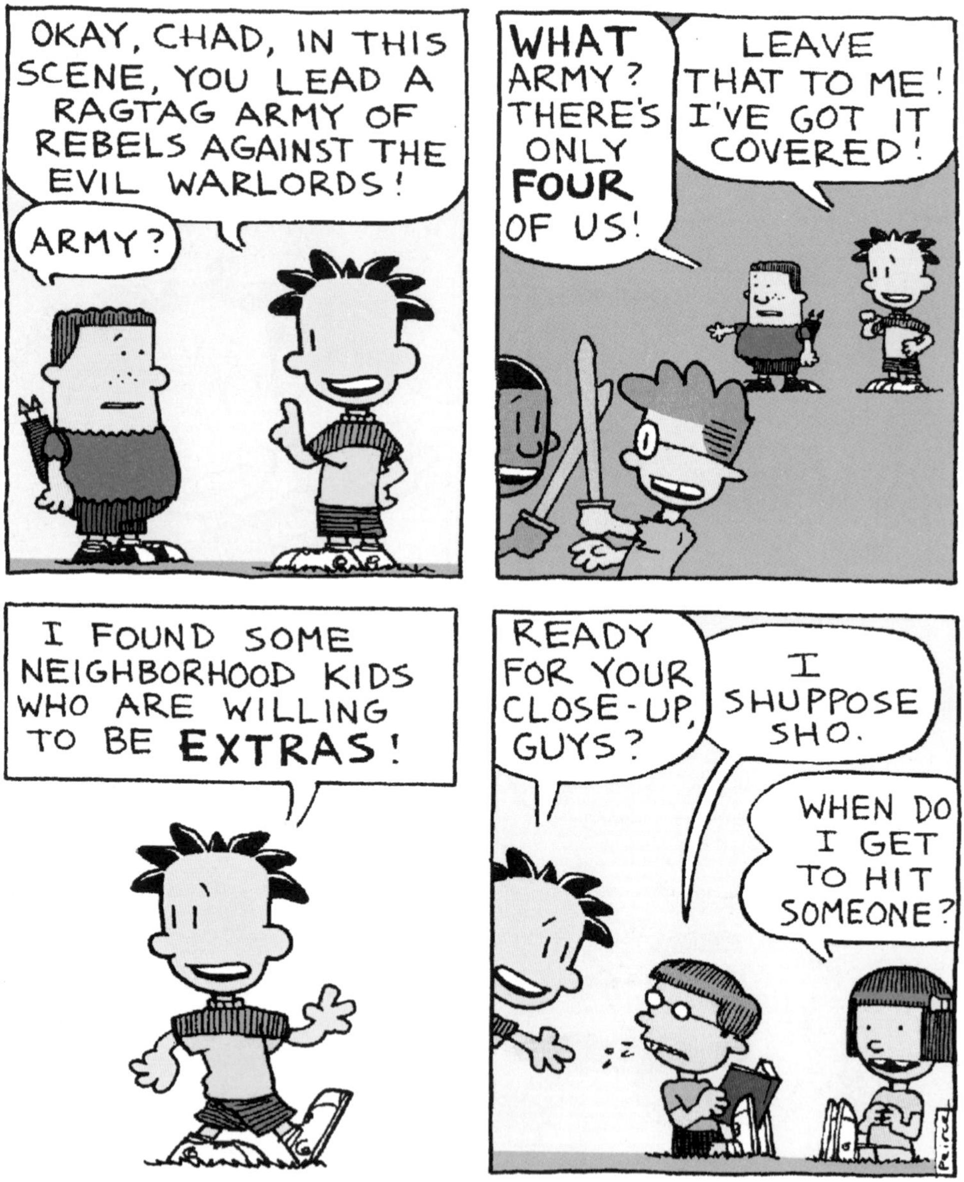

OKAY, CHAD, IN THIS SCENE, YOU LEAD A RAGTAG ARMY OF REBELS AGAINST THE EVIL WARLORDS!
ARMY?
WHAT ARMY? THERE'S ONLY FOUR OF US!
LEAVE THAT TO ME! I'VE GOT IT COVERED!
I FOUND SOME NEIGHBORHOOD KIDS WHO ARE WILLING TO BE EXTRAS!
READY FOR YOUR CLOSE-UP, GUYS?
I SHUPPOSE SHO.
WHEN DO I GET TO HIT SOMEONE?

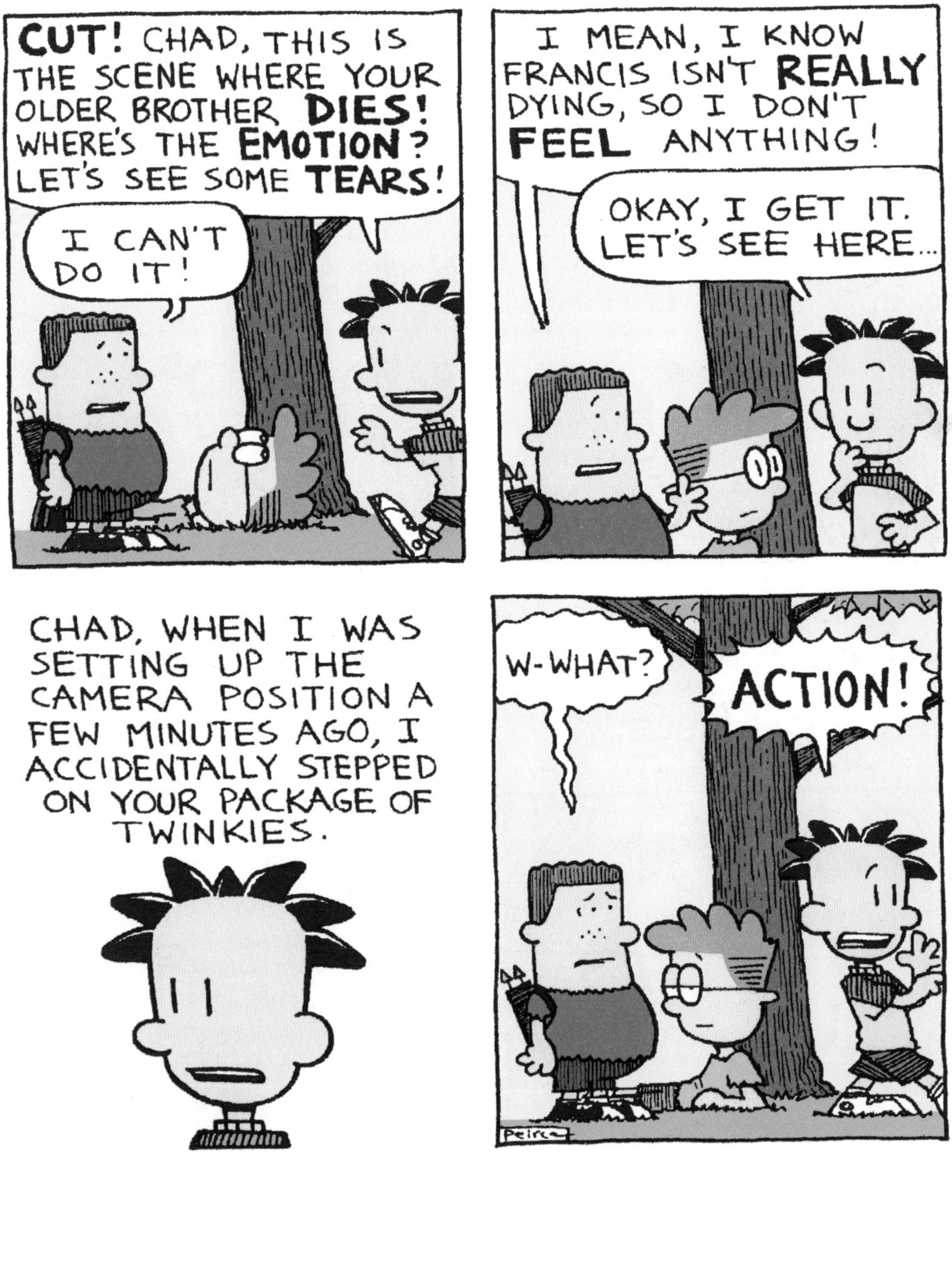
CUT! CHAD, THIS IS THE SCENE WHERE YOUR OLDER BROTHER DIES! WHERE'S THE EMOTION? LET'S SEE SOME TEARS!
I CAN'T DO IT!
I MEAN, I KNOW FRANCIS ISN'T REALLY DYING, SO I DON'T FEEL ANYTHING!
OKAY, I GET IT. LET'S SEE HERE...
CHAD, WHEN I WAS SETTING UP THE CAMERA POSITION A FEW MINUTES AGO, I ACCIDENTALLY STEPPED ON YOUR PACKAGE OF TWINKIES.
W-WHAT?
ACTION!
Peirce

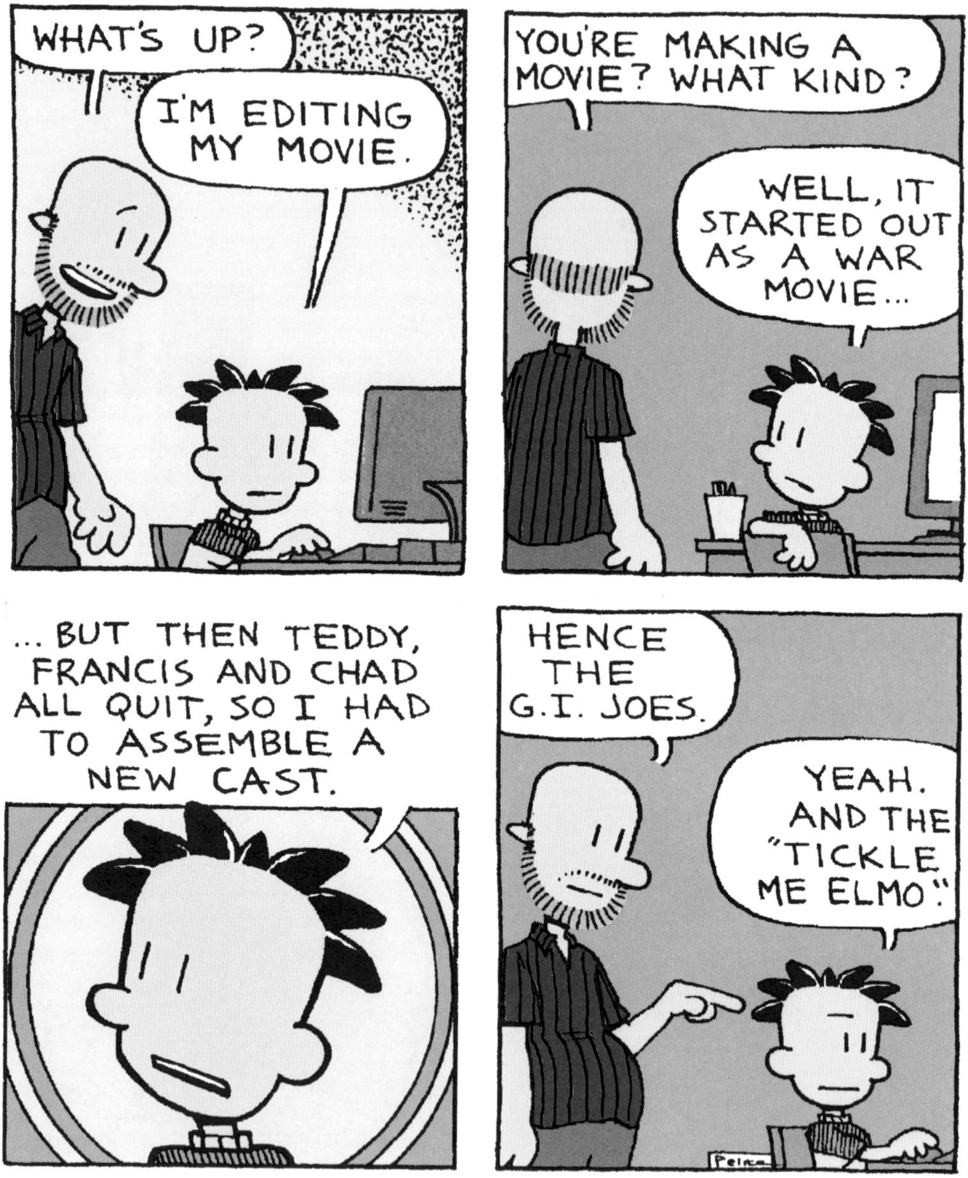
WHAT'S UP?
I'M EDITING MY MOVIE.
YOU'RE MAKING A MOVIE? WHAT KIND?
WELL, IT STARTED OUT AS A WAR MOVIE...
...BUT THEN TEDDY, FRANCIS AND CHAD ALL QUIT, SO I HAD TO ASSEMBLE A NEW CAST.
HENCE THE G.I. JOES.
YEAH. AND THE "TICKLE ME ELMO."

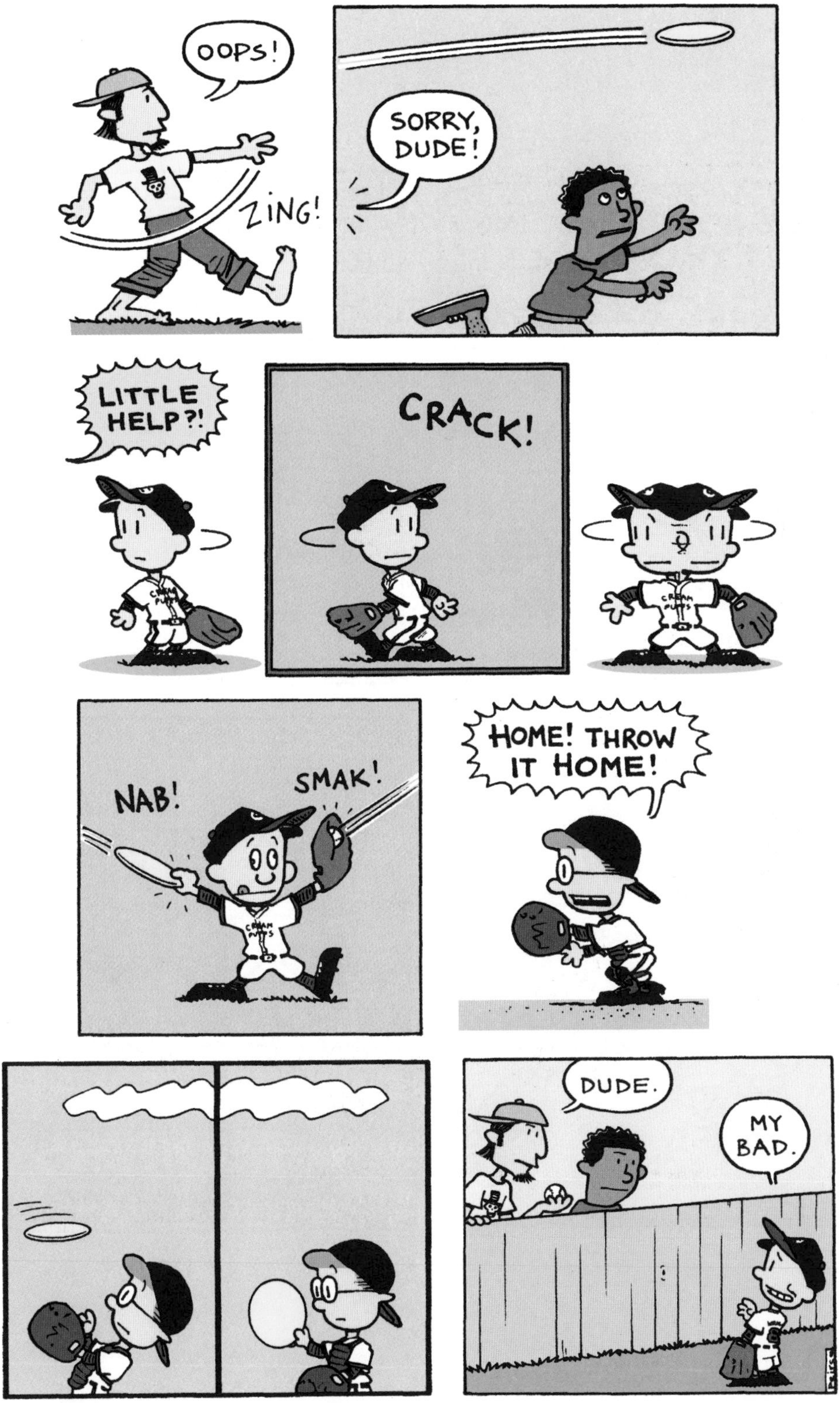
OOPS!
ZING!
SORRY, DUDE!
LITTLE HELP?!
CRACK!
NAB!
SMAK!
HOME! THROW IT HOME!
DUDE.
MY BAD.

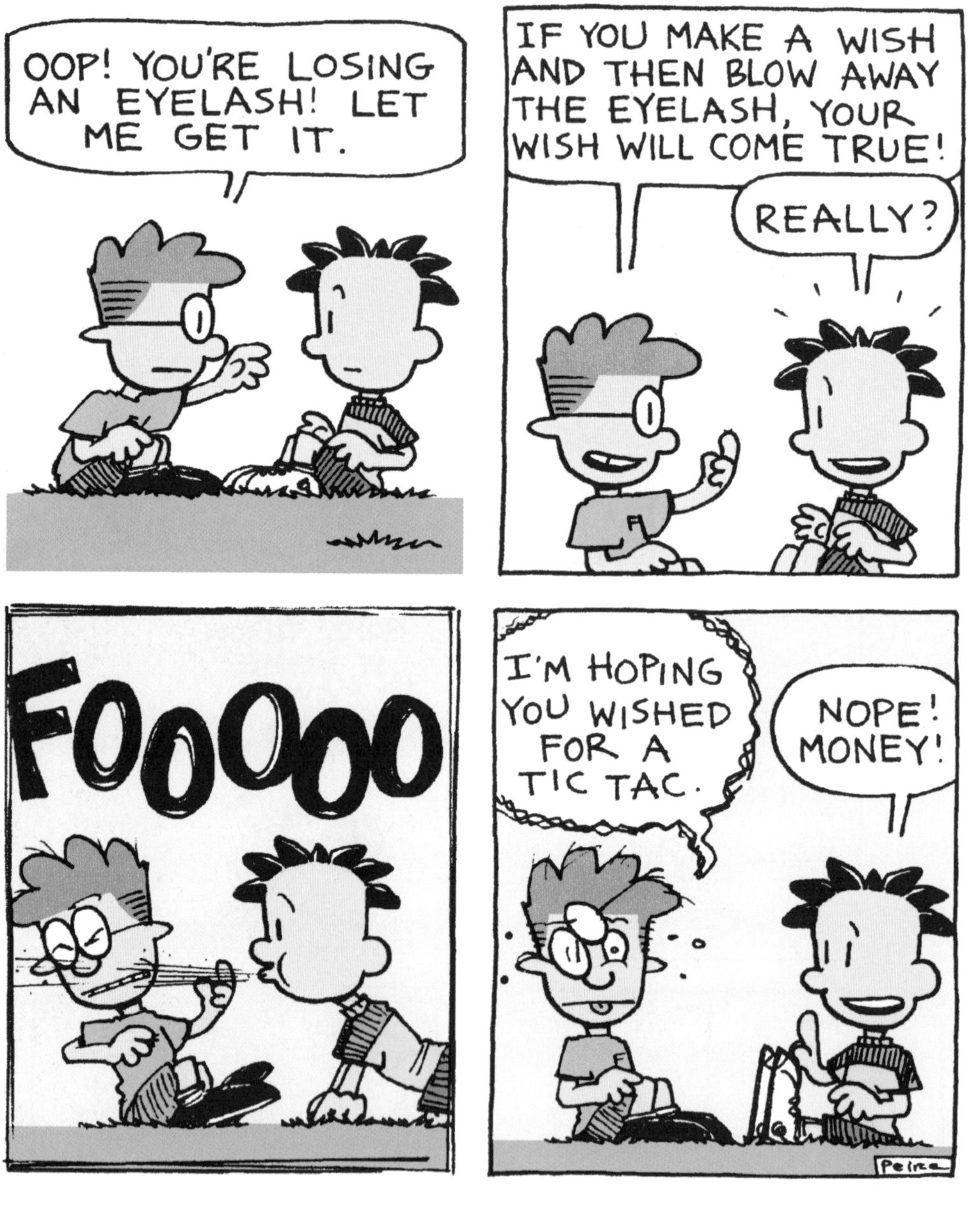
OOP! YOU'RE LOSING AN EYELASH! LET ME GET IT.
IF YOU MAKE A WISH AND THEN BLOW AWAY THE EYELASH, YOUR WISH WILL COME TRUE!
REALLY?
FOOOOO
I'M HOPING YOU WISHED FOR A TIC TAC.
NOPE! MONEY!
Peirce

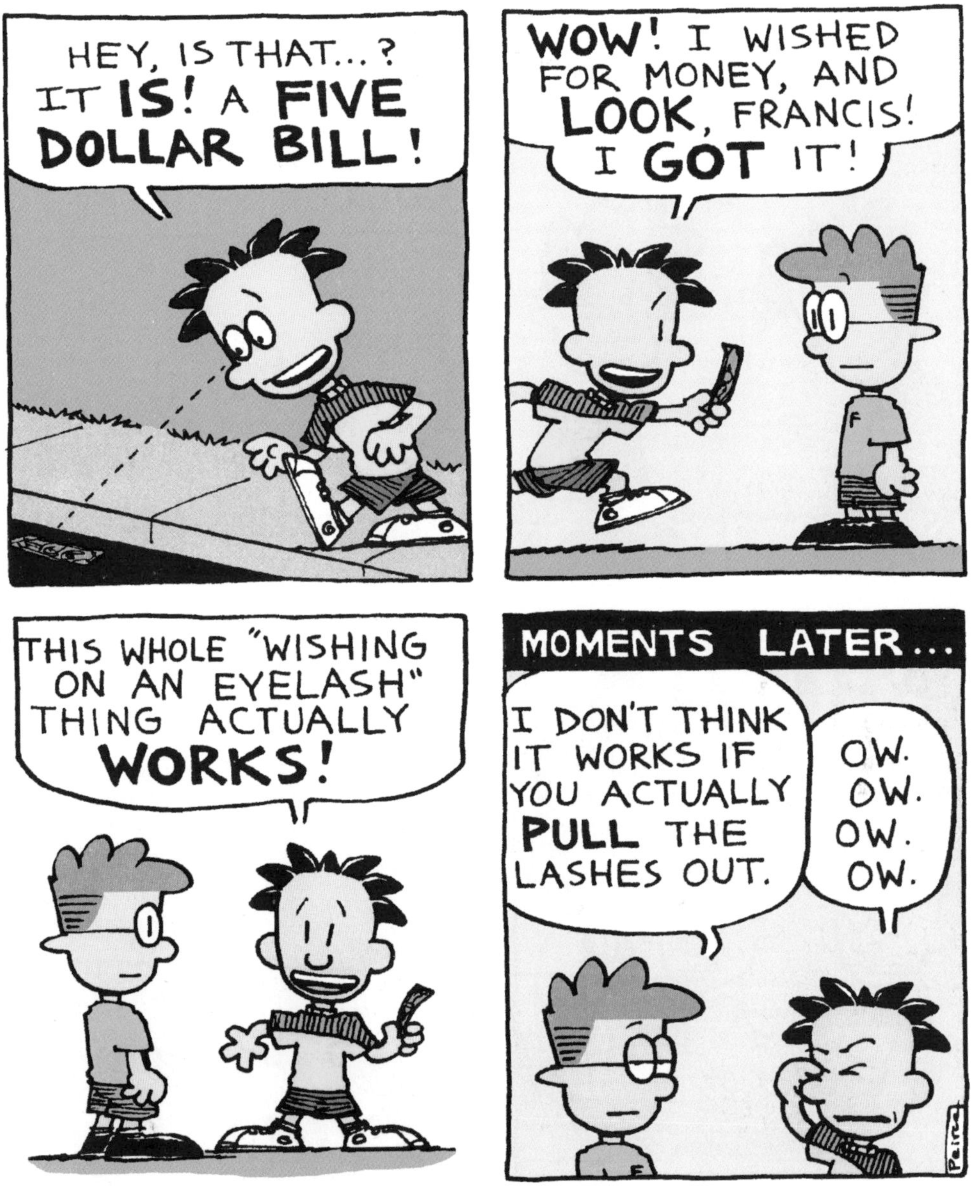
HEY, IS THAT...? IT IS! A FIVE DOLLAR BILL!
WOW! I WISHED FOR MONEY, AND LOOK, FRANCIS! I GOT IT!
THIS WHOLE "WISHING ON AN EYELASH" THING ACTUALLY WORKS!
MOMENTS LATER...
I DON'T THINK IT WORKS IF YOU ACTUALLY PULL THE LASHES OUT.
OW. OW. OW. OW.
Peirce

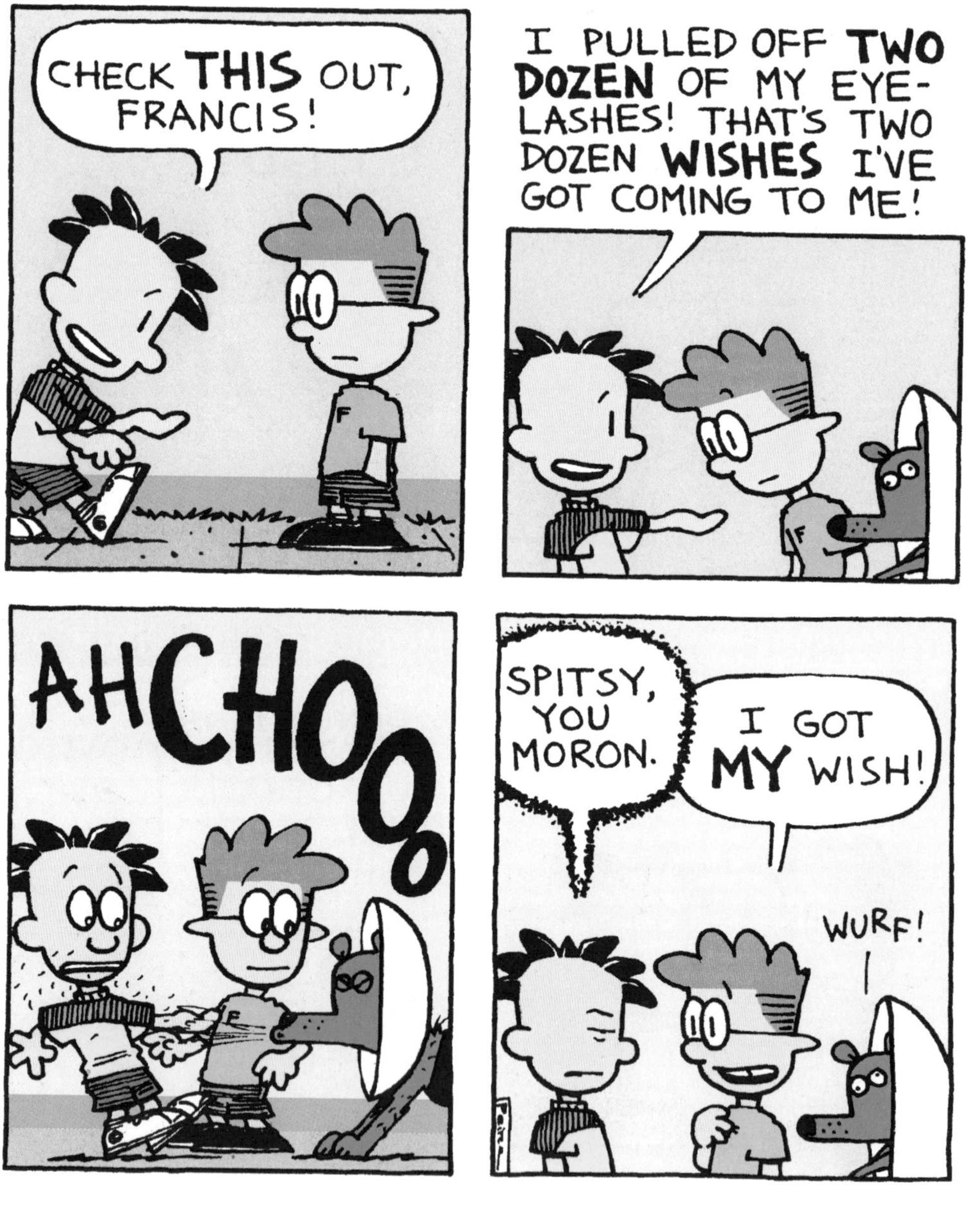
CHECK **THIS** OUT, FRANCIS!
I PULLED OFF **TWO DOZEN** OF MY EYE-LASHES! THAT'S TWO DOZEN **WISHES** I'VE GOT COMING TO ME!
AHCHOOO
SPITSY, YOU MORON.
I GOT **MY** WISH!
WURF!

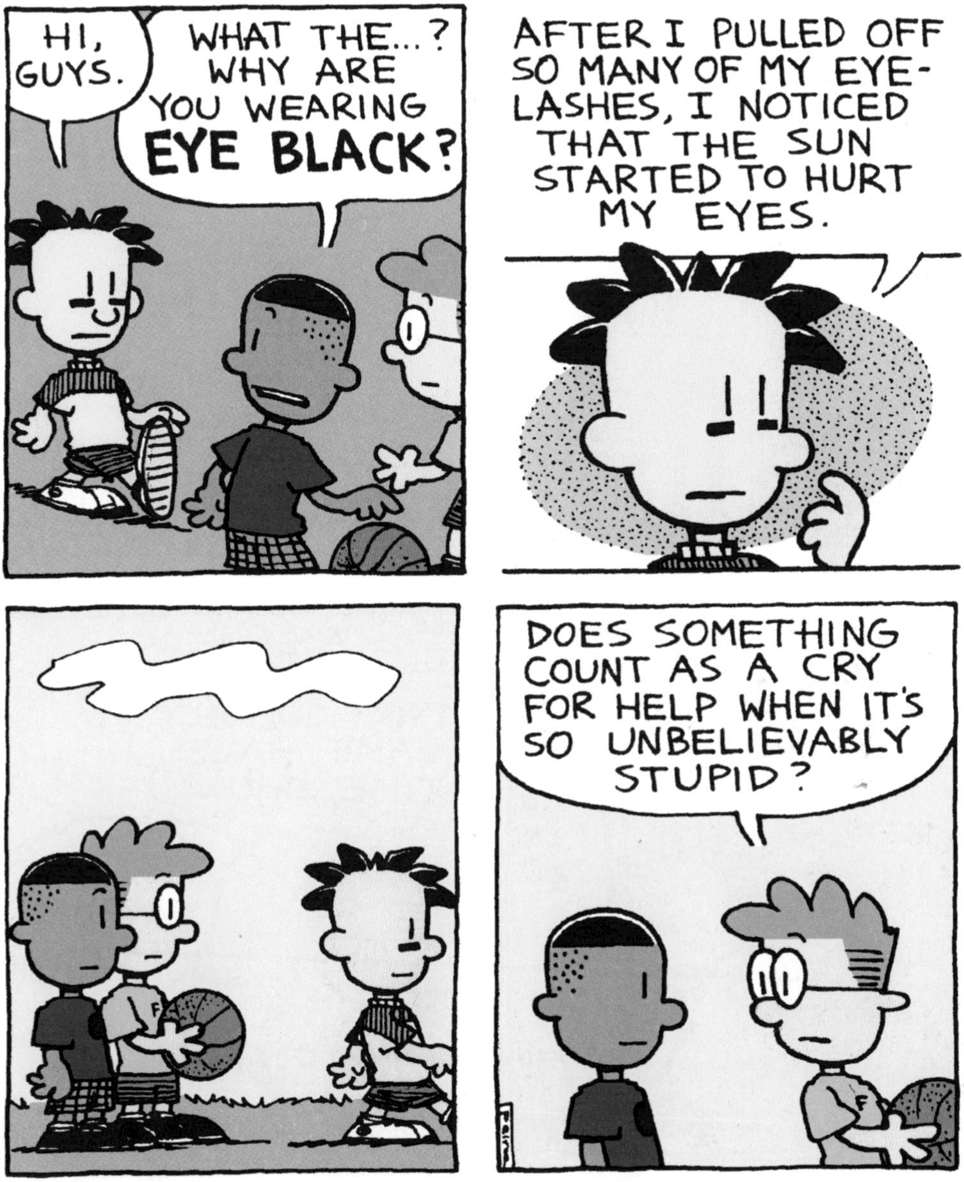
HI, GUYS.
WHAT THE...? WHY ARE YOU WEARING EYE BLACK?
AFTER I PULLED OFF SO MANY OF MY EYE-LASHES, I NOTICED THAT THE SUN STARTED TO HURT MY EYES.
DOES SOMETHING COUNT AS A CRY FOR HELP WHEN IT'S SO UNBELIEVABLY STUPID?

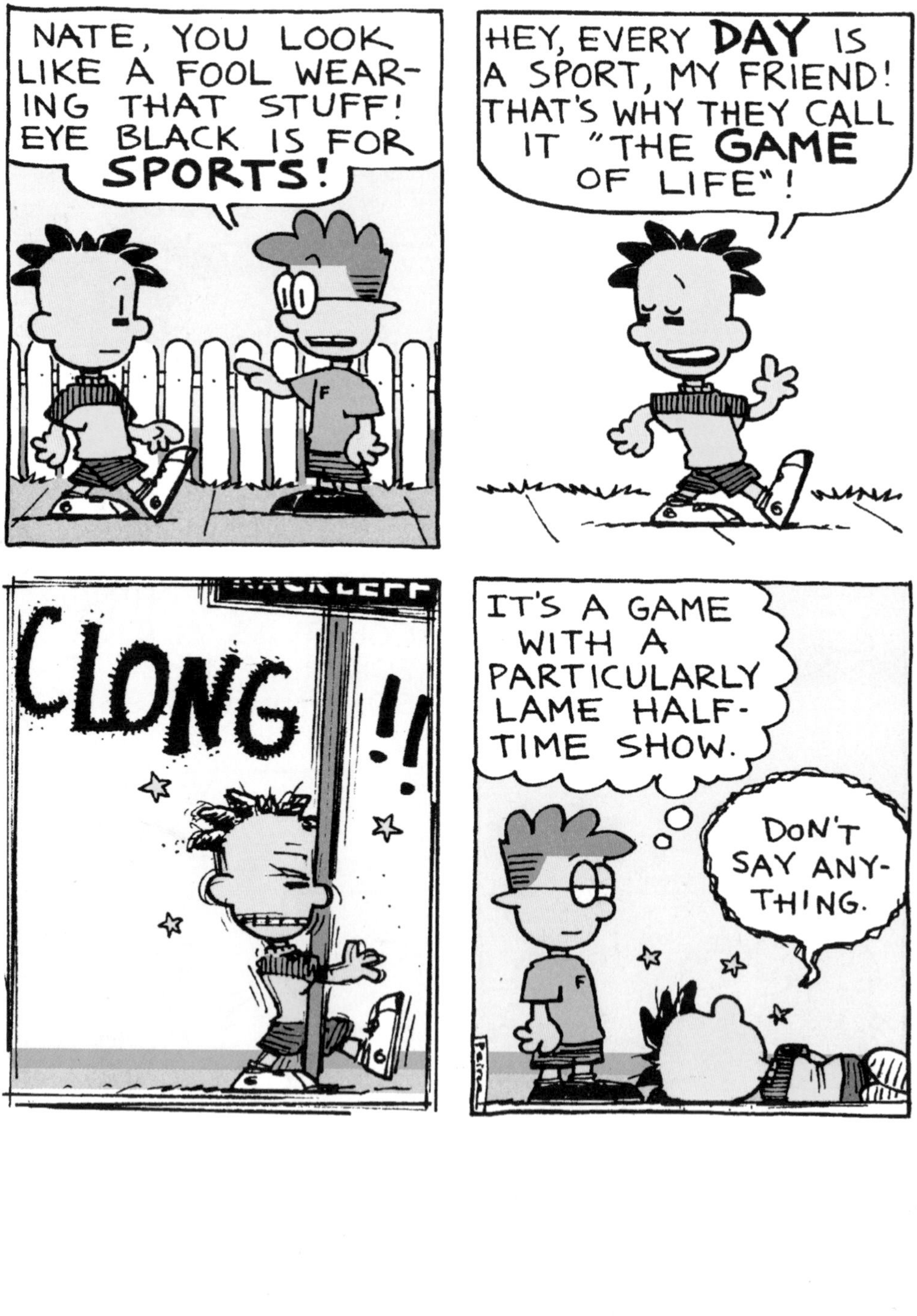
NATE, YOU LOOK LIKE A FOOL WEARING THAT STUFF! EYE BLACK IS FOR **SPORTS**!
HEY, EVERY **DAY** IS A SPORT, MY FRIEND! THAT'S WHY THEY CALL IT "THE **GAME** OF LIFE"!
CLONG!!
IT'S A GAME WITH A PARTICULARLY LAME HALF-TIME SHOW.
DON'T SAY ANYTHING.

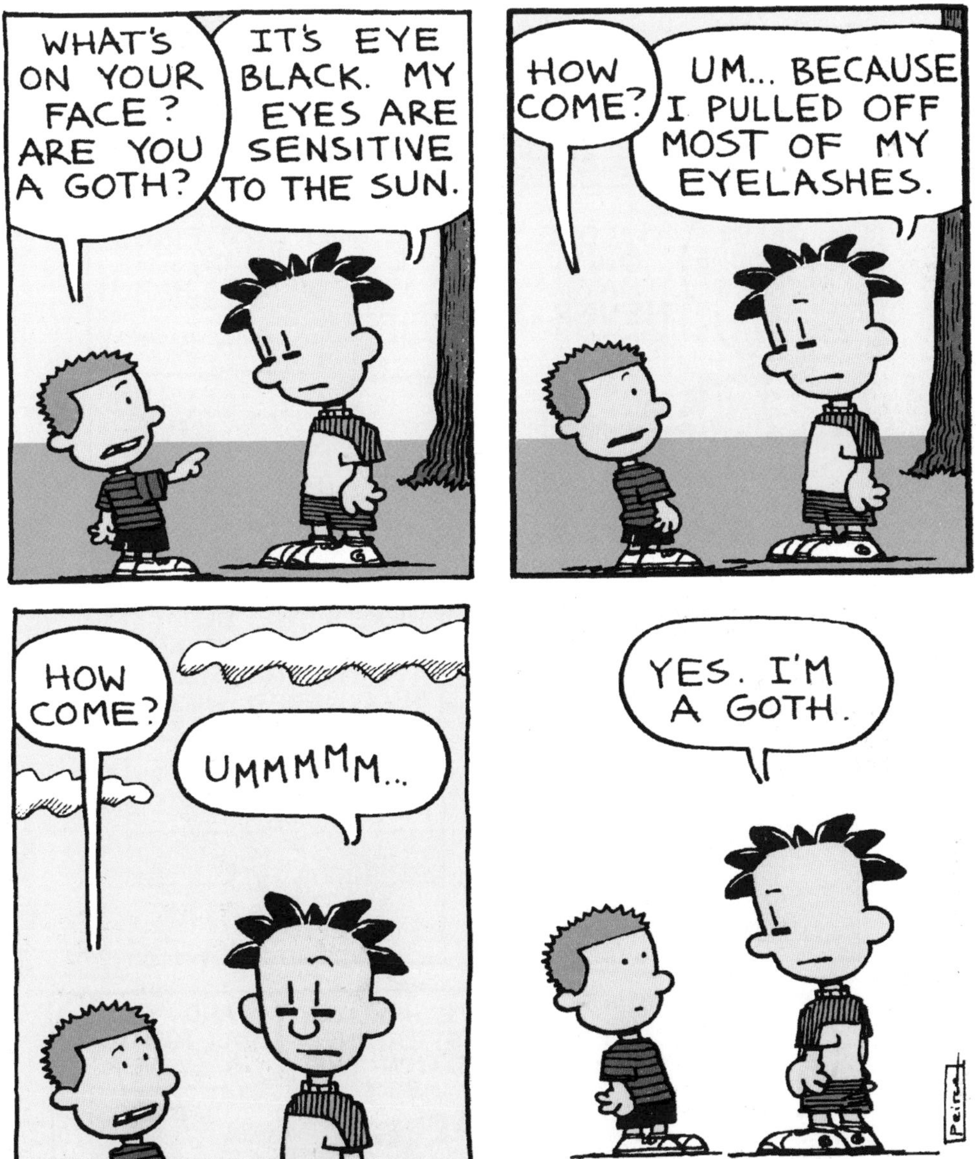
WHAT'S ON YOUR FACE? ARE YOU A GOTH?
IT'S EYE BLACK. MY EYES ARE SENSITIVE TO THE SUN.
HOW COME?
UM... BECAUSE I PULLED OFF MOST OF MY EYELASHES.
HOW COME?
UMMMMM...
YES. I'M A GOTH.
Peirce

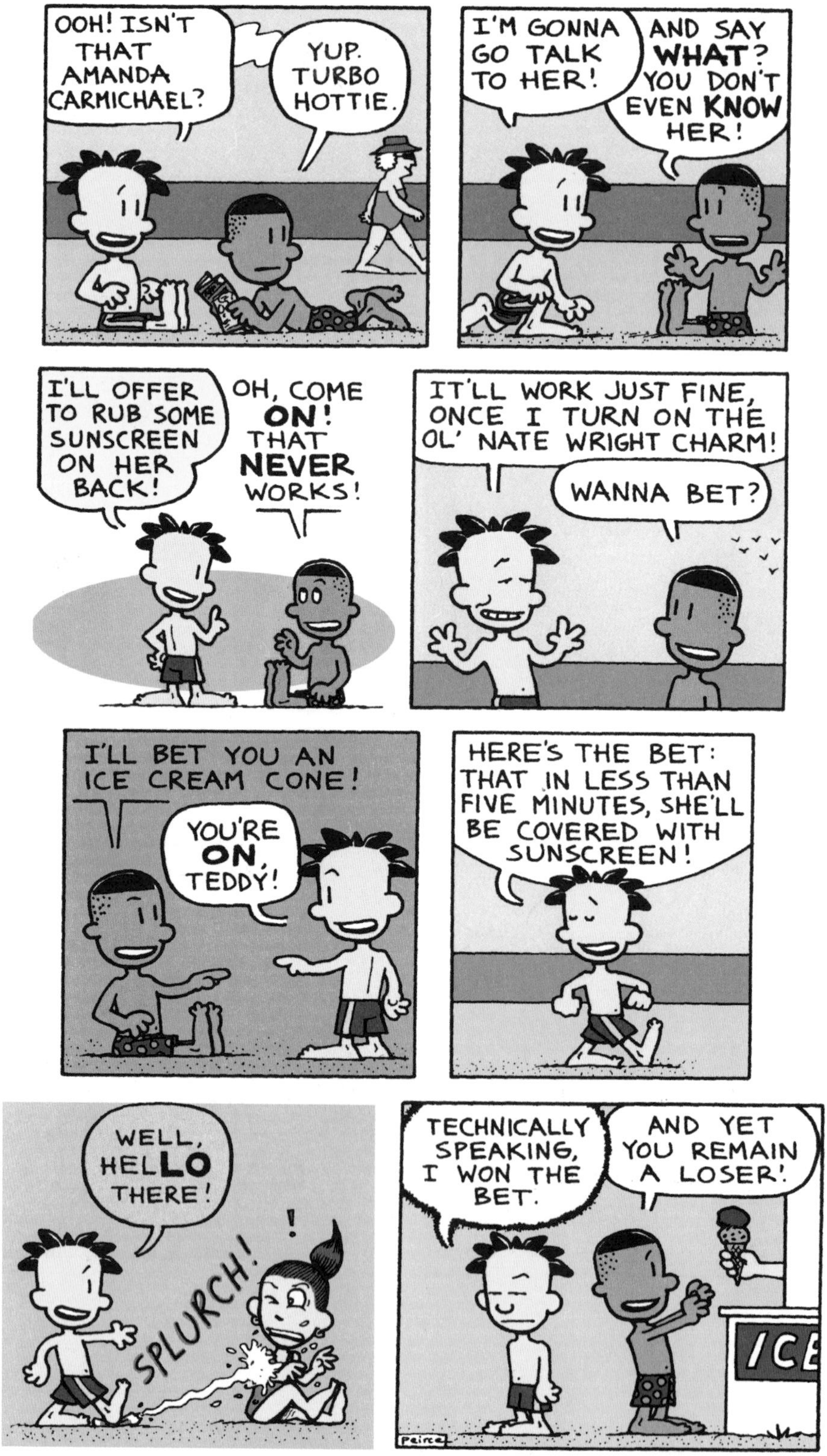
OOH! ISN'T THAT AMANDA CARMICHAEL?
YUP. TURBO HOTTIE.
I'M GONNA GO TALK TO HER!
AND SAY WHAT? YOU DON'T EVEN KNOW HER!
I'LL OFFER TO RUB SOME SUNSCREEN ON HER BACK!
OH, COME ON! THAT NEVER WORKS!
IT'LL WORK JUST FINE, ONCE I TURN ON THE OL' NATE WRIGHT CHARM!
WANNA BET?
I'LL BET YOU AN ICE CREAM CONE!
YOU'RE ON, TEDDY!
HERE'S THE BET: THAT IN LESS THAN FIVE MINUTES, SHE'LL BE COVERED WITH SUNSCREEN!
WELL, HELLO THERE!
SPLURCH!
!
TECHNICALLY SPEAKING, I WON THE BET.
AND YET YOU REMAIN A LOSER!
ICE
peirce

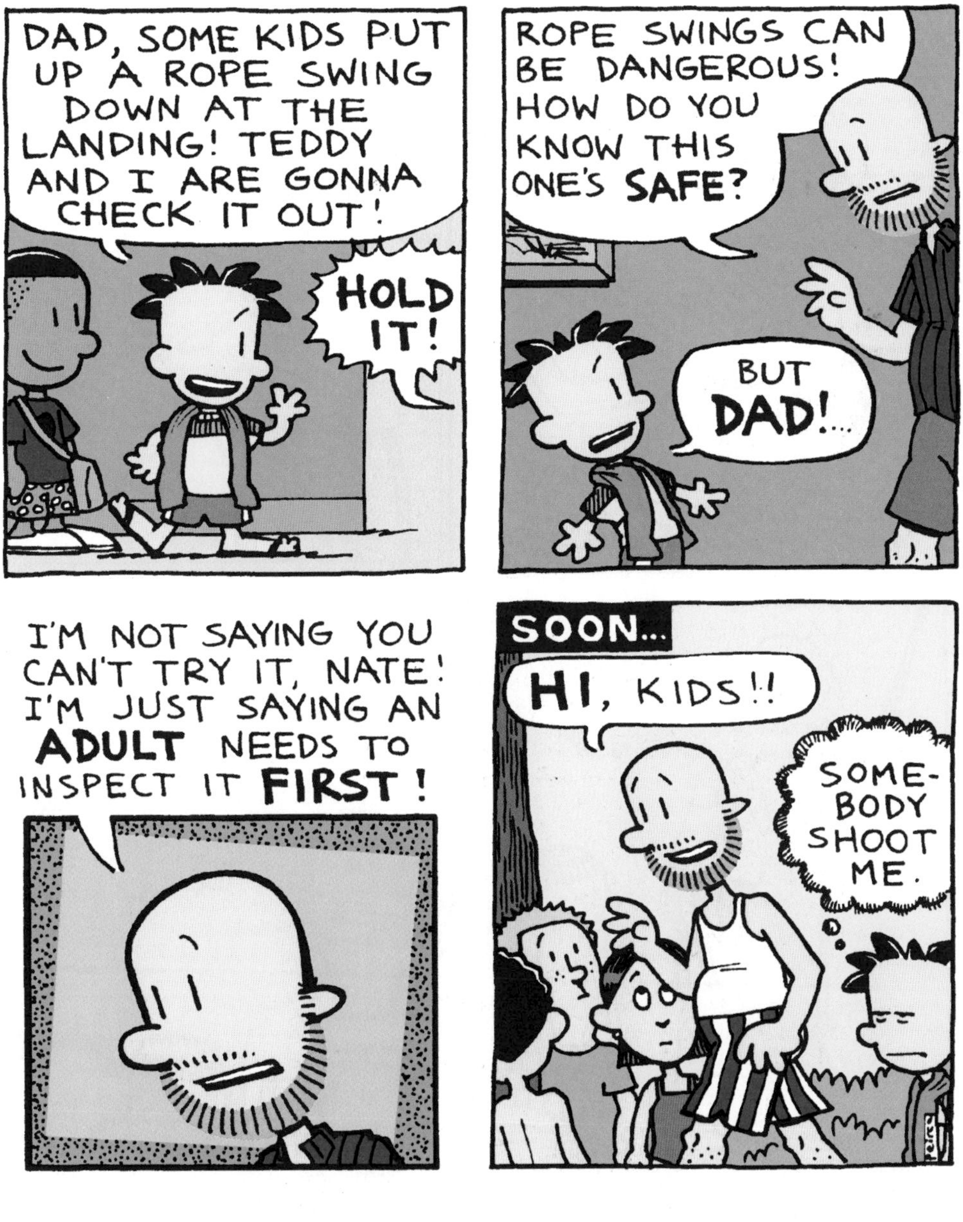
DAD, SOME KIDS PUT UP A ROPE SWING DOWN AT THE LANDING! TEDDY AND I ARE GONNA CHECK IT OUT!
HOLD IT!
ROPE SWINGS CAN BE DANGEROUS! HOW DO YOU KNOW THIS ONE'S SAFE?
BUT DAD!...
I'M NOT SAYING YOU CAN'T TRY IT, NATE! I'M JUST SAYING AN ADULT NEEDS TO INSPECT IT FIRST!
SOON...
HI, KIDS!!
SOME-BODY SHOOT ME.

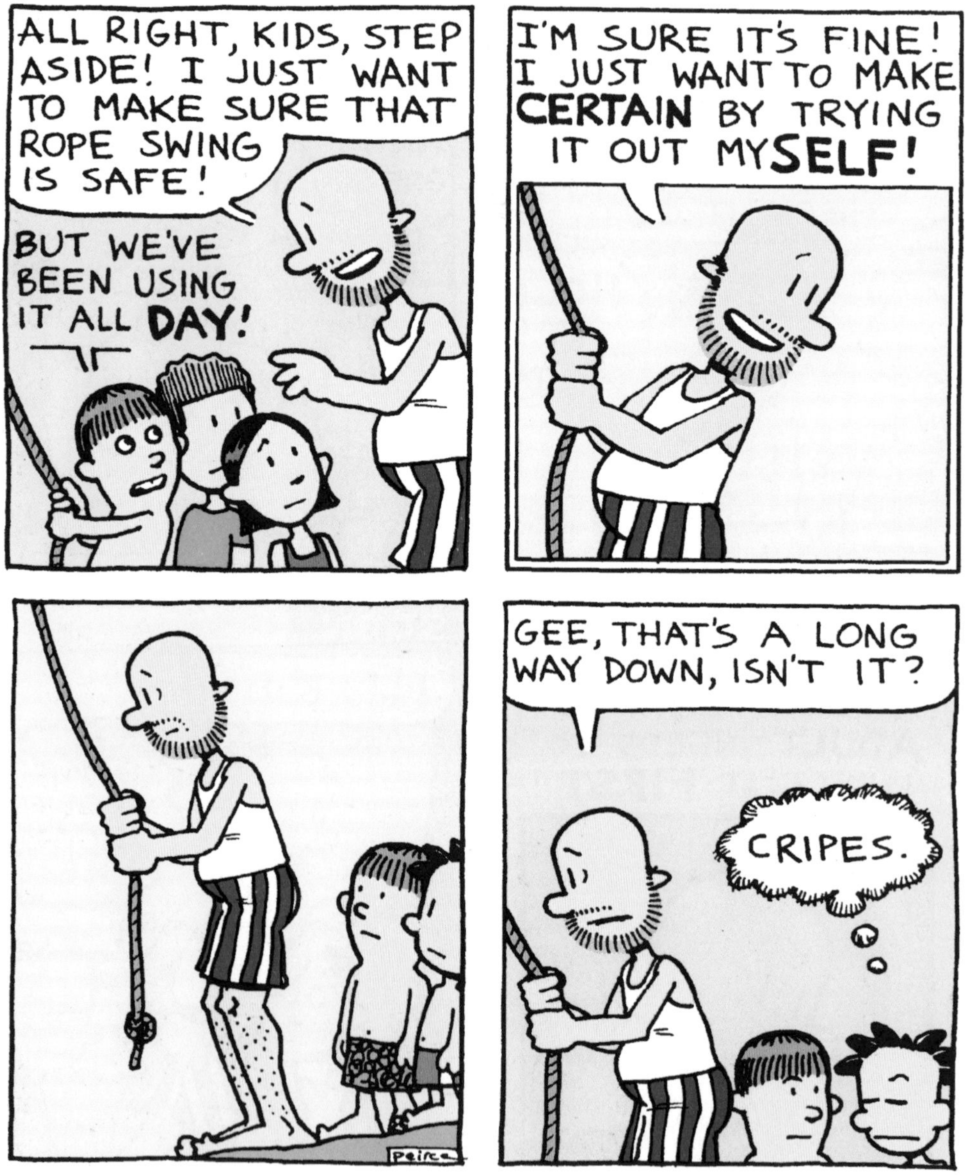
ALL RIGHT, KIDS, STEP ASIDE! I JUST WANT TO MAKE SURE THAT ROPE SWING IS SAFE!
BUT WE'VE BEEN USING IT ALL DAY!
I'M SURE IT'S FINE! I JUST WANT TO MAKE CERTAIN BY TRYING IT OUT MYSELF!
GEE, THAT'S A LONG WAY DOWN, ISN'T IT?
CRIPES.
Peirce

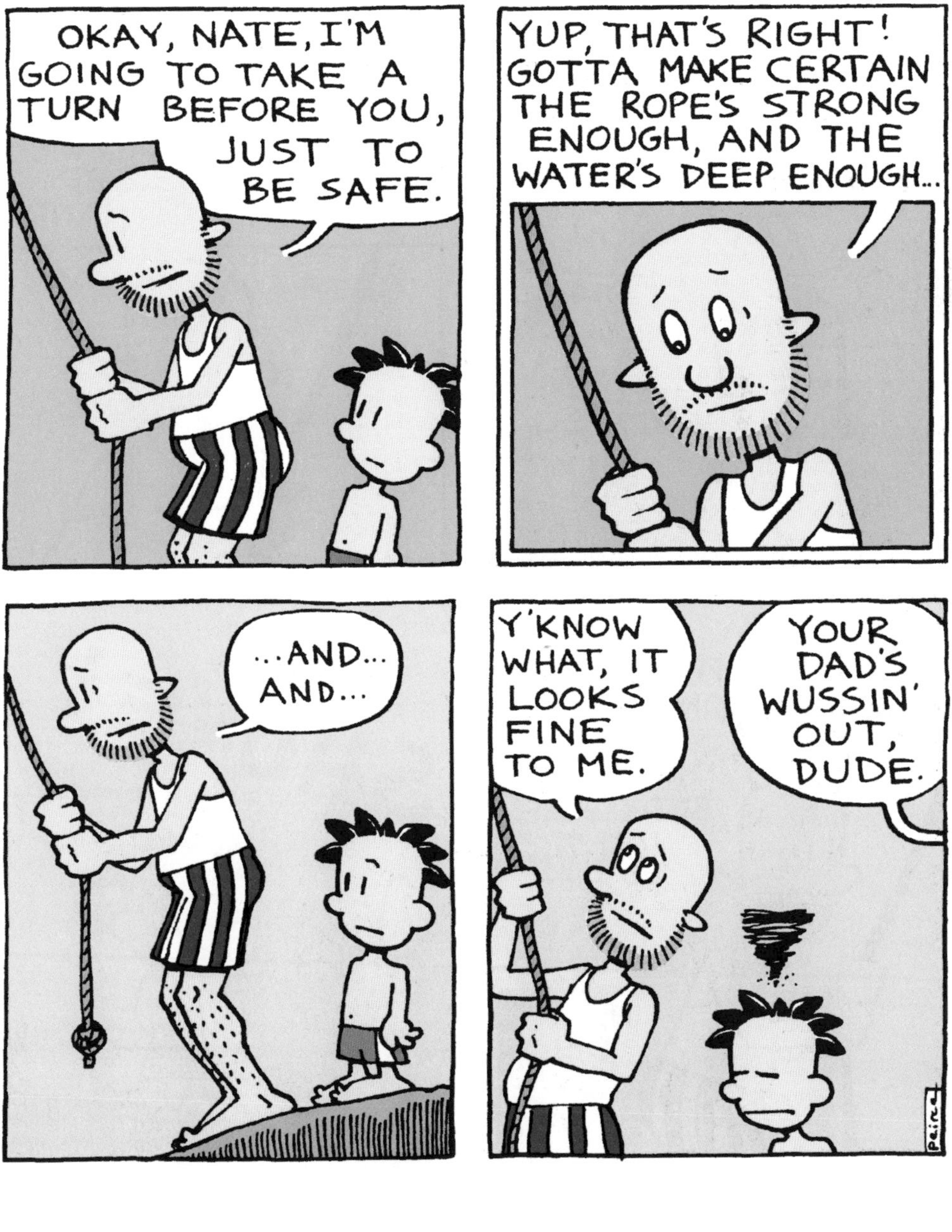
OKAY, NATE, I'M GOING TO TAKE A TURN BEFORE YOU, JUST TO BE SAFE.
YUP, THAT'S RIGHT! GOTTA MAKE CERTAIN THE ROPE'S STRONG ENOUGH, AND THE WATER'S DEEP ENOUGH...
...AND... AND...
Y'KNOW WHAT, IT LOOKS FINE TO ME.
YOUR DAD'S WUSSIN' OUT, DUDE.

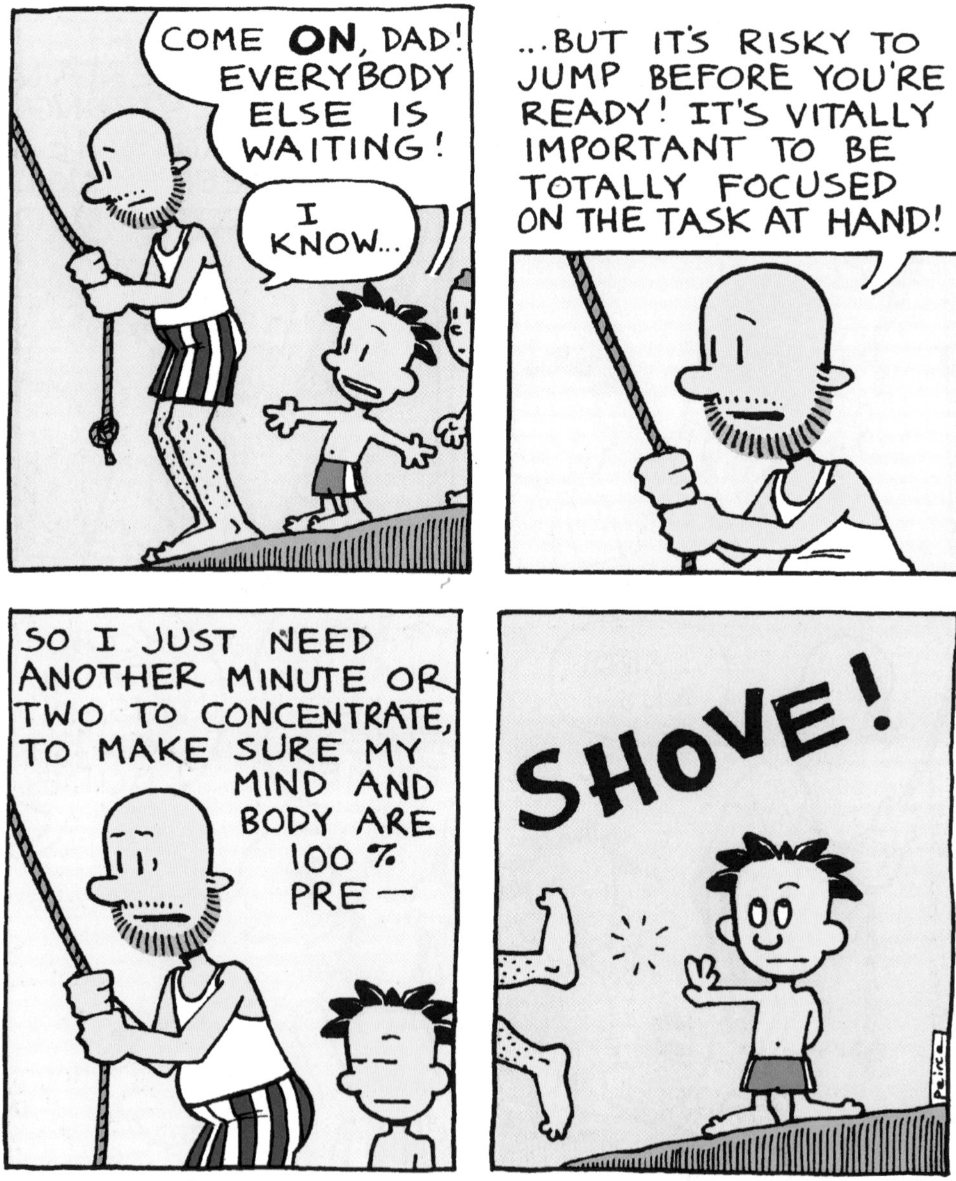
COME **ON**, DAD! EVERYBODY ELSE IS WAITING!
I KNOW...
...BUT IT'S RISKY TO JUMP BEFORE YOU'RE READY! IT'S VITALLY IMPORTANT TO BE TOTALLY FOCUSED ON THE TASK AT HAND!
SO I JUST NEED ANOTHER MINUTE OR TWO TO CONCENTRATE, TO MAKE SURE MY MIND AND BODY ARE 100% PRE—
SHOVE!
Peirce

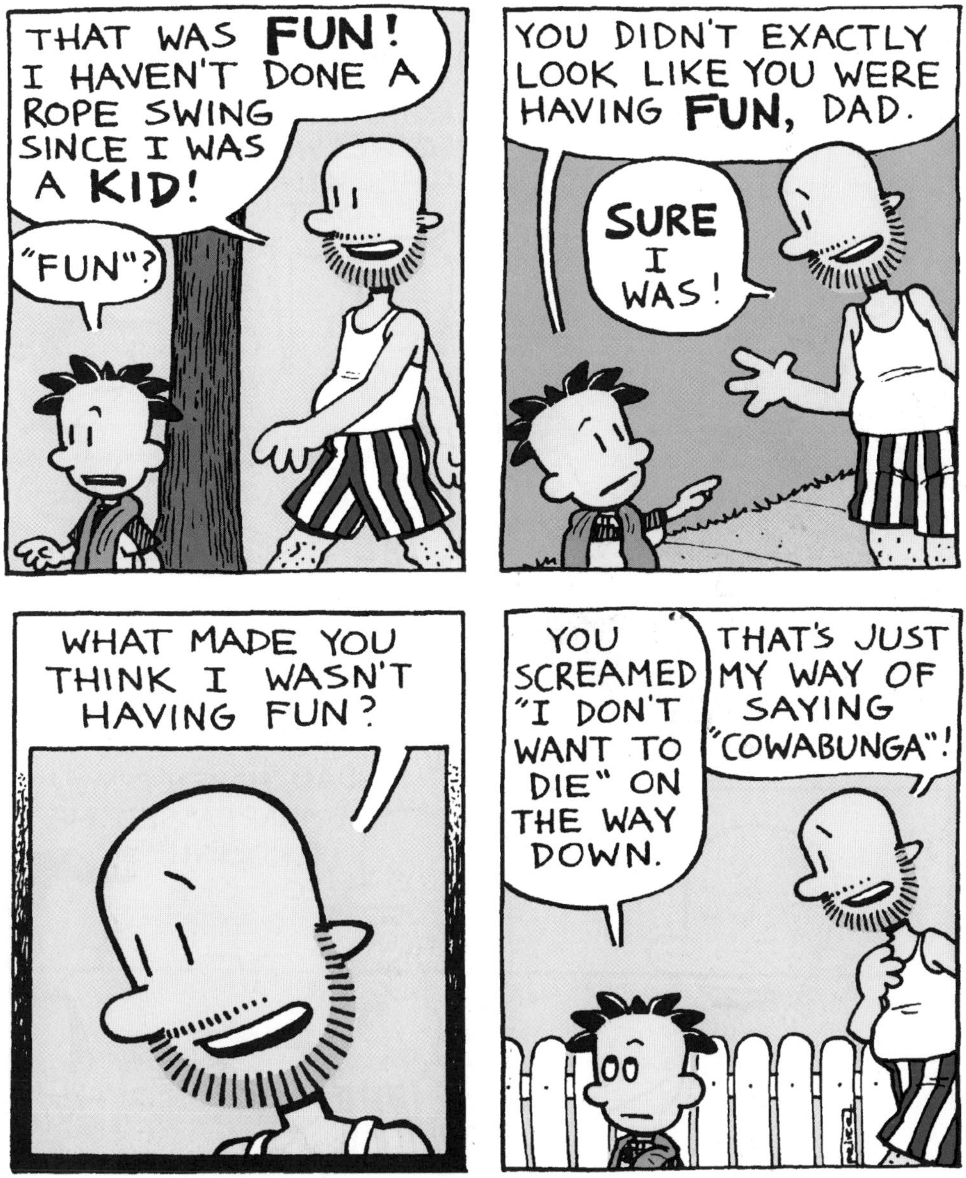
THAT WAS **FUN**! I HAVEN'T DONE A ROPE SWING SINCE I WAS A **KID**!
"FUN"?
YOU DIDN'T EXACTLY LOOK LIKE YOU WERE HAVING **FUN**, DAD.
SURE I WAS!
WHAT MADE YOU THINK I WASN'T HAVING FUN?
YOU SCREAMED "I DON'T WANT TO DIE" ON THE WAY DOWN.
THAT'S JUST MY WAY OF SAYING "COWABUNGA"!

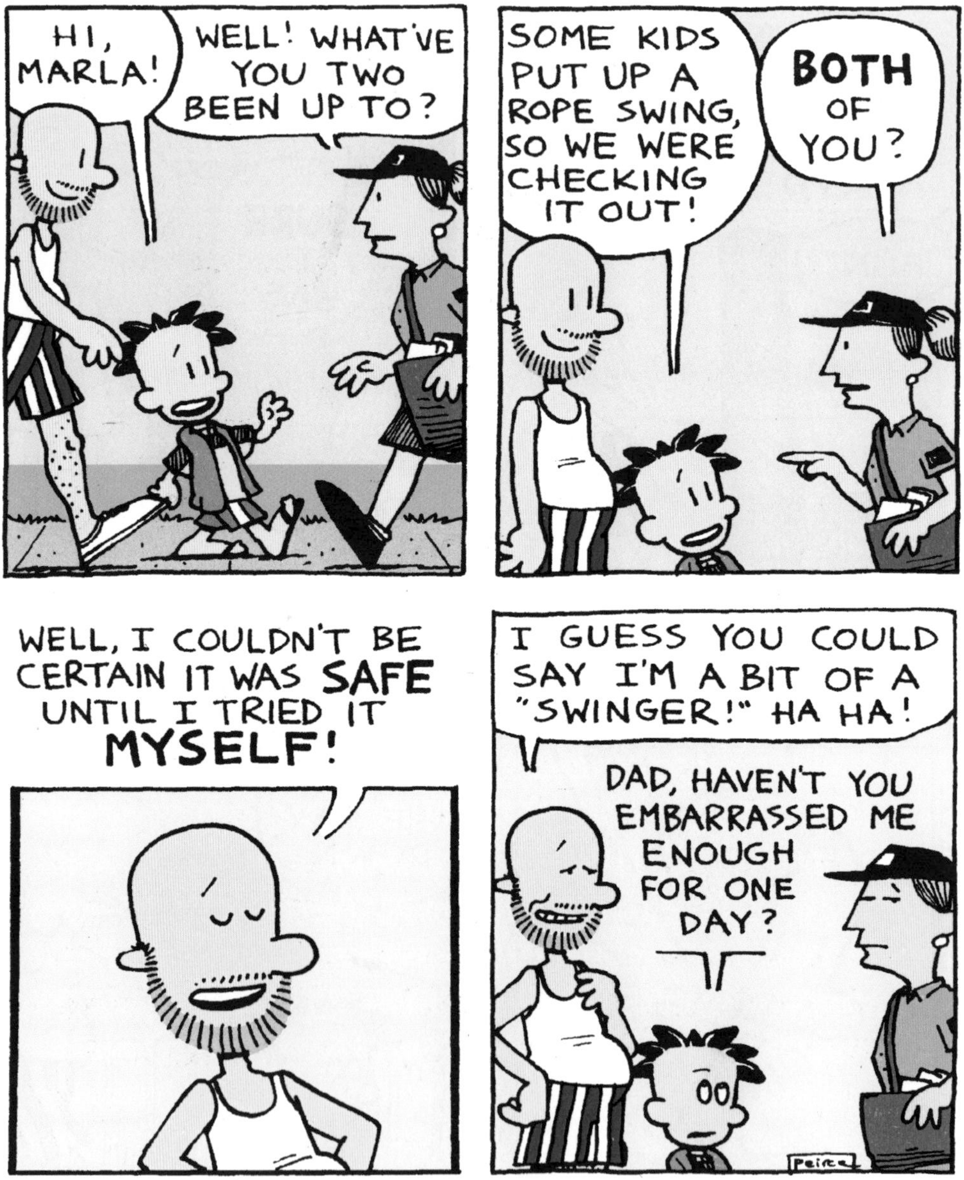
HI, MARLA!
WELL! WHAT'VE YOU TWO BEEN UP TO?
SOME KIDS PUT UP A ROPE SWING, SO WE WERE CHECKING IT OUT!
BOTH OF YOU?
WELL, I COULDN'T BE CERTAIN IT WAS SAFE UNTIL I TRIED IT MYSELF!
I GUESS YOU COULD SAY I'M A BIT OF A "SWINGER!" HA HA!
DAD, HAVEN'T YOU EMBARRASSED ME ENOUGH FOR ONE DAY?
Peirce

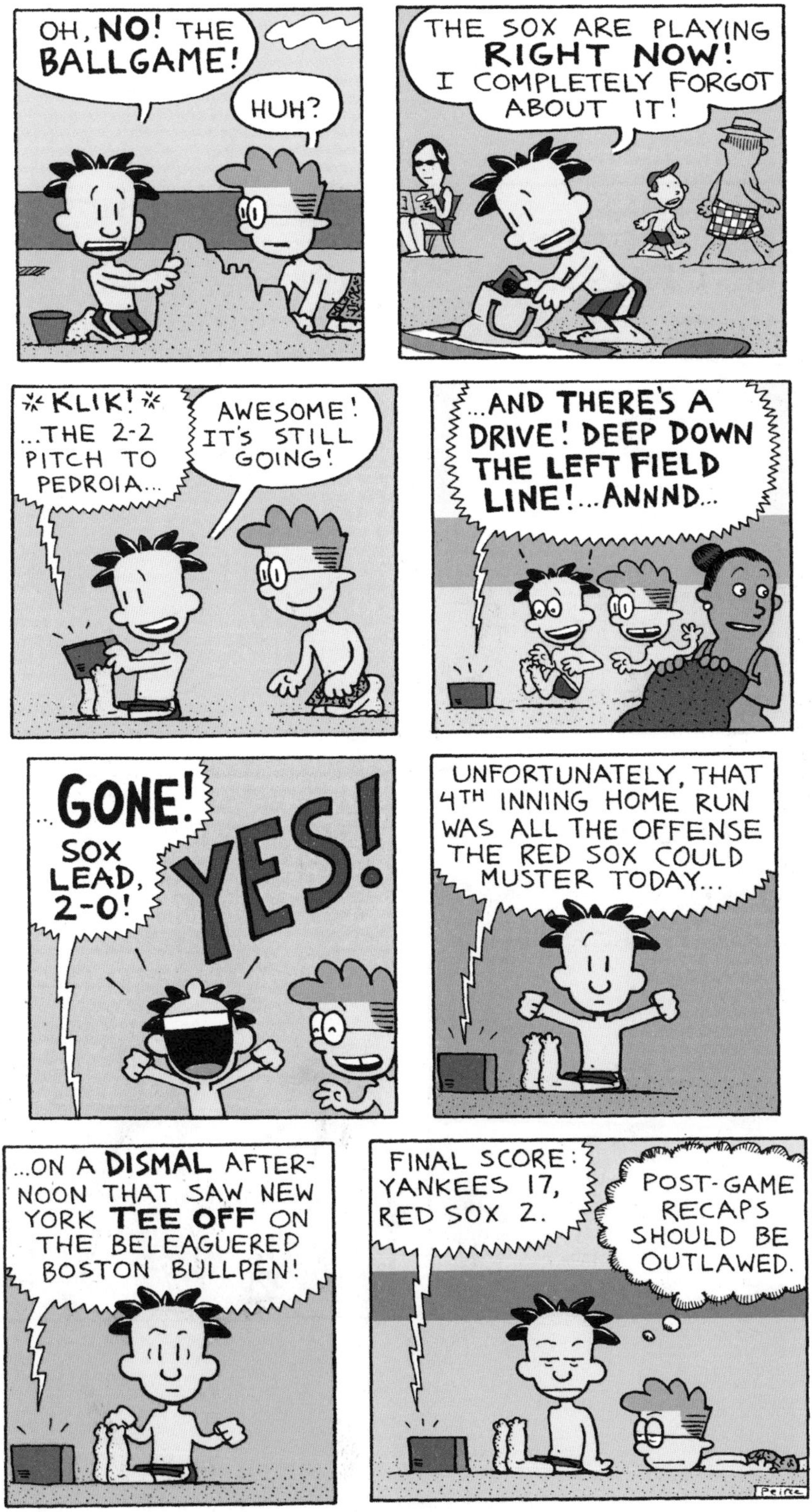

OH, NO! THE BALLGAME!
HUH?
THE SOX ARE PLAYING RIGHT NOW! I COMPLETELY FORGOT ABOUT IT!
KLIK! ...THE 2-2 PITCH TO PEDROIA...
AWESOME! IT'S STILL GOING!
...AND THERE'S A DRIVE! DEEP DOWN THE LEFT FIELD LINE!...ANNND...
...GONE! SOX LEAD, 2-0!
YES!
UNFORTUNATELY, THAT 4TH INNING HOME RUN WAS ALL THE OFFENSE THE RED SOX COULD MUSTER TODAY...
...ON A DISMAL AFTER-NOON THAT SAW NEW YORK TEE OFF ON THE BELEAGUERED BOSTON BULLPEN!
FINAL SCORE: YANKEES 17, RED SOX 2.
POST-GAME RECAPS SHOULD BE OUTLAWED.
Peirce

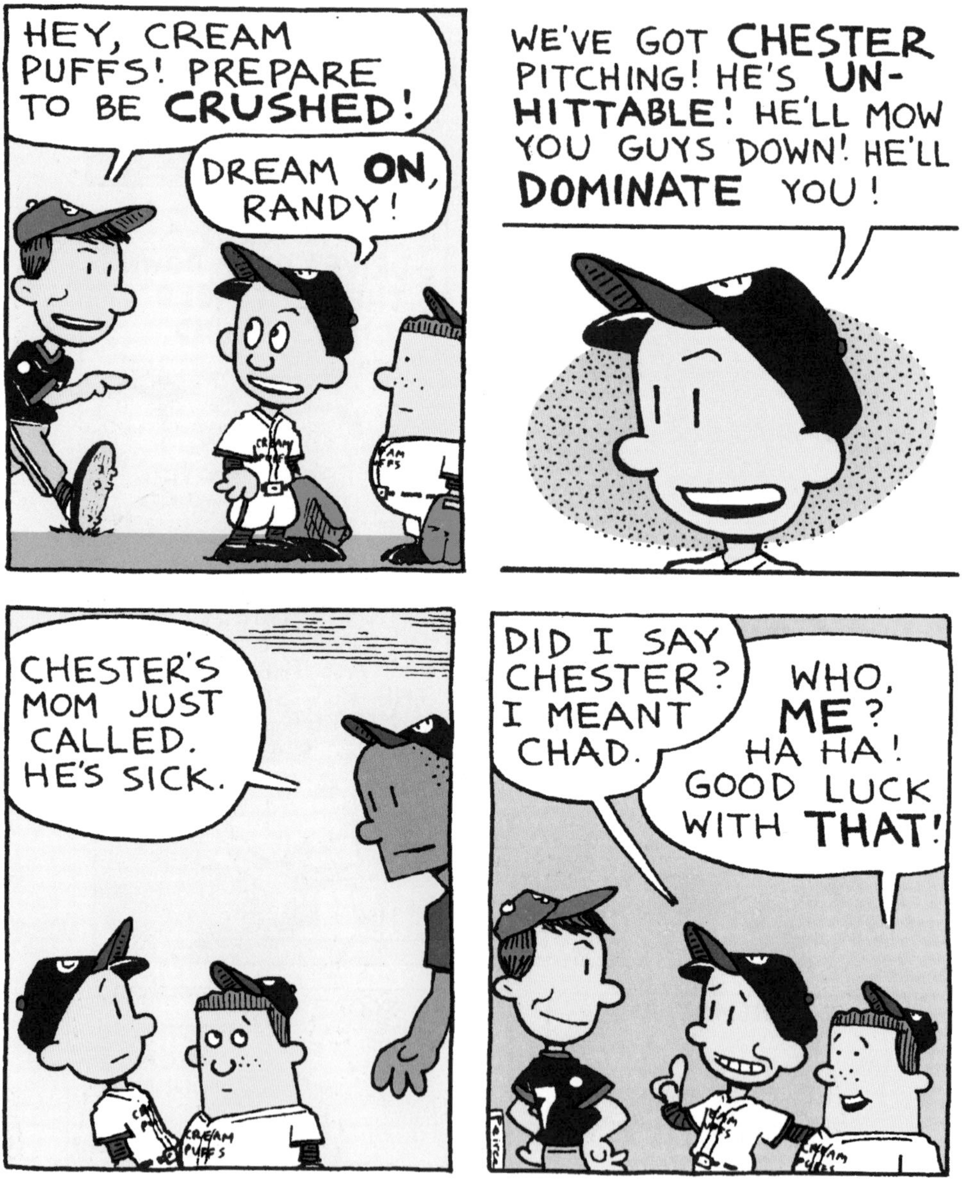
HEY, CREAM PUFFS! PREPARE TO BE CRUSHED!
DREAM ON, RANDY!
WE'VE GOT CHESTER PITCHING! HE'S UN-HITTABLE! HE'LL MOW YOU GUYS DOWN! HE'LL DOMINATE YOU!
CHESTER'S MOM JUST CALLED. HE'S SICK.
DID I SAY CHESTER? I MEANT CHAD.
WHO, ME? HA HA! GOOD LUCK WITH THAT!

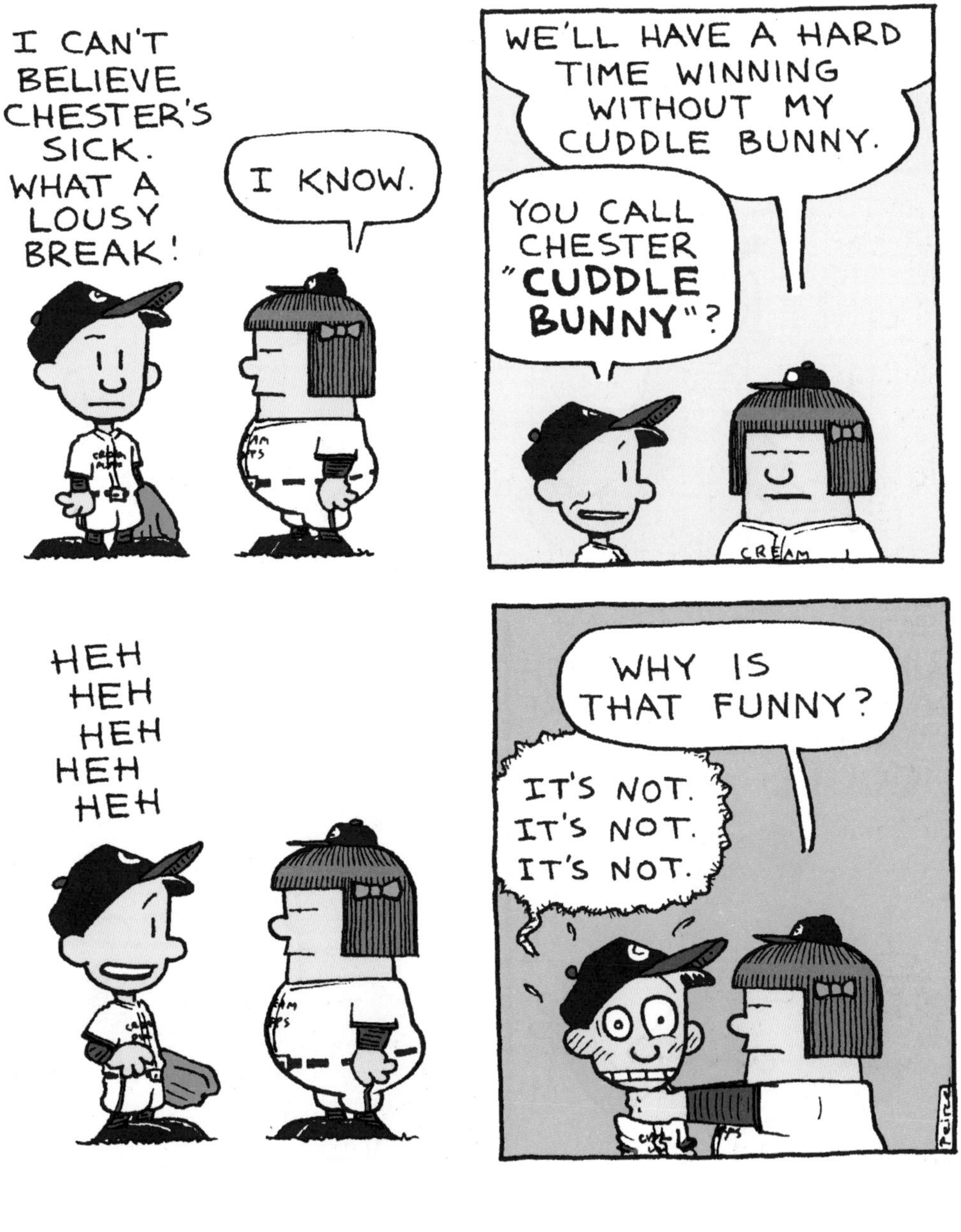
I CAN'T BELIEVE CHESTER'S SICK. WHAT A LOUSY BREAK!
I KNOW.
WE'LL HAVE A HARD TIME WINNING WITHOUT MY CUDDLE BUNNY.
YOU CALL CHESTER "CUDDLE BUNNY"?
CREAM
HEH HEH HEH HEH HEH
WHY IS THAT FUNNY?
IT'S NOT. IT'S NOT. IT'S NOT.

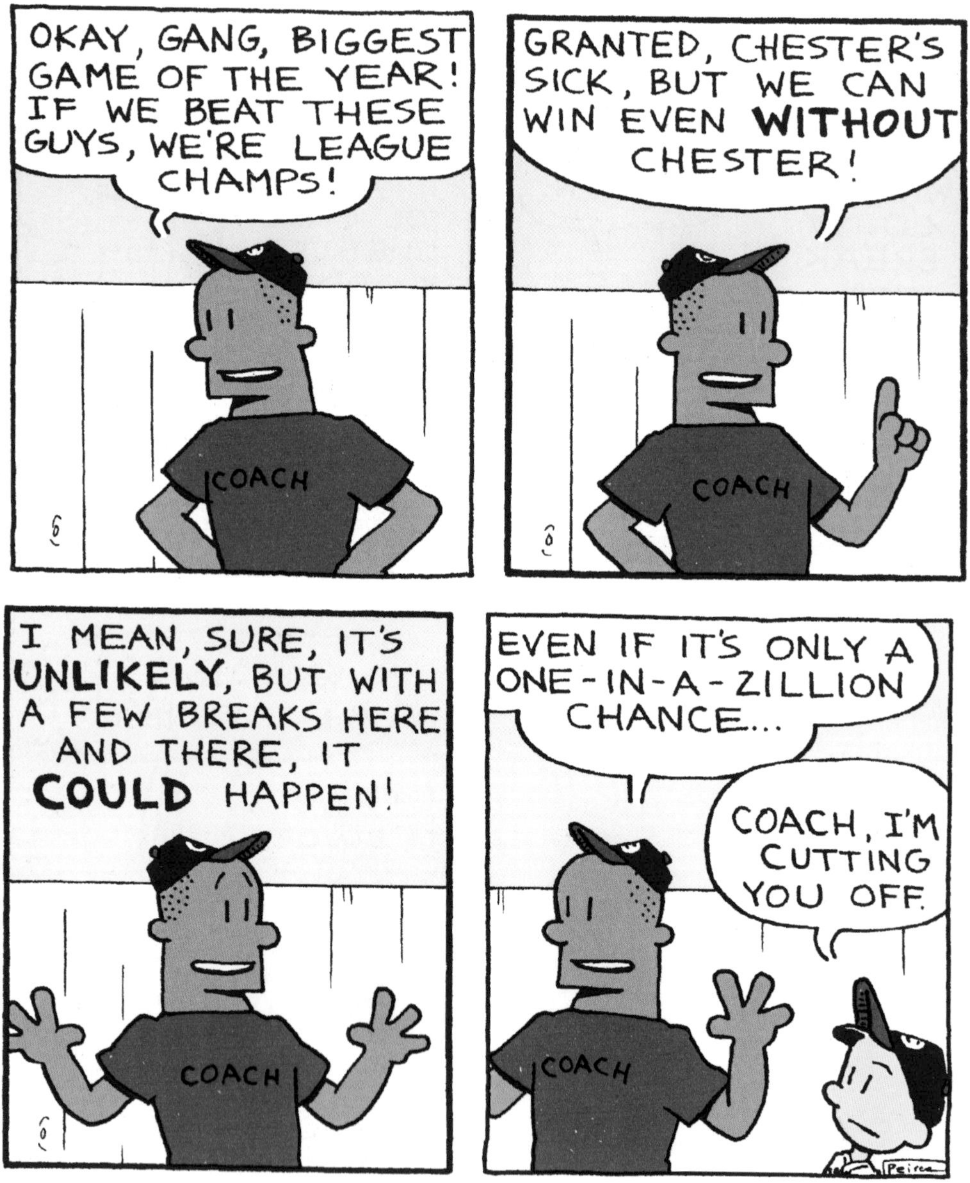
OKAY, GANG, BIGGEST GAME OF THE YEAR! IF WE BEAT THESE GUYS, WE'RE LEAGUE CHAMPS!
COACH
GRANTED, CHESTER'S SICK, BUT WE CAN WIN EVEN WITHOUT CHESTER!
COACH
I MEAN, SURE, IT'S UNLIKELY, BUT WITH A FEW BREAKS HERE AND THERE, IT COULD HAPPEN!
COACH
EVEN IF IT'S ONLY A ONE-IN-A-ZILLION CHANCE...
COACH, I'M CUTTING YOU OFF.
COACH
Peirce

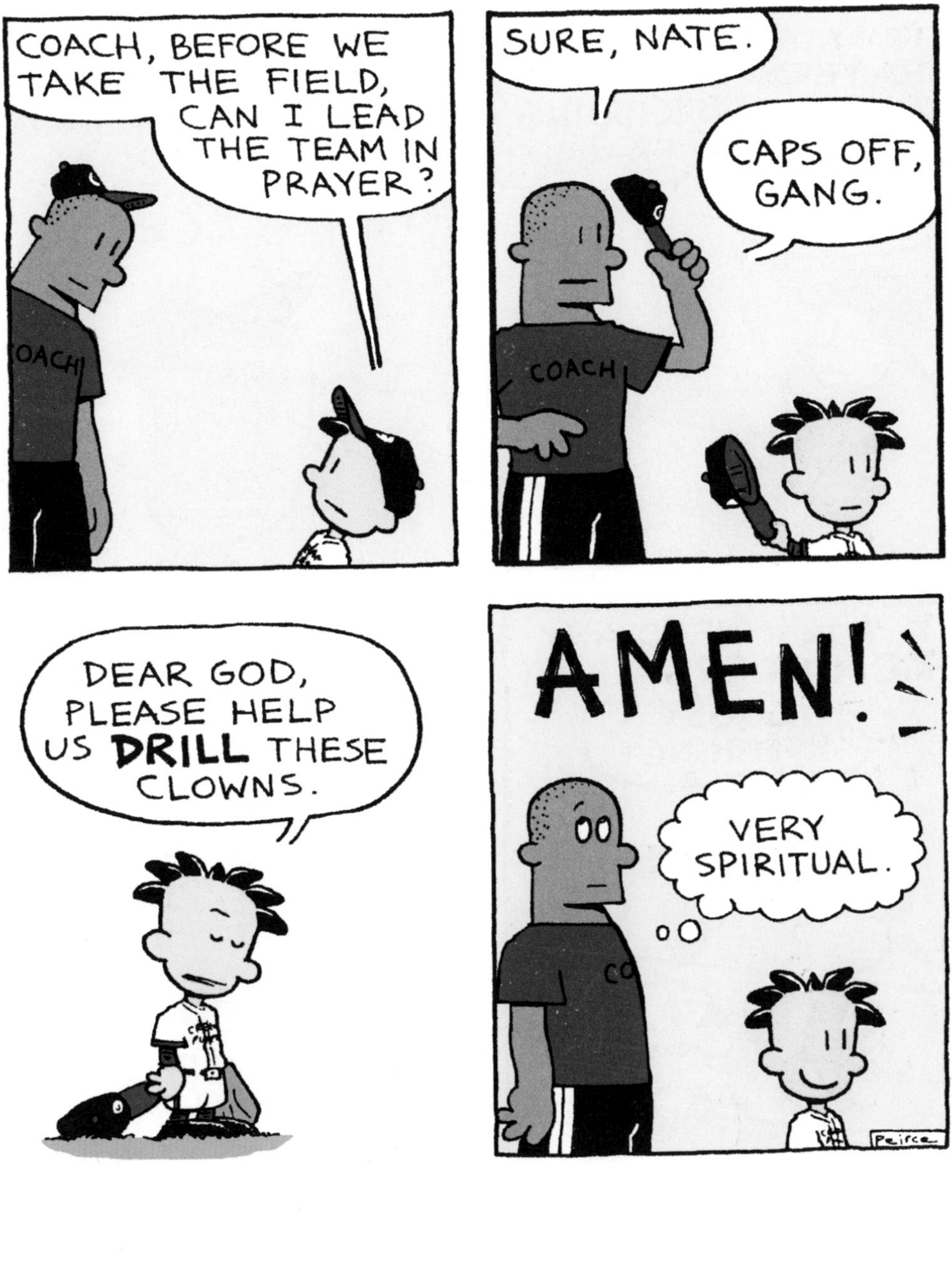
COACH, BEFORE WE TAKE THE FIELD, CAN I LEAD THE TEAM IN PRAYER?
COACH
SURE, NATE.
CAPS OFF, GANG.
COACH
DEAR GOD, PLEASE HELP US **DRILL** THESE CLOWNS.
AMEN!
VERY SPIRITUAL.
Peirce

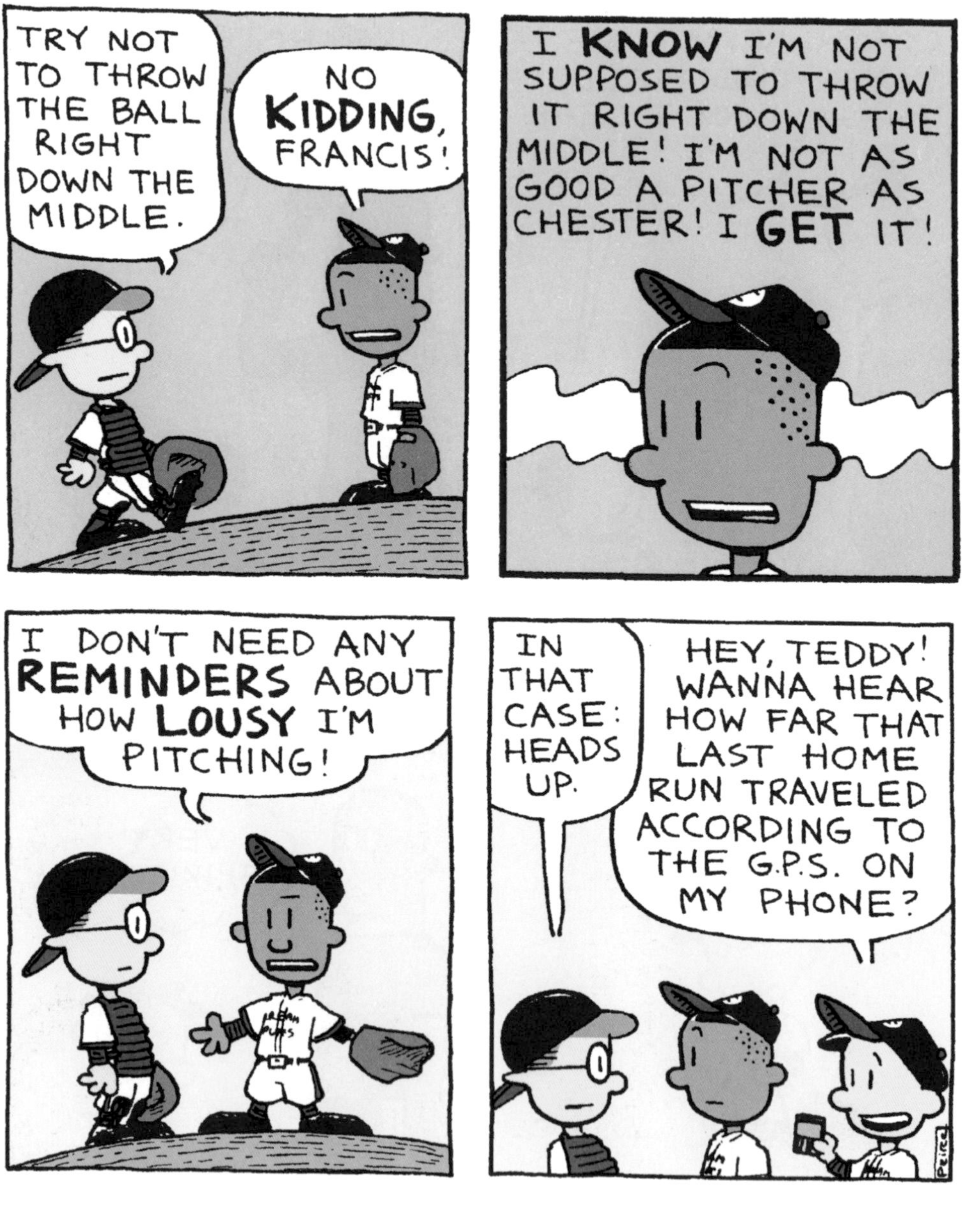
TRY NOT TO THROW THE BALL RIGHT DOWN THE MIDDLE.
NO KIDDING, FRANCIS!
I KNOW I'M NOT SUPPOSED TO THROW IT RIGHT DOWN THE MIDDLE! I'M NOT AS GOOD A PITCHER AS CHESTER! I GET IT!
I DON'T NEED ANY REMINDERS ABOUT HOW LOUSY I'M PITCHING!
HEY, TEDDY! WANNA HEAR HOW FAR THAT LAST HOME RUN TRAVELED ACCORDING TO THE G.P.S. ON MY PHONE?
IN THAT CASE: HEADS UP.
PEIRCE

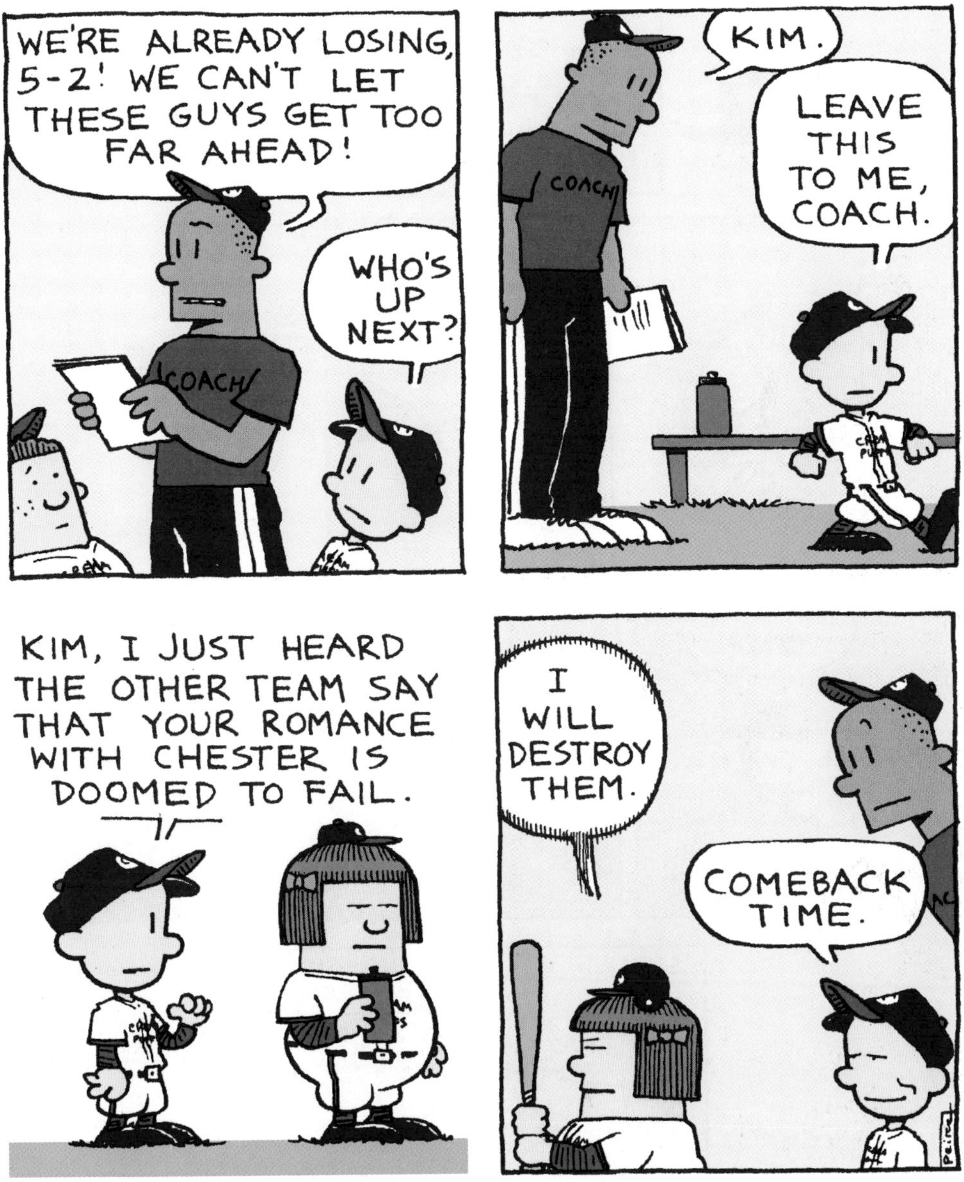
WE'RE ALREADY LOSING, 5-2! WE CAN'T LET THESE GUYS GET TOO FAR AHEAD!
WHO'S UP NEXT?
KIM.
LEAVE THIS TO ME, COACH.
KIM, I JUST HEARD THE OTHER TEAM SAY THAT YOUR ROMANCE WITH CHESTER IS DOOMED TO FAIL.
I WILL DESTROY THEM.
COMEBACK TIME.

KRAK!

BUMP!

OH, COME **ON!**

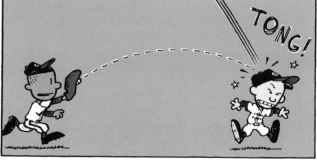

TONG!

SHOULD I GIVE NATE AN ASSIST FOR THAT?

...AND AN ICE PACK.

COACH

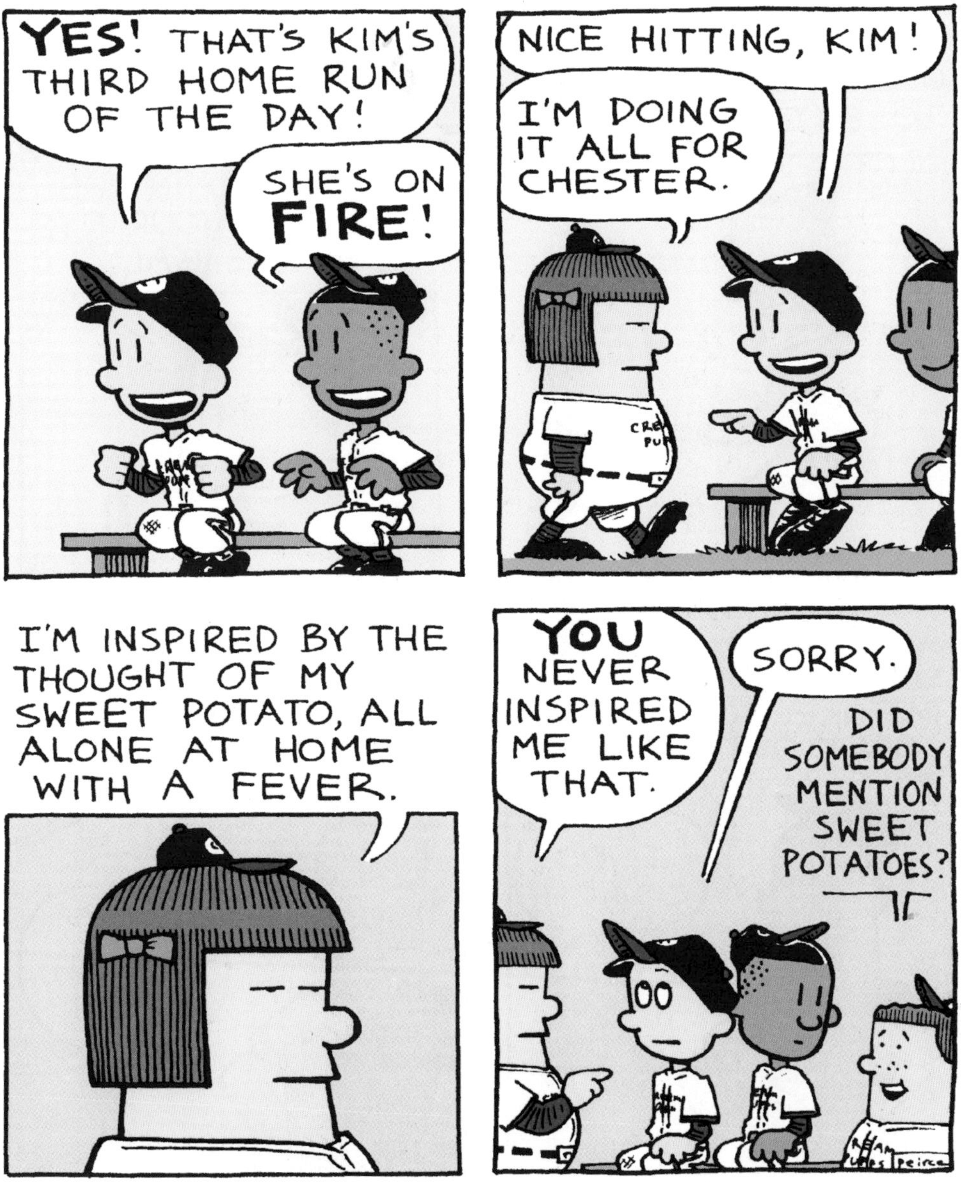
YES! THAT'S KIM'S THIRD HOME RUN OF THE DAY!
SHE'S ON FIRE!
NICE HITTING, KIM!
I'M DOING IT ALL FOR CHESTER.
I'M INSPIRED BY THE THOUGHT OF MY SWEET POTATO, ALL ALONE AT HOME WITH A FEVER.
YOU NEVER INSPIRED ME LIKE THAT.
SORRY.
DID SOMEBODY MENTION SWEET POTATOES?
peirce

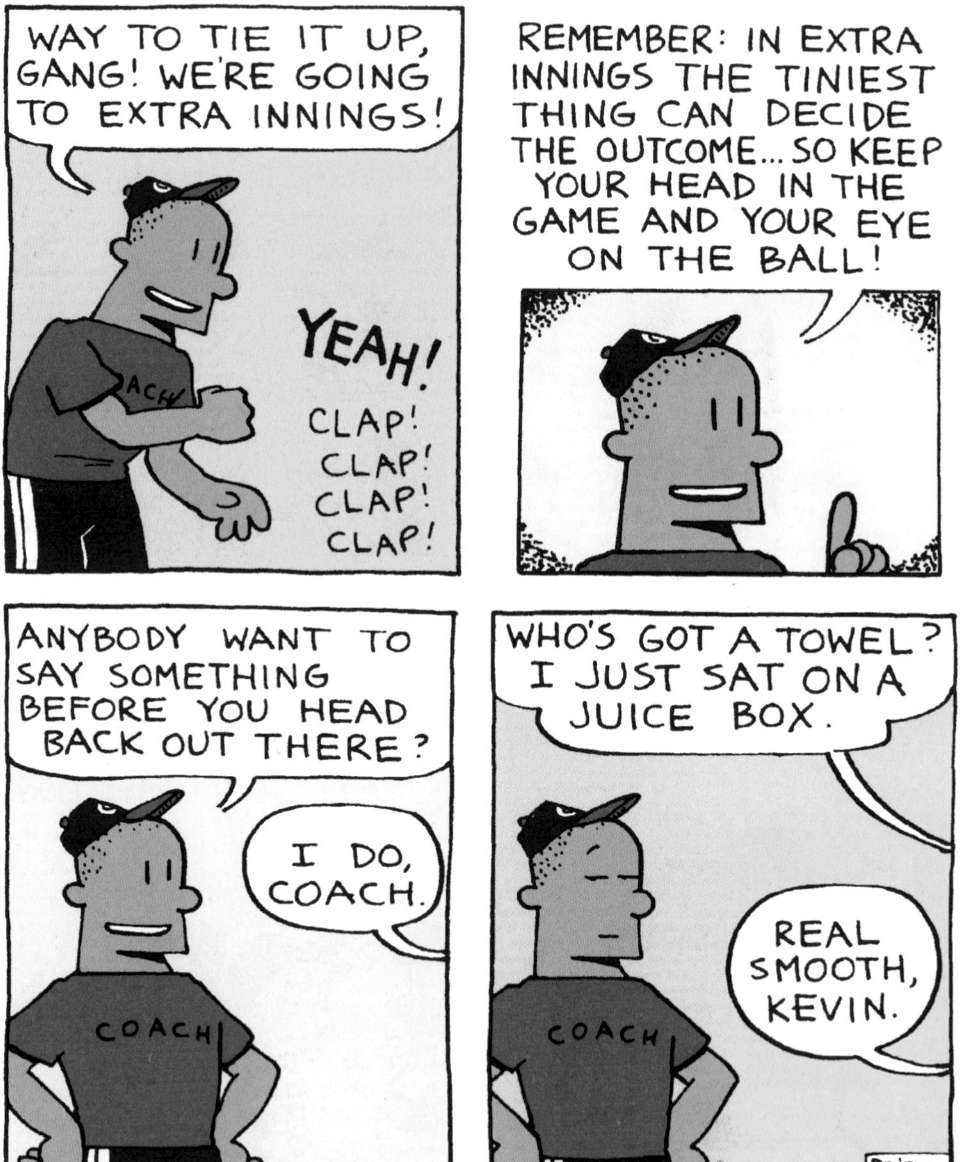
WAY TO TIE IT UP, GANG! WE'RE GOING TO EXTRA INNINGS!
YEAH!
CLAP! CLAP! CLAP! CLAP!
REMEMBER: IN EXTRA INNINGS THE TINIEST THING CAN DECIDE THE OUTCOME... SO KEEP YOUR HEAD IN THE GAME AND YOUR EYE ON THE BALL!
ANYBODY WANT TO SAY SOMETHING BEFORE YOU HEAD BACK OUT THERE?
I DO, COACH.
COACH
WHO'S GOT A TOWEL? I JUST SAT ON A JUICE BOX.
REAL SMOOTH, KEVIN.
COACH
Peirce

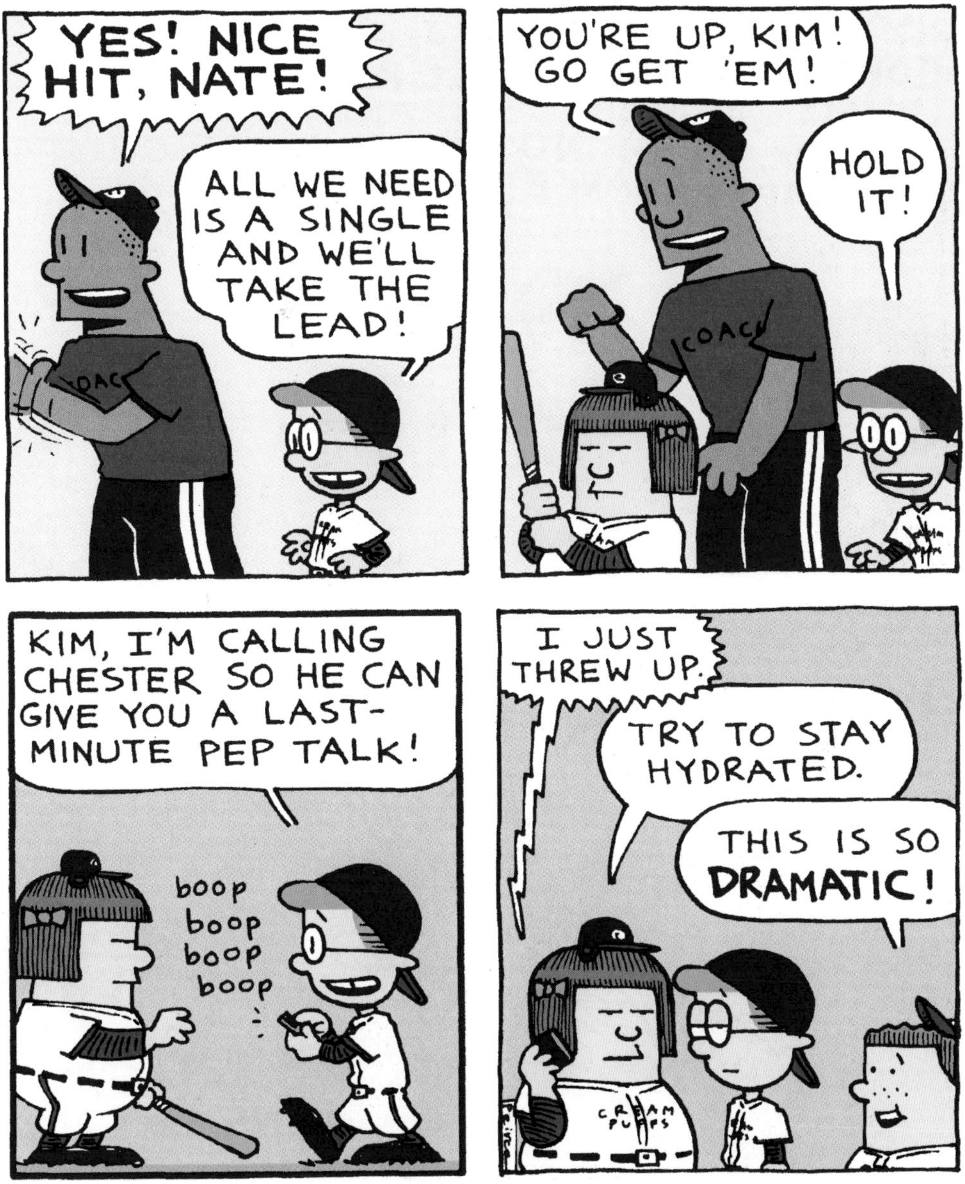
YES! NICE HIT, NATE!
ALL WE NEED IS A SINGLE AND WE'LL TAKE THE LEAD!
YOU'RE UP, KIM! GO GET 'EM!
HOLD IT!
KIM, I'M CALLING CHESTER SO HE CAN GIVE YOU A LAST-MINUTE PEP TALK!
boop boop boop boop
I JUST THREW UP.
TRY TO STAY HYDRATED.
THIS IS SO DRAMATIC!

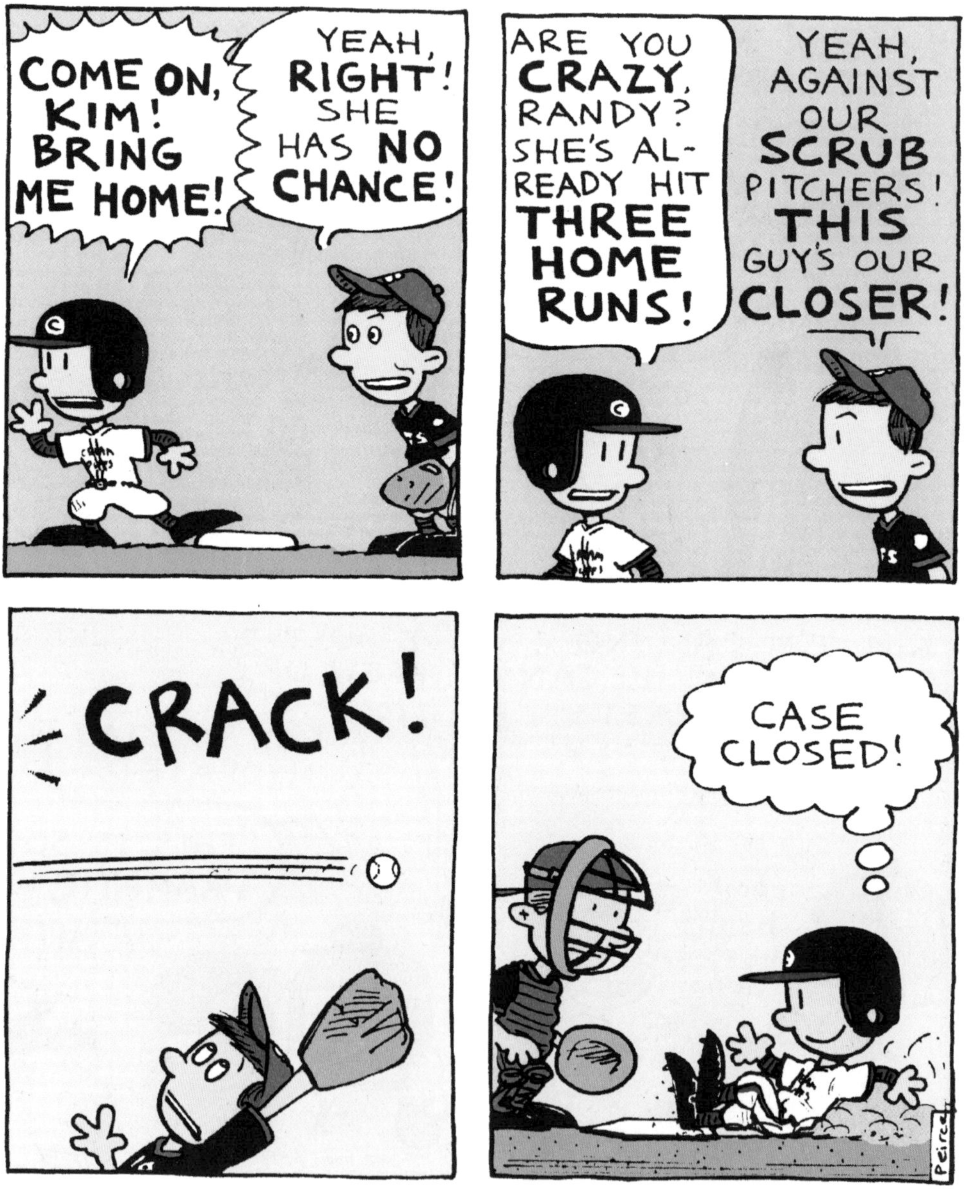
COME ON, KIM! BRING ME HOME!
YEAH, RIGHT! SHE HAS NO CHANCE!
ARE YOU CRAZY, RANDY? SHE'S AL-READY HIT THREE HOME RUNS!
YEAH, AGAINST OUR SCRUB PITCHERS! THIS GUY'S OUR CLOSER!
CRACK!
CASE CLOSED!
Peirce

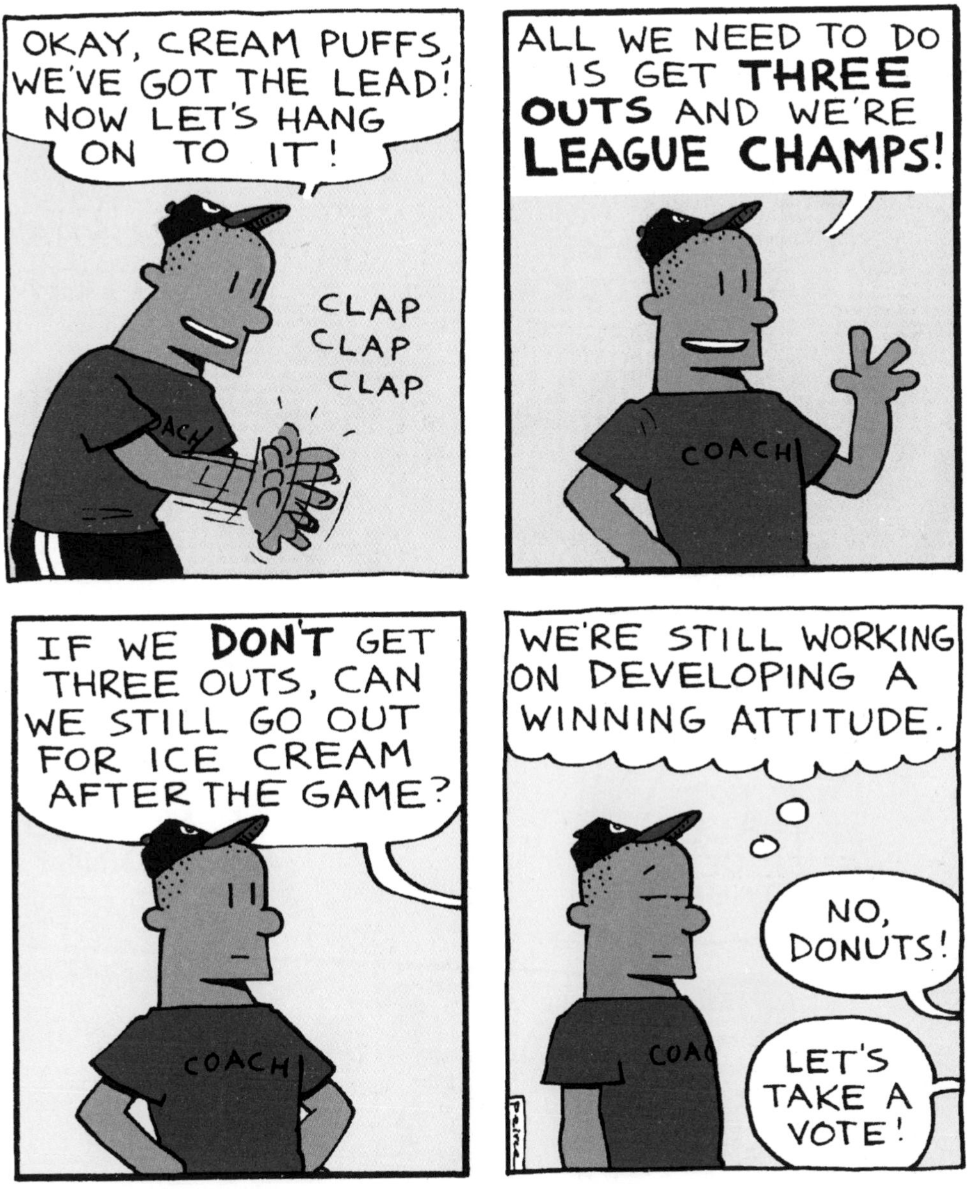
OKAY, CREAM PUFFS, WE'VE GOT THE LEAD! NOW LET'S HANG ON TO IT!
CLAP CLAP CLAP
COACH
ALL WE NEED TO DO IS GET THREE OUTS AND WE'RE LEAGUE CHAMPS!
COACH
IF WE DON'T GET THREE OUTS, CAN WE STILL GO OUT FOR ICE CREAM AFTER THE GAME?
COACH
WE'RE STILL WORKING ON DEVELOPING A WINNING ATTITUDE.
NO, DONUTS!
LET'S TAKE A VOTE!

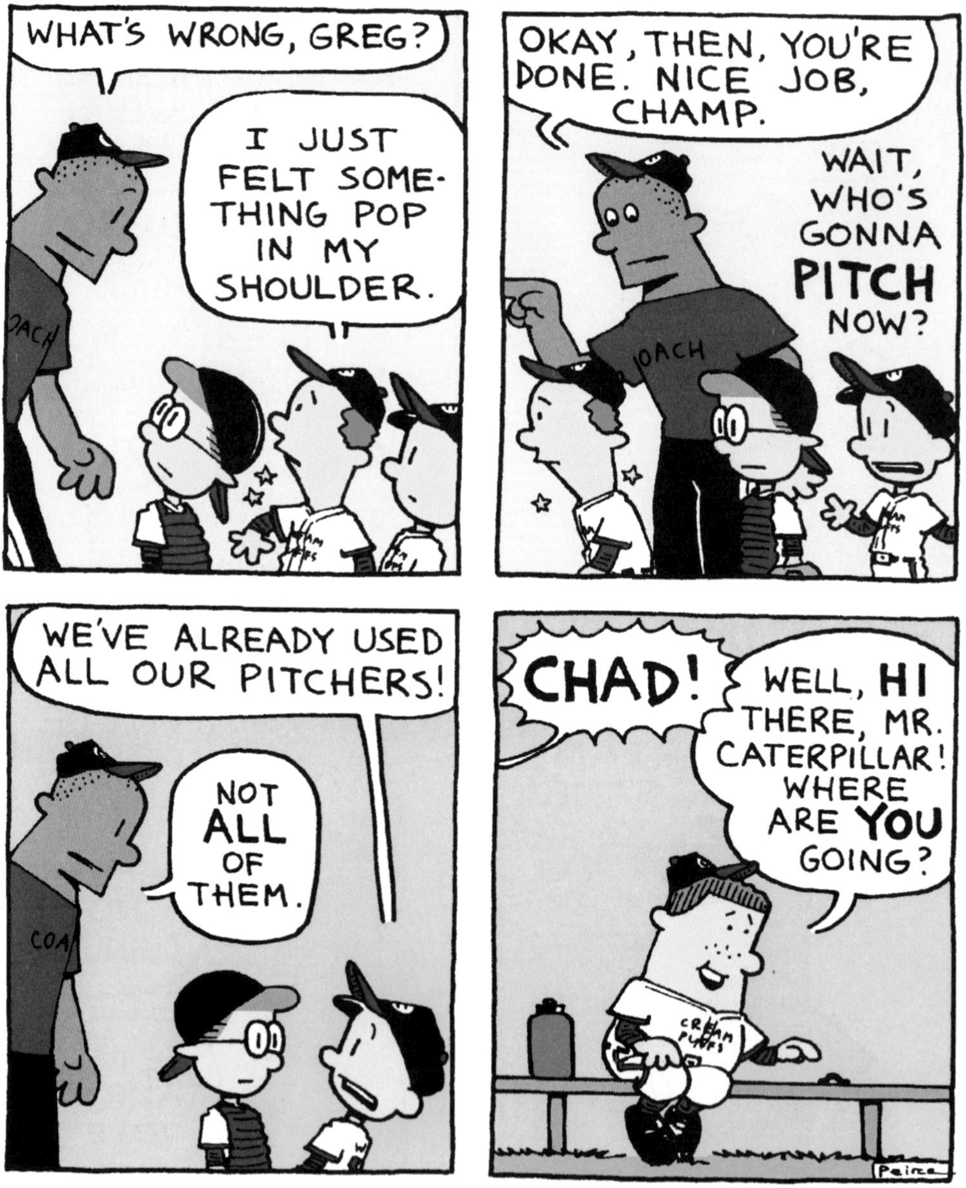
WHAT'S WRONG, GREG?
I JUST FELT SOMETHING POP IN MY SHOULDER.
OKAY, THEN, YOU'RE DONE. NICE JOB, CHAMP.
WAIT, WHO'S GONNA PITCH NOW?
WE'VE ALREADY USED ALL OUR PITCHERS!
NOT ALL OF THEM.
CHAD!
WELL, HI THERE, MR. CATERPILLAR! WHERE ARE YOU GOING?

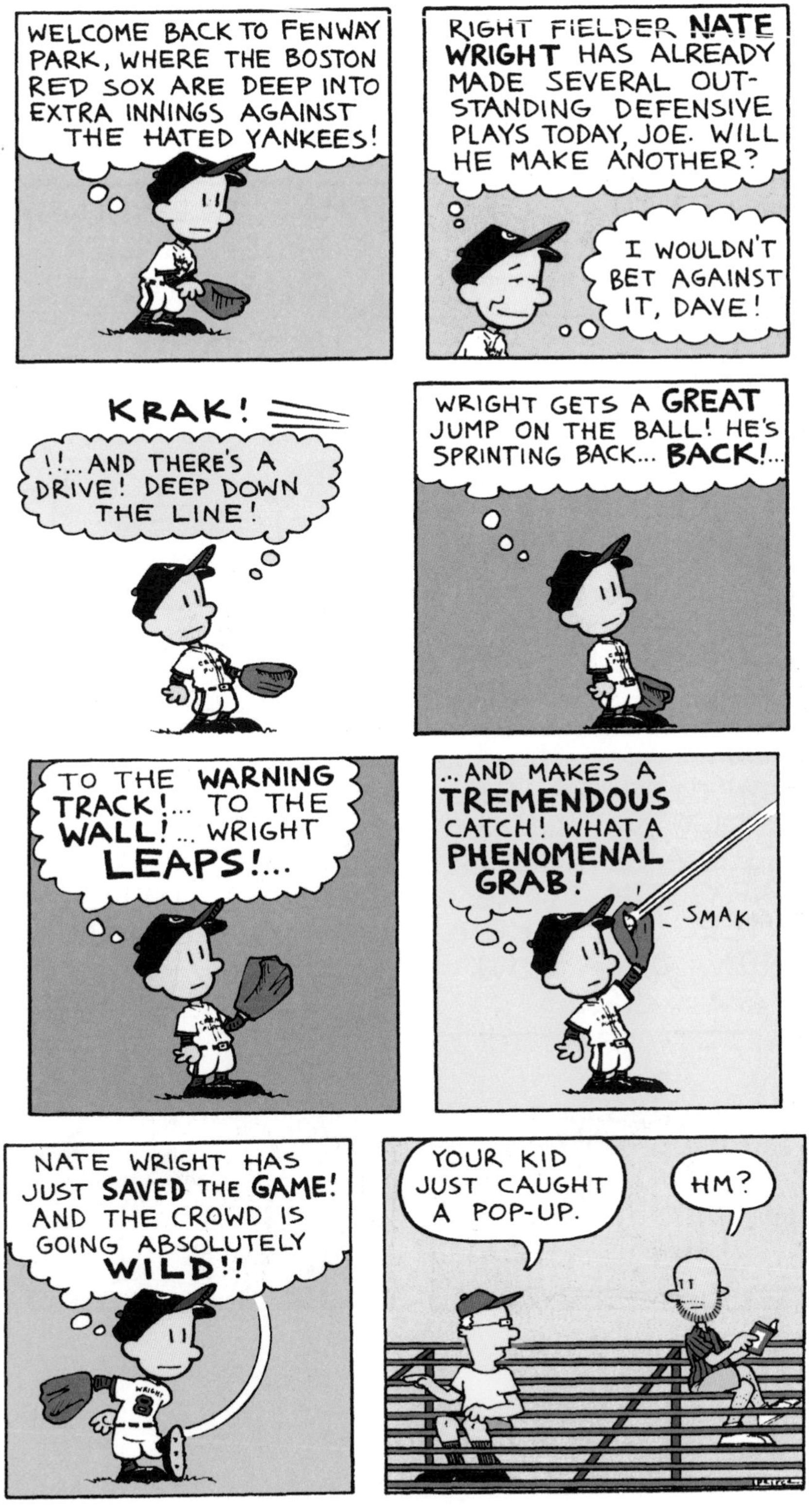
WELCOME BACK TO FENWAY PARK, WHERE THE BOSTON RED SOX ARE DEEP INTO EXTRA INNINGS AGAINST THE HATED YANKEES!
RIGHT FIELDER NATE WRIGHT HAS ALREADY MADE SEVERAL OUT-STANDING DEFENSIVE PLAYS TODAY, JOE. WILL HE MAKE ANOTHER?
I WOULDN'T BET AGAINST IT, DAVE!
KRAK!
!!... AND THERE'S A DRIVE! DEEP DOWN THE LINE!
WRIGHT GETS A GREAT JUMP ON THE BALL! HE'S SPRINTING BACK... BACK!...
TO THE WARNING TRACK!... TO THE WALL!... WRIGHT LEAPS!...
... AND MAKES A TREMENDOUS CATCH! WHAT A PHENOMENAL GRAB!
SMAK
NATE WRIGHT HAS JUST SAVED THE GAME! AND THE CROWD IS GOING ABSOLUTELY WILD!!
YOUR KID JUST CAUGHT A POP-UP.
HM?

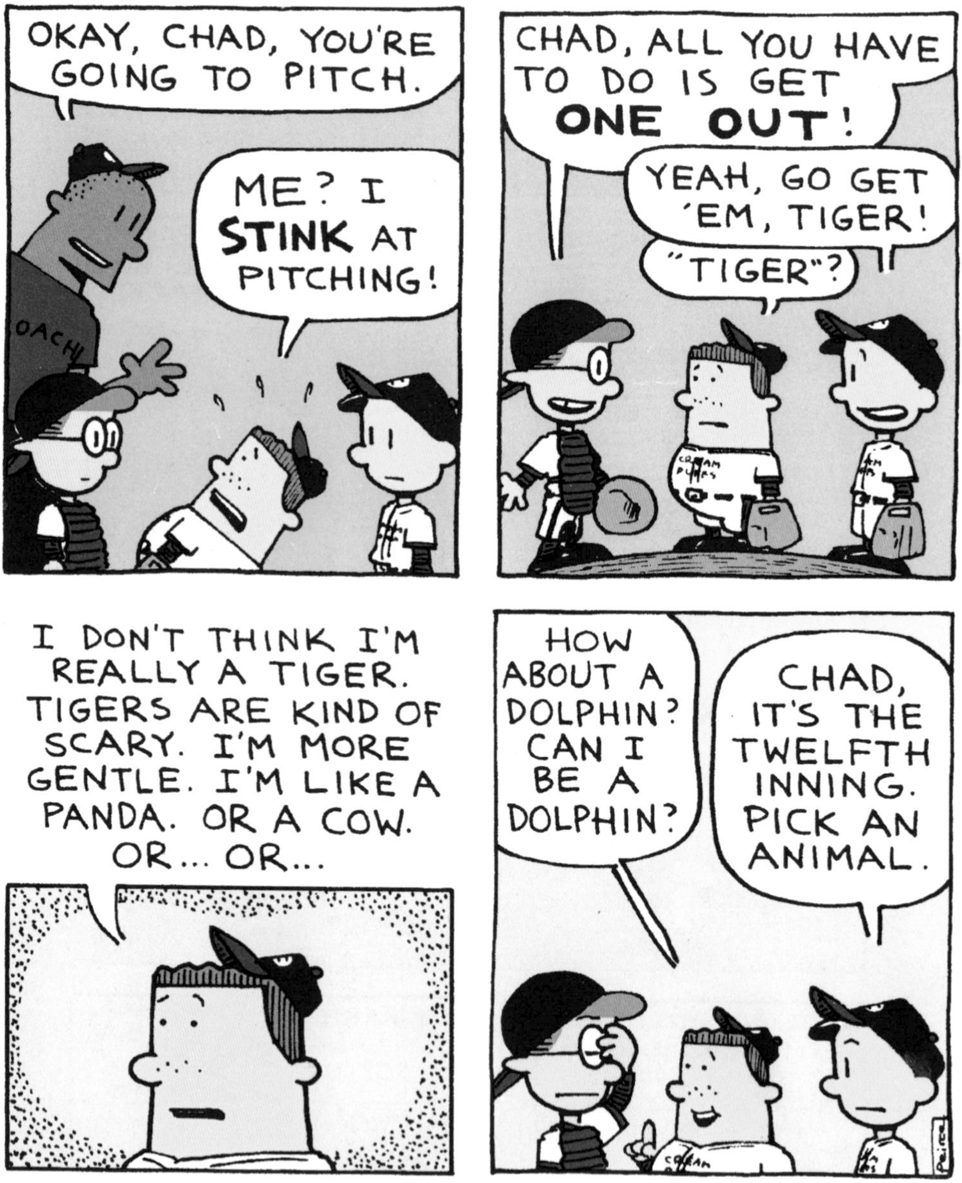
OKAY, CHAD, YOU'RE GOING TO PITCH.
ME? I **STINK** AT PITCHING!
CHAD, ALL YOU HAVE TO DO IS GET **ONE OUT**!
YEAH, GO GET 'EM, TIGER!
"TIGER"?
I DON'T THINK I'M REALLY A TIGER. TIGERS ARE KIND OF SCARY. I'M MORE GENTLE. I'M LIKE A PANDA. OR A COW. OR... OR...
HOW ABOUT A DOLPHIN? CAN I BE A DOLPHIN?
CHAD, IT'S THE TWELFTH INNING. PICK AN ANIMAL.

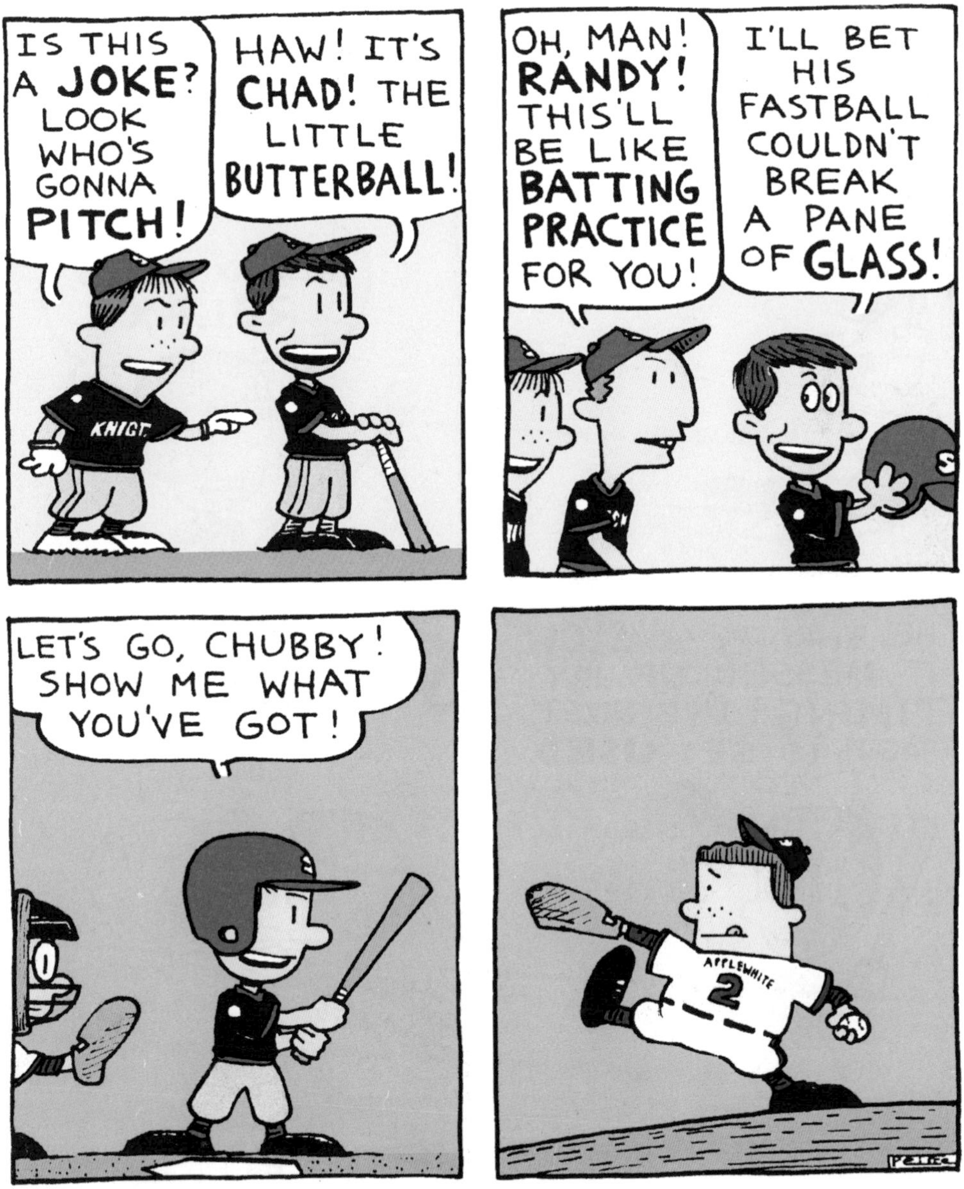
IS THIS A JOKE? LOOK WHO'S GONNA PITCH!
HAW! IT'S CHAD! THE LITTLE BUTTERBALL!
OH, MAN! RANDY! THIS'LL BE LIKE BATTING PRACTICE FOR YOU!
I'LL BET HIS FASTBALL COULDN'T BREAK A PANE OF GLASS!
LET'S GO, CHUBBY! SHOW ME WHAT YOU'VE GOT!
APPLEWHITE
2

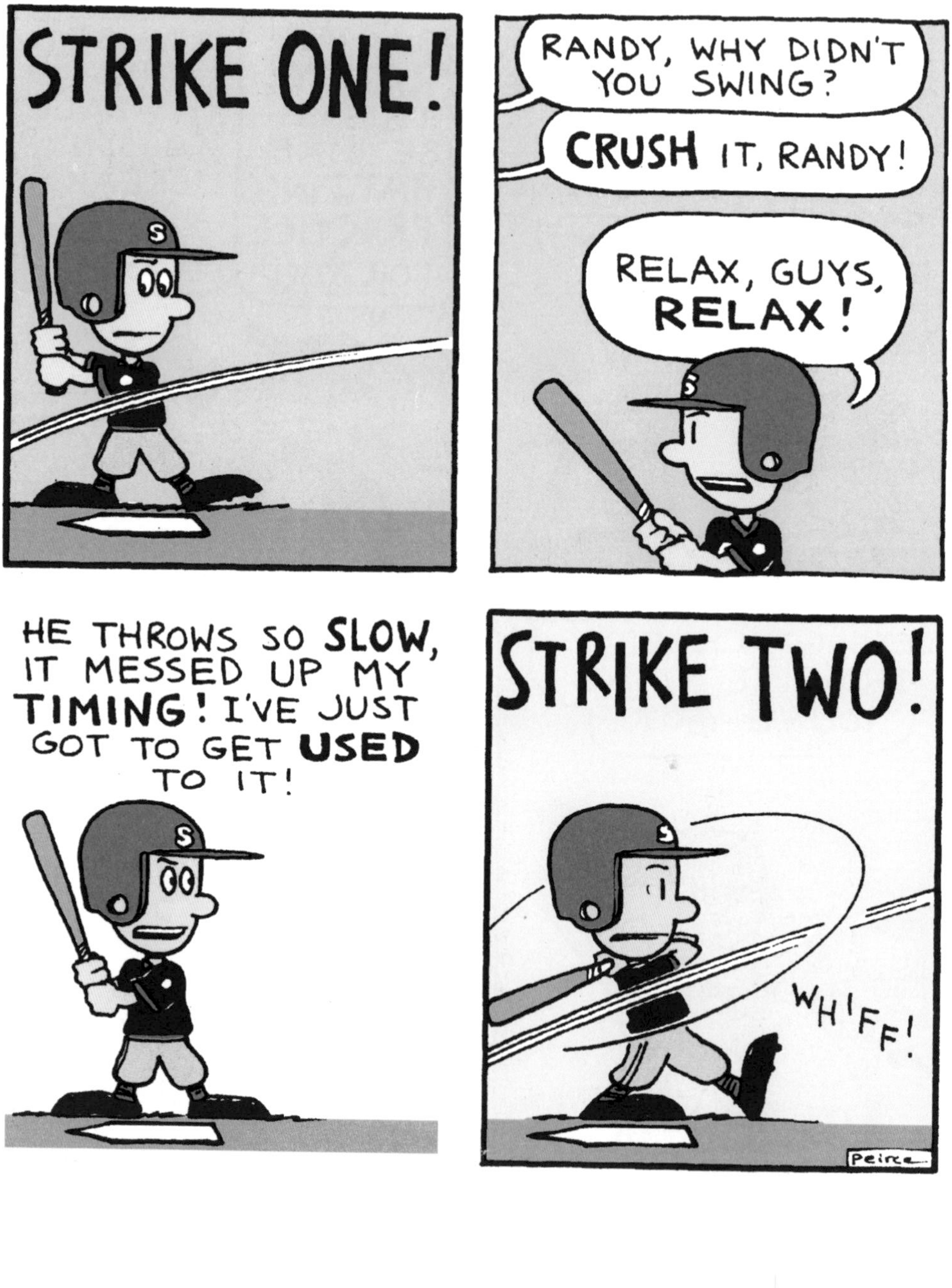
STRIKE ONE!
RANDY, WHY DIDN'T YOU SWING?
CRUSH IT, RANDY!
RELAX, GUYS, RELAX!
HE THROWS SO SLOW, IT MESSED UP MY TIMING! I'VE JUST GOT TO GET USED TO IT!
STRIKE TWO!
WHIFF!
Peirce

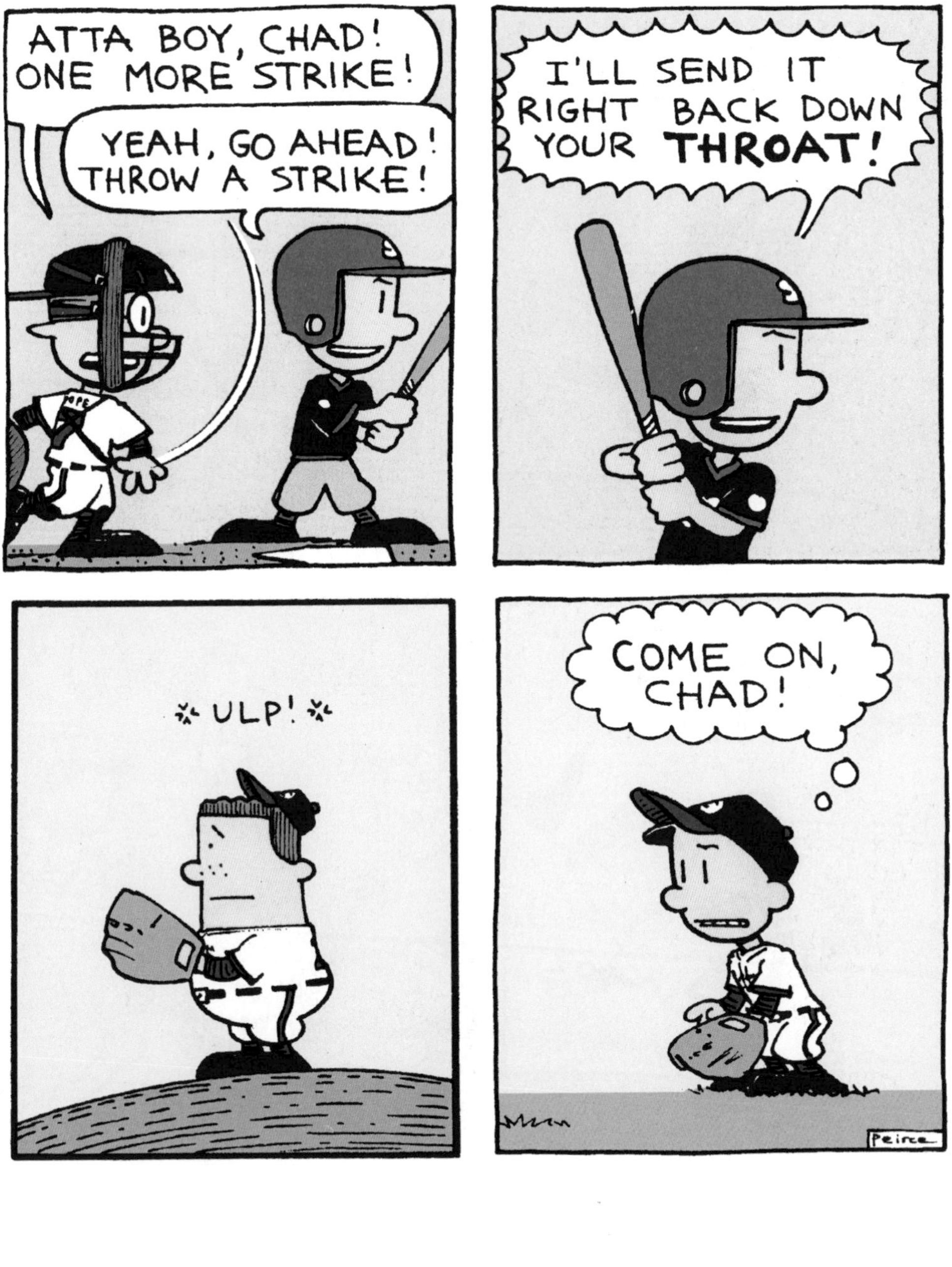
ATTA BOY, CHAD! ONE MORE STRIKE!
YEAH, GO AHEAD! THROW A STRIKE!
I'LL SEND IT RIGHT BACK DOWN YOUR THROAT!
ULP!
COME ON, CHAD!
Peirce

POW!
SMAK!
Peirce

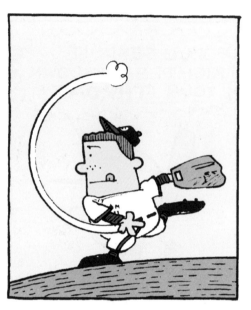

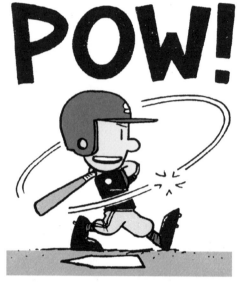

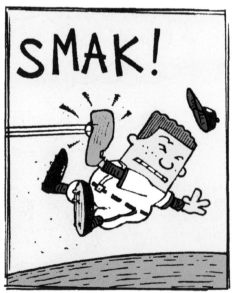

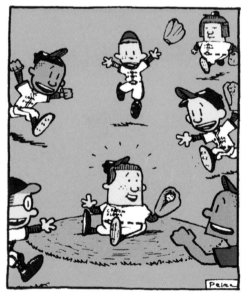

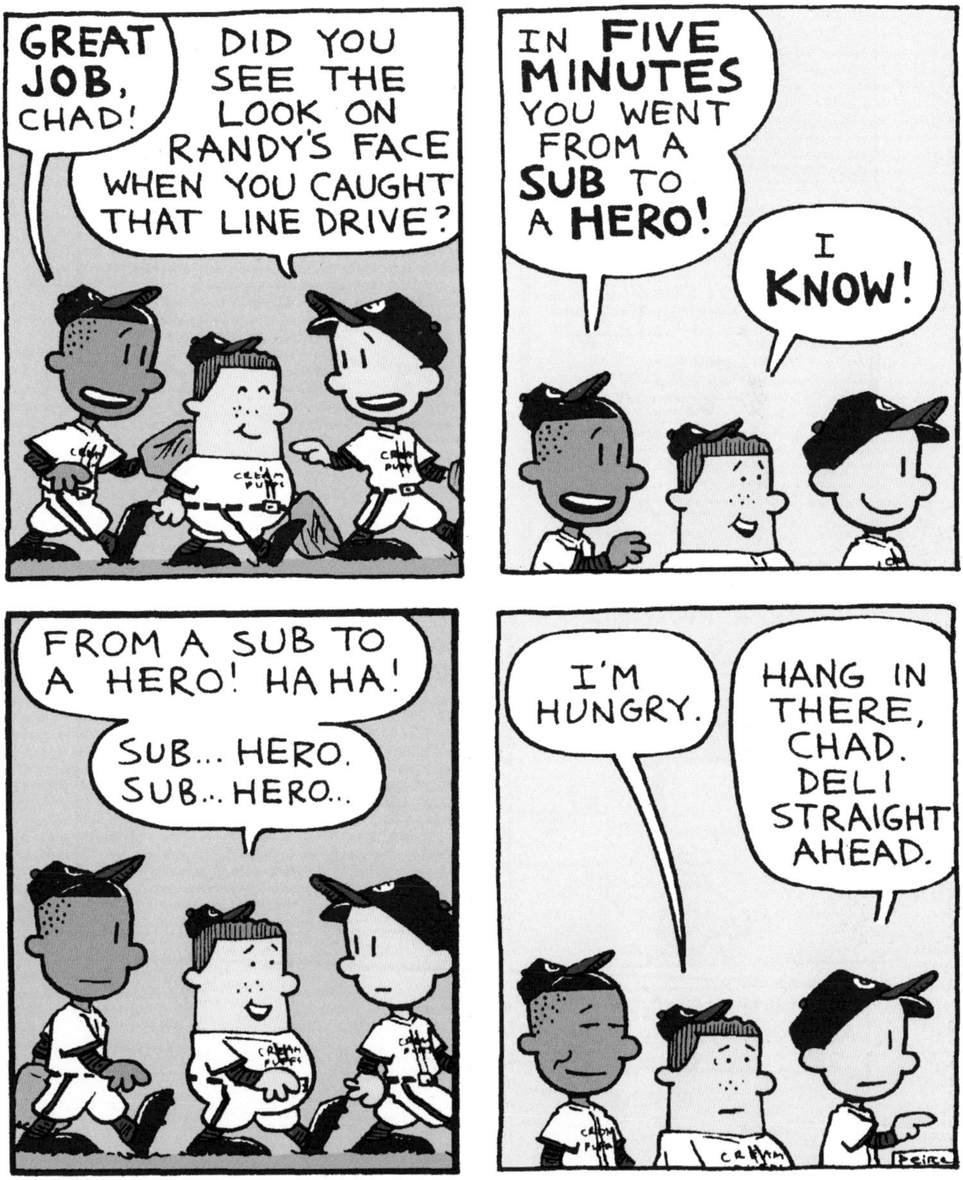
GREAT JOB, CHAD!
DID YOU SEE THE LOOK ON RANDY'S FACE WHEN YOU CAUGHT THAT LINE DRIVE?
IN FIVE MINUTES YOU WENT FROM A SUB TO A HERO!
I KNOW!
FROM A SUB TO A HERO! HA HA!
SUB... HERO. SUB... HERO...
I'M HUNGRY.
HANG IN THERE, CHAD. DELI STRAIGHT AHEAD.
Peirce

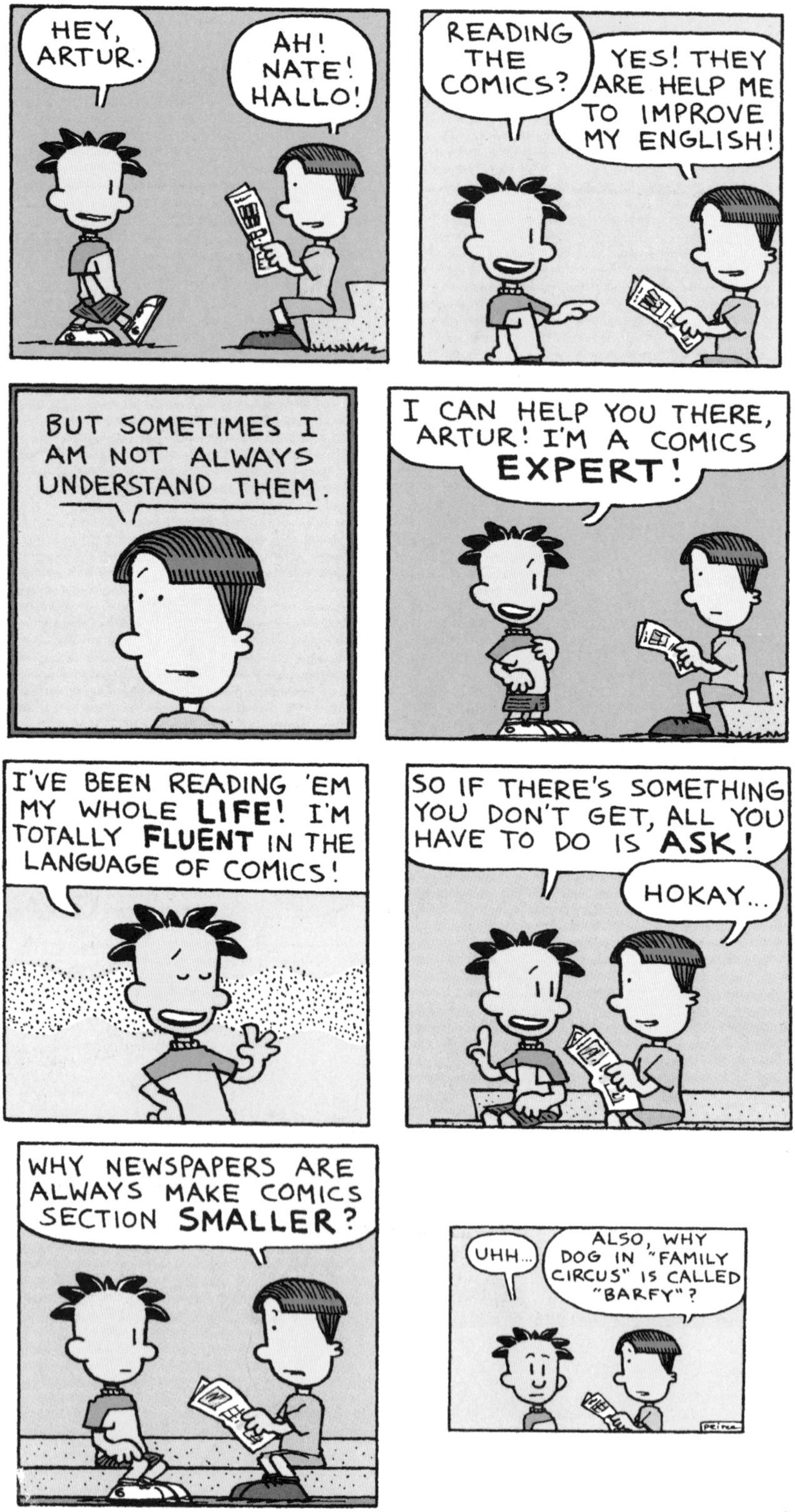
HEY, ARTUR.
AH! NATE! HALLO!
READING THE COMICS?
YES! THEY ARE HELP ME TO IMPROVE MY ENGLISH!
BUT SOMETIMES I AM NOT ALWAYS UNDERSTAND THEM.
I CAN HELP YOU THERE, ARTUR! I'M A COMICS EXPERT!
I'VE BEEN READING 'EM MY WHOLE LIFE! I'M TOTALLY FLUENT IN THE LANGUAGE OF COMICS!
SO IF THERE'S SOMETHING YOU DON'T GET, ALL YOU HAVE TO DO IS ASK!
HOKAY...
WHY NEWSPAPERS ARE ALWAYS MAKE COMICS SECTION SMALLER?
UHH...
ALSO, WHY DOG IN "FAMILY CIRCUS" IS CALLED "BARFY"?
peirce

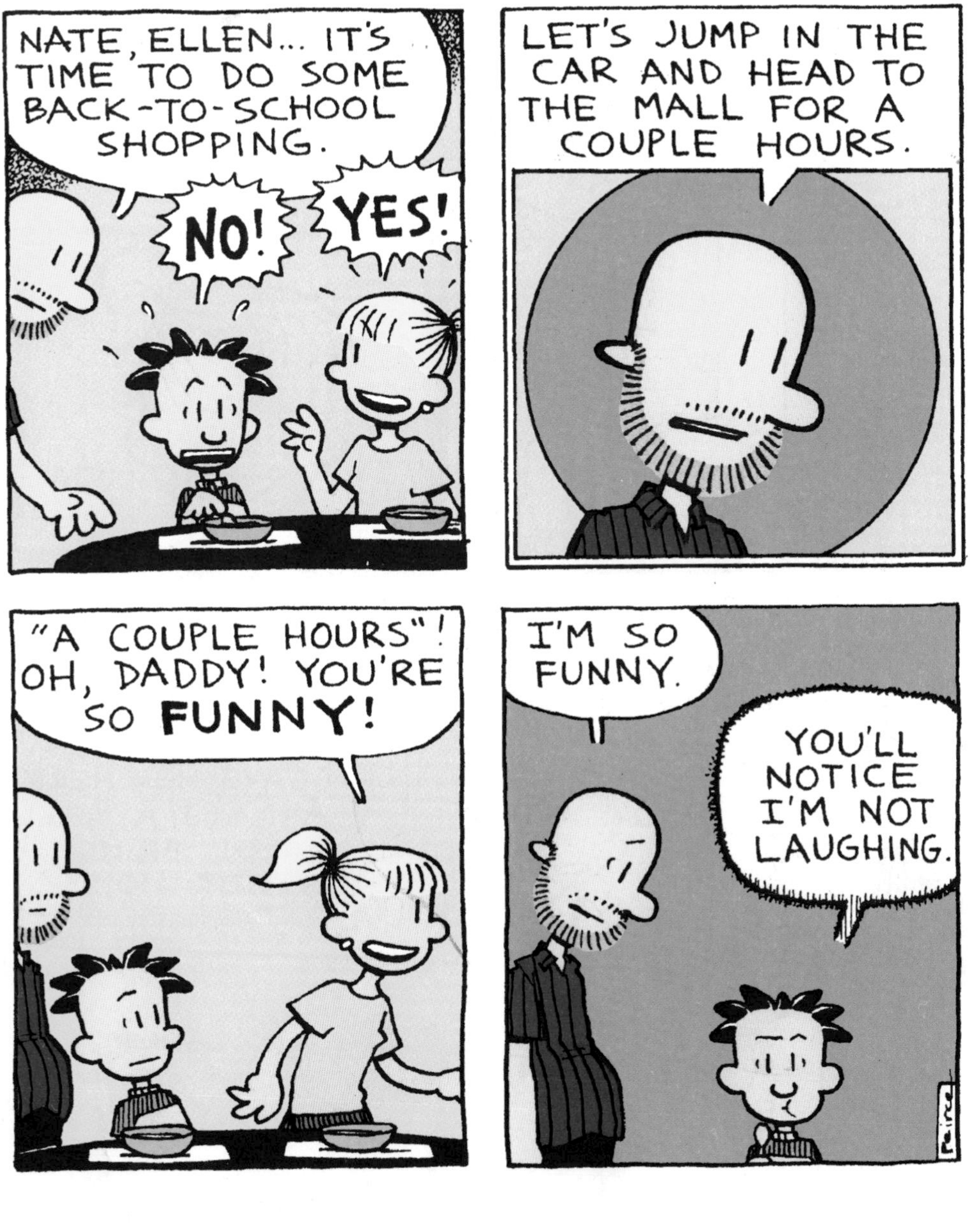
NATE, ELLEN... IT'S TIME TO DO SOME BACK-TO-SCHOOL SHOPPING.
NO!
YES!
LET'S JUMP IN THE CAR AND HEAD TO THE MALL FOR A COUPLE HOURS.
"A COUPLE HOURS"! OH, DADDY! YOU'RE SO FUNNY!
I'M SO FUNNY.
YOU'LL NOTICE I'M NOT LAUGHING.
Peirce

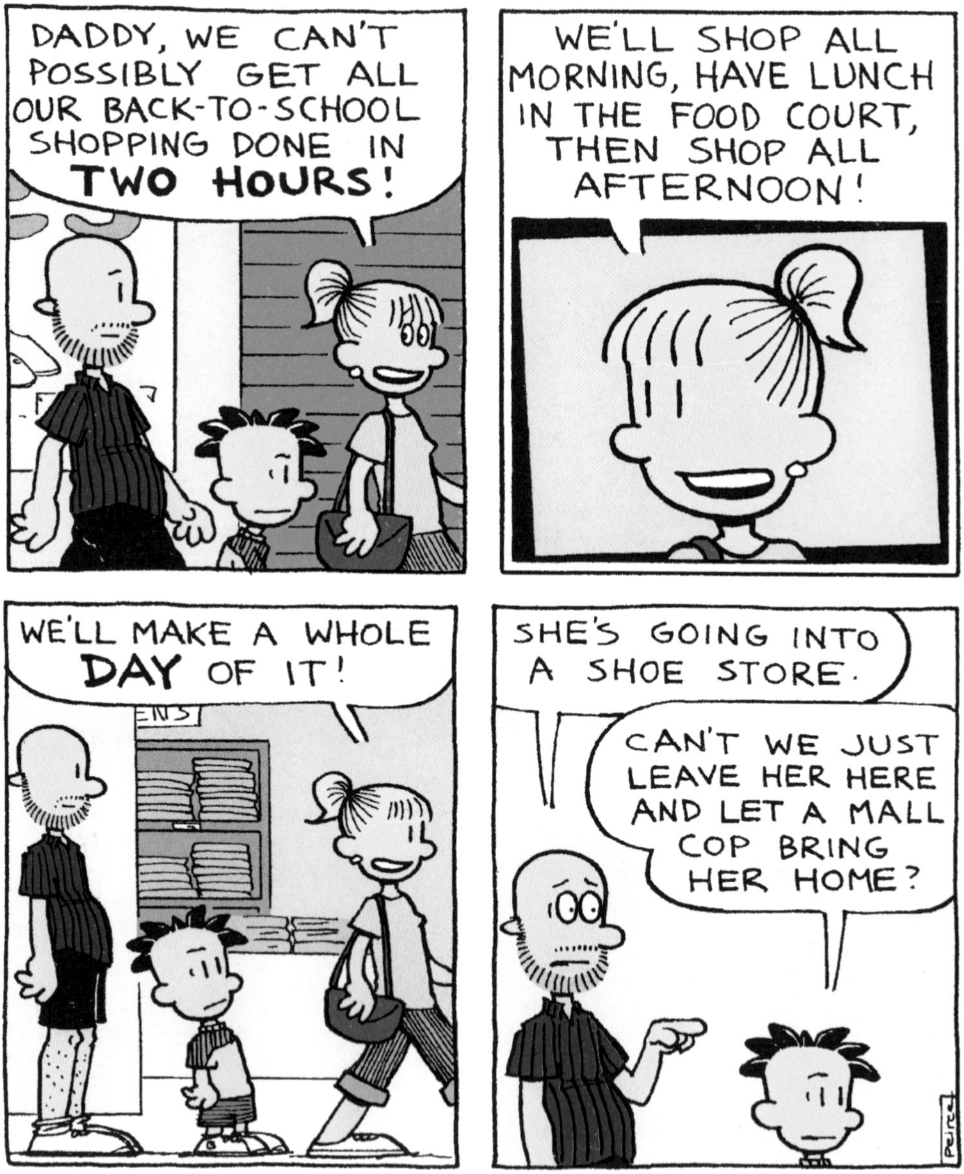
DADDY, WE CAN'T POSSIBLY GET ALL OUR BACK-TO-SCHOOL SHOPPING DONE IN TWO HOURS!
WE'LL SHOP ALL MORNING, HAVE LUNCH IN THE FOOD COURT, THEN SHOP ALL AFTERNOON!
WE'LL MAKE A WHOLE DAY OF IT!
SHE'S GOING INTO A SHOE STORE.
CAN'T WE JUST LEAVE HER HERE AND LET A MALL COP BRING HER HOME?
Peirce

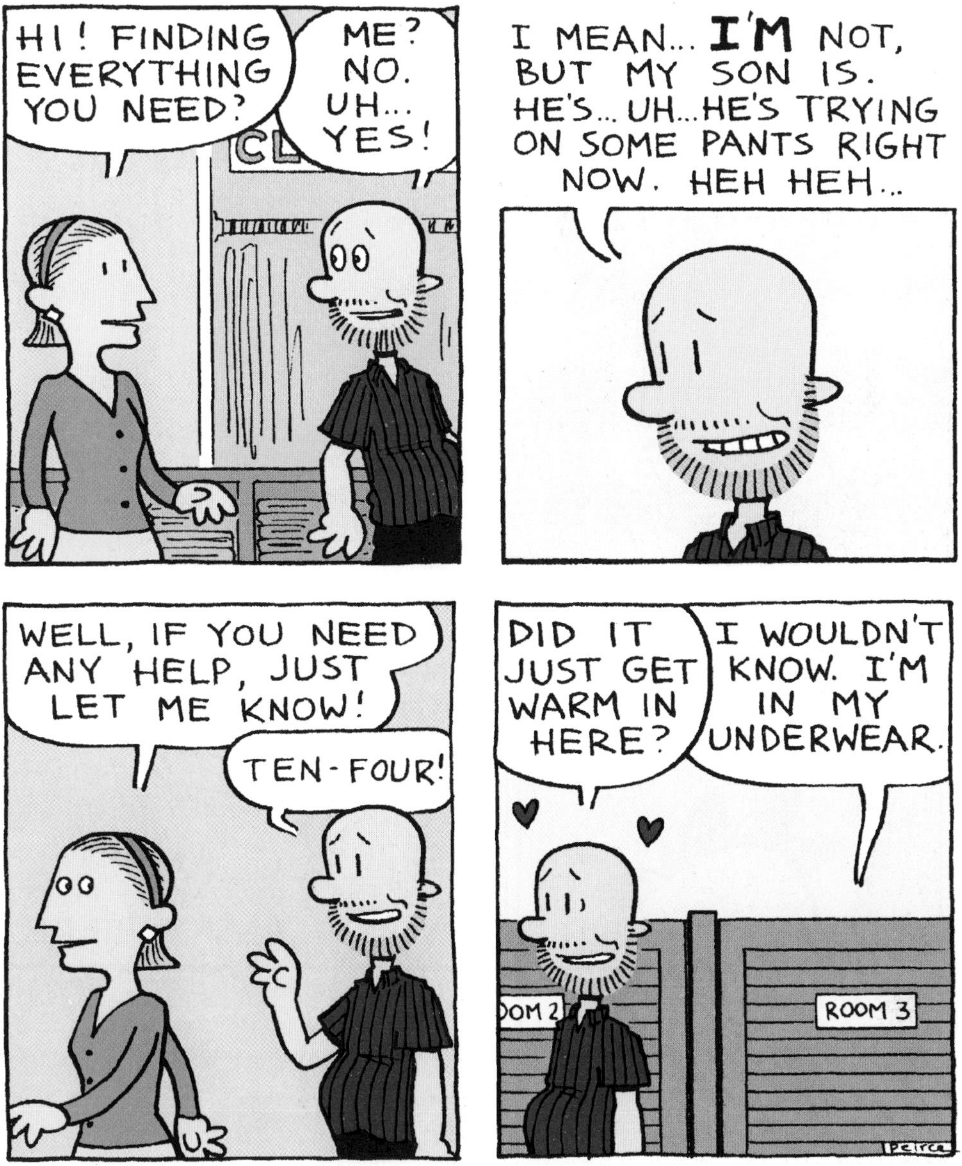
HI! FINDING EVERYTHING YOU NEED?
ME? NO. UH... YES!
I MEAN... **I'M** NOT, BUT MY SON IS. HE'S... UH... HE'S TRYING ON SOME PANTS RIGHT NOW. HEH HEH...
WELL, IF YOU NEED ANY HELP, JUST LET ME KNOW!
TEN-FOUR!
DID IT JUST GET WARM IN HERE?
I WOULDN'T KNOW. I'M IN MY UNDERWEAR.
ROOM 3

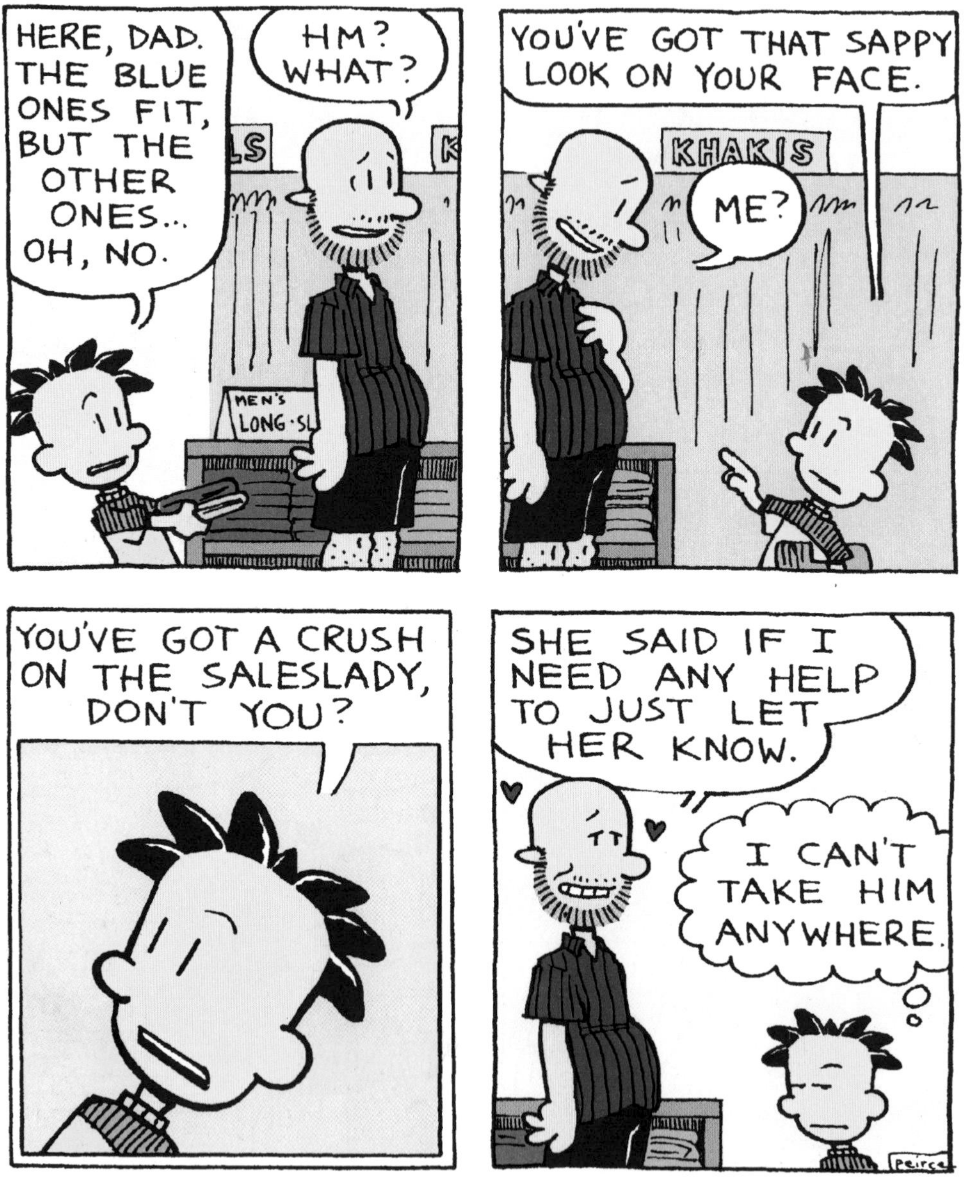
HERE, DAD. THE BLUE ONES FIT, BUT THE OTHER ONES... OH, NO.
HM? WHAT?
MEN'S LONG·SL
YOU'VE GOT THAT SAPPY LOOK ON YOUR FACE.
KHAKIS
ME?
YOU'VE GOT A CRUSH ON THE SALESLADY, DON'T YOU?
SHE SAID IF I NEED ANY HELP TO JUST LET HER KNOW.
I CAN'T TAKE HIM ANYWHERE.
PEIRCE

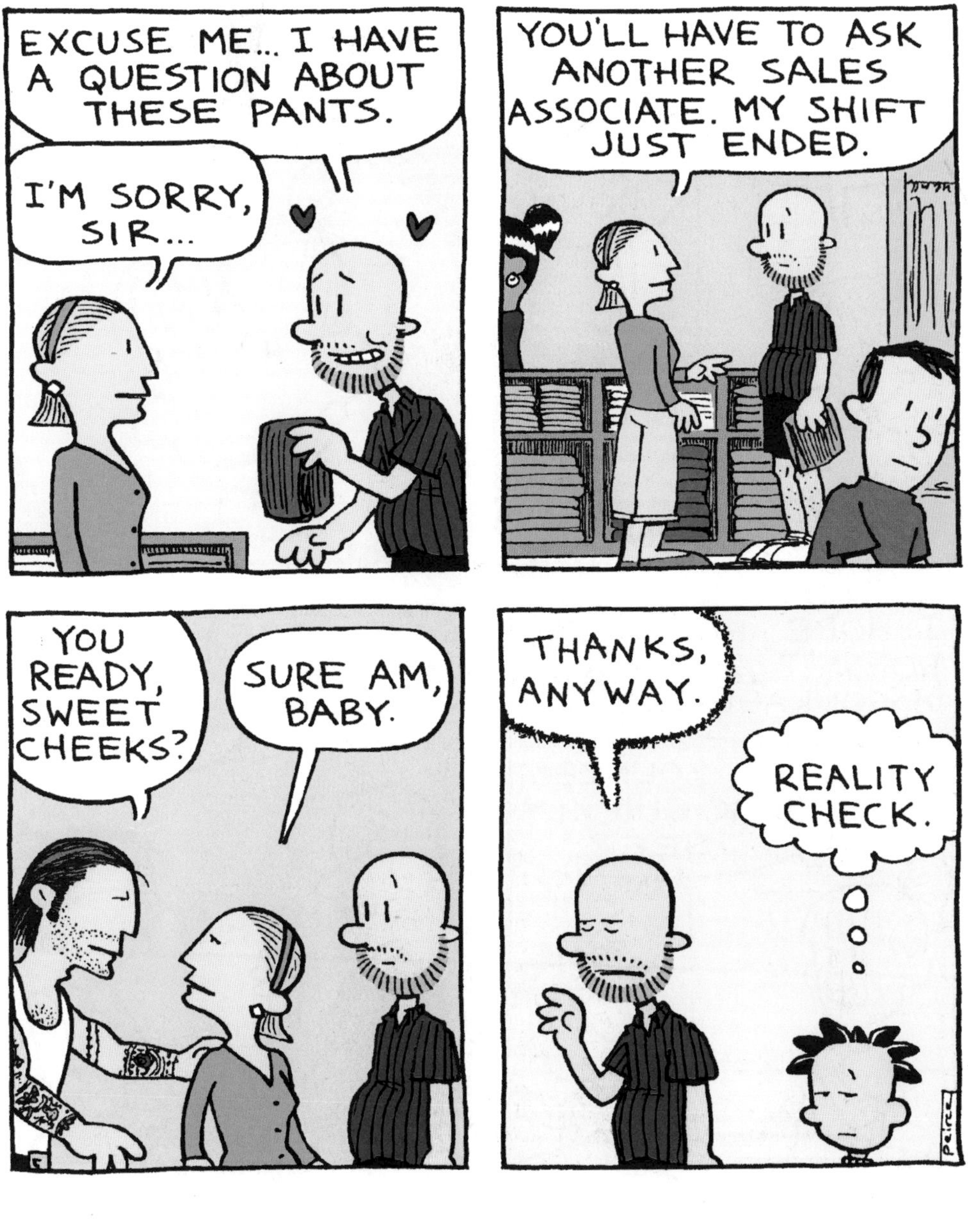
EXCUSE ME... I HAVE A QUESTION ABOUT THESE PANTS.
I'M SORRY, SIR...
YOU'LL HAVE TO ASK ANOTHER SALES ASSOCIATE. MY SHIFT JUST ENDED.
YOU READY, SWEET CHEEKS?
SURE AM, BABY.
THANKS, ANYWAY.
REALITY CHECK.
peirce

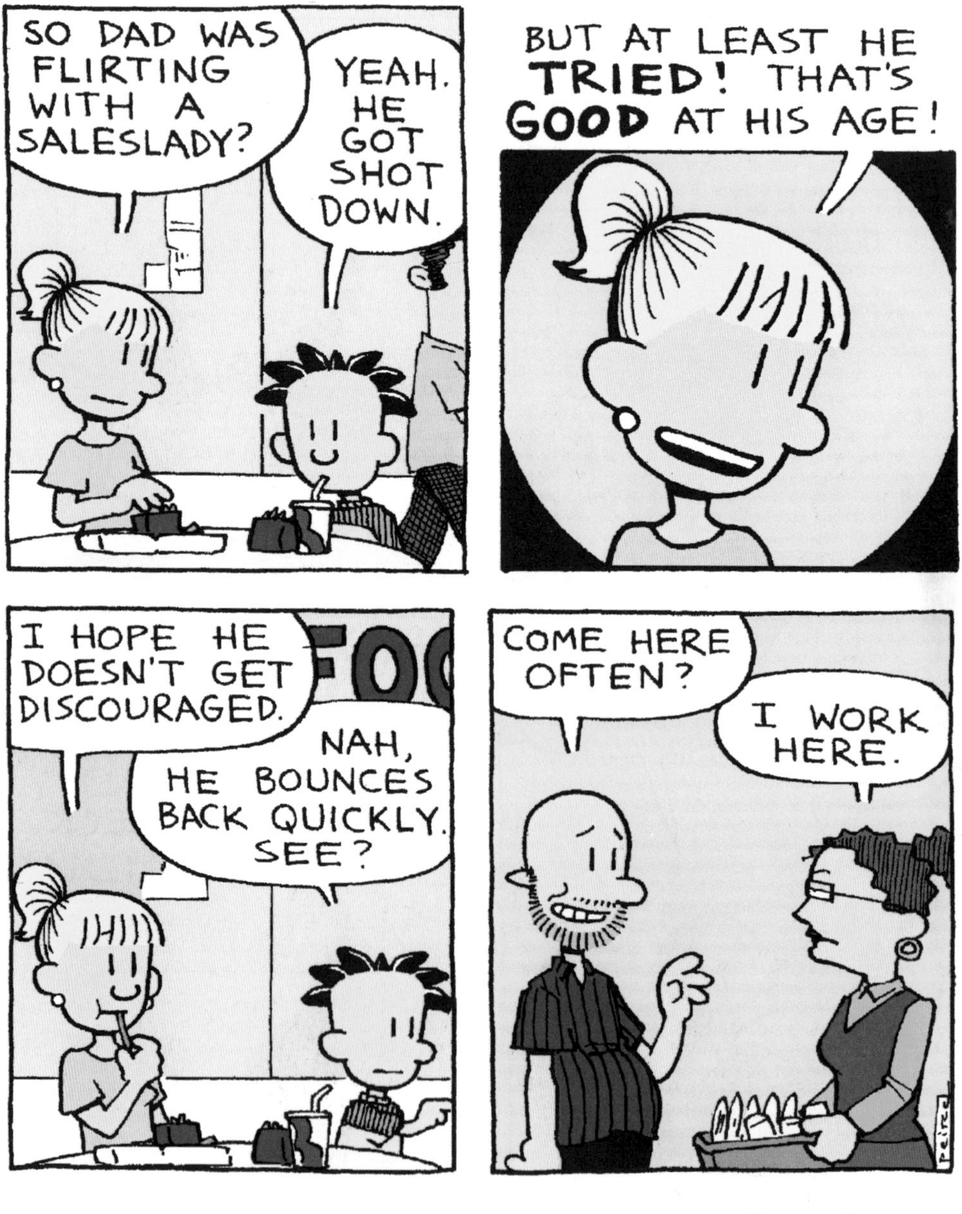
SO DAD WAS FLIRTING WITH A SALESLADY?
YEAH. HE GOT SHOT DOWN.
BUT AT LEAST HE TRIED! THAT'S GOOD AT HIS AGE!
I HOPE HE DOESN'T GET DISCOURAGED.
NAH, HE BOUNCES BACK QUICKLY. SEE?
COME HERE OFTEN?
I WORK HERE.
peirce

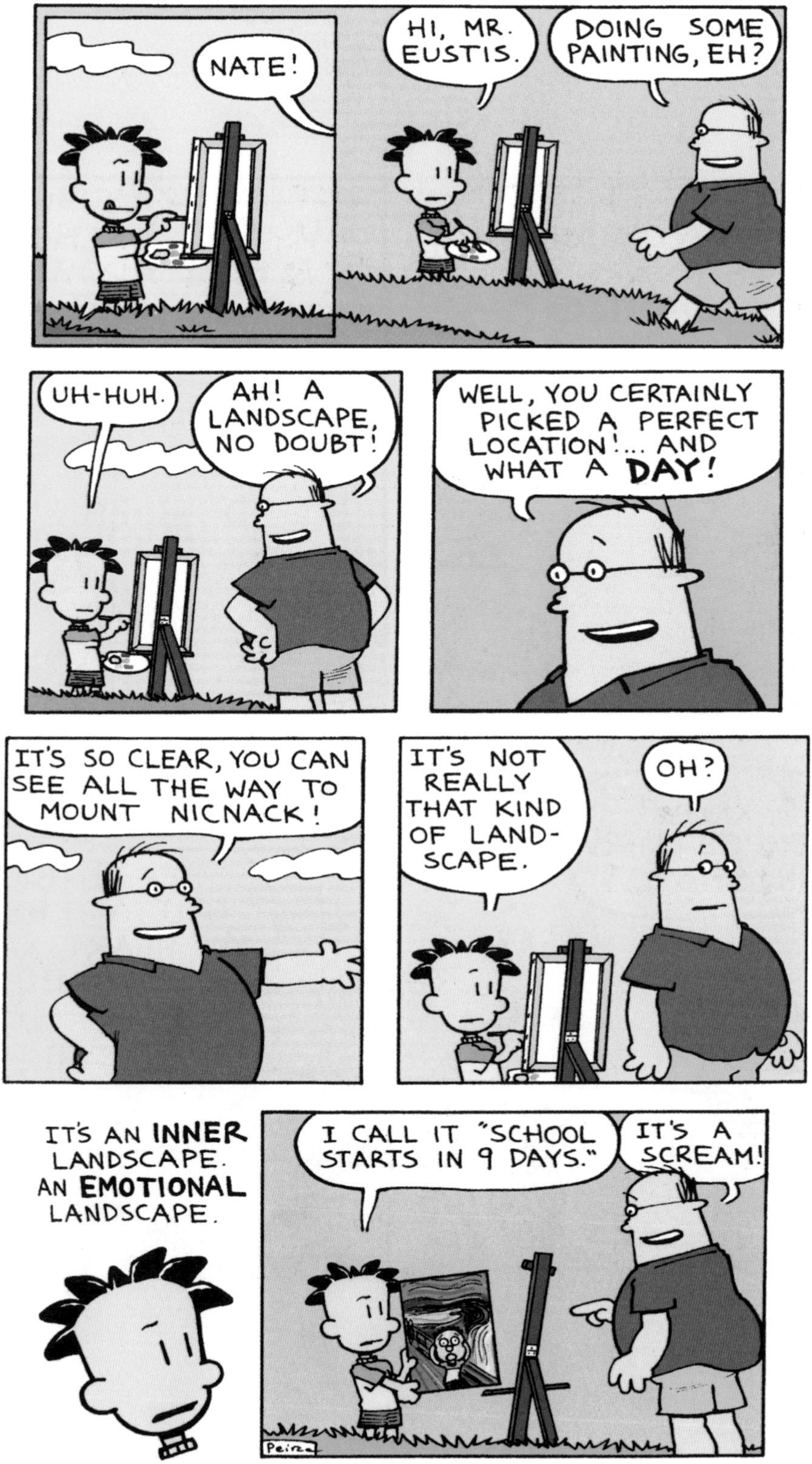
NATE!
HI, MR. EUSTIS.
DOING SOME PAINTING, EH?
UH-HUH.
AH! A LANDSCAPE, NO DOUBT!
WELL, YOU CERTAINLY PICKED A PERFECT LOCATION!... AND WHAT A DAY!
IT'S SO CLEAR, YOU CAN SEE ALL THE WAY TO MOUNT NICNACK!
IT'S NOT REALLY THAT KIND OF LAND-SCAPE.
OH?
IT'S AN INNER LANDSCAPE. AN EMOTIONAL LANDSCAPE.
I CALL IT "SCHOOL STARTS IN 9 DAYS."
IT'S A SCREAM!
Peirce

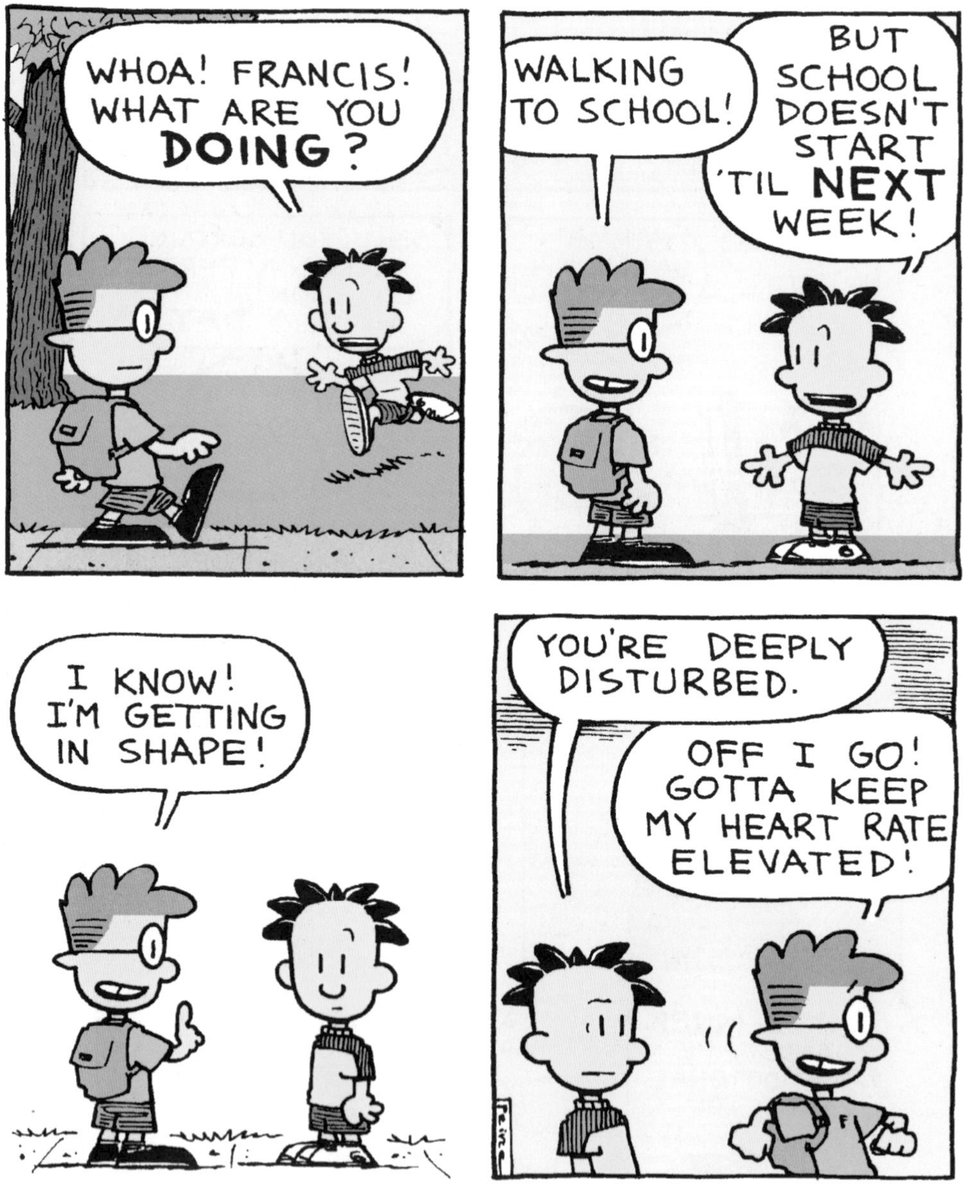
WHOA! FRANCIS! WHAT ARE YOU DOING?
WALKING TO SCHOOL!
BUT SCHOOL DOESN'T START 'TIL NEXT WEEK!
I KNOW! I'M GETTING IN SHAPE!
YOU'RE DEEPLY DISTURBED.
OFF I GO! GOTTA KEEP MY HEART RATE ELEVATED!

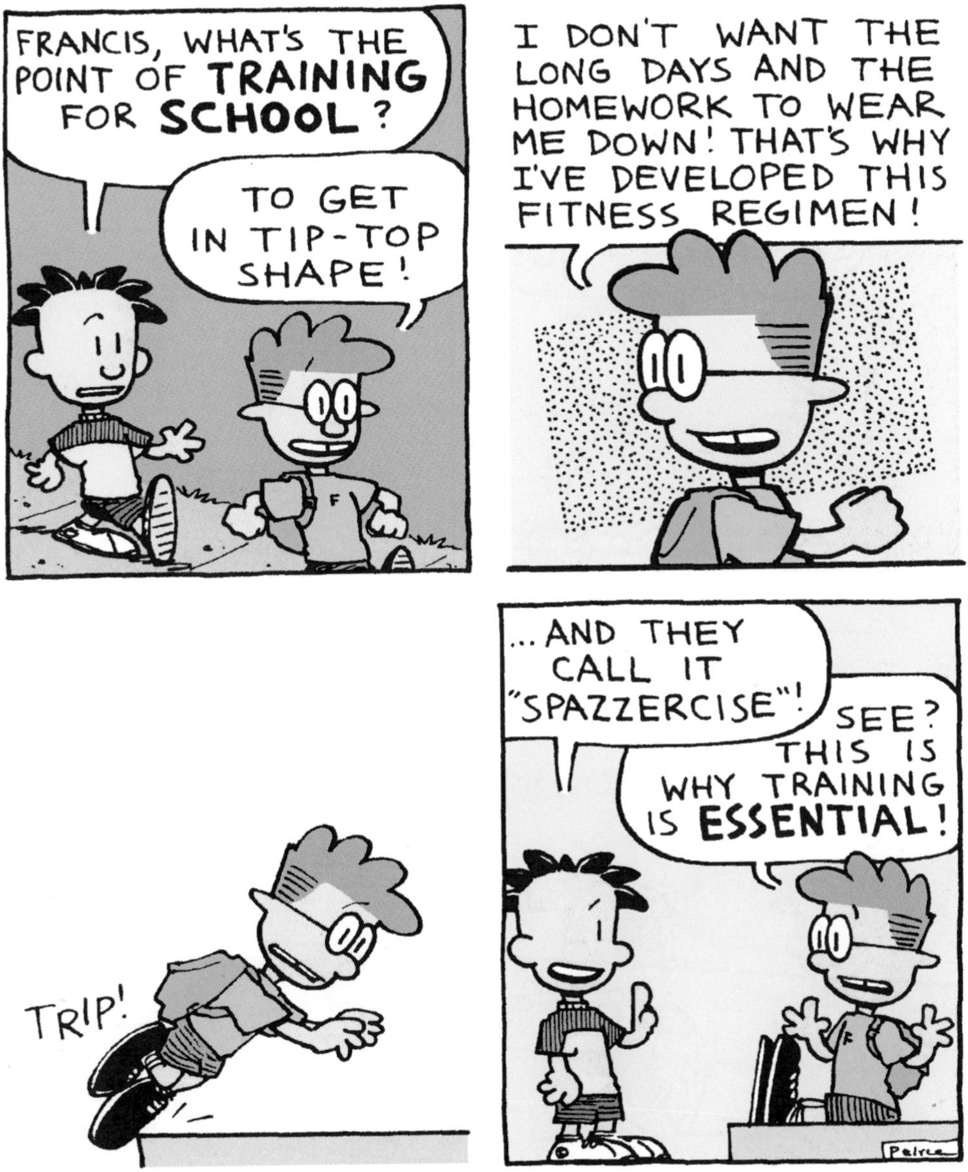
FRANCIS, WHAT'S THE POINT OF **TRAINING** FOR **SCHOOL**?
TO GET IN TIP-TOP SHAPE!
I DON'T WANT THE LONG DAYS AND THE HOMEWORK TO WEAR ME DOWN! THAT'S WHY I'VE DEVELOPED THIS FITNESS REGIMEN!
TRIP!
...AND THEY CALL IT "SPAZZERCISE"!
SEE? THIS IS WHY TRAINING IS **ESSENTIAL**!
Peirce

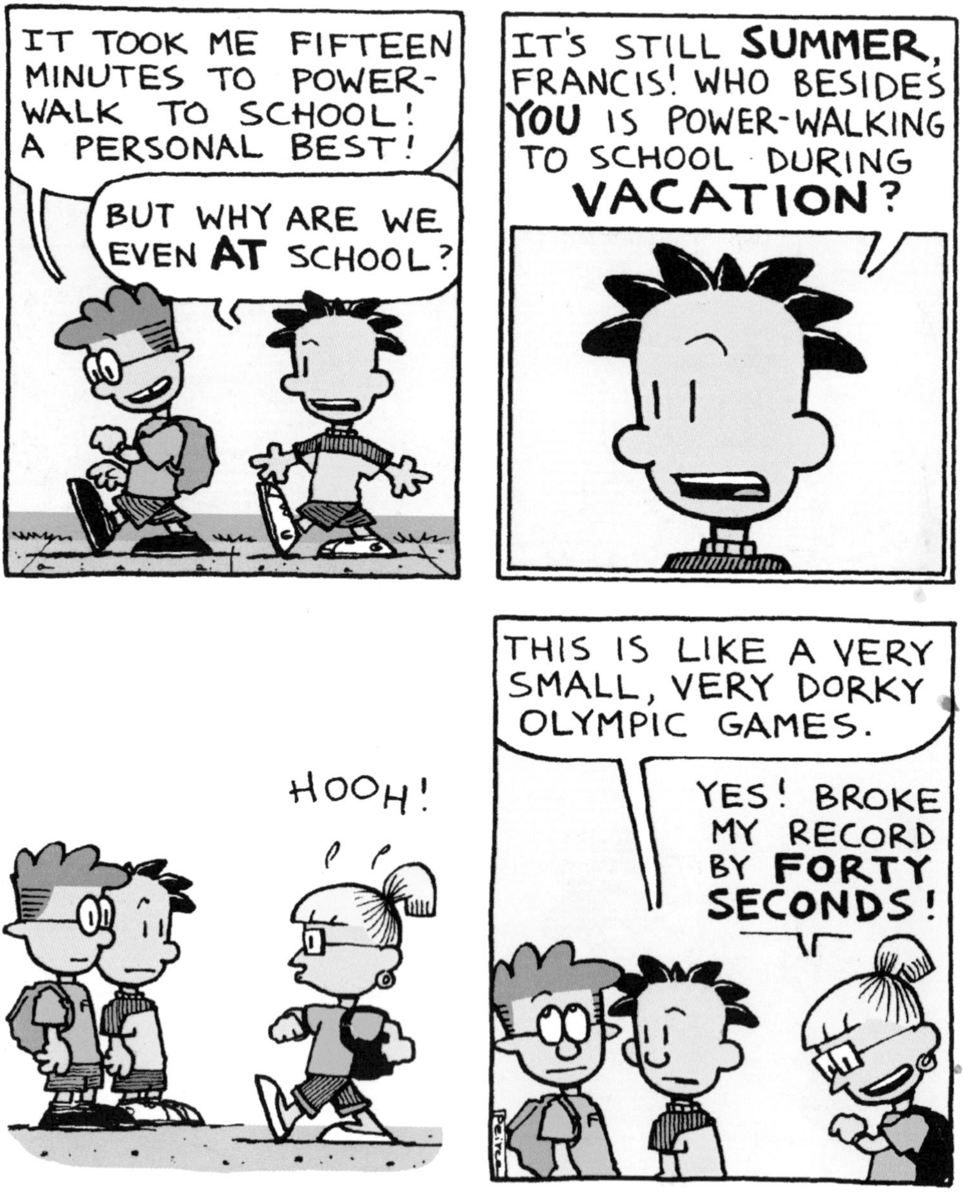
IT TOOK ME FIFTEEN MINUTES TO POWER-WALK TO SCHOOL! A PERSONAL BEST!
BUT WHY ARE WE EVEN AT SCHOOL?
IT'S STILL SUMMER, FRANCIS! WHO BESIDES YOU IS POWER-WALKING TO SCHOOL DURING VACATION?
HOOH!
THIS IS LIKE A VERY SMALL, VERY DORKY OLYMPIC GAMES.
YES! BROKE MY RECORD BY FORTY SECONDS!
PEIRCE

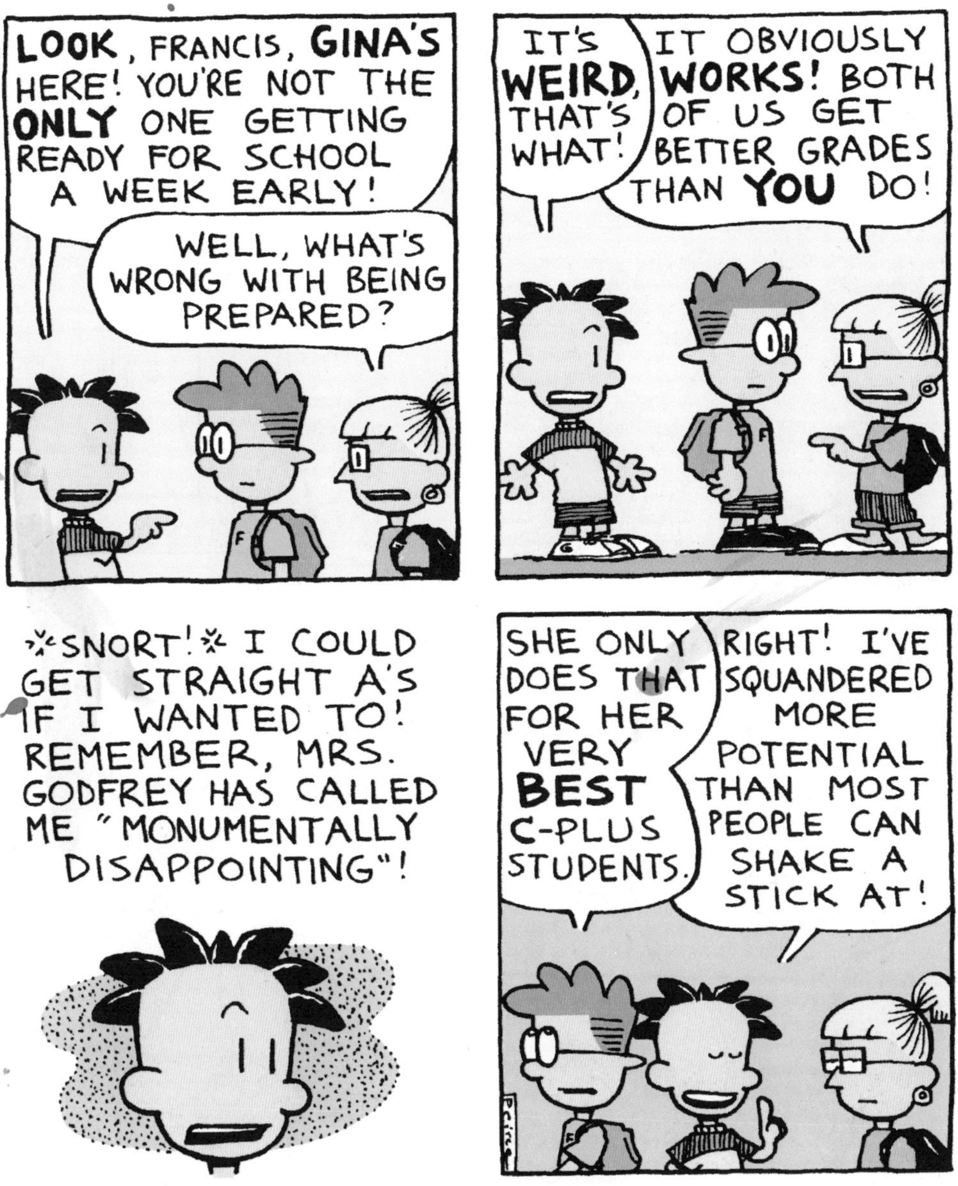
LOOK, FRANCIS, GINA'S HERE! YOU'RE NOT THE ONLY ONE GETTING READY FOR SCHOOL A WEEK EARLY!
WELL, WHAT'S WRONG WITH BEING PREPARED?
IT'S WEIRD, THAT'S WHAT!
IT OBVIOUSLY WORKS! BOTH OF US GET BETTER GRADES THAN YOU DO!
SNORT! I COULD GET STRAIGHT A'S IF I WANTED TO! REMEMBER, MRS. GODFREY HAS CALLED ME "MONUMENTALLY DISAPPOINTING"!
SHE ONLY DOES THAT FOR HER VERY BEST C-PLUS STUDENTS.
RIGHT! I'VE SQUANDERED MORE POTENTIAL THAN MOST PEOPLE CAN SHAKE A STICK AT!

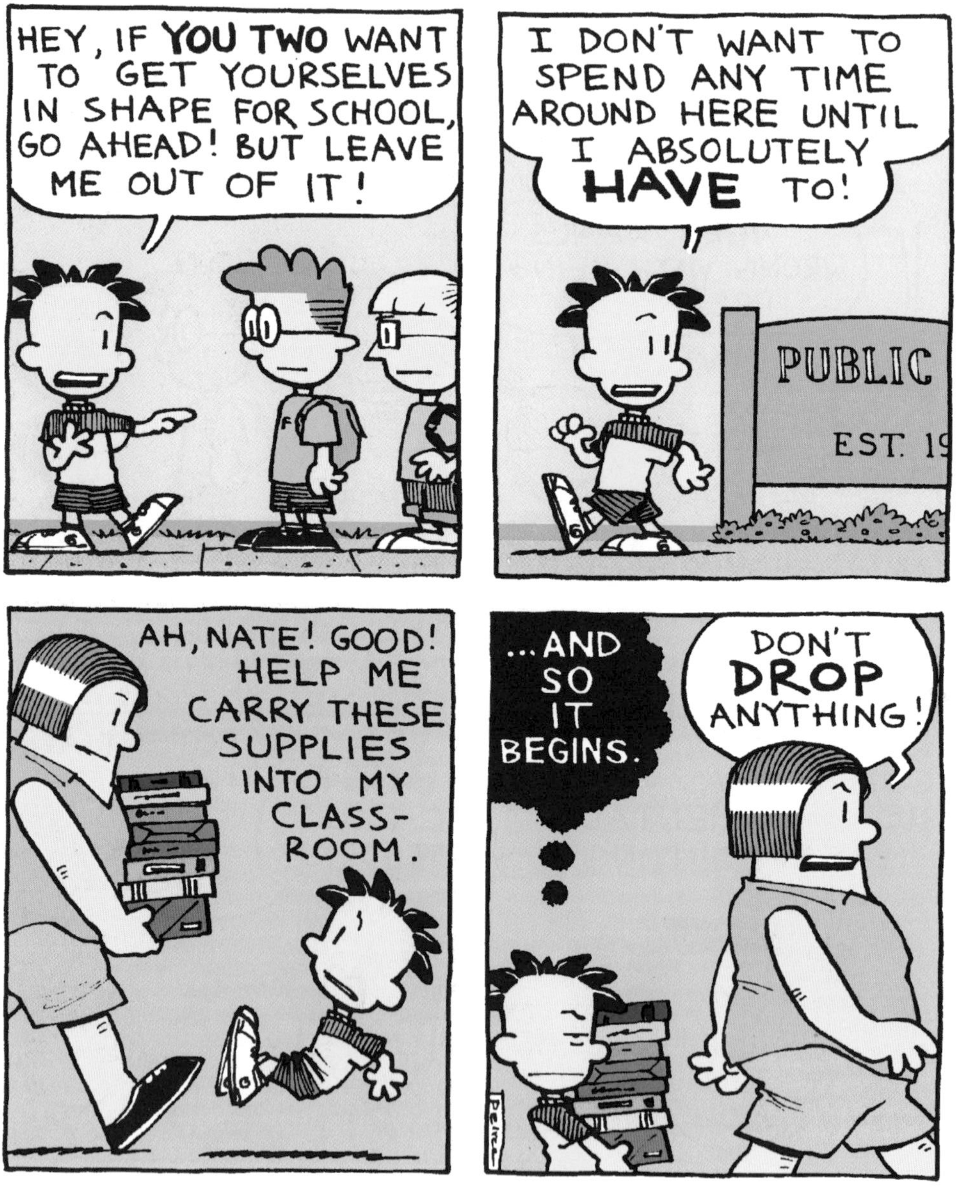
HEY, IF YOU TWO WANT TO GET YOURSELVES IN SHAPE FOR SCHOOL, GO AHEAD! BUT LEAVE ME OUT OF IT!
I DON'T WANT TO SPEND ANY TIME AROUND HERE UNTIL I ABSOLUTELY HAVE TO!
PUBLIC
EST. 19
AH, NATE! GOOD! HELP ME CARRY THESE SUPPLIES INTO MY CLASS-ROOM.
...AND SO IT BEGINS.
DON'T DROP ANYTHING!

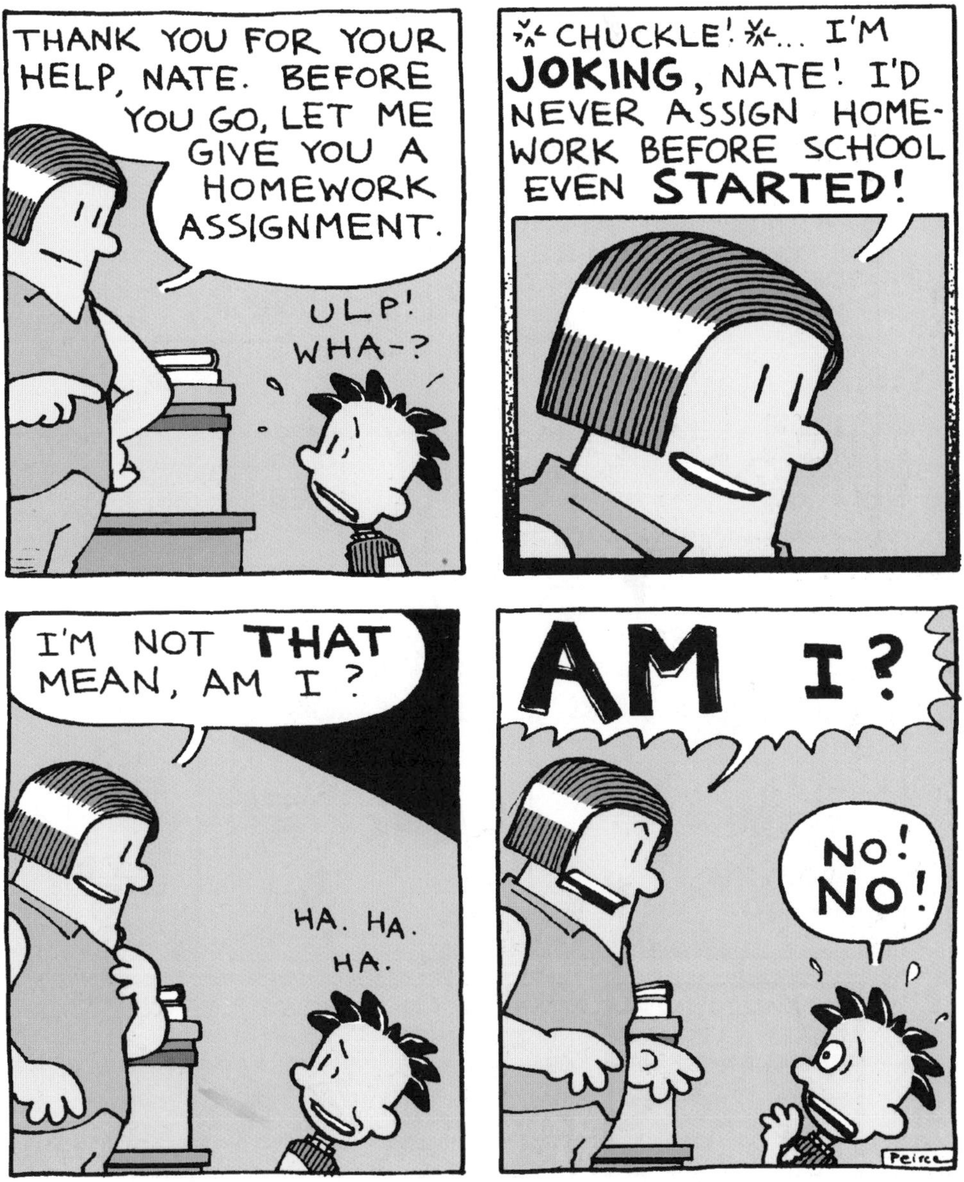
THANK YOU FOR YOUR HELP, NATE. BEFORE YOU GO, LET ME GIVE YOU A HOMEWORK ASSIGNMENT.
ULP! WHA-?
CHUCKLE!... I'M JOKING, NATE! I'D NEVER ASSIGN HOME-WORK BEFORE SCHOOL EVEN STARTED!
I'M NOT THAT MEAN, AM I?
HA. HA. HA.
AM I?
NO! NO!
Peirce

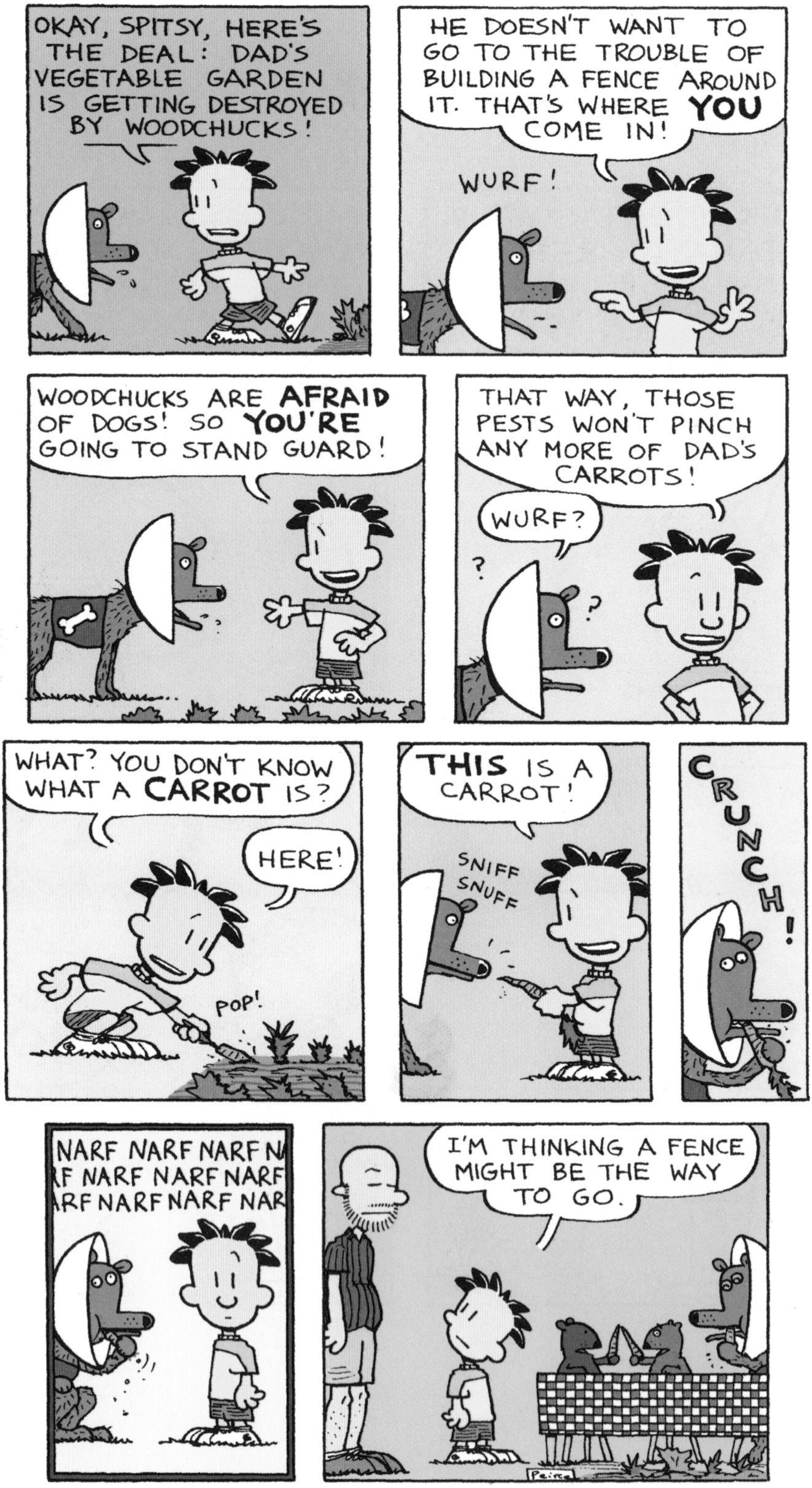
OKAY, SPITSY, HERE'S THE DEAL: DAD'S VEGETABLE GARDEN IS GETTING DESTROYED BY WOODCHUCKS!
HE DOESN'T WANT TO GO TO THE TROUBLE OF BUILDING A FENCE AROUND IT. THAT'S WHERE YOU COME IN!
WURF!
WOODCHUCKS ARE AFRAID OF DOGS! SO YOU'RE GOING TO STAND GUARD!
THAT WAY, THOSE PESTS WON'T PINCH ANY MORE OF DAD'S CARROTS!
WURF?
?
?
WHAT? YOU DON'T KNOW WHAT A CARROT IS?
HERE!
POP!
THIS IS A CARROT!
SNIFF SNUFF
CRUNCH!
NARF NARF NARF NA
RF NARF NARF NARF
ARF NARF NARF NAR
I'M THINKING A FENCE MIGHT BE THE WAY TO GO.
Peirce

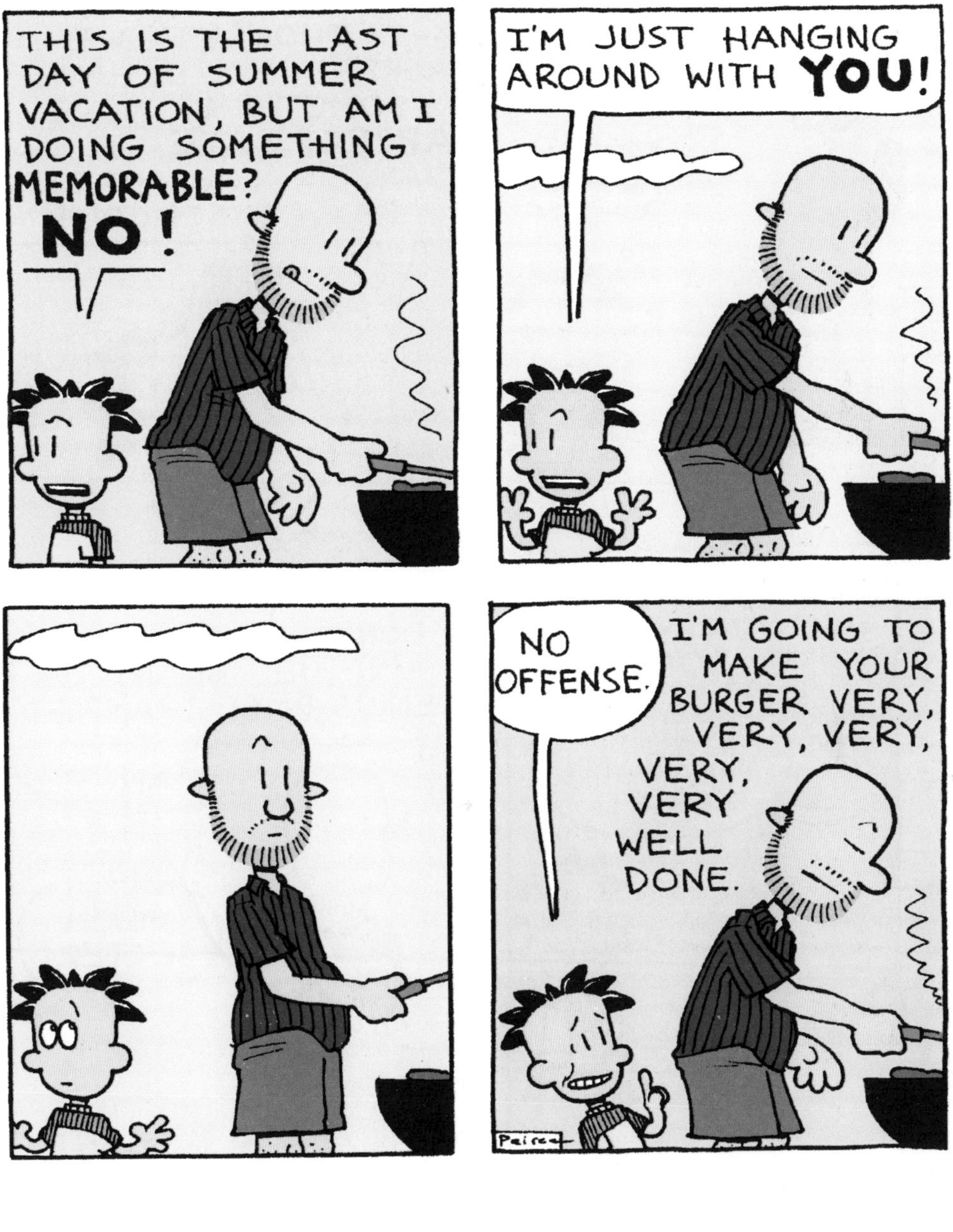
THIS IS THE LAST DAY OF SUMMER VACATION, BUT AM I DOING SOMETHING MEMORABLE? NO!
I'M JUST HANGING AROUND WITH YOU!
NO OFFENSE.
I'M GOING TO MAKE YOUR BURGER VERY, VERY, VERY, VERY, VERY WELL DONE.
Peirce

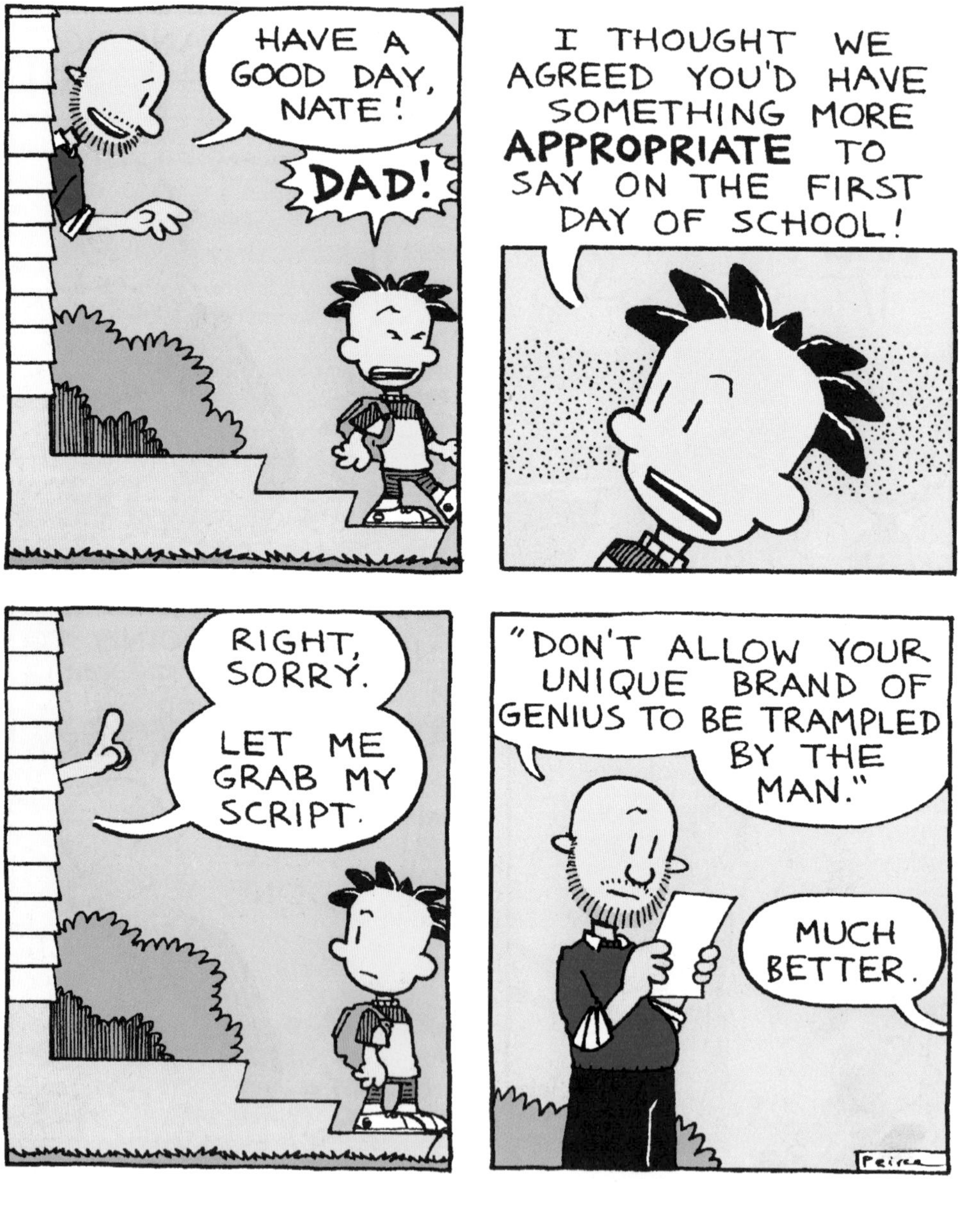
HAVE A GOOD DAY, NATE!
DAD!
I THOUGHT WE AGREED YOU'D HAVE SOMETHING MORE **APPROPRIATE** TO SAY ON THE FIRST DAY OF SCHOOL!
RIGHT, SORRY.
LET ME GRAB MY SCRIPT.
"DON'T ALLOW YOUR UNIQUE BRAND OF GENIUS TO BE TRAMPLED BY THE MAN."
MUCH BETTER.
Peirce

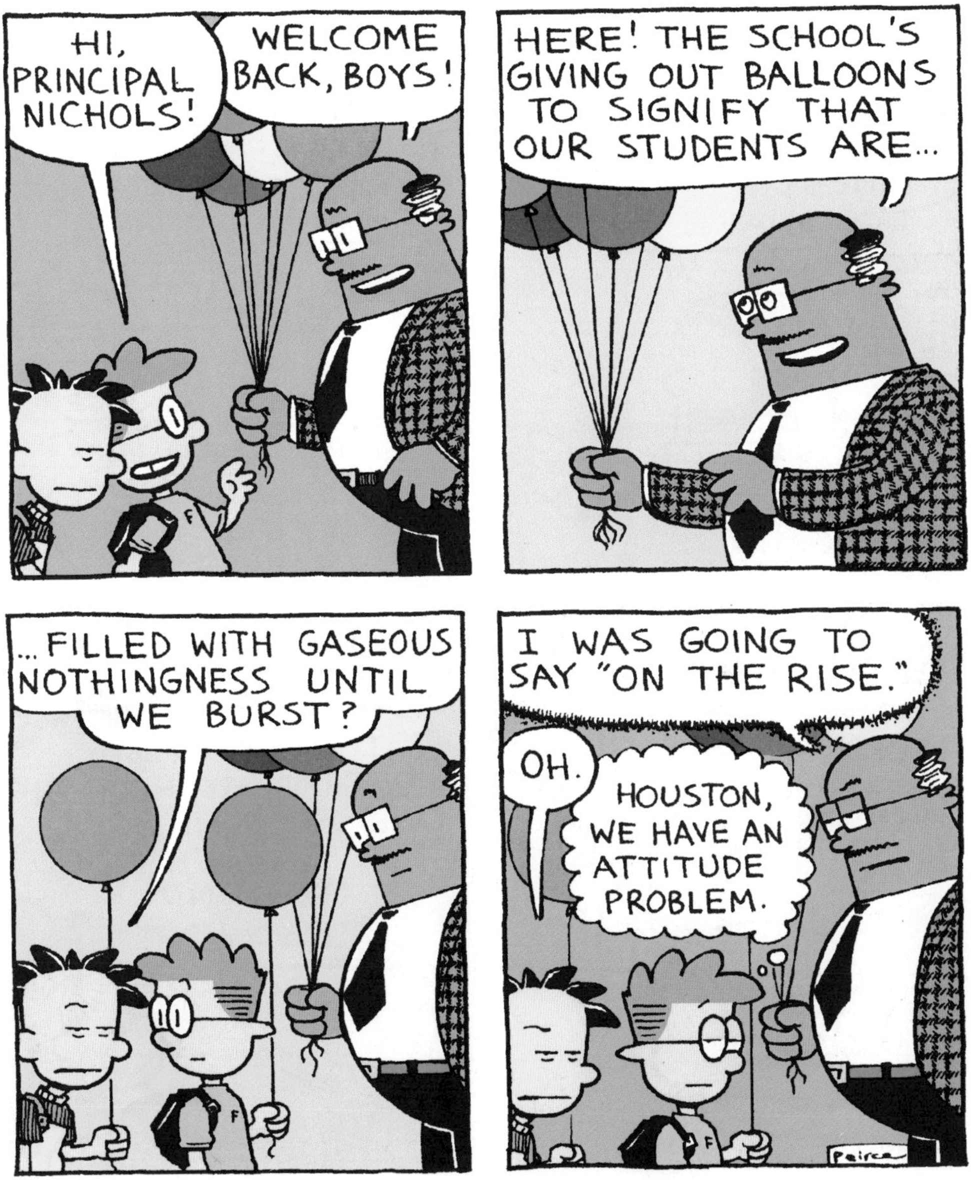
HI, PRINCIPAL NICHOLS!
WELCOME BACK, BOYS!
HERE! THE SCHOOL'S GIVING OUT BALLOONS TO SIGNIFY THAT OUR STUDENTS ARE...
...FILLED WITH GASEOUS NOTHINGNESS UNTIL WE BURST?
I WAS GOING TO SAY "ON THE RISE."
OH.
HOUSTON, WE HAVE AN ATTITUDE PROBLEM.
Peirce

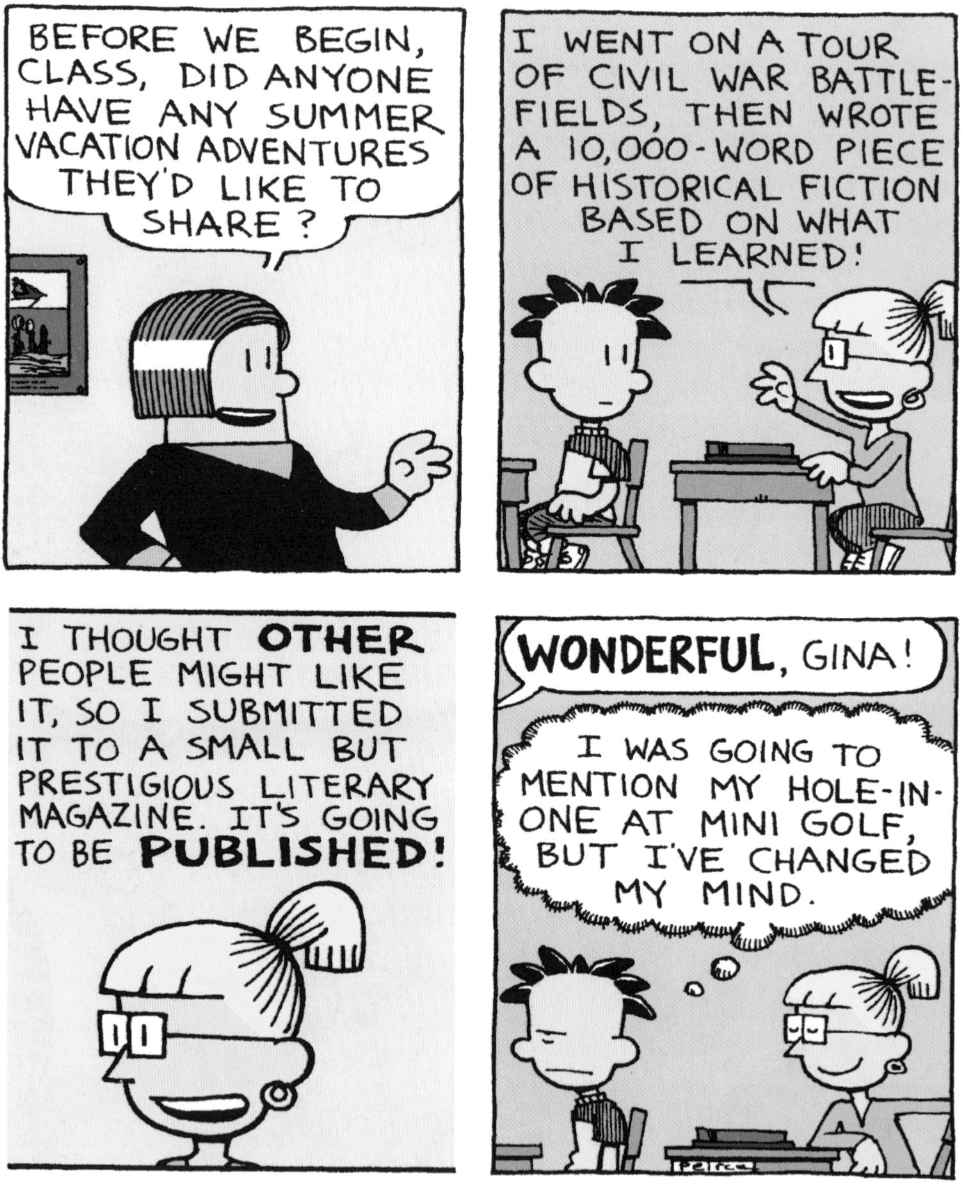
BEFORE WE BEGIN, CLASS, DID ANYONE HAVE ANY SUMMER VACATION ADVENTURES THEY'D LIKE TO SHARE?
I WENT ON A TOUR OF CIVIL WAR BATTLE-FIELDS, THEN WROTE A 10,000-WORD PIECE OF HISTORICAL FICTION BASED ON WHAT I LEARNED!
I THOUGHT **OTHER** PEOPLE MIGHT LIKE IT, SO I SUBMITTED IT TO A SMALL BUT PRESTIGIOUS LITERARY MAGAZINE. IT'S GOING TO BE **PUBLISHED**!
WONDERFUL, GINA!
I WAS GOING TO MENTION MY HOLE-IN-ONE AT MINI GOLF, BUT I'VE CHANGED MY MIND.

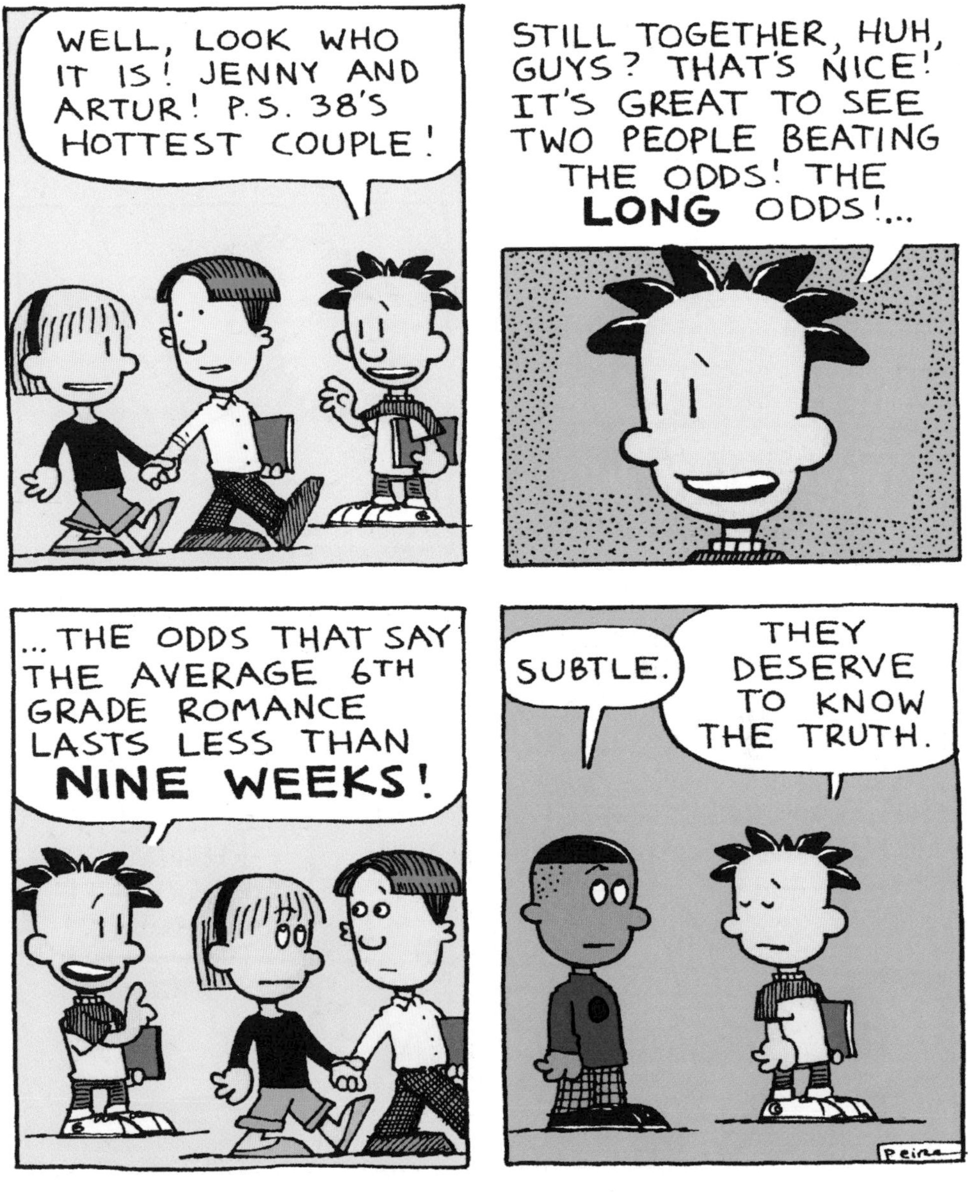
WELL, LOOK WHO IT IS! JENNY AND ARTUR! P.S. 38'S HOTTEST COUPLE!
STILL TOGETHER, HUH, GUYS? THAT'S NICE! IT'S GREAT TO SEE TWO PEOPLE BEATING THE ODDS! THE **LONG** ODDS!...
... THE ODDS THAT SAY THE AVERAGE 6TH GRADE ROMANCE LASTS LESS THAN **NINE WEEKS!**
SUBTLE.
THEY DESERVE TO KNOW THE TRUTH.
PEIRCE

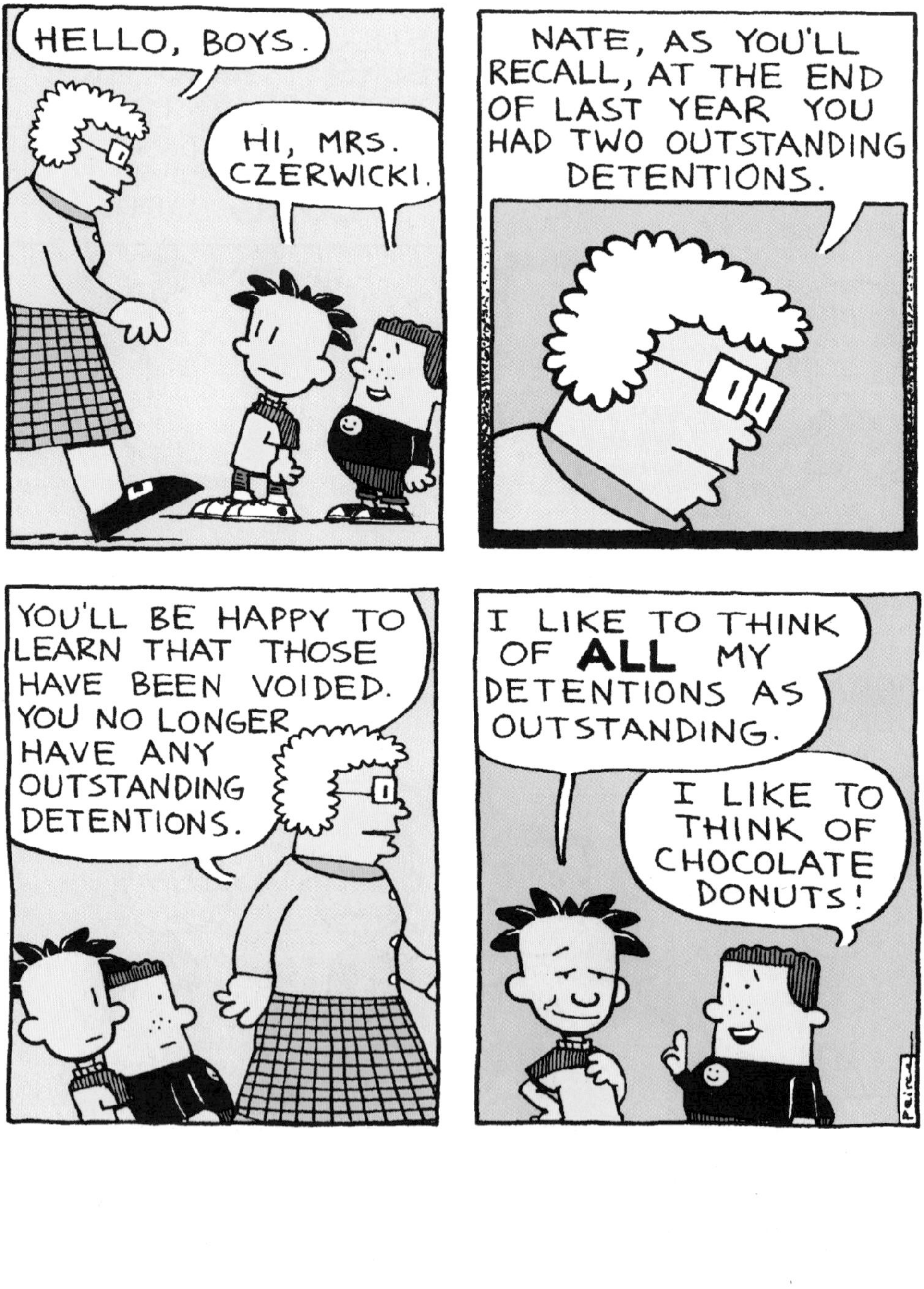
HELLO, BOYS.
HI, MRS. CZERWICKI.
NATE, AS YOU'LL RECALL, AT THE END OF LAST YEAR YOU HAD TWO OUTSTANDING DETENTIONS.
YOU'LL BE HAPPY TO LEARN THAT THOSE HAVE BEEN VOIDED. YOU NO LONGER HAVE ANY OUTSTANDING DETENTIONS.
I LIKE TO THINK OF ALL MY DETENTIONS AS OUTSTANDING.
I LIKE TO THINK OF CHOCOLATE DONUTS!
PEIRCE

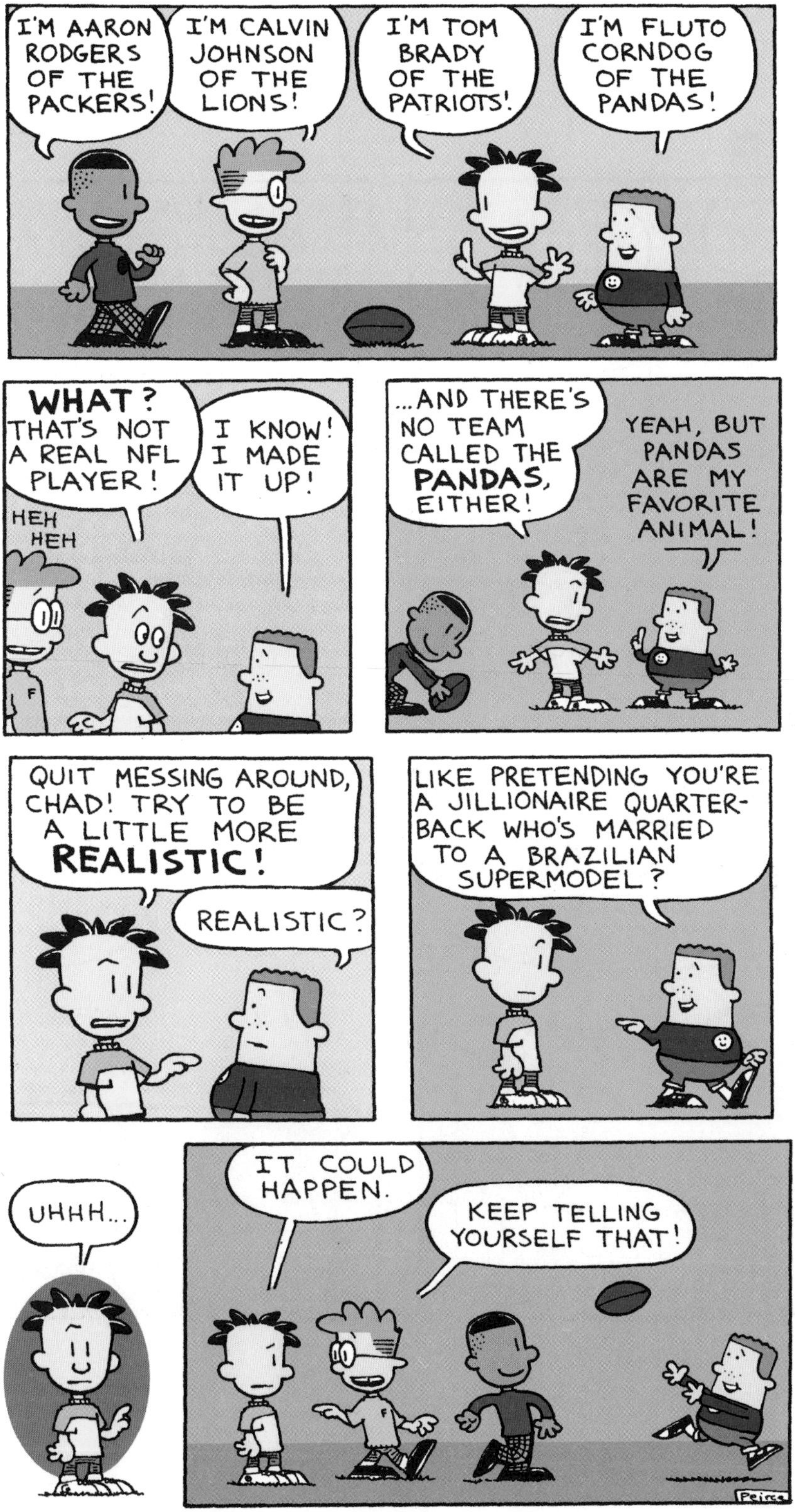
I'M AARON RODGERS OF THE PACKERS!
I'M CALVIN JOHNSON OF THE LIONS!
I'M TOM BRADY OF THE PATRIOTS!
I'M FLUTO CORNDOG OF THE PANDAS!
WHAT? THAT'S NOT A REAL NFL PLAYER!
I KNOW! I MADE IT UP!
HEH HEH
...AND THERE'S NO TEAM CALLED THE PANDAS, EITHER!
YEAH, BUT PANDAS ARE MY FAVORITE ANIMAL!
QUIT MESSING AROUND, CHAD! TRY TO BE A LITTLE MORE REALISTIC!
REALISTIC?
LIKE PRETENDING YOU'RE A JILLIONAIRE QUARTER-BACK WHO'S MARRIED TO A BRAZILIAN SUPERMODEL?
UHHH...
IT COULD HAPPEN.
KEEP TELLING YOURSELF THAT!
Peirce

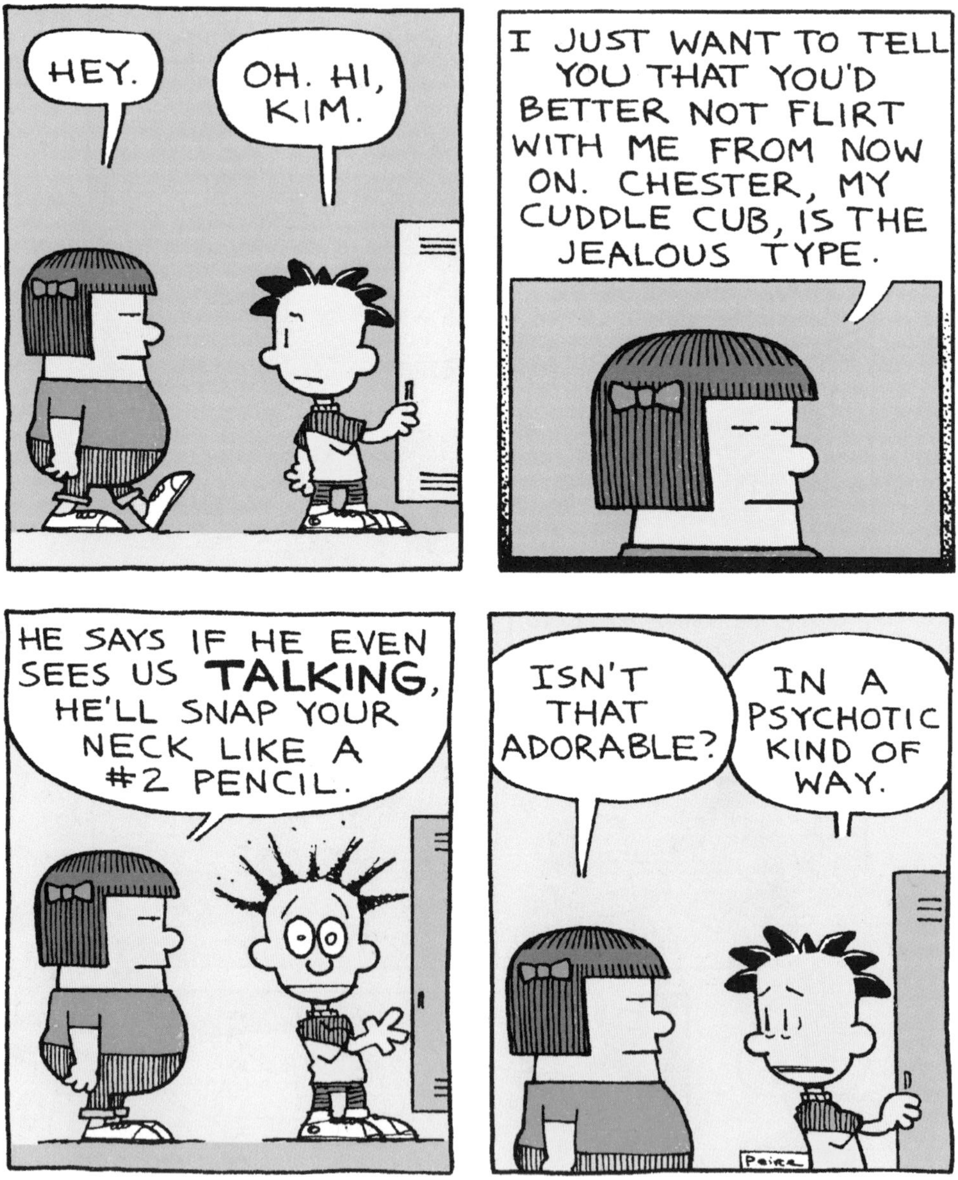
HEY.
OH. HI, KIM.
I JUST WANT TO TELL YOU THAT YOU'D BETTER NOT FLIRT WITH ME FROM NOW ON. CHESTER, MY CUDDLE CUB, IS THE JEALOUS TYPE.
HE SAYS IF HE EVEN SEES US TALKING, HE'LL SNAP YOUR NECK LIKE A #2 PENCIL.
ISN'T THAT ADORABLE?
IN A PSYCHOTIC KIND OF WAY.
Peirce

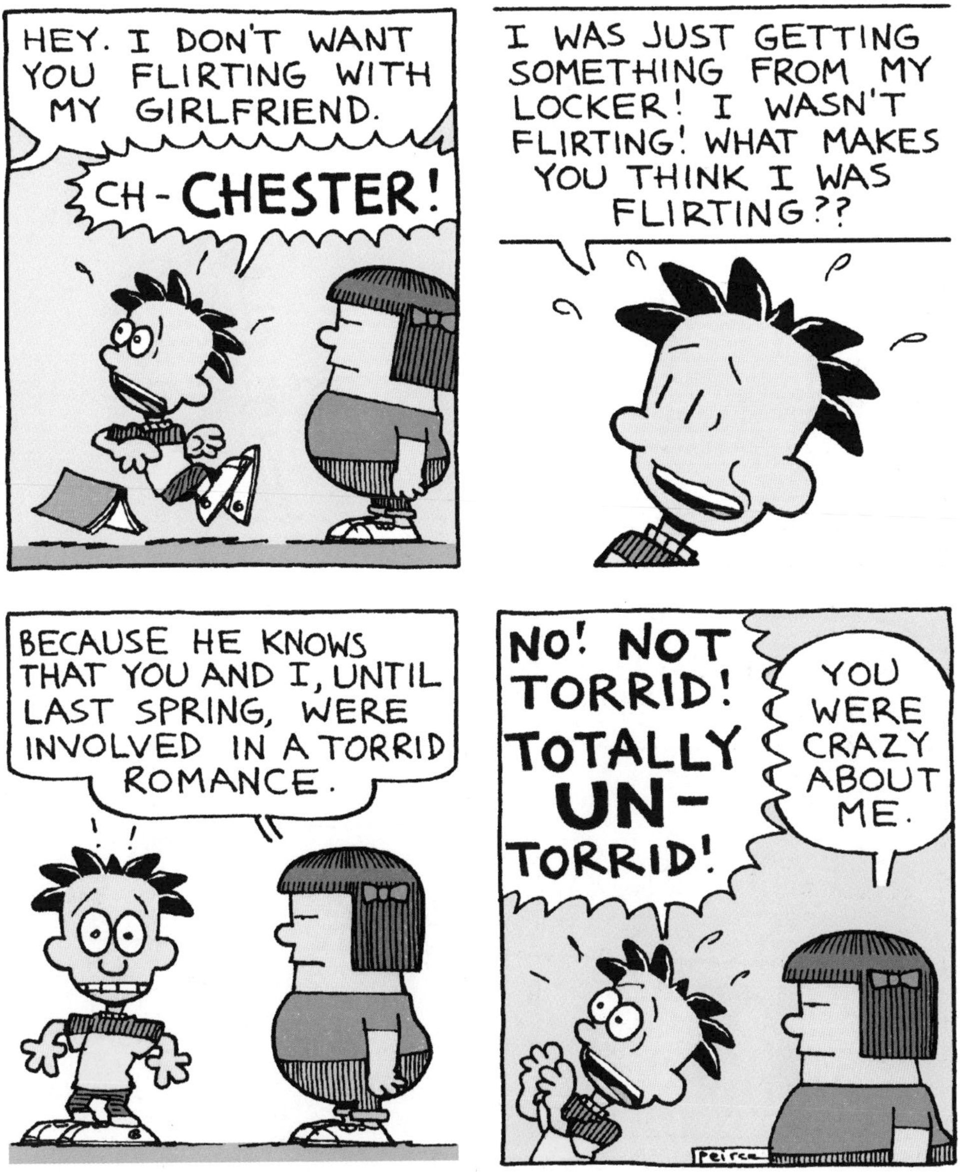
HEY. I DON'T WANT YOU FLIRTING WITH MY GIRLFRIEND.
CH-CHESTER!
I WAS JUST GETTING SOMETHING FROM MY LOCKER! I WASN'T FLIRTING! WHAT MAKES YOU THINK I WAS FLIRTING??
BECAUSE HE KNOWS THAT YOU AND I, UNTIL LAST SPRING, WERE INVOLVED IN A TORRID ROMANCE.
NO! NOT TORRID! TOTALLY UN-TORRID!
YOU WERE CRAZY ABOUT ME.
peirce

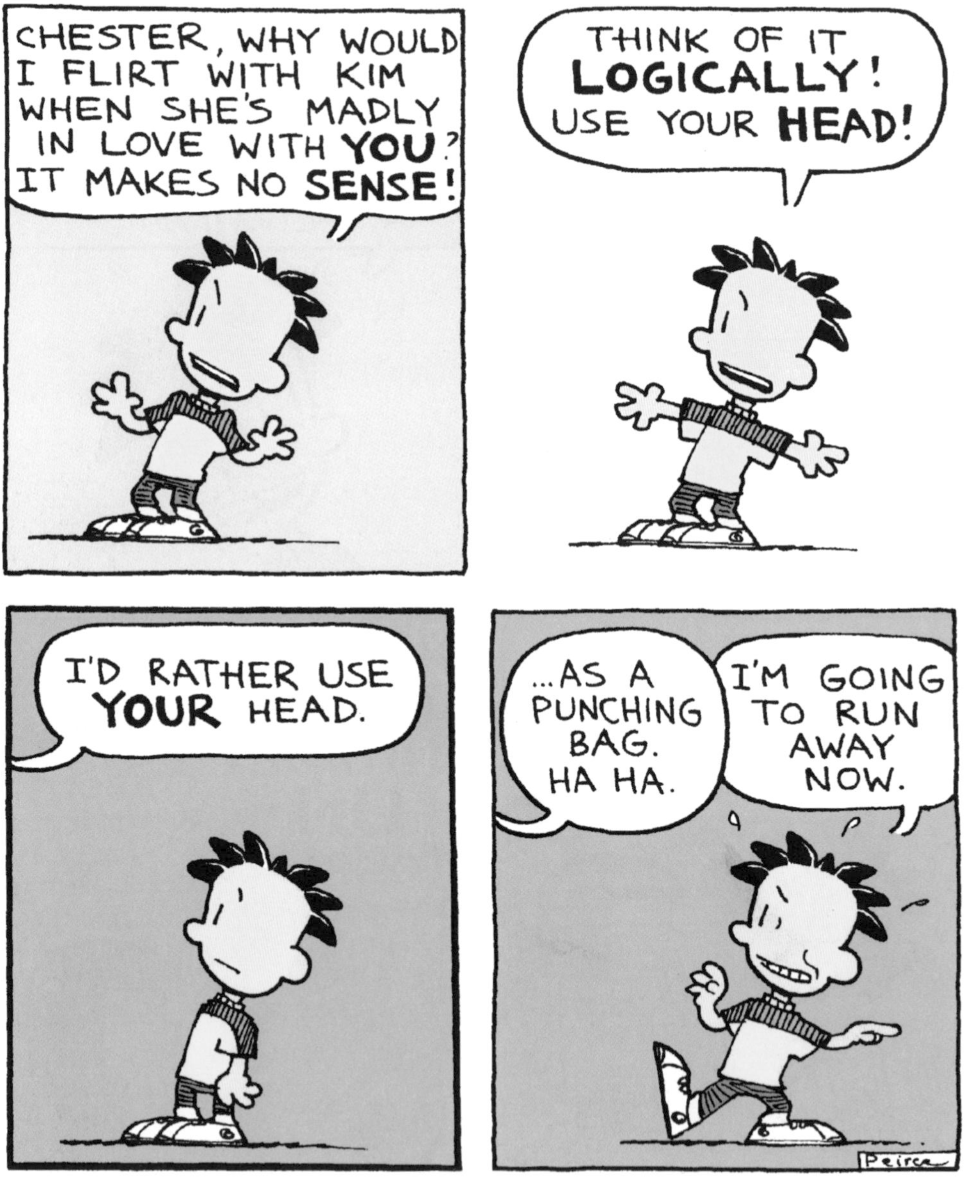
CHESTER, WHY WOULD I FLIRT WITH KIM WHEN SHE'S MADLY IN LOVE WITH **YOU**? IT MAKES NO **SENSE**!
THINK OF IT **LOGICALLY**! USE YOUR **HEAD**!
I'D RATHER USE **YOUR** HEAD.
...AS A PUNCHING BAG. HA HA.
I'M GOING TO RUN AWAY NOW.
Peirce

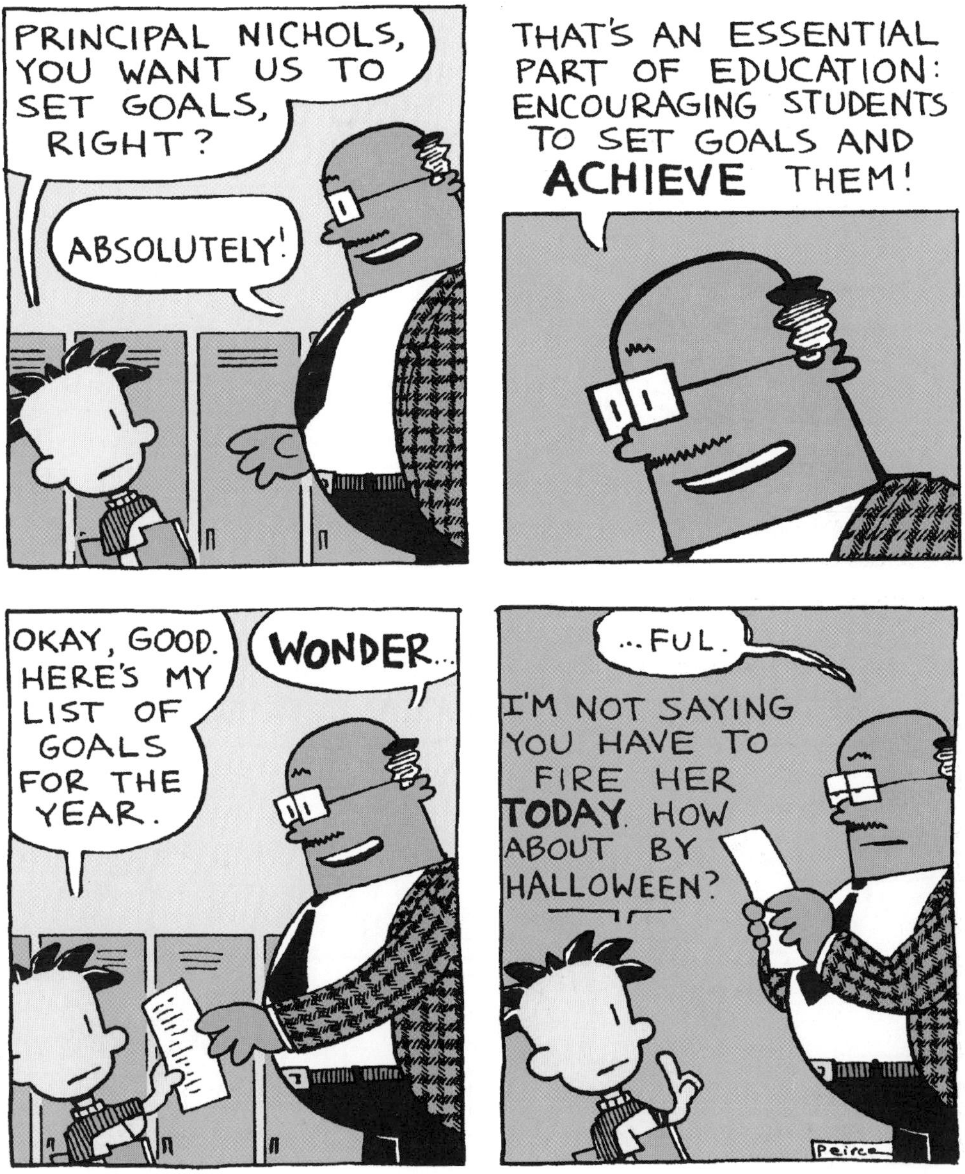
PRINCIPAL NICHOLS, YOU WANT US TO SET GOALS, RIGHT?
ABSOLUTELY!
THAT'S AN ESSENTIAL PART OF EDUCATION: ENCOURAGING STUDENTS TO SET GOALS AND ACHIEVE THEM!
OKAY, GOOD. HERE'S MY LIST OF GOALS FOR THE YEAR.
WONDER...
...FUL.
I'M NOT SAYING YOU HAVE TO FIRE HER TODAY. HOW ABOUT BY HALLOWEEN?
Peirce

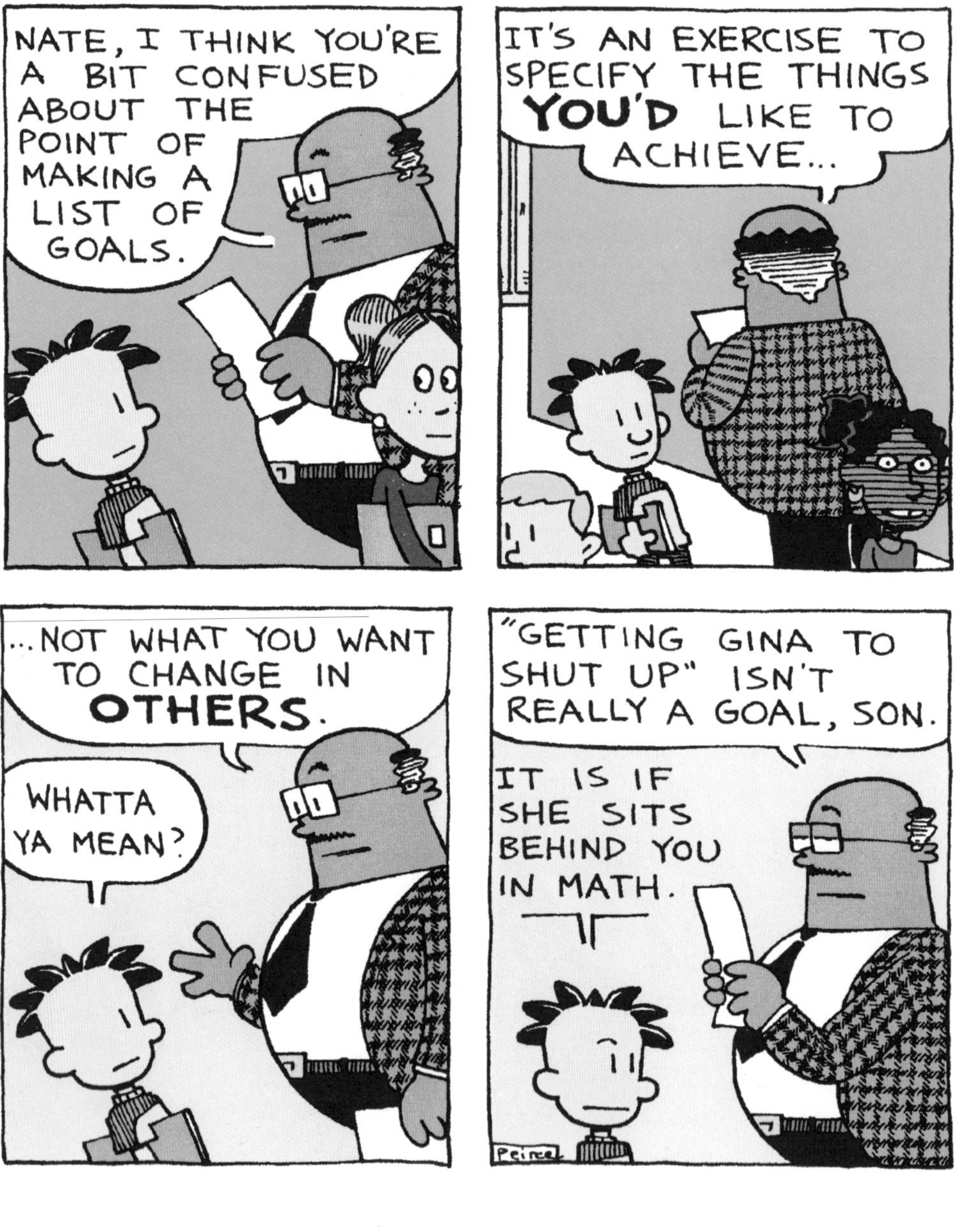
NATE, I THINK YOU'RE A BIT CONFUSED ABOUT THE POINT OF MAKING A LIST OF GOALS.
IT'S AN EXERCISE TO SPECIFY THE THINGS **YOU'D** LIKE TO ACHIEVE...
...NOT WHAT YOU WANT TO CHANGE IN **OTHERS**.
WHATTA YA MEAN?
"GETTING GINA TO SHUT UP" ISN'T REALLY A GOAL, SON.
IT IS IF SHE SITS BEHIND YOU IN MATH.
Peirce

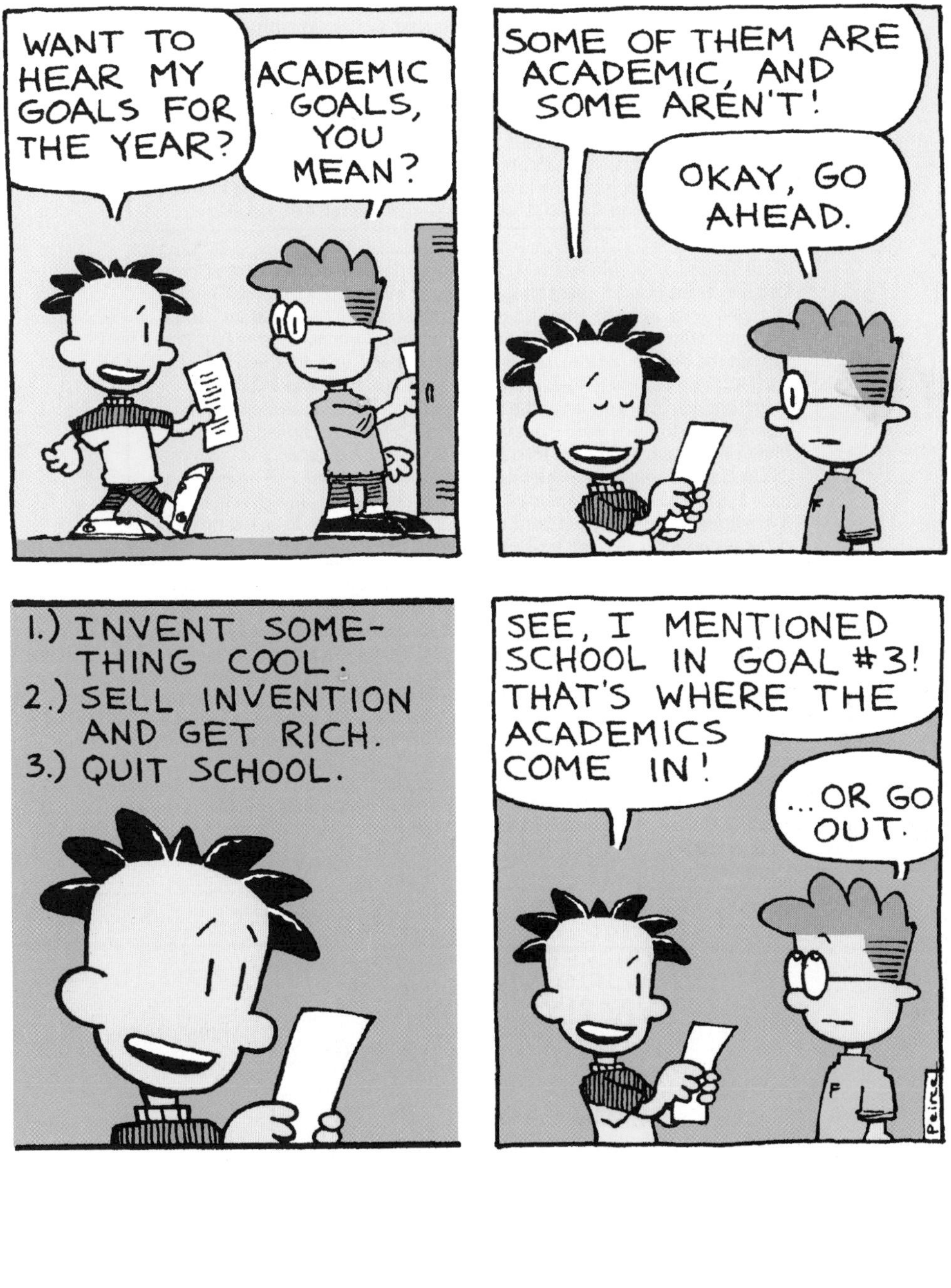
WANT TO HEAR MY GOALS FOR THE YEAR?
ACADEMIC GOALS, YOU MEAN?
SOME OF THEM ARE ACADEMIC, AND SOME AREN'T!
OKAY, GO AHEAD.
1.) INVENT SOMETHING COOL.
2.) SELL INVENTION AND GET RICH.
3.) QUIT SCHOOL.
SEE, I MENTIONED SCHOOL IN GOAL #3! THAT'S WHERE THE ACADEMICS COME IN!
...OR GO OUT.
Peirce

GEORGE WASHINGTON, FATHER OF OUR COUNTRY
By Nate Wright

People sometimes call George Washington the father of our country. I think those people are right, because indeed, George Washington truly WAS the father of our country, which as we all know is called the United States of America. But HOW did a shy young man from the humble little town of Wakefield, Virginia, grow up to become our first president? Well, allow me to give you some of the startling facts that will PROVE my point, which is that George Washington is the real father of our country. When young George was born, on February 22nd, 1732, he was just a baby. But soon, as so often happens, he grew up. Then George got smallpox, which was a disease back in the old days. As a result, George had bad skin.

Then his dad died. Oh, by the way, George's dad was named Augustine and his mother had the very simple name of Mary. Heartbroken, George chopped down a cherry tree and became a surveyor. After that he joined the army, which was in the middle of a war with France. George fought against the French in Ohio, which is kind of weird, and got them to surrender some forts. For example: one of those forts was called Fort Duquesne. George got out of the army and decided it was time to get married. He found a widow named Martha Custis who agreed to marry him even though he had wooden teeth. So they got married and went to live at George's mansion, which is called Mount Vernon. It is open 365 days a year and contains a museum, orientation center, and gift shop. Everything was going great until England came along and started raising taxes. George got so mad, he declared WAR ON ENGLAND!!

George was made commander of the Continental Army, and then he crossed the Delaware to fight the British at Valley Forge. There were many fierce battles, but thanks to George and his very, very good leadership, the British eventually gave up and went back to England. George wanted to retire to Mount Vernon, but the rest of the country was like: we don't THINK so. So they elected George as the first president.

George was inaugurated on April 30th, 1789, in New York City. Why New York City? Because George had not invented the city of Washington, DC yet. Pretty soon he did, though, and he made it the capital of the whole country. That was the first of many impressive accomplishments he accomplished as president. Most of them he did while he was alive, but some he achieved when he was dead, like getting his face carved into Mount Rushmore. On December 14th, 1799, tragedy struck. George went horseback riding in the snow, came down with acute laryngitis, and died. But what a very amazing life he led. As the first president and father of our country, George Washington definitely made history.

THE END

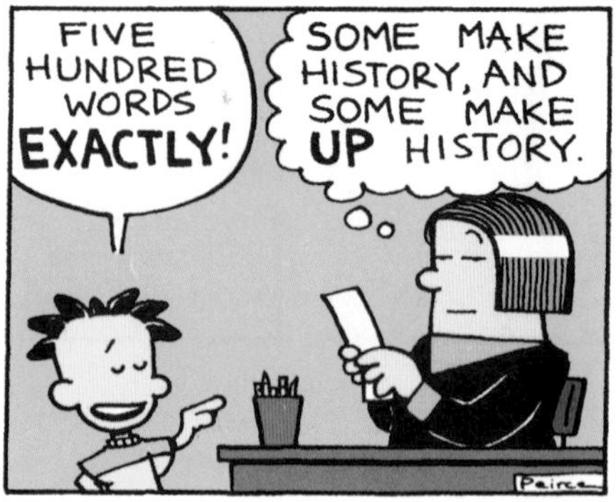
FIVE HUNDRED WORDS **EXACTLY!**
SOME MAKE HISTORY, AND SOME MAKE **UP** HISTORY.
Peirce

CLASS, HERE'S HOW YOUR GRADE FOR THE SEMESTER WILL BE DETERMINED:

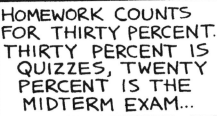

HOMEWORK COUNTS FOR THIRTY PERCENT. THIRTY PERCENT IS QUIZZES, TWENTY PERCENT IS THE MIDTERM EXAM...

...AND THE REMAINING TWENTY PERCENT IS...

...CLASS PARTICIPATION!

Z

WHA-?...YES! NO! BEN FRANKLIN!

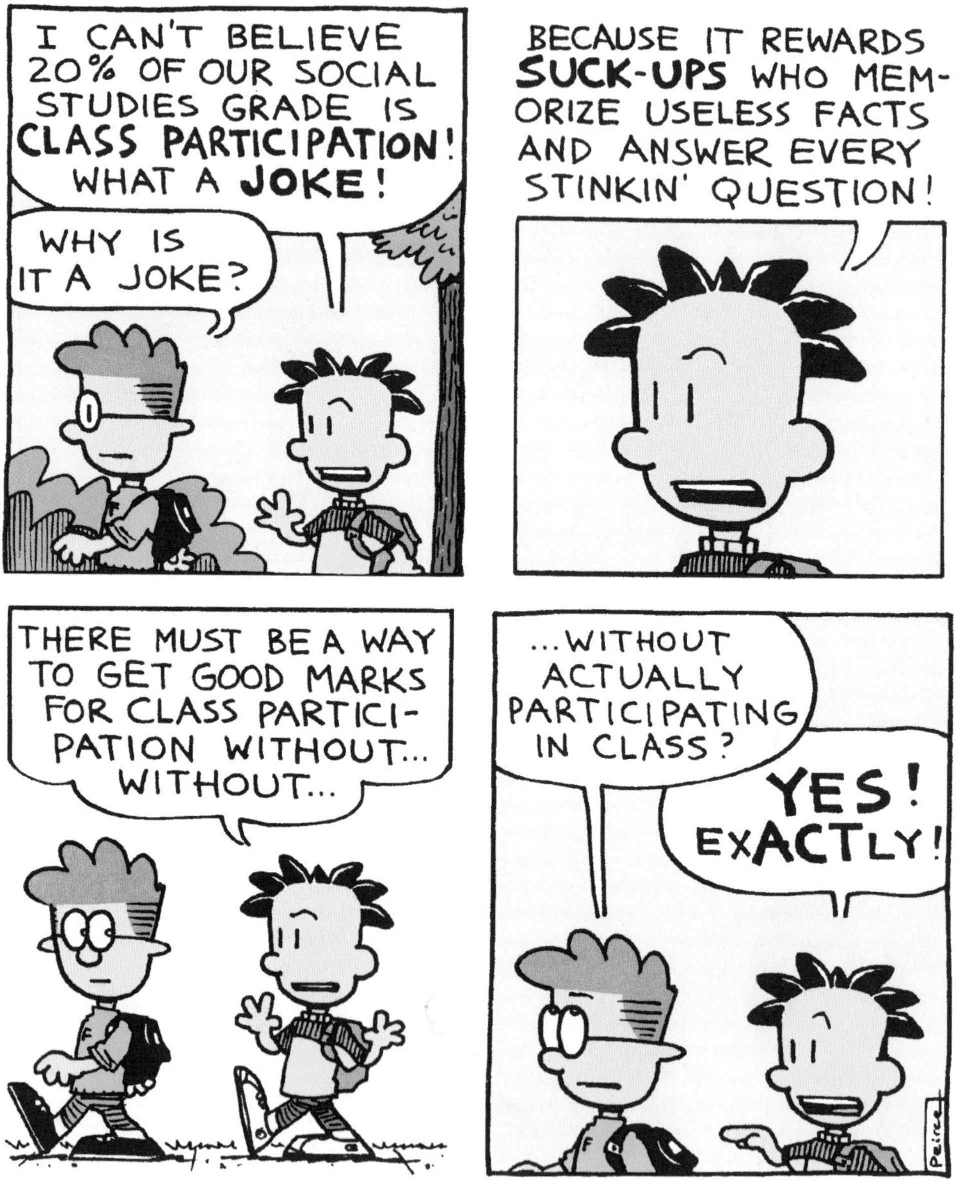
I CAN'T BELIEVE 20% OF OUR SOCIAL STUDIES GRADE IS CLASS PARTICIPATION! WHAT A JOKE!
WHY IS IT A JOKE?
BECAUSE IT REWARDS SUCK-UPS WHO MEMORIZE USELESS FACTS AND ANSWER EVERY STINKIN' QUESTION!
THERE MUST BE A WAY TO GET GOOD MARKS FOR CLASS PARTICIPATION WITHOUT... WITHOUT...
...WITHOUT ACTUALLY PARTICIPATING IN CLASS?
YES! EXACTLY!
Peirce

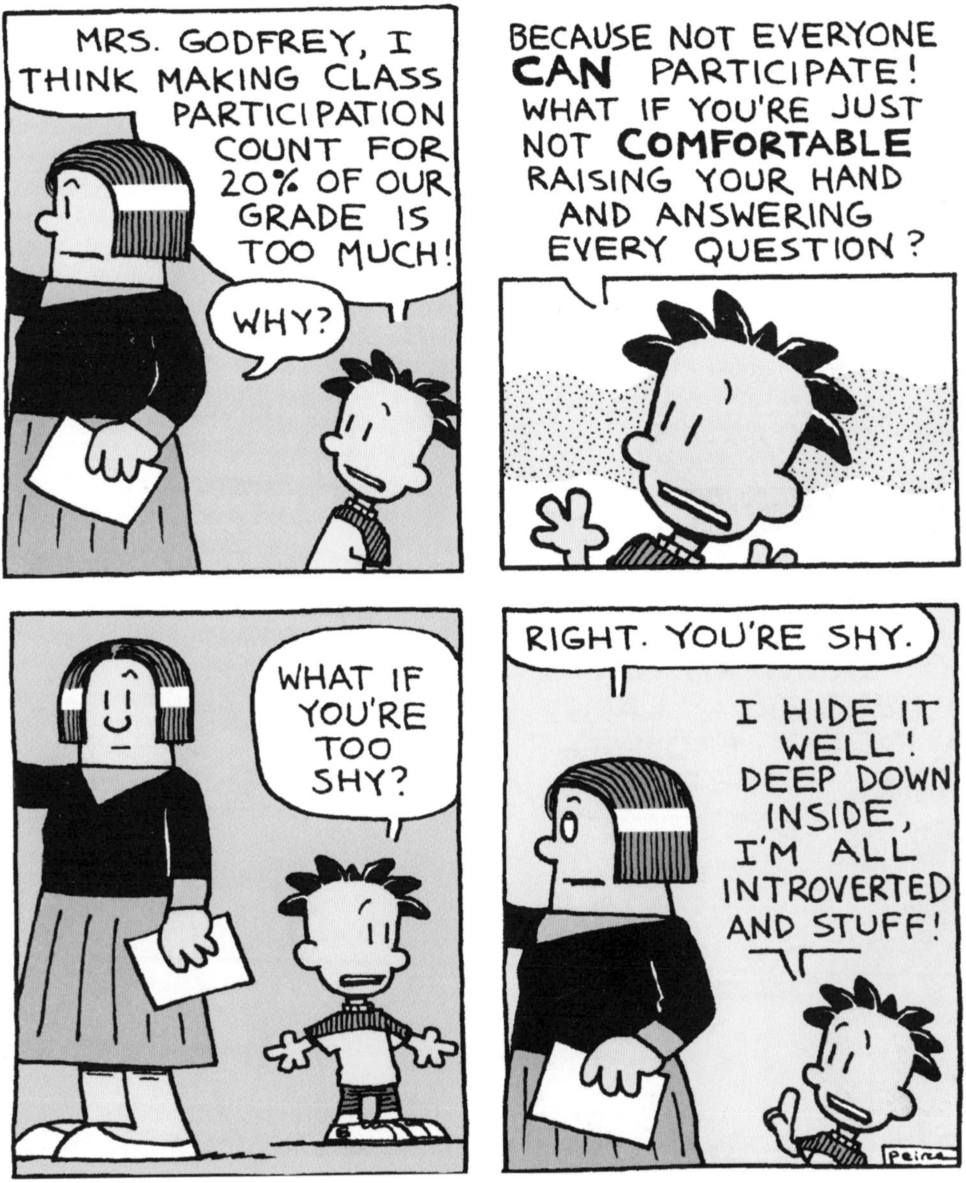
MRS. GODFREY, I THINK MAKING CLASS PARTICIPATION COUNT FOR 20% OF OUR GRADE IS TOO MUCH!
WHY?
BECAUSE NOT EVERYONE **CAN** PARTICIPATE! WHAT IF YOU'RE JUST NOT **COMFORTABLE** RAISING YOUR HAND AND ANSWERING EVERY QUESTION?
WHAT IF YOU'RE TOO SHY?
RIGHT. YOU'RE SHY.
I HIDE IT WELL! DEEP DOWN INSIDE, I'M ALL INTROVERTED AND STUFF!
peirce

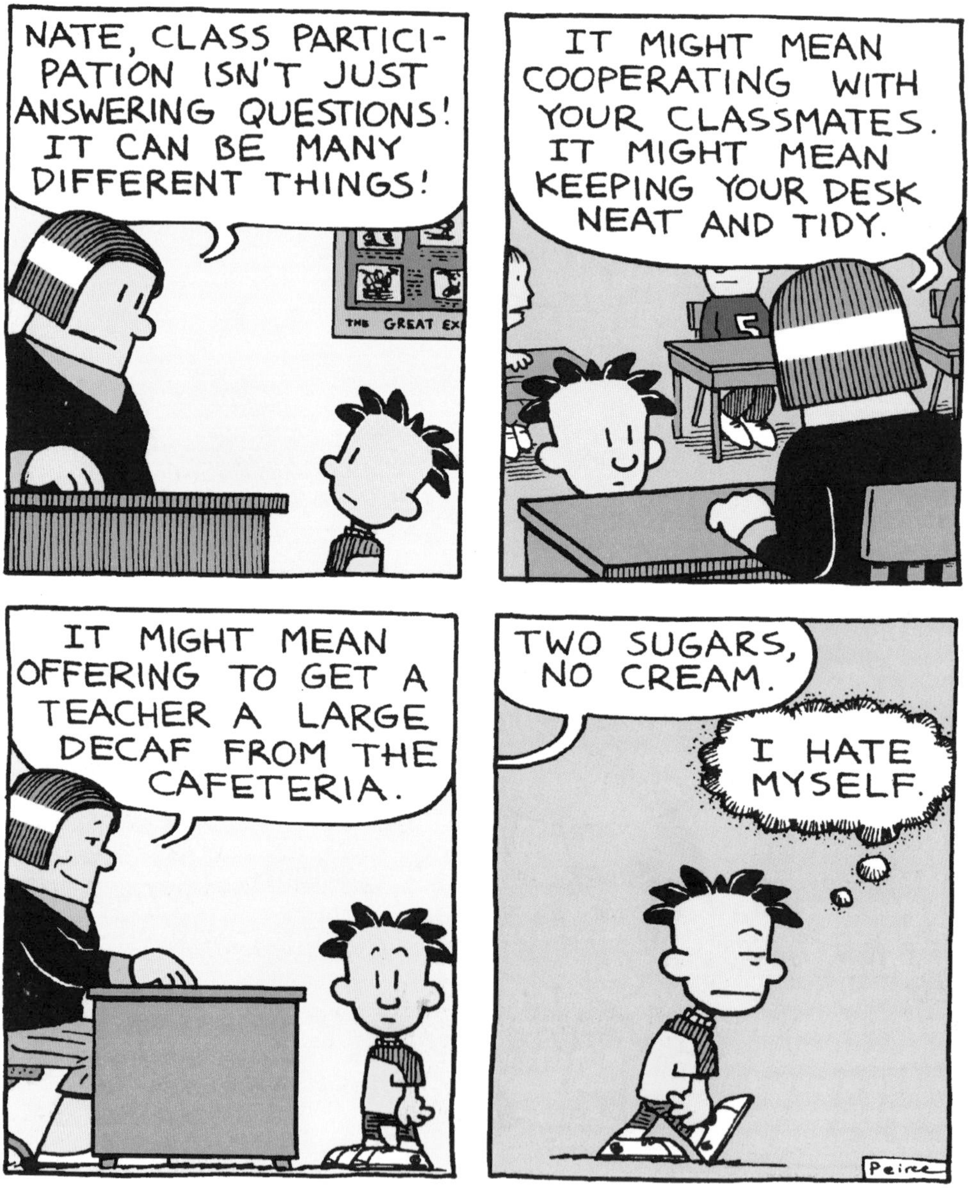
NATE, CLASS PARTICIPATION ISN'T JUST ANSWERING QUESTIONS! IT CAN BE MANY DIFFERENT THINGS!
THE GREAT EX
IT MIGHT MEAN COOPERATING WITH YOUR CLASSMATES. IT MIGHT MEAN KEEPING YOUR DESK NEAT AND TIDY.
IT MIGHT MEAN OFFERING TO GET A TEACHER A LARGE DECAF FROM THE CAFETERIA.
TWO SUGARS, NO CREAM.
I HATE MYSELF.
Peirce

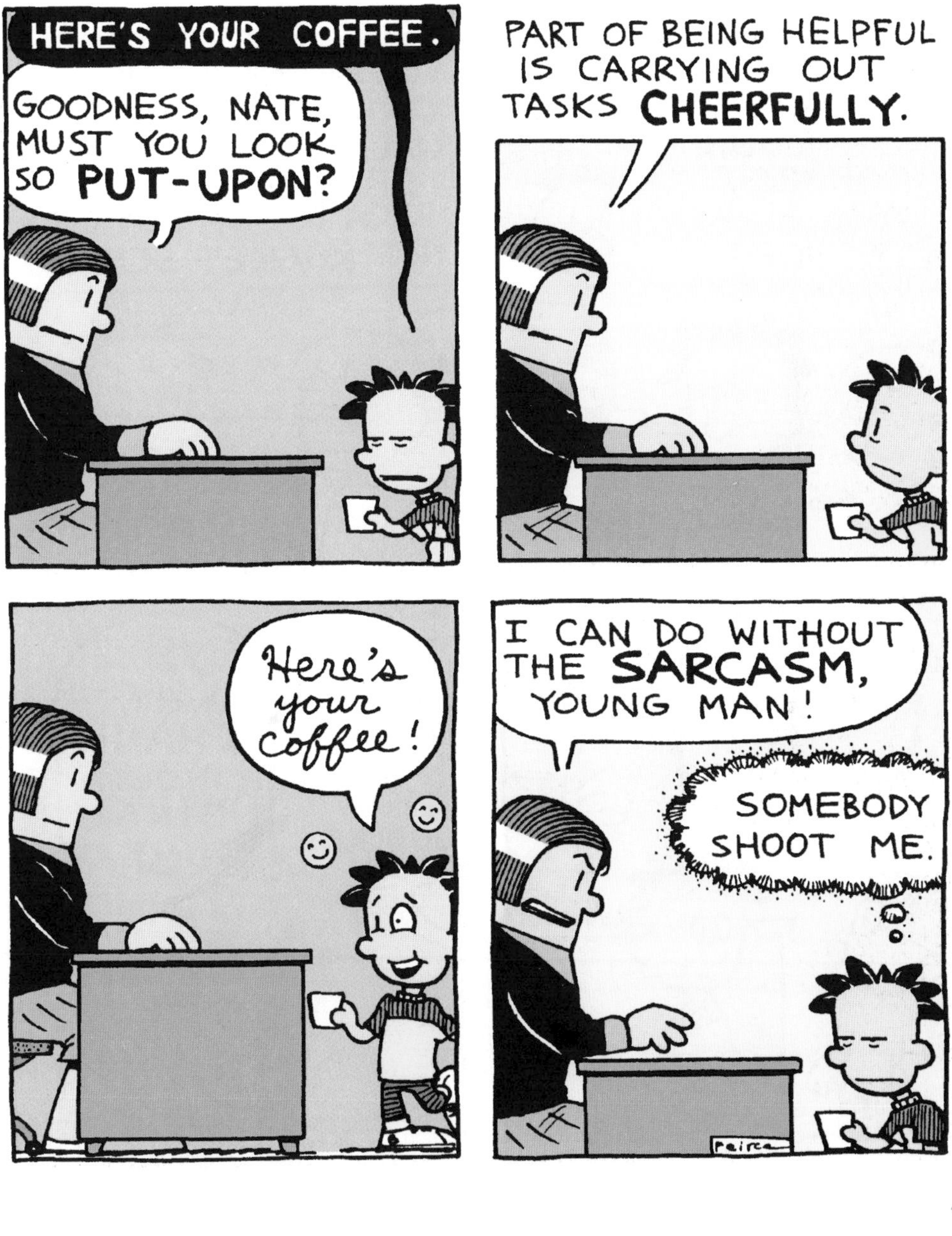
HERE'S YOUR COFFEE.
GOODNESS, NATE, MUST YOU LOOK SO PUT-UPON?
PART OF BEING HELPFUL IS CARRYING OUT TASKS CHEERFULLY.
Here's your coffee!
I CAN DO WITHOUT THE SARCASM, YOUNG MAN!
SOMEBODY SHOOT ME.
Peirce

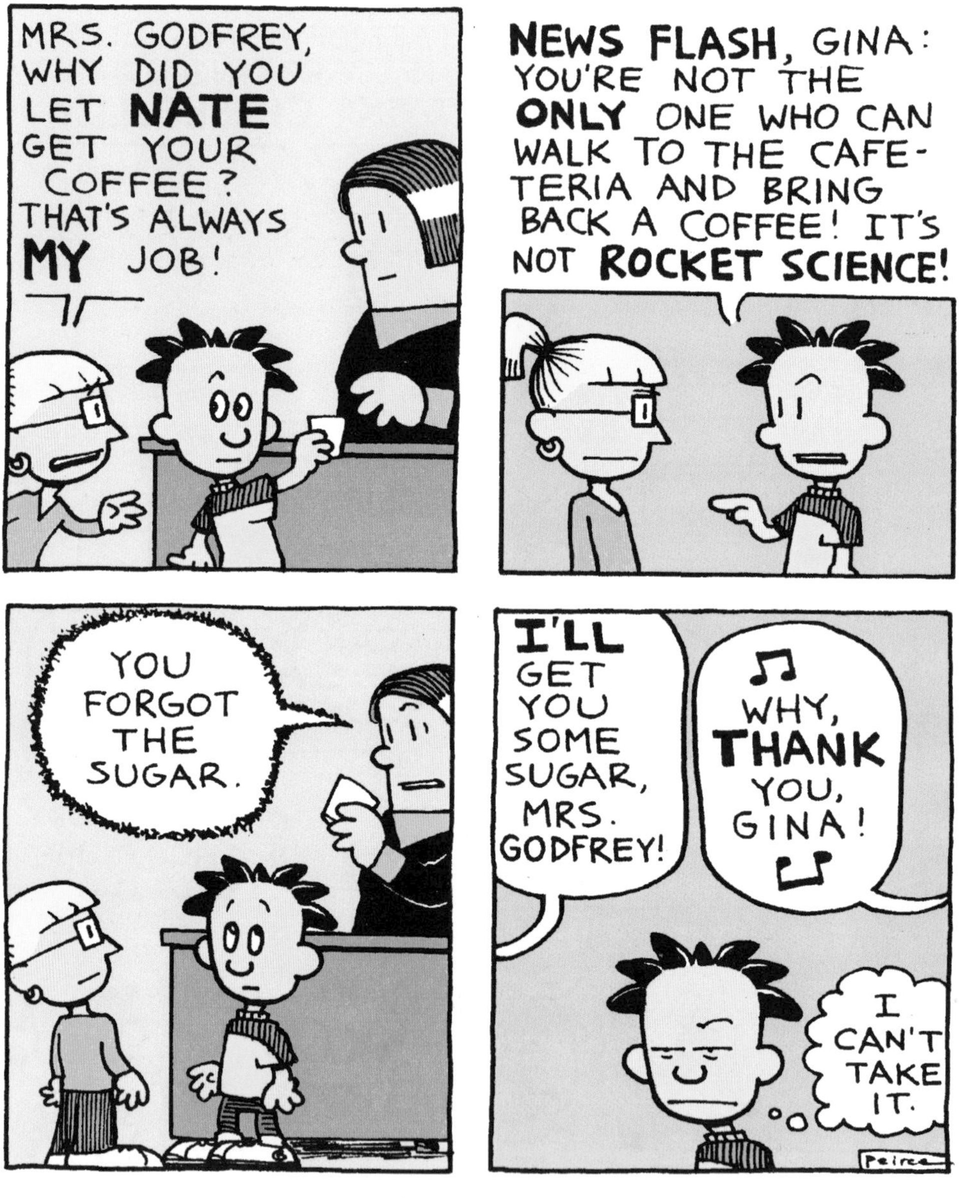
MRS. GODFREY, WHY DID YOU LET NATE GET YOUR COFFEE? THAT'S ALWAYS MY JOB!
NEWS FLASH, GINA: YOU'RE NOT THE ONLY ONE WHO CAN WALK TO THE CAFETERIA AND BRING BACK A COFFEE! IT'S NOT ROCKET SCIENCE!
YOU FORGOT THE SUGAR.
I'LL GET YOU SOME SUGAR, MRS. GODFREY!
WHY, THANK YOU, GINA!
I CAN'T TAKE IT.
Peirce

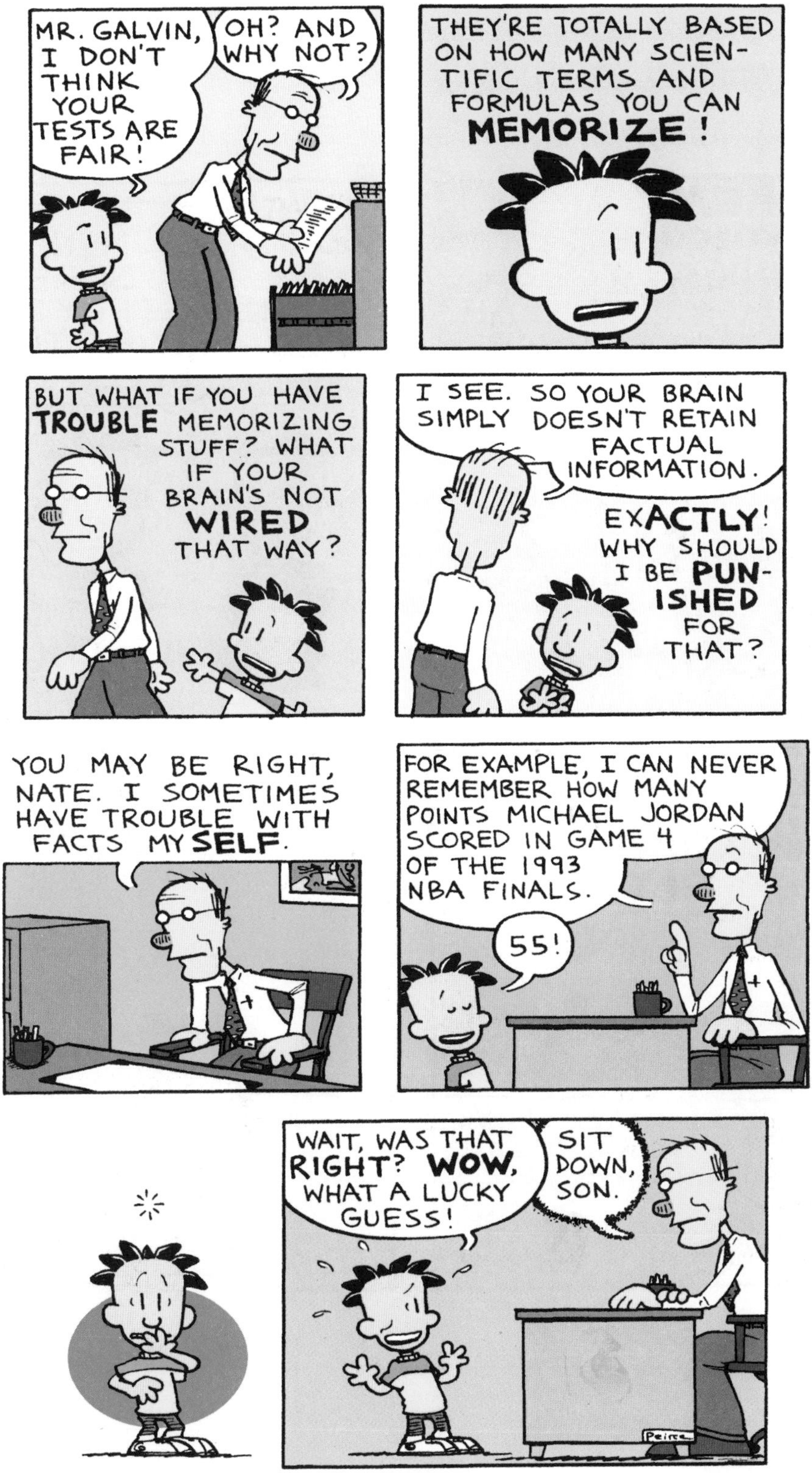
MR. GALVIN, I DON'T THINK YOUR TESTS ARE FAIR!
OH? AND WHY NOT?
THEY'RE TOTALLY BASED ON HOW MANY SCIENTIFIC TERMS AND FORMULAS YOU CAN MEMORIZE!
BUT WHAT IF YOU HAVE TROUBLE MEMORIZING STUFF? WHAT IF YOUR BRAIN'S NOT WIRED THAT WAY?
I SEE. SO YOUR BRAIN SIMPLY DOESN'T RETAIN FACTUAL INFORMATION.
EXACTLY! WHY SHOULD I BE PUNISHED FOR THAT?
YOU MAY BE RIGHT, NATE. I SOMETIMES HAVE TROUBLE WITH FACTS MYSELF.
FOR EXAMPLE, I CAN NEVER REMEMBER HOW MANY POINTS MICHAEL JORDAN SCORED IN GAME 4 OF THE 1993 NBA FINALS.
55!
WAIT, WAS THAT RIGHT? WOW, WHAT A LUCKY GUESS!
SIT DOWN, SON.
Peirce

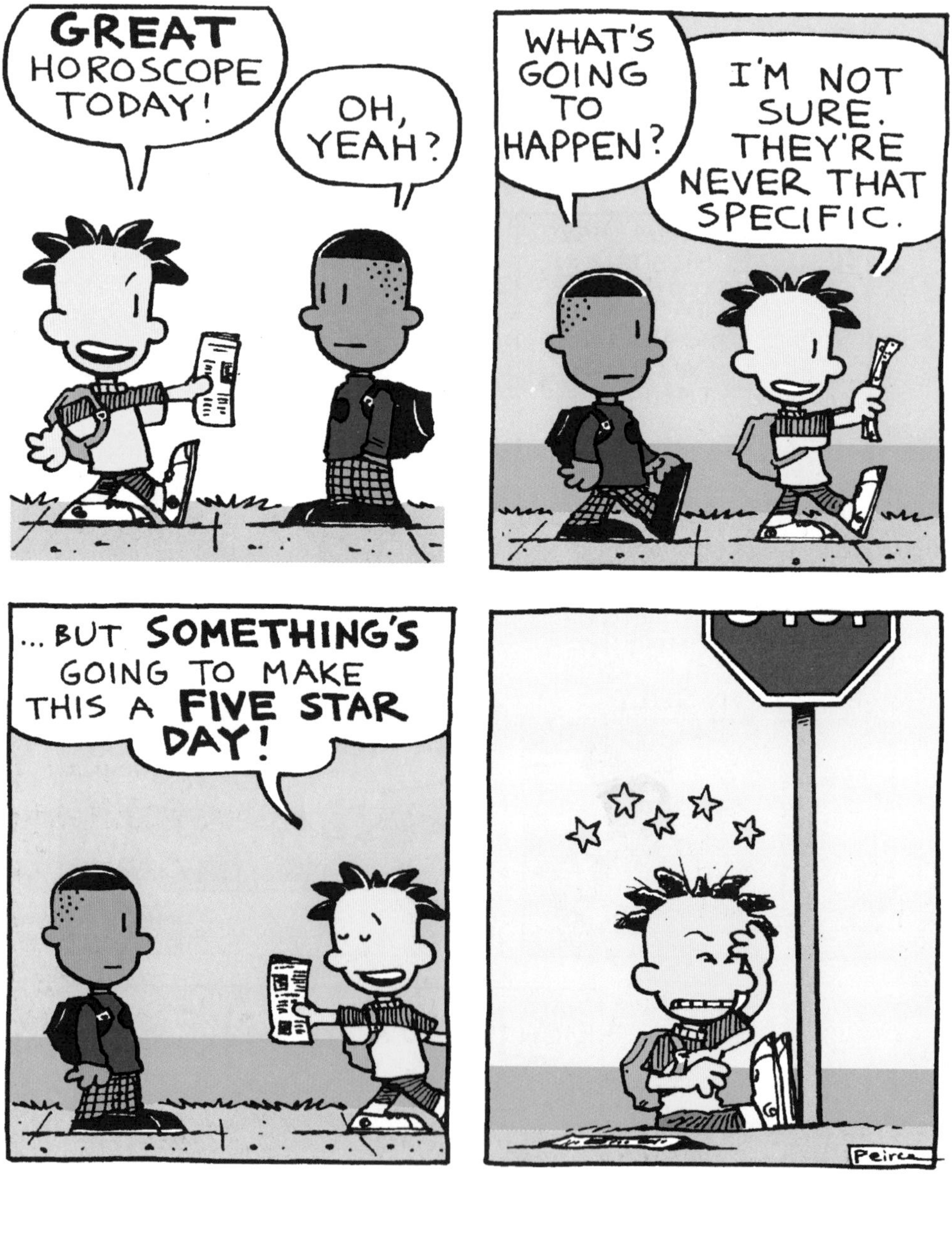
GREAT HOROSCOPE TODAY!
OH, YEAH?
WHAT'S GOING TO HAPPEN?
I'M NOT SURE. THEY'RE NEVER THAT SPECIFIC.
...BUT SOMETHING'S GOING TO MAKE THIS A FIVE STAR DAY!
Peirce

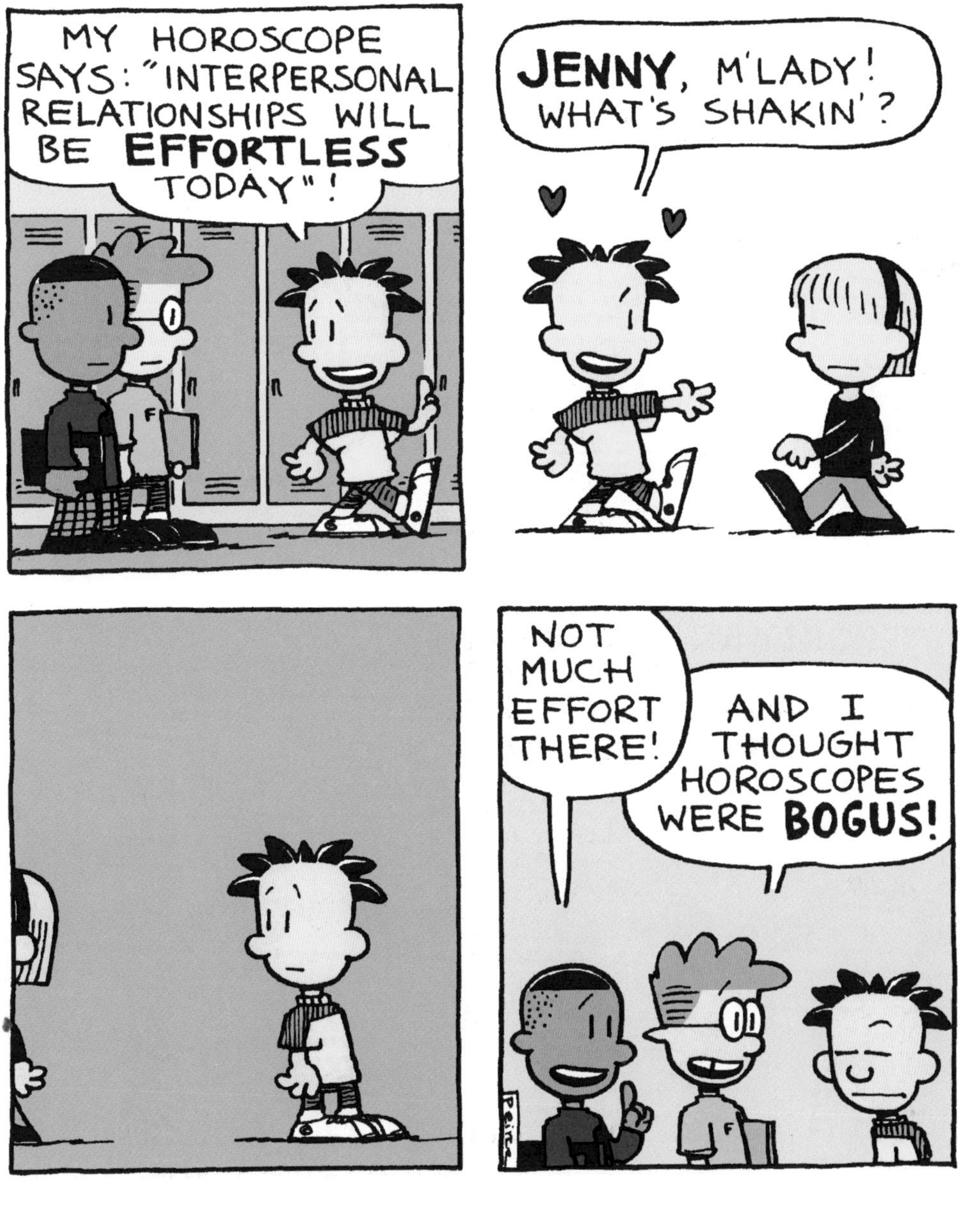
MY HOROSCOPE SAYS: "INTERPERSONAL RELATIONSHIPS WILL BE **EFFORTLESS** TODAY"!
JENNY, M'LADY! WHAT'S SHAKIN'?
NOT MUCH EFFORT THERE!
AND I THOUGHT HOROSCOPES WERE **BOGUS**!
PEIRCE

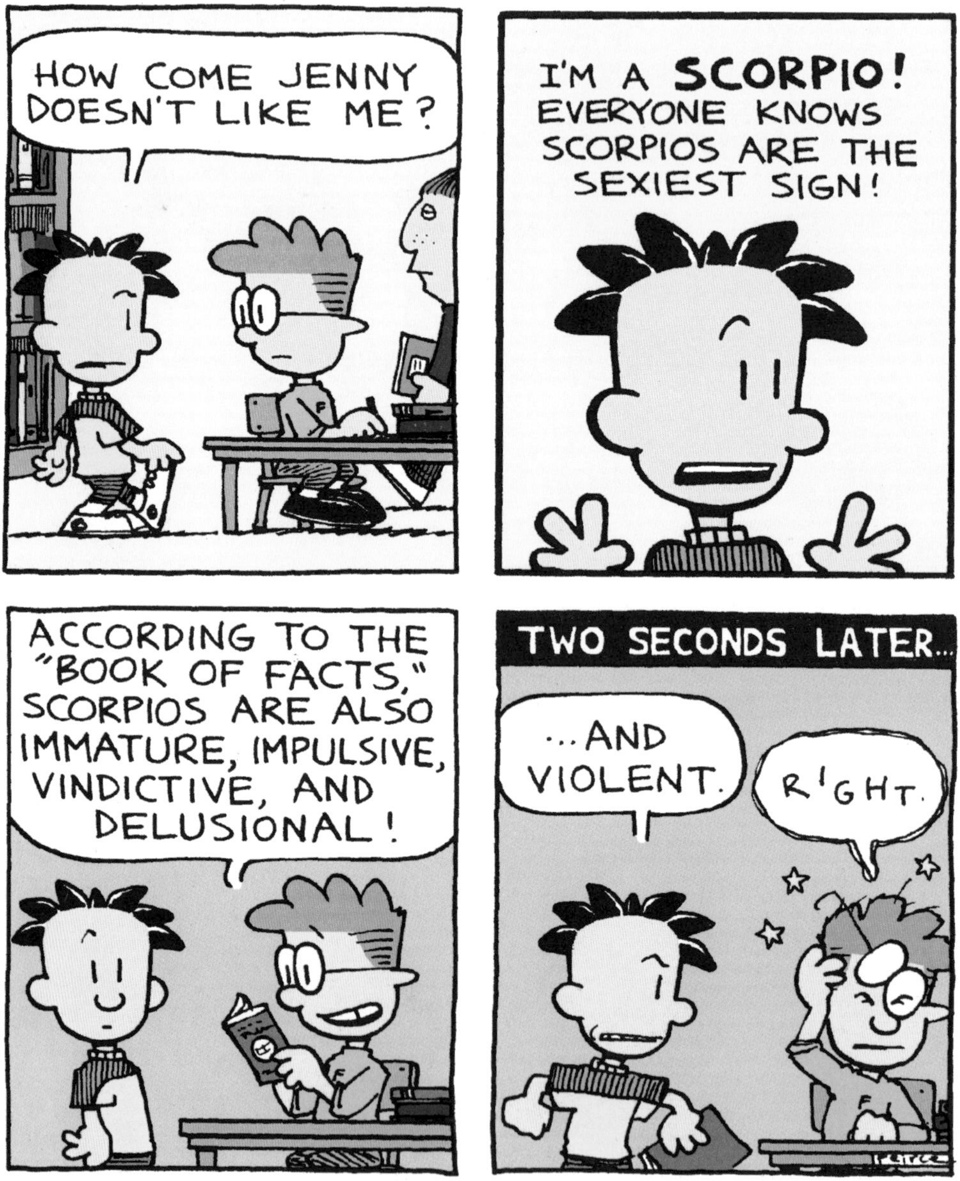
HOW COME JENNY DOESN'T LIKE ME?
I'M A **SCORPIO!** EVERYONE KNOWS SCORPIOS ARE THE SEXIEST SIGN!
ACCORDING TO THE "BOOK OF FACTS," SCORPIOS ARE ALSO IMMATURE, IMPULSIVE, VINDICTIVE, AND DELUSIONAL!
TWO SECONDS LATER...
...AND VIOLENT.
RIGHT.

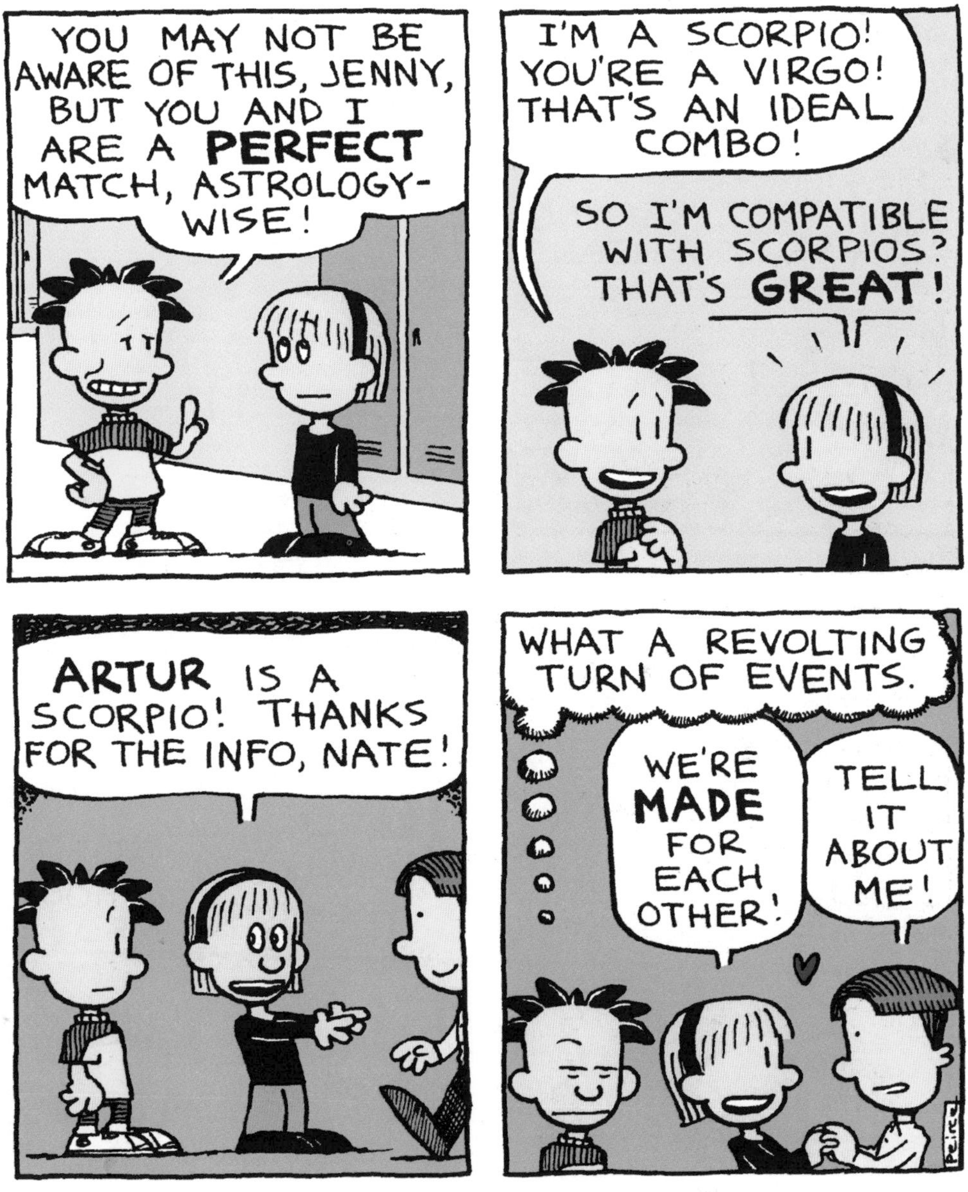
YOU MAY NOT BE AWARE OF THIS, JENNY, BUT YOU AND I ARE A PERFECT MATCH, ASTROLOGY-WISE!
I'M A SCORPIO! YOU'RE A VIRGO! THAT'S AN IDEAL COMBO!
SO I'M COMPATIBLE WITH SCORPIOS? THAT'S GREAT!
ARTUR IS A SCORPIO! THANKS FOR THE INFO, NATE!
WHAT A REVOLTING TURN OF EVENTS.
WE'RE MADE FOR EACH OTHER!
TELL IT ABOUT ME!
PEIRCE

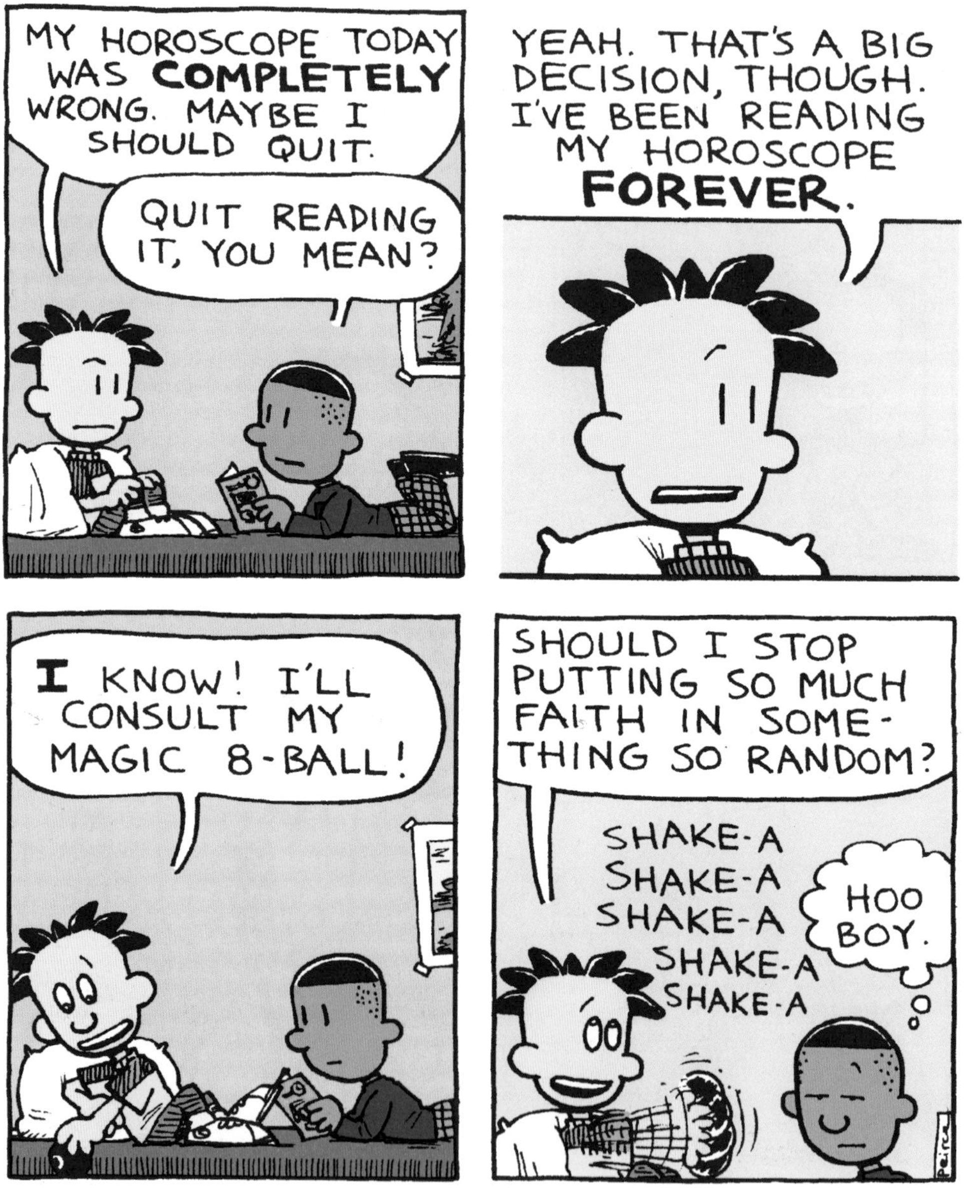
MY HOROSCOPE TODAY WAS COMPLETELY WRONG. MAYBE I SHOULD QUIT.
QUIT READING IT, YOU MEAN?
YEAH. THAT'S A BIG DECISION, THOUGH. I'VE BEEN READING MY HOROSCOPE FOREVER.
I KNOW! I'LL CONSULT MY MAGIC 8-BALL!
SHOULD I STOP PUTTING SO MUCH FAITH IN SOME-THING SO RANDOM?
SHAKE-A SHAKE-A SHAKE-A SHAKE-A SHAKE-A
HOO BOY.
Peirce

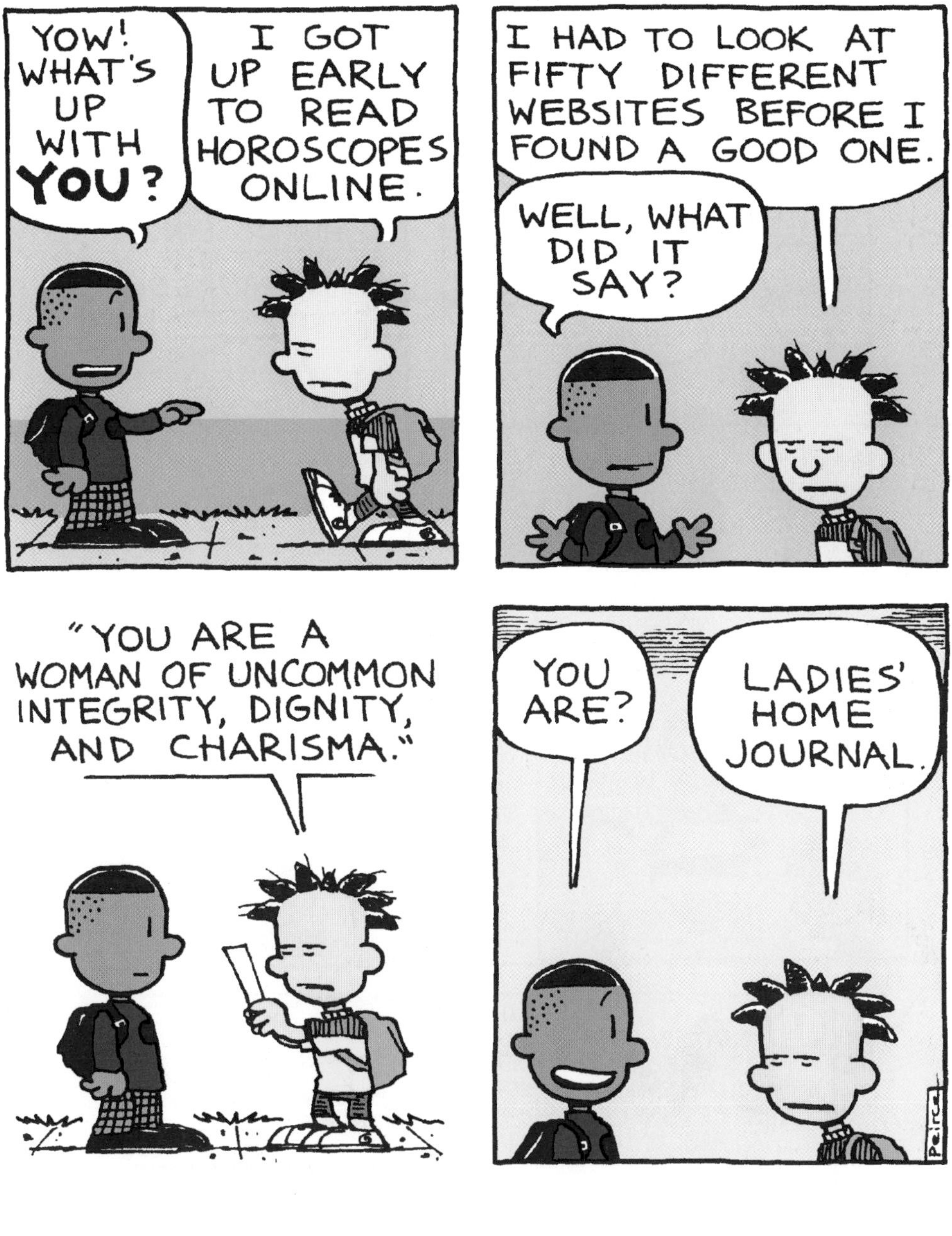
YOW! WHAT'S UP WITH YOU?
I GOT UP EARLY TO READ HOROSCOPES ONLINE.
I HAD TO LOOK AT FIFTY DIFFERENT WEBSITES BEFORE I FOUND A GOOD ONE.
WELL, WHAT DID IT SAY?
"YOU ARE A WOMAN OF UNCOMMON INTEGRITY, DIGNITY, AND CHARISMA."
YOU ARE?
LADIES' HOME JOURNAL.
Peirce

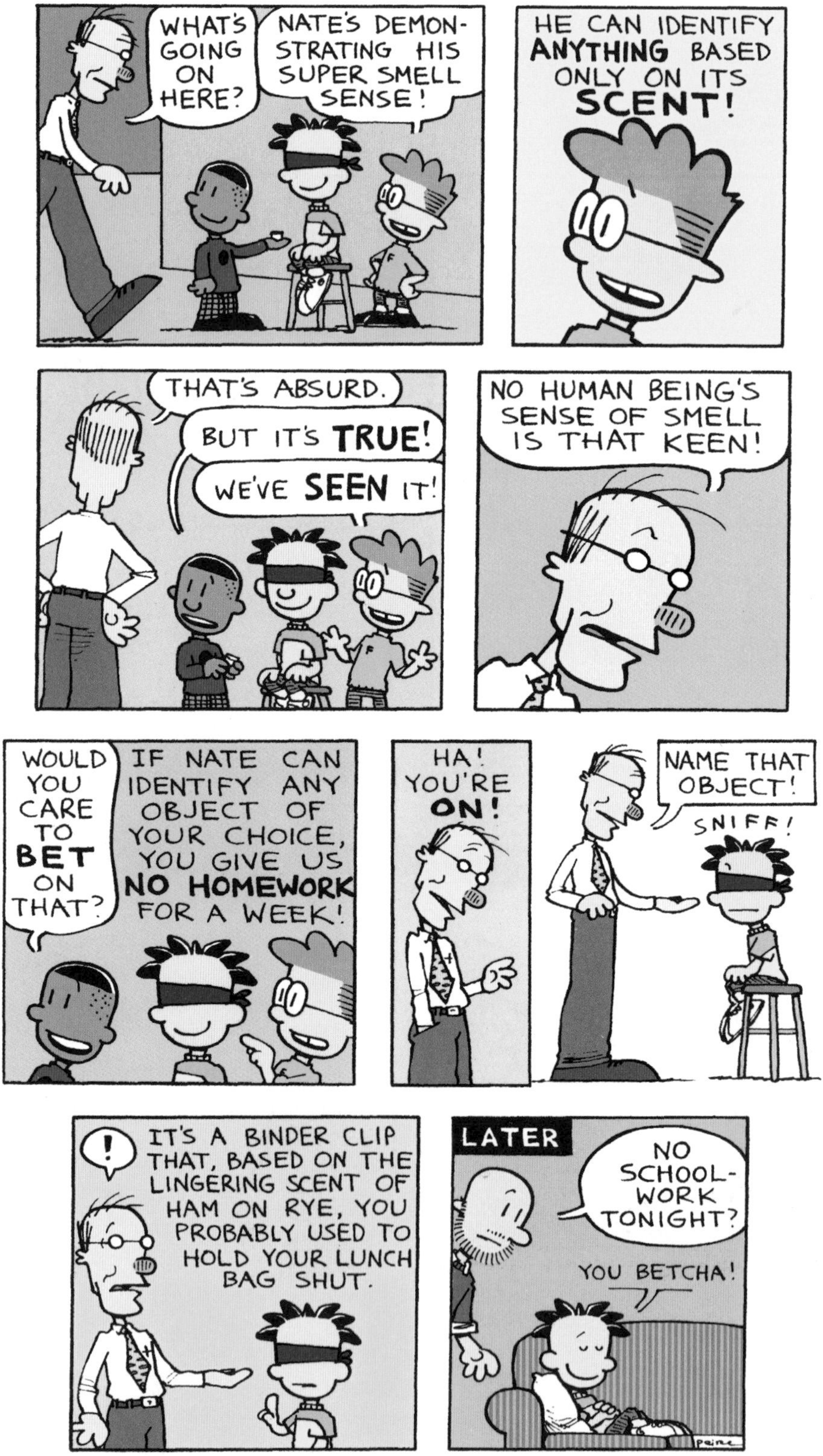
WHAT'S GOING ON HERE?
NATE'S DEMON-STRATING HIS SUPER SMELL SENSE!
HE CAN IDENTIFY ANYTHING BASED ONLY ON ITS SCENT!
THAT'S ABSURD.
BUT IT'S TRUE!
WE'VE SEEN IT!
NO HUMAN BEING'S SENSE OF SMELL IS THAT KEEN!
WOULD YOU CARE TO BET ON THAT?
IF NATE CAN IDENTIFY ANY OBJECT OF YOUR CHOICE, YOU GIVE US NO HOMEWORK FOR A WEEK!
HA! YOU'RE ON!
NAME THAT OBJECT!
SNIFF!
!
IT'S A BINDER CLIP THAT, BASED ON THE LINGERING SCENT OF HAM ON RYE, YOU PROBABLY USED TO HOLD YOUR LUNCH BAG SHUT.
LATER
NO SCHOOL-WORK TONIGHT?
YOU BETCHA!

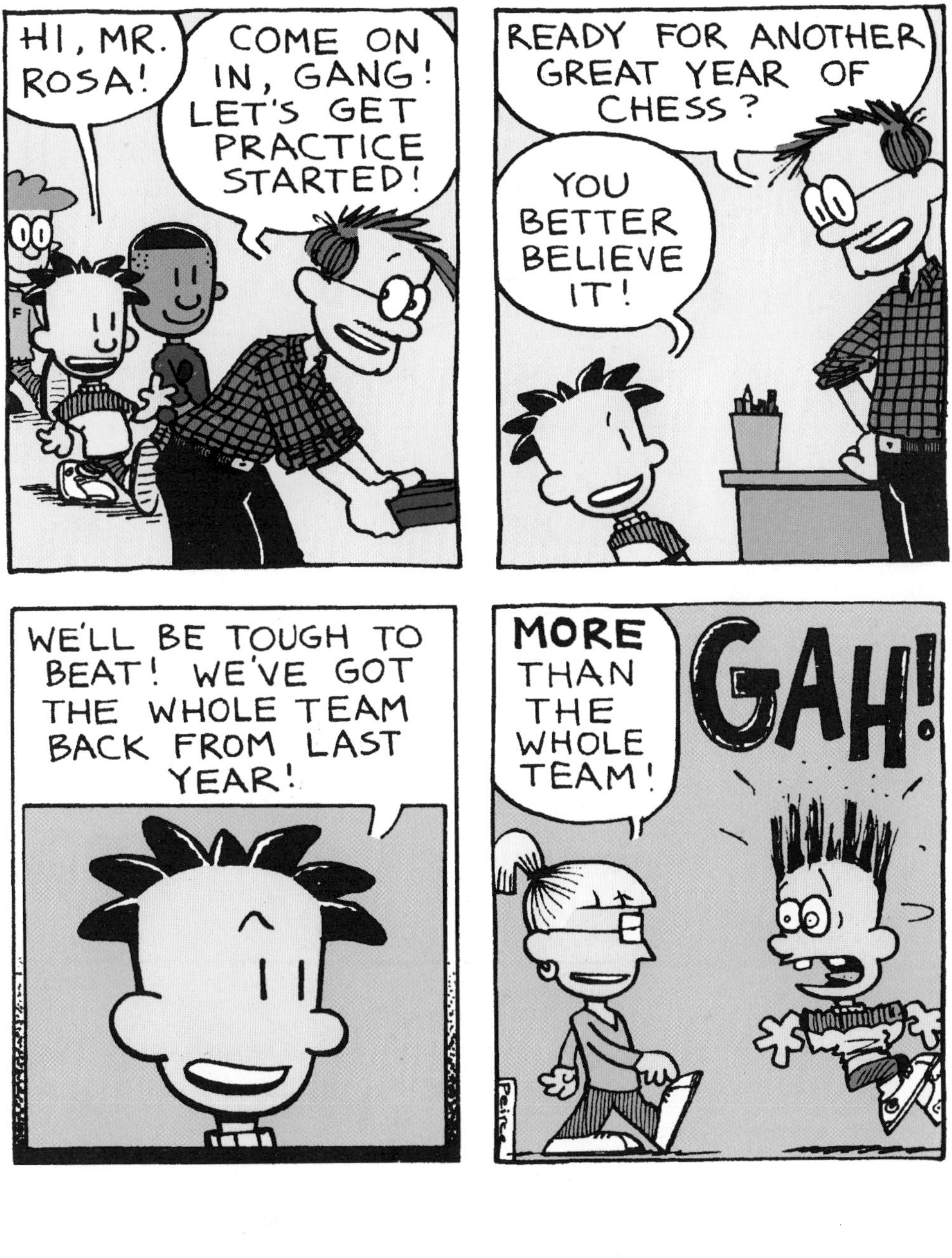
HI, MR. ROSA!
COME ON IN, GANG! LET'S GET PRACTICE STARTED!
READY FOR ANOTHER GREAT YEAR OF CHESS?
YOU BETTER BELIEVE IT!
WE'LL BE TOUGH TO BEAT! WE'VE GOT THE WHOLE TEAM BACK FROM LAST YEAR!
MORE THAN THE WHOLE TEAM!
GAH!
Peirce

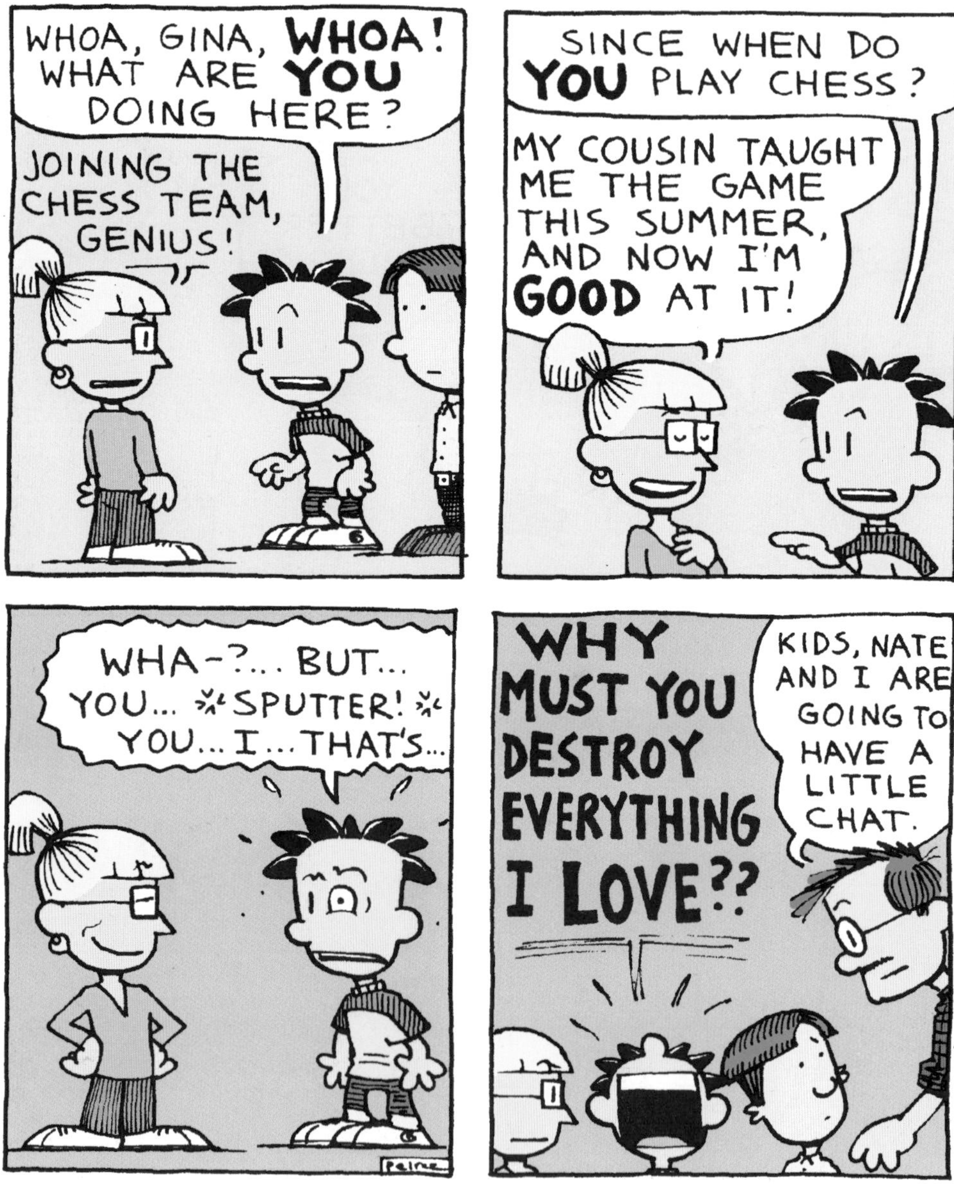
WHOA, GINA, WHOA! WHAT ARE YOU DOING HERE?
JOINING THE CHESS TEAM, GENIUS!
SINCE WHEN DO YOU PLAY CHESS?
MY COUSIN TAUGHT ME THE GAME THIS SUMMER, AND NOW I'M GOOD AT IT!
WHA-?... BUT... YOU... SPUTTER! YOU... I... THAT'S...
WHY MUST YOU DESTROY EVERYTHING I LOVE??
KIDS, NATE AND I ARE GOING TO HAVE A LITTLE CHAT.
Peirce

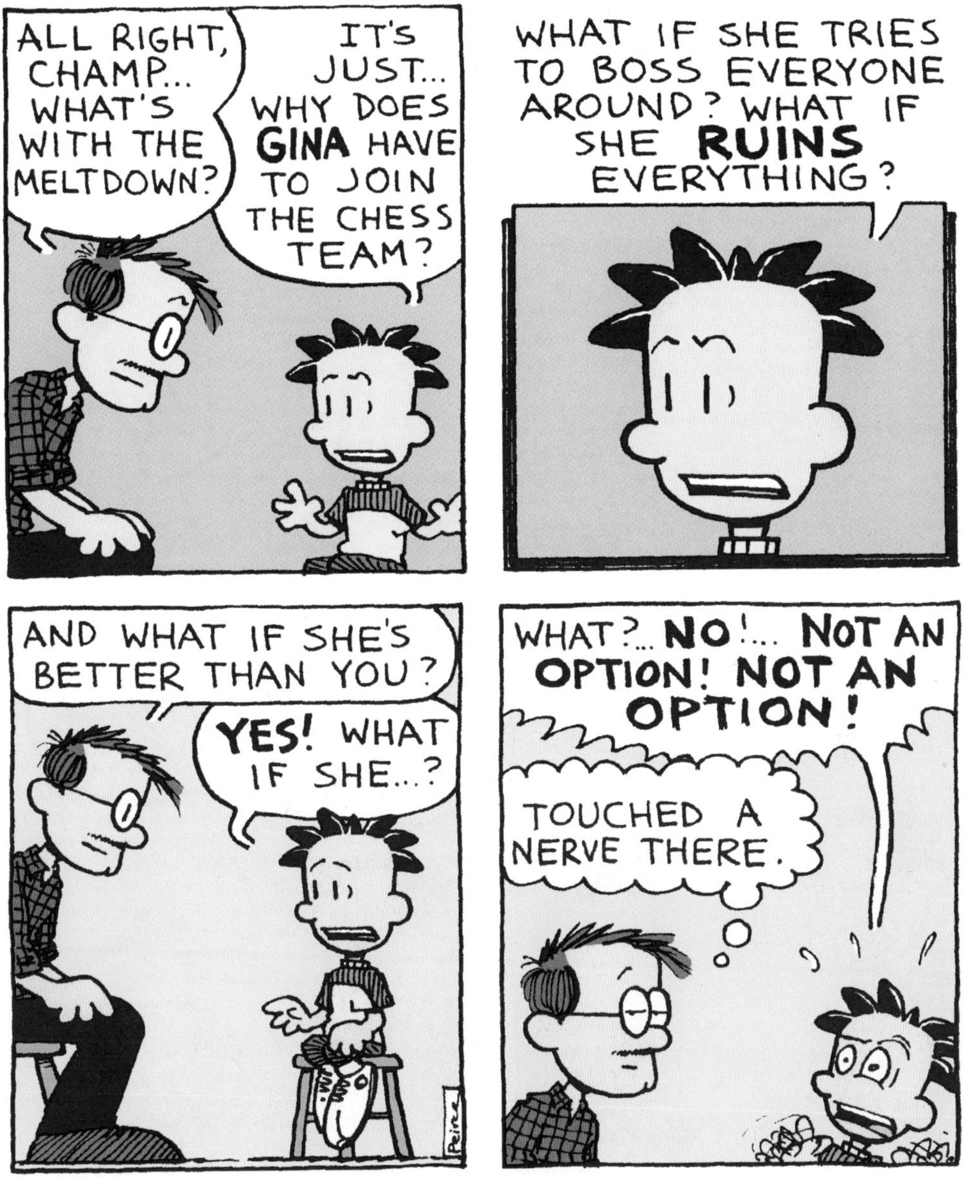
ALL RIGHT, CHAMP... WHAT'S WITH THE MELTDOWN?
IT'S JUST... WHY DOES **GINA** HAVE TO JOIN THE CHESS TEAM?
WHAT IF SHE TRIES TO BOSS EVERYONE AROUND? WHAT IF SHE **RUINS** EVERYTHING?
AND WHAT IF SHE'S BETTER THAN YOU?
YES! WHAT IF SHE...?
WHAT?... **NO!... NOT AN OPTION! NOT AN OPTION!**
TOUCHED A NERVE THERE.

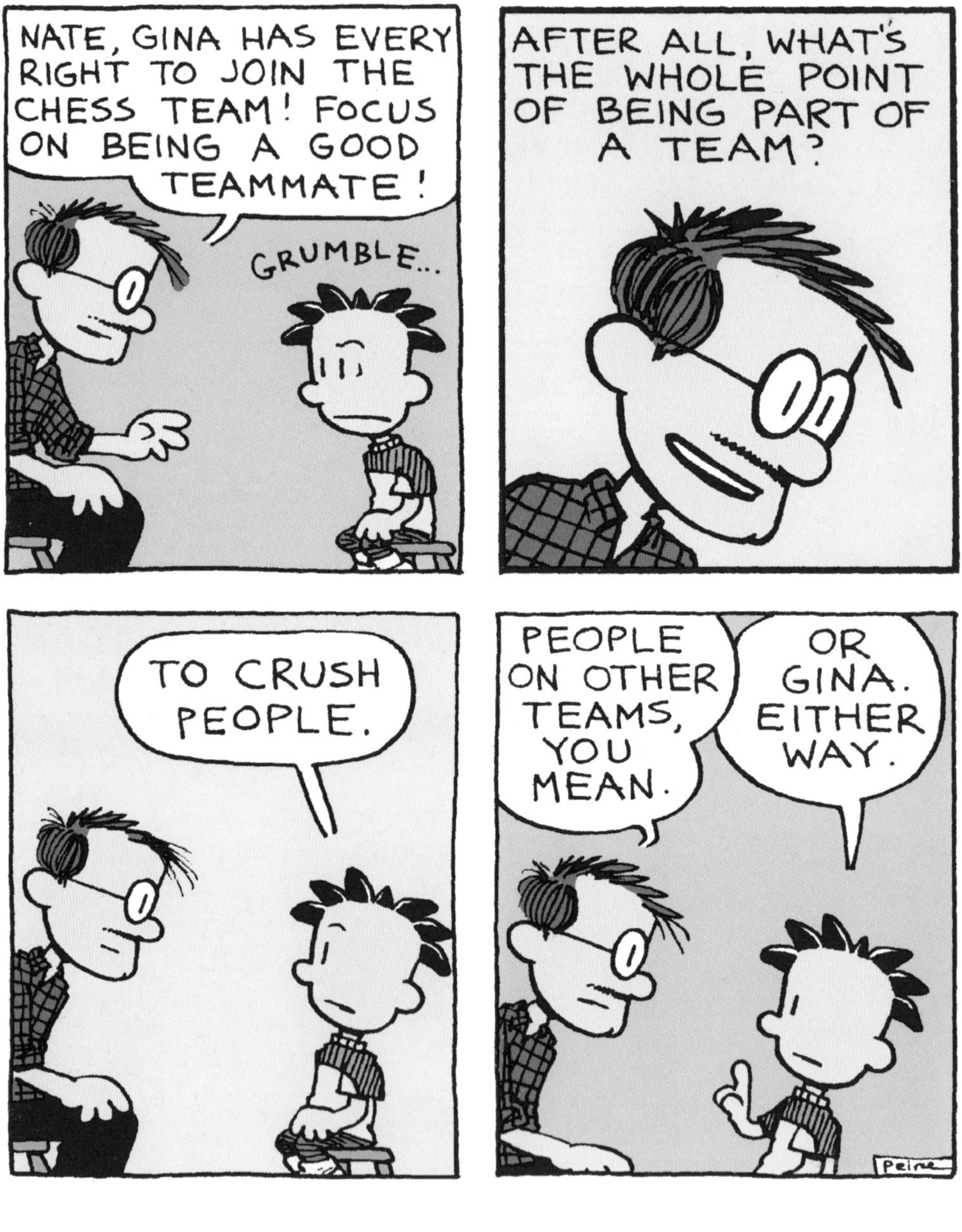
NATE, GINA HAS EVERY RIGHT TO JOIN THE CHESS TEAM! FOCUS ON BEING A GOOD TEAMMATE!
GRUMBLE...
AFTER ALL, WHAT'S THE WHOLE POINT OF BEING PART OF A TEAM?
TO CRUSH PEOPLE.
PEOPLE ON OTHER TEAMS, YOU MEAN.
OR GINA. EITHER WAY.
Peirce

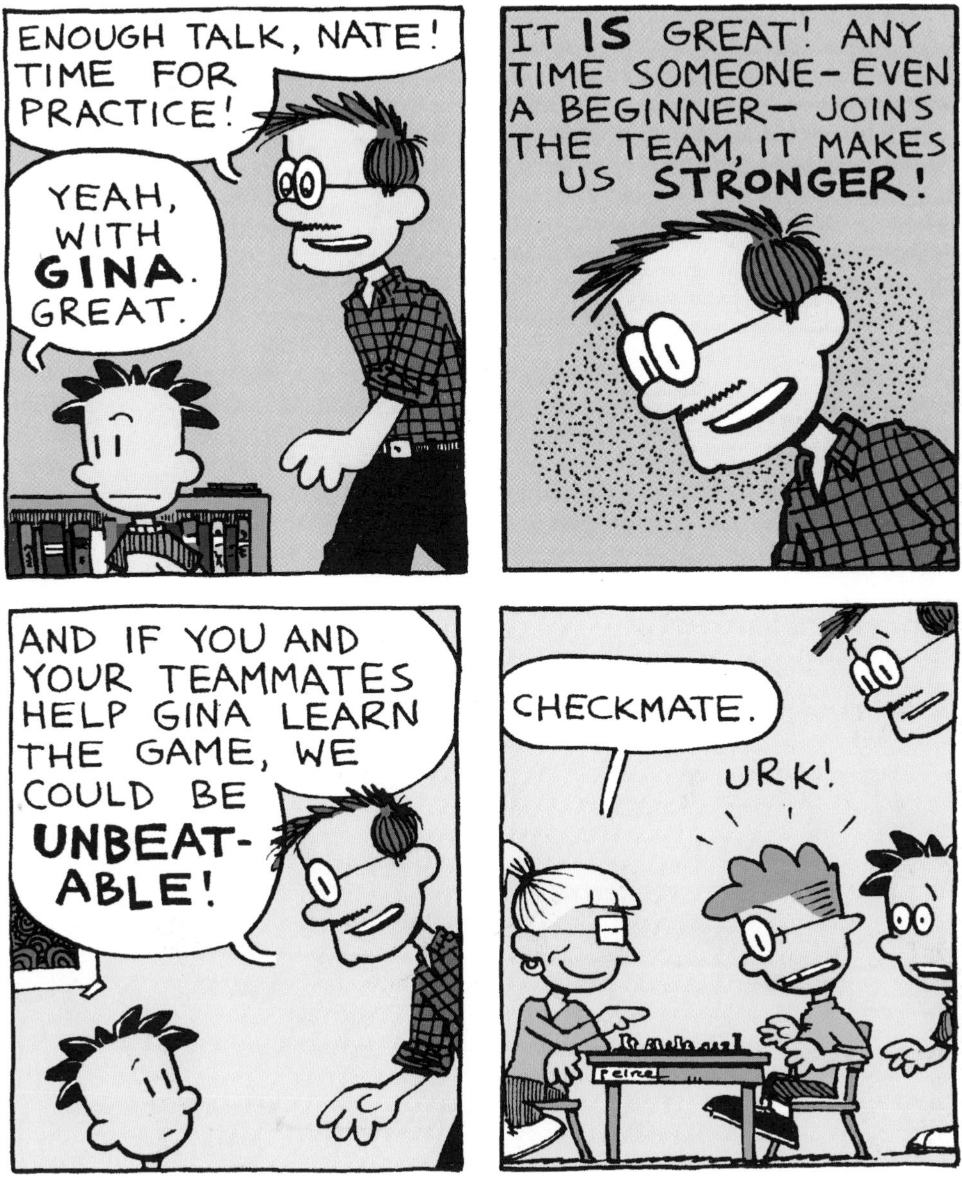
ENOUGH TALK, NATE! TIME FOR PRACTICE!
YEAH, WITH **GINA**. GREAT.
IT **IS** GREAT! ANY TIME SOMEONE–EVEN A BEGINNER–JOINS THE TEAM, IT MAKES US **STRONGER**!
AND IF YOU AND YOUR TEAMMATES HELP GINA LEARN THE GAME, WE COULD BE **UNBEATABLE**!
CHECKMATE.
URK!

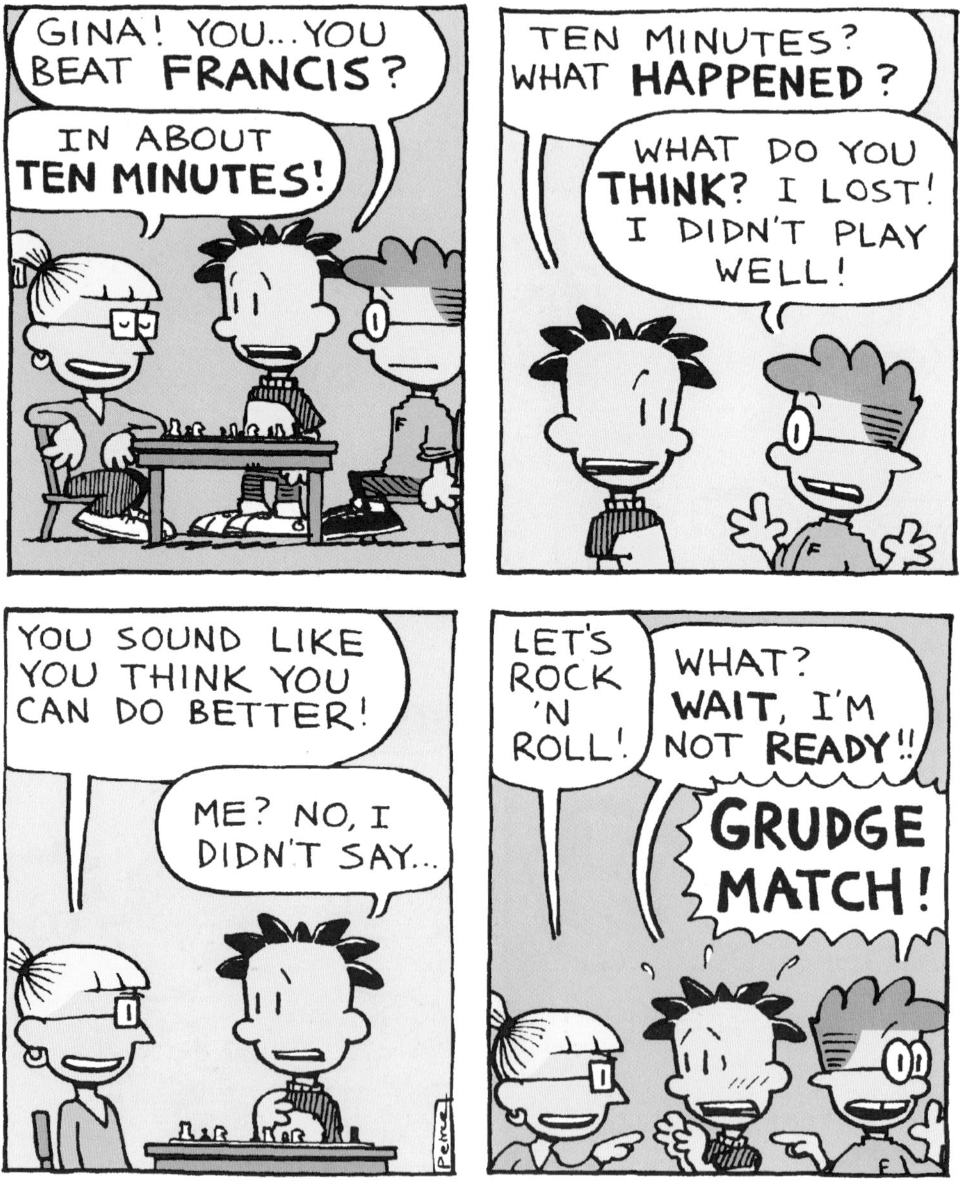
GINA! YOU... YOU BEAT FRANCIS?
IN ABOUT TEN MINUTES!
TEN MINUTES? WHAT HAPPENED?
WHAT DO YOU THINK? I LOST! I DIDN'T PLAY WELL!
YOU SOUND LIKE YOU THINK YOU CAN DO BETTER!
ME? NO, I DIDN'T SAY...
LET'S ROCK 'N ROLL!
WHAT? WAIT, I'M NOT READY!!
GRUDGE MATCH!
Peirce

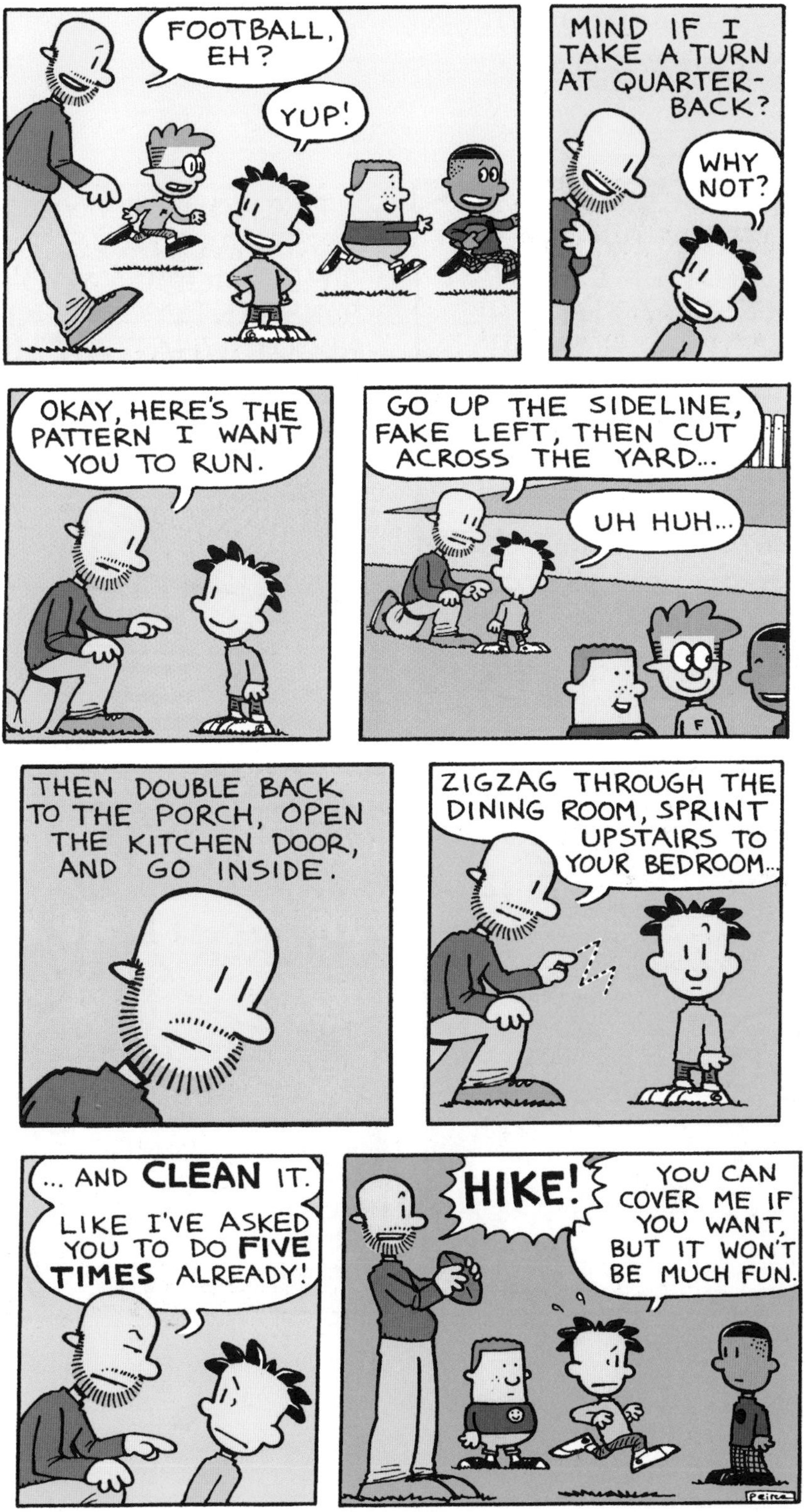
FOOTBALL, EH?
YUP!
MIND IF I TAKE A TURN AT QUARTER-BACK?
WHY NOT?
OKAY, HERE'S THE PATTERN I WANT YOU TO RUN.
GO UP THE SIDELINE, FAKE LEFT, THEN CUT ACROSS THE YARD...
UH HUH...
THEN DOUBLE BACK TO THE PORCH, OPEN THE KITCHEN DOOR, AND GO INSIDE.
ZIGZAG THROUGH THE DINING ROOM, SPRINT UPSTAIRS TO YOUR BEDROOM...
... AND **CLEAN** IT.
LIKE I'VE ASKED YOU TO DO **FIVE TIMES** ALREADY!
HIKE!
YOU CAN COVER ME IF YOU WANT, BUT IT WON'T BE MUCH FUN.
Peirce

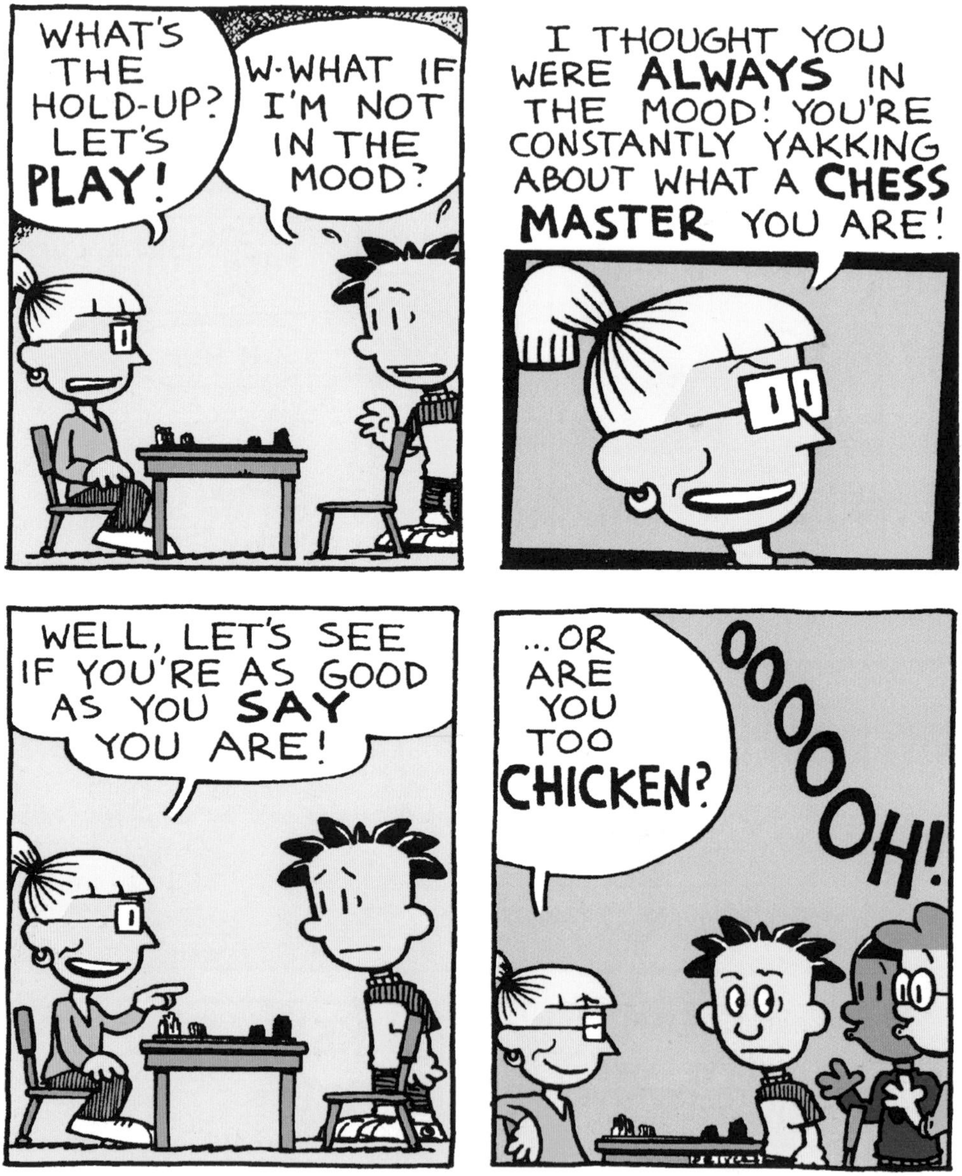
WHAT'S THE HOLD-UP? LET'S PLAY!
W-WHAT IF I'M NOT IN THE MOOD?
I THOUGHT YOU WERE ALWAYS IN THE MOOD! YOU'RE CONSTANTLY YAKKING ABOUT WHAT A CHESS MASTER YOU ARE!
WELL, LET'S SEE IF YOU'RE AS GOOD AS YOU SAY YOU ARE!
...OR ARE YOU TOO CHICKEN?
OOOOOOH!

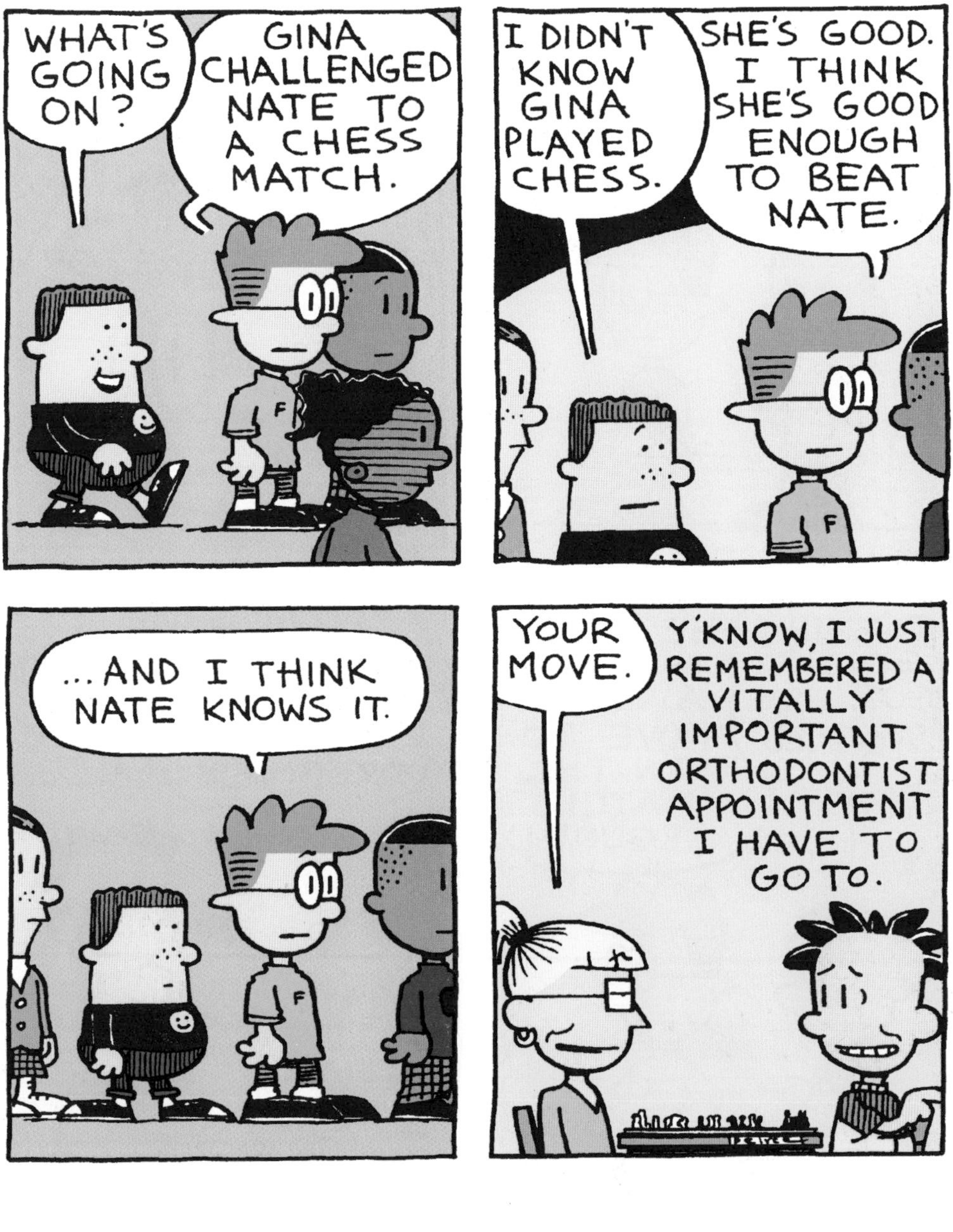
WHAT'S GOING ON?
GINA CHALLENGED NATE TO A CHESS MATCH.
I DIDN'T KNOW GINA PLAYED CHESS.
SHE'S GOOD. I THINK SHE'S GOOD ENOUGH TO BEAT NATE.
...AND I THINK NATE KNOWS IT.
YOUR MOVE.
Y'KNOW, I JUST REMEMBERED A VITALLY IMPORTANT ORTHODONTIST APPOINTMENT I HAVE TO GO TO.

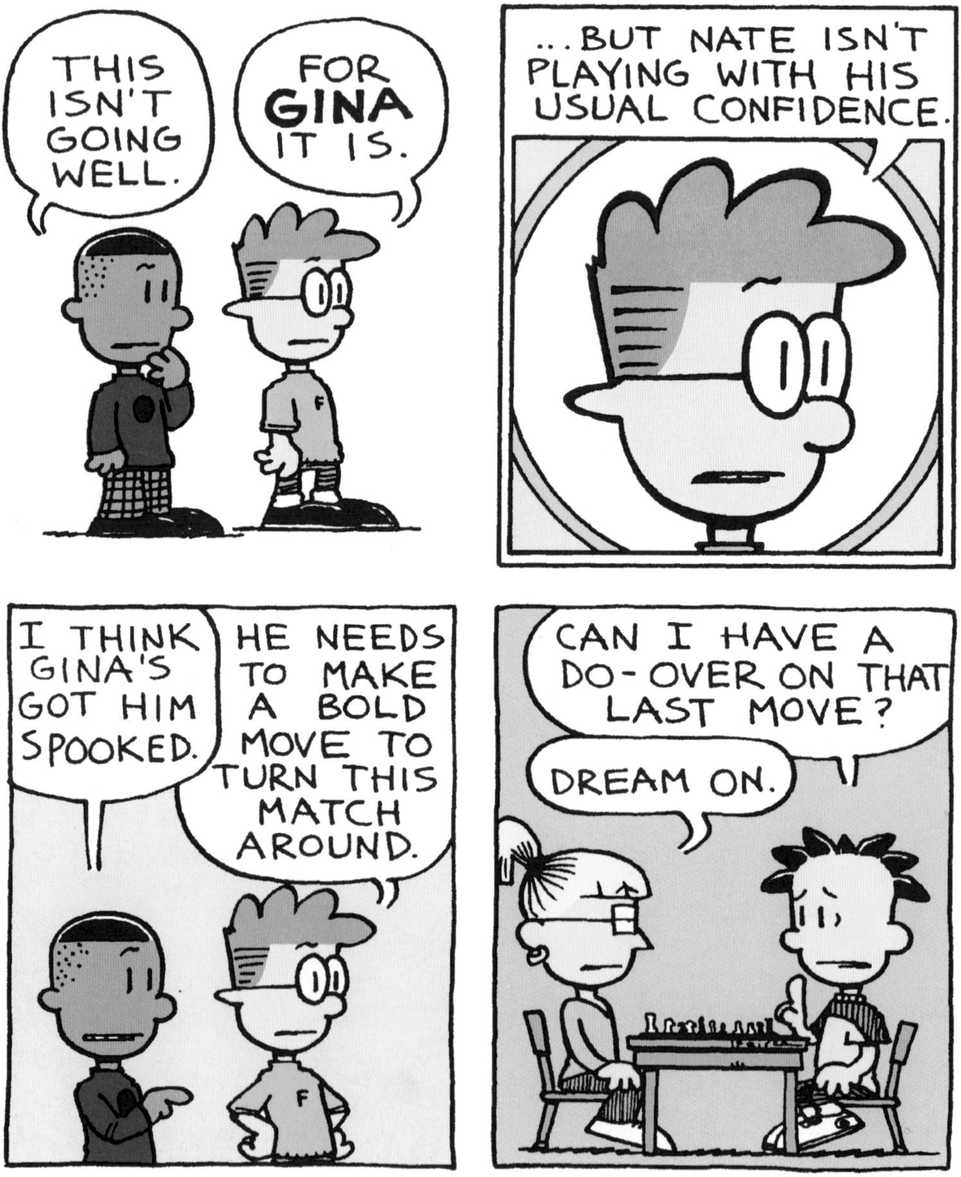
THIS ISN'T GOING WELL.
FOR GINA IT IS.
...BUT NATE ISN'T PLAYING WITH HIS USUAL CONFIDENCE.
I THINK GINA'S GOT HIM SPOOKED.
HE NEEDS TO MAKE A BOLD MOVE TO TURN THIS MATCH AROUND.
CAN I HAVE A DO-OVER ON THAT LAST MOVE?
DREAM ON.

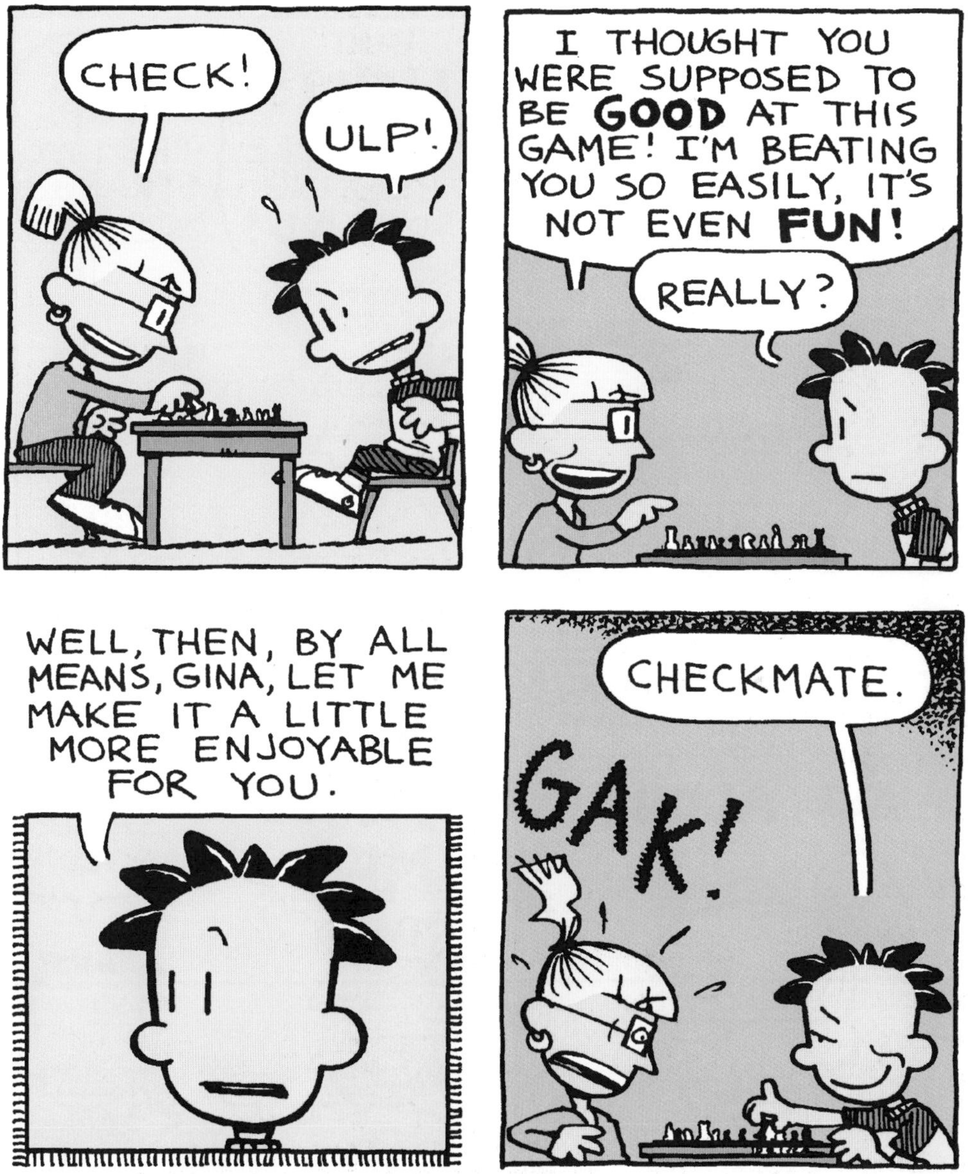
CHECK!
ULP!
I THOUGHT YOU WERE SUPPOSED TO BE **GOOD** AT THIS GAME! I'M BEATING YOU SO EASILY, IT'S NOT EVEN **FUN**!
REALLY?
WELL, THEN, BY ALL MEANS, GINA, LET ME MAKE IT A LITTLE MORE ENJOYABLE FOR YOU.
CHECKMATE.
GAK!

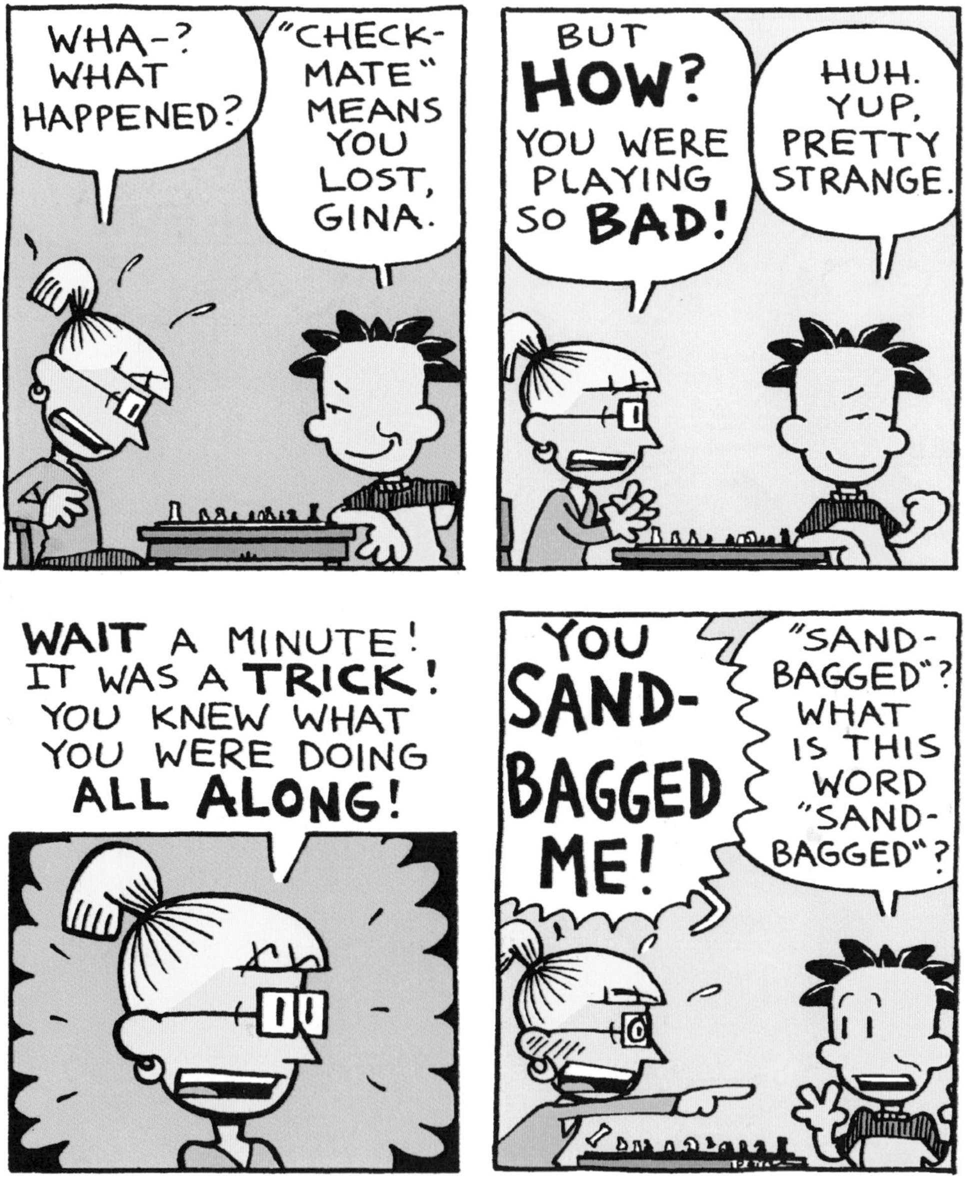
WHA-? WHAT HAPPENED?
"CHECK-MATE" MEANS YOU LOST, GINA.
BUT HOW? YOU WERE PLAYING SO BAD!
HUH. YUP, PRETTY STRANGE.
WAIT A MINUTE! IT WAS A TRICK! YOU KNEW WHAT YOU WERE DOING ALL ALONG!
YOU SAND-BAGGED ME!
"SAND-BAGGED"? WHAT IS THIS WORD "SAND-BAGGED"?

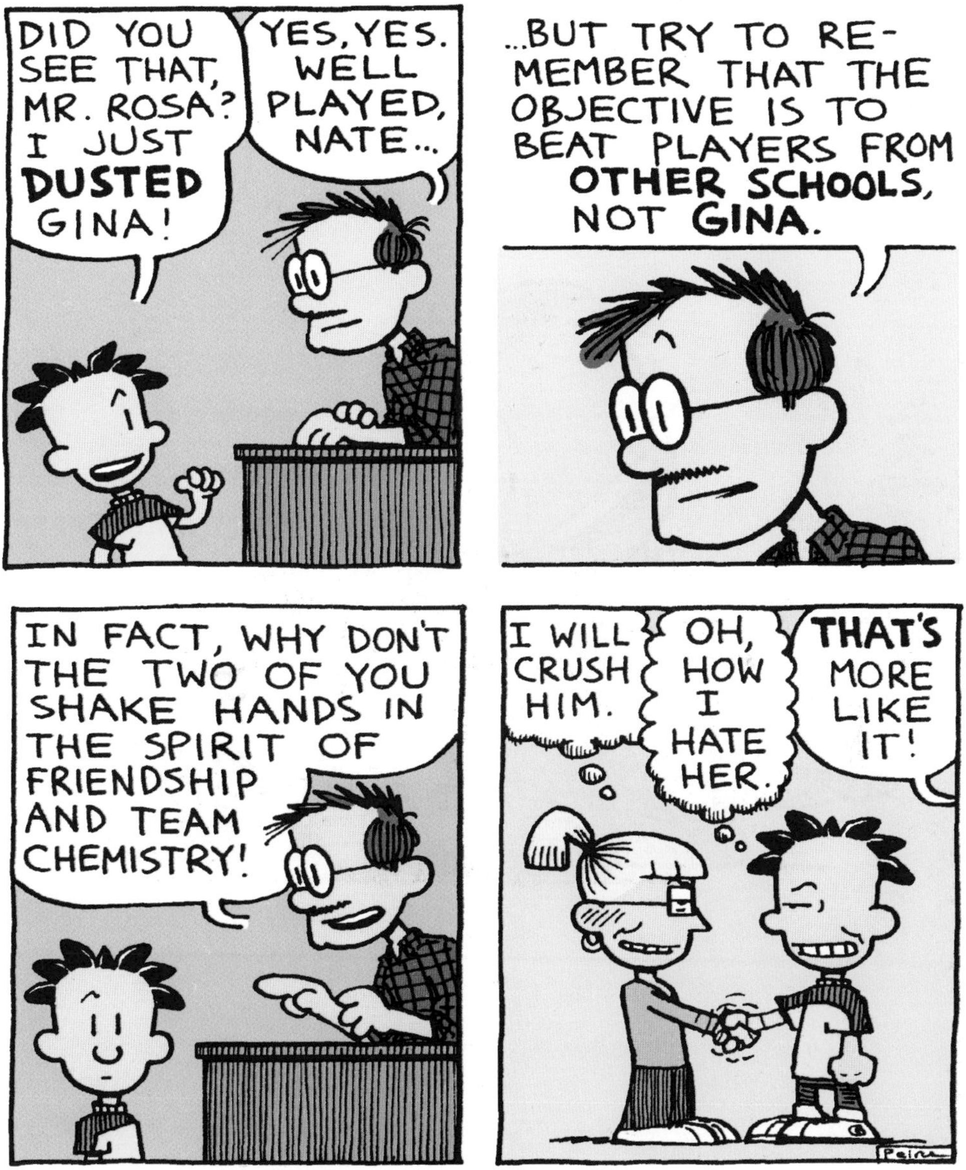
DID YOU SEE THAT, MR. ROSA? I JUST **DUSTED** GINA!
YES, YES. WELL PLAYED, NATE...
...BUT TRY TO RE-MEMBER THAT THE OBJECTIVE IS TO BEAT PLAYERS FROM **OTHER SCHOOLS**, NOT **GINA**.
IN FACT, WHY DON'T THE TWO OF YOU SHAKE HANDS IN THE SPIRIT OF FRIENDSHIP AND TEAM CHEMISTRY!
I WILL CRUSH HIM.
OH, HOW I HATE HER.
THAT'S MORE LIKE IT!

big

NATE

WHAT'S A LITTLE NOOGIE BETWEEN FRIENDS?

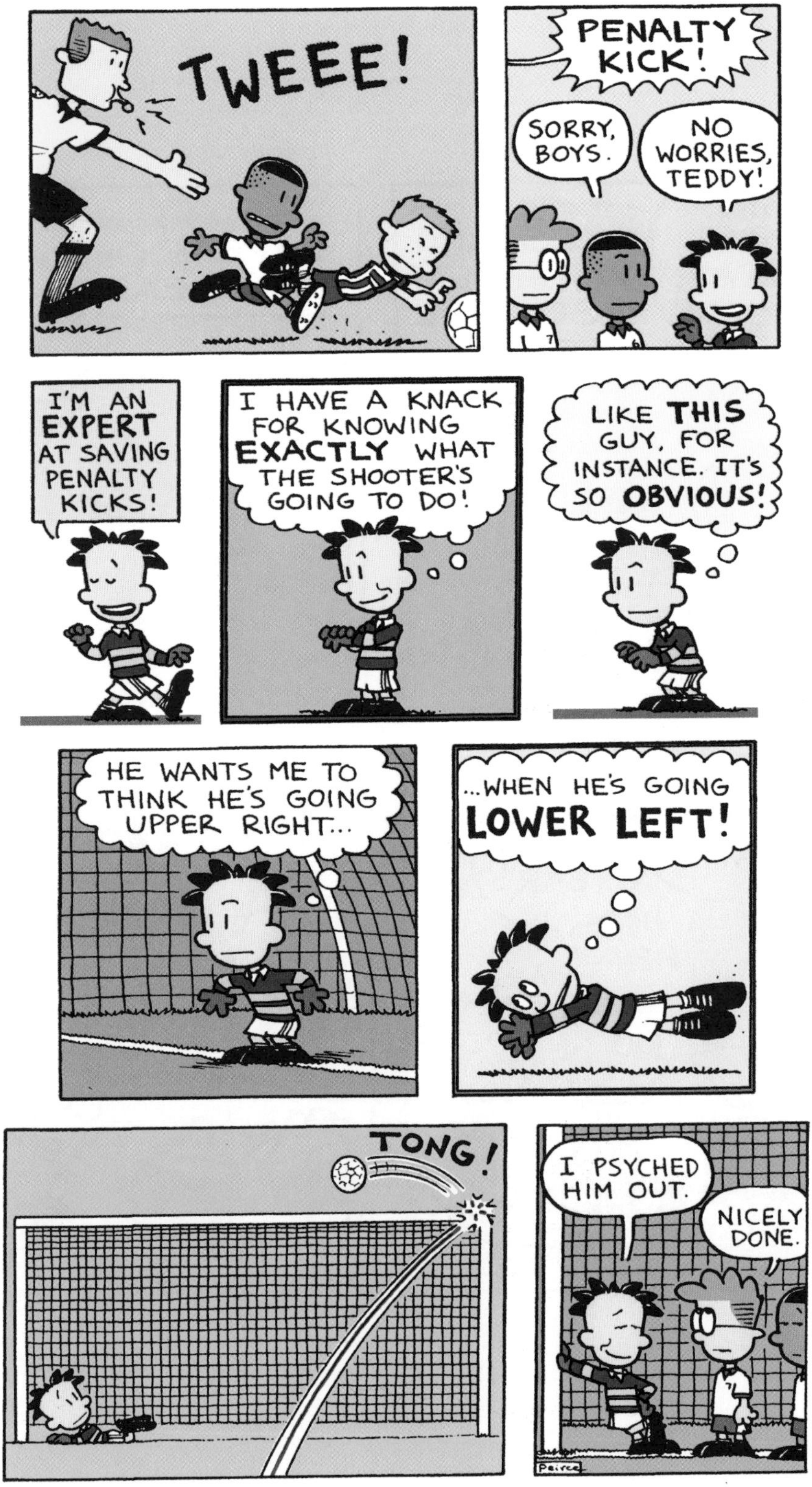
TWEEE!
PENALTY KICK!
SORRY, BOYS.
NO WORRIES, TEDDY!
I'M AN EXPERT AT SAVING PENALTY KICKS!
I HAVE A KNACK FOR KNOWING EXACTLY WHAT THE SHOOTER'S GOING TO DO!
LIKE THIS GUY, FOR INSTANCE. IT'S SO OBVIOUS!
HE WANTS ME TO THINK HE'S GOING UPPER RIGHT...
...WHEN HE'S GOING LOWER LEFT!
TONG!
I PSYCHED HIM OUT.
NICELY DONE.
Peirce

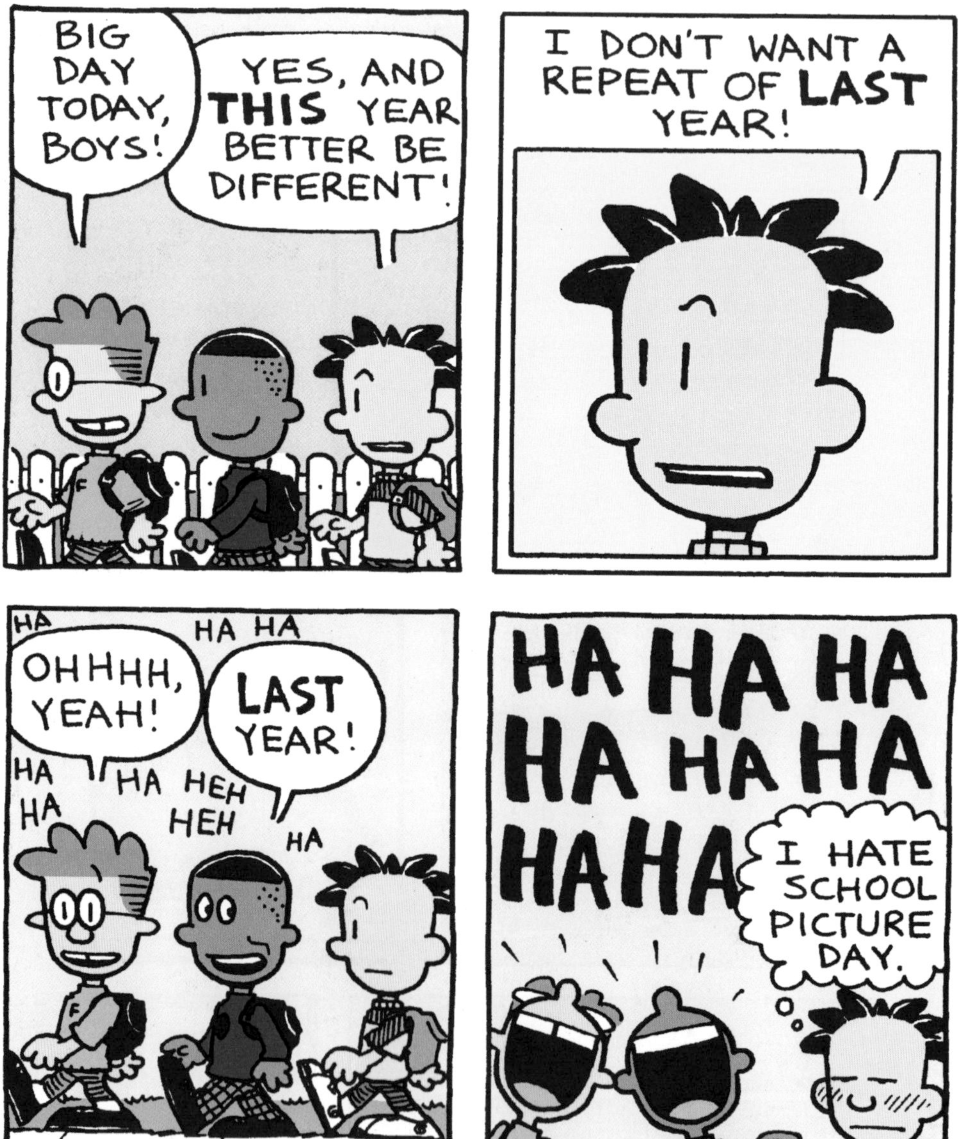
BIG DAY TODAY, BOYS!
YES, AND THIS YEAR BETTER BE DIFFERENT!
I DON'T WANT A REPEAT OF LAST YEAR!
HA
HA HA
OHHHH, YEAH!
LAST YEAR!
HA
HA
HA HEH
HEH
HA
HA HA HA
HA HA HA
HAHA
I HATE SCHOOL PICTURE DAY.
Peirce

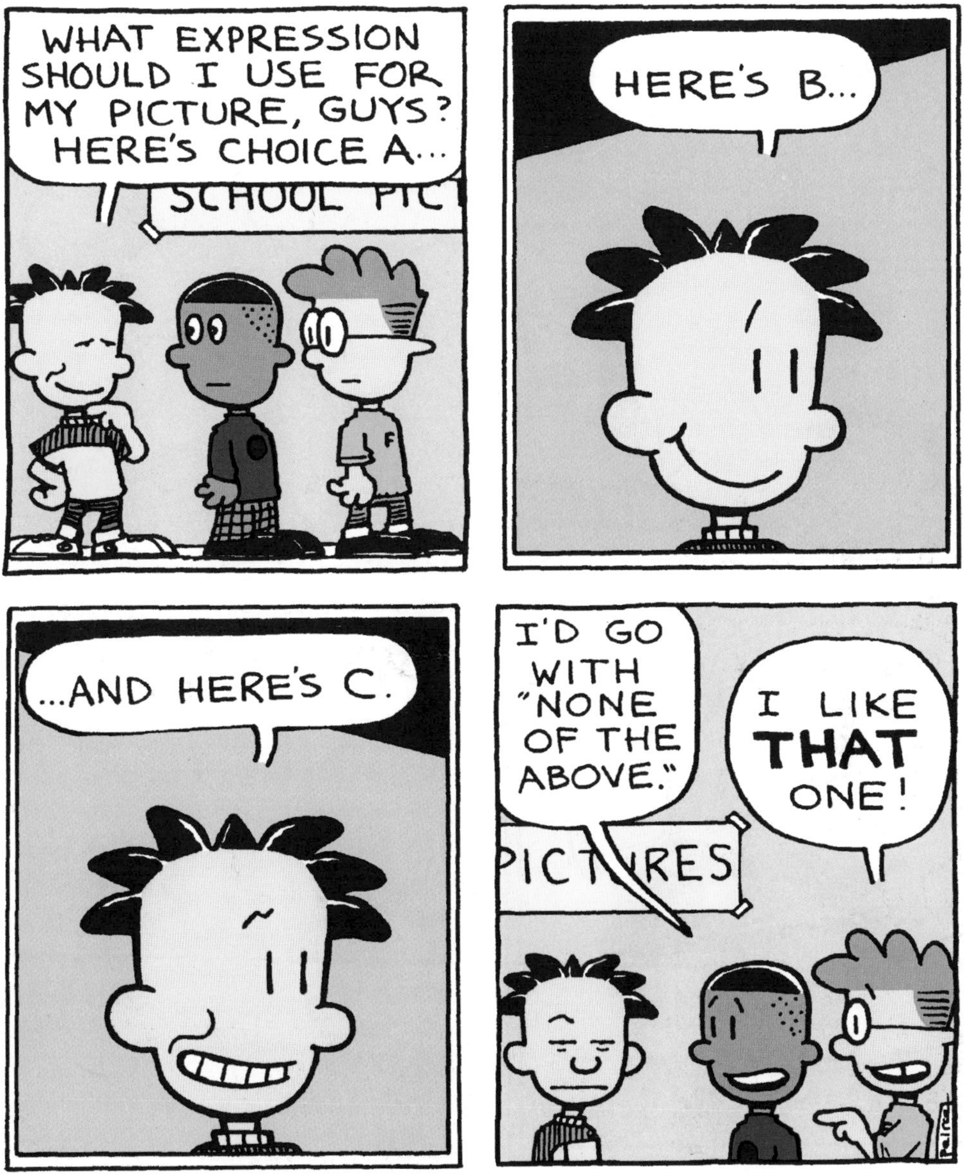
WHAT EXPRESSION SHOULD I USE FOR MY PICTURE, GUYS? HERE'S CHOICE A...
SCHOOL PIC
HERE'S B...
...AND HERE'S C.
I'D GO WITH "NONE OF THE ABOVE."
I LIKE **THAT** ONE!
PICTURES
Peirce

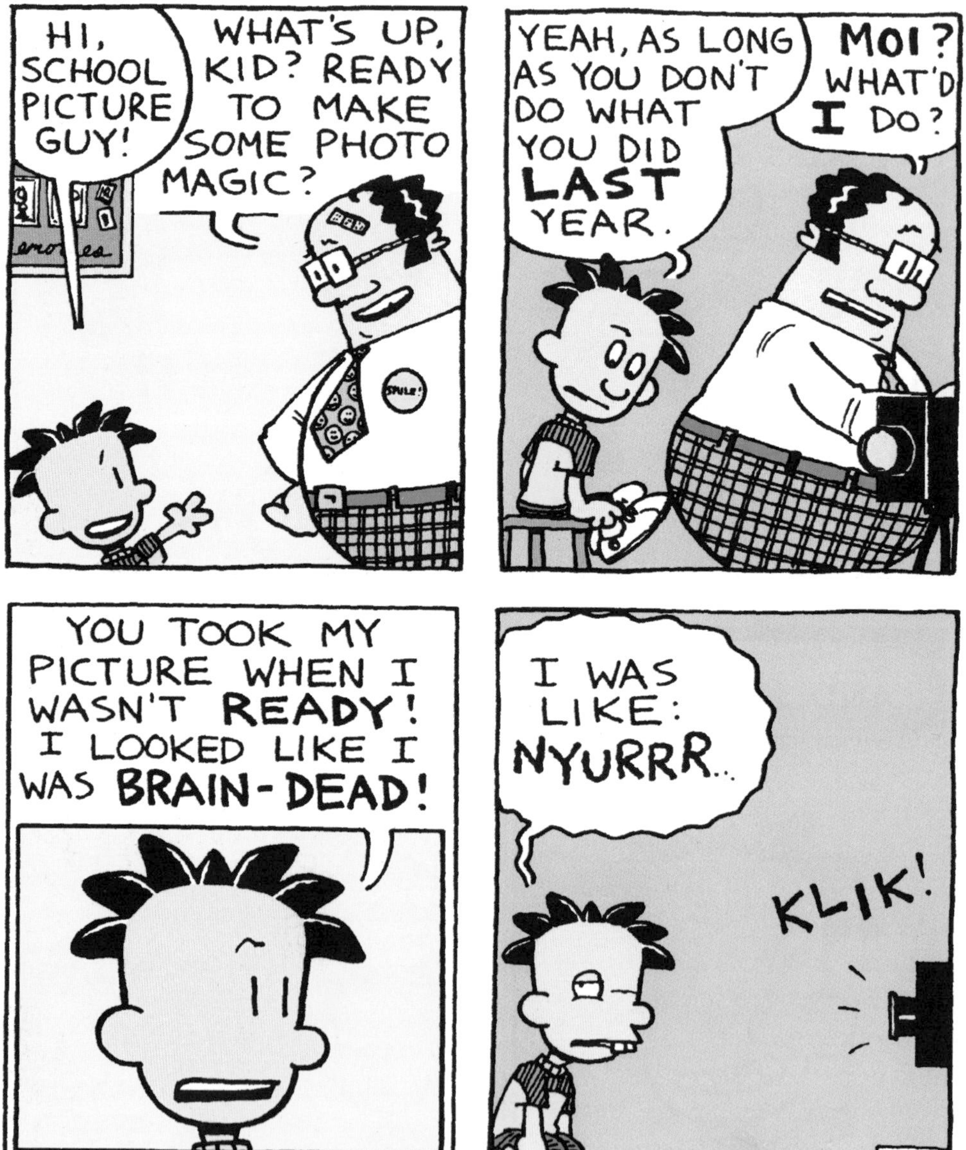
HI, SCHOOL PICTURE GUY!
WHAT'S UP, KID? READY TO MAKE SOME PHOTO MAGIC?
SMILE!
YEAH, AS LONG AS YOU DON'T DO WHAT YOU DID LAST YEAR.
MOI? WHAT'D I DO?
YOU TOOK MY PICTURE WHEN I WASN'T READY! I LOOKED LIKE I WAS BRAIN-DEAD!
I WAS LIKE: NYURRR...
KLIK!
PEIRCE

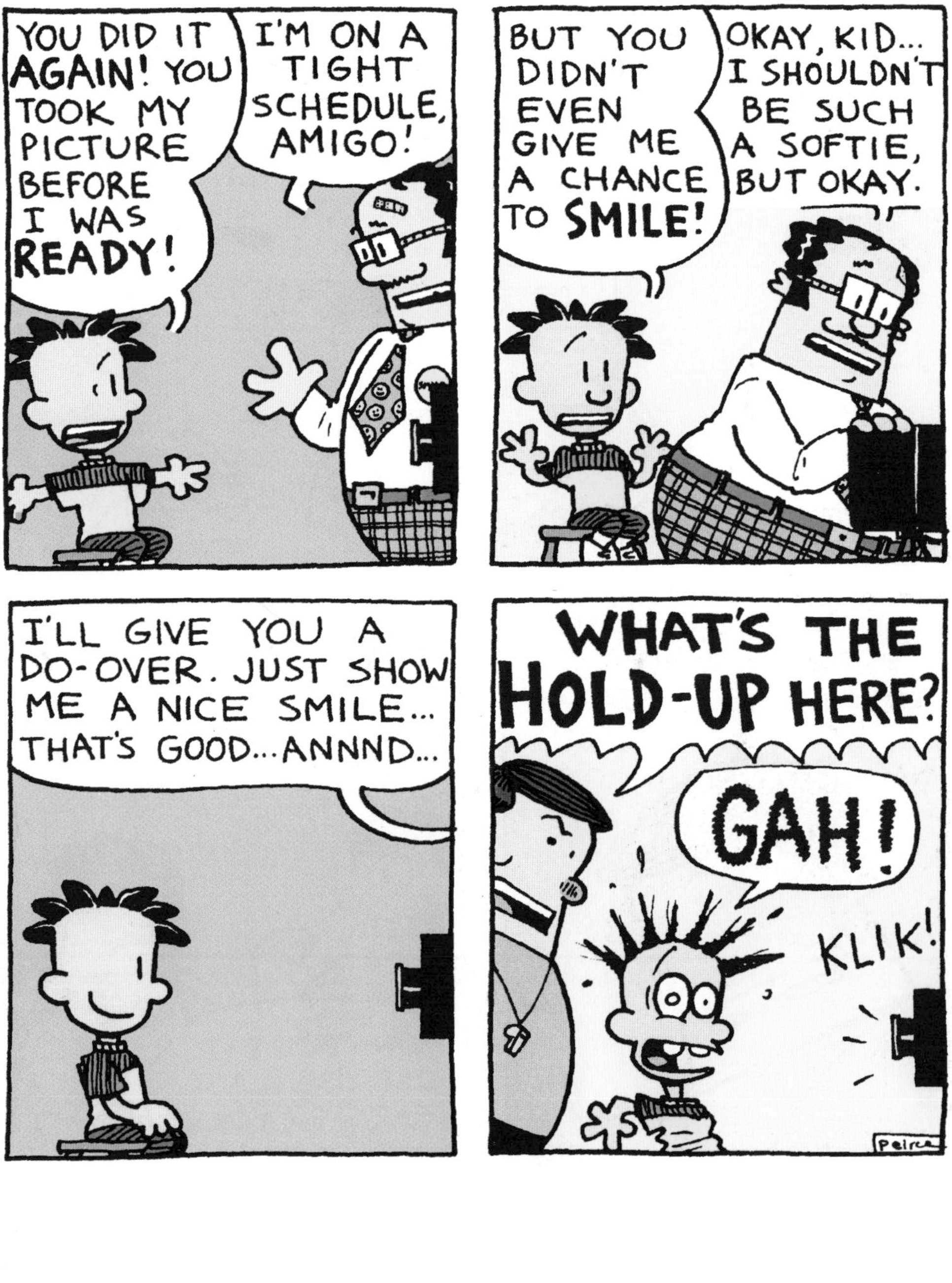
YOU DID IT AGAIN! YOU TOOK MY PICTURE BEFORE I WAS READY!
I'M ON A TIGHT SCHEDULE, AMIGO!
BUT YOU DIDN'T EVEN GIVE ME A CHANCE TO SMILE!
OKAY, KID... I SHOULDN'T BE SUCH A SOFTIE, BUT OKAY.
I'LL GIVE YOU A DO-OVER. JUST SHOW ME A NICE SMILE... THAT'S GOOD... ANNND...
WHAT'S THE HOLD-UP HERE?
GAH!
KLIK!
Peirce

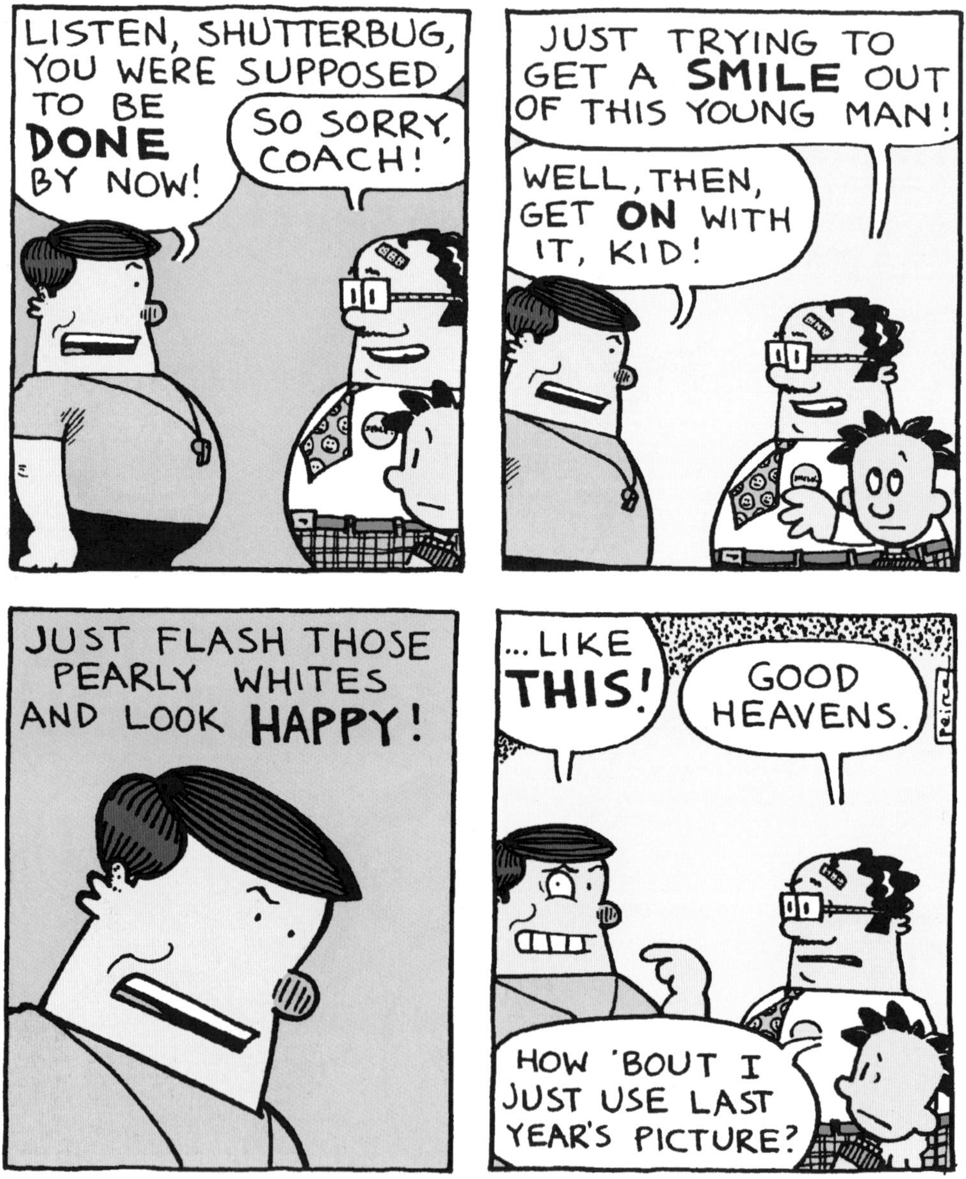
LISTEN, SHUTTERBUG, YOU WERE SUPPOSED TO BE DONE BY NOW!
SO SORRY, COACH!
JUST TRYING TO GET A SMILE OUT OF THIS YOUNG MAN!
WELL, THEN, GET ON WITH IT, KID!
JUST FLASH THOSE PEARLY WHITES AND LOOK HAPPY!
...LIKE THIS!
GOOD HEAVENS.
HOW 'BOUT I JUST USE LAST YEAR'S PICTURE?
Peirce

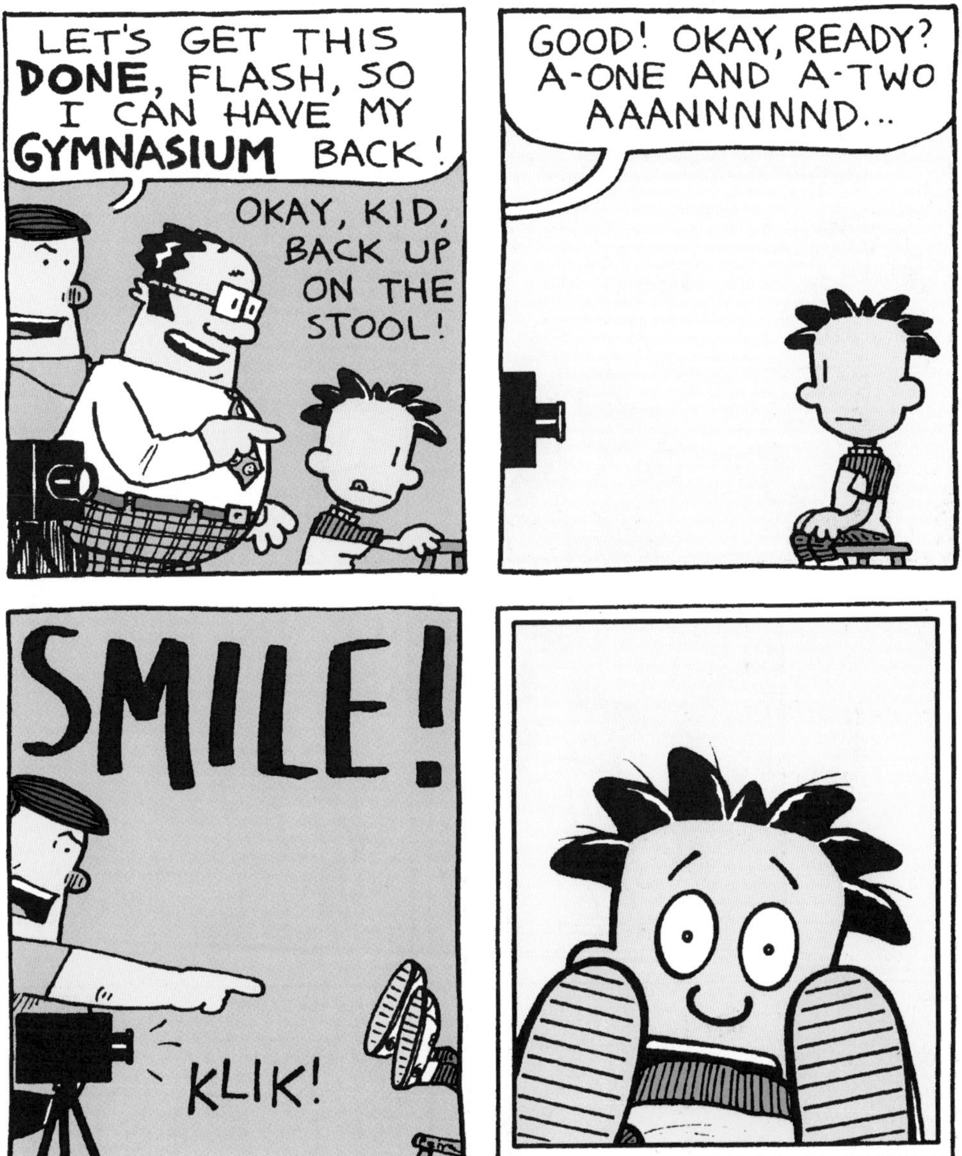
LET'S GET THIS DONE, FLASH, SO I CAN HAVE MY GYMNASIUM BACK!
OKAY, KID, BACK UP ON THE STOOL!
GOOD! OKAY, READY? A-ONE AND A-TWO AAANNNNND...
SMILE!
KLIK!

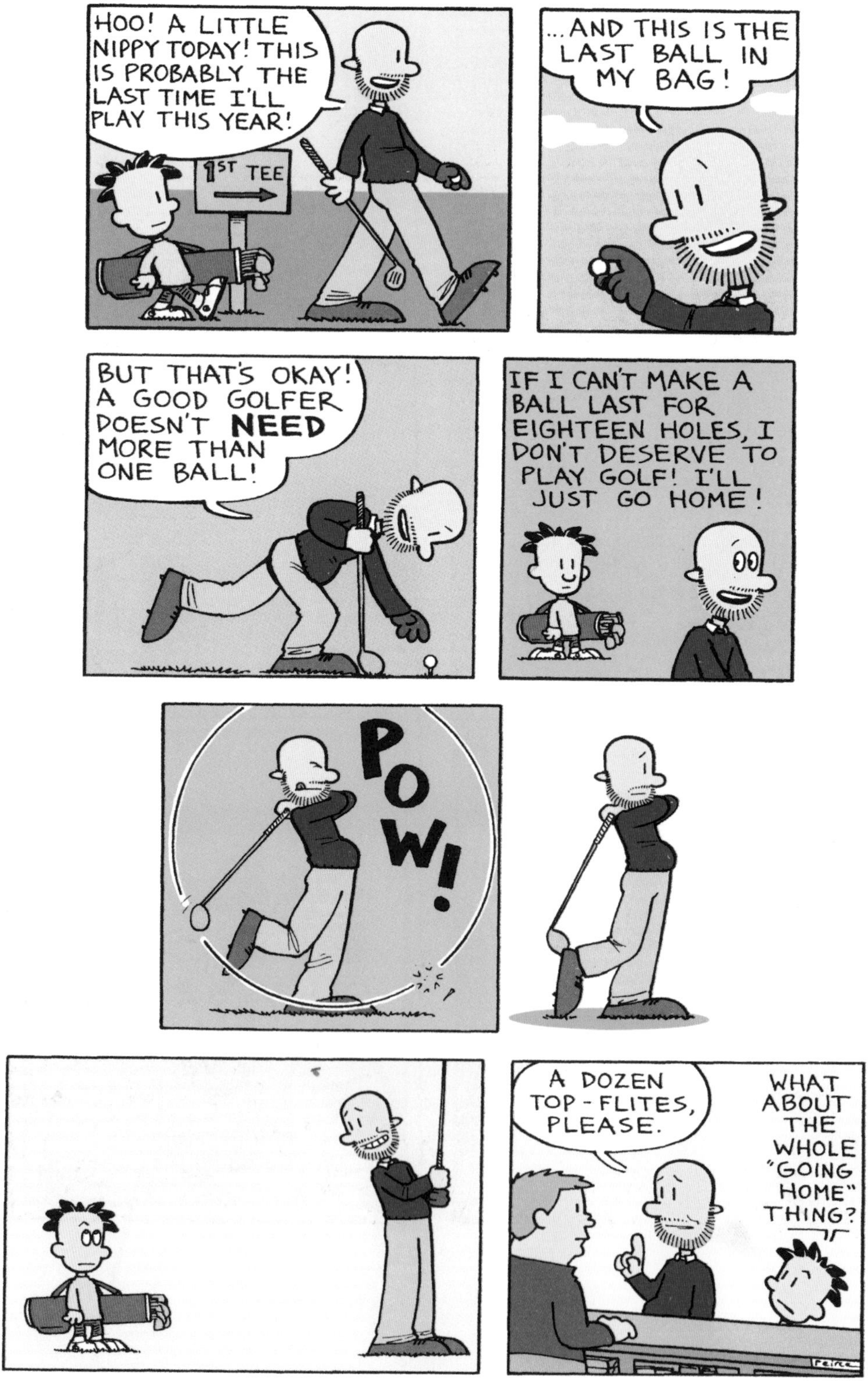
HOO! A LITTLE NIPPY TODAY! THIS IS PROBABLY THE LAST TIME I'LL PLAY THIS YEAR!
1ST TEE
...AND THIS IS THE LAST BALL IN MY BAG!
BUT THAT'S OKAY! A GOOD GOLFER DOESN'T NEED MORE THAN ONE BALL!
IF I CAN'T MAKE A BALL LAST FOR EIGHTEEN HOLES, I DON'T DESERVE TO PLAY GOLF! I'LL JUST GO HOME!
POW!
A DOZEN TOP-FLITES, PLEASE.
WHAT ABOUT THE WHOLE "GOING HOME" THING?

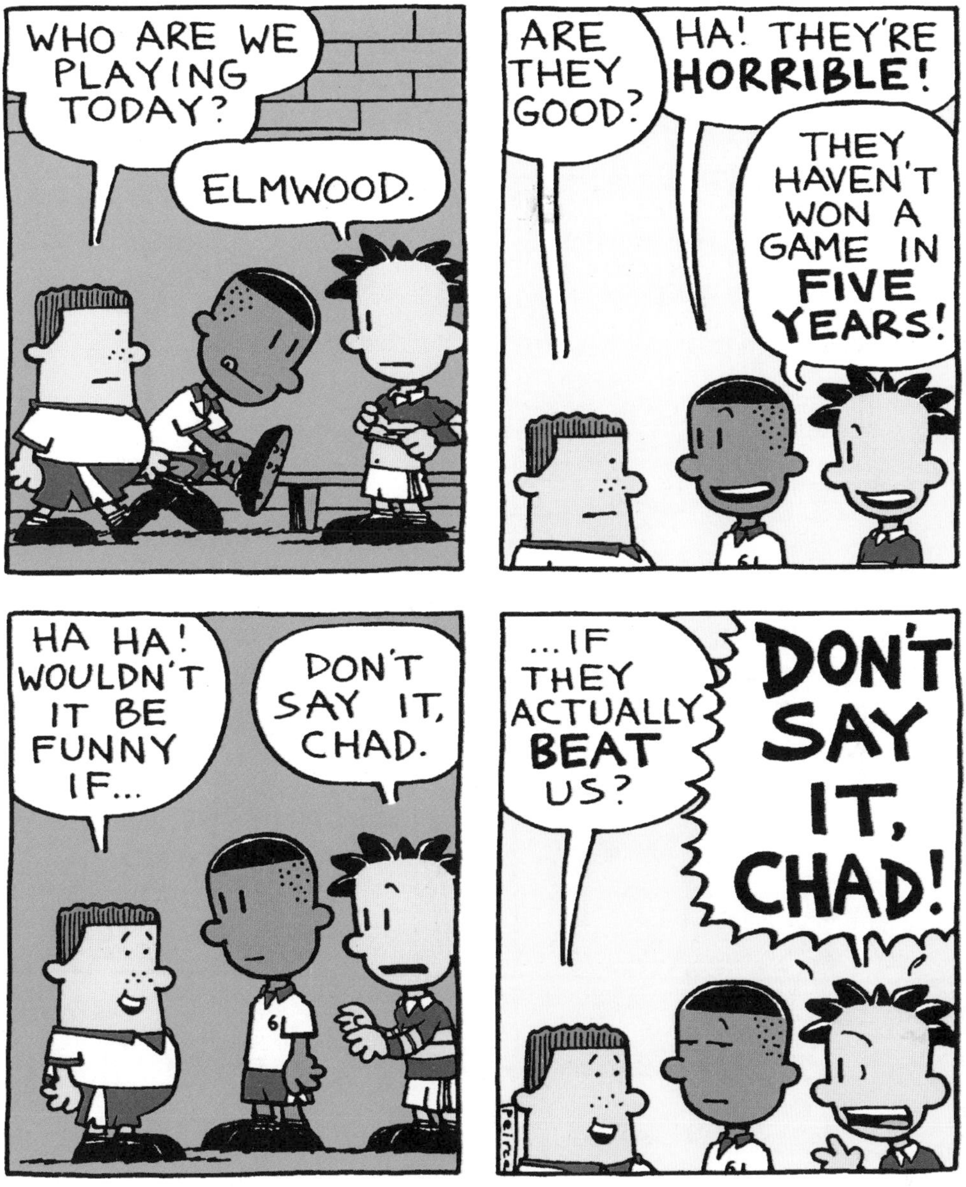
WHO ARE WE PLAYING TODAY?
ELMWOOD.
ARE THEY GOOD?
HA! THEY'RE **HORRIBLE**!
THEY HAVEN'T WON A GAME IN **FIVE YEARS**!
HA HA! WOULDN'T IT BE FUNNY IF...
DON'T SAY IT, CHAD.
...IF THEY ACTUALLY **BEAT** US?
DON'T SAY IT, CHAD!
PEIRCE

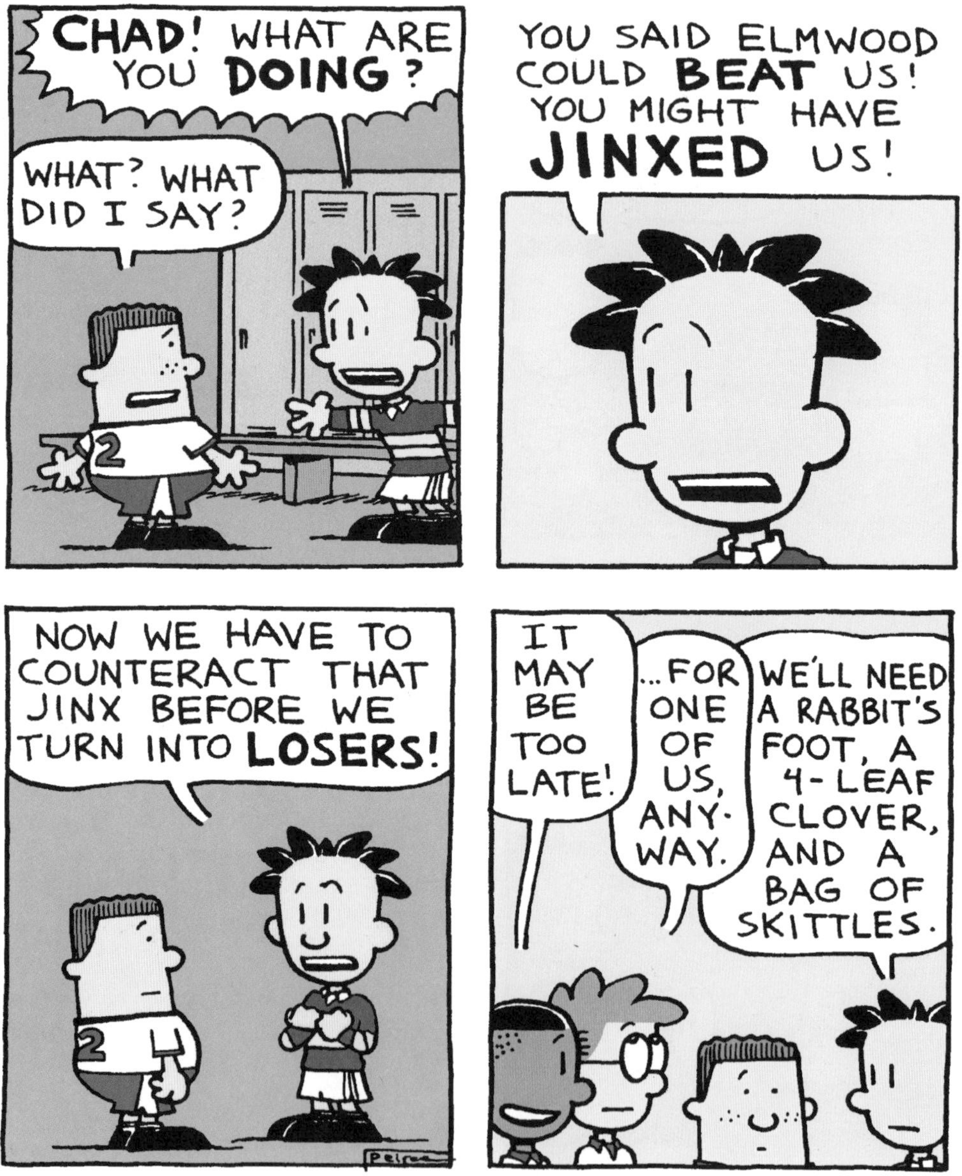
CHAD! WHAT ARE YOU DOING?
WHAT? WHAT DID I SAY?
YOU SAID ELMWOOD COULD BEAT US! YOU MIGHT HAVE JINXED US!
NOW WE HAVE TO COUNTERACT THAT JINX BEFORE WE TURN INTO LOSERS!
IT MAY BE TOO LATE!
...FOR ONE OF US, ANYWAY.
WE'LL NEED A RABBIT'S FOOT, A 4-LEAF CLOVER, AND A BAG OF SKITTLES.

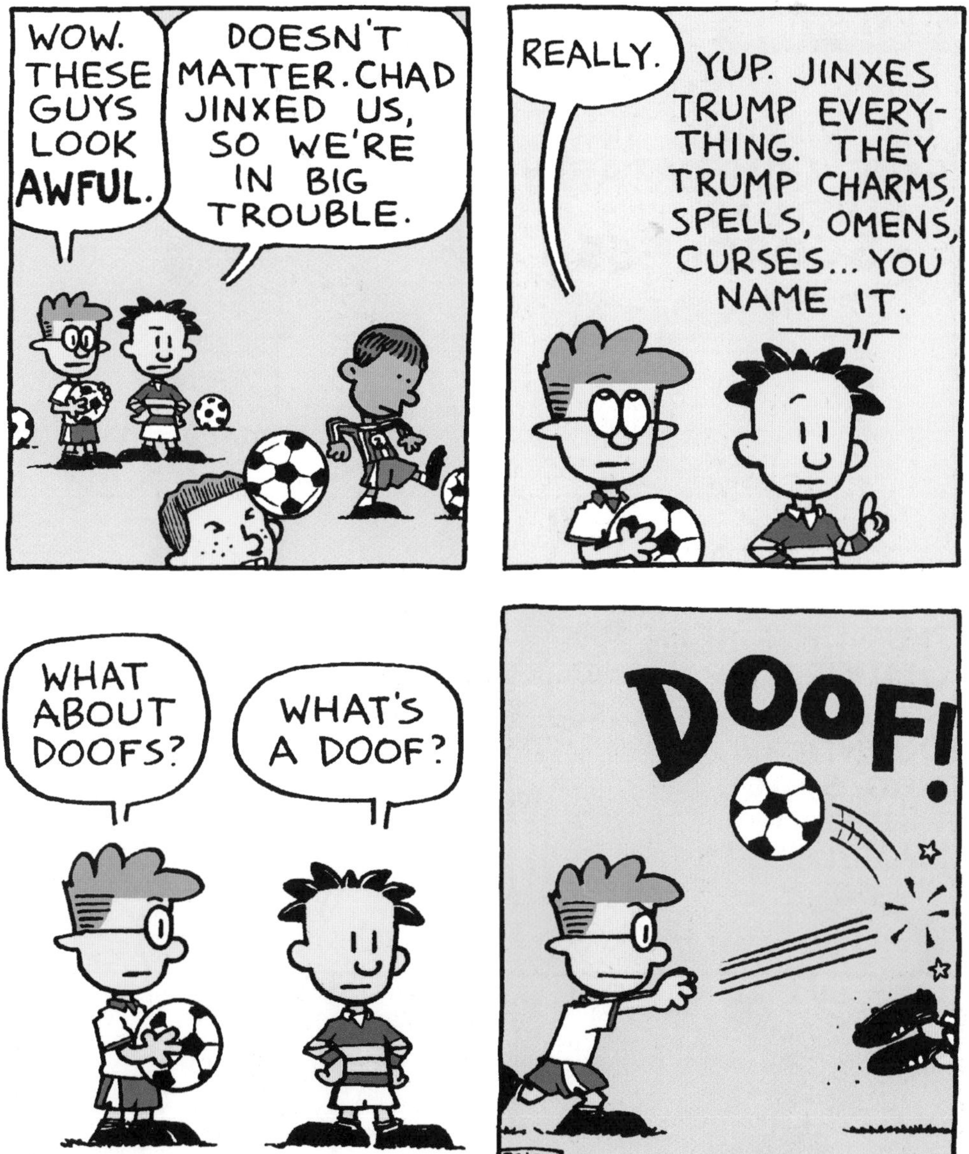
WOW. THESE GUYS LOOK **AWFUL**.
DOESN'T MATTER. CHAD JINXED US, SO WE'RE IN BIG TROUBLE.
REALLY.
YUP. JINXES TRUMP EVERYTHING. THEY TRUMP CHARMS, SPELLS, OMENS, CURSES... YOU NAME IT.
WHAT ABOUT DOOFS?
WHAT'S A DOOF?
DOOF!
Peirce

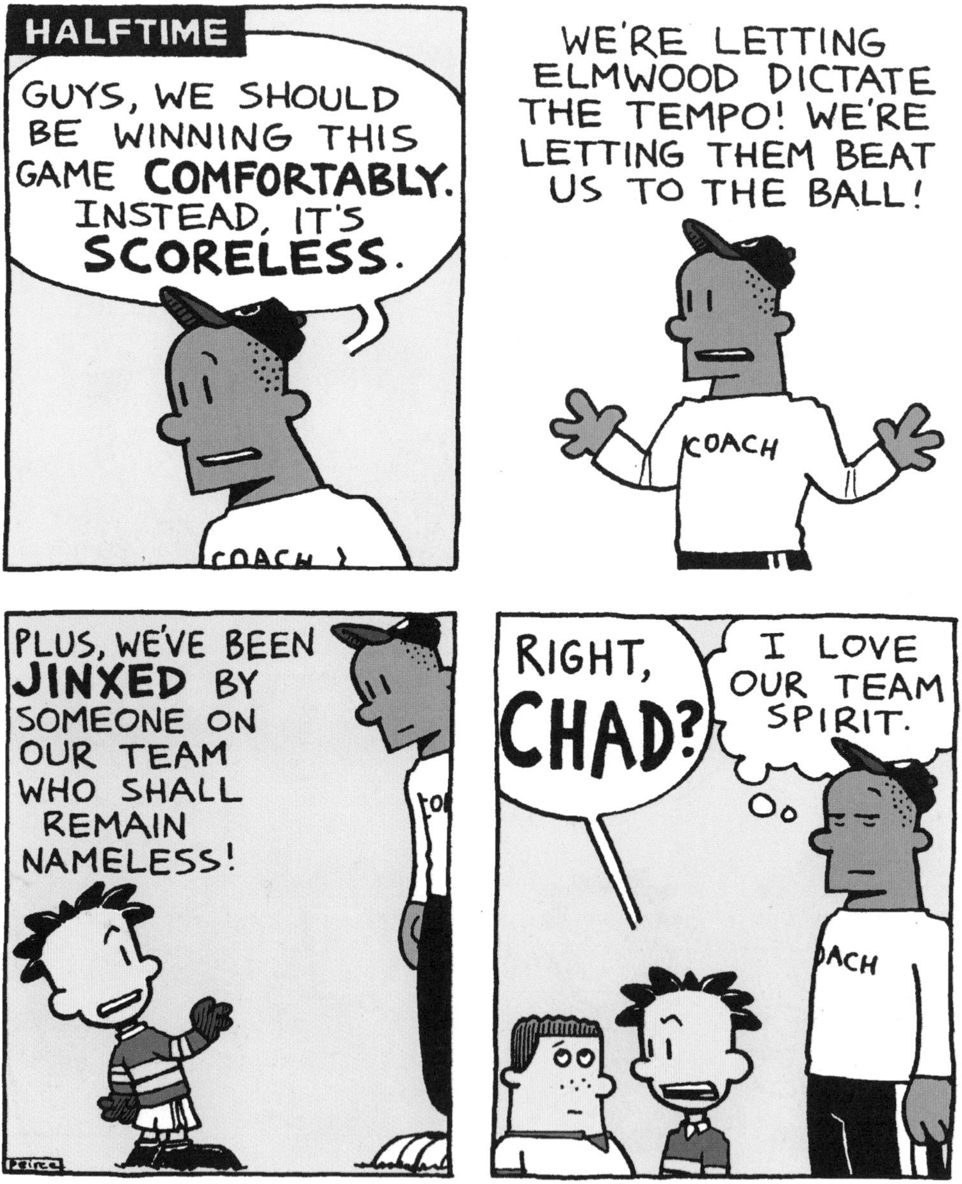
HALFTIME
GUYS, WE SHOULD BE WINNING THIS GAME COMFORTABLY. INSTEAD, IT'S SCORELESS.
COACH
WE'RE LETTING ELMWOOD DICTATE THE TEMPO! WE'RE LETTING THEM BEAT US TO THE BALL!
COACH
PLUS, WE'VE BEEN JINXED BY SOMEONE ON OUR TEAM WHO SHALL REMAIN NAMELESS!
RIGHT, CHAD?
I LOVE OUR TEAM SPIRIT.

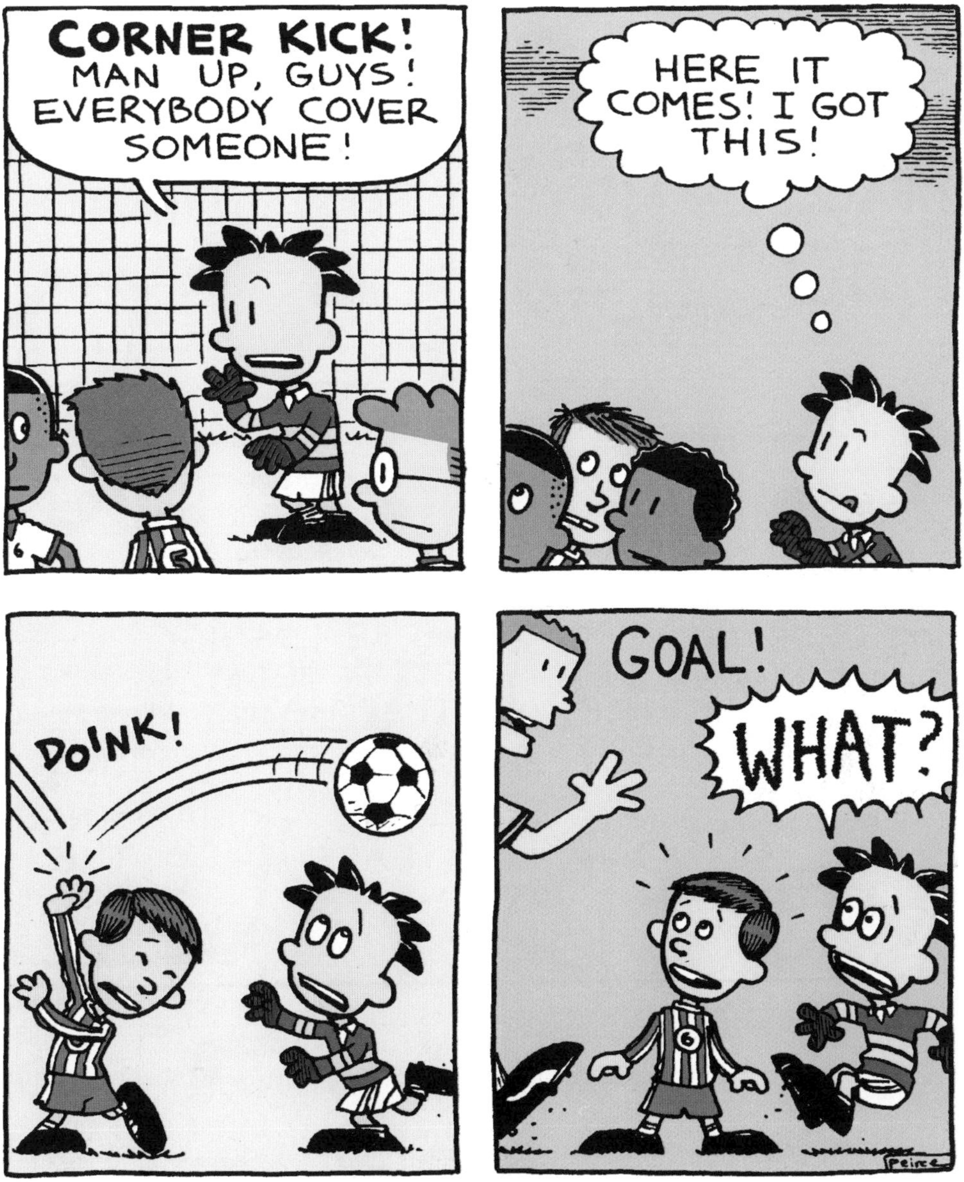
CORNER KICK! MAN UP, GUYS! EVERYBODY COVER SOMEONE!
HERE IT COMES! I GOT THIS!
DOINK!
GOAL!
WHAT?
Peirce

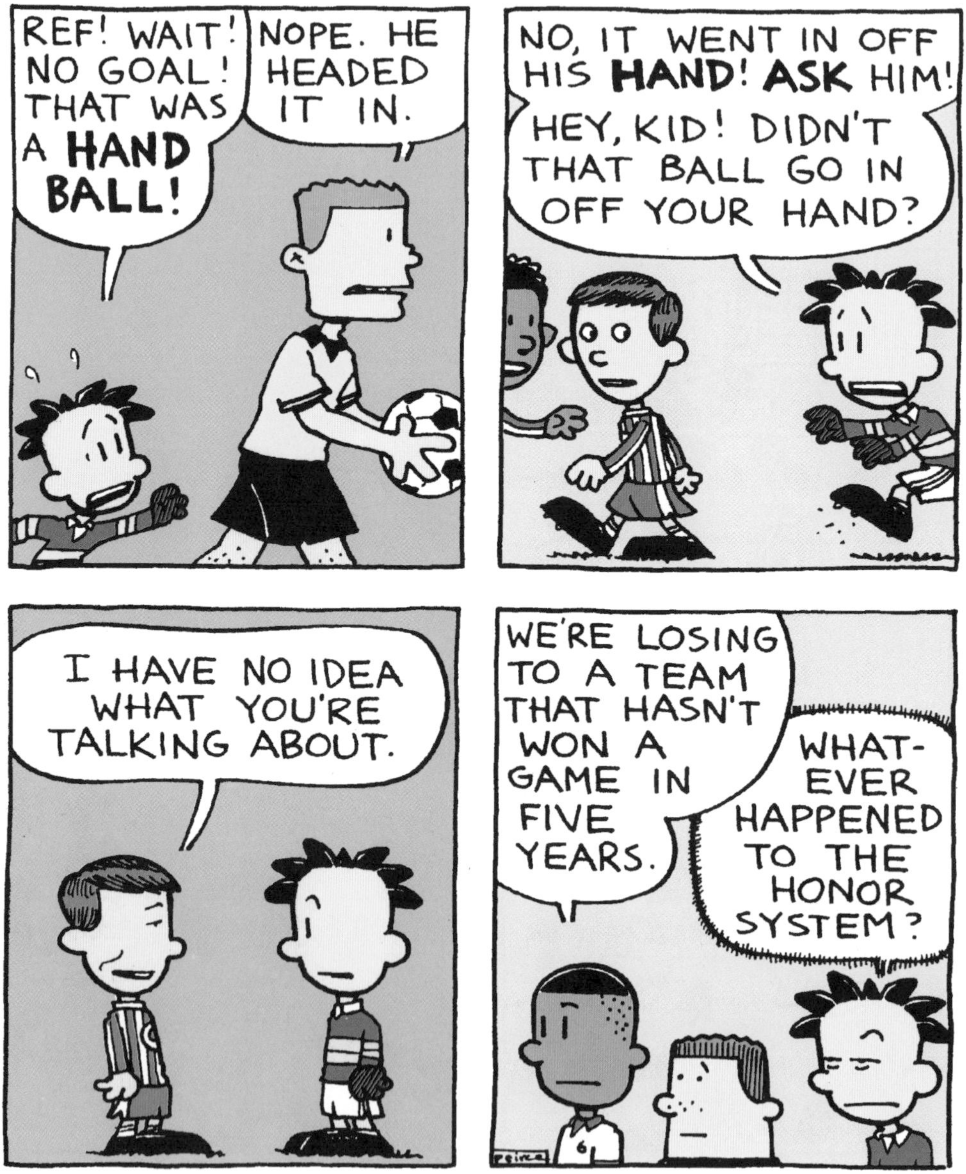

REF! WAIT! NO GOAL! THAT WAS A **HAND BALL**!
NOPE. HE HEADED IT IN.
NO, IT WENT IN OFF HIS **HAND**! **ASK** HIM!
HEY, KID! DIDN'T THAT BALL GO IN OFF YOUR HAND?
I HAVE NO IDEA WHAT YOU'RE TALKING ABOUT.
WE'RE LOSING TO A TEAM THAT HASN'T WON A GAME IN FIVE YEARS.
WHAT-EVER HAPPENED TO THE HONOR SYSTEM?

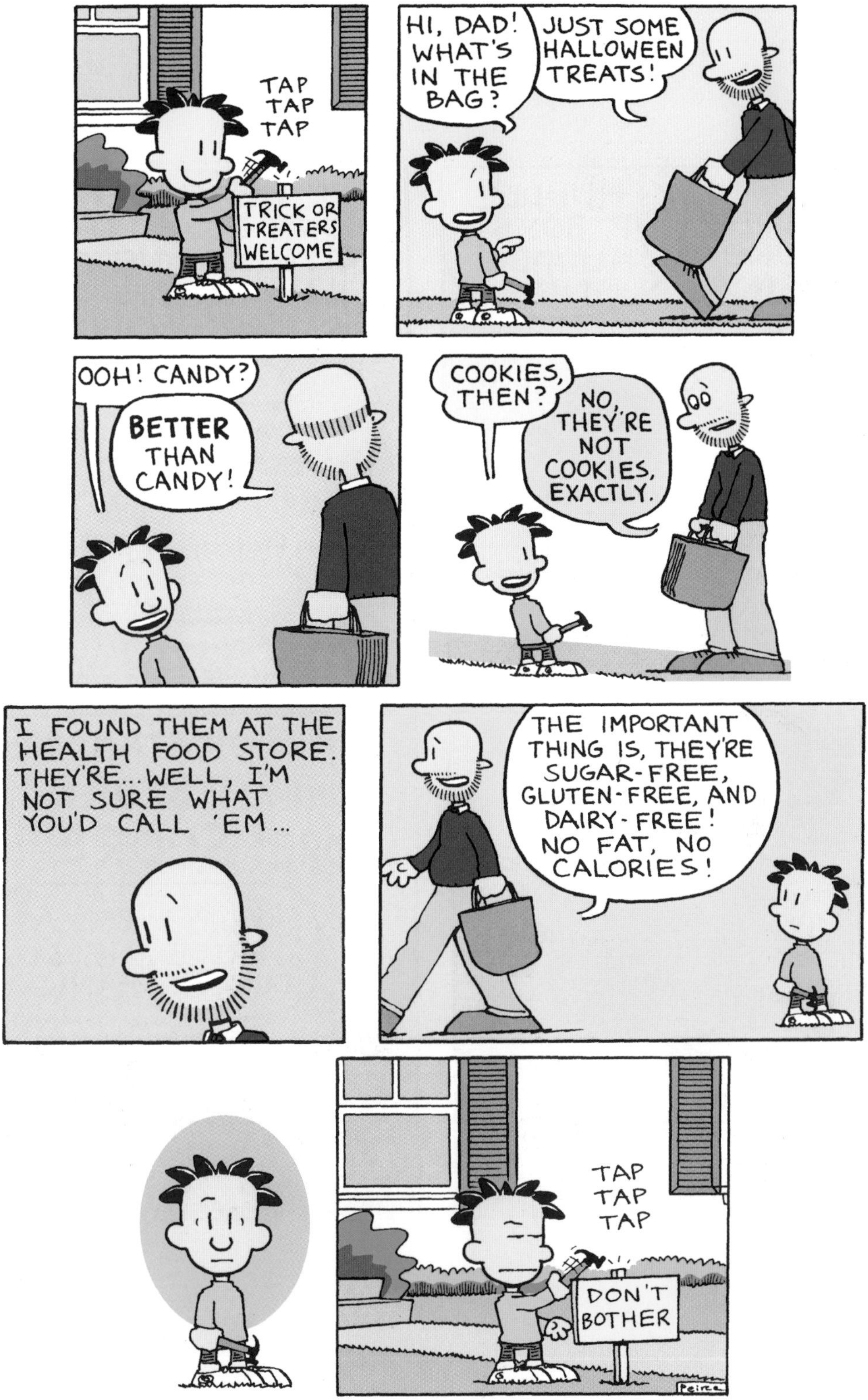
TAP
TAP
TAP
TRICK OR TREATERS WELCOME
HI, DAD! WHAT'S IN THE BAG?
JUST SOME HALLOWEEN TREATS!
OOH! CANDY?
BETTER THAN CANDY!
COOKIES, THEN?
NO, THEY'RE NOT COOKIES, EXACTLY.
I FOUND THEM AT THE HEALTH FOOD STORE. THEY'RE...WELL, I'M NOT SURE WHAT YOU'D CALL 'EM...
THE IMPORTANT THING IS, THEY'RE SUGAR-FREE, GLUTEN-FREE, AND DAIRY-FREE! NO FAT, NO CALORIES!
TAP
TAP
TAP
DON'T BOTHER
Peirce

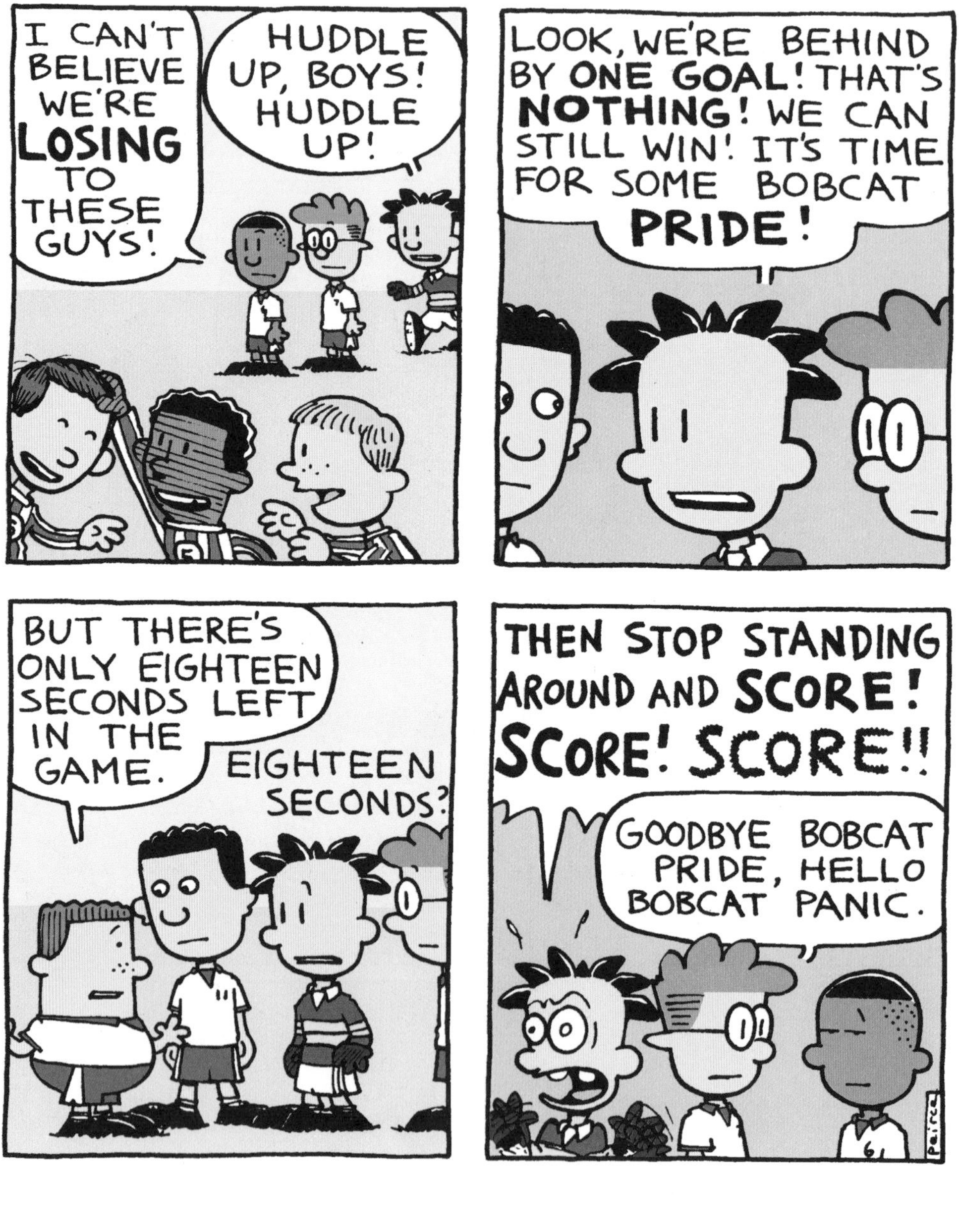
I CAN'T BELIEVE WE'RE **LOSING** TO THESE GUYS!
HUDDLE UP, BOYS! HUDDLE UP!
LOOK, WE'RE BEHIND BY **ONE GOAL**! THAT'S **NOTHING**! WE CAN STILL WIN! IT'S TIME FOR SOME BOBCAT **PRIDE**!
BUT THERE'S ONLY EIGHTEEN SECONDS LEFT IN THE GAME.
EIGHTEEN SECONDS?
THEN STOP STANDING AROUND AND SCORE! SCORE! SCORE!!
GOODBYE BOBCAT PRIDE, HELLO BOBCAT PANIC.

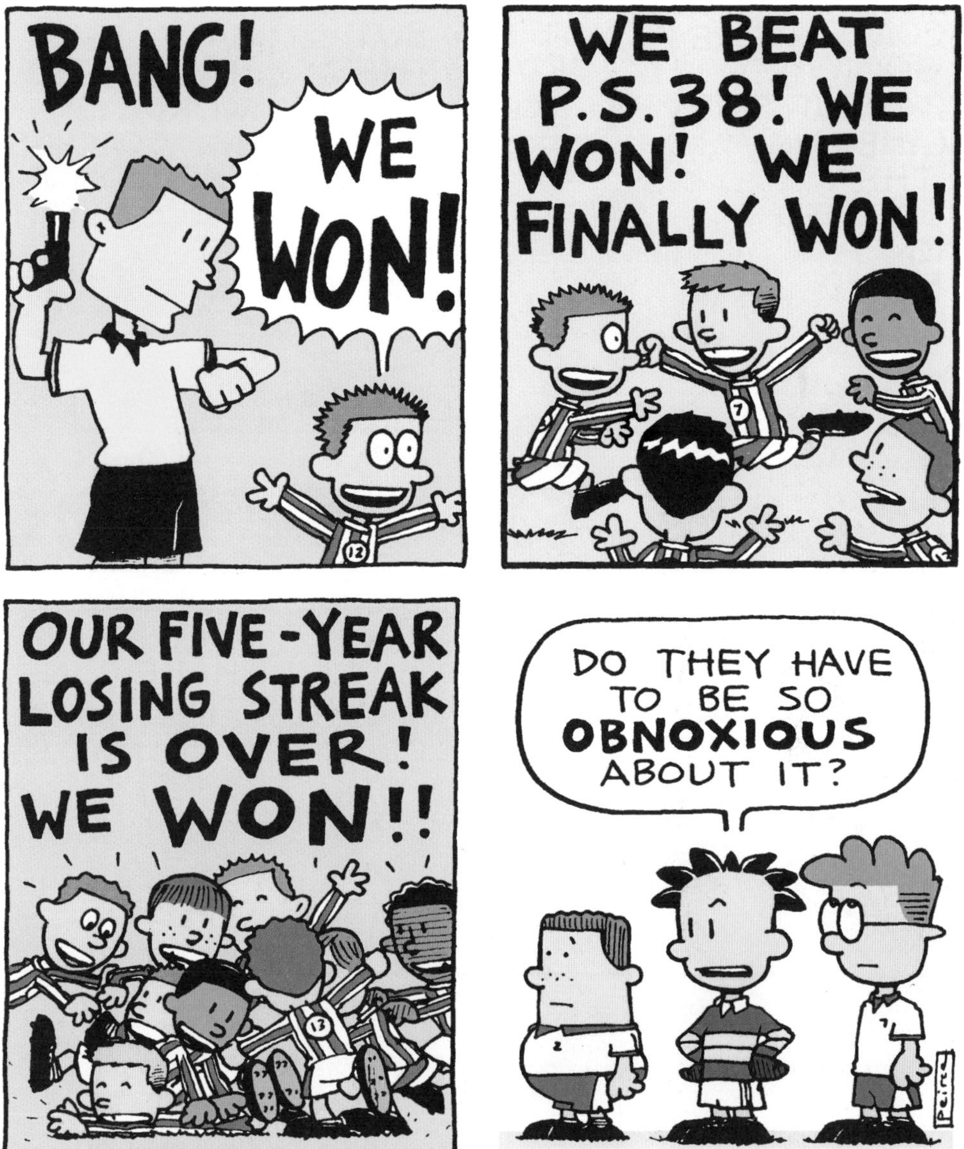
BANG!
WE WON!
WE BEAT P.S. 38! WE WON! WE FINALLY WON!
OUR FIVE-YEAR LOSING STREAK IS OVER! WE WON!!
DO THEY HAVE TO BE SO **OBNOXIOUS** ABOUT IT?

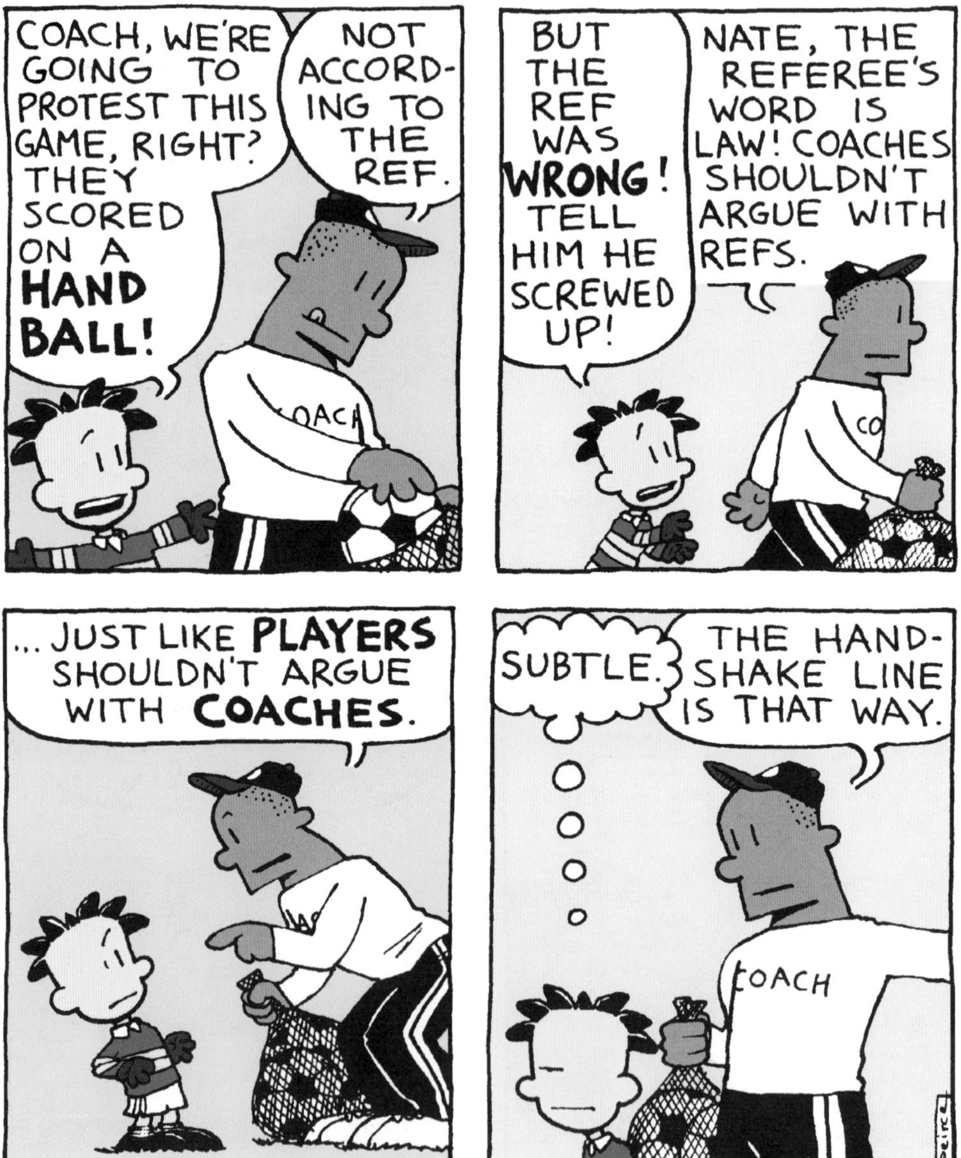
COACH, WE'RE GOING TO PROTEST THIS GAME, RIGHT? THEY SCORED ON A **HAND BALL**!
NOT ACCORDING TO THE REF.
BUT THE REF WAS **WRONG**! TELL HIM HE SCREWED UP!
NATE, THE REFEREE'S WORD IS LAW! COACHES SHOULDN'T ARGUE WITH REFS.
... JUST LIKE **PLAYERS** SHOULDN'T ARGUE WITH **COACHES**.
SUBTLE.
THE HANDSHAKE LINE IS THAT WAY.

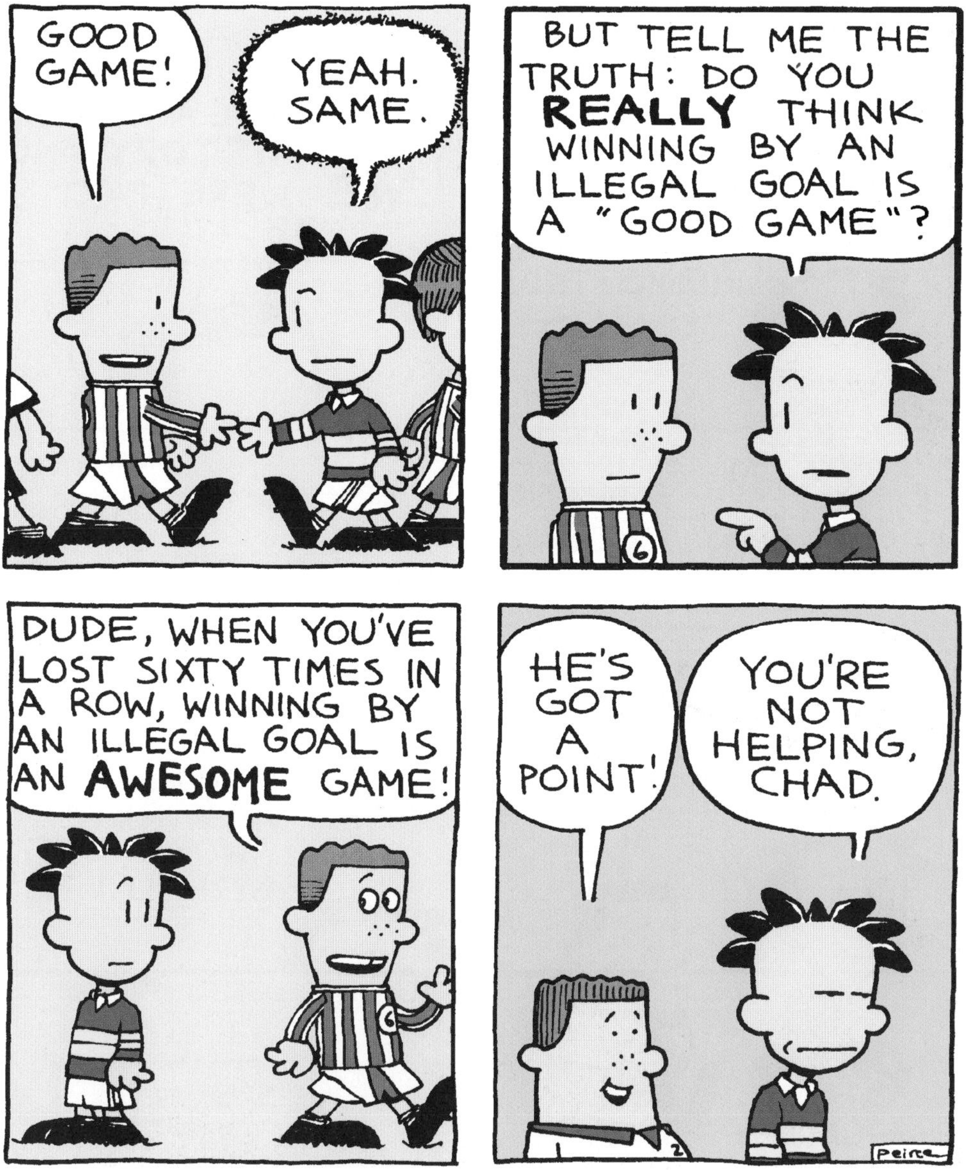
GOOD GAME!
YEAH. SAME.
BUT TELL ME THE TRUTH: DO YOU REALLY THINK WINNING BY AN ILLEGAL GOAL IS A "GOOD GAME"?
DUDE, WHEN YOU'VE LOST SIXTY TIMES IN A ROW, WINNING BY AN ILLEGAL GOAL IS AN AWESOME GAME!
HE'S GOT A POINT!
YOU'RE NOT HELPING, CHAD.
Peirce

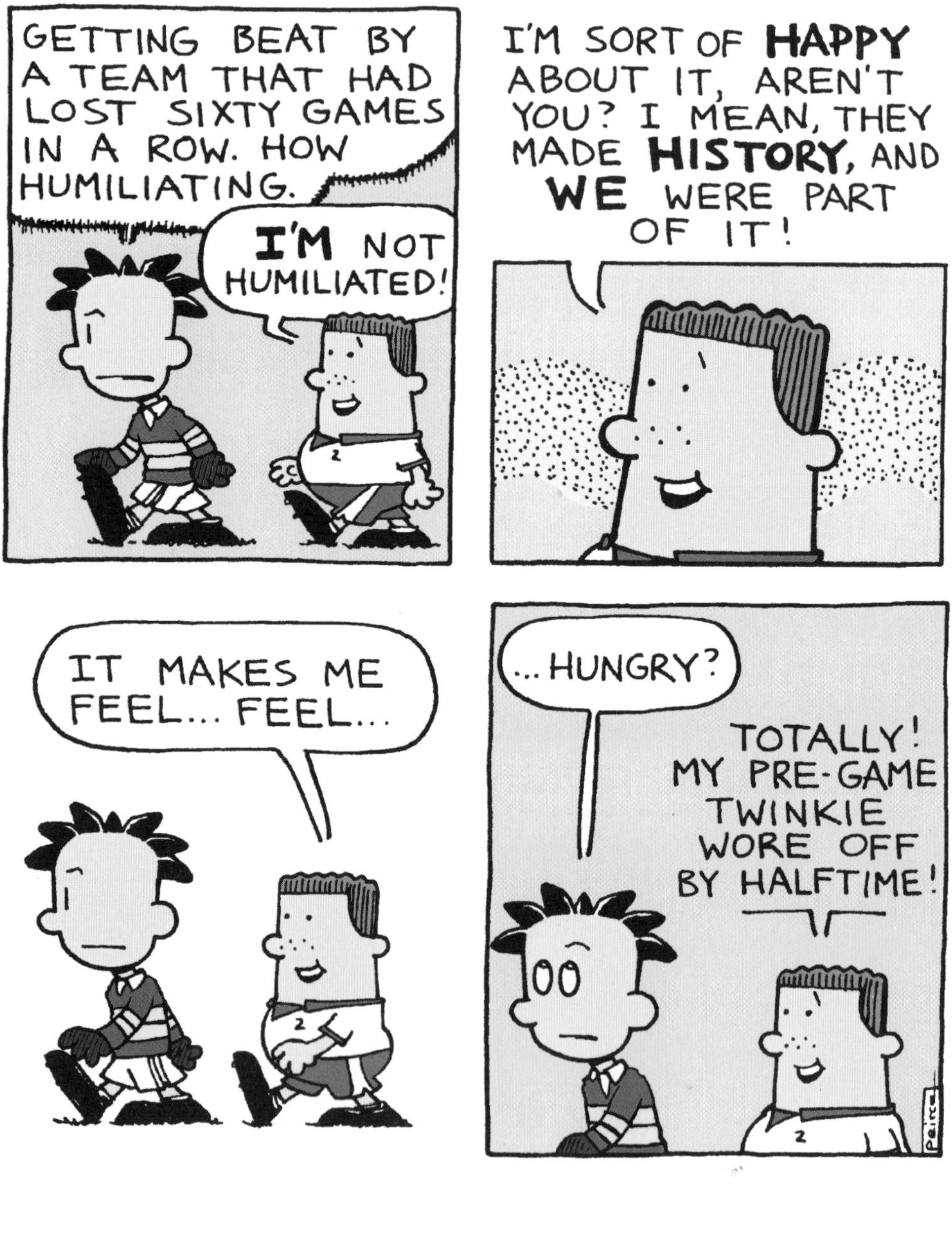
GETTING BEAT BY A TEAM THAT HAD LOST SIXTY GAMES IN A ROW. HOW HUMILIATING.
I'M NOT HUMILIATED!
I'M SORT OF HAPPY ABOUT IT, AREN'T YOU? I MEAN, THEY MADE HISTORY, AND WE WERE PART OF IT!
IT MAKES ME FEEL... FEEL...
...HUNGRY?
TOTALLY! MY PRE-GAME TWINKIE WORE OFF BY HALFTIME!

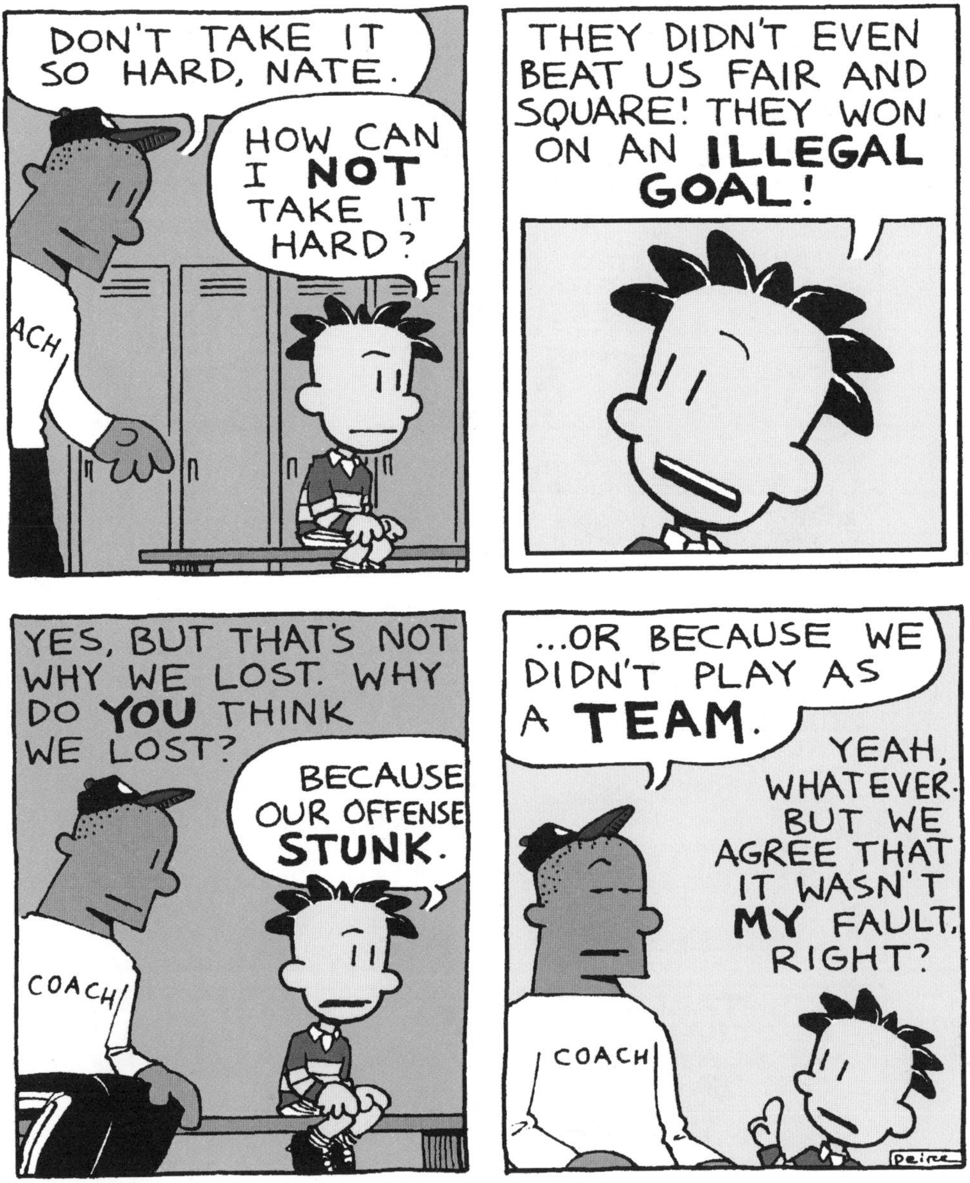
DON'T TAKE IT SO HARD, NATE.
HOW CAN I **NOT** TAKE IT HARD?
ACH
THEY DIDN'T EVEN BEAT US FAIR AND SQUARE! THEY WON ON AN **ILLEGAL GOAL**!
YES, BUT THAT'S NOT WHY WE LOST. WHY DO **YOU** THINK WE LOST?
BECAUSE OUR OFFENSE **STUNK**.
COACH
...OR BECAUSE WE DIDN'T PLAY AS A **TEAM**.
YEAH, WHATEVER. BUT WE AGREE THAT IT WASN'T **MY** FAULT, RIGHT?
COACH
peirce

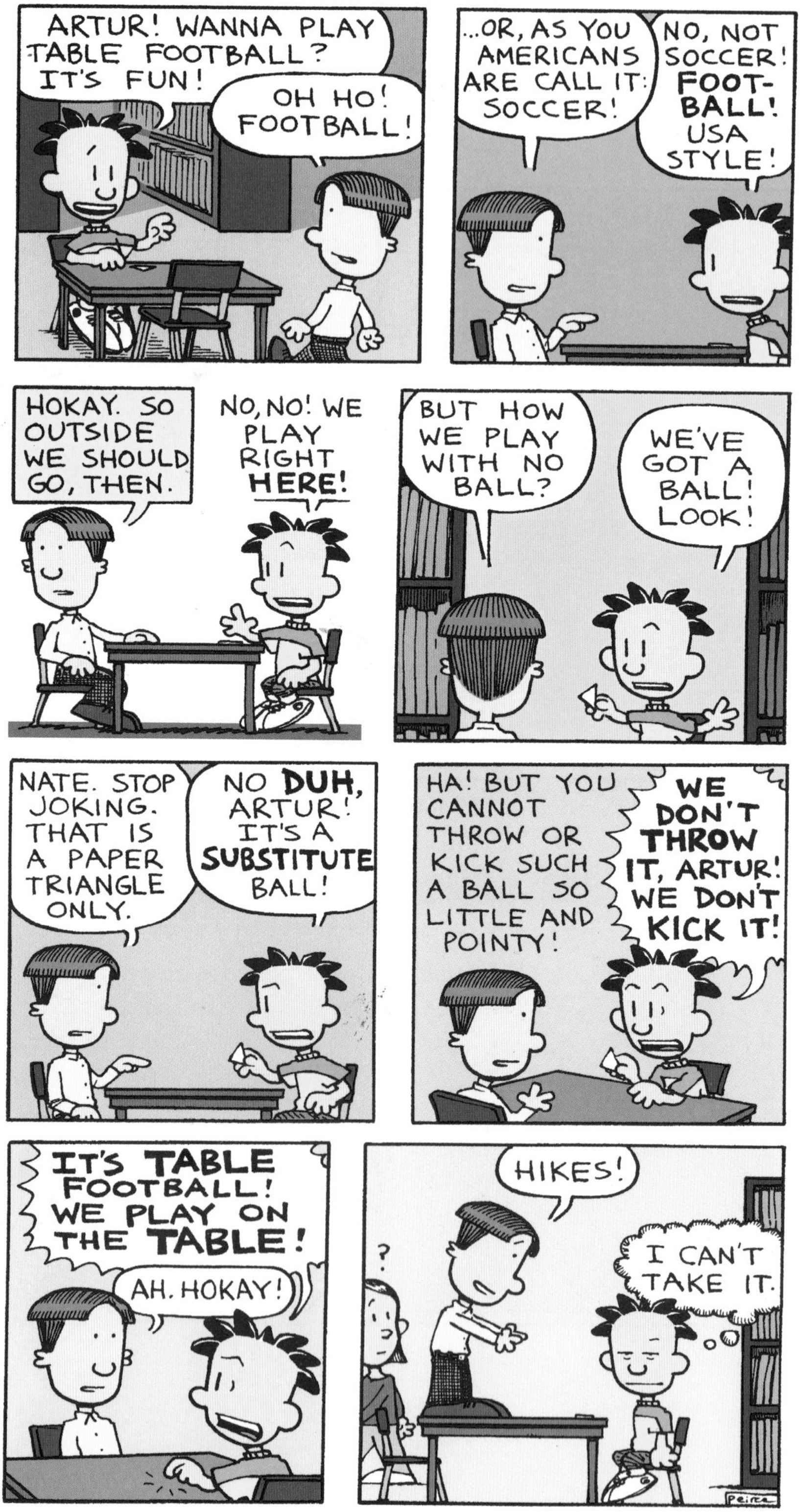
ARTUR! WANNA PLAY TABLE FOOTBALL? IT'S FUN!
OH HO! FOOTBALL!
...OR, AS YOU AMERICANS ARE CALL IT: SOCCER!
NO, NOT SOCCER! FOOT-BALL! USA STYLE!
HOKAY. SO OUTSIDE WE SHOULD GO, THEN.
NO, NO! WE PLAY RIGHT HERE!
BUT HOW WE PLAY WITH NO BALL?
WE'VE GOT A BALL! LOOK!
NATE. STOP JOKING. THAT IS A PAPER TRIANGLE ONLY.
NO DUH, ARTUR! IT'S A SUBSTITUTE BALL!
HA! BUT YOU CANNOT THROW OR KICK SUCH A BALL SO LITTLE AND POINTY!
WE DON'T THROW IT, ARTUR! WE DON'T KICK IT!
IT'S TABLE FOOTBALL! WE PLAY ON THE TABLE!
AH. HOKAY!
HIKES!
?
I CAN'T TAKE IT.
Peirce

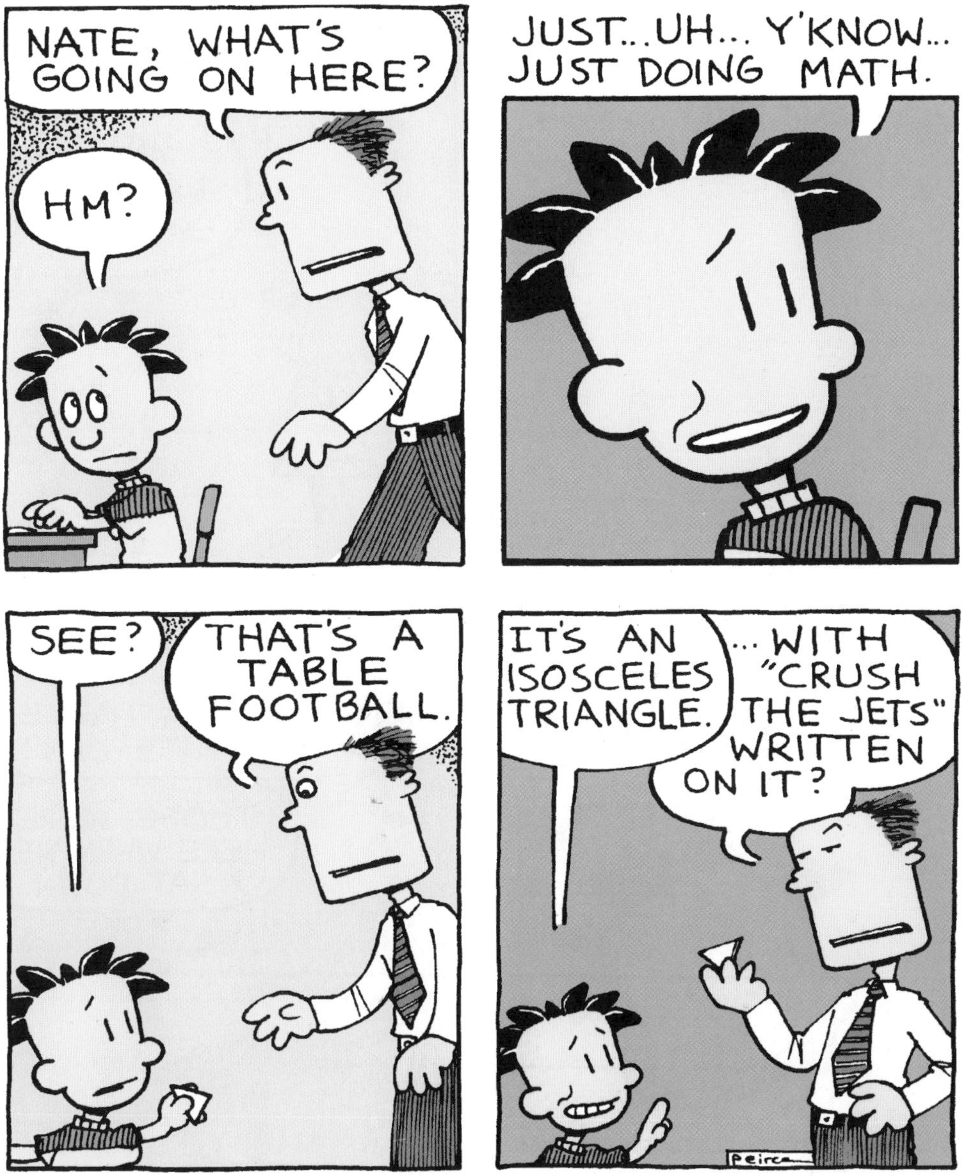
NATE, WHAT'S GOING ON HERE?
HM?
JUST...UH... Y'KNOW... JUST DOING MATH.
SEE?
THAT'S A TABLE FOOTBALL.
IT'S AN ISOSCELES TRIANGLE.
...WITH "CRUSH THE JETS" WRITTEN ON IT?
Peirce

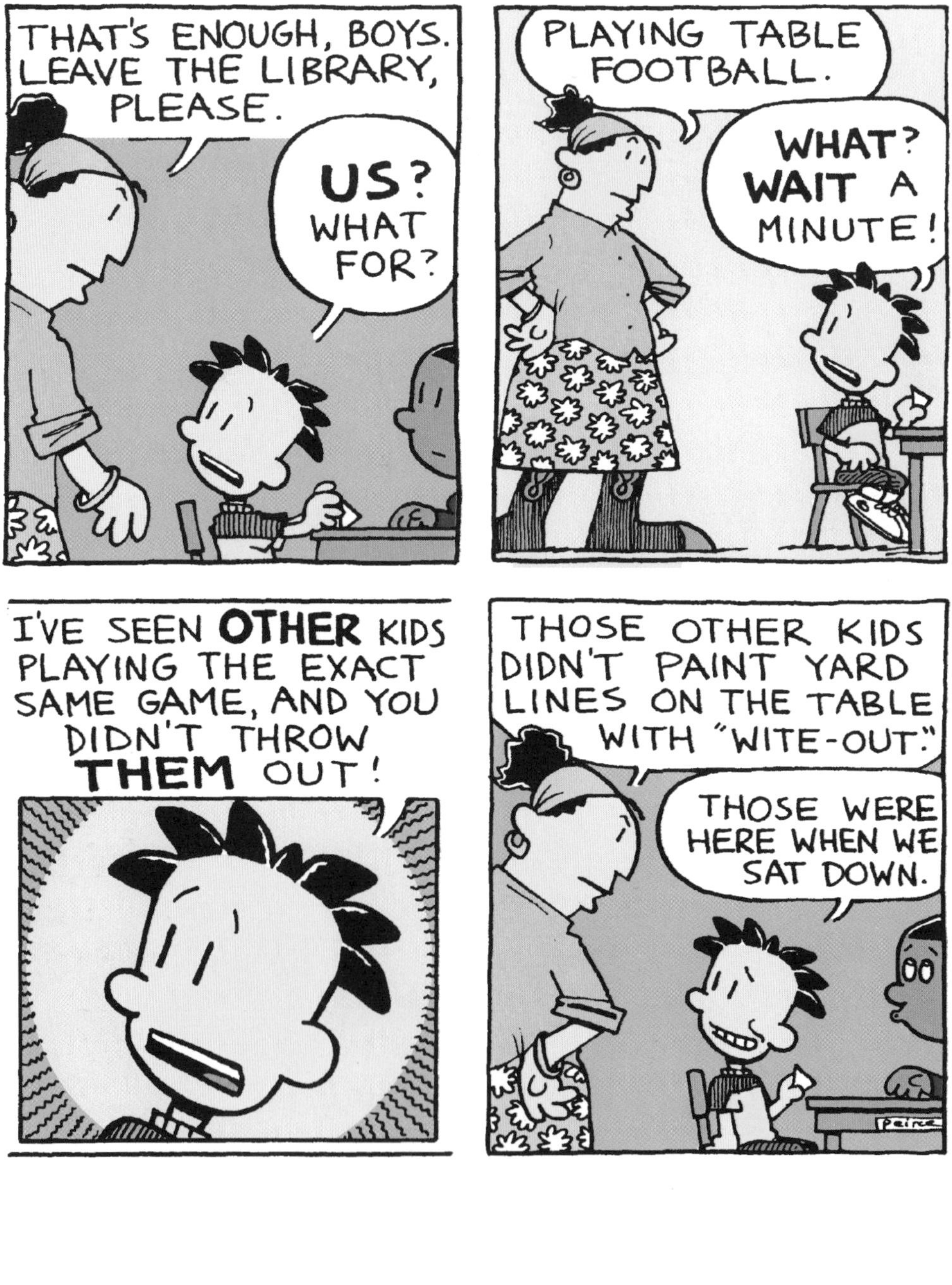
THAT'S ENOUGH, BOYS. LEAVE THE LIBRARY, PLEASE.
US? WHAT FOR?
PLAYING TABLE FOOTBALL.
WHAT? WAIT A MINUTE!
I'VE SEEN OTHER KIDS PLAYING THE EXACT SAME GAME, AND YOU DIDN'T THROW THEM OUT!
THOSE OTHER KIDS DIDN'T PAINT YARD LINES ON THE TABLE WITH "WITE-OUT."
THOSE WERE HERE WHEN WE SAT DOWN.
PEIRCE

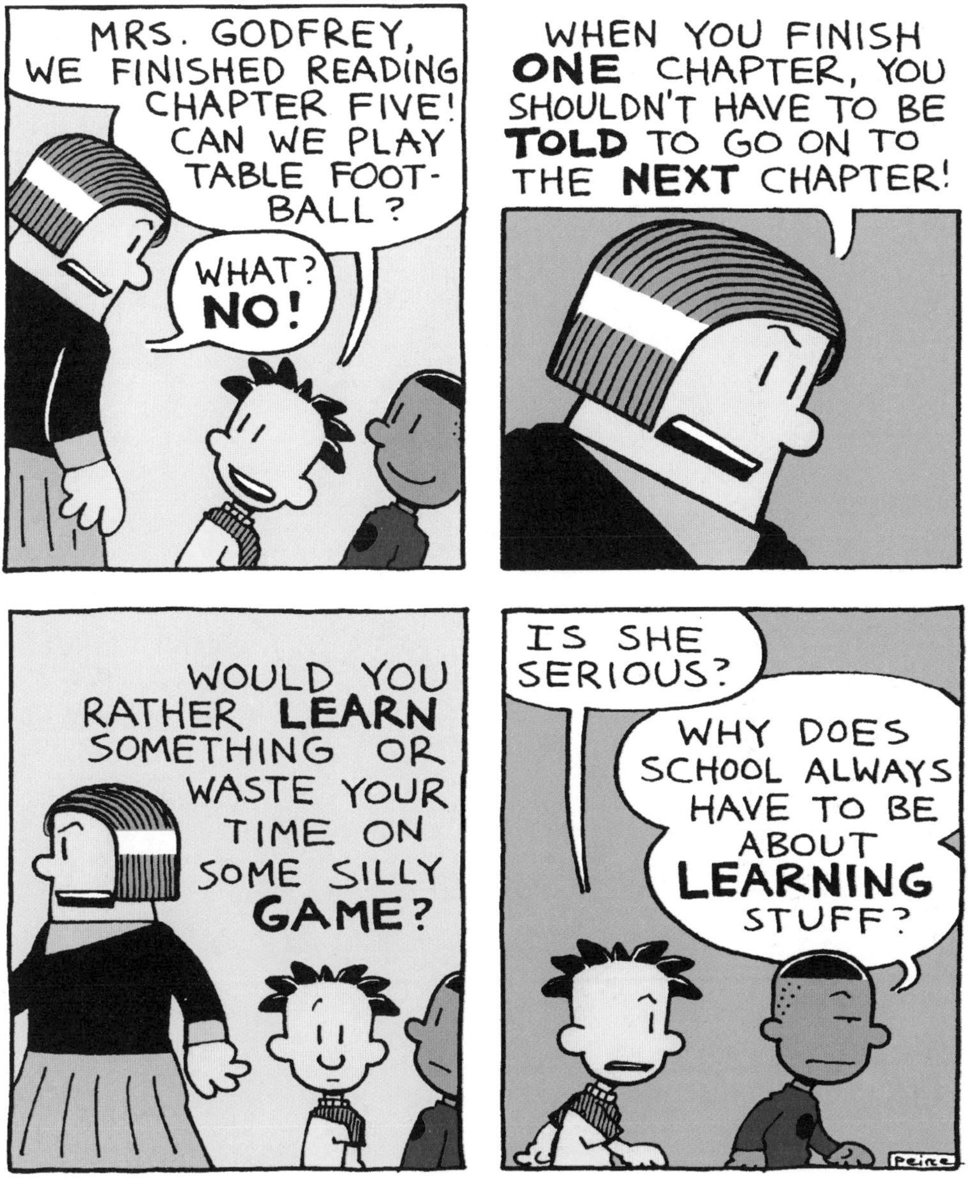
MRS. GODFREY, WE FINISHED READING CHAPTER FIVE! CAN WE PLAY TABLE FOOT-BALL?
WHAT? NO!
WHEN YOU FINISH ONE CHAPTER, YOU SHOULDN'T HAVE TO BE TOLD TO GO ON TO THE NEXT CHAPTER!
WOULD YOU RATHER LEARN SOMETHING OR WASTE YOUR TIME ON SOME SILLY GAME?
IS SHE SERIOUS?
WHY DOES SCHOOL ALWAYS HAVE TO BE ABOUT LEARNING STUFF?
PEIRCE

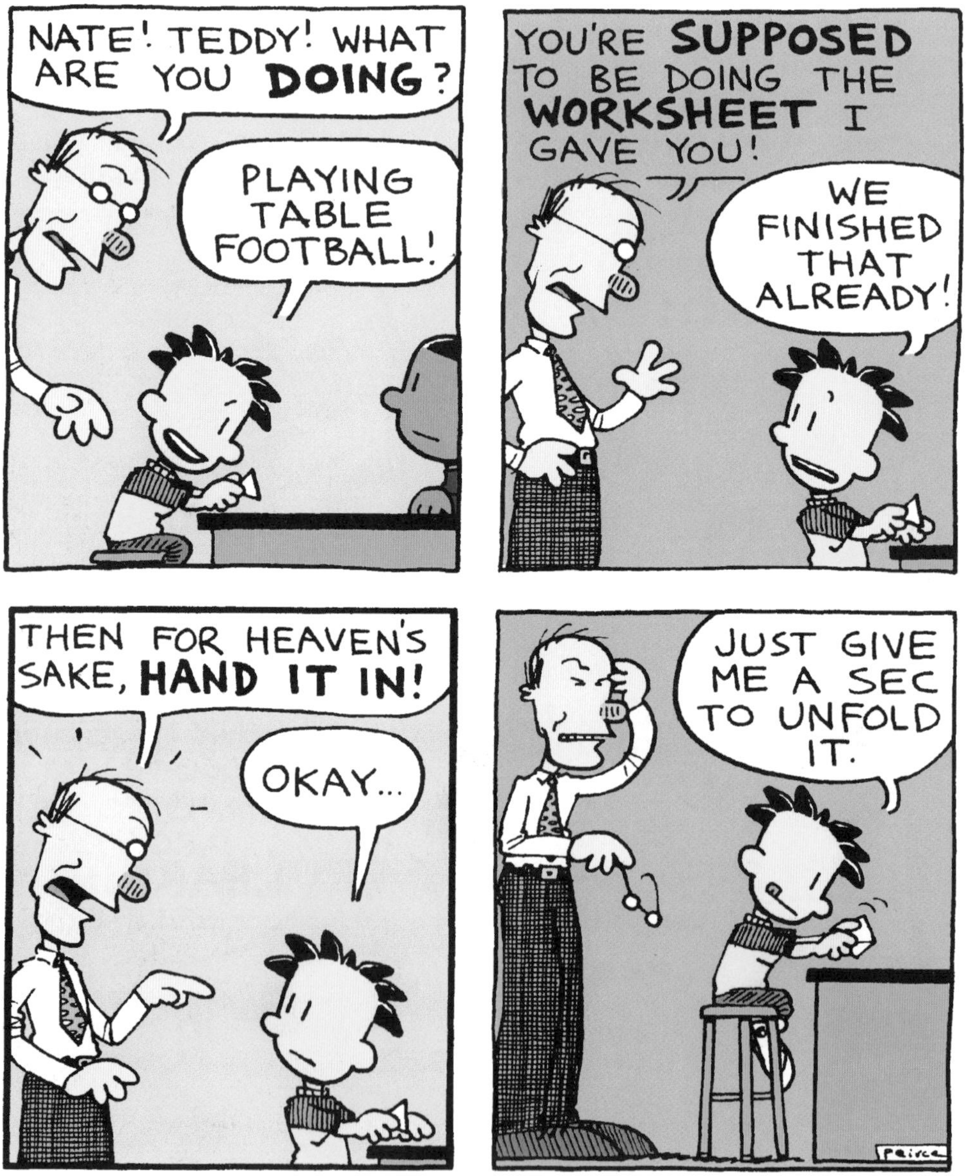
NATE! TEDDY! WHAT ARE YOU **DOING**?
PLAYING TABLE FOOTBALL!
YOU'RE **SUPPOSED** TO BE DOING THE **WORKSHEET** I GAVE YOU!
WE FINISHED THAT ALREADY!
THEN FOR HEAVEN'S SAKE, **HAND IT IN!**
OKAY...
JUST GIVE ME A SEC TO UNFOLD IT.
PEIRCE

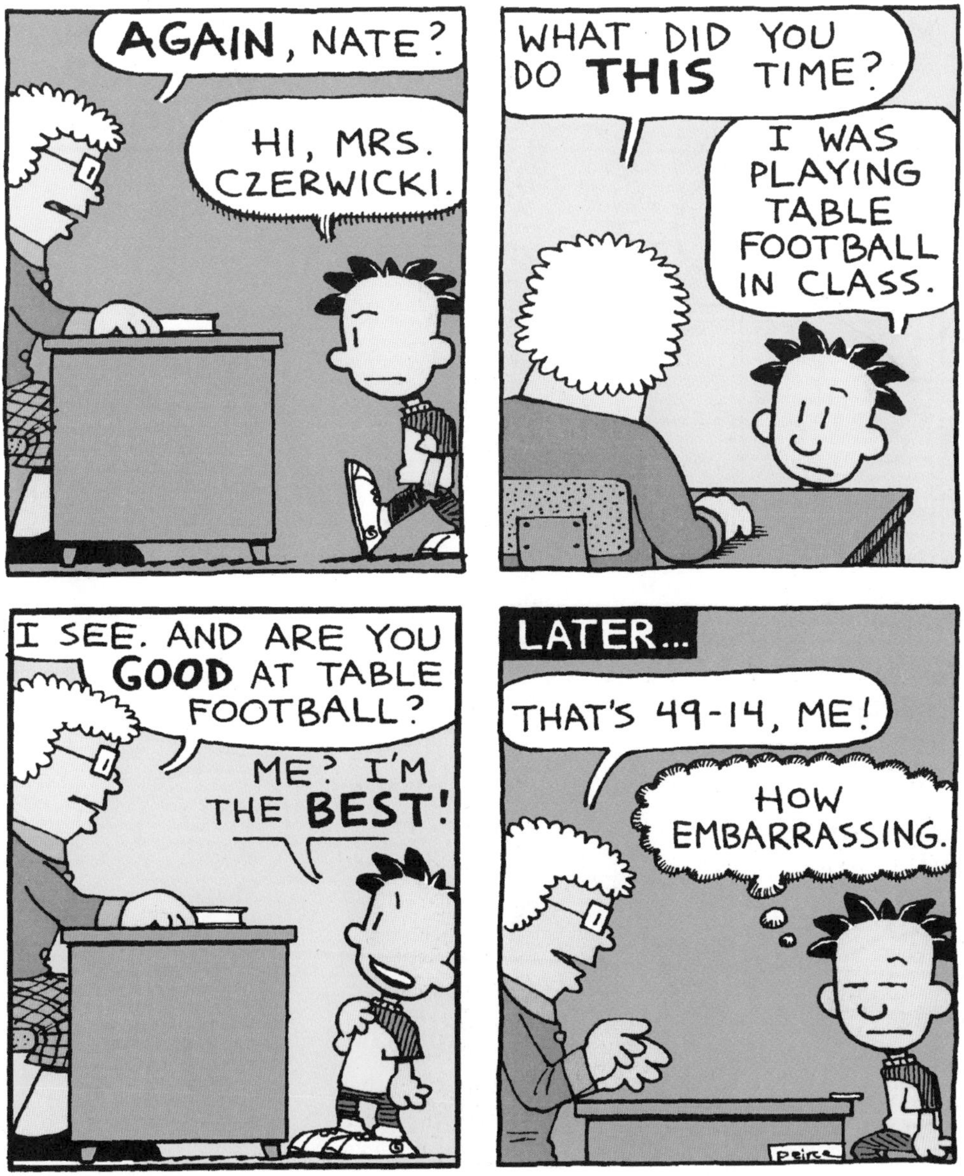
AGAIN, NATE?
HI, MRS. CZERWICKI.
WHAT DID YOU DO THIS TIME?
I WAS PLAYING TABLE FOOTBALL IN CLASS.
I SEE. AND ARE YOU GOOD AT TABLE FOOTBALL?
ME? I'M THE BEST!
LATER...
THAT'S 49-14, ME!
HOW EMBARRASSING.
peirce

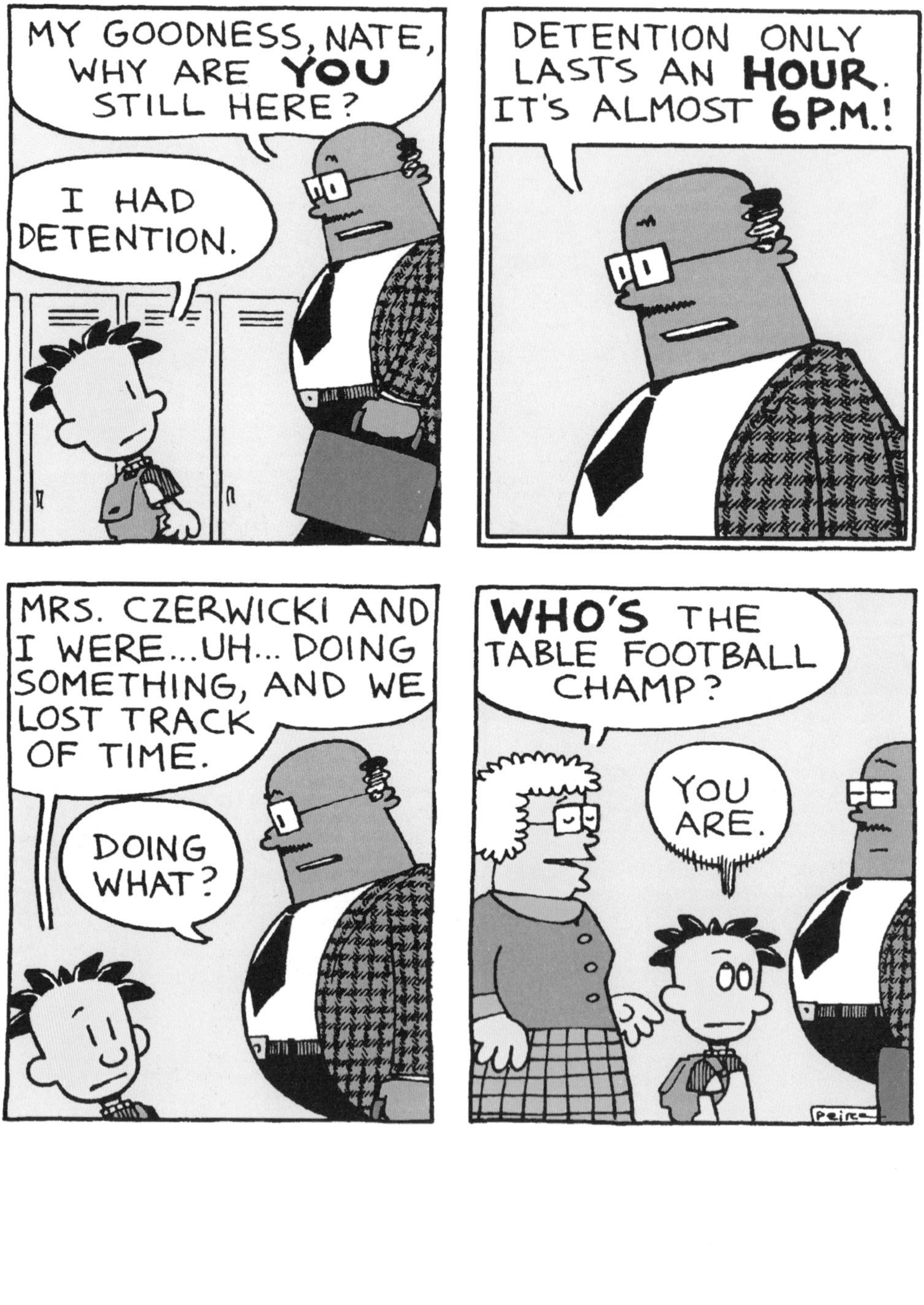
MY GOODNESS, NATE, WHY ARE YOU STILL HERE?
I HAD DETENTION.
DETENTION ONLY LASTS AN HOUR. IT'S ALMOST 6 P.M.!
MRS. CZERWICKI AND I WERE... UH... DOING SOMETHING, AND WE LOST TRACK OF TIME.
DOING WHAT?
WHO'S THE TABLE FOOTBALL CHAMP?
YOU ARE.

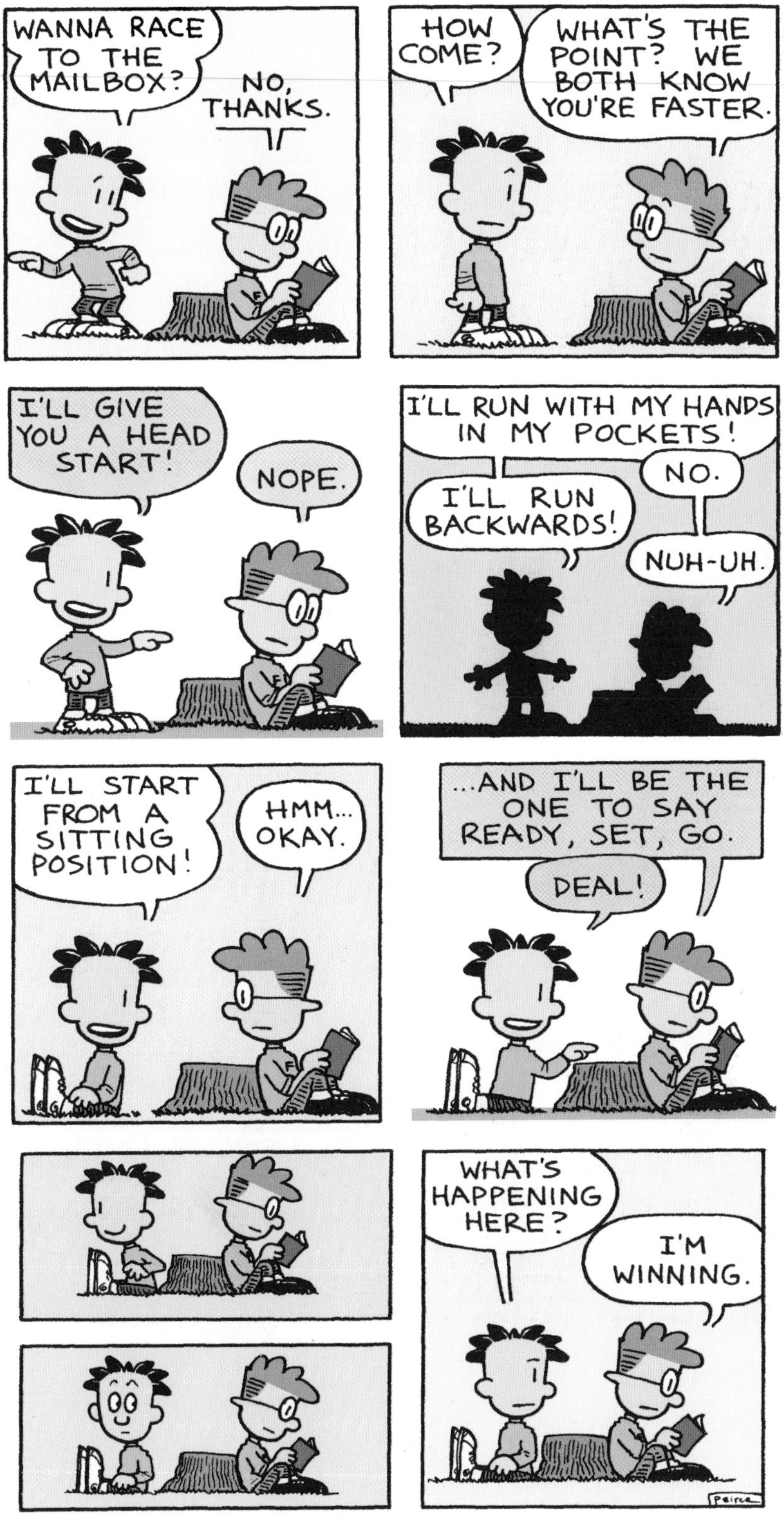
WANNA RACE TO THE MAILBOX?
NO, THANKS.
HOW COME?
WHAT'S THE POINT? WE BOTH KNOW YOU'RE FASTER.
I'LL GIVE YOU A HEAD START!
NOPE.
I'LL RUN WITH MY HANDS IN MY POCKETS!
NO.
I'LL RUN BACKWARDS!
NUH-UH.
I'LL START FROM A SITTING POSITION!
HMM... OKAY.
...AND I'LL BE THE ONE TO SAY READY, SET, GO.
DEAL!
WHAT'S HAPPENING HERE?
I'M WINNING.
Peirce

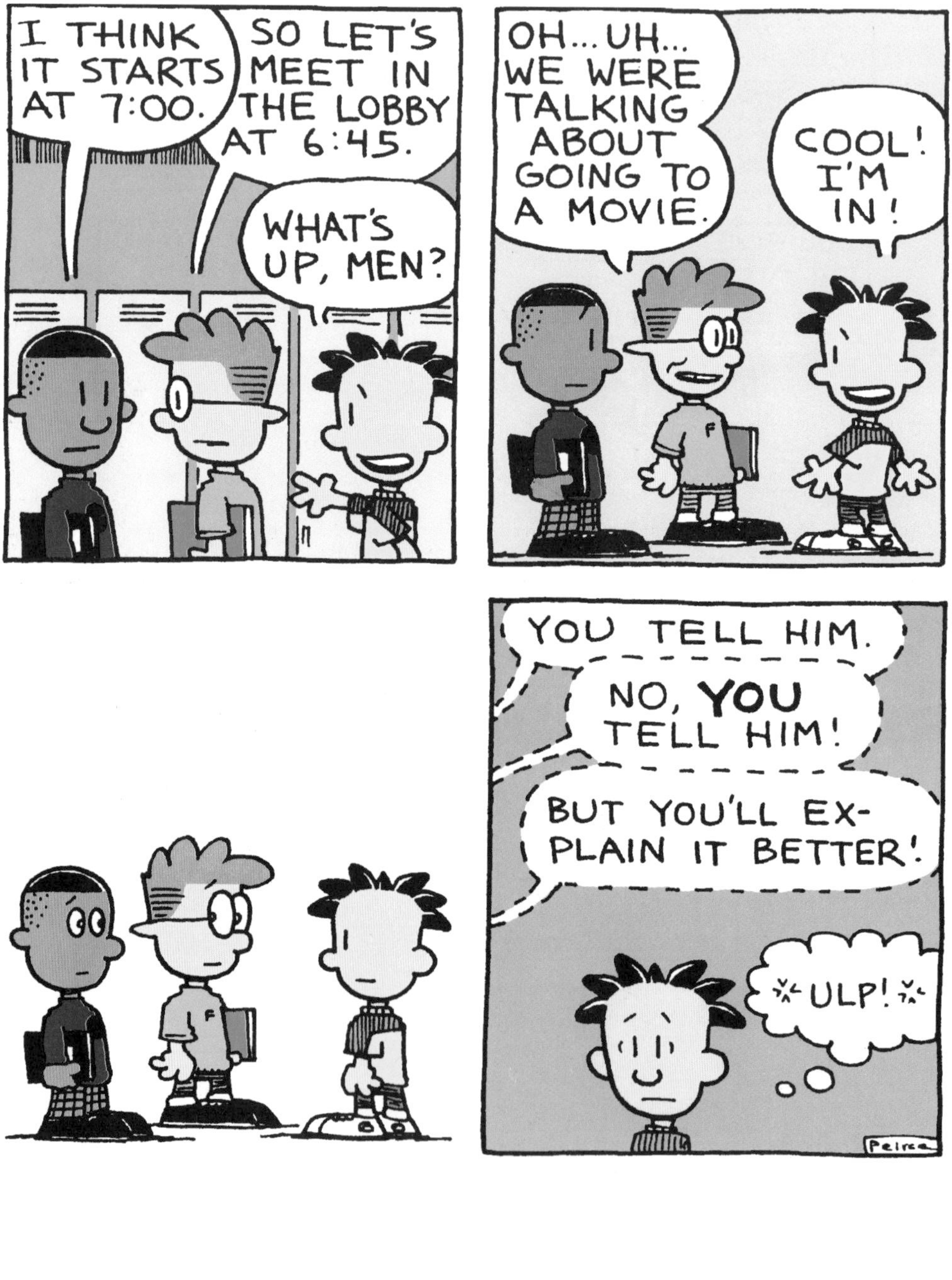
I THINK IT STARTS AT 7:00.
SO LET'S MEET IN THE LOBBY AT 6:45.
WHAT'S UP, MEN?
OH... UH... WE WERE TALKING ABOUT GOING TO A MOVIE.
COOL! I'M IN!
YOU TELL HIM.
NO, **YOU** TELL HIM!
BUT YOU'LL EX-PLAIN IT BETTER!
ULP!
Peirce

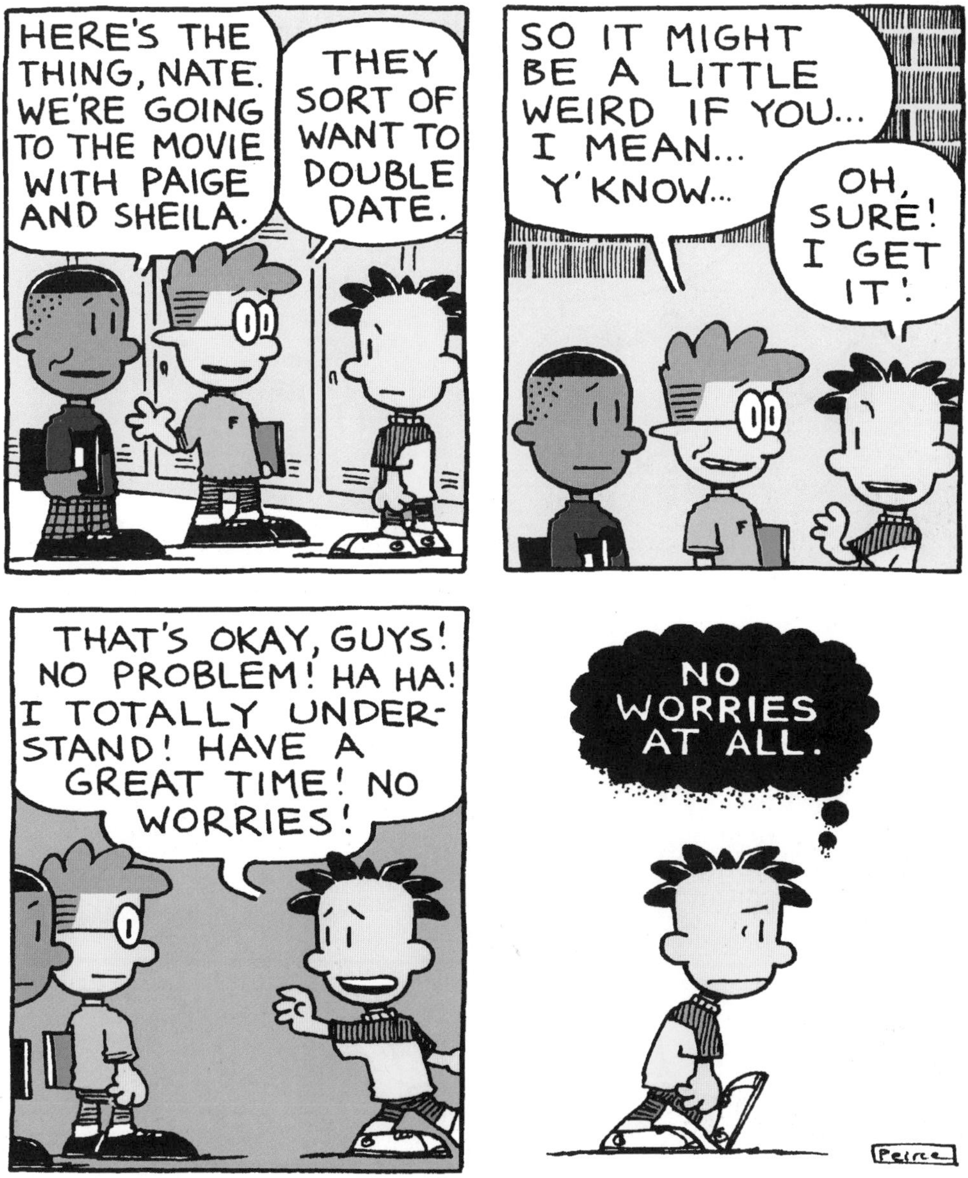
HERE'S THE THING, NATE. WE'RE GOING TO THE MOVIE WITH PAIGE AND SHEILA.
THEY SORT OF WANT TO DOUBLE DATE.
SO IT MIGHT BE A LITTLE WEIRD IF YOU... I MEAN... Y'KNOW...
OH, SURE! I GET IT!
THAT'S OKAY, GUYS! NO PROBLEM! HA HA! I TOTALLY UNDERSTAND! HAVE A GREAT TIME! NO WORRIES!
NO WORRIES AT ALL.
Peirce

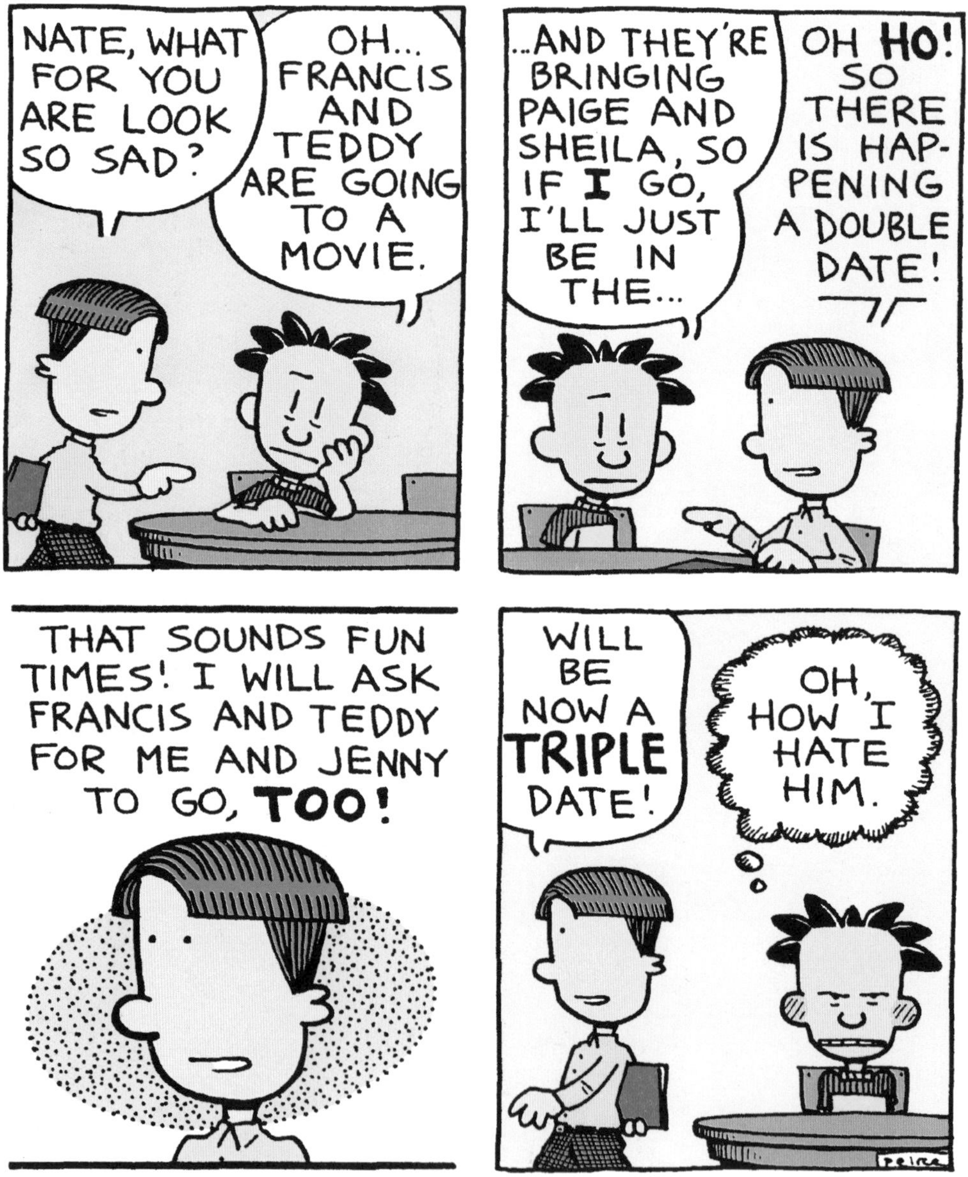
NATE, WHAT FOR YOU ARE LOOK SO SAD?
OH... FRANCIS AND TEDDY ARE GOING TO A MOVIE.
...AND THEY'RE BRINGING PAIGE AND SHEILA, SO IF **I** GO, I'LL JUST BE IN THE...
OH **HO**! SO THERE IS HAPPENING A DOUBLE DATE!
THAT SOUNDS FUN TIMES! I WILL ASK FRANCIS AND TEDDY FOR ME AND JENNY TO GO, **TOO**!
WILL BE NOW A **TRIPLE** DATE!
OH, HOW I HATE HIM.
PEIRCE

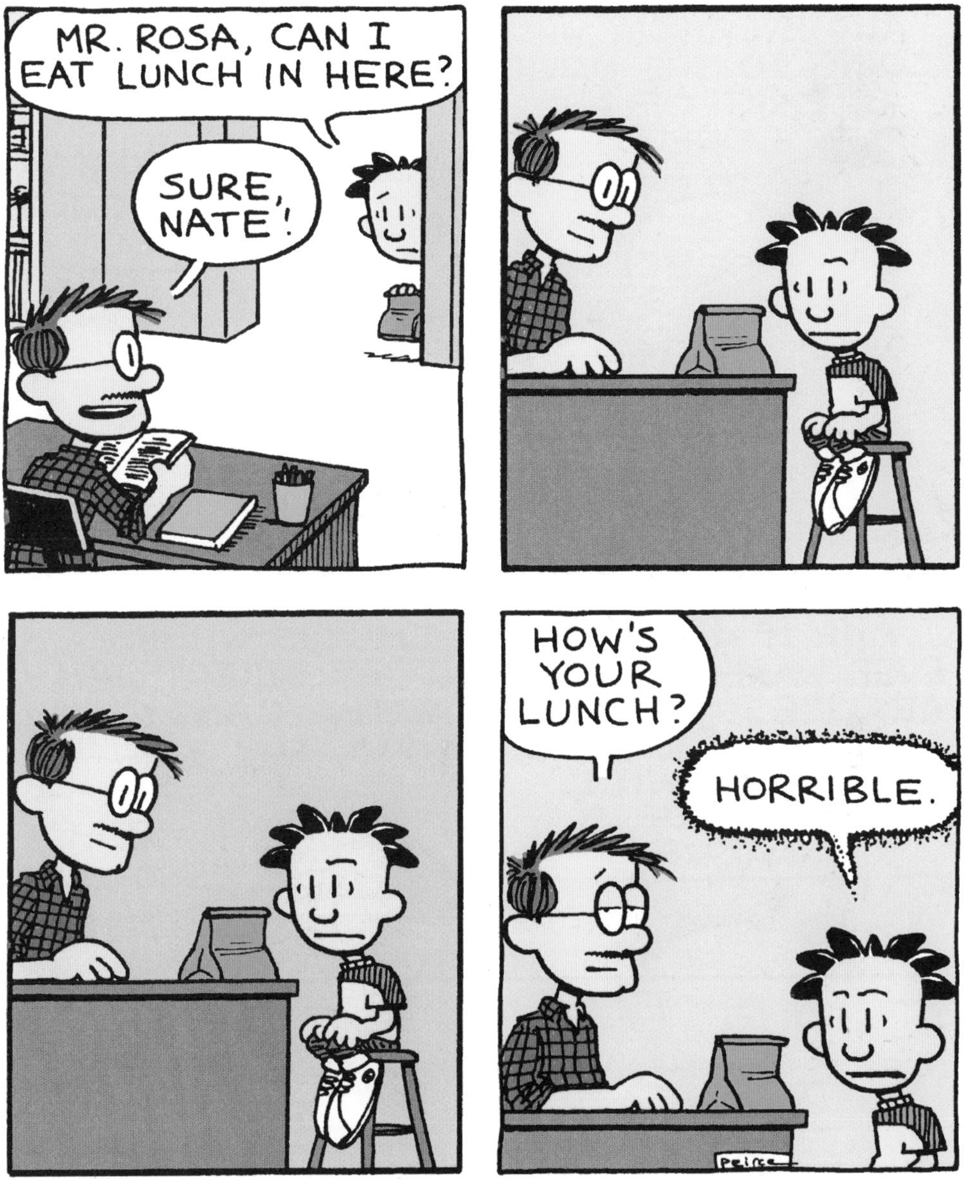
MR. ROSA, CAN I EAT LUNCH IN HERE?
SURE, NATE!
HOW'S YOUR LUNCH?
HORRIBLE.
PEIRCE

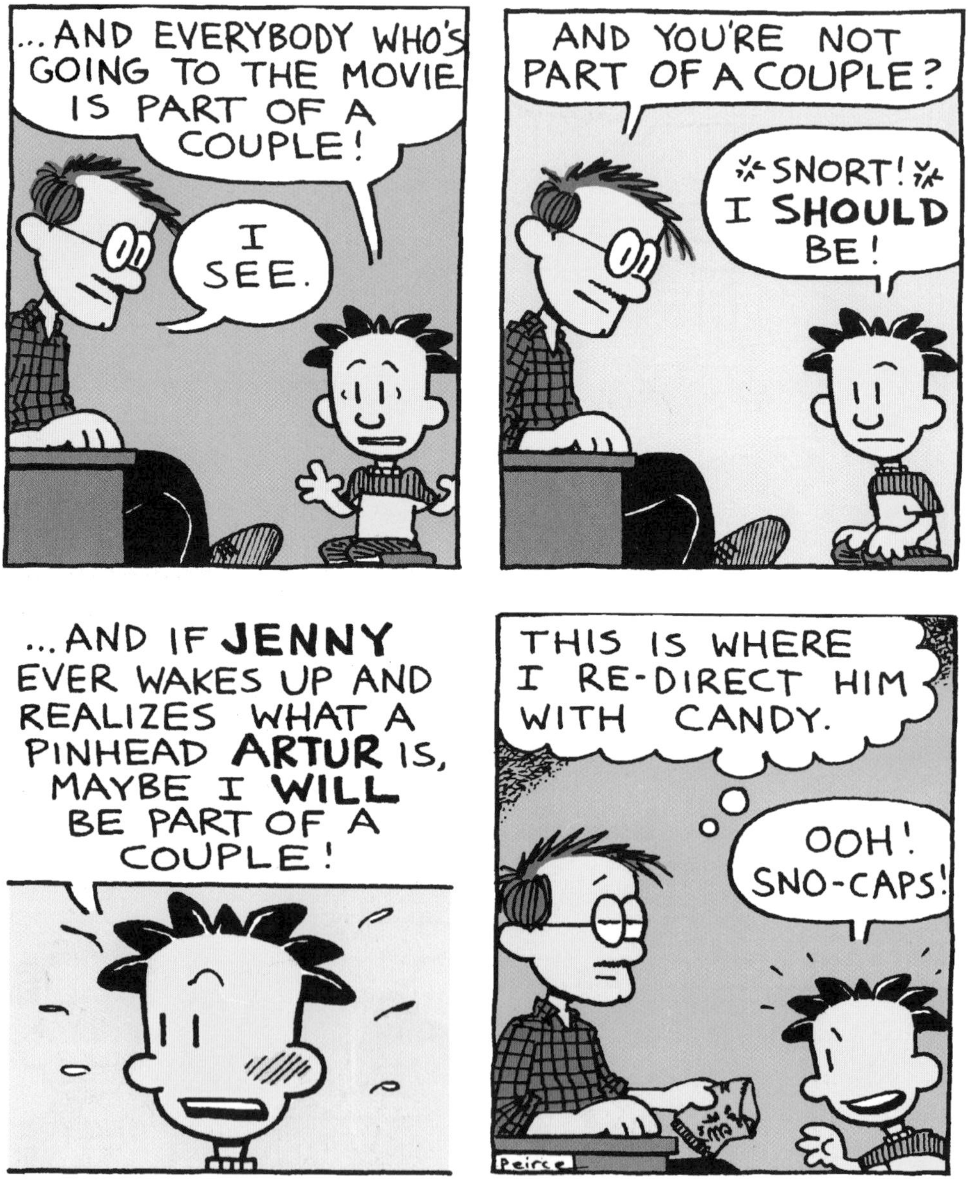
...AND EVERYBODY WHO'S GOING TO THE MOVIE IS PART OF A COUPLE!
I SEE.
AND YOU'RE NOT PART OF A COUPLE?
SNORT! I **SHOULD** BE!
...AND IF **JENNY** EVER WAKES UP AND REALIZES WHAT A PINHEAD **ARTUR** IS, MAYBE I **WILL** BE PART OF A COUPLE!
THIS IS WHERE I RE-DIRECT HIM WITH CANDY.
OOH! SNO-CAPS!
Peirce

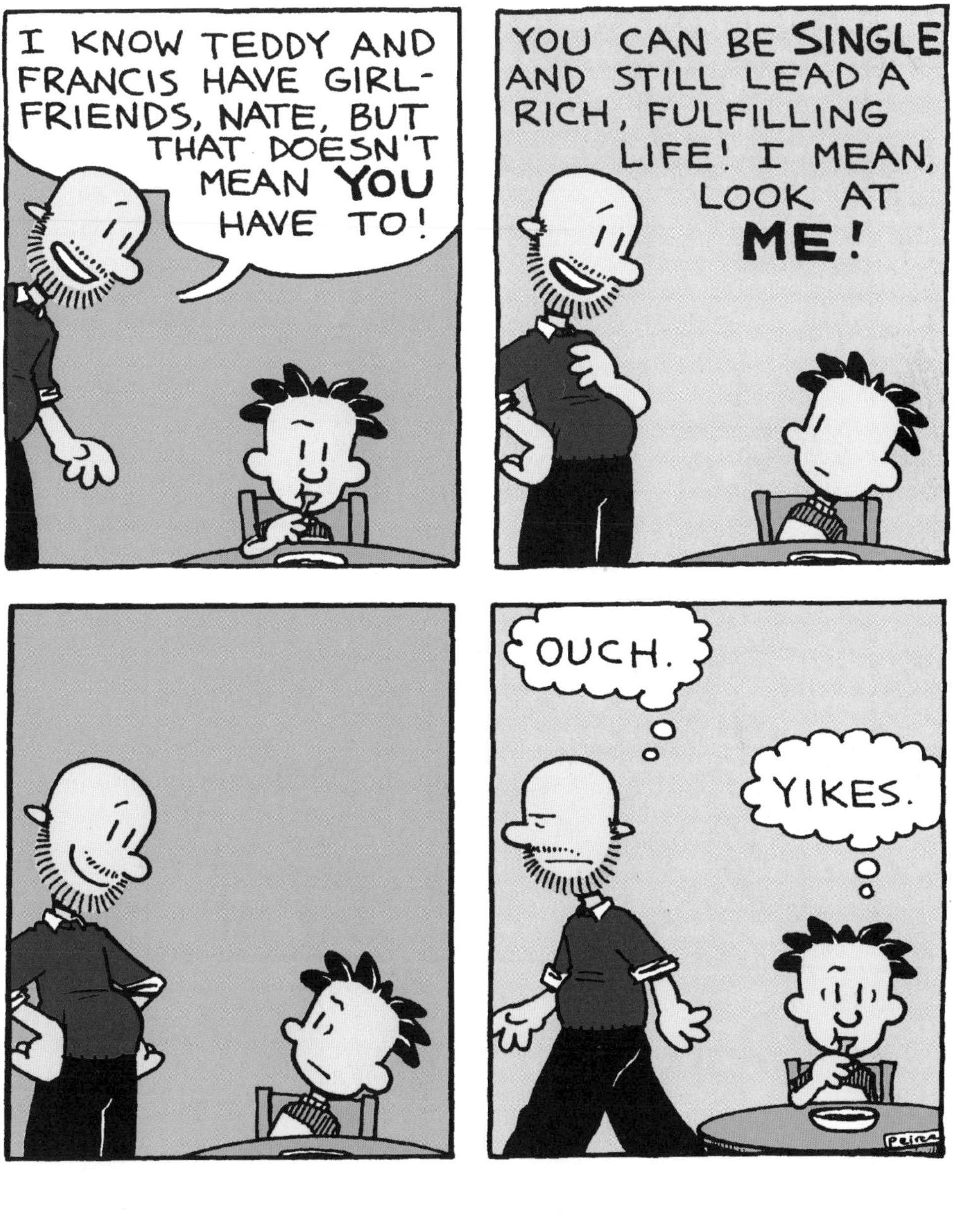
I KNOW TEDDY AND FRANCIS HAVE GIRL-FRIENDS, NATE, BUT THAT DOESN'T MEAN YOU HAVE TO!
YOU CAN BE SINGLE AND STILL LEAD A RICH, FULFILLING LIFE! I MEAN, LOOK AT ME!
OUCH.
YIKES.

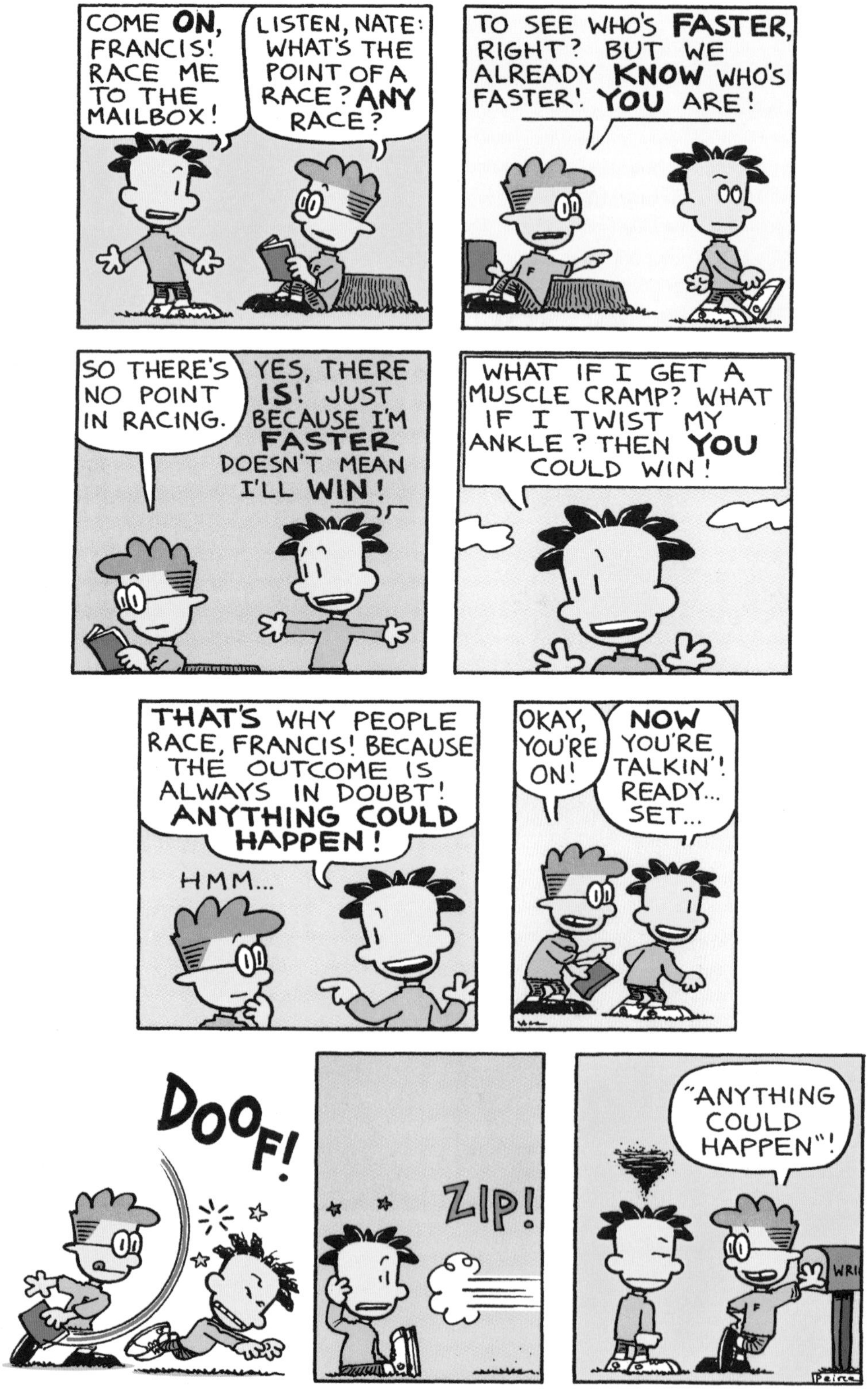
COME ON, FRANCIS! RACE ME TO THE MAILBOX!
LISTEN, NATE: WHAT'S THE POINT OF A RACE? ANY RACE?
TO SEE WHO'S FASTER, RIGHT? BUT WE ALREADY KNOW WHO'S FASTER! YOU ARE!
SO THERE'S NO POINT IN RACING.
YES, THERE IS! JUST BECAUSE I'M FASTER DOESN'T MEAN I'LL WIN!
WHAT IF I GET A MUSCLE CRAMP? WHAT IF I TWIST MY ANKLE? THEN YOU COULD WIN!
THAT'S WHY PEOPLE RACE, FRANCIS! BECAUSE THE OUTCOME IS ALWAYS IN DOUBT! ANYTHING COULD HAPPEN!
HMM...
OKAY, YOU'RE ON!
NOW YOU'RE TALKIN'! READY... SET...
DOOF!
ZIP!
"ANYTHING COULD HAPPEN"!

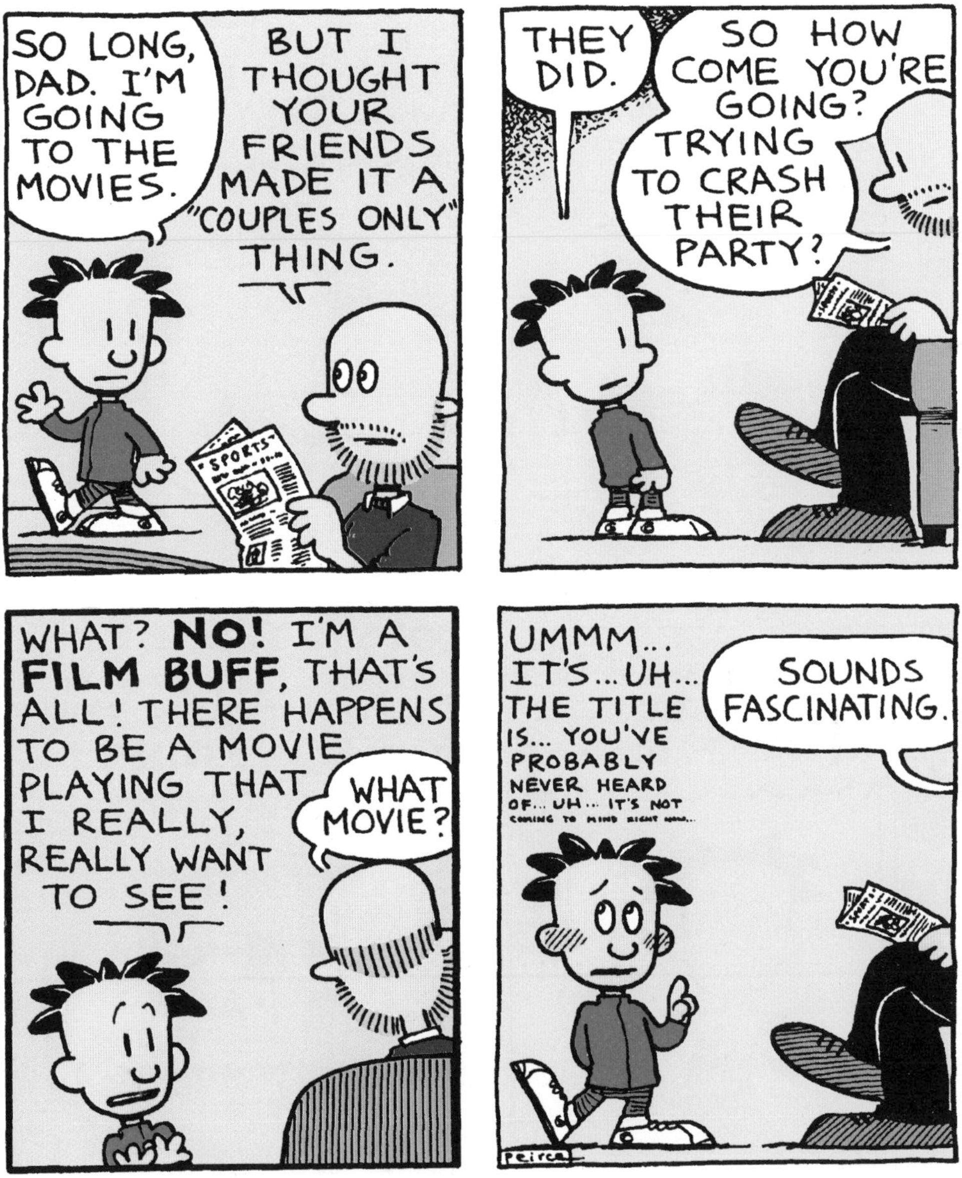

SO LONG, DAD. I'M GOING TO THE MOVIES.
BUT I THOUGHT YOUR FRIENDS MADE IT A "COUPLES ONLY" THING.
SPORTS
THEY DID.
SO HOW COME YOU'RE GOING? TRYING TO CRASH THEIR PARTY?
WHAT? **NO!** I'M A **FILM BUFF**, THAT'S ALL! THERE HAPPENS TO BE A MOVIE PLAYING THAT I REALLY, REALLY WANT TO SEE!
WHAT MOVIE?
UMMM... IT'S... UH... THE TITLE IS... YOU'VE PROBABLY NEVER HEARD OF... UH... IT'S NOT COMING TO MIND RIGHT NOW...
SOUNDS FASCINATING.
peirce

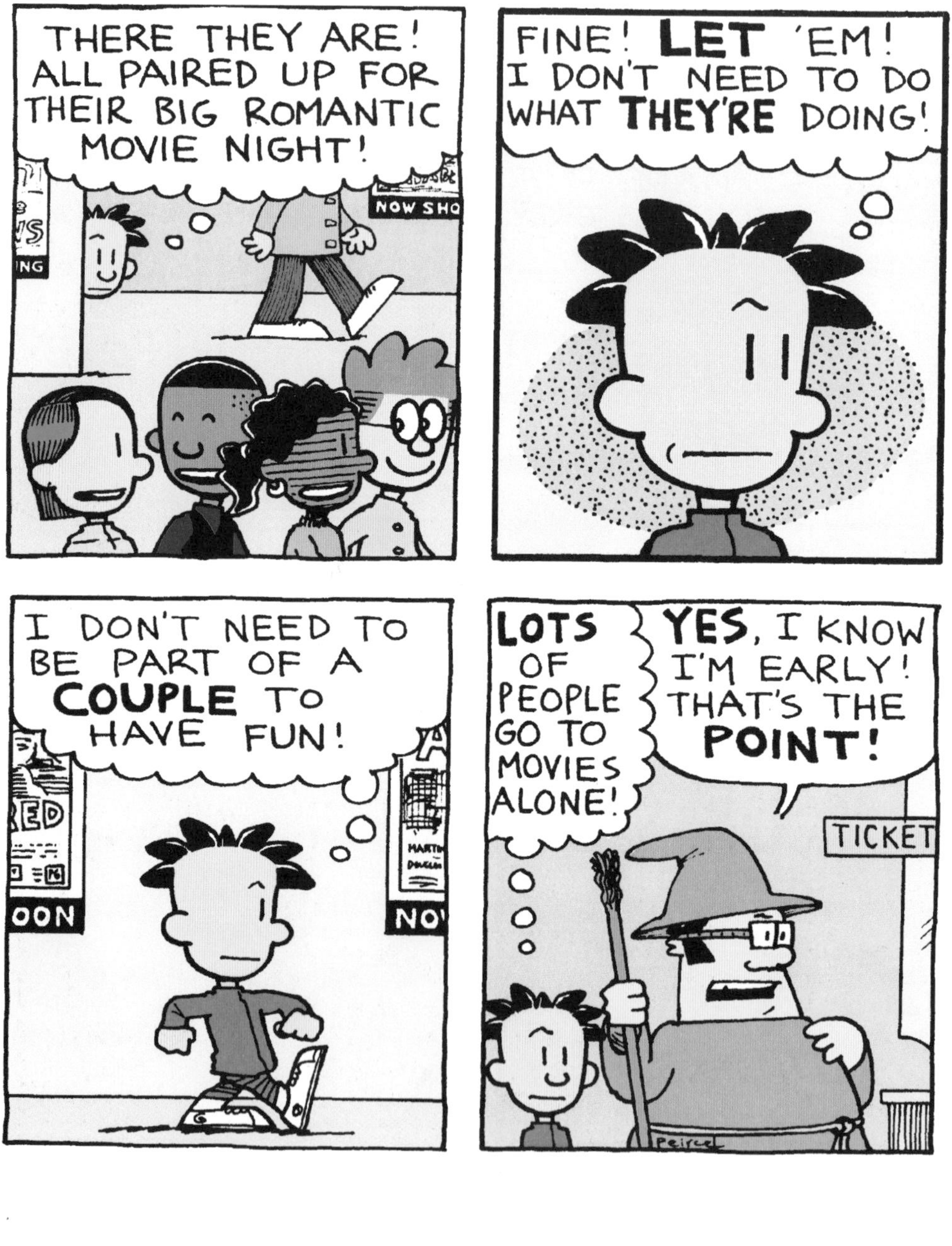
THERE THEY ARE! ALL PAIRED UP FOR THEIR BIG ROMANTIC MOVIE NIGHT!
NOW SHO
FINE! LET 'EM! I DON'T NEED TO DO WHAT THEY'RE DOING!
I DON'T NEED TO BE PART OF A COUPLE TO HAVE FUN!
OON
LOTS OF PEOPLE GO TO MOVIES ALONE!
YES, I KNOW I'M EARLY! THAT'S THE POINT!
TICKET
Peirce

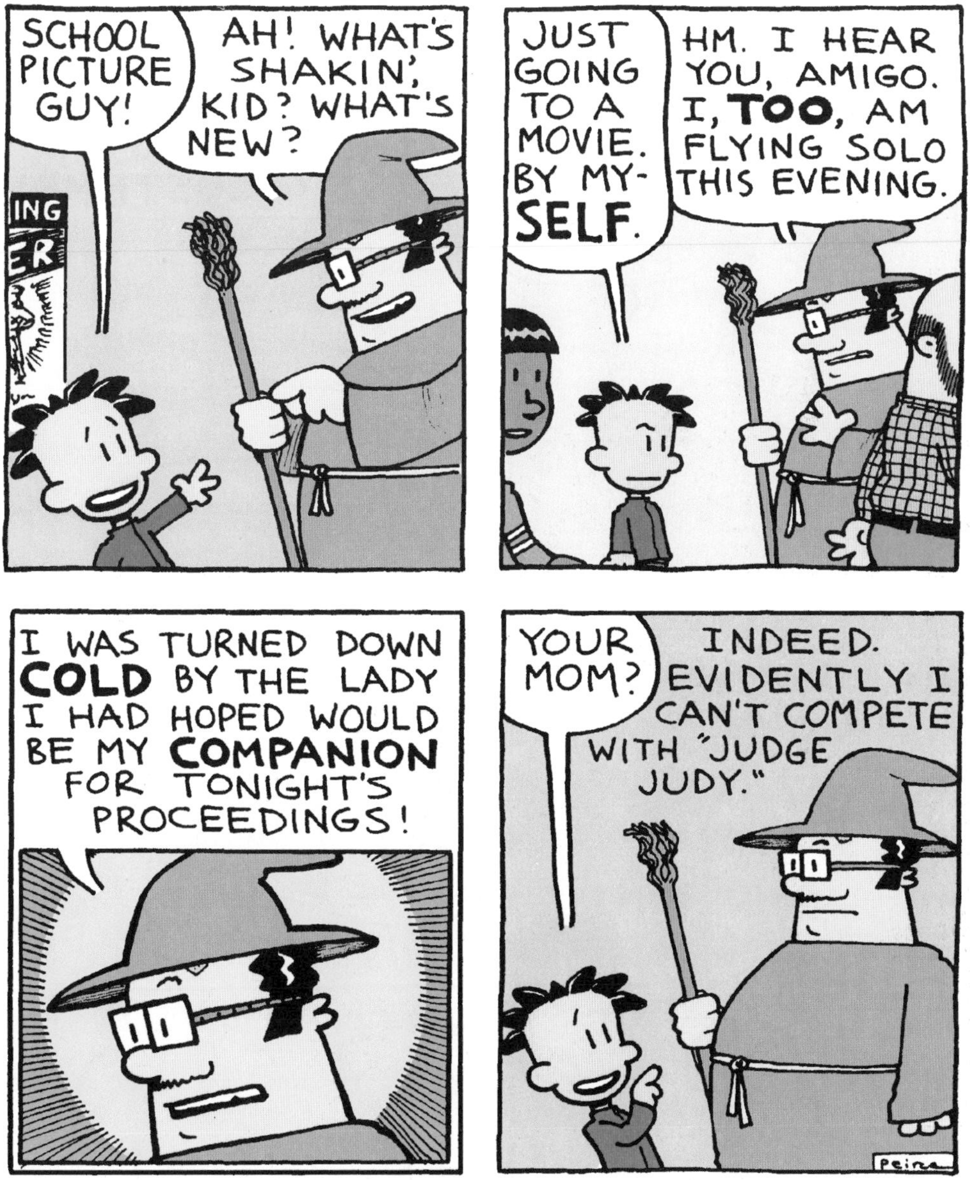
SCHOOL PICTURE GUY!
AH! WHAT'S SHAKIN', KID? WHAT'S NEW?
JUST GOING TO A MOVIE. BY MY-**SELF**.
HM. I HEAR YOU, AMIGO. I, **TOO**, AM FLYING SOLO THIS EVENING.
I WAS TURNED DOWN **COLD** BY THE LADY I HAD HOPED WOULD BE MY **COMPANION** FOR TONIGHT'S PROCEEDINGS!
YOUR MOM?
INDEED. EVIDENTLY I CAN'T COMPETE WITH "JUDGE JUDY."

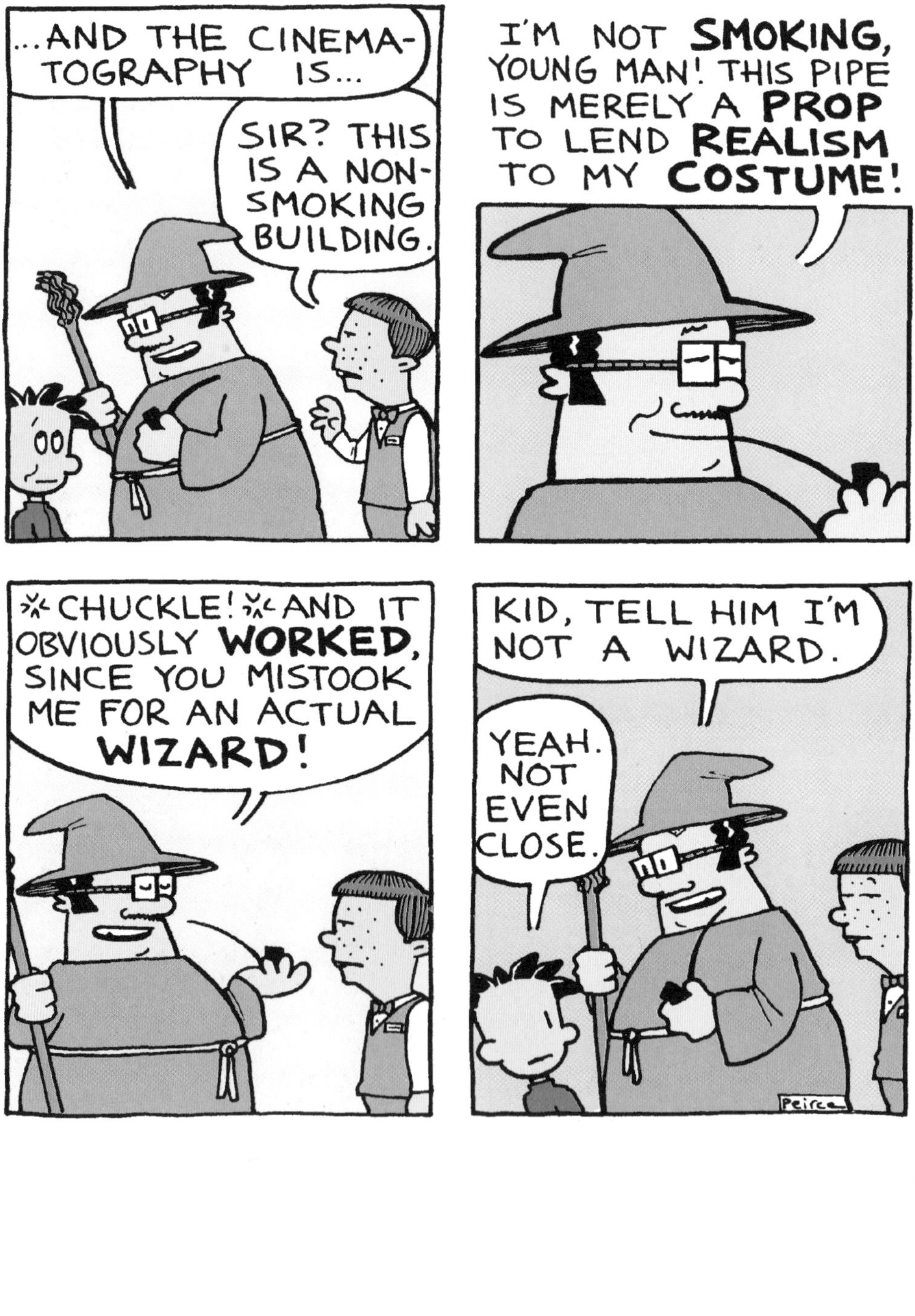
...AND THE CINEMATOGRAPHY IS...
SIR? THIS IS A NON-SMOKING BUILDING.
I'M NOT **SMOKING**, YOUNG MAN! THIS PIPE IS MERELY A **PROP** TO LEND **REALISM** TO MY **COSTUME**!
CHUCKLE! AND IT OBVIOUSLY **WORKED**, SINCE YOU MISTOOK ME FOR AN ACTUAL **WIZARD**!
KID, TELL HIM I'M NOT A WIZARD.
YEAH. NOT EVEN CLOSE.
Peirce

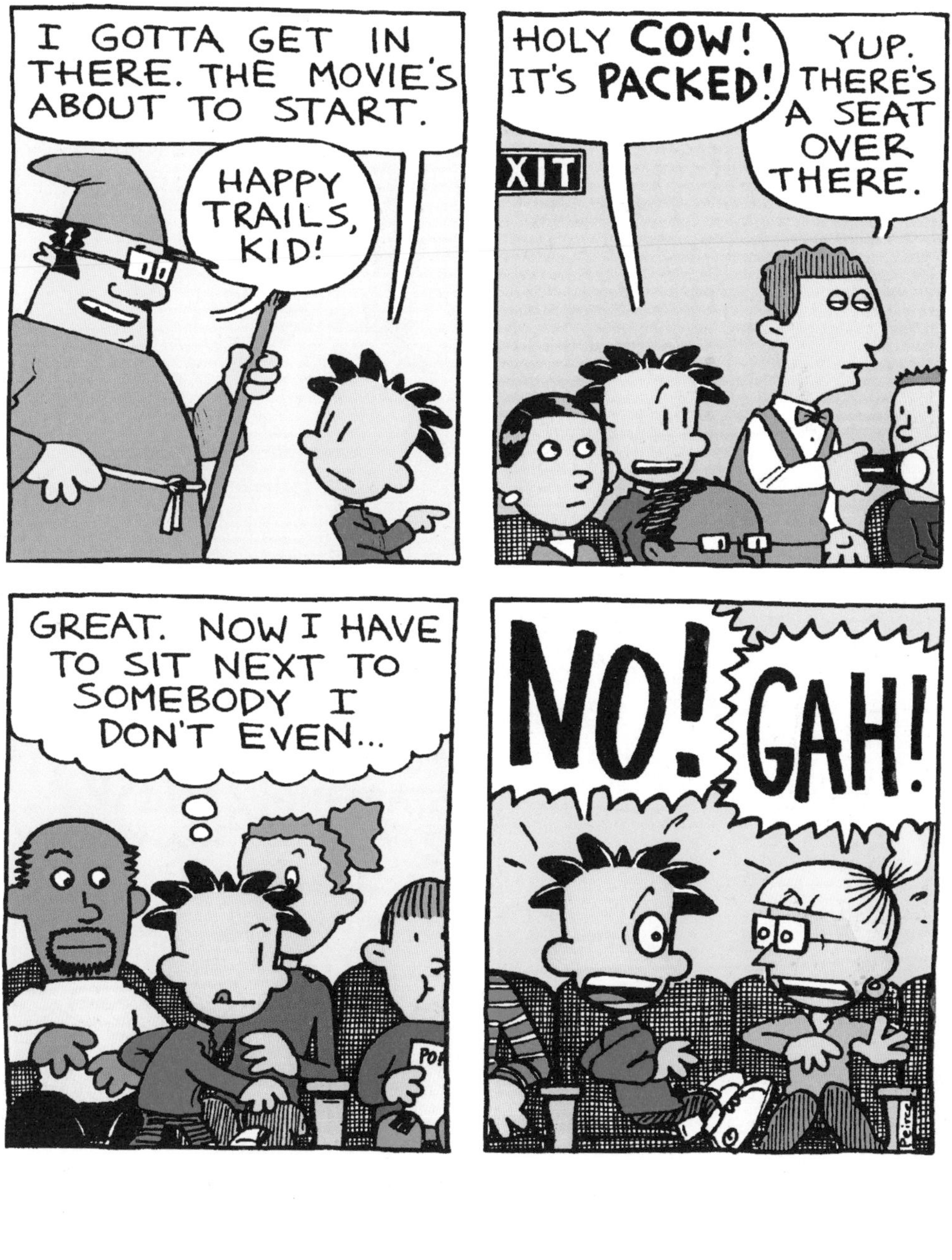
I GOTTA GET IN THERE. THE MOVIE'S ABOUT TO START.
HAPPY TRAILS, KID!
HOLY COW! IT'S PACKED!
XIT
YUP. THERE'S A SEAT OVER THERE.
GREAT. NOW I HAVE TO SIT NEXT TO SOMEBODY I DON'T EVEN...
POP
NO!
GAH!
Peirce

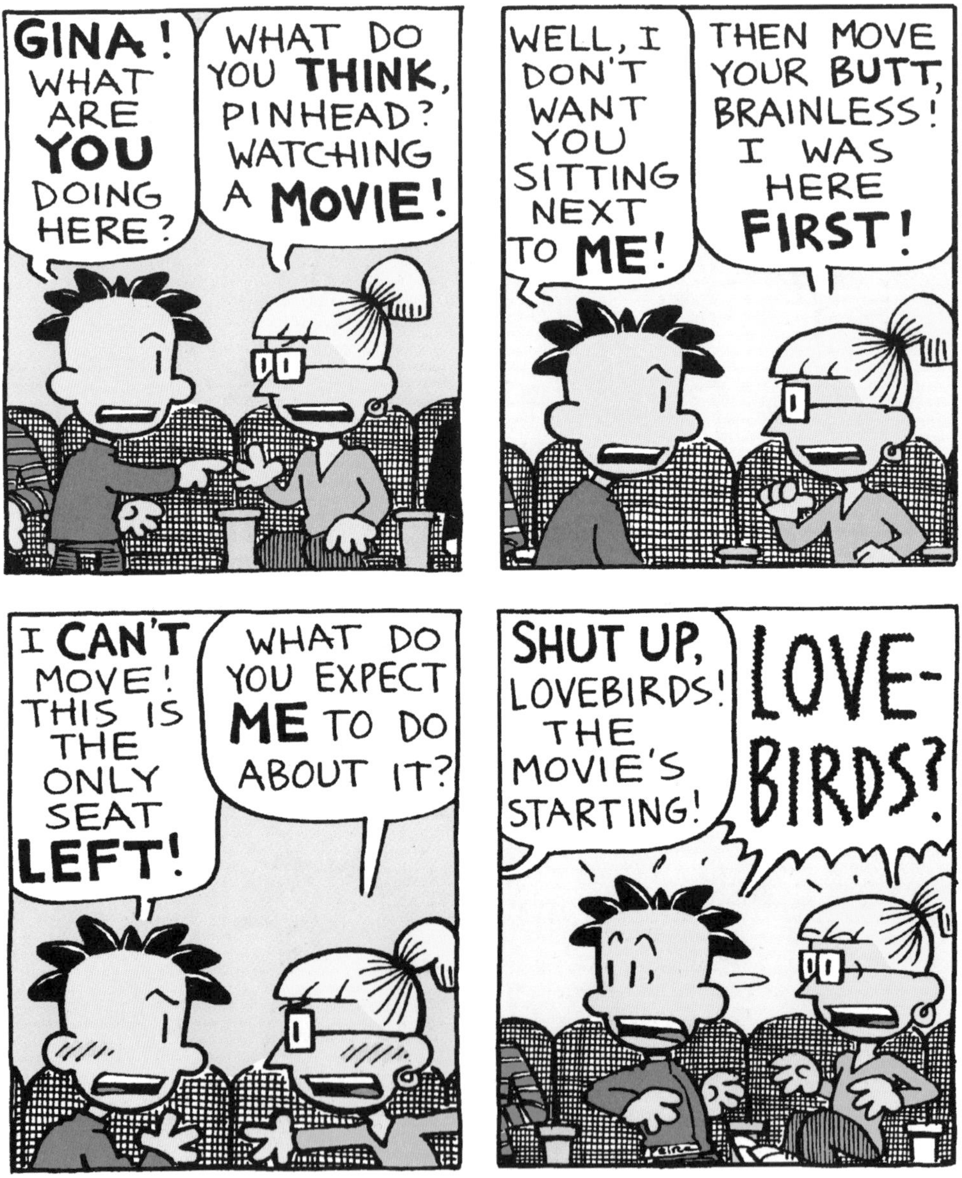
GINA! WHAT ARE YOU DOING HERE?
WHAT DO YOU THINK, PINHEAD? WATCHING A MOVIE!
WELL, I DON'T WANT YOU SITTING NEXT TO ME!
THEN MOVE YOUR BUTT, BRAINLESS! I WAS HERE FIRST!
I CAN'T MOVE! THIS IS THE ONLY SEAT LEFT!
WHAT DO YOU EXPECT ME TO DO ABOUT IT?
SHUT UP, LOVEBIRDS! THE MOVIE'S STARTING!
LOVE-BIRDS?

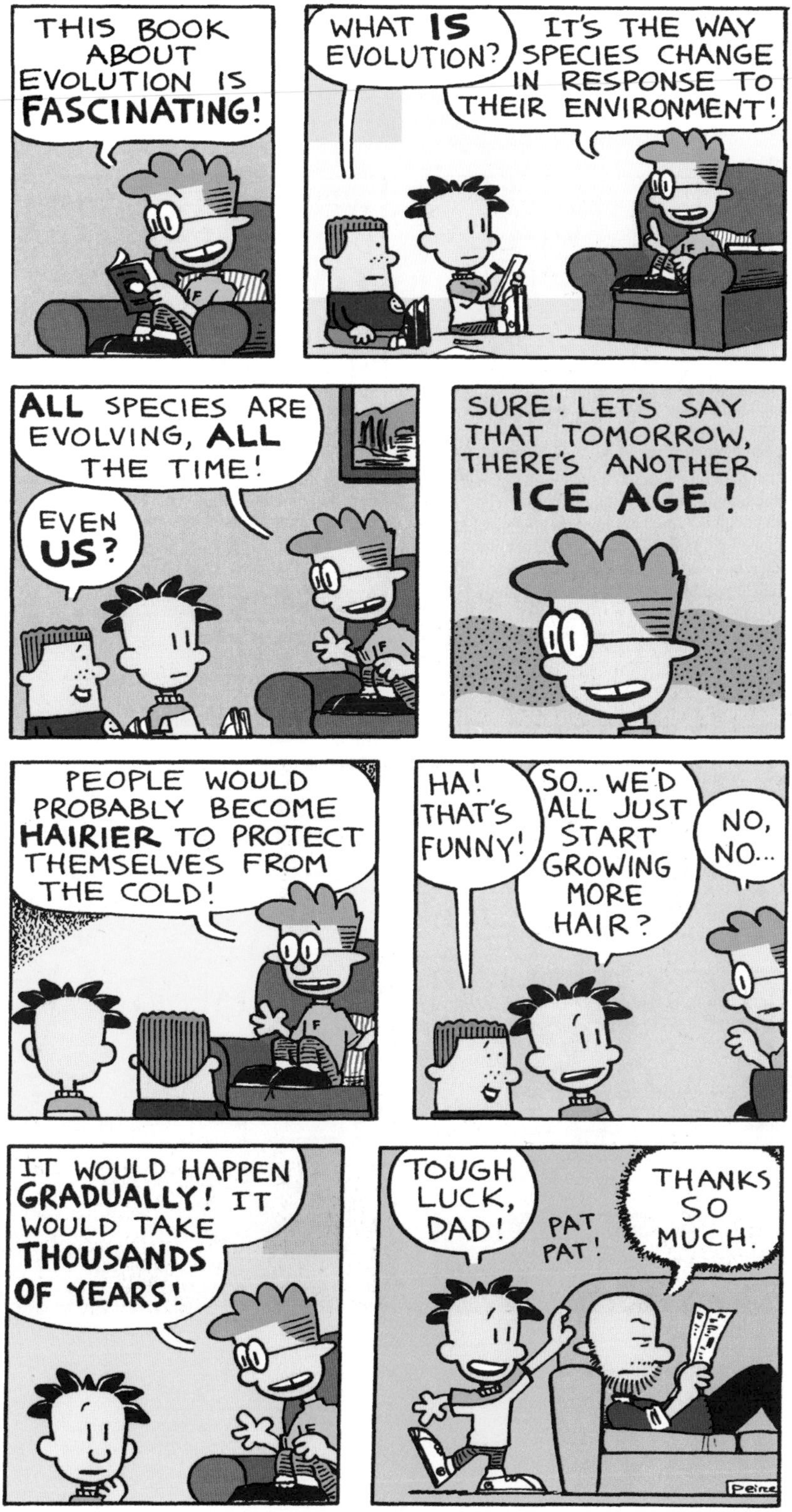
THIS BOOK ABOUT EVOLUTION IS FASCINATING!
WHAT IS EVOLUTION?
IT'S THE WAY SPECIES CHANGE IN RESPONSE TO THEIR ENVIRONMENT!
ALL SPECIES ARE EVOLVING, ALL THE TIME!
EVEN US?
SURE! LET'S SAY THAT TOMORROW, THERE'S ANOTHER ICE AGE!
PEOPLE WOULD PROBABLY BECOME HAIRIER TO PROTECT THEMSELVES FROM THE COLD!
HA! THAT'S FUNNY!
SO... WE'D ALL JUST START GROWING MORE HAIR?
NO, NO...
IT WOULD HAPPEN GRADUALLY! IT WOULD TAKE THOUSANDS OF YEARS!
TOUGH LUCK, DAD!
PAT PAT!
THANKS SO MUCH.
Peirce

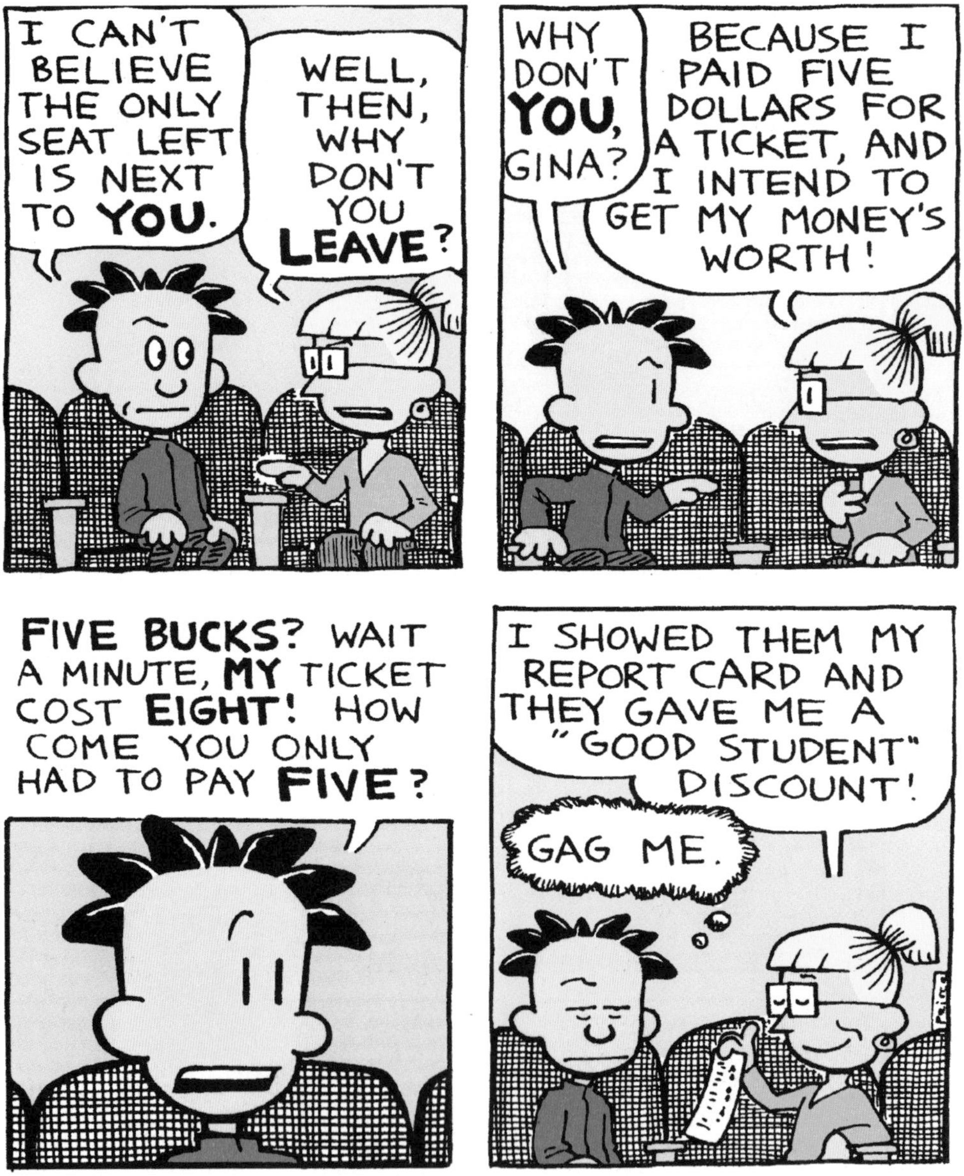
I CAN'T BELIEVE THE ONLY SEAT LEFT IS NEXT TO YOU.
WELL, THEN, WHY DON'T YOU LEAVE?
WHY DON'T YOU, GINA?
BECAUSE I PAID FIVE DOLLARS FOR A TICKET, AND I INTEND TO GET MY MONEY'S WORTH!
FIVE BUCKS? WAIT A MINUTE, MY TICKET COST EIGHT! HOW COME YOU ONLY HAD TO PAY FIVE?
I SHOWED THEM MY REPORT CARD AND THEY GAVE ME A "GOOD STUDENT" DISCOUNT!
GAG ME.

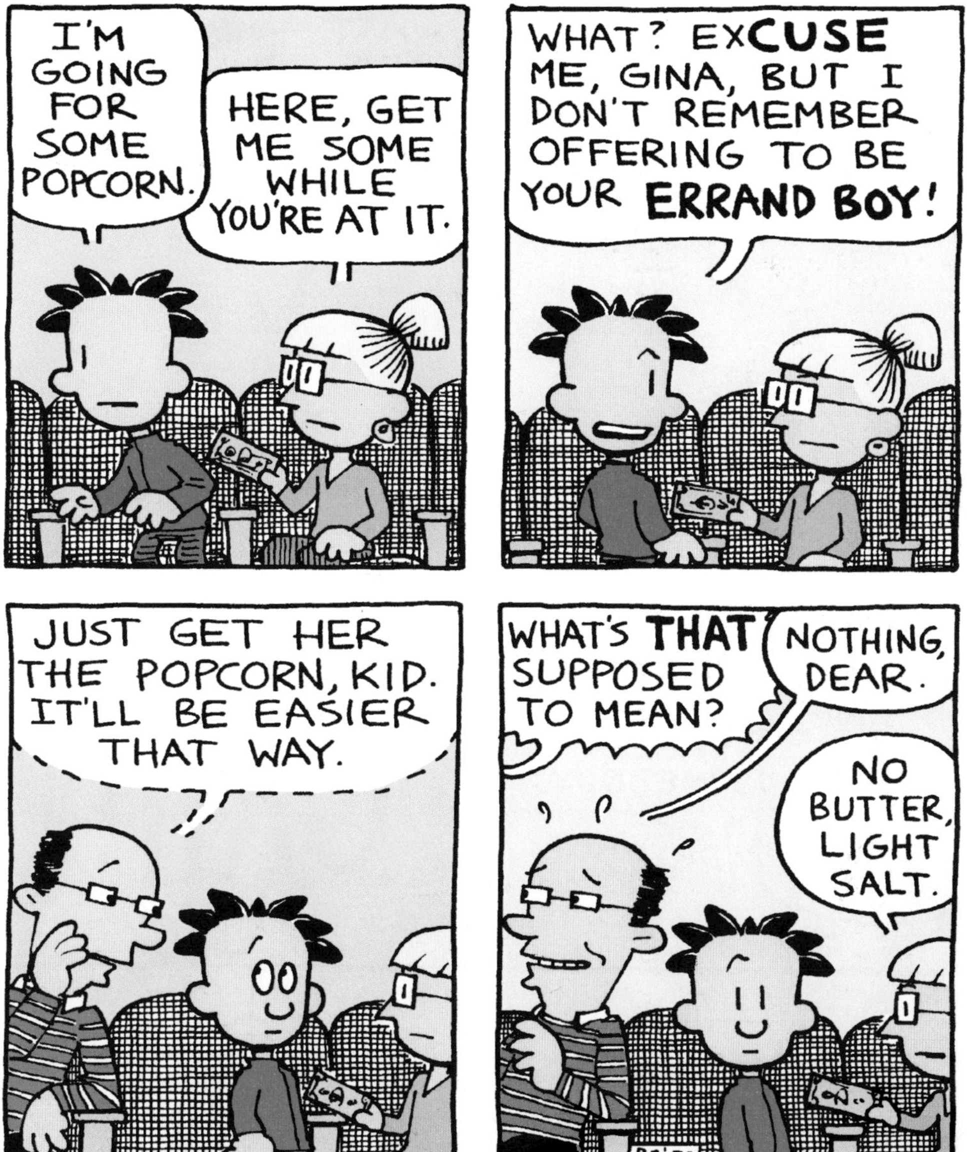
I'M GOING FOR SOME POPCORN.
HERE, GET ME SOME WHILE YOU'RE AT IT.
WHAT? EXCUSE ME, GINA, BUT I DON'T REMEMBER OFFERING TO BE YOUR ERRAND BOY!
JUST GET HER THE POPCORN, KID. IT'LL BE EASIER THAT WAY.
WHAT'S THAT SUPPOSED TO MEAN?
NOTHING, DEAR.
NO BUTTER, LIGHT SALT.
PEIRCE

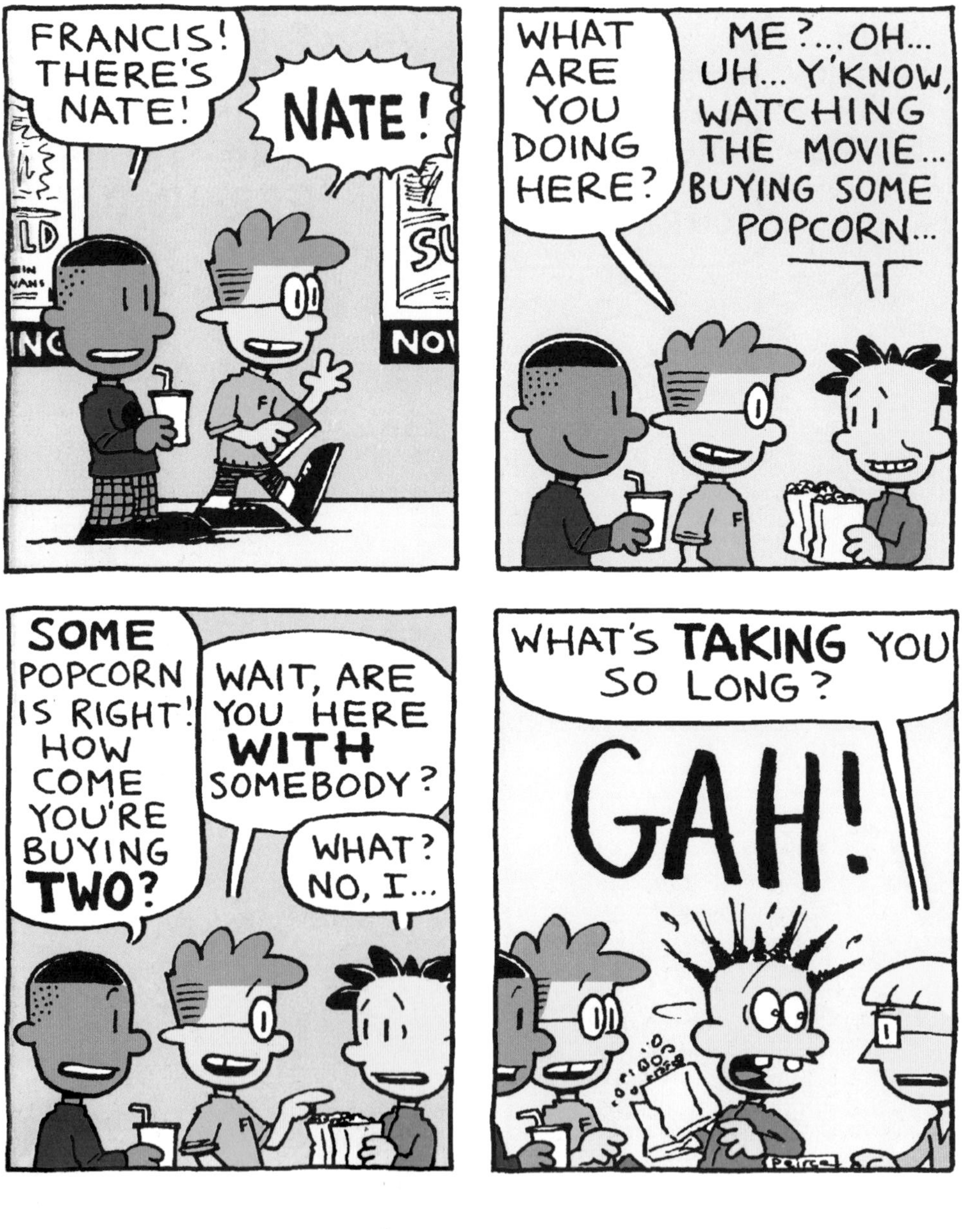
FRANCIS! THERE'S NATE!
NATE!
WHAT ARE YOU DOING HERE?
ME?... OH... UH... Y'KNOW, WATCHING THE MOVIE... BUYING SOME POPCORN...
SOME POPCORN IS RIGHT! HOW COME YOU'RE BUYING TWO?
WAIT, ARE YOU HERE WITH SOMEBODY?
WHAT? NO, I...
WHAT'S TAKING YOU SO LONG?
GAH!

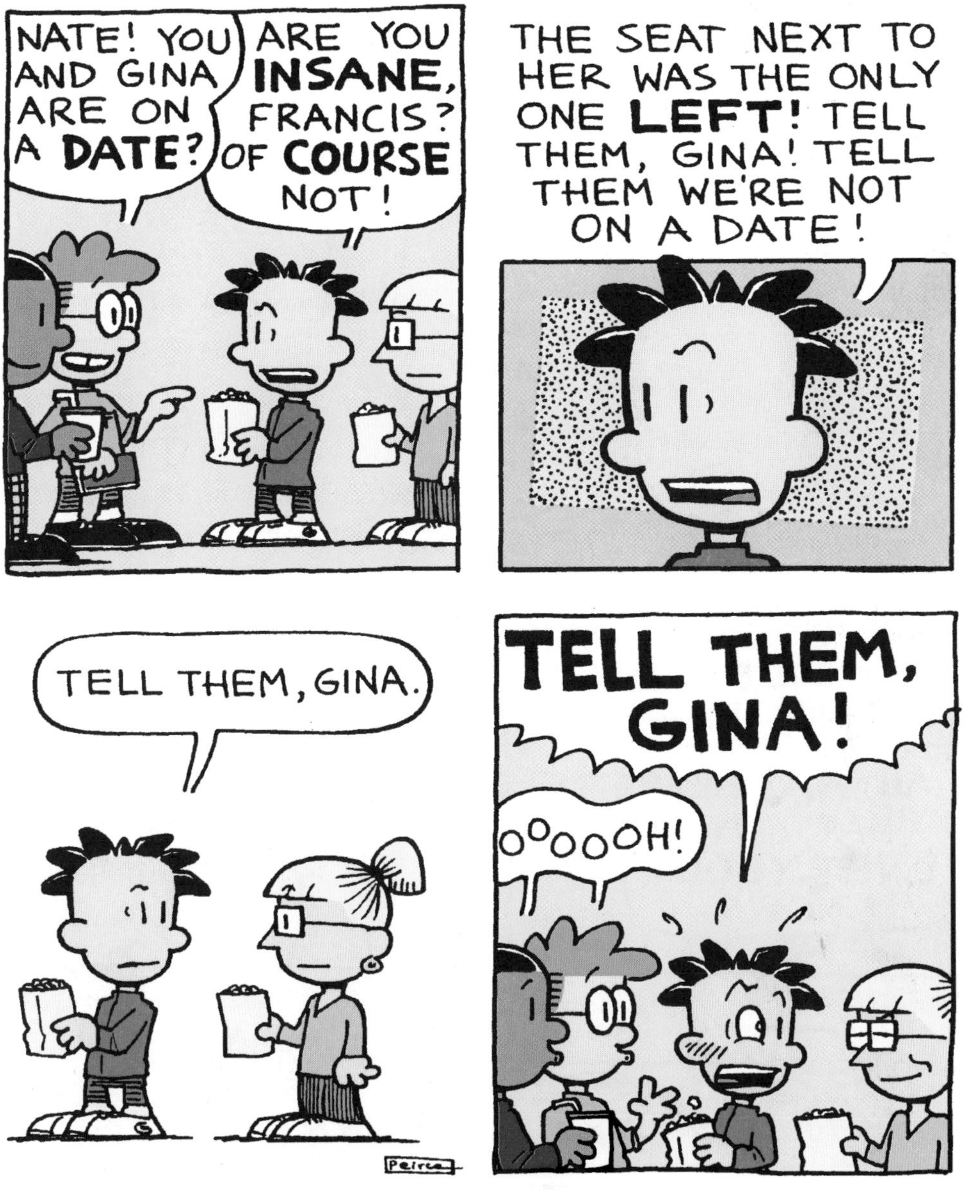
NATE! YOU AND GINA ARE ON A **DATE**?
ARE YOU **INSANE**, FRANCIS? OF **COURSE** NOT!
THE SEAT NEXT TO HER WAS THE ONLY ONE **LEFT!** TELL THEM, GINA! TELL THEM WE'RE NOT ON A DATE!
TELL THEM, GINA.
TELL THEM, GINA!
OOOOOH!
Peirce

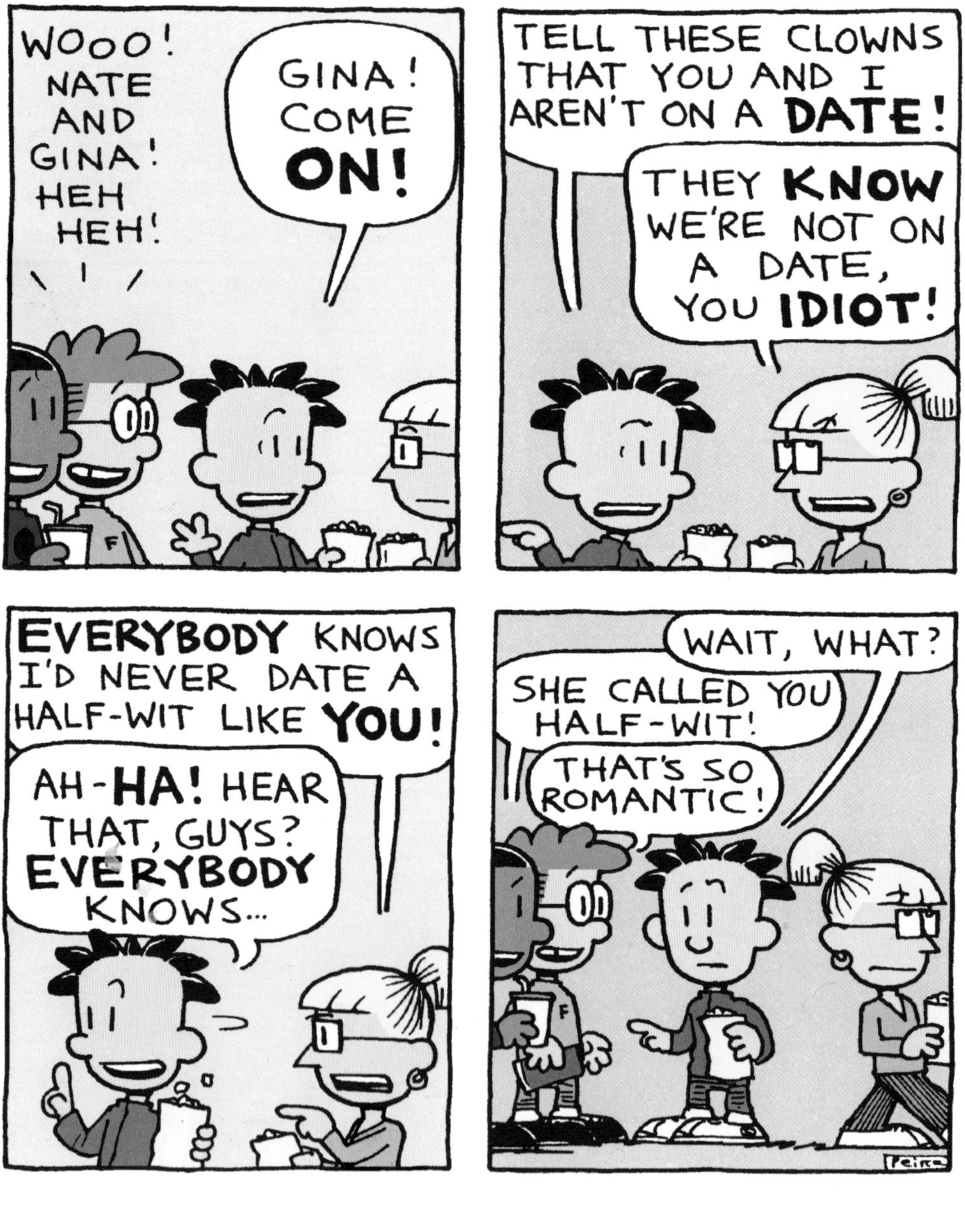
WOOO! NATE AND GINA! HEH HEH!
GINA! COME ON!
TELL THESE CLOWNS THAT YOU AND I AREN'T ON A DATE!
THEY KNOW WE'RE NOT ON A DATE, YOU IDIOT!
EVERYBODY KNOWS I'D NEVER DATE A HALF-WIT LIKE YOU!
AH-HA! HEAR THAT, GUYS? EVERYBODY KNOWS...
WAIT, WHAT?
SHE CALLED YOU HALF-WIT!
THAT'S SO ROMANTIC!

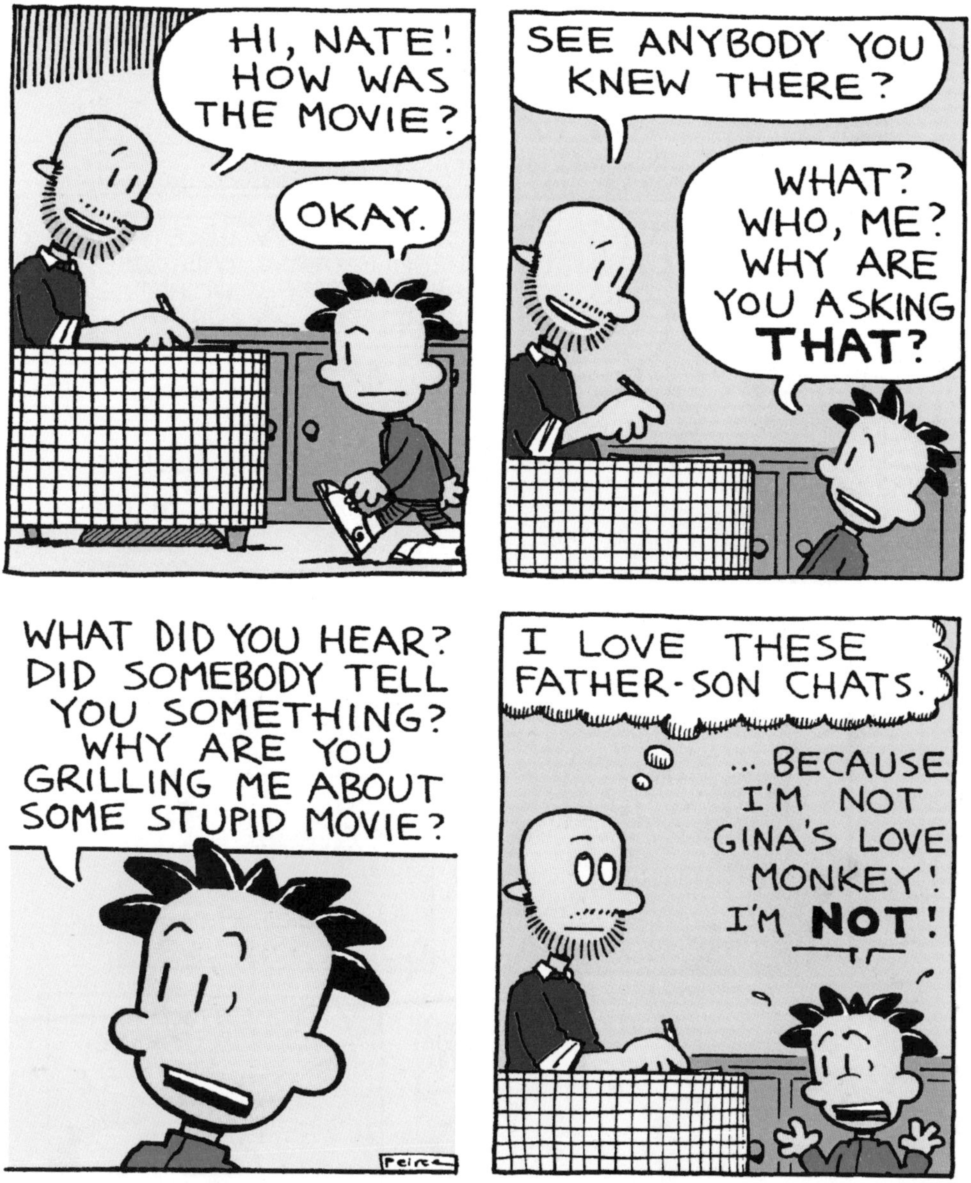
HI, NATE! HOW WAS THE MOVIE?
OKAY.
SEE ANYBODY YOU KNEW THERE?
WHAT? WHO, ME? WHY ARE YOU ASKING **THAT**?
WHAT DID YOU HEAR? DID SOMEBODY TELL YOU SOMETHING? WHY ARE YOU GRILLING ME ABOUT SOME STUPID MOVIE?
I LOVE THESE FATHER-SON CHATS.
... BECAUSE I'M NOT GINA'S LOVE MONKEY! I'M **NOT**!
PEIRCE

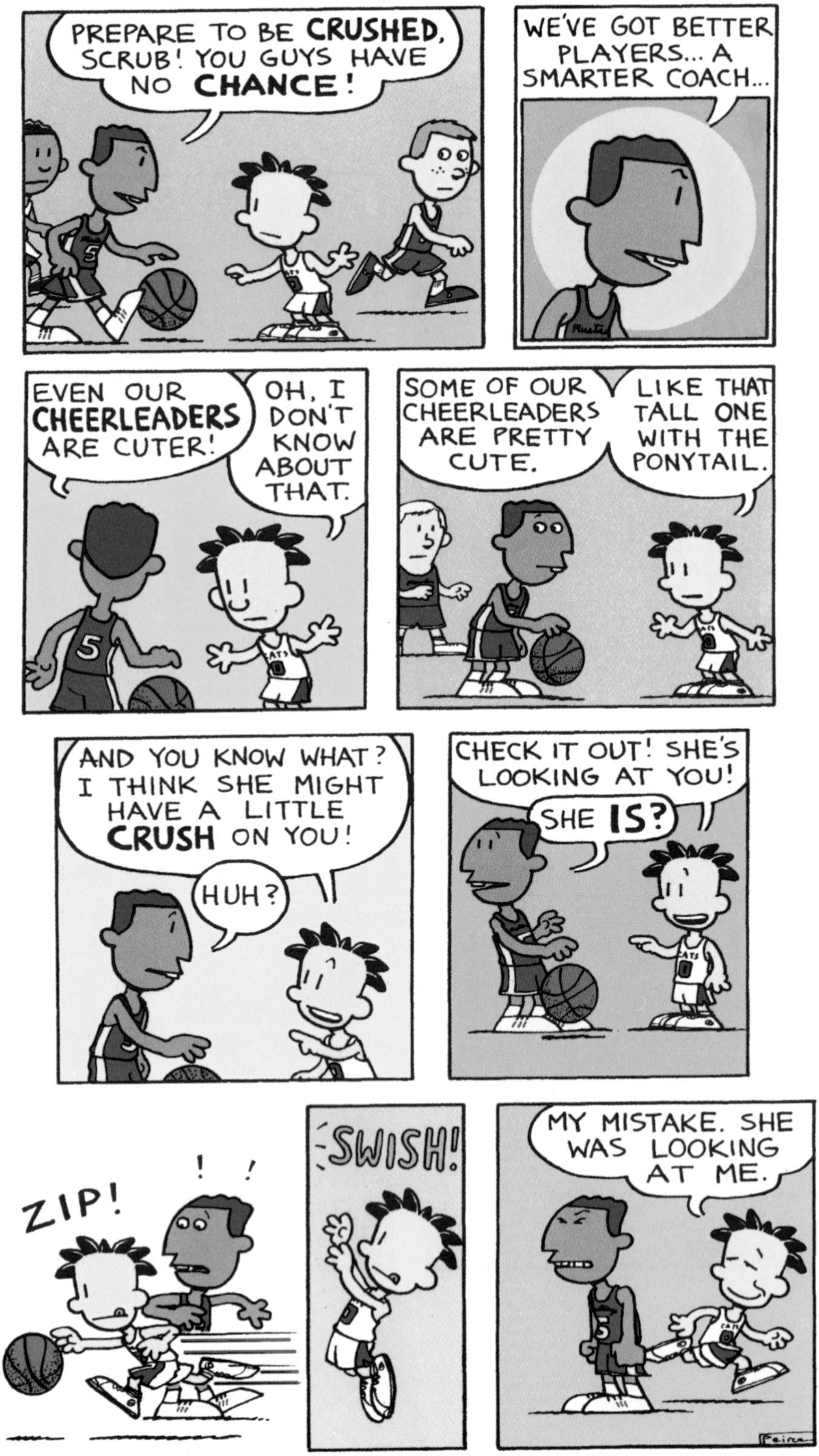
PREPARE TO BE CRUSHED, SCRUB! YOU GUYS HAVE NO CHANCE!
WE'VE GOT BETTER PLAYERS... A SMARTER COACH...
EVEN OUR CHEERLEADERS ARE CUTER!
OH, I DON'T KNOW ABOUT THAT.
SOME OF OUR CHEERLEADERS ARE PRETTY CUTE.
LIKE THAT TALL ONE WITH THE PONYTAIL.
AND YOU KNOW WHAT? I THINK SHE MIGHT HAVE A LITTLE CRUSH ON YOU!
HUH?
CHECK IT OUT! SHE'S LOOKING AT YOU!
SHE IS?
ZIP!
! !
SWISH!
MY MISTAKE. SHE WAS LOOKING AT ME.

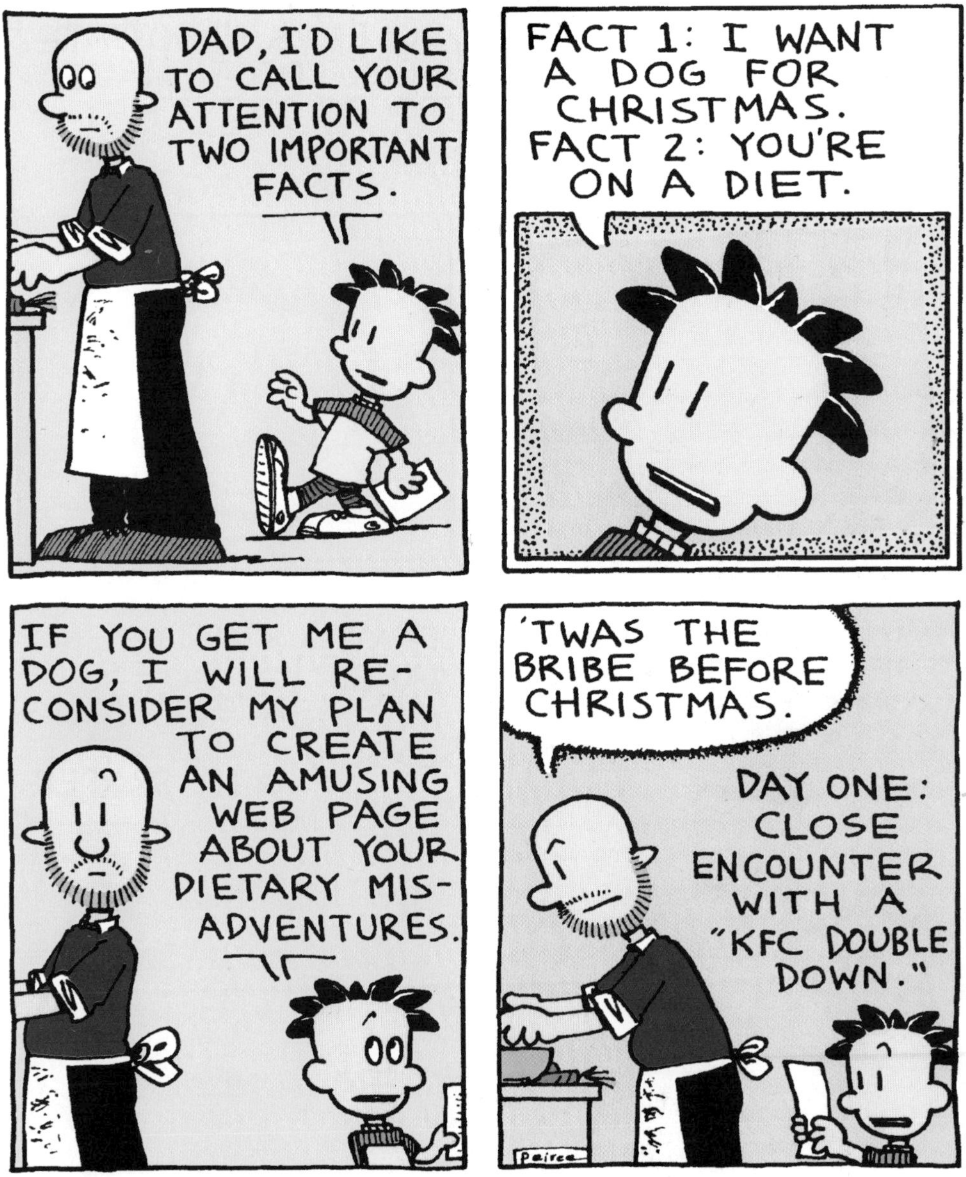
DAD, I'D LIKE TO CALL YOUR ATTENTION TO TWO IMPORTANT FACTS.
FACT 1: I WANT A DOG FOR CHRISTMAS. FACT 2: YOU'RE ON A DIET.
IF YOU GET ME A DOG, I WILL RE-CONSIDER MY PLAN TO CREATE AN AMUSING WEB PAGE ABOUT YOUR DIETARY MIS-ADVENTURES.
'TWAS THE BRIBE BEFORE CHRISTMAS.
DAY ONE: CLOSE ENCOUNTER WITH A "KFC DOUBLE DOWN."
Peirce

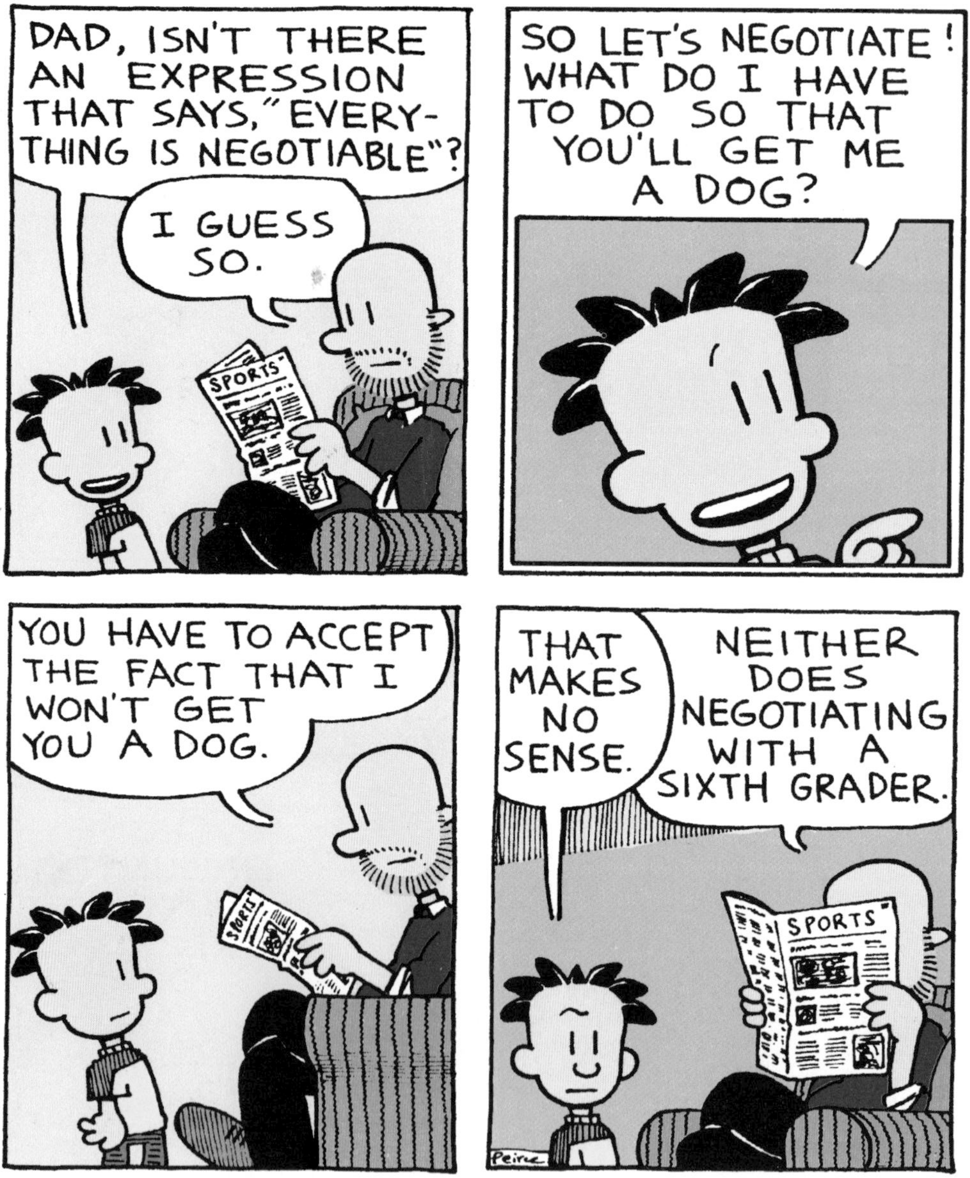
DAD, ISN'T THERE AN EXPRESSION THAT SAYS, "EVERYTHING IS NEGOTIABLE"?
I GUESS SO.
SPORTS
SO LET'S NEGOTIATE! WHAT DO I HAVE TO DO SO THAT YOU'LL GET ME A DOG?
YOU HAVE TO ACCEPT THE FACT THAT I WON'T GET YOU A DOG.
SPORTS
THAT MAKES NO SENSE.
NEITHER DOES NEGOTIATING WITH A SIXTH GRADER.
SPORTS
Peirce

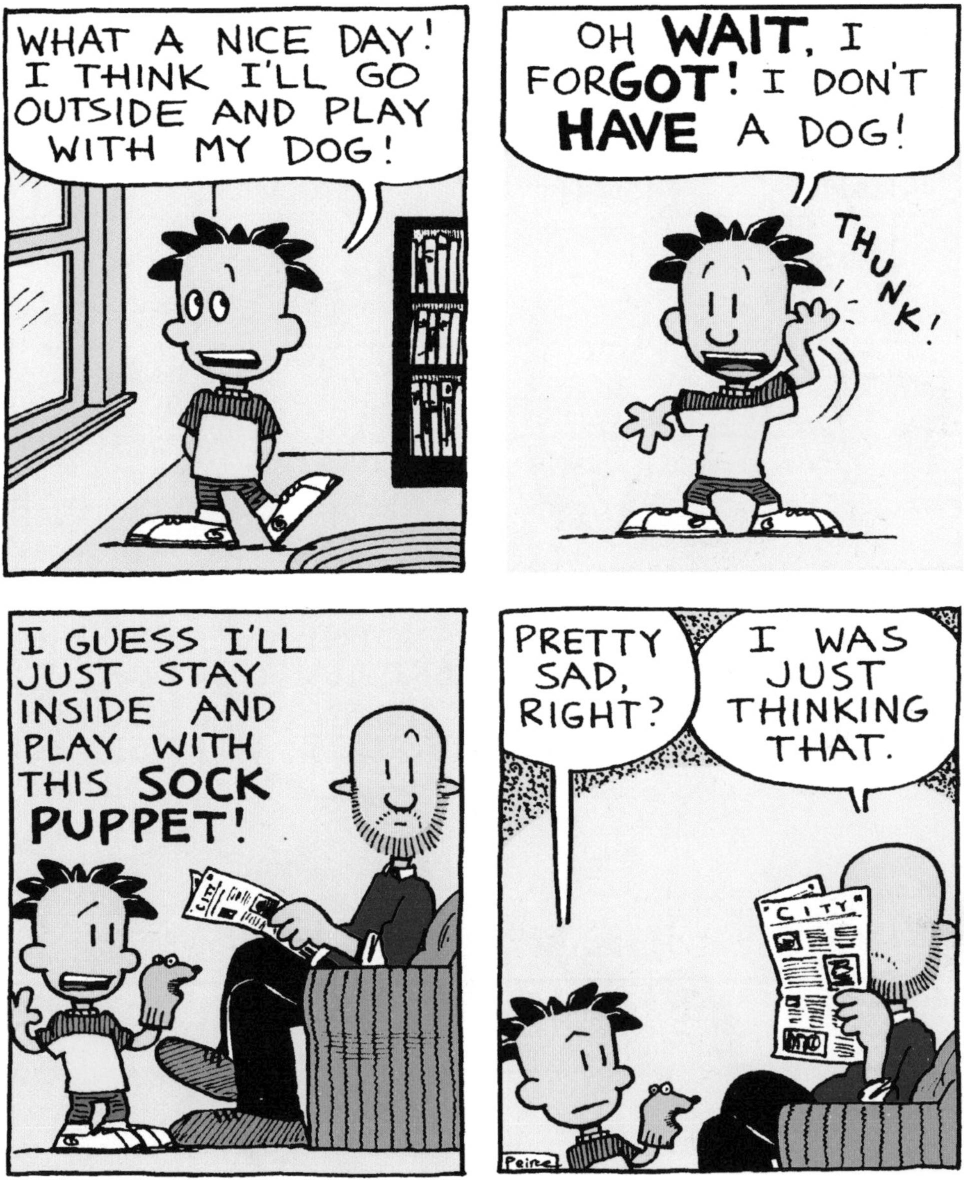
WHAT A NICE DAY! I THINK I'LL GO OUTSIDE AND PLAY WITH MY DOG!
OH **WAIT**, I FOR**GOT**! I DON'T **HAVE** A DOG!
THUNK!
I GUESS I'LL JUST STAY INSIDE AND PLAY WITH THIS **SOCK PUPPET**!
CITY
PRETTY SAD, RIGHT?
I WAS JUST THINKING THAT.
CITY
Peirce

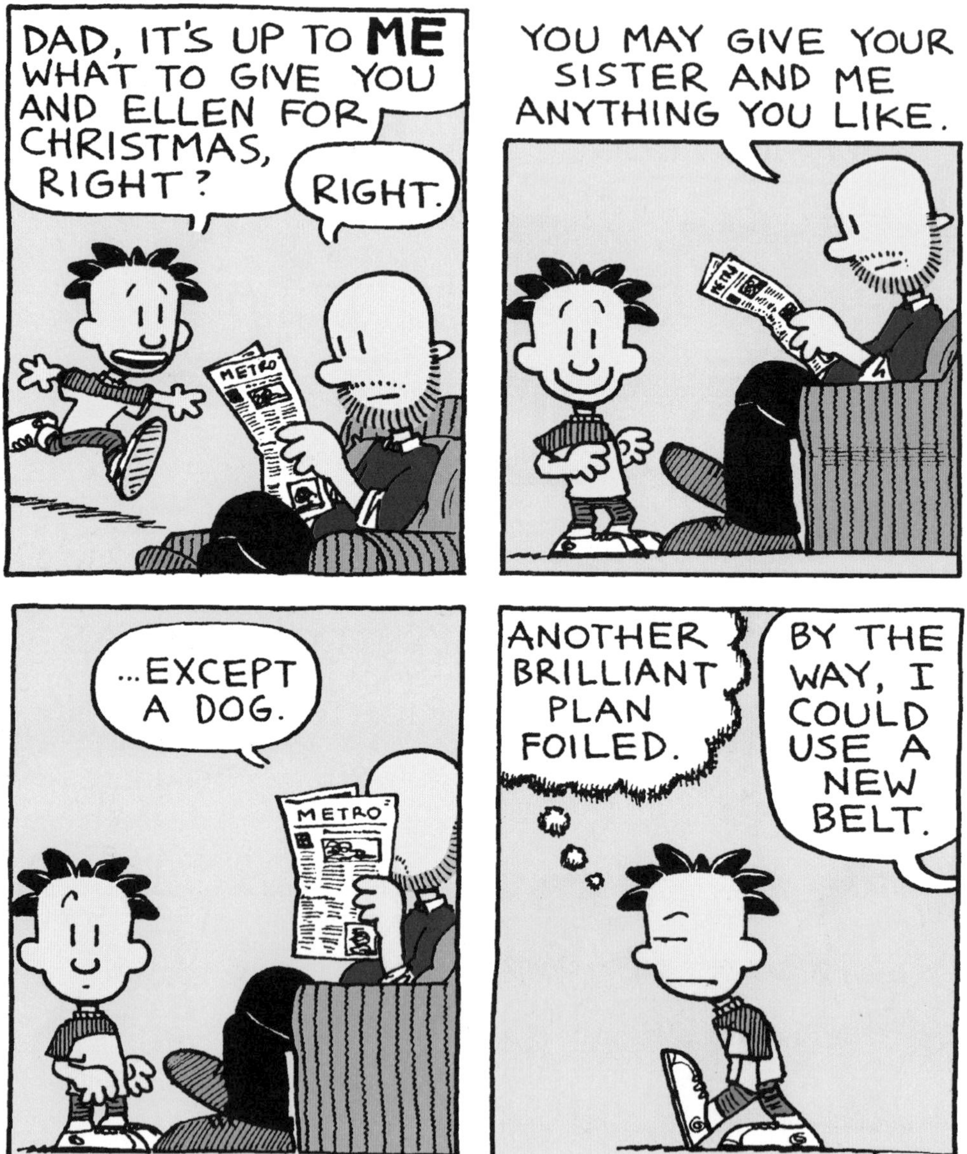
DAD, IT'S UP TO ME WHAT TO GIVE YOU AND ELLEN FOR CHRISTMAS, RIGHT?
RIGHT.
YOU MAY GIVE YOUR SISTER AND ME ANYTHING YOU LIKE.
METRO
...EXCEPT A DOG.
METRO
ANOTHER BRILLIANT PLAN FOILED.
BY THE WAY, I COULD USE A NEW BELT.
Peirce

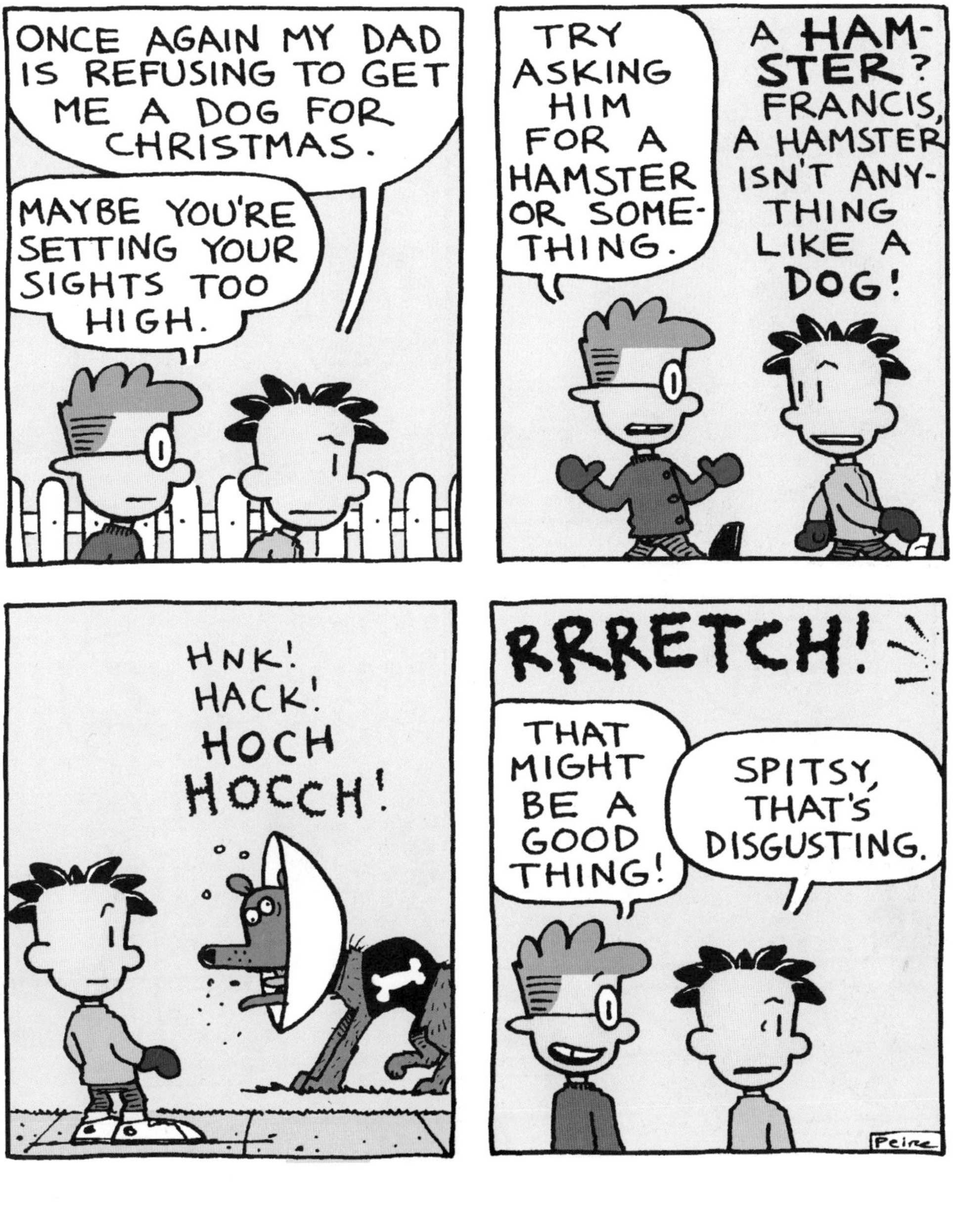
ONCE AGAIN MY DAD IS REFUSING TO GET ME A DOG FOR CHRISTMAS.
MAYBE YOU'RE SETTING YOUR SIGHTS TOO HIGH.
TRY ASKING HIM FOR A HAMSTER OR SOMETHING.
A HAMSTER? FRANCIS, A HAMSTER ISN'T ANYTHING LIKE A DOG!
HNK! HACK! HOCH HOCCH!
RRRETCH!
THAT MIGHT BE A GOOD THING!
SPITSY, THAT'S DISGUSTING.
Peirce

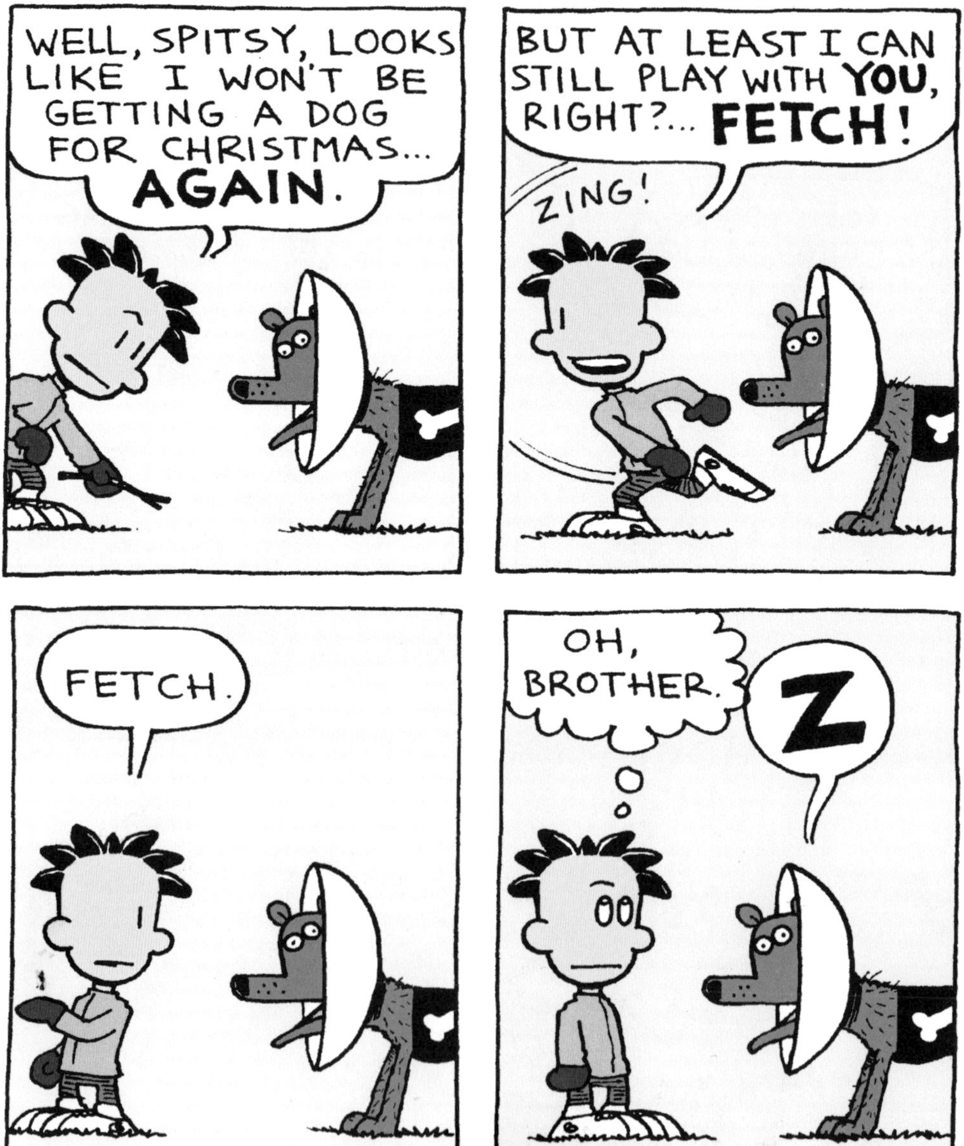
WELL, SPITSY, LOOKS LIKE I WON'T BE GETTING A DOG FOR CHRISTMAS... AGAIN.
BUT AT LEAST I CAN STILL PLAY WITH YOU, RIGHT?... FETCH!
ZING!
FETCH.
OH, BROTHER.
Z
Peirce

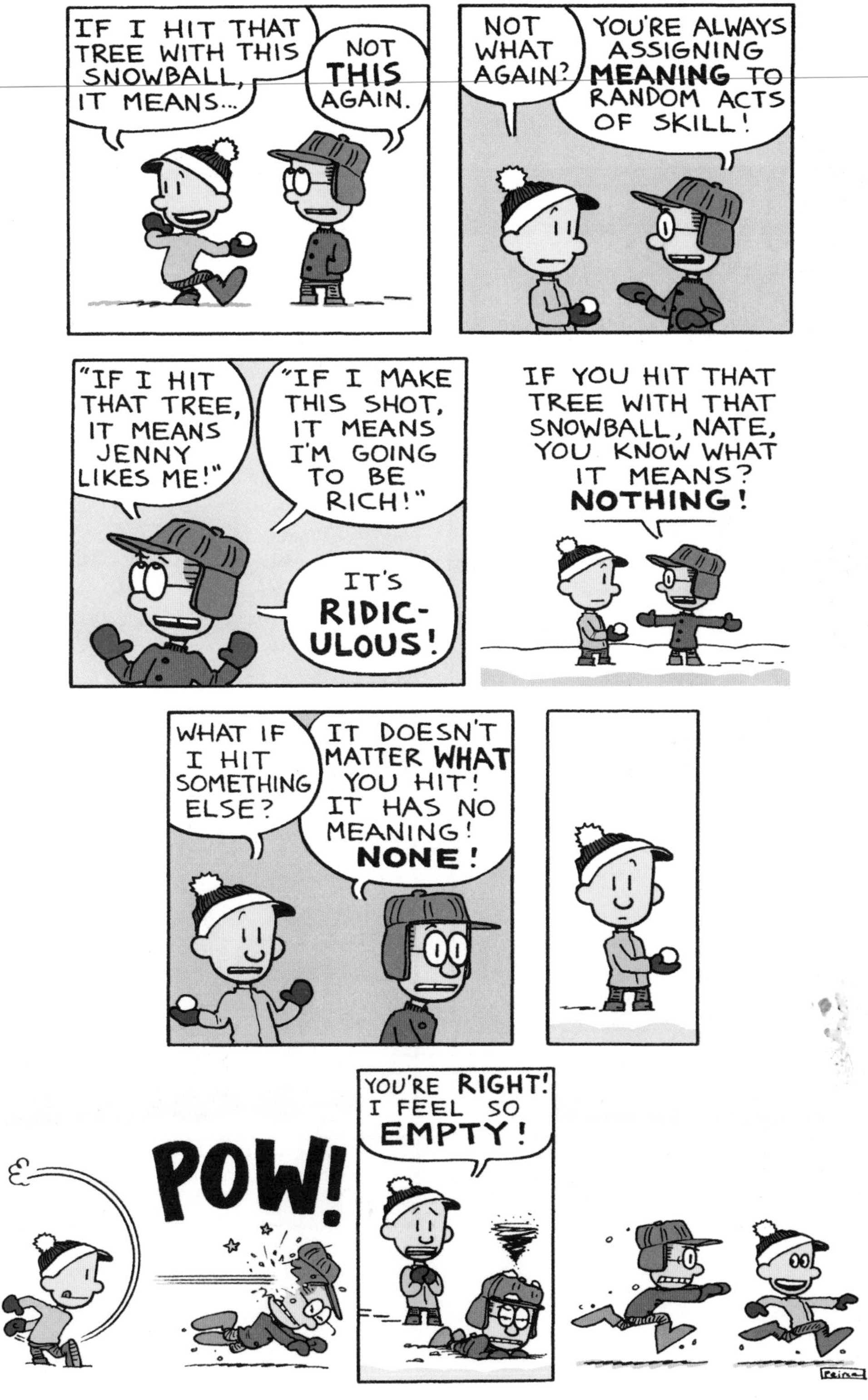
IF I HIT THAT TREE WITH THIS SNOWBALL, IT MEANS...
NOT THIS AGAIN.
NOT WHAT AGAIN?
YOU'RE ALWAYS ASSIGNING MEANING TO RANDOM ACTS OF SKILL!
"IF I HIT THAT TREE, IT MEANS JENNY LIKES ME!"
"IF I MAKE THIS SHOT, IT MEANS I'M GOING TO BE RICH!"
IT'S RIDIC-ULOUS!
IF YOU HIT THAT TREE WITH THAT SNOWBALL, NATE, YOU KNOW WHAT IT MEANS? NOTHING!
WHAT IF I HIT SOMETHING ELSE?
IT DOESN'T MATTER WHAT YOU HIT! IT HAS NO MEANING! NONE!
POW!
YOU'RE RIGHT! I FEEL SO EMPTY!
PEIRCE

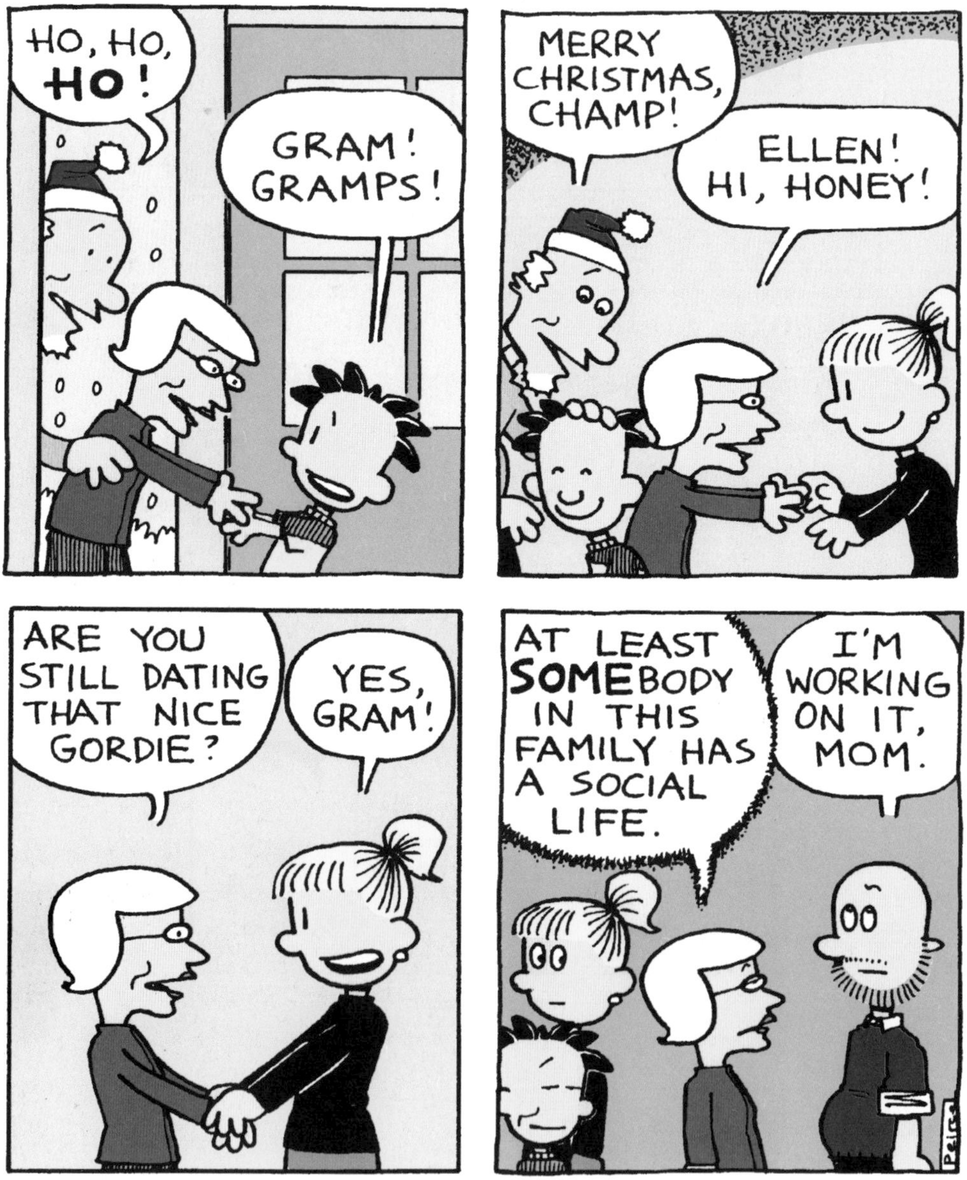
HO, HO, **HO**!
GRAM! GRAMPS!
MERRY CHRISTMAS, CHAMP!
ELLEN! HI, HONEY!
ARE YOU STILL DATING THAT NICE GORDIE?
YES, GRAM!
AT LEAST **SOME**BODY IN THIS FAMILY HAS A SOCIAL LIFE.
I'M WORKING ON IT, MOM.
Peirce

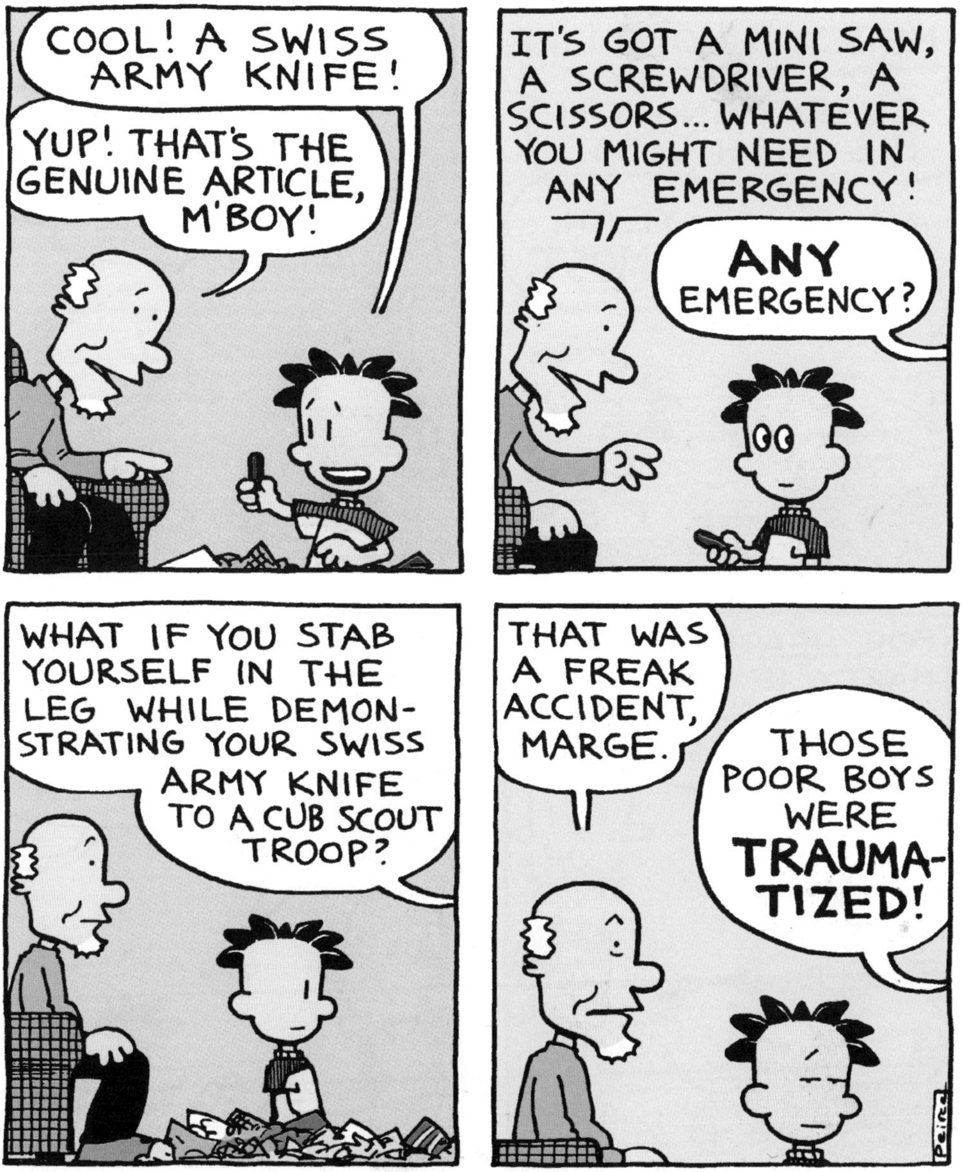
COOL! A SWISS ARMY KNIFE!
YUP! THAT'S THE GENUINE ARTICLE, M'BOY!
IT'S GOT A MINI SAW, A SCREWDRIVER, A SCISSORS... WHATEVER YOU MIGHT NEED IN ANY EMERGENCY!
ANY EMERGENCY?
WHAT IF YOU STAB YOURSELF IN THE LEG WHILE DEMON-STRATING YOUR SWISS ARMY KNIFE TO A CUB SCOUT TROOP?
THAT WAS A FREAK ACCIDENT, MARGE.
THOSE POOR BOYS WERE **TRAUMA-TIZED!**
Peirce

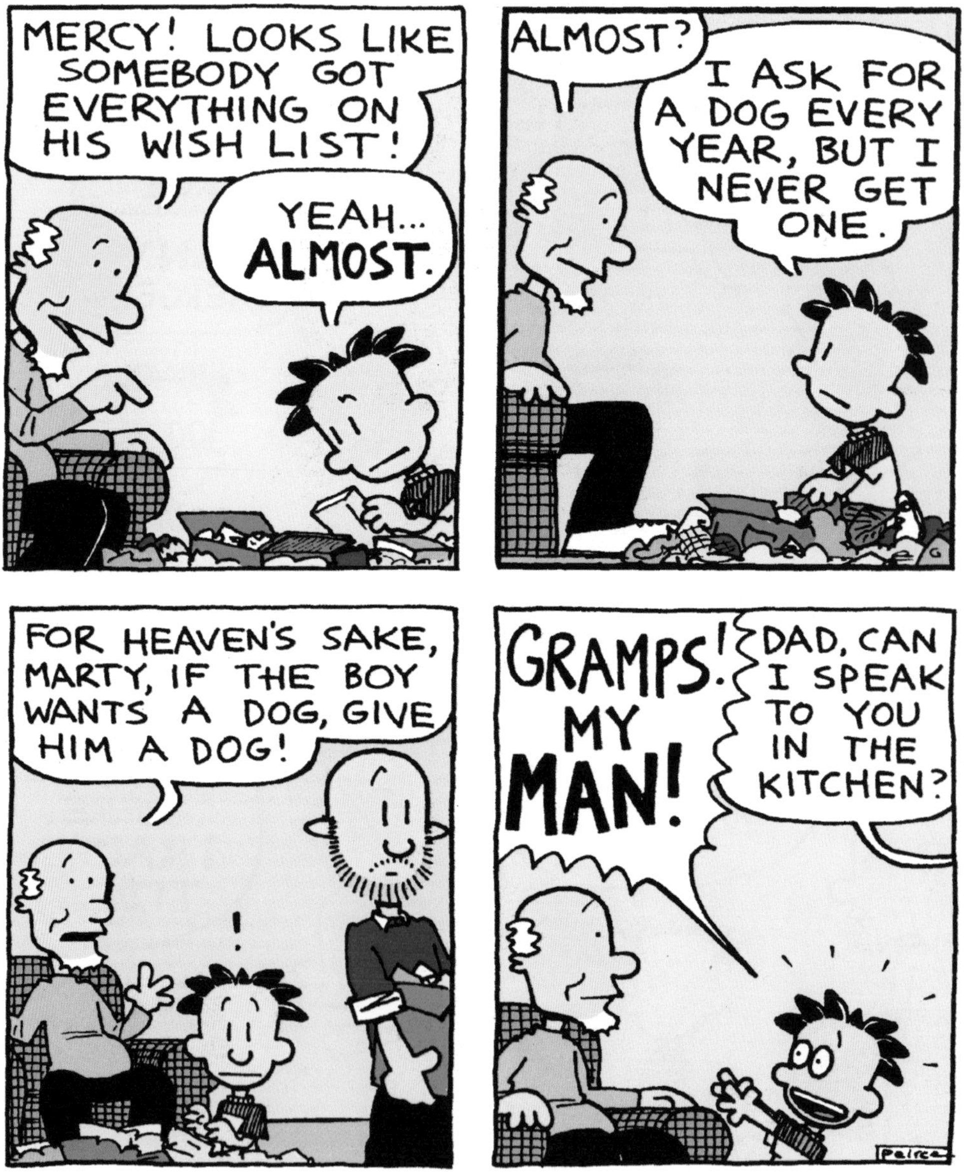
MERCY! LOOKS LIKE SOMEBODY GOT EVERYTHING ON HIS WISH LIST!
YEAH... ALMOST.
ALMOST?
I ASK FOR A DOG EVERY YEAR, BUT I NEVER GET ONE.
FOR HEAVEN'S SAKE, MARTY, IF THE BOY WANTS A DOG, GIVE HIM A DOG!
!
GRAMPS! MY MAN!
DAD, CAN I SPEAK TO YOU IN THE KITCHEN?

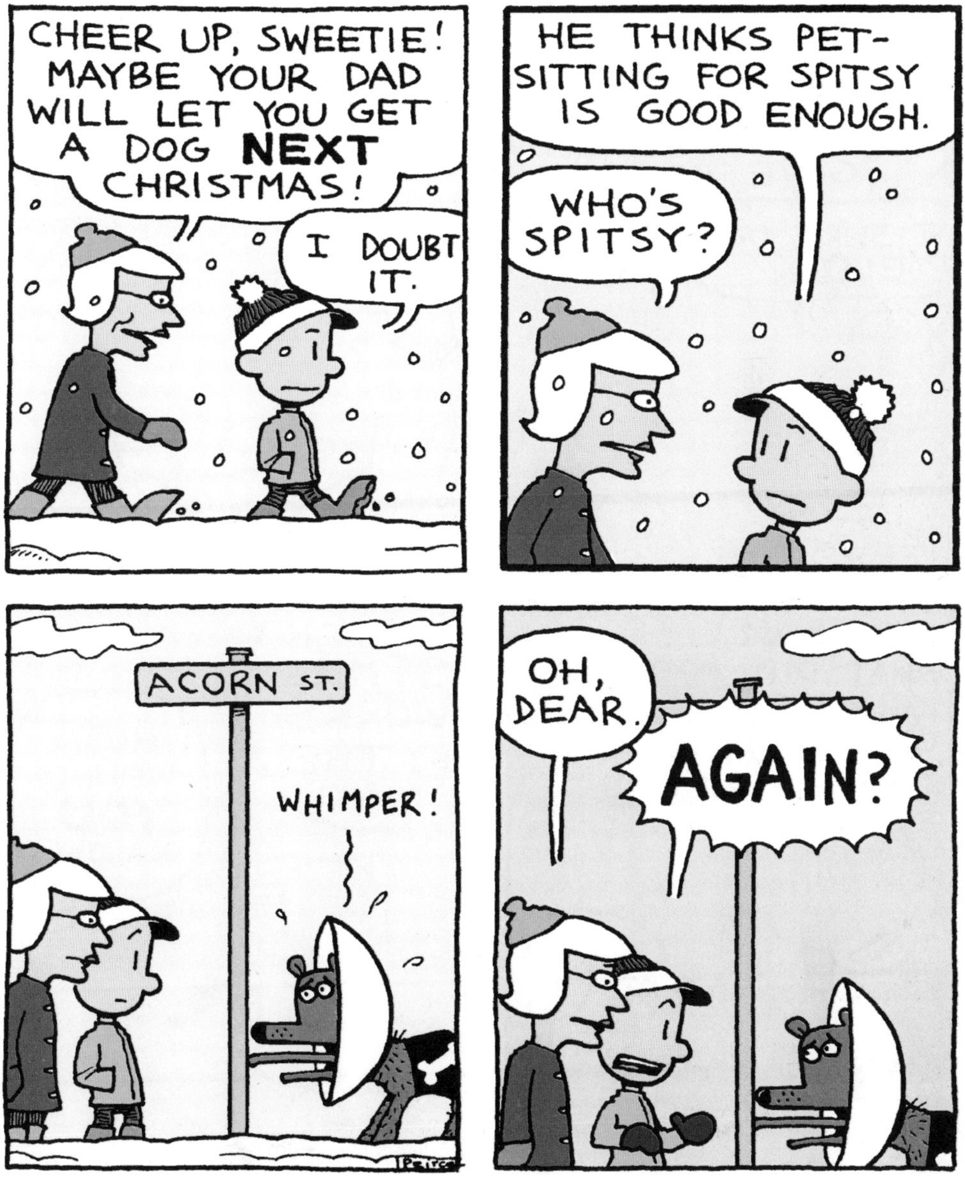
CHEER UP, SWEETIE! MAYBE YOUR DAD WILL LET YOU GET A DOG **NEXT** CHRISTMAS!
I DOUBT IT.
HE THINKS PET-SITTING FOR SPITSY IS GOOD ENOUGH.
WHO'S SPITSY?
ACORN ST.
WHIMPER!
OH, DEAR.
AGAIN?

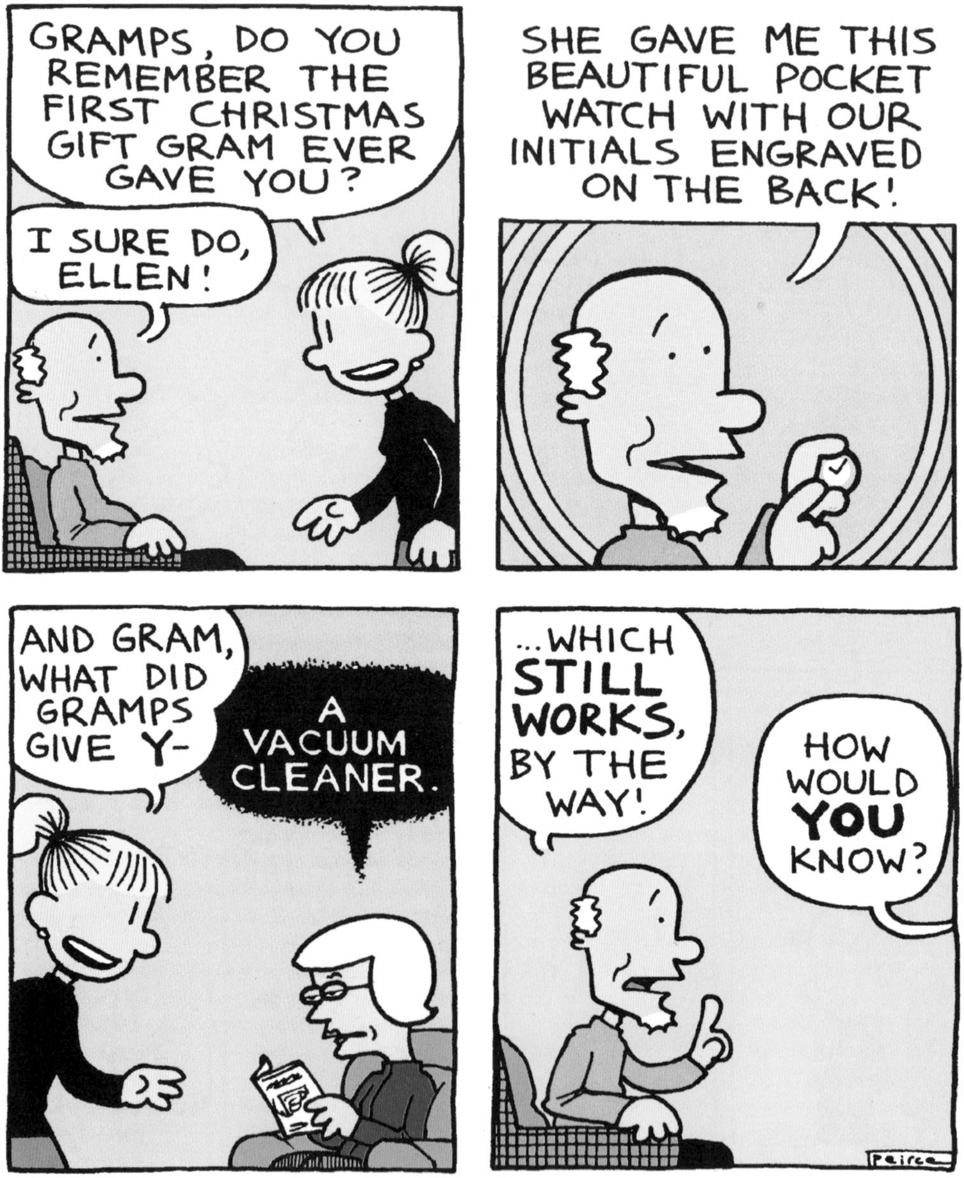
GRAMPS, DO YOU REMEMBER THE FIRST CHRISTMAS GIFT GRAM EVER GAVE YOU?
I SURE DO, ELLEN!
SHE GAVE ME THIS BEAUTIFUL POCKET WATCH WITH OUR INITIALS ENGRAVED ON THE BACK!
AND GRAM, WHAT DID GRAMPS GIVE Y-
A VACUUM CLEANER.
...WHICH STILL WORKS, BY THE WAY!
HOW WOULD YOU KNOW?
Peirce

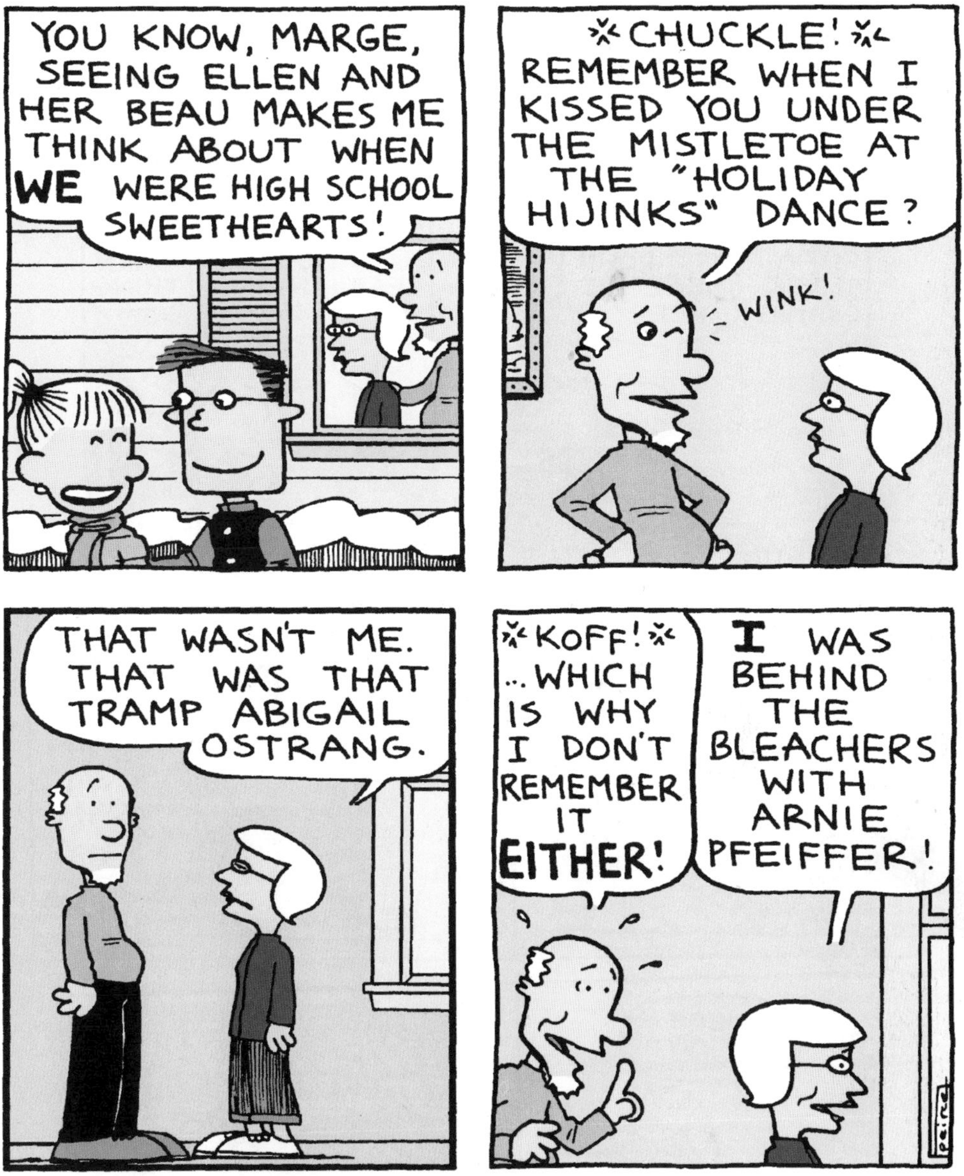
YOU KNOW, MARGE, SEEING ELLEN AND HER BEAU MAKES ME THINK ABOUT WHEN **WE** WERE HIGH SCHOOL SWEETHEARTS!
CHUCKLE! REMEMBER WHEN I KISSED YOU UNDER THE MISTLETOE AT THE "HOLIDAY HIJINKS" DANCE?
WINK!
THAT WASN'T ME. THAT WAS THAT TRAMP ABIGAIL OSTRANG.
KOFF! ...WHICH IS WHY I DON'T REMEMBER IT **EITHER**!
I WAS BEHIND THE BLEACHERS WITH ARNIE PFEIFFER!
PEIRCE

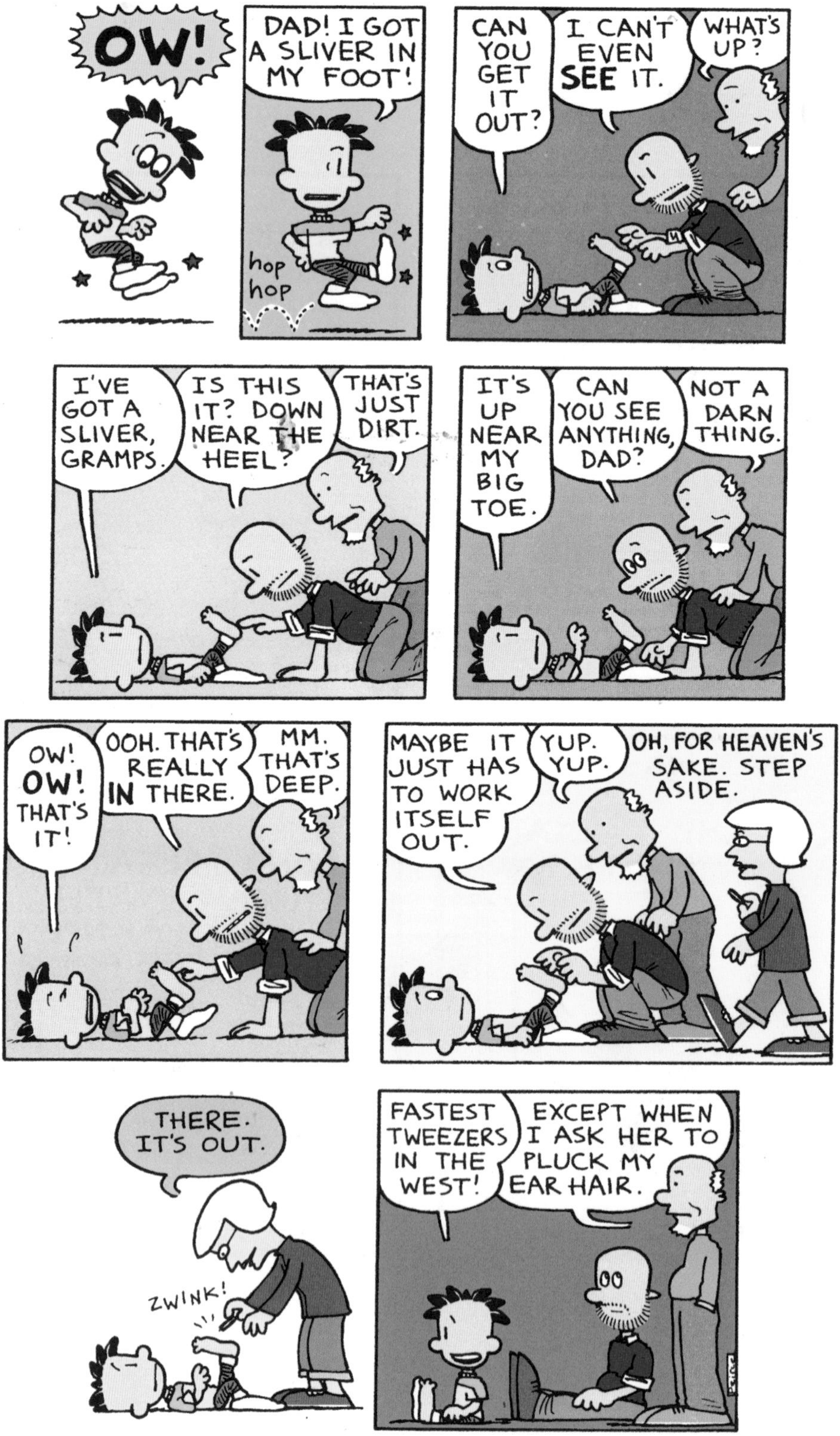
OW!
DAD! I GOT A SLIVER IN MY FOOT!
hop hop
CAN YOU GET IT OUT?
I CAN'T EVEN **SEE** IT.
WHAT'S UP?
I'VE GOT A SLIVER, GRAMPS.
IS THIS IT? DOWN NEAR THE HEEL?
THAT'S JUST DIRT.
IT'S UP NEAR MY BIG TOE.
CAN YOU SEE ANYTHING, DAD?
NOT A DARN THING.
OW! **OW!** THAT'S IT!
OOH. THAT'S REALLY **IN** THERE.
MM. THAT'S DEEP.
MAYBE IT JUST HAS TO WORK ITSELF OUT.
YUP. YUP.
OH, FOR HEAVEN'S SAKE. STEP ASIDE.
THERE. IT'S OUT.
ZWINK!
FASTEST TWEEZERS IN THE WEST!
EXCEPT WHEN I ASK HER TO PLUCK MY EAR HAIR.

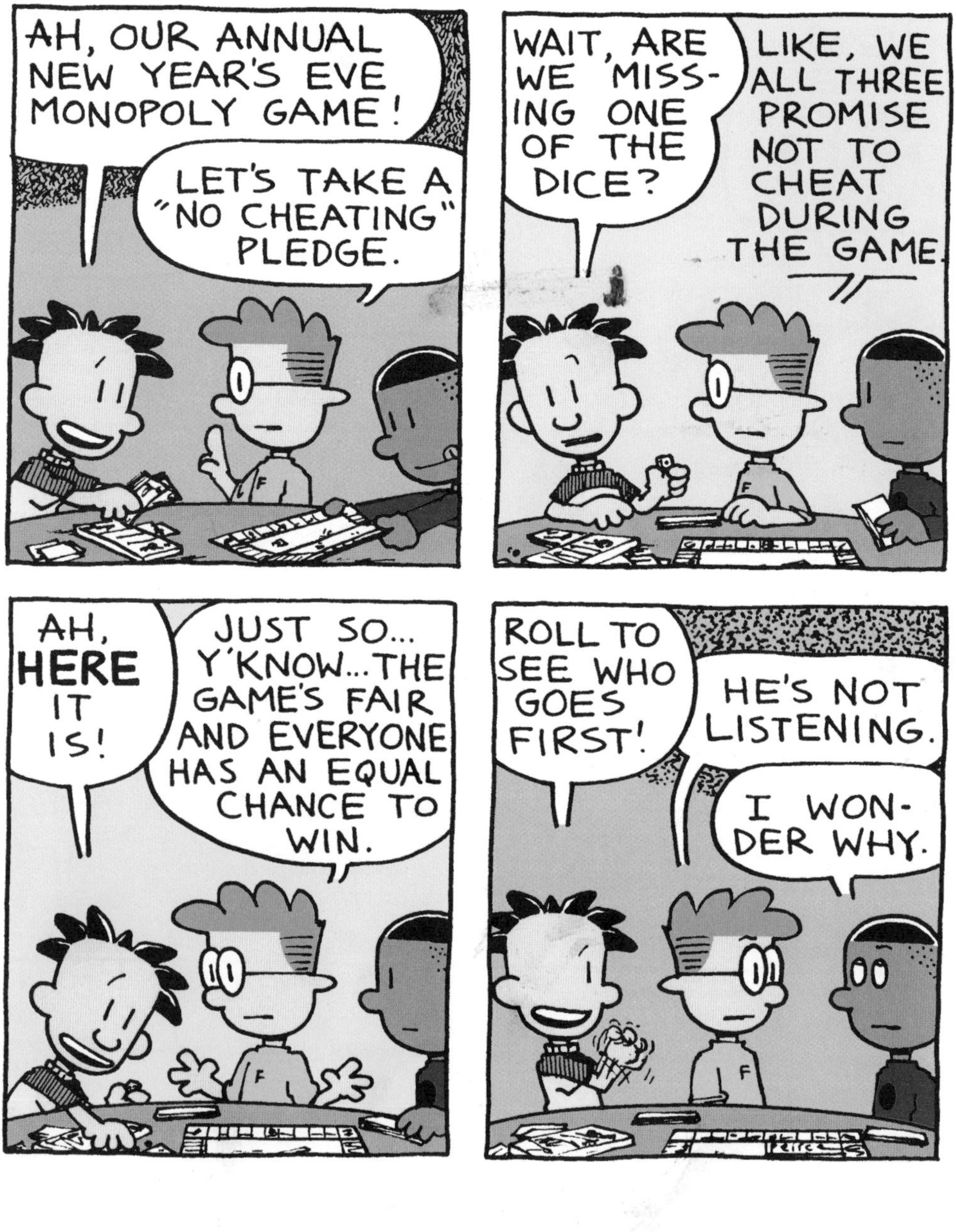
AH, OUR ANNUAL NEW YEAR'S EVE MONOPOLY GAME!
LET'S TAKE A "NO CHEATING" PLEDGE.
WAIT, ARE WE MISSING ONE OF THE DICE?
LIKE, WE ALL THREE PROMISE NOT TO CHEAT DURING THE GAME.
AH, **HERE** IT IS!
JUST SO... Y'KNOW... THE GAME'S FAIR AND EVERYONE HAS AN EQUAL CHANCE TO WIN.
ROLL TO SEE WHO GOES FIRST!
HE'S NOT LISTENING.
I WONDER WHY.

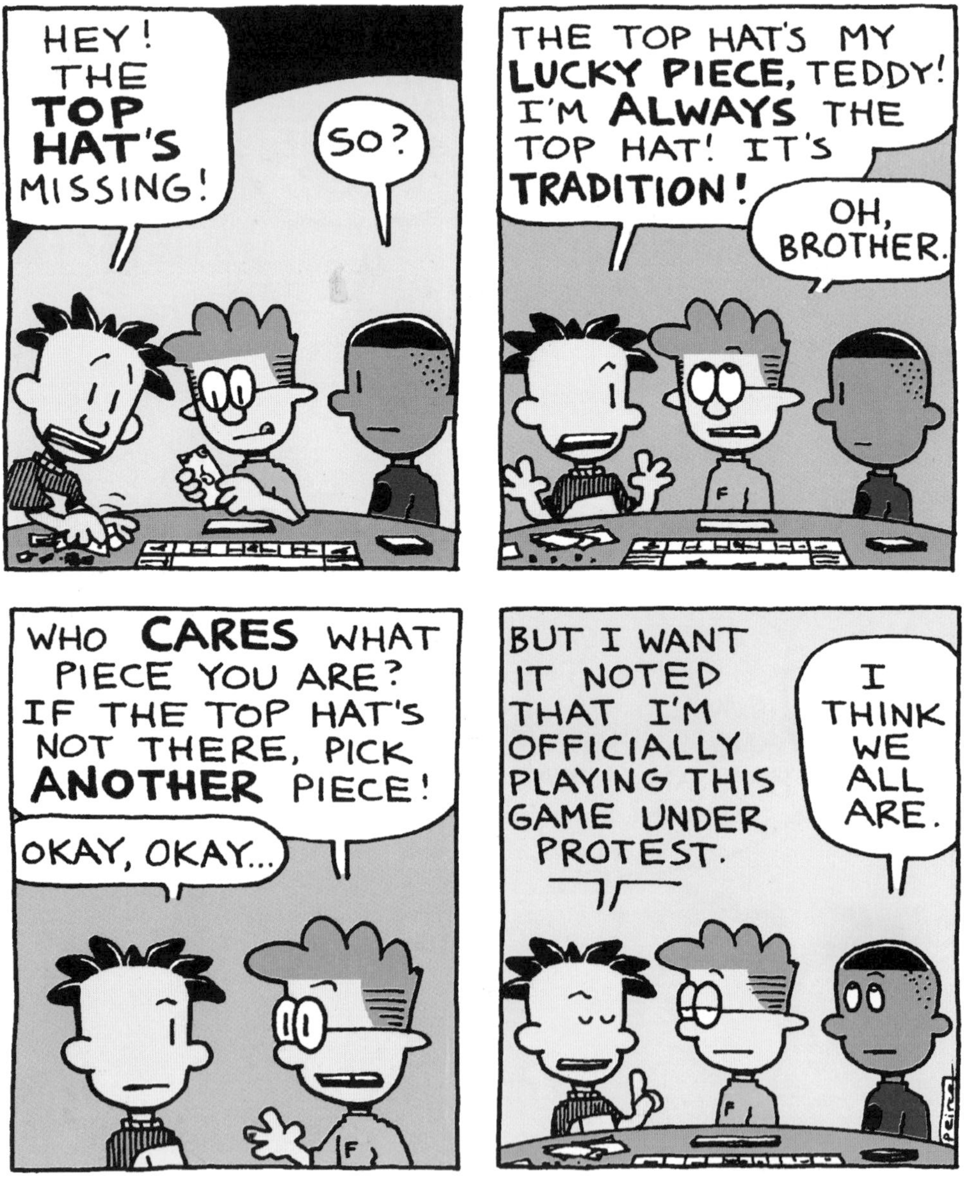
HEY! THE TOP HAT'S MISSING!
SO?
THE TOP HAT'S MY LUCKY PIECE, TEDDY! I'M ALWAYS THE TOP HAT! IT'S TRADITION!
OH, BROTHER.
WHO CARES WHAT PIECE YOU ARE? IF THE TOP HAT'S NOT THERE, PICK ANOTHER PIECE!
OKAY, OKAY...
BUT I WANT IT NOTED THAT I'M OFFICIALLY PLAYING THIS GAME UNDER PROTEST.
I THINK WE ALL ARE.
PEIRCE

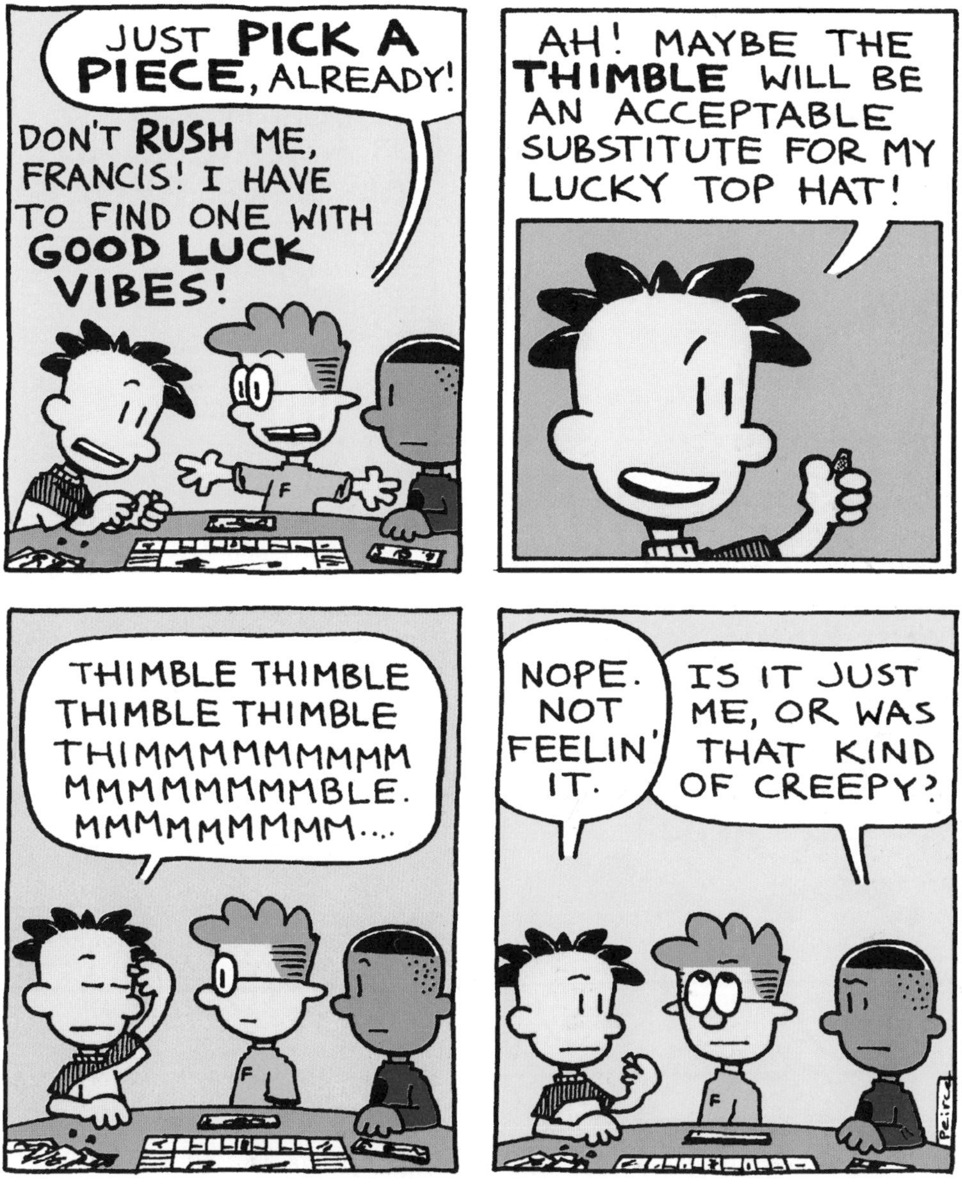
JUST PICK A PIECE, ALREADY!
DON'T RUSH ME, FRANCIS! I HAVE TO FIND ONE WITH GOOD LUCK VIBES!
AH! MAYBE THE THIMBLE WILL BE AN ACCEPTABLE SUBSTITUTE FOR MY LUCKY TOP HAT!
THIMBLE THIMBLE THIMBLE THIMBLE THIMMMMMMMMM MMMMMMMMBLE. MMMMMMMM....
NOPE. NOT FEELIN' IT.
IS IT JUST ME, OR WAS THAT KIND OF CREEPY?
F
F
F
Peirce

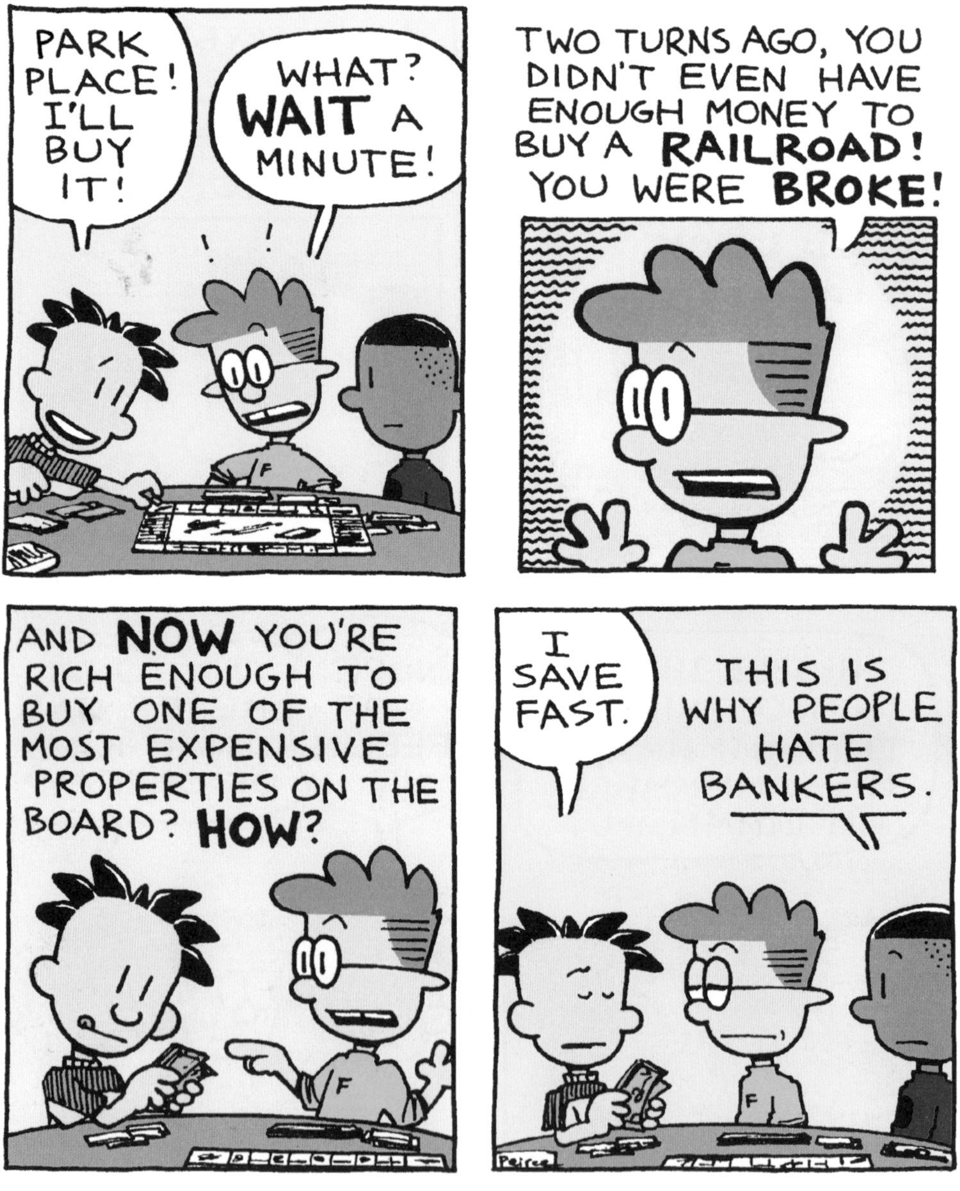
PARK PLACE! I'LL BUY IT!
WHAT? WAIT A MINUTE!
TWO TURNS AGO, YOU DIDN'T EVEN HAVE ENOUGH MONEY TO BUY A RAILROAD! YOU WERE BROKE!
AND NOW YOU'RE RICH ENOUGH TO BUY ONE OF THE MOST EXPENSIVE PROPERTIES ON THE BOARD? HOW?
I SAVE FAST.
THIS IS WHY PEOPLE HATE BANKERS.
Peirce

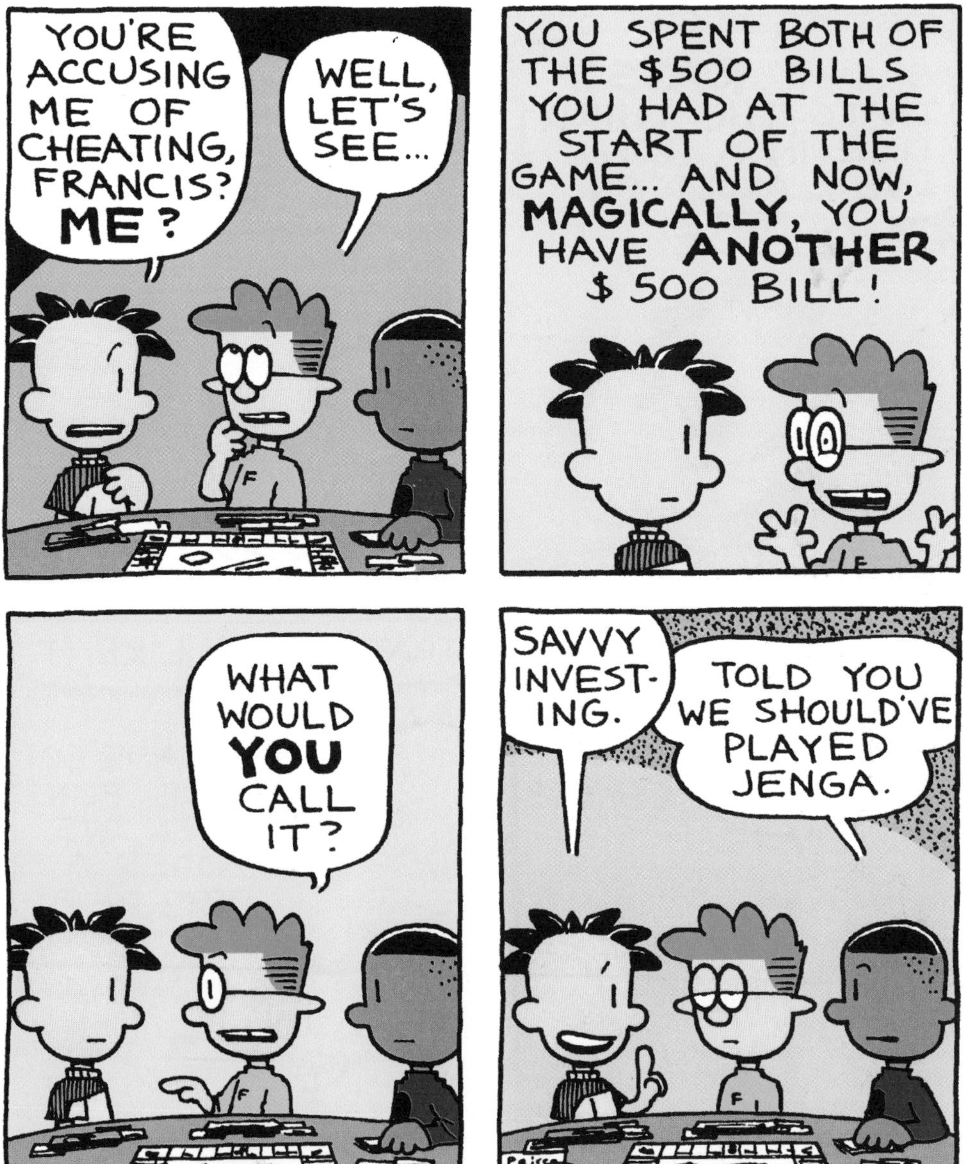
YOU'RE ACCUSING ME OF CHEATING, FRANCIS? ME?
WELL, LET'S SEE...
YOU SPENT BOTH OF THE $500 BILLS YOU HAD AT THE START OF THE GAME... AND NOW, MAGICALLY, YOU HAVE ANOTHER $500 BILL!
WHAT WOULD YOU CALL IT?
SAVVY INVEST-ING.
TOLD YOU WE SHOULD'VE PLAYED JENGA.
Peirce

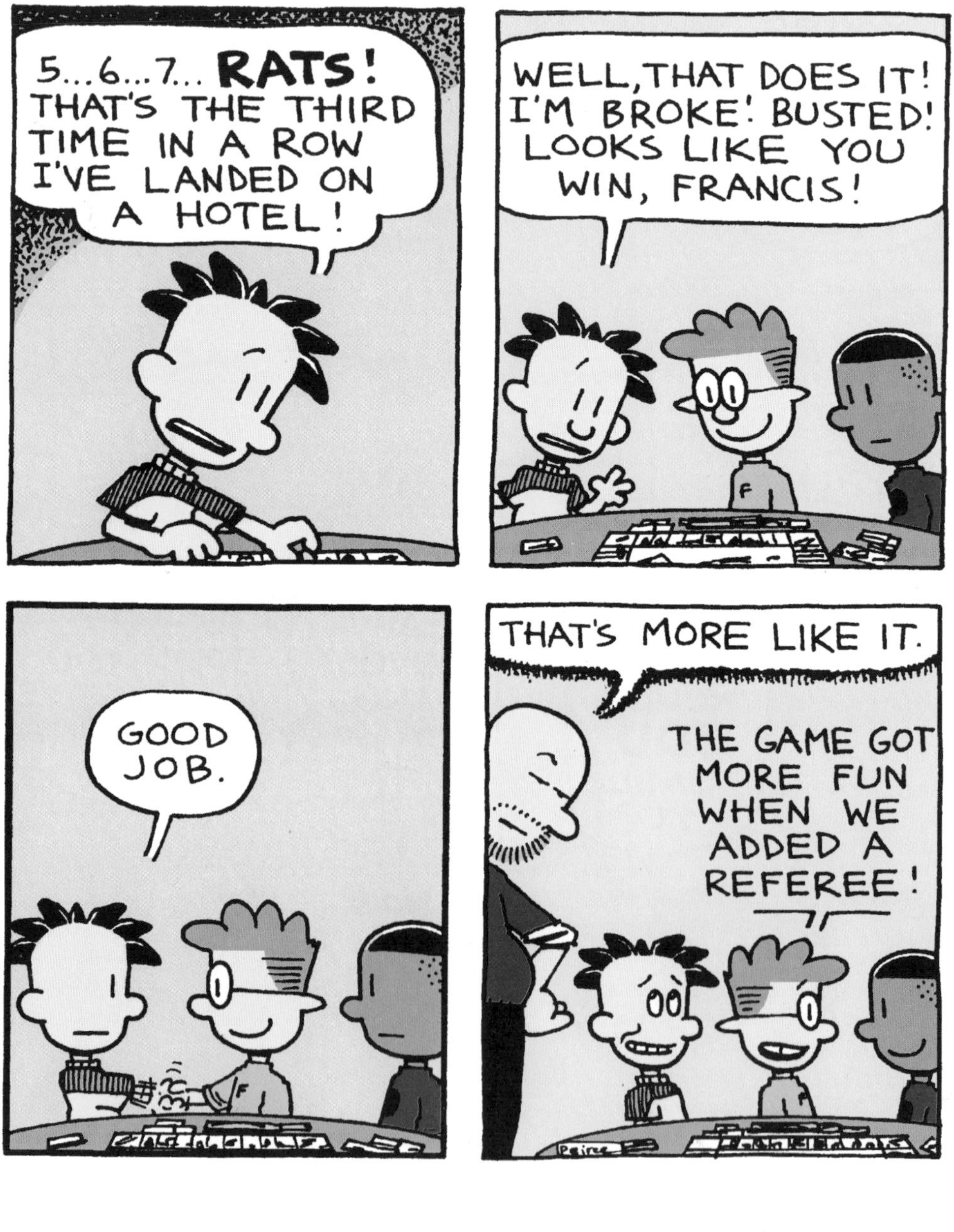
5...6...7... RATS!
THAT'S THE THIRD TIME IN A ROW I'VE LANDED ON A HOTEL!
WELL, THAT DOES IT! I'M BROKE! BUSTED! LOOKS LIKE YOU WIN, FRANCIS!
GOOD JOB.
THAT'S MORE LIKE IT.
THE GAME GOT MORE FUN WHEN WE ADDED A REFEREE!
Peirce

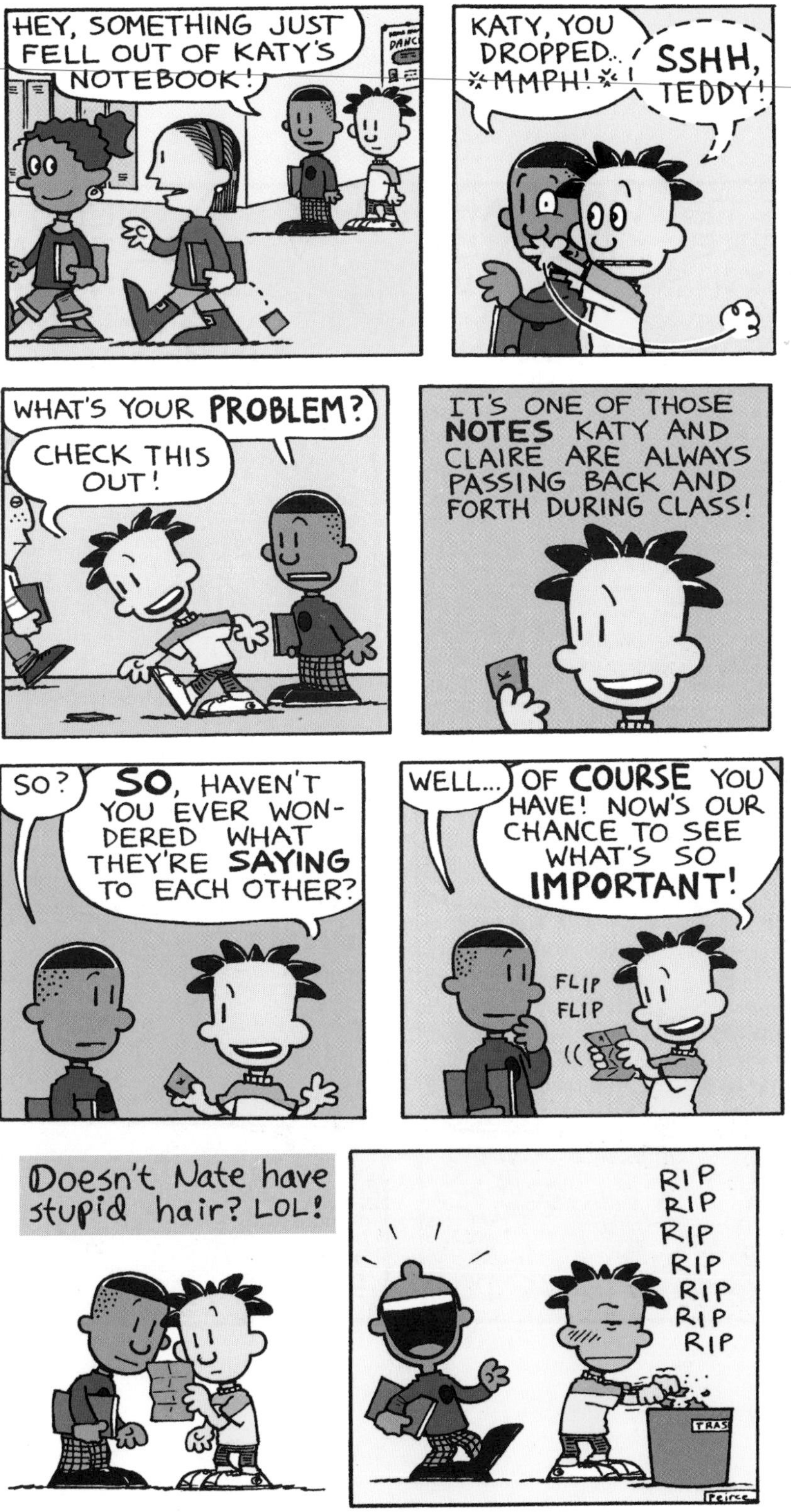
HEY, SOMETHING JUST FELL OUT OF KATY'S NOTEBOOK!
DANCE
KATY, YOU DROPPED.. MMPH!
SSHH, TEDDY!
WHAT'S YOUR PROBLEM?
CHECK THIS OUT!
IT'S ONE OF THOSE NOTES KATY AND CLAIRE ARE ALWAYS PASSING BACK AND FORTH DURING CLASS!
SO?
SO, HAVEN'T YOU EVER WONDERED WHAT THEY'RE SAYING TO EACH OTHER?
WELL...
OF COURSE YOU HAVE! NOW'S OUR CHANCE TO SEE WHAT'S SO IMPORTANT!
FLIP FLIP
Doesn't Nate have stupid hair? LOL!
RIP RIP RIP RIP RIP RIP RIP
TRAS
Peirce

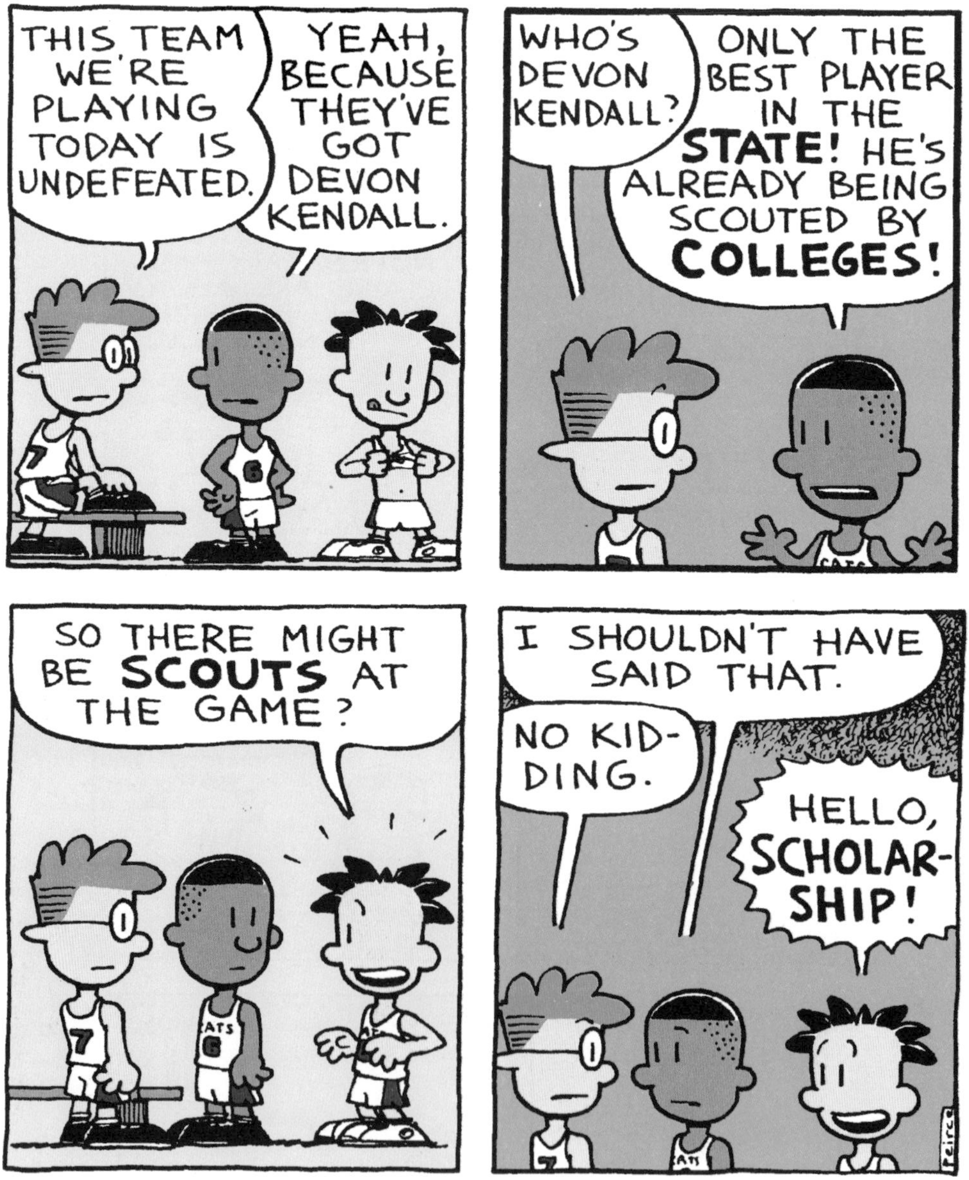
THIS TEAM WE'RE PLAYING TODAY IS UNDEFEATED.
YEAH, BECAUSE THEY'VE GOT DEVON KENDALL.
WHO'S DEVON KENDALL?
ONLY THE BEST PLAYER IN THE STATE! HE'S ALREADY BEING SCOUTED BY COLLEGES!
SO THERE MIGHT BE SCOUTS AT THE GAME?
I SHOULDN'T HAVE SAID THAT.
NO KID-DING.
HELLO, SCHOLAR-SHIP!
Peirce

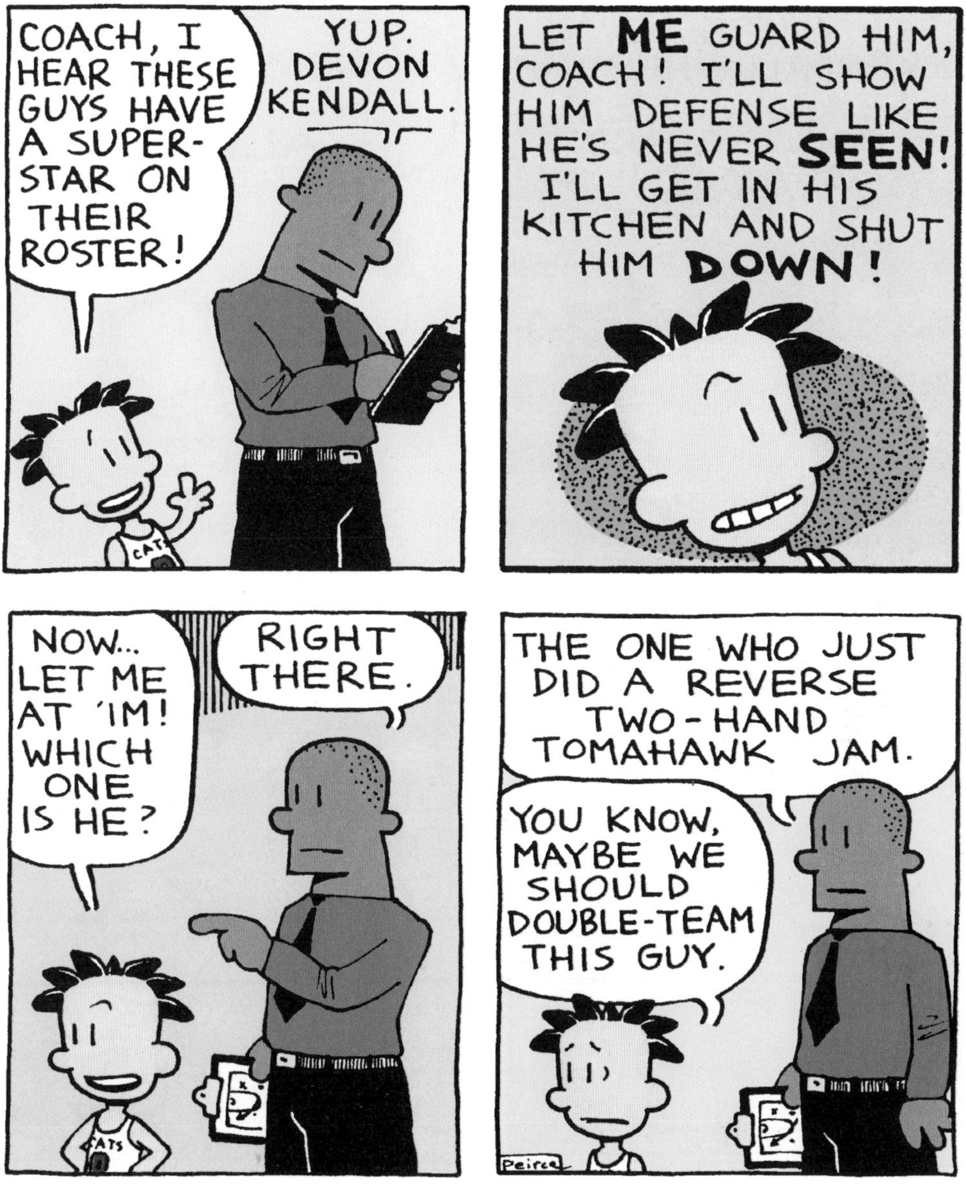
COACH, I HEAR THESE GUYS HAVE A SUPER-STAR ON THEIR ROSTER!
YUP. DEVON KENDALL.
CATS
LET **ME** GUARD HIM, COACH! I'LL SHOW HIM DEFENSE LIKE HE'S NEVER **SEEN**! I'LL GET IN HIS KITCHEN AND SHUT HIM **DOWN**!
NOW... LET ME AT 'IM! WHICH ONE IS HE?
RIGHT THERE.
CATS
THE ONE WHO JUST DID A REVERSE TWO-HAND TOMAHAWK JAM.
YOU KNOW, MAYBE WE SHOULD DOUBLE-TEAM THIS GUY.
Peirce

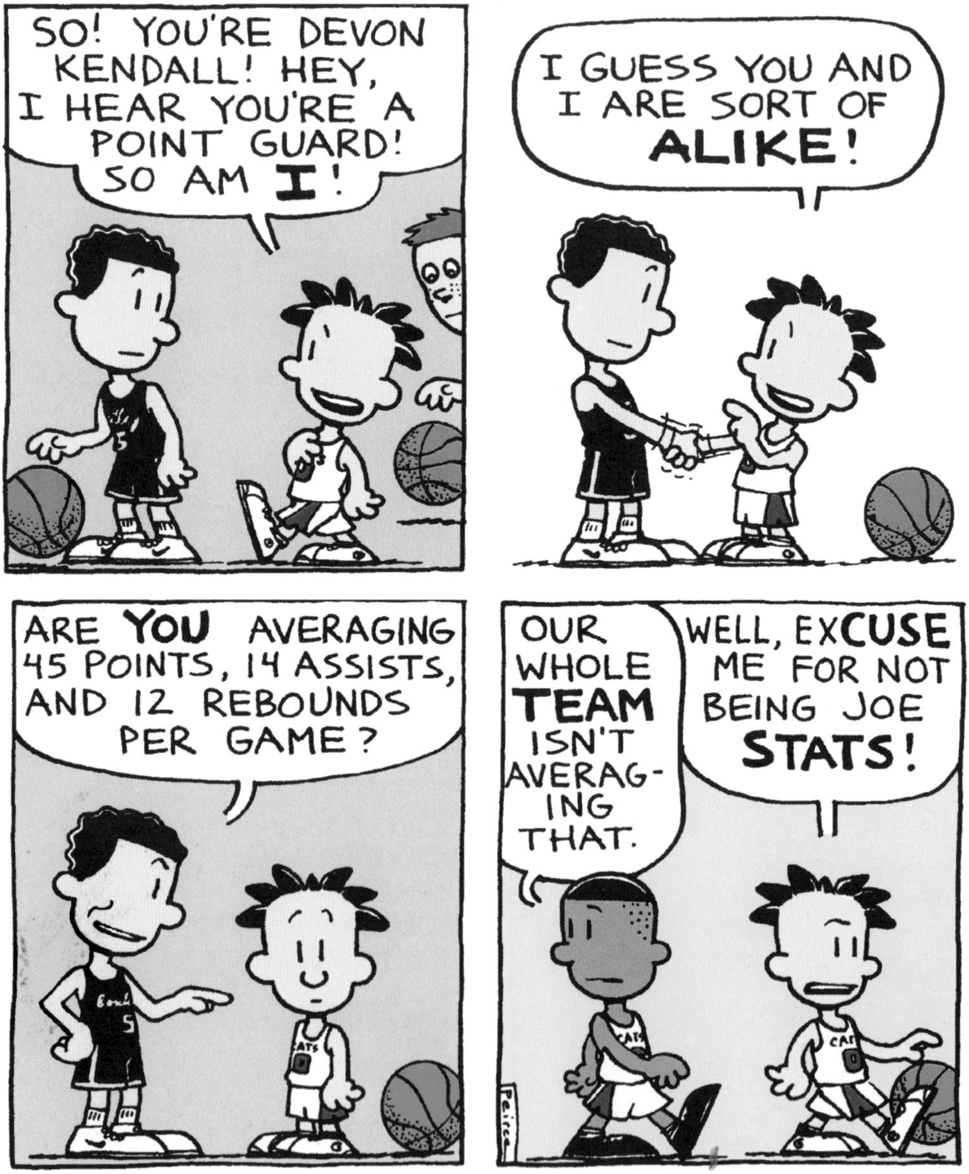
SO! YOU'RE DEVON KENDALL! HEY, I HEAR YOU'RE A POINT GUARD! SO AM I!
I GUESS YOU AND I ARE SORT OF ALIKE!
ARE YOU AVERAGING 45 POINTS, 14 ASSISTS, AND 12 REBOUNDS PER GAME?
OUR WHOLE TEAM ISN'T AVERAGING THAT.
WELL, EXCUSE ME FOR NOT BEING JOE STATS!

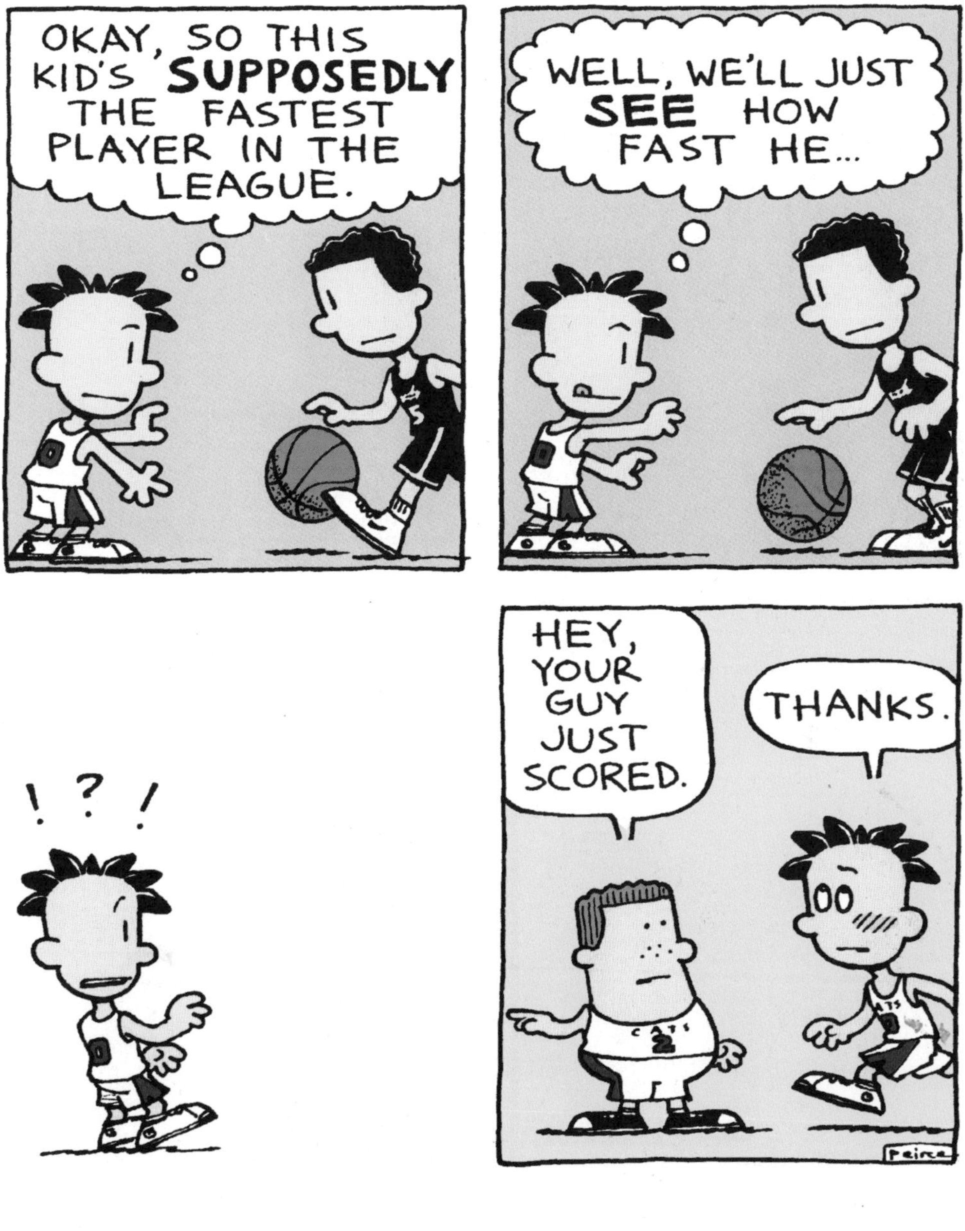
OKAY, SO THIS KID'S **SUPPOSEDLY** THE FASTEST PLAYER IN THE LEAGUE.
WELL, WE'LL JUST **SEE** HOW FAST HE...
! ? !
HEY, YOUR GUY JUST SCORED.
THANKS.
Peirce

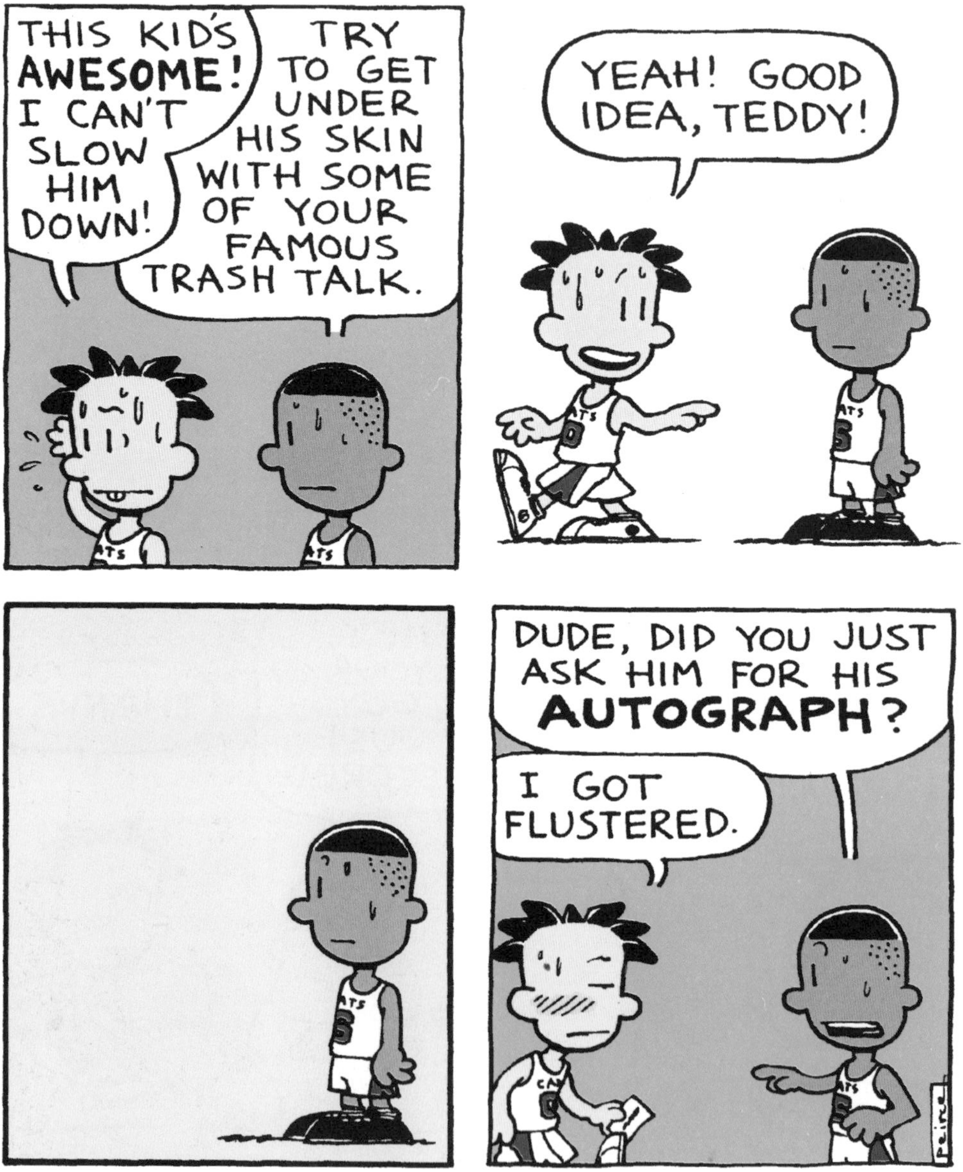
THIS KID'S AWESOME! I CAN'T SLOW HIM DOWN!
TRY TO GET UNDER HIS SKIN WITH SOME OF YOUR FAMOUS TRASH TALK.
YEAH! GOOD IDEA, TEDDY!
DUDE, DID YOU JUST ASK HIM FOR HIS AUTOGRAPH?
I GOT FLUSTERED.
peirce

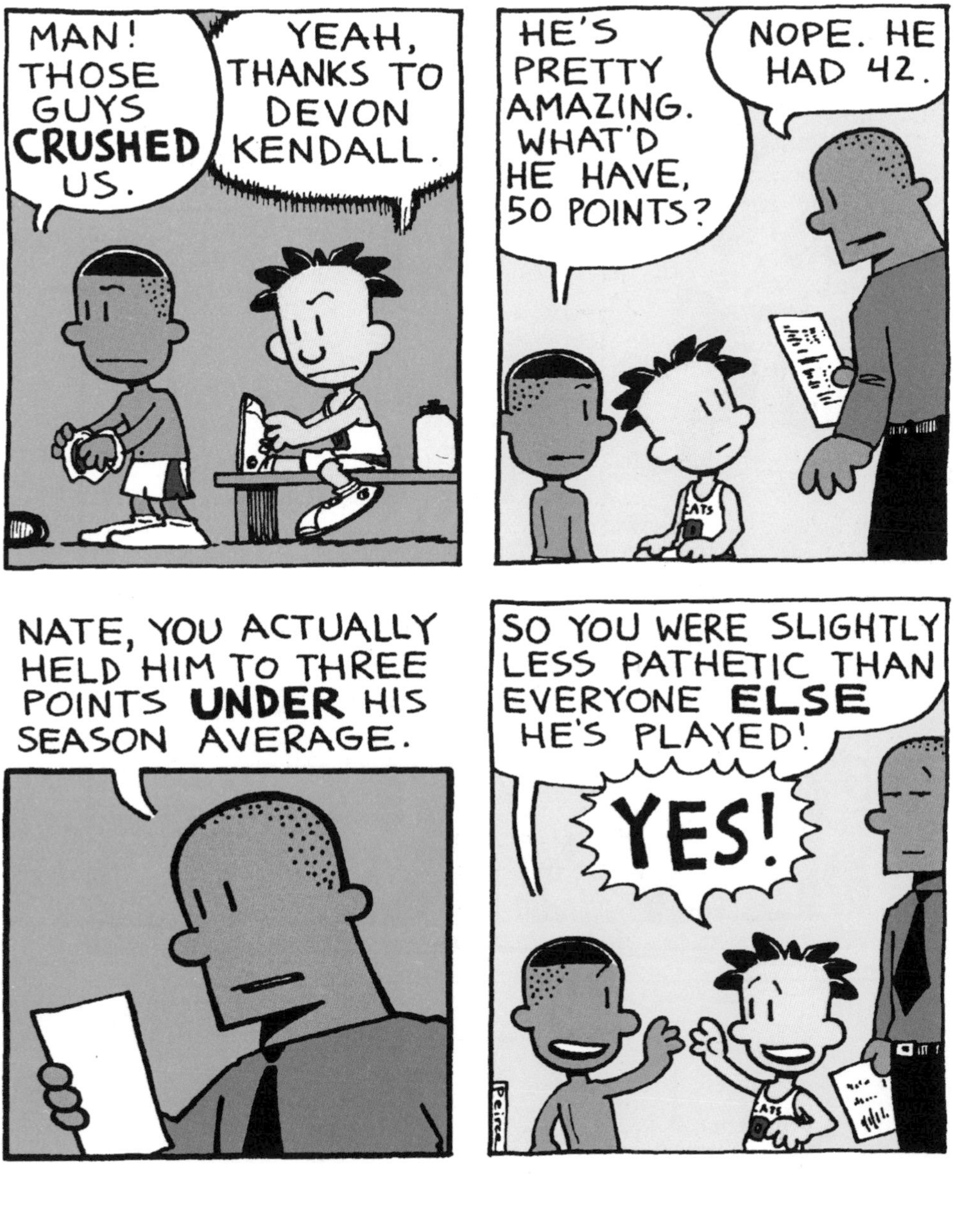
MAN! THOSE GUYS **CRUSHED** US.
YEAH, THANKS TO DEVON KENDALL.
HE'S PRETTY AMAZING. WHAT'D HE HAVE, 50 POINTS?
NOPE. HE HAD 42.
NATE, YOU ACTUALLY HELD HIM TO THREE POINTS **UNDER** HIS SEASON AVERAGE.
SO YOU WERE SLIGHTLY LESS PATHETIC THAN EVERYONE **ELSE** HE'S PLAYED!
YES!
Peirce

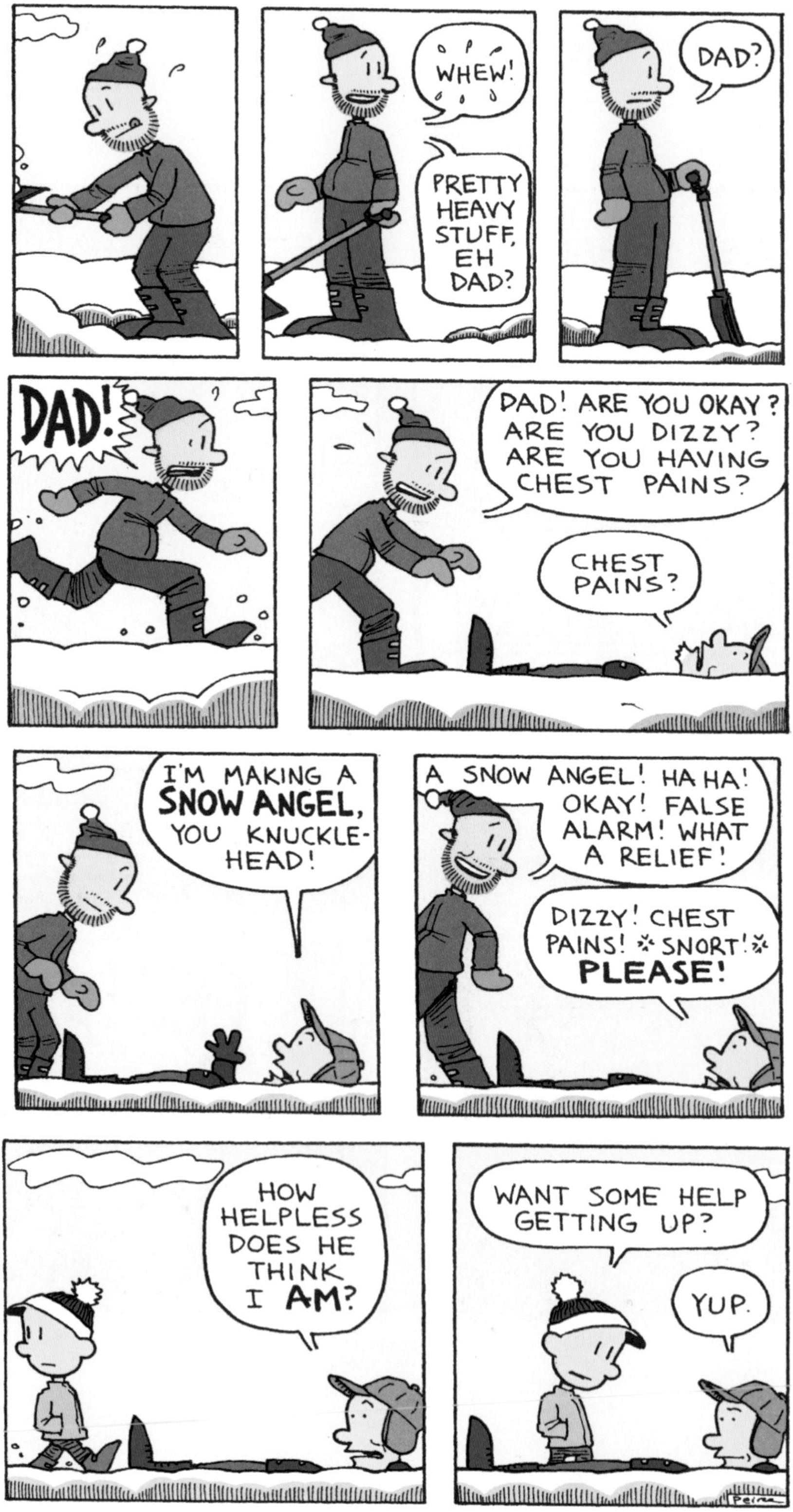
WHEW!
PRETTY HEAVY STUFF, EH DAD?
DAD?
DAD!
DAD! ARE YOU OKAY? ARE YOU DIZZY? ARE YOU HAVING CHEST PAINS?
CHEST PAINS?
I'M MAKING A **SNOW ANGEL**, YOU KNUCKLE-HEAD!
A SNOW ANGEL! HA HA! OKAY! FALSE ALARM! WHAT A RELIEF!
DIZZY! CHEST PAINS! *SNORT!* **PLEASE!**
HOW HELPLESS DOES HE THINK I **AM**?
WANT SOME HELP GETTING UP?
YUP.
Peirce

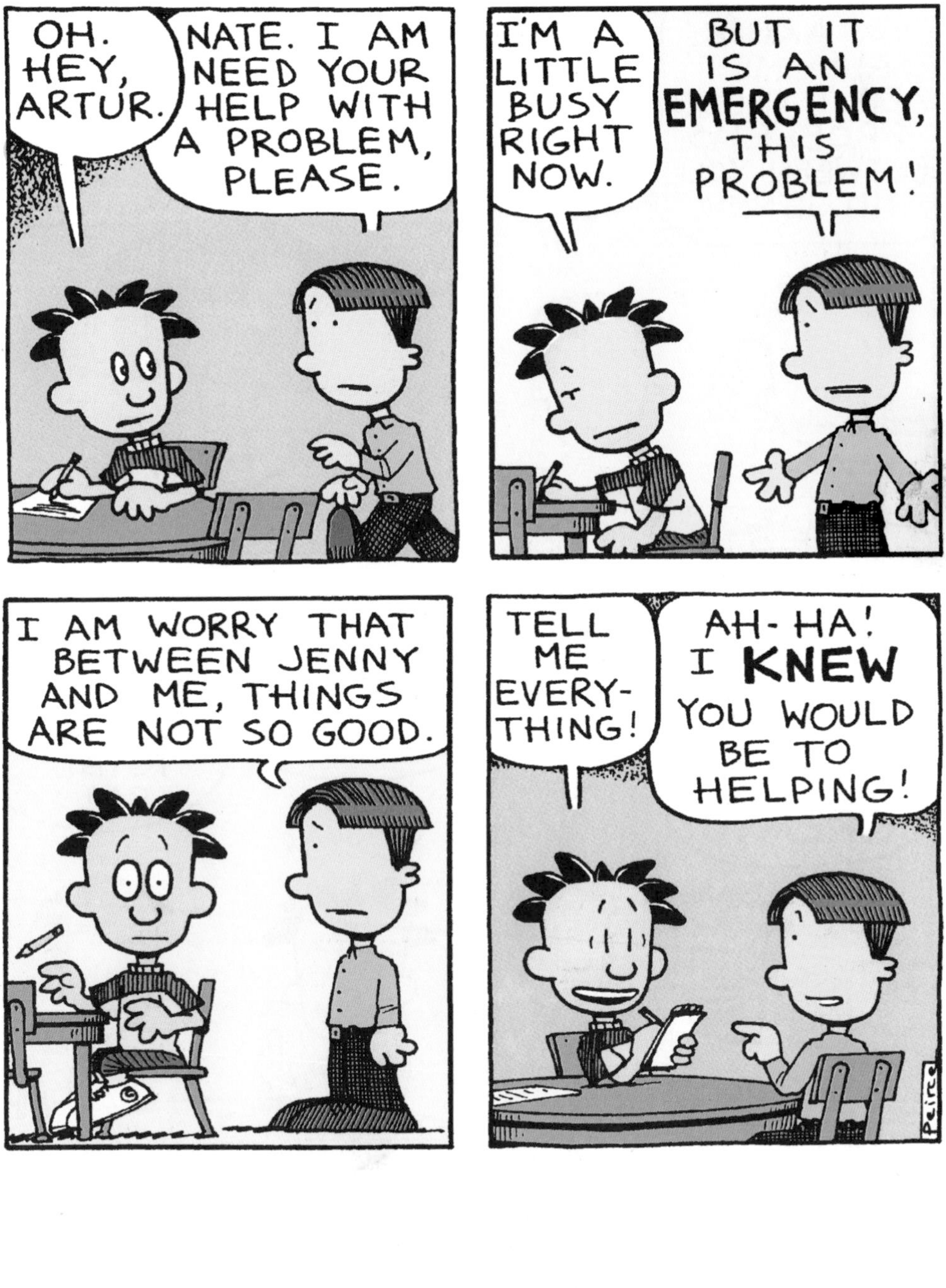
OH. HEY, ARTUR.
NATE. I AM NEED YOUR HELP WITH A PROBLEM, PLEASE.
I'M A LITTLE BUSY RIGHT NOW.
BUT IT IS AN EMERGENCY, THIS PROBLEM!
I AM WORRY THAT BETWEEN JENNY AND ME, THINGS ARE NOT SO GOOD.
TELL ME EVERY-THING!
AH-HA! I KNEW YOU WOULD BE TO HELPING!
Peirce

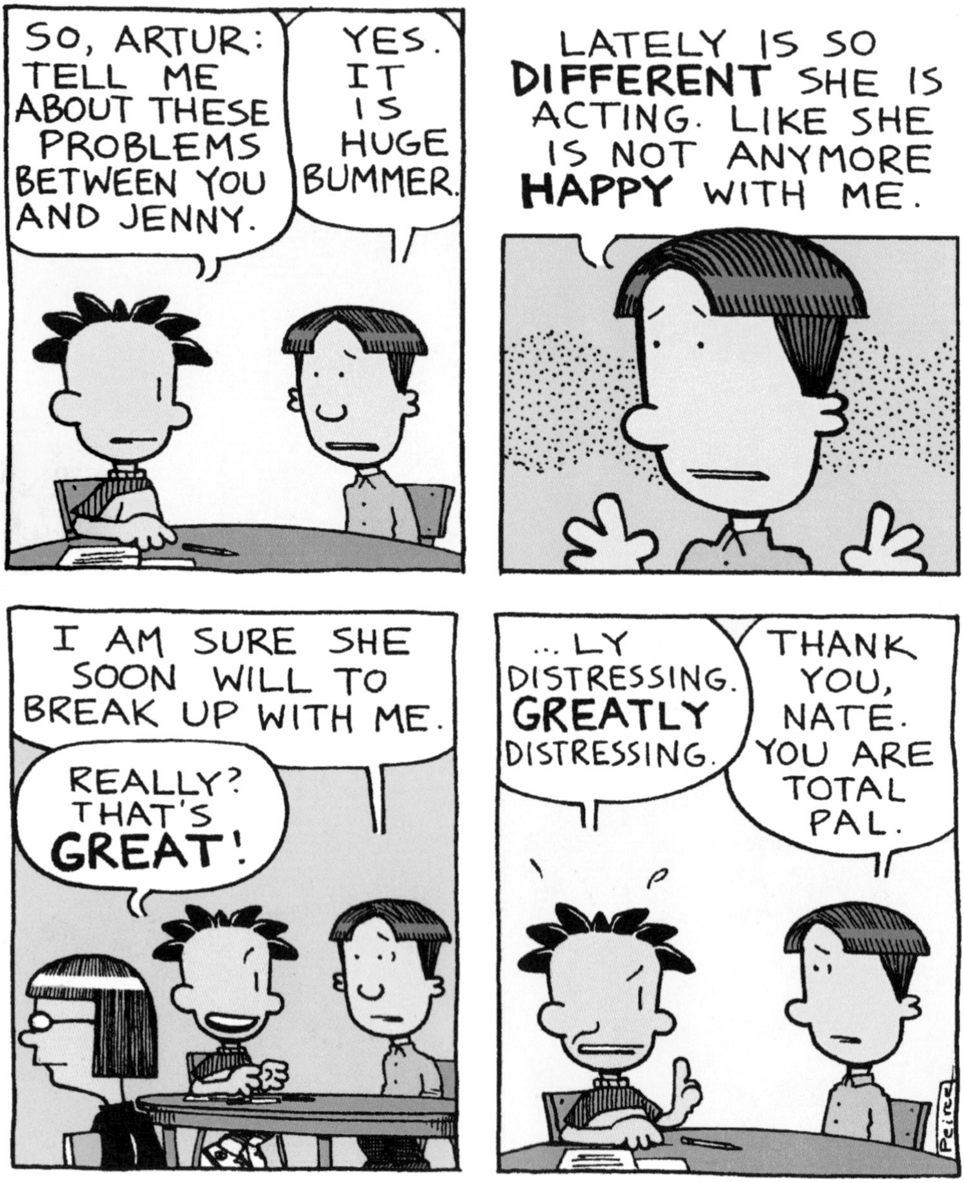
SO, ARTUR: TELL ME ABOUT THESE PROBLEMS BETWEEN YOU AND JENNY.
YES. IT IS HUGE BUMMER.
LATELY IS SO DIFFERENT SHE IS ACTING. LIKE SHE IS NOT ANYMORE HAPPY WITH ME.
I AM SURE SHE SOON WILL TO BREAK UP WITH ME.
REALLY? THAT'S GREAT!
...LY DISTRESSING. GREATLY DISTRESSING.
THANK YOU, NATE. YOU ARE TOTAL PAL.
PEIRCE

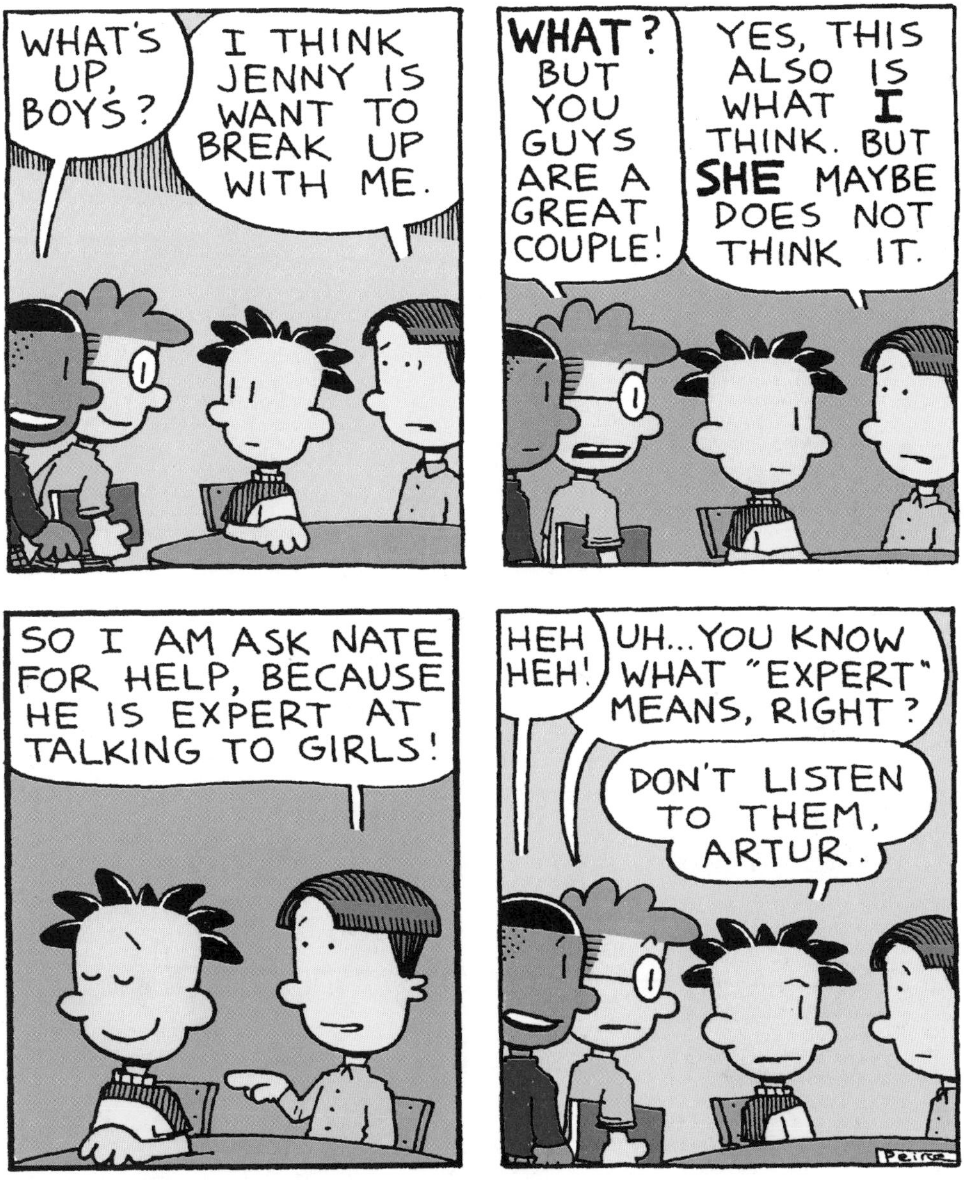
WHAT'S UP, BOYS?
I THINK JENNY IS WANT TO BREAK UP WITH ME.
WHAT? BUT YOU GUYS ARE A GREAT COUPLE!
YES, THIS ALSO IS WHAT I THINK. BUT SHE MAYBE DOES NOT THINK IT.
SO I AM ASK NATE FOR HELP, BECAUSE HE IS EXPERT AT TALKING TO GIRLS!
HEH HEH!
UH... YOU KNOW WHAT "EXPERT" MEANS, RIGHT?
DON'T LISTEN TO THEM, ARTUR.
Peirce

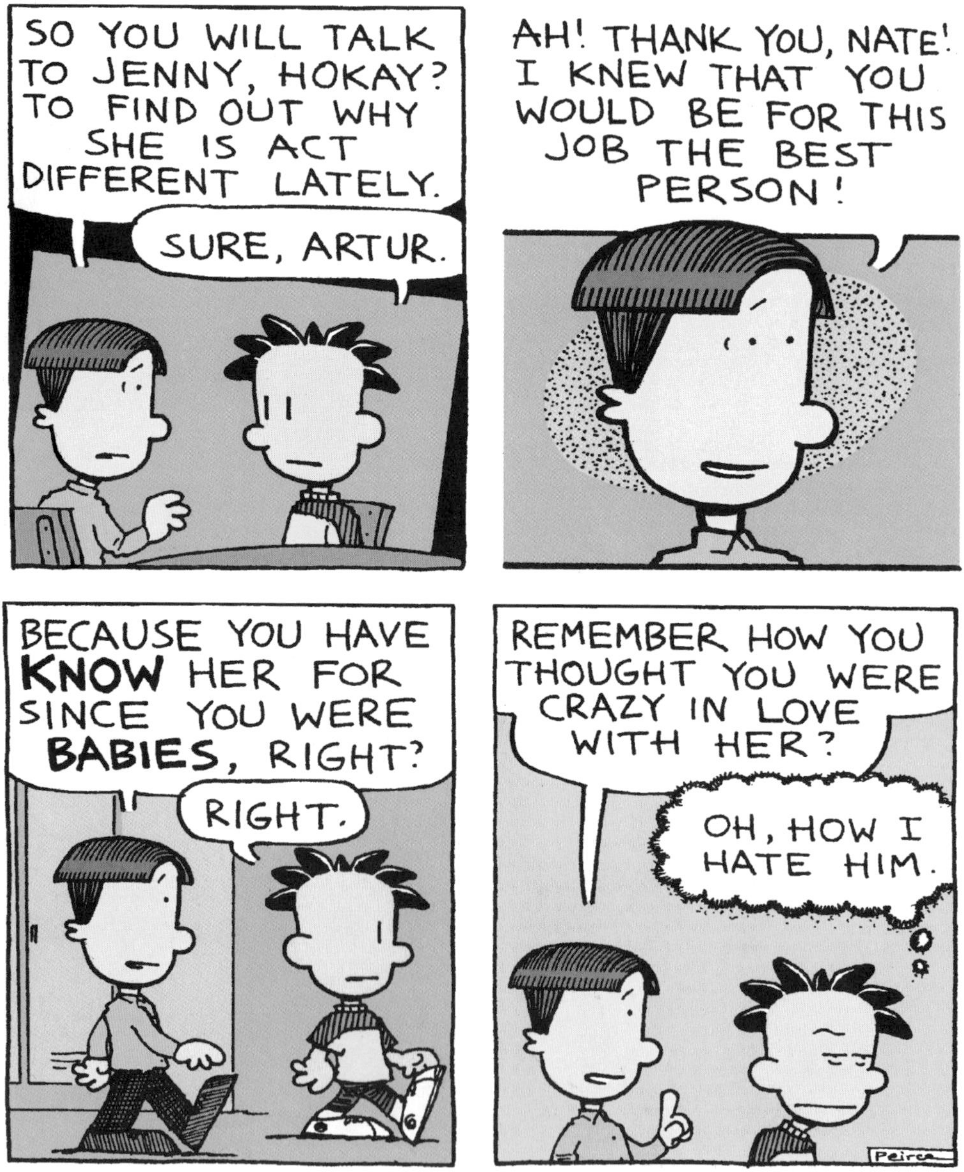
SO YOU WILL TALK TO JENNY, HOKAY? TO FIND OUT WHY SHE IS ACT DIFFERENT LATELY.
SURE, ARTUR.
AH! THANK YOU, NATE! I KNEW THAT YOU WOULD BE FOR THIS JOB THE BEST PERSON!
BECAUSE YOU HAVE **KNOW** HER FOR SINCE YOU WERE **BABIES**, RIGHT?
RIGHT.
REMEMBER HOW YOU THOUGHT YOU WERE CRAZY IN LOVE WITH HER?
OH, HOW I HATE HIM.
Peirce

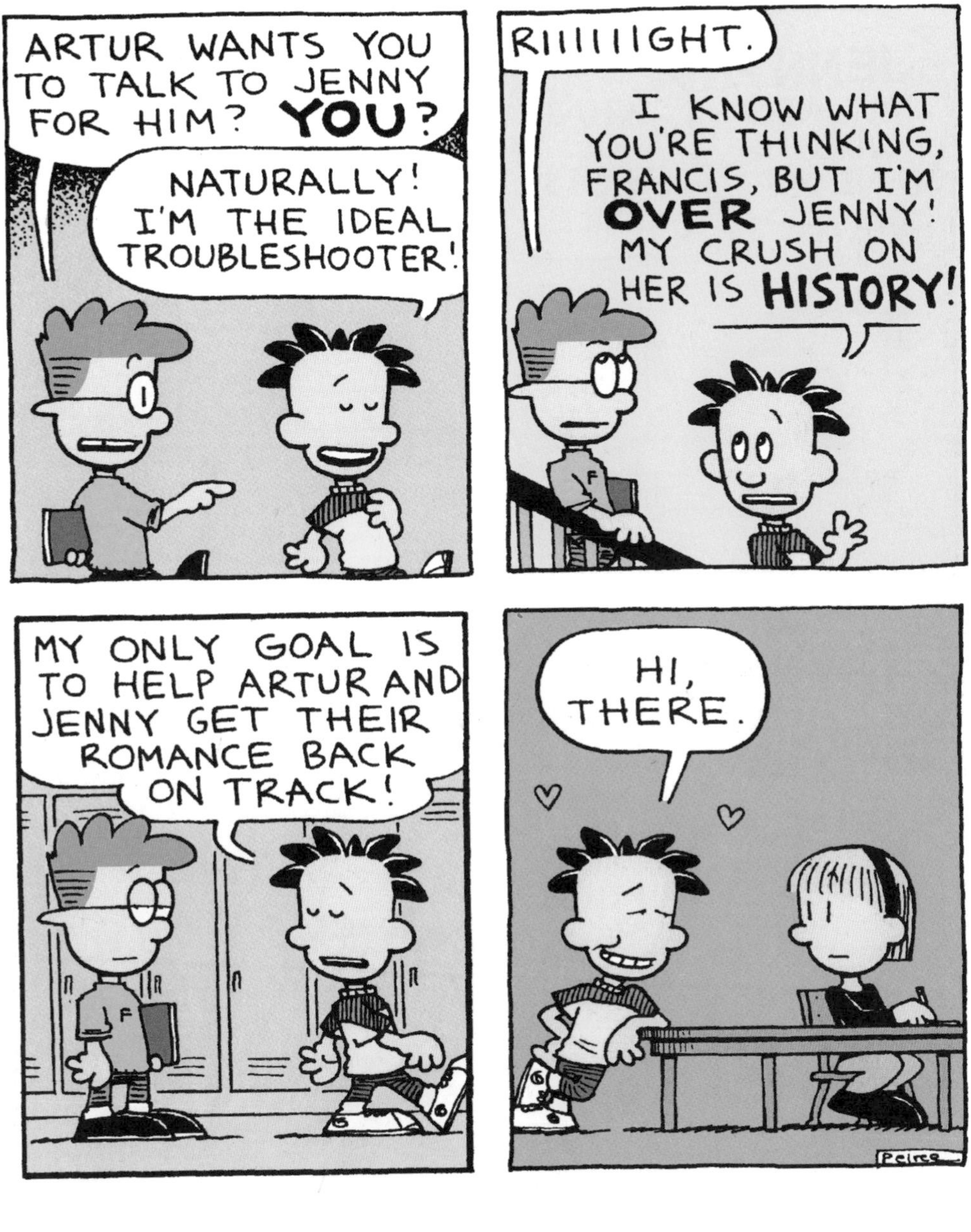
ARTUR WANTS YOU TO TALK TO JENNY FOR HIM? YOU?
NATURALLY! I'M THE IDEAL TROUBLESHOOTER!
RIIIIIIGHT.
I KNOW WHAT YOU'RE THINKING, FRANCIS, BUT I'M OVER JENNY! MY CRUSH ON HER IS HISTORY!
MY ONLY GOAL IS TO HELP ARTUR AND JENNY GET THEIR ROMANCE BACK ON TRACK!
HI, THERE.
PEIRCE

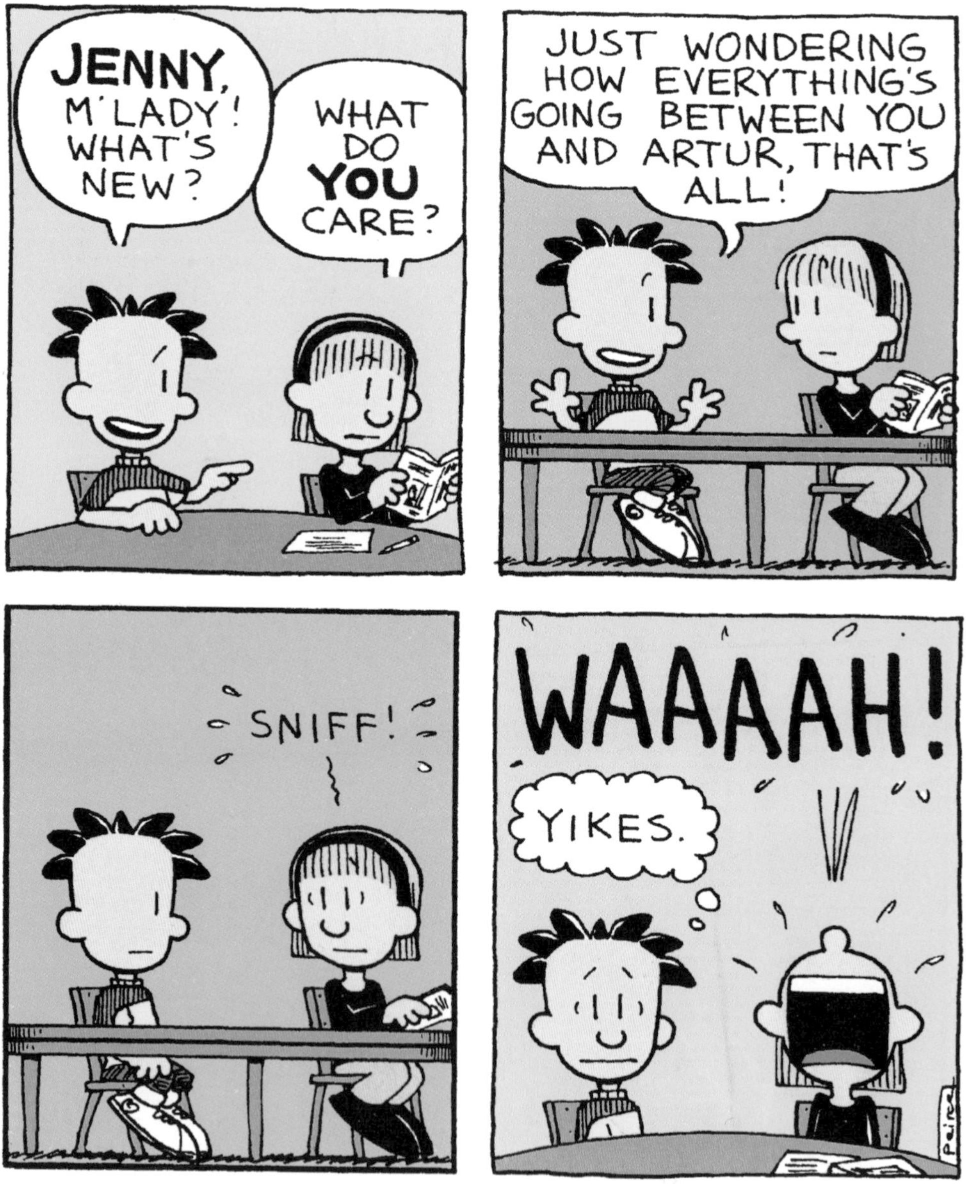
JENNY, M'LADY! WHAT'S NEW?
WHAT DO YOU CARE?
JUST WONDERING HOW EVERYTHING'S GOING BETWEEN YOU AND ARTUR, THAT'S ALL!
SNIFF!
WAAAAH!
YIKES.
peirce

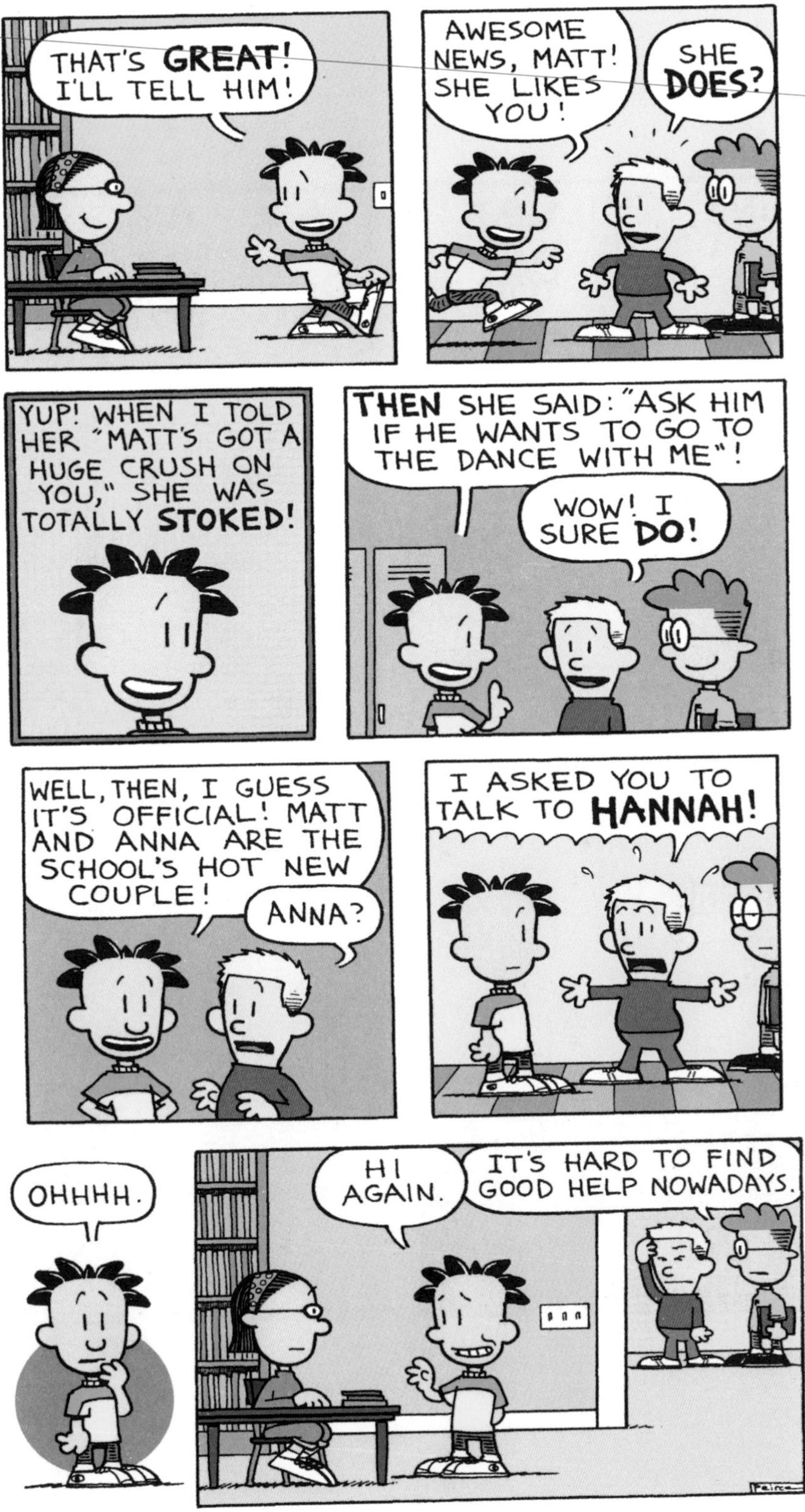
THAT'S **GREAT**! I'LL TELL HIM!
AWESOME NEWS, MATT! SHE LIKES YOU!
SHE **DOES**?
YUP! WHEN I TOLD HER "MATT'S GOT A HUGE CRUSH ON YOU," SHE WAS TOTALLY **STOKED**!
THEN SHE SAID: "ASK HIM IF HE WANTS TO GO TO THE DANCE WITH ME"!
WOW! I SURE **DO**!
WELL, THEN, I GUESS IT'S OFFICIAL! MATT AND ANNA ARE THE SCHOOL'S HOT NEW COUPLE!
ANNA?
I ASKED YOU TO TALK TO **HANNAH**!
OHHHH.
HI AGAIN.
IT'S HARD TO FIND GOOD HELP NOWADAYS.
Peirce

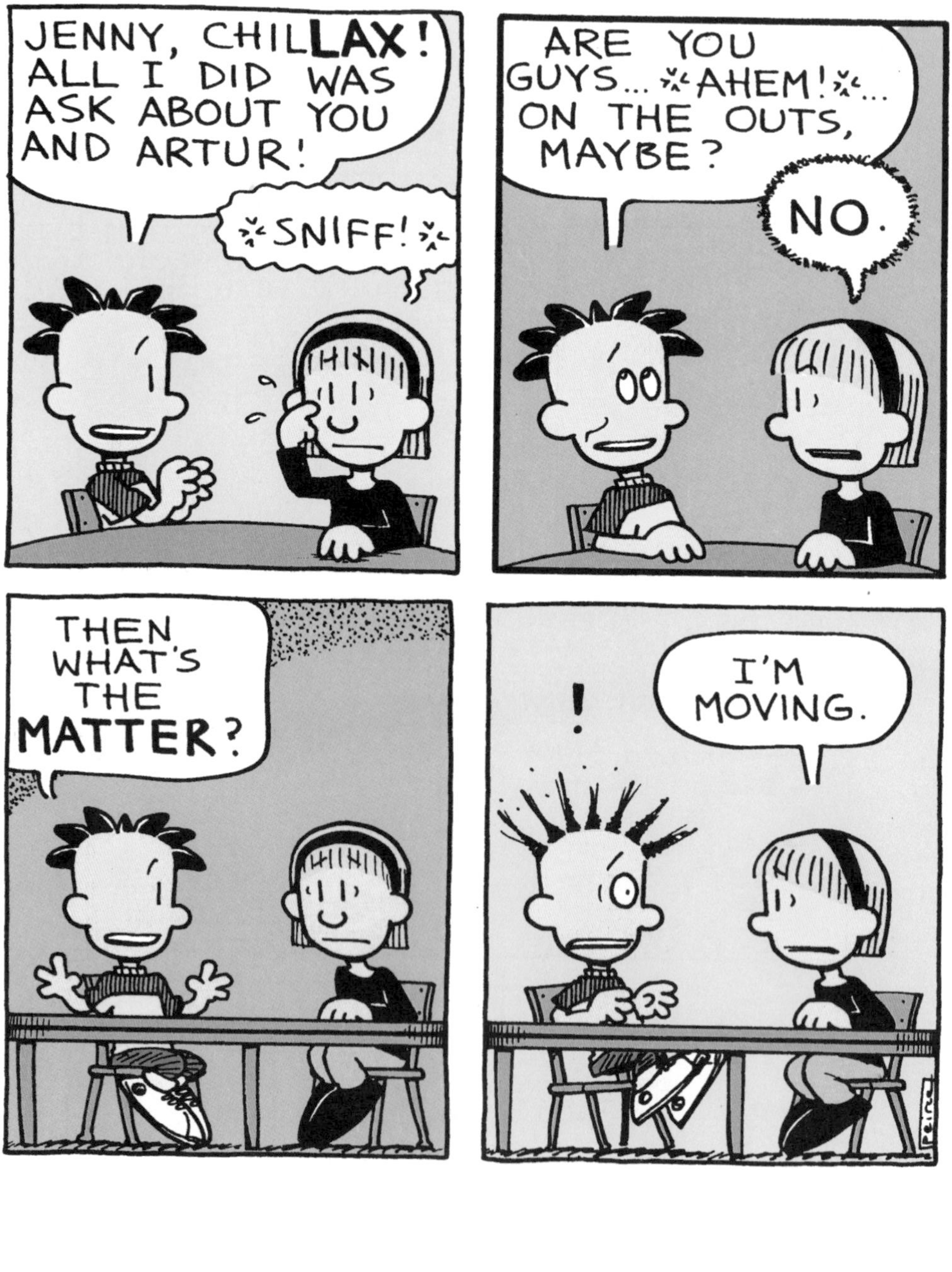
JENNY, CHILLAX! ALL I DID WAS ASK ABOUT YOU AND ARTUR!
SNIFF!
ARE YOU GUYS... *AHEM!*... ON THE OUTS, MAYBE?
NO.
THEN WHAT'S THE MATTER?
!
I'M MOVING.

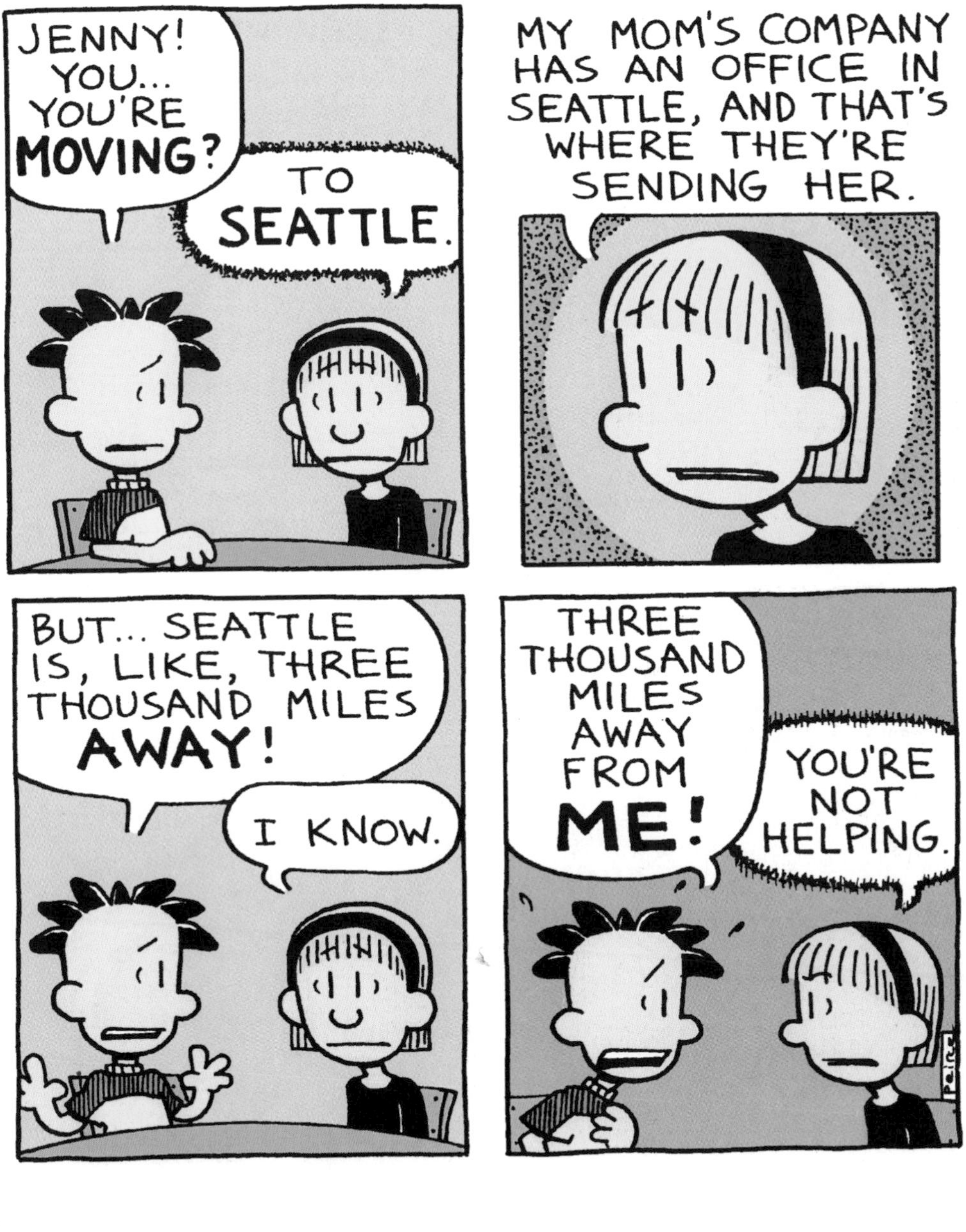
JENNY! YOU... YOU'RE MOVING?
TO SEATTLE.
MY MOM'S COMPANY HAS AN OFFICE IN SEATTLE, AND THAT'S WHERE THEY'RE SENDING HER.
BUT... SEATTLE IS, LIKE, THREE THOUSAND MILES AWAY!
I KNOW.
THREE THOUSAND MILES AWAY FROM ME!
YOU'RE NOT HELPING.

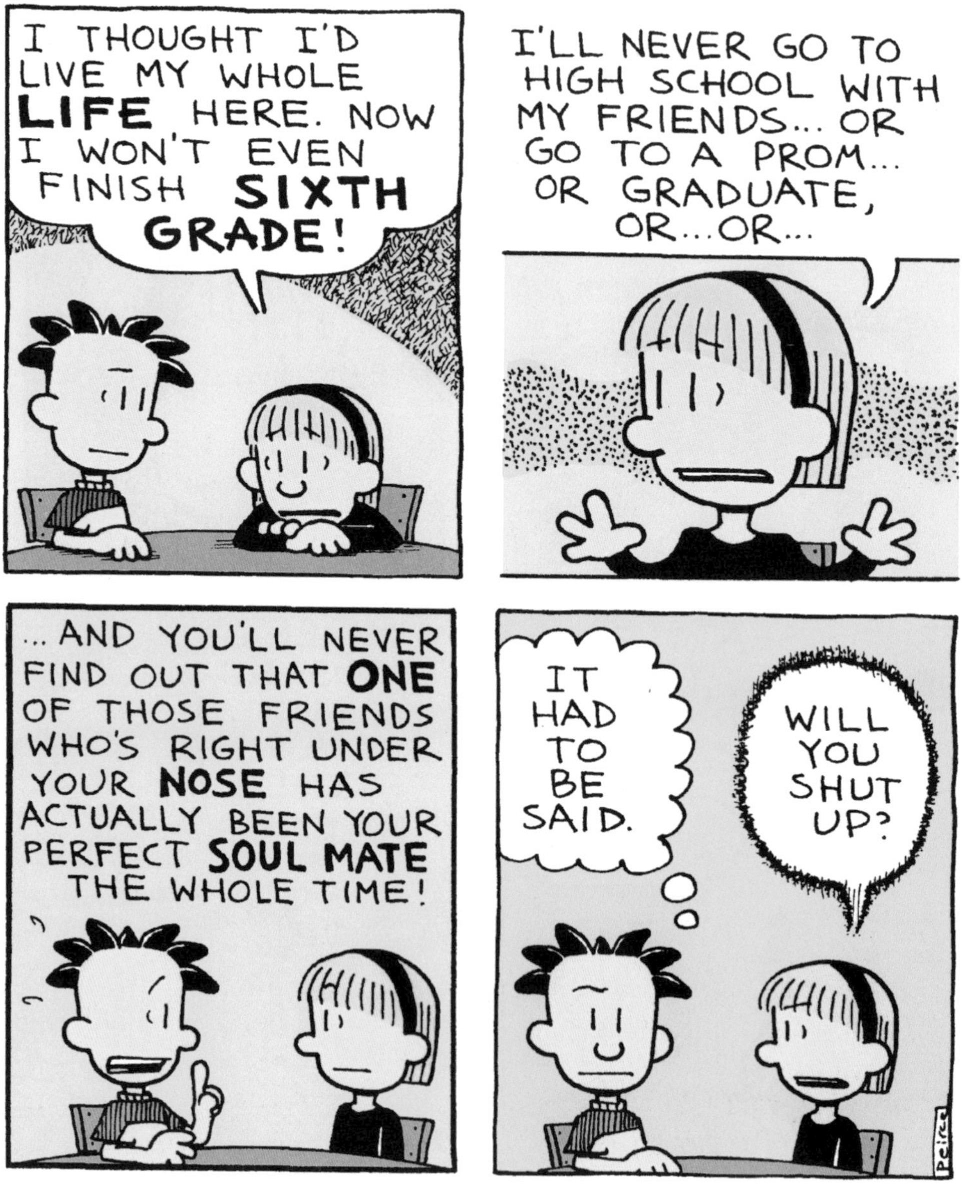
I THOUGHT I'D LIVE MY WHOLE LIFE HERE. NOW I WON'T EVEN FINISH SIXTH GRADE!
I'LL NEVER GO TO HIGH SCHOOL WITH MY FRIENDS... OR GO TO A PROM... OR GRADUATE, OR...OR...
...AND YOU'LL NEVER FIND OUT THAT ONE OF THOSE FRIENDS WHO'S RIGHT UNDER YOUR NOSE HAS ACTUALLY BEEN YOUR PERFECT SOUL MATE THE WHOLE TIME!
IT HAD TO BE SAID.
WILL YOU SHUT UP?
peirce

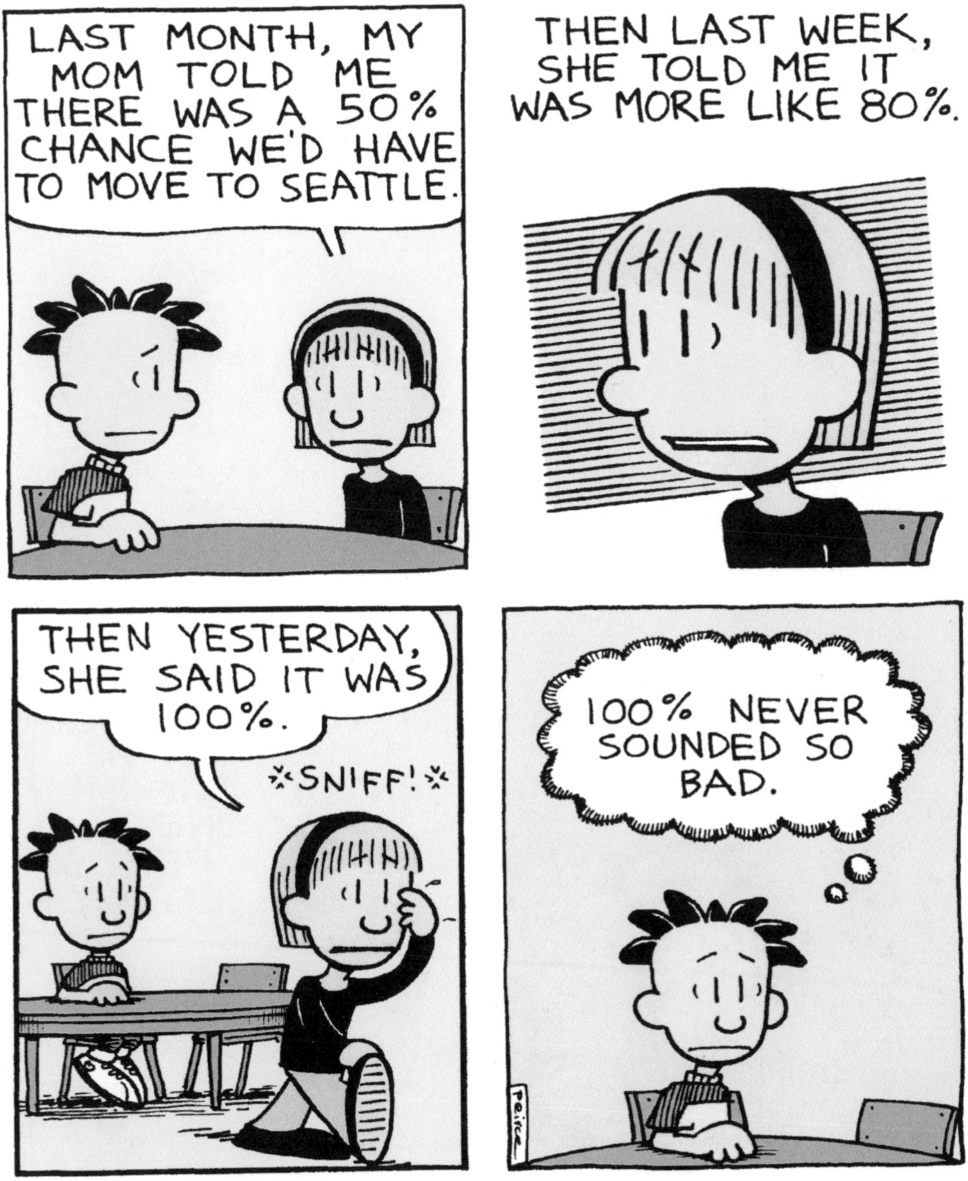
LAST MONTH, MY MOM TOLD ME THERE WAS A 50% CHANCE WE'D HAVE TO MOVE TO SEATTLE.
THEN LAST WEEK, SHE TOLD ME IT WAS MORE LIKE 80%.
THEN YESTERDAY, SHE SAID IT WAS 100%.
SNIFF!
100% NEVER SOUNDED SO BAD.
PEIRCE

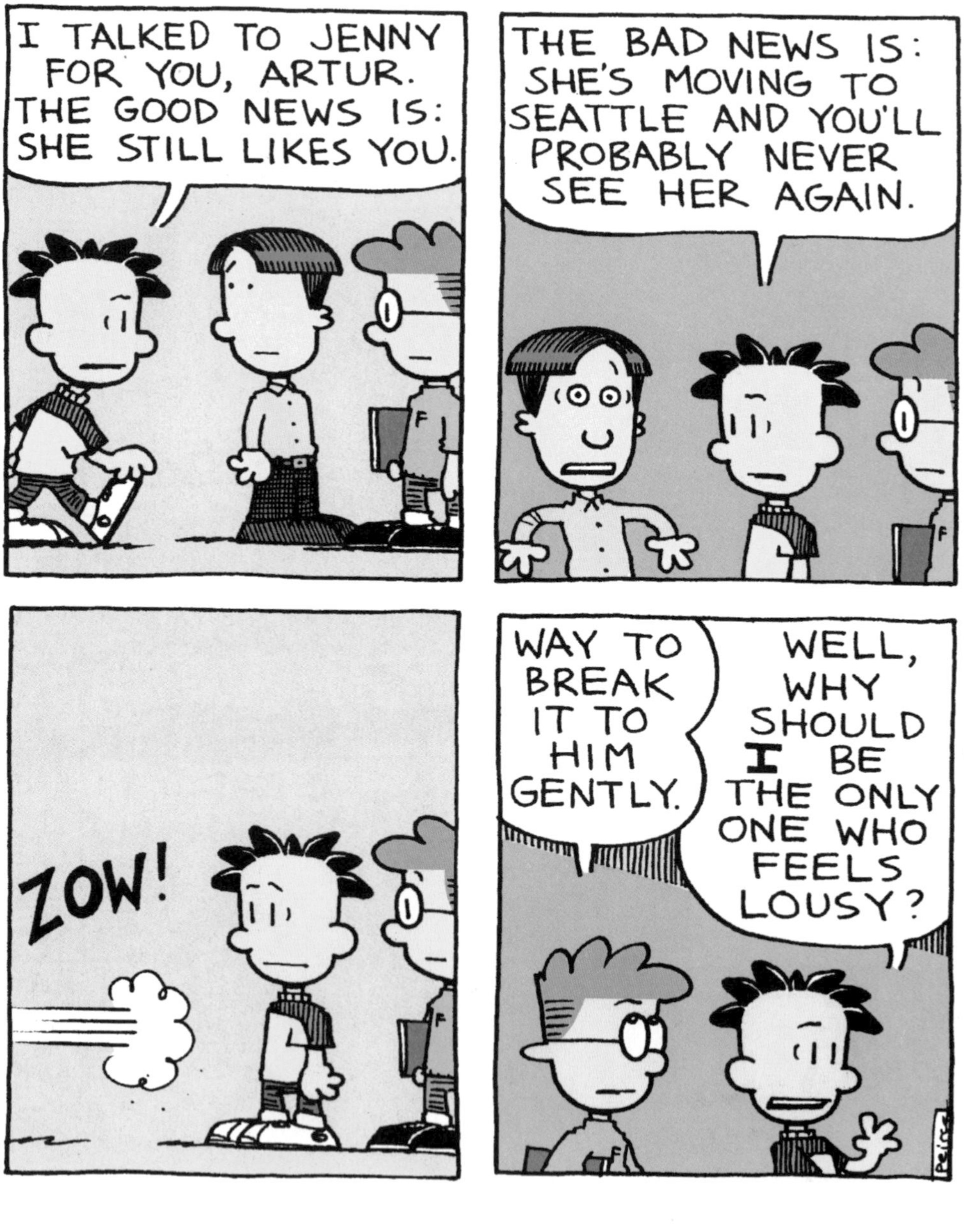
I TALKED TO JENNY FOR YOU, ARTUR. THE GOOD NEWS IS: SHE STILL LIKES YOU.
THE BAD NEWS IS: SHE'S MOVING TO SEATTLE AND YOU'LL PROBABLY NEVER SEE HER AGAIN.
ZOW!
WAY TO BREAK IT TO HIM GENTLY.
WELL, WHY SHOULD I BE THE ONLY ONE WHO FEELS LOUSY?
PEIRCE

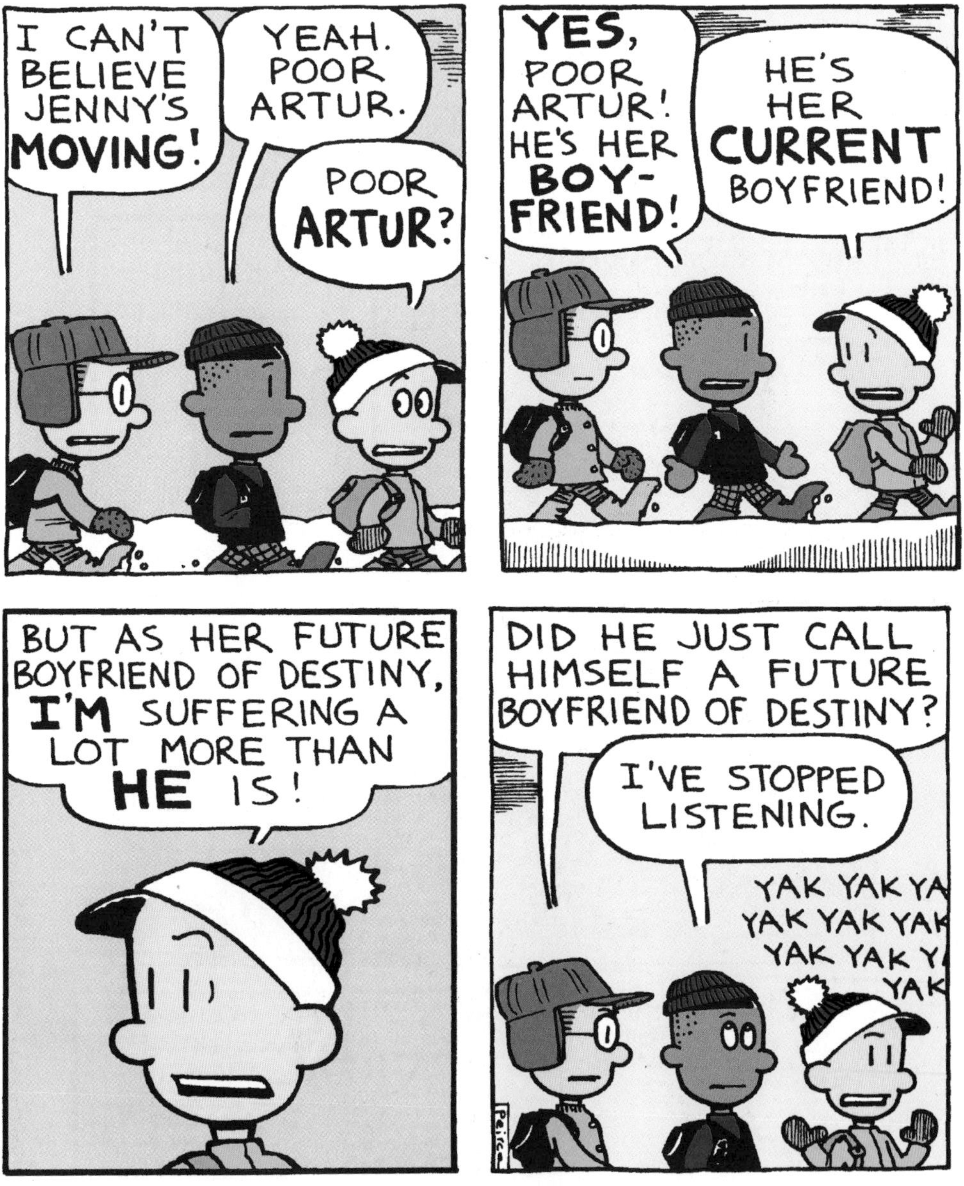
I CAN'T BELIEVE JENNY'S MOVING!
YEAH. POOR ARTUR.
POOR ARTUR?
YES, POOR ARTUR! HE'S HER BOY-FRIEND!
HE'S HER CURRENT BOYFRIEND!
BUT AS HER FUTURE BOYFRIEND OF DESTINY, I'M SUFFERING A LOT MORE THAN HE IS!
DID HE JUST CALL HIMSELF A FUTURE BOYFRIEND OF DESTINY?
I'VE STOPPED LISTENING.
YAK YAK YA
YAK YAK YAK
YAK YAK Y
YAK
Peirce

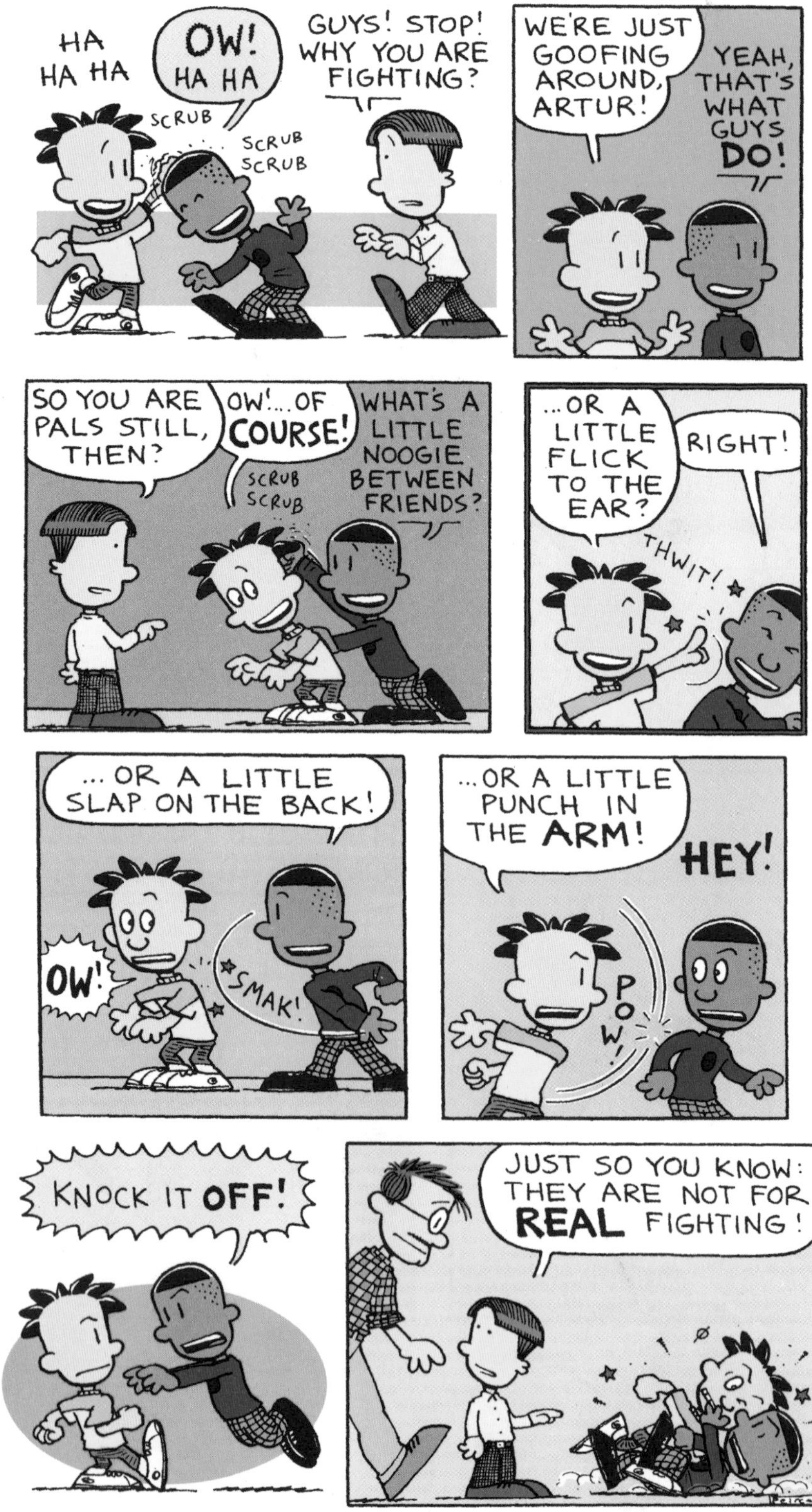
HA HA HA
OW! HA HA
SCRUB
SCRUB SCRUB
GUYS! STOP! WHY YOU ARE FIGHTING?
WE'RE JUST GOOFING AROUND, ARTUR!
YEAH, THAT'S WHAT GUYS DO!
SO YOU ARE PALS STILL, THEN?
OW!... OF COURSE!
SCRUB SCRUB
WHAT'S A LITTLE NOOGIE BETWEEN FRIENDS?
...OR A LITTLE FLICK TO THE EAR?
RIGHT!
THWIT!
... OR A LITTLE SLAP ON THE BACK!
OW!
SMAK!
...OR A LITTLE PUNCH IN THE ARM!
HEY!
POW!
KNOCK IT OFF!
JUST SO YOU KNOW: THEY ARE NOT FOR REAL FIGHTING!

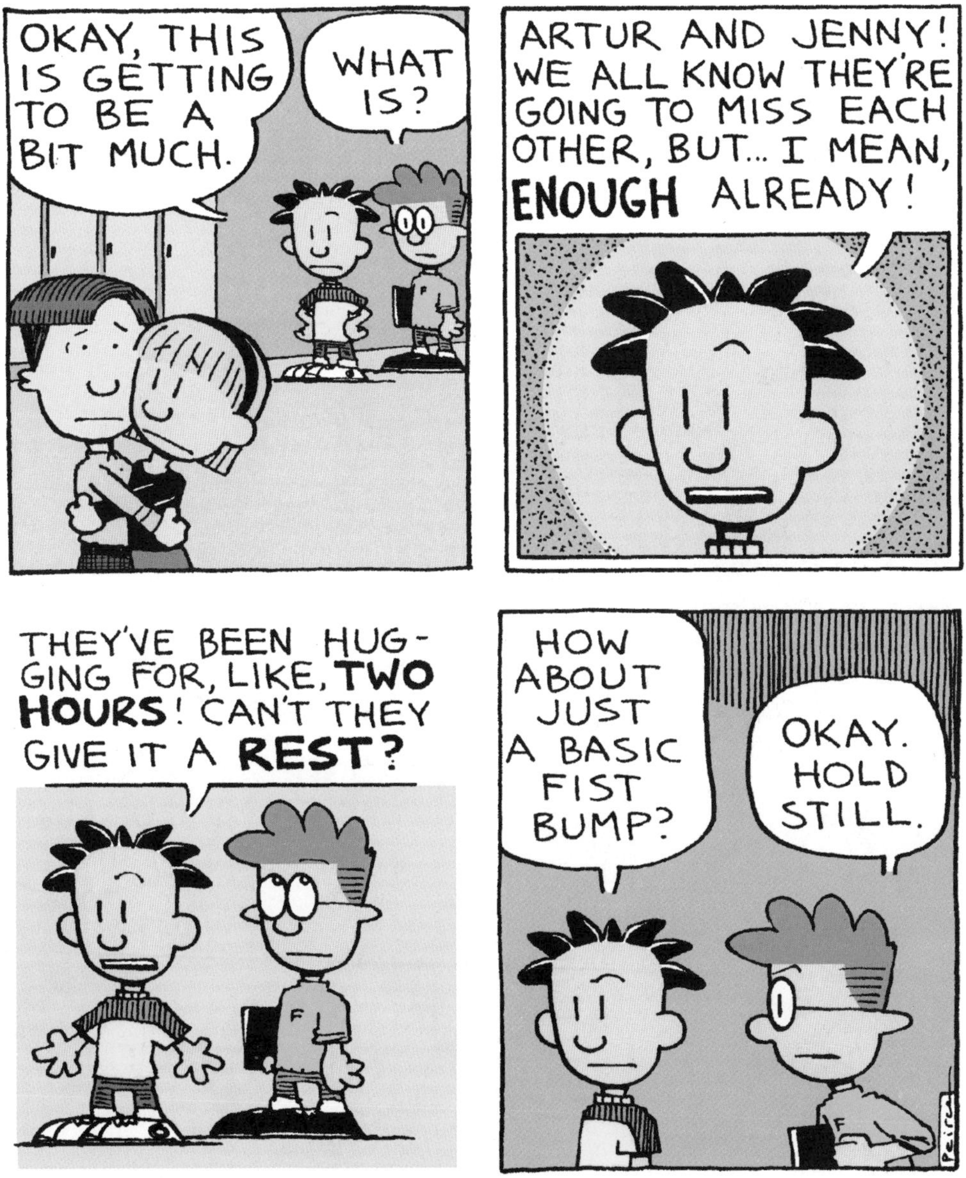
OKAY, THIS IS GETTING TO BE A BIT MUCH.
WHAT IS?
ARTUR AND JENNY! WE ALL KNOW THEY'RE GOING TO MISS EACH OTHER, BUT... I MEAN, ENOUGH ALREADY!
THEY'VE BEEN HUGGING FOR, LIKE, TWO HOURS! CAN'T THEY GIVE IT A REST?
HOW ABOUT JUST A BASIC FIST BUMP?
OKAY. HOLD STILL.
Peirce

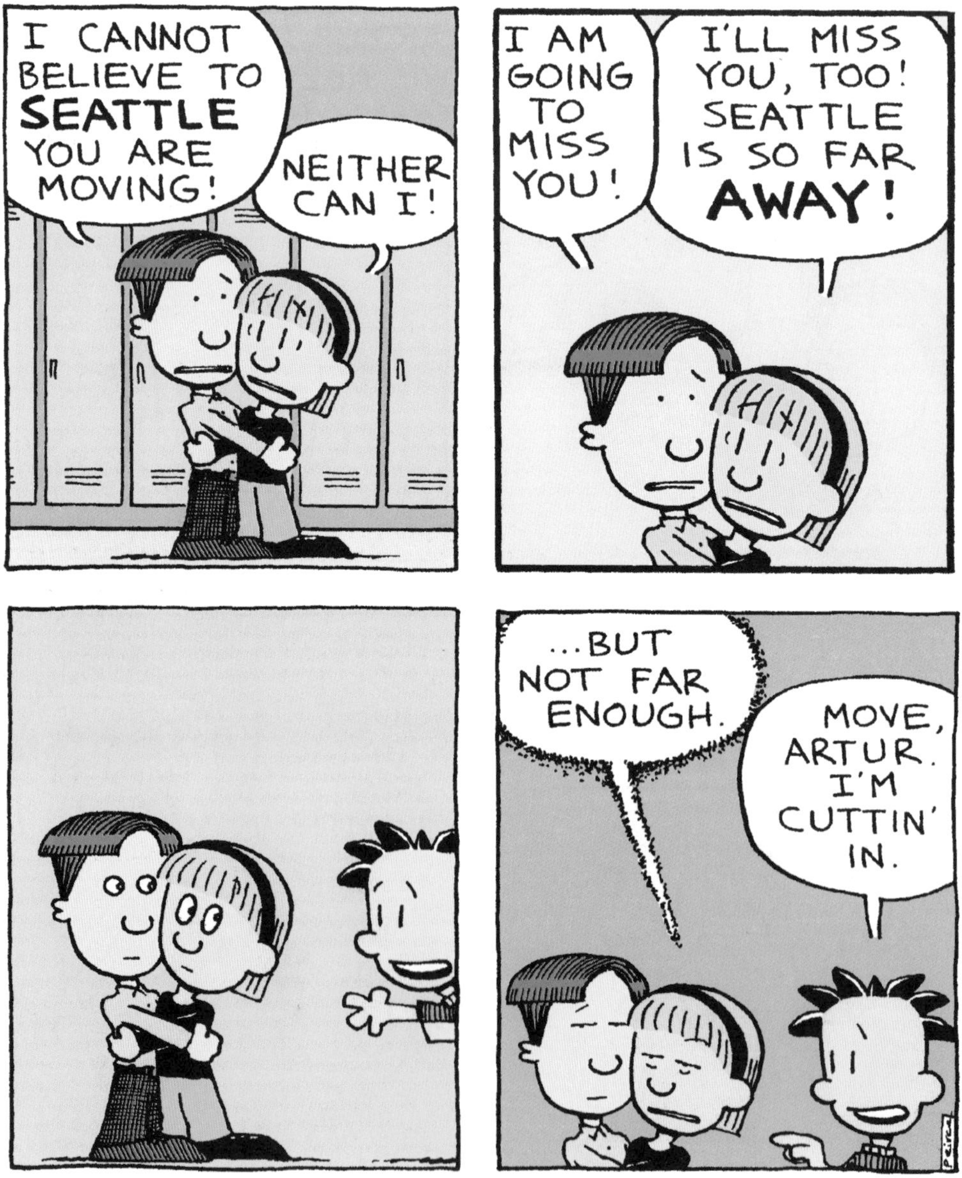
I CANNOT BELIEVE TO **SEATTLE** YOU ARE MOVING!
NEITHER CAN I!
I AM GOING TO MISS YOU!
I'LL MISS YOU, TOO! SEATTLE IS SO FAR **AWAY!**
...BUT NOT FAR ENOUGH.
MOVE, ARTUR. I'M CUTTIN' IN.
PEIRCE

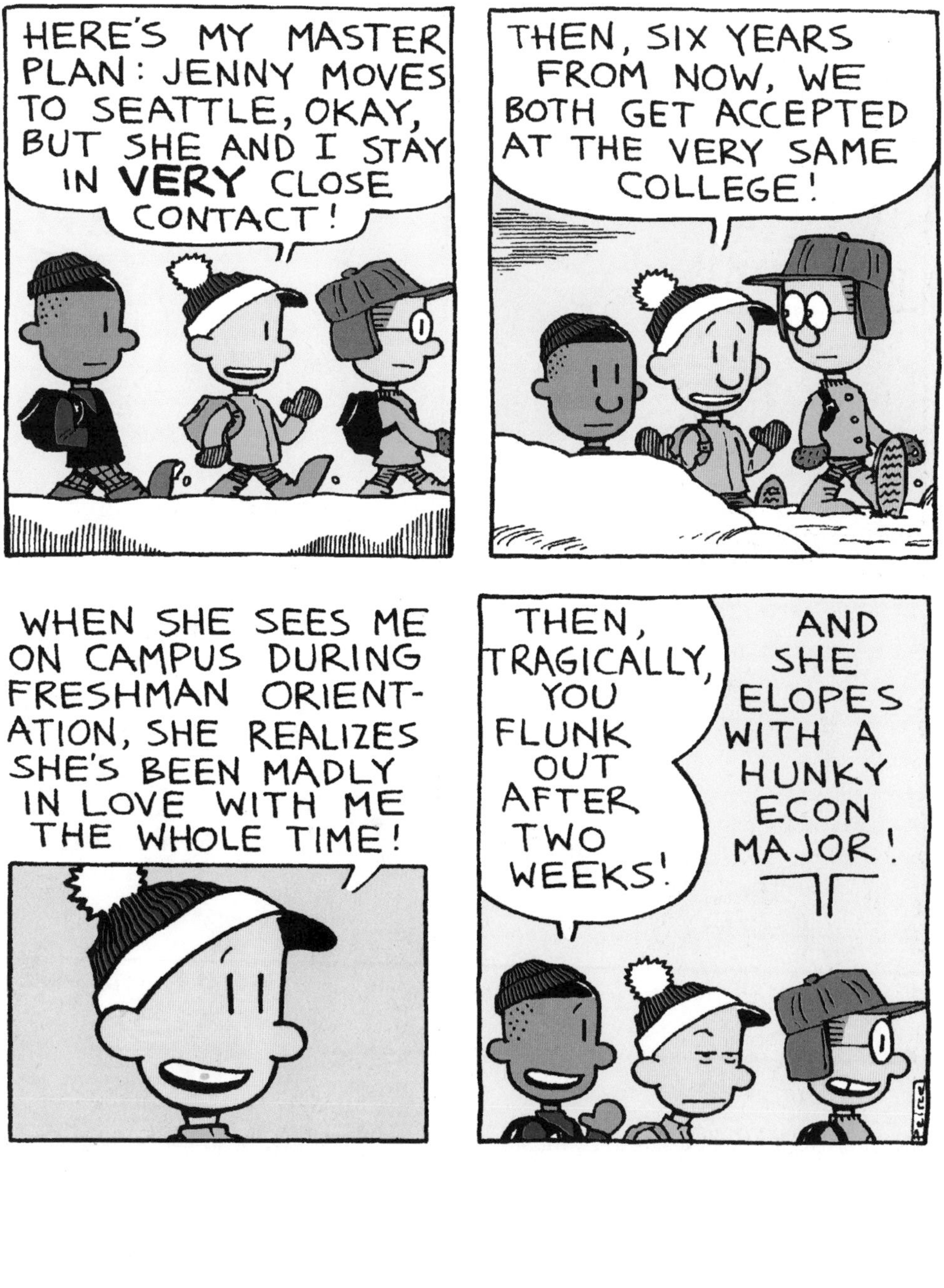
HERE'S MY MASTER PLAN: JENNY MOVES TO SEATTLE, OKAY, BUT SHE AND I STAY IN **VERY** CLOSE CONTACT!
THEN, SIX YEARS FROM NOW, WE BOTH GET ACCEPTED AT THE VERY SAME COLLEGE!
WHEN SHE SEES ME ON CAMPUS DURING FRESHMAN ORIENT-ATION, SHE REALIZES SHE'S BEEN MADLY IN LOVE WITH ME THE WHOLE TIME!
THEN, TRAGICALLY, YOU FLUNK OUT AFTER TWO WEEKS!
AND SHE ELOPES WITH A HUNKY ECON MAJOR!

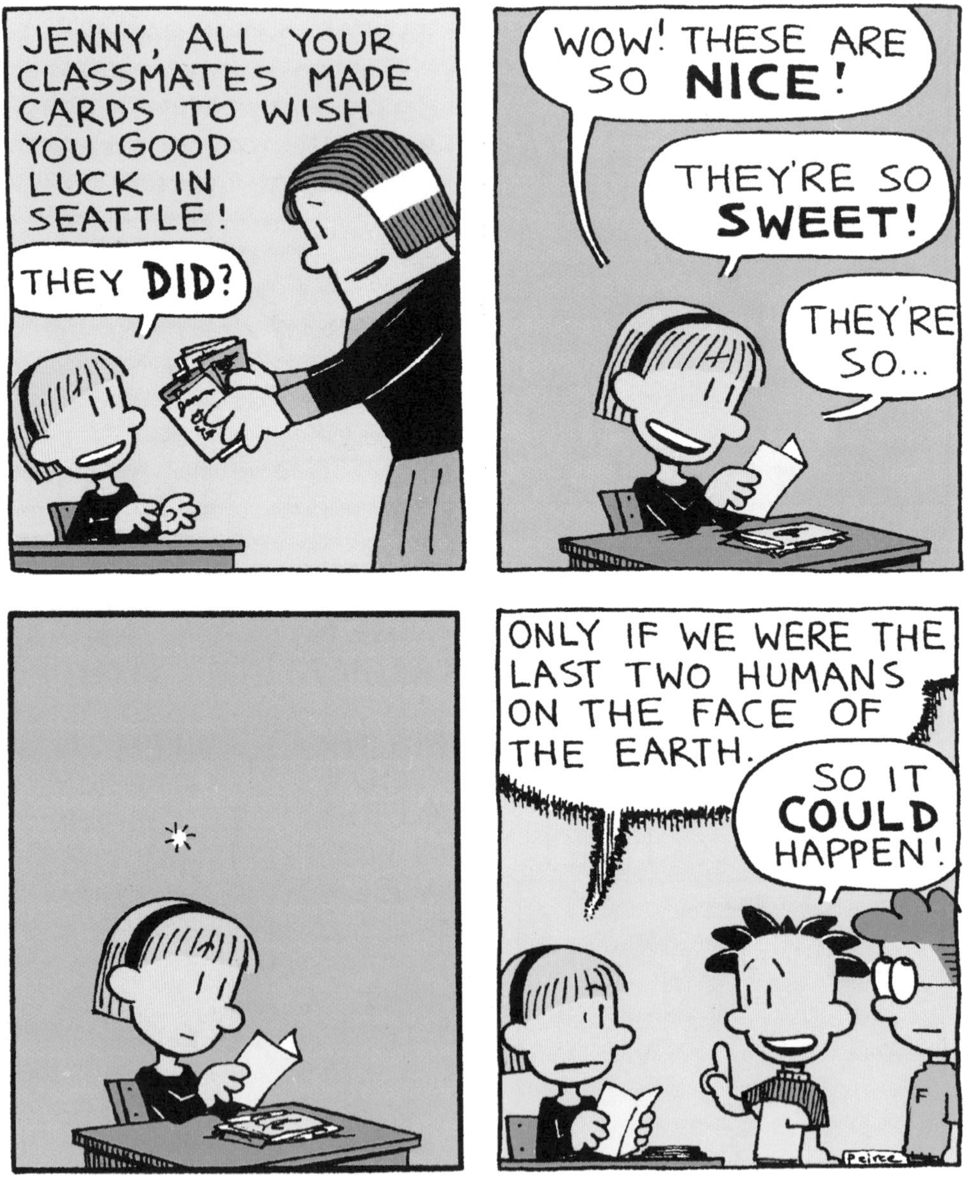
JENNY, ALL YOUR CLASSMATES MADE CARDS TO WISH YOU GOOD LUCK IN SEATTLE!
THEY **DID**?
WOW! THESE ARE SO **NICE**!
THEY'RE SO **SWEET!**
THEY'RE SO...
ONLY IF WE WERE THE LAST TWO HUMANS ON THE FACE OF THE EARTH.
SO IT **COULD** HAPPEN!
Peirce

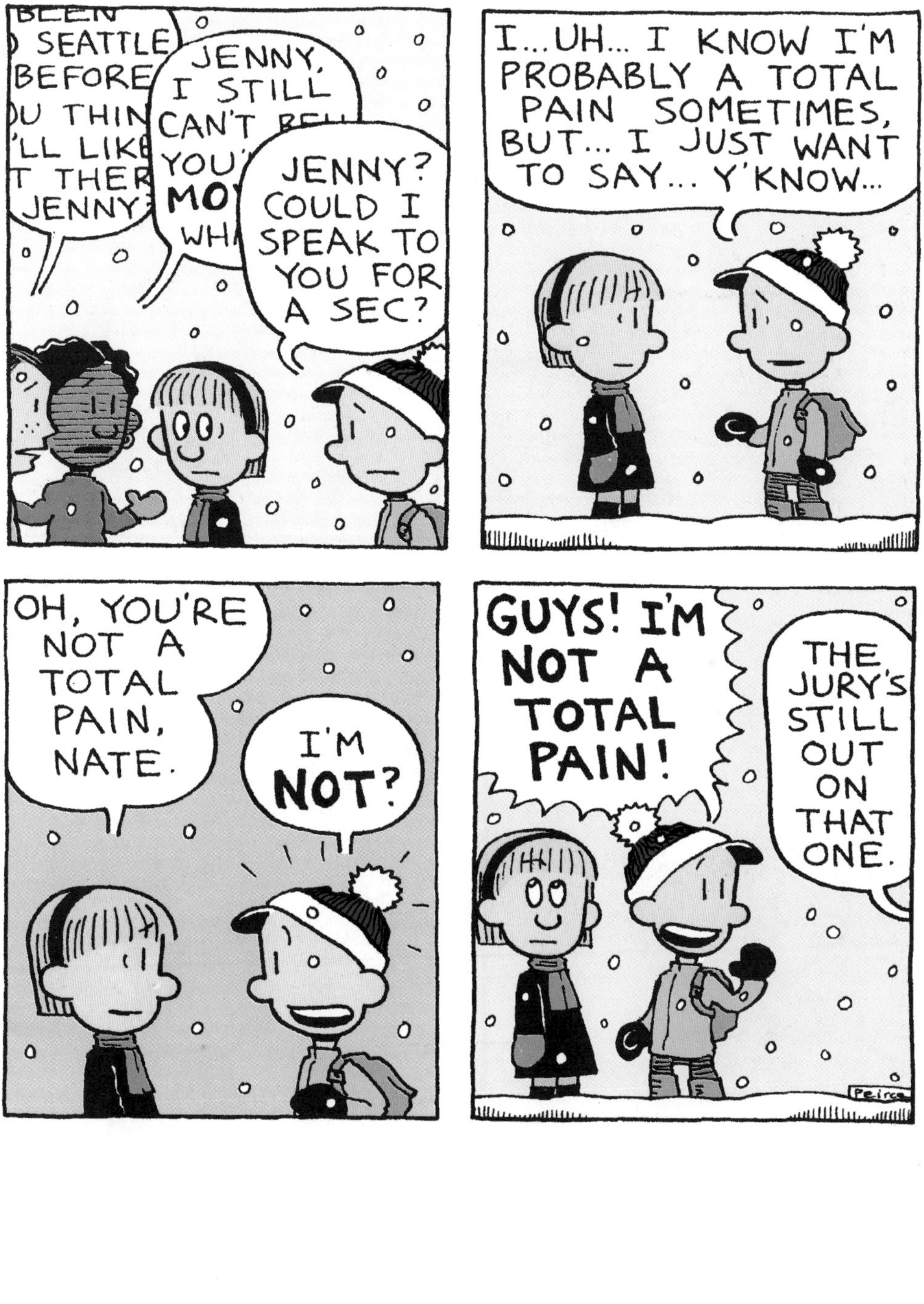
SEATTLE BEFORE ... JENNY?
JENNY, I STILL CAN'T ...
JENNY? COULD I SPEAK TO YOU FOR A SEC?
I...UH... I KNOW I'M PROBABLY A TOTAL PAIN SOMETIMES, BUT... I JUST WANT TO SAY... Y'KNOW...
OH, YOU'RE NOT A TOTAL PAIN, NATE.
I'M **NOT**?
GUYS! I'M NOT A TOTAL PAIN!
THE JURY'S STILL OUT ON THAT ONE.
Peirce

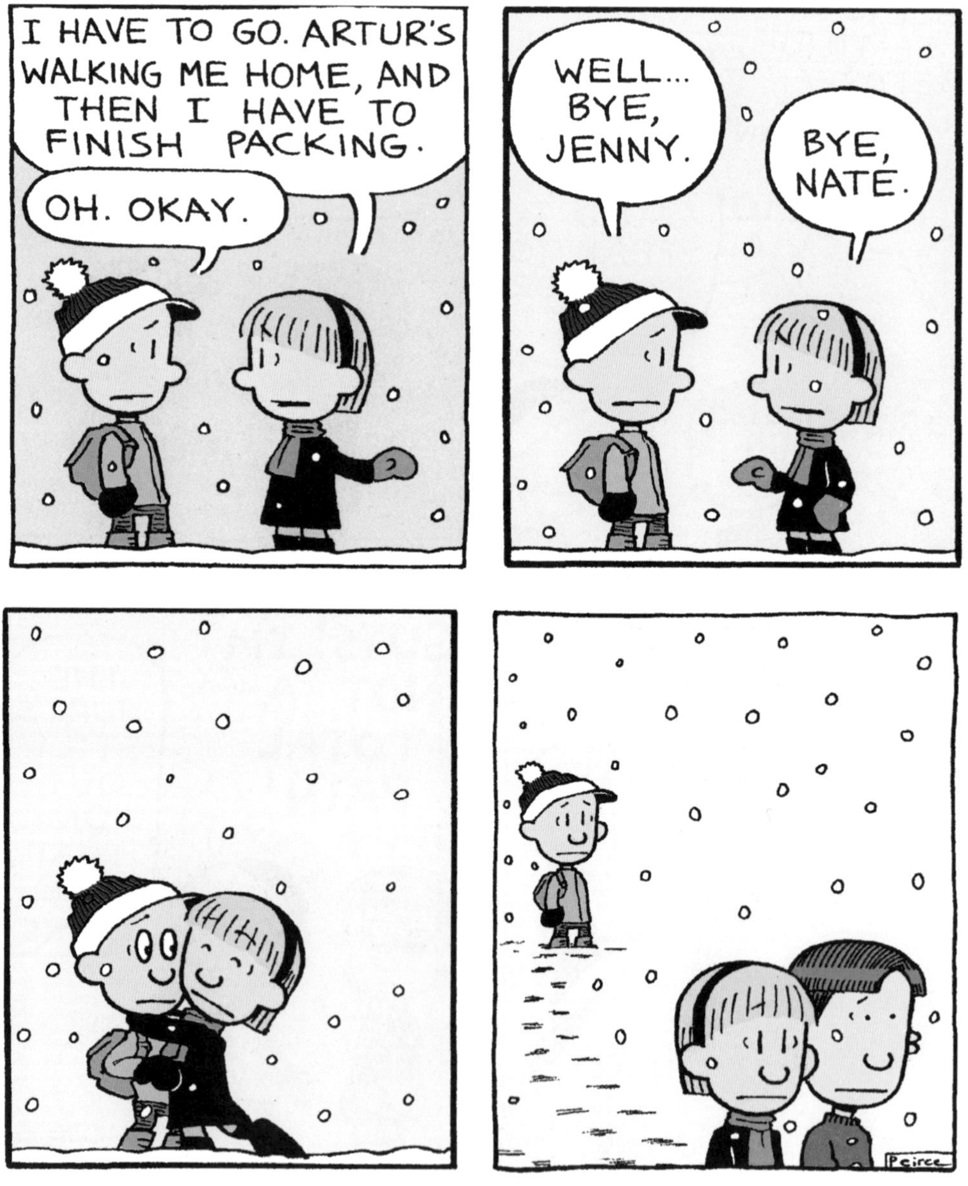
I HAVE TO GO. ARTUR'S WALKING ME HOME, AND THEN I HAVE TO FINISH PACKING.
OH. OKAY.
WELL... BYE, JENNY.
BYE, NATE.
Peirce

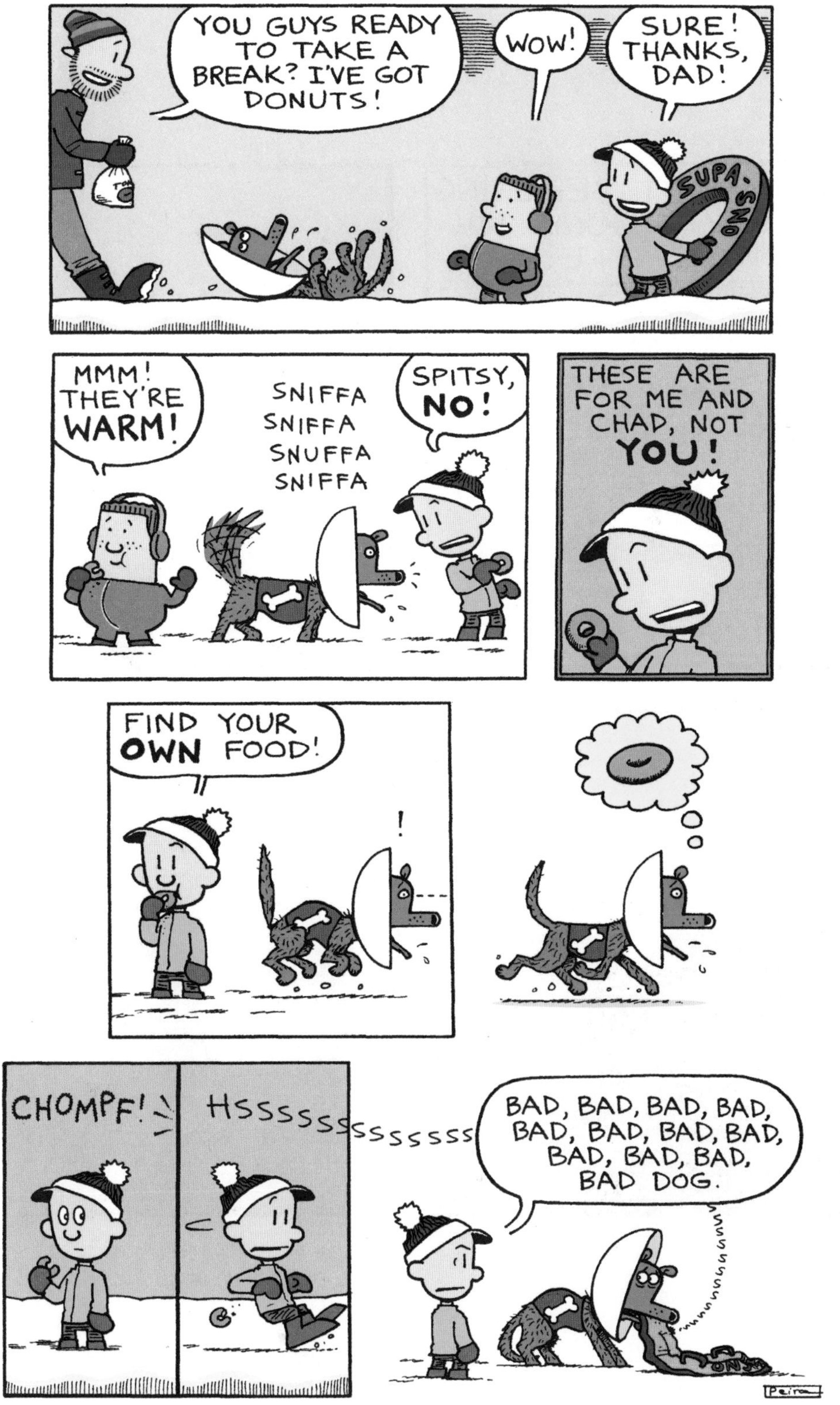

YOU GUYS READY TO TAKE A BREAK? I'VE GOT DONUTS!
WOW!
SURE! THANKS, DAD!
SUPA-SNO
MMM! THEY'RE WARM!
SNIFFA SNIFFA SNUFFA SNIFFA
SPITSY, NO!
THESE ARE FOR ME AND CHAD, NOT YOU!
FIND YOUR OWN FOOD!
!
CHOMPF!
HSSSSSSSSSSSSS
BAD, BAD, BAD, BAD, BAD, BAD, BAD, BAD, BAD, BAD, BAD, BAD DOG.
Peirce

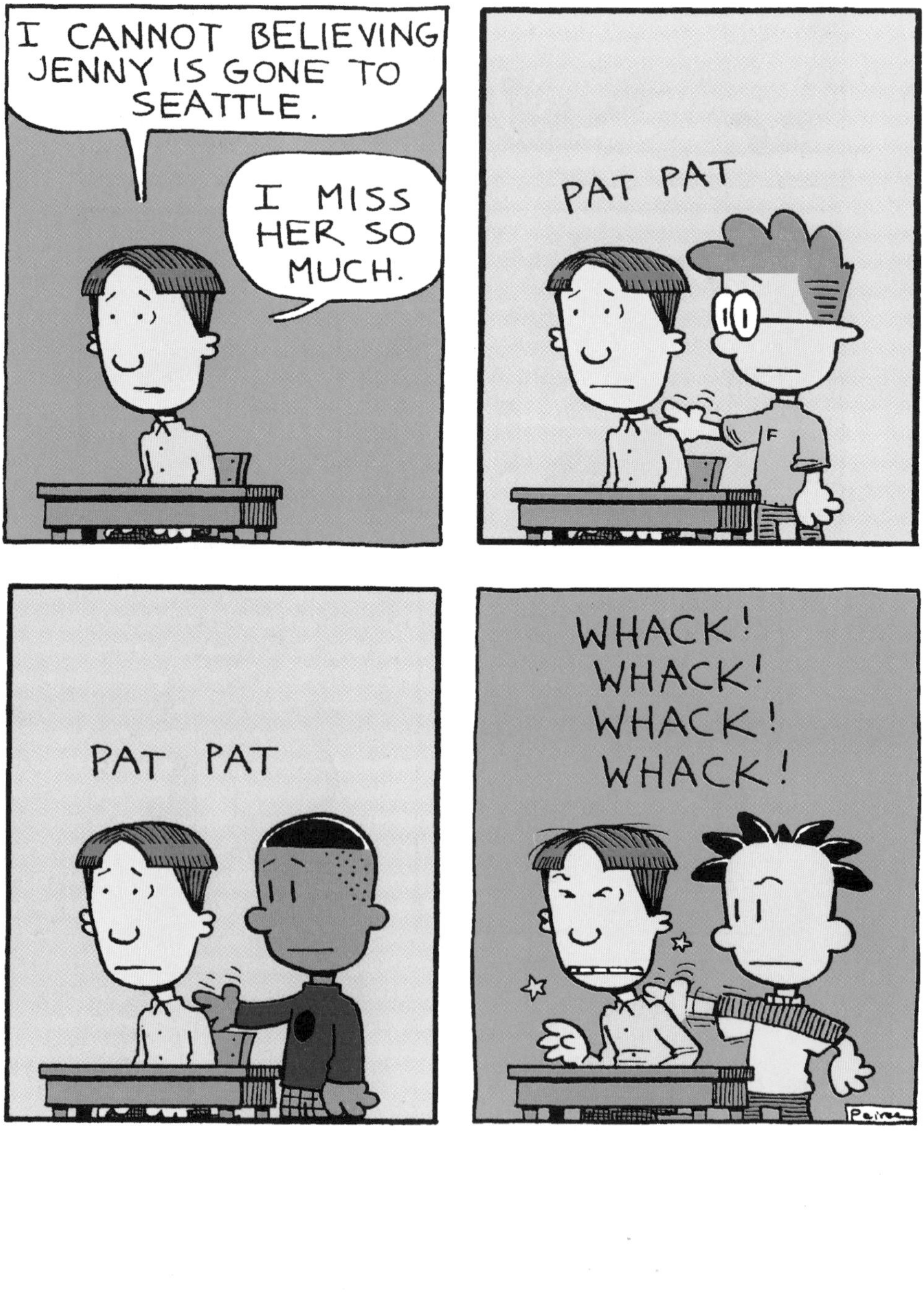
I CANNOT BELIEVING JENNY IS GONE TO SEATTLE.
I MISS HER SO MUCH.
PAT PAT
F
PAT PAT
WHACK! WHACK! WHACK! WHACK!
Peirce

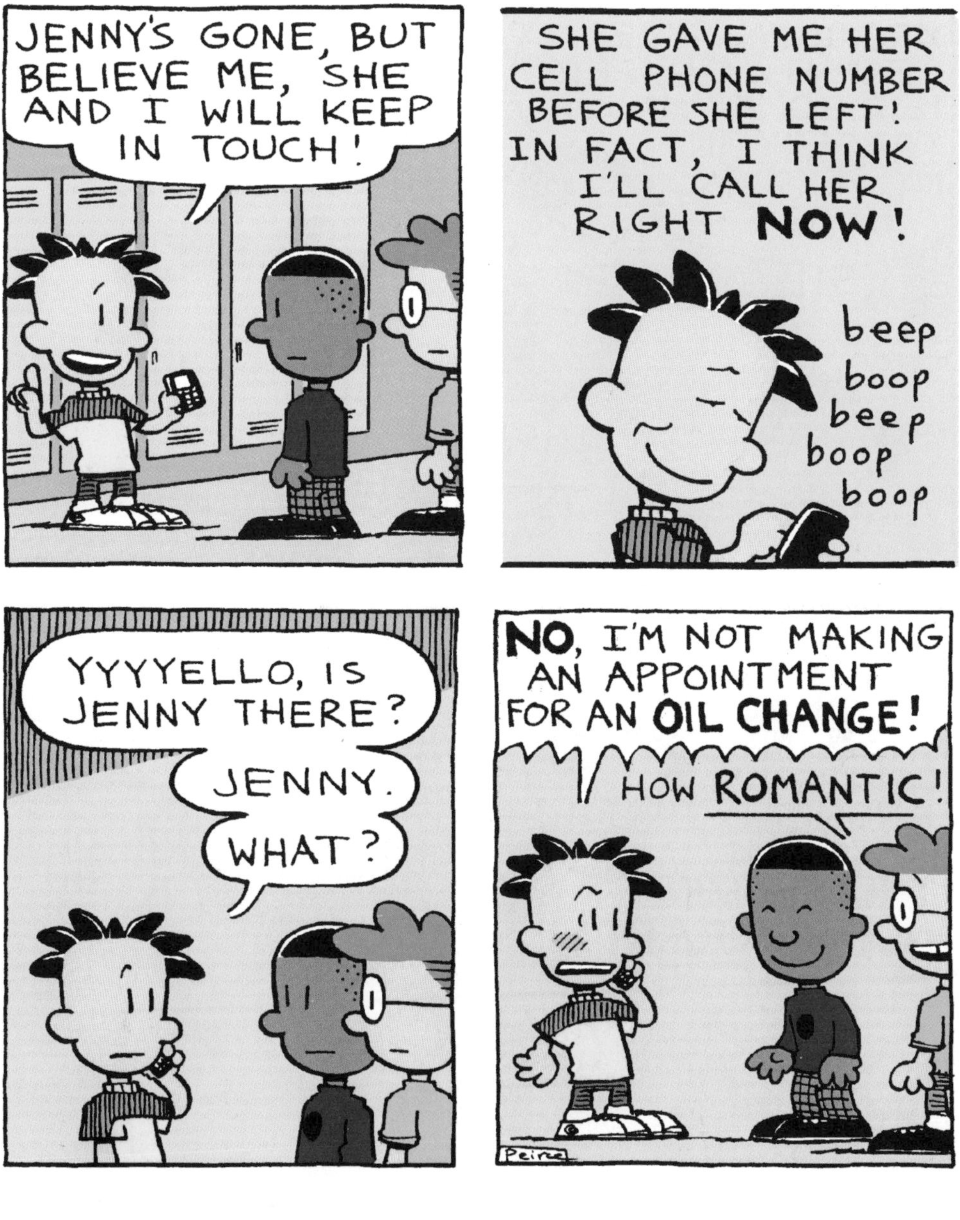
JENNY'S GONE, BUT BELIEVE ME, SHE AND I WILL KEEP IN TOUCH!
SHE GAVE ME HER CELL PHONE NUMBER BEFORE SHE LEFT! IN FACT, I THINK I'LL CALL HER RIGHT NOW!
beep boop beep boop boop
YYYYELLO, IS JENNY THERE?
JENNY.
WHAT?
NO, I'M NOT MAKING AN APPOINTMENT FOR AN OIL CHANGE!
HOW ROMANTIC!
Peirce

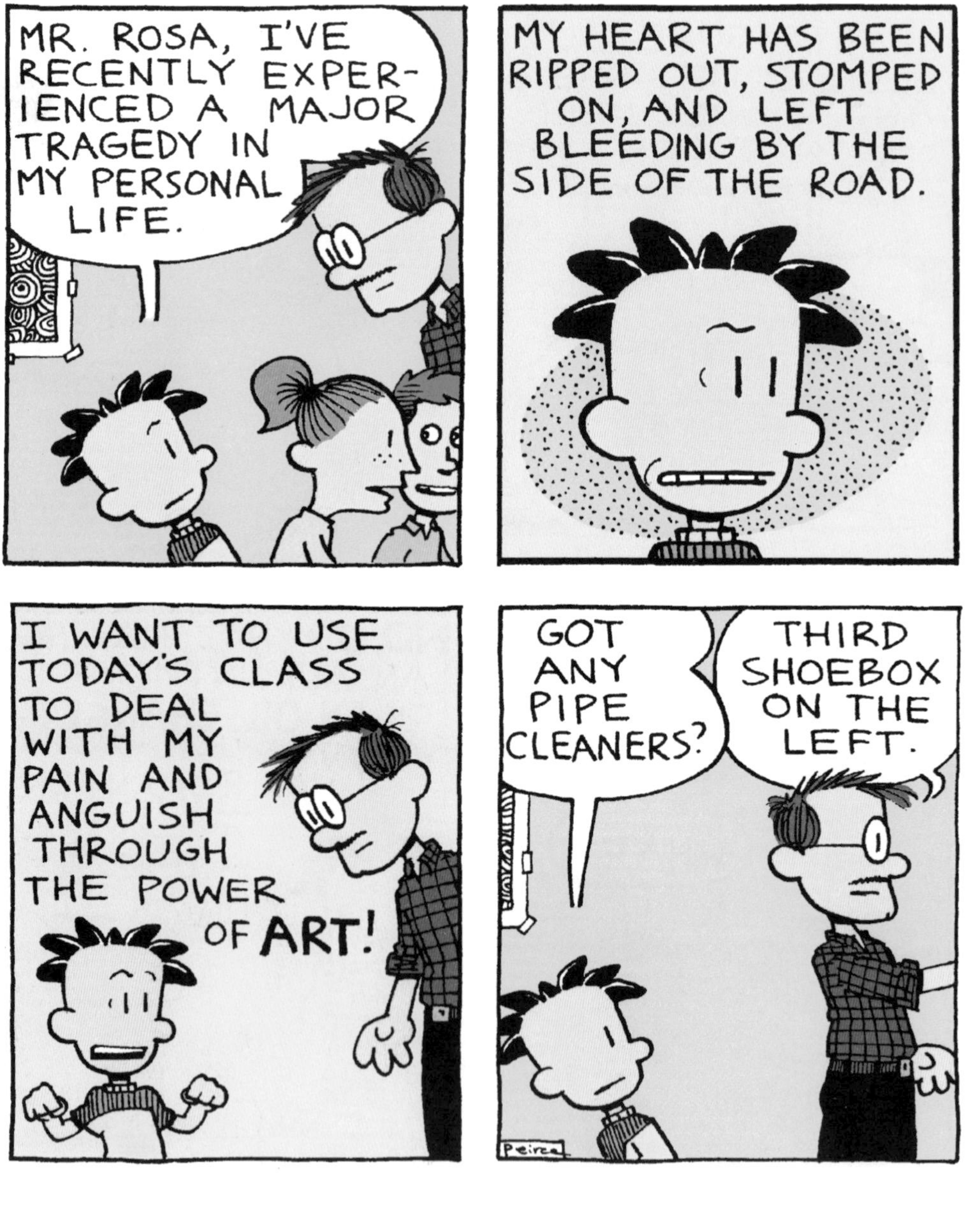
MR. ROSA, I'VE RECENTLY EXPERIENCED A MAJOR TRAGEDY IN MY PERSONAL LIFE.
MY HEART HAS BEEN RIPPED OUT, STOMPED ON, AND LEFT BLEEDING BY THE SIDE OF THE ROAD.
I WANT TO USE TODAY'S CLASS TO DEAL WITH MY PAIN AND ANGUISH THROUGH THE POWER OF ART!
GOT ANY PIPE CLEANERS?
THIRD SHOEBOX ON THE LEFT.
Peirce

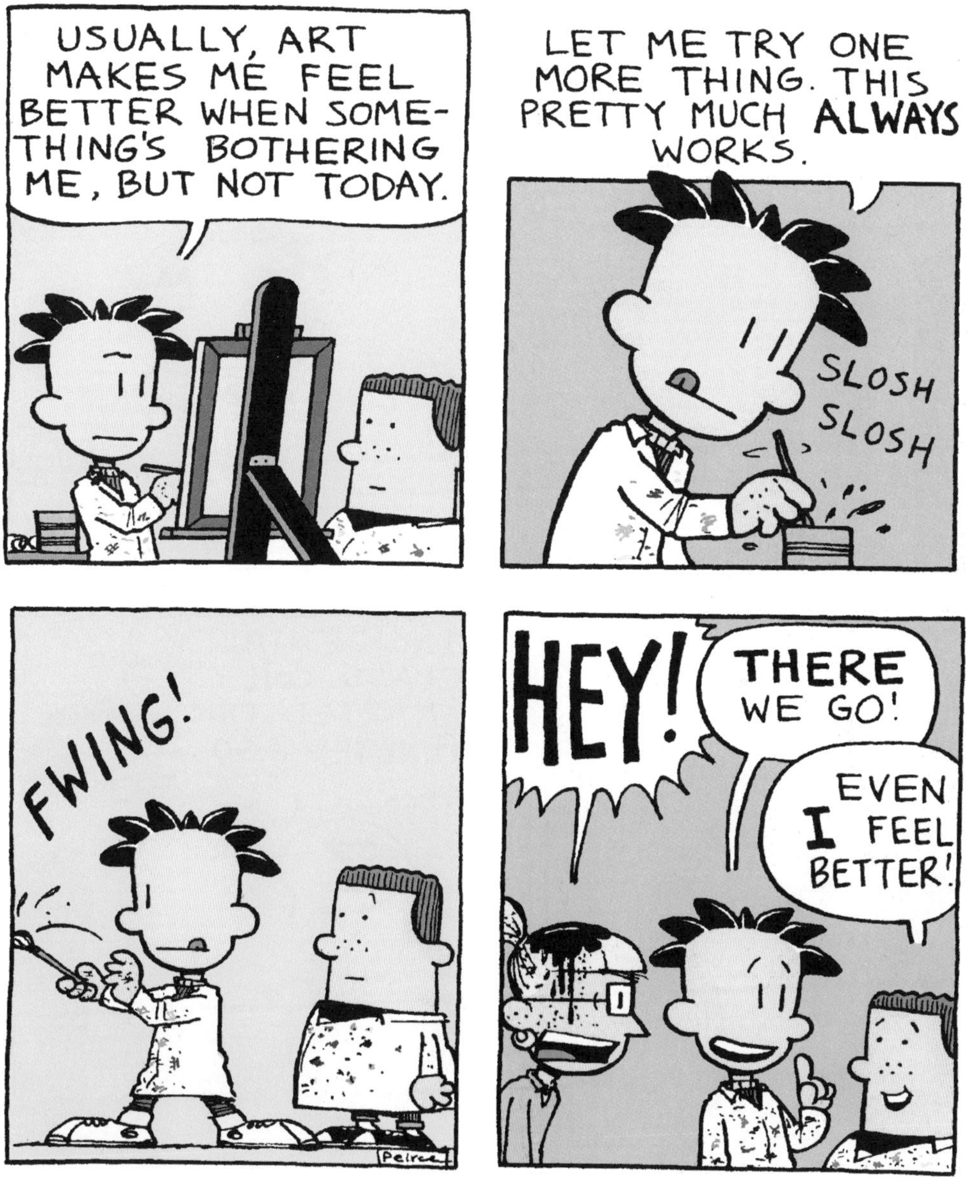
USUALLY, ART MAKES ME FEEL BETTER WHEN SOME-THING'S BOTHERING ME, BUT NOT TODAY.
LET ME TRY ONE MORE THING. THIS PRETTY MUCH ALWAYS WORKS.
SLOSH SLOSH
FWING!
HEY!
THERE WE GO!
EVEN I FEEL BETTER!

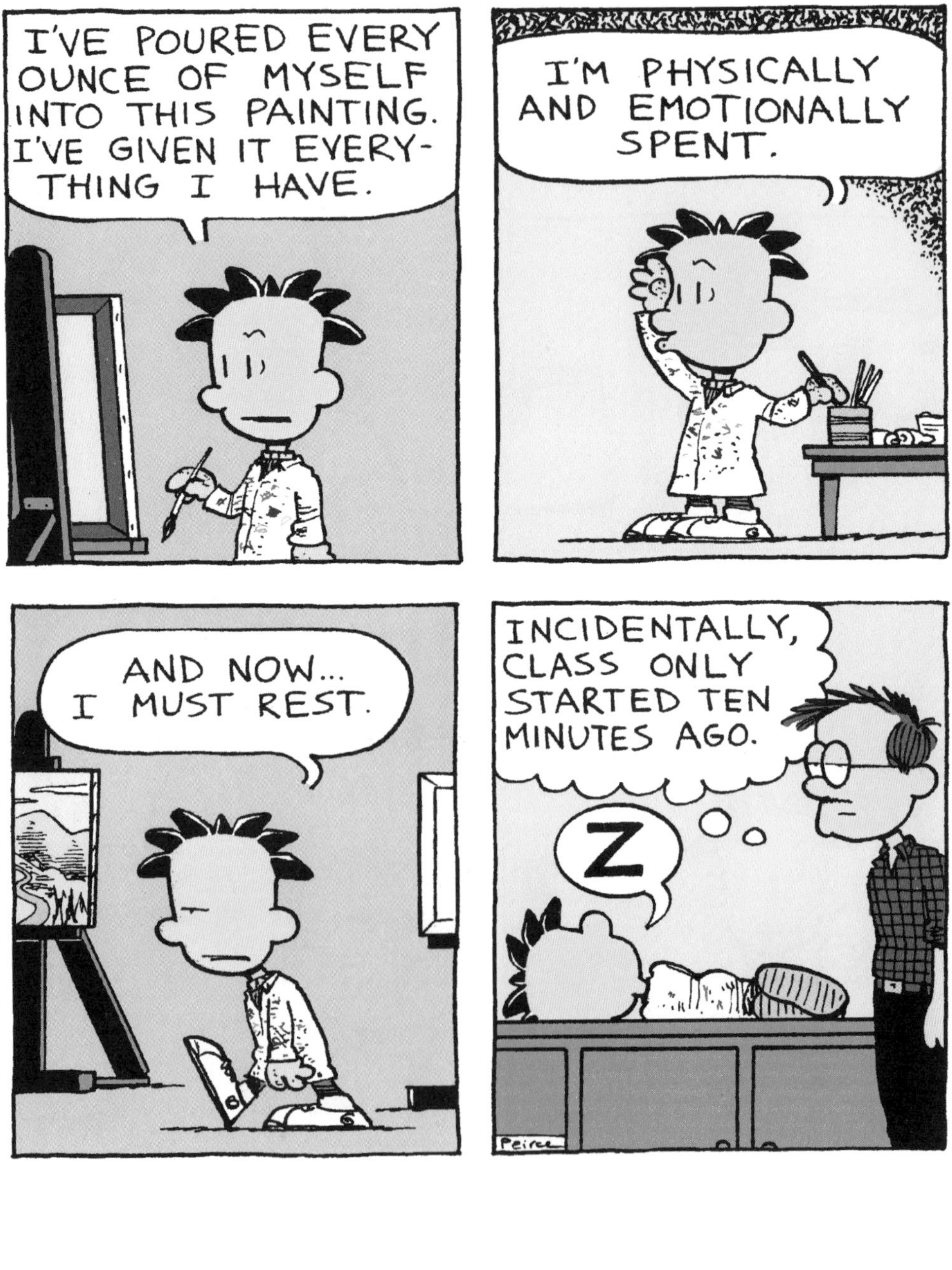
I'VE POURED EVERY OUNCE OF MYSELF INTO THIS PAINTING. I'VE GIVEN IT EVERYTHING I HAVE.
I'M PHYSICALLY AND EMOTIONALLY SPENT.
AND NOW... I MUST REST.
INCIDENTALLY, CLASS ONLY STARTED TEN MINUTES AGO.
Z
Peirce

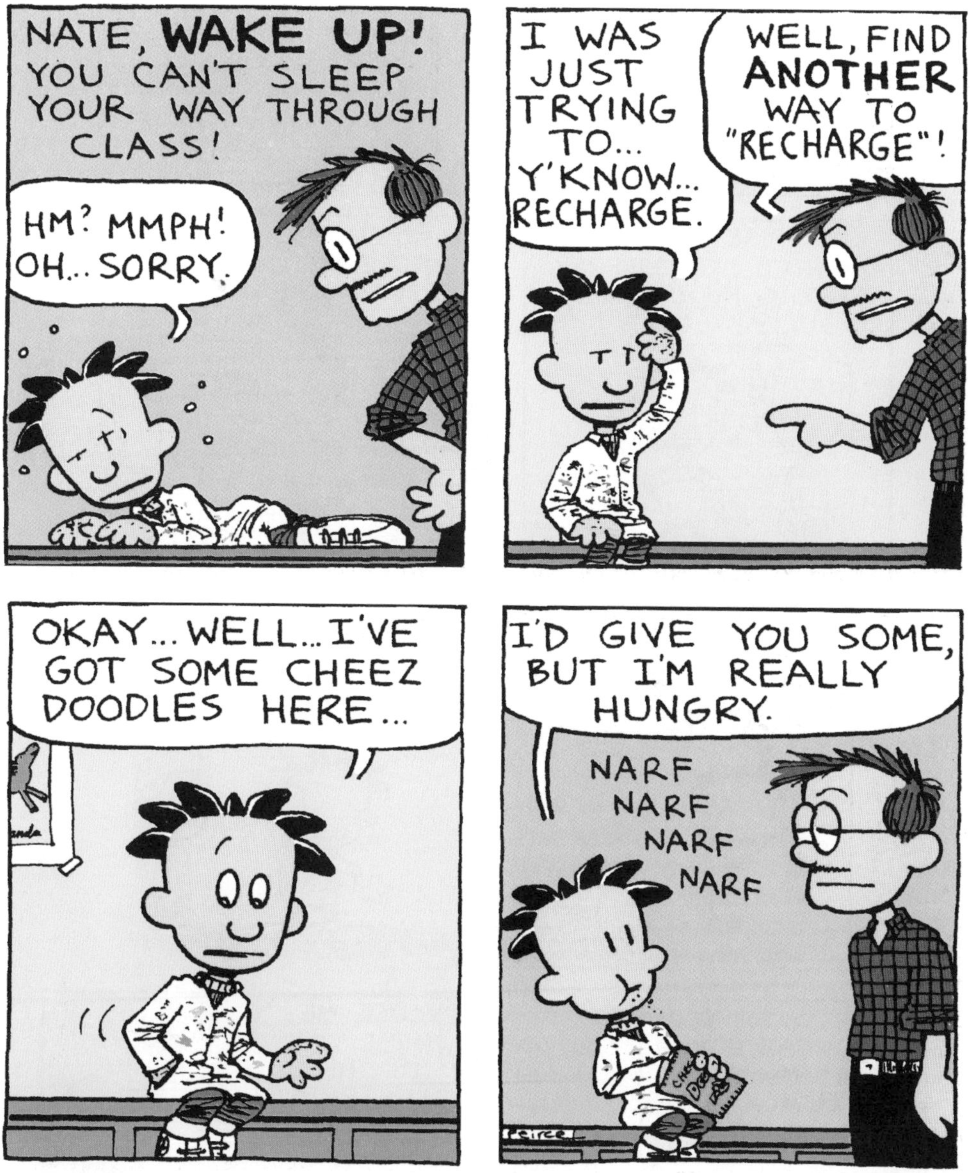
NATE, **WAKE UP!** YOU CAN'T SLEEP YOUR WAY THROUGH CLASS!
HM? MMPH! OH... SORRY.
I WAS JUST TRYING TO... Y'KNOW... RECHARGE.
WELL, FIND **ANOTHER** WAY TO "RECHARGE"!
OKAY... WELL... I'VE GOT SOME CHEEZ DOODLES HERE...
I'D GIVE YOU SOME, BUT I'M REALLY HUNGRY.
NARF NARF NARF NARF

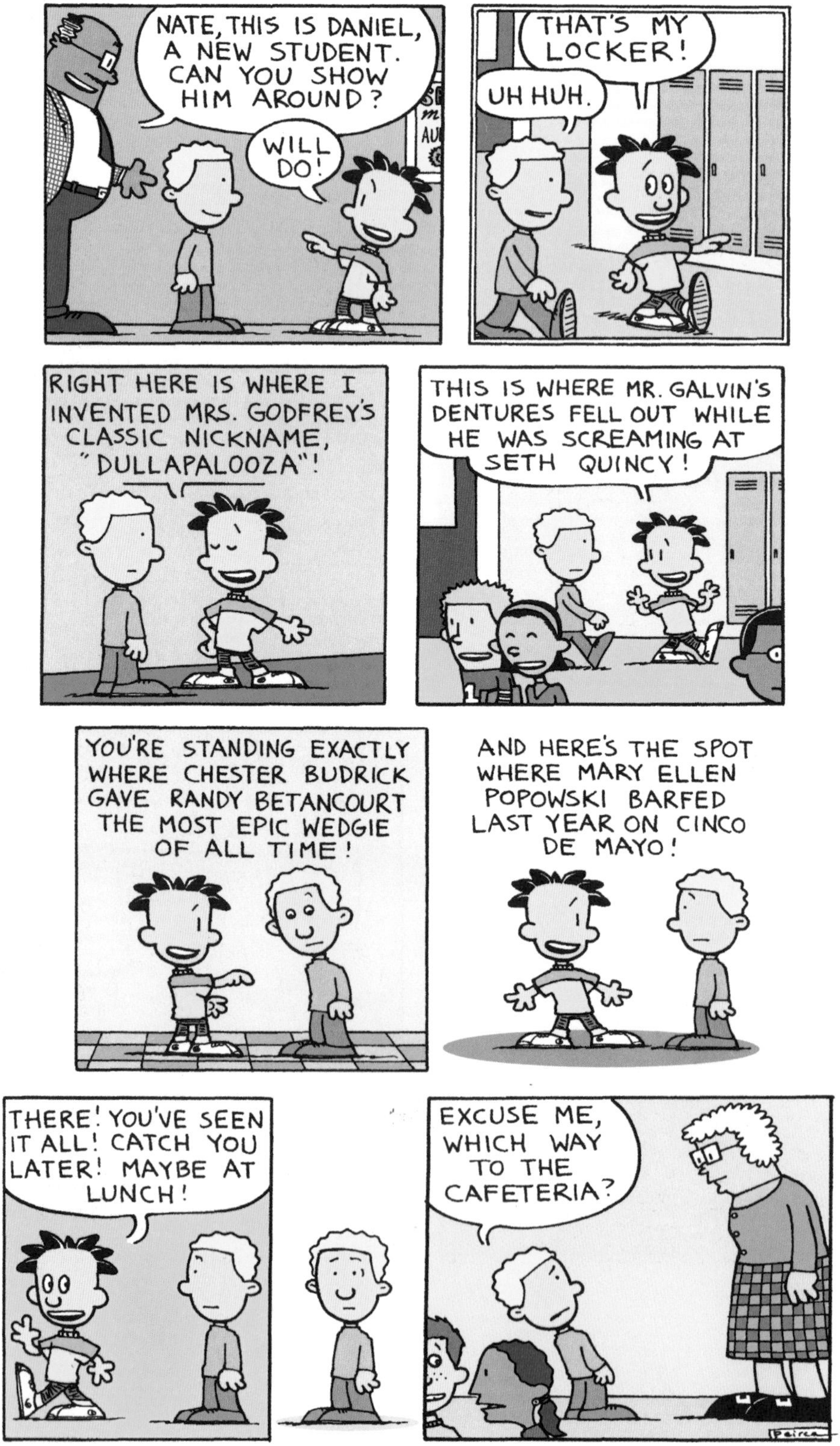
NATE, THIS IS DANIEL, A NEW STUDENT. CAN YOU SHOW HIM AROUND?
WILL DO!
THAT'S MY LOCKER!
UH HUH.
RIGHT HERE IS WHERE I INVENTED MRS. GODFREY'S CLASSIC NICKNAME, "DULLAPALOOZA"!
THIS IS WHERE MR. GALVIN'S DENTURES FELL OUT WHILE HE WAS SCREAMING AT SETH QUINCY!
YOU'RE STANDING EXACTLY WHERE CHESTER BUDRICK GAVE RANDY BETANCOURT THE MOST EPIC WEDGIE OF ALL TIME!
AND HERE'S THE SPOT WHERE MARY ELLEN POPOWSKI BARFED LAST YEAR ON CINCO DE MAYO!
THERE! YOU'VE SEEN IT ALL! CATCH YOU LATER! MAYBE AT LUNCH!
EXCUSE ME, WHICH WAY TO THE CAFETERIA?

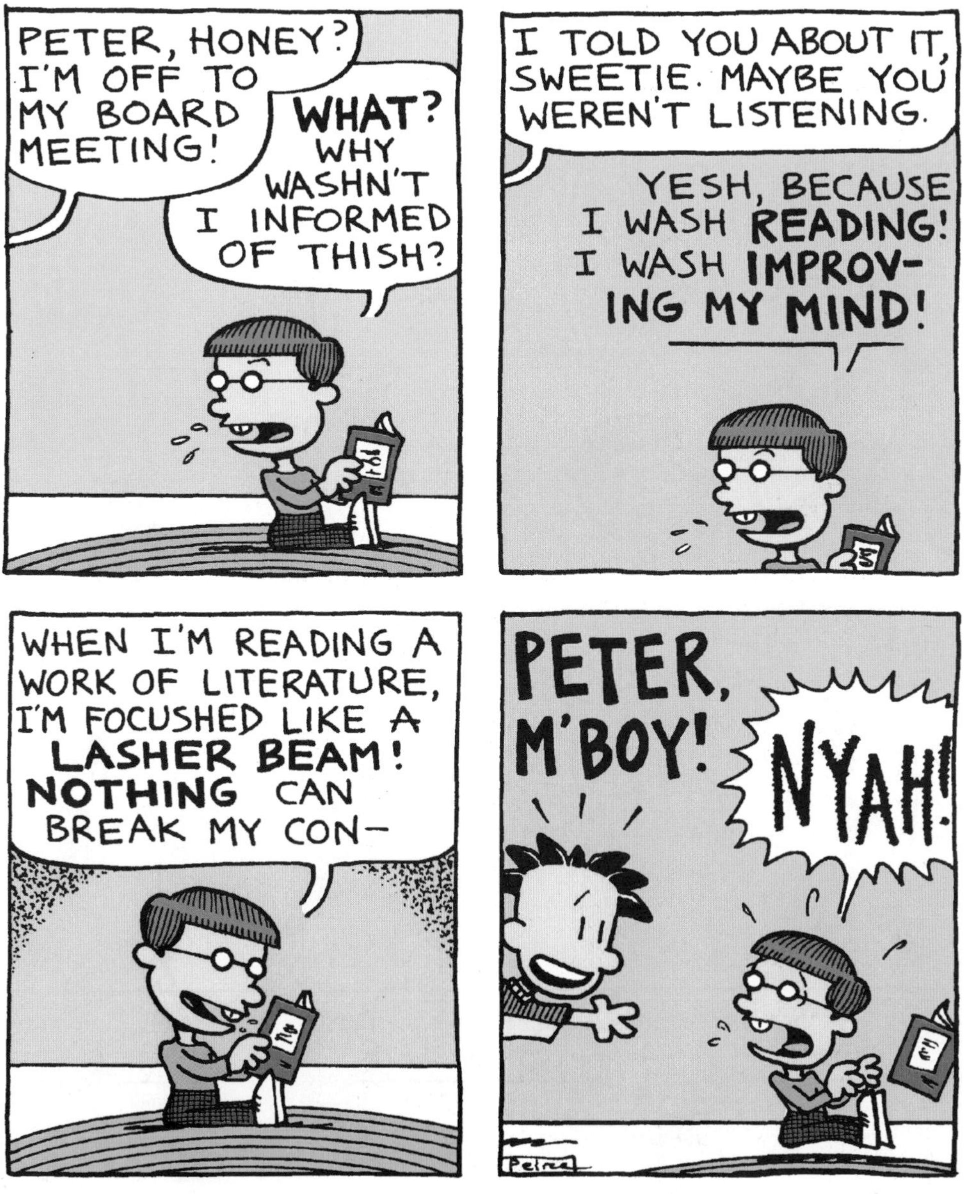
PETER, HONEY? I'M OFF TO MY BOARD MEETING!
WHAT? WHY WASHN'T I INFORMED OF THISH?
I TOLD YOU ABOUT IT, SWEETIE. MAYBE YOU WEREN'T LISTENING.
YESH, BECAUSE I WASH READING! I WASH IMPROVING MY MIND!
WHEN I'M READING A WORK OF LITERATURE, I'M FOCUSHED LIKE A LASHER BEAM! NOTHING CAN BREAK MY CON—
PETER, M'BOY!
NYAH!
Peirce

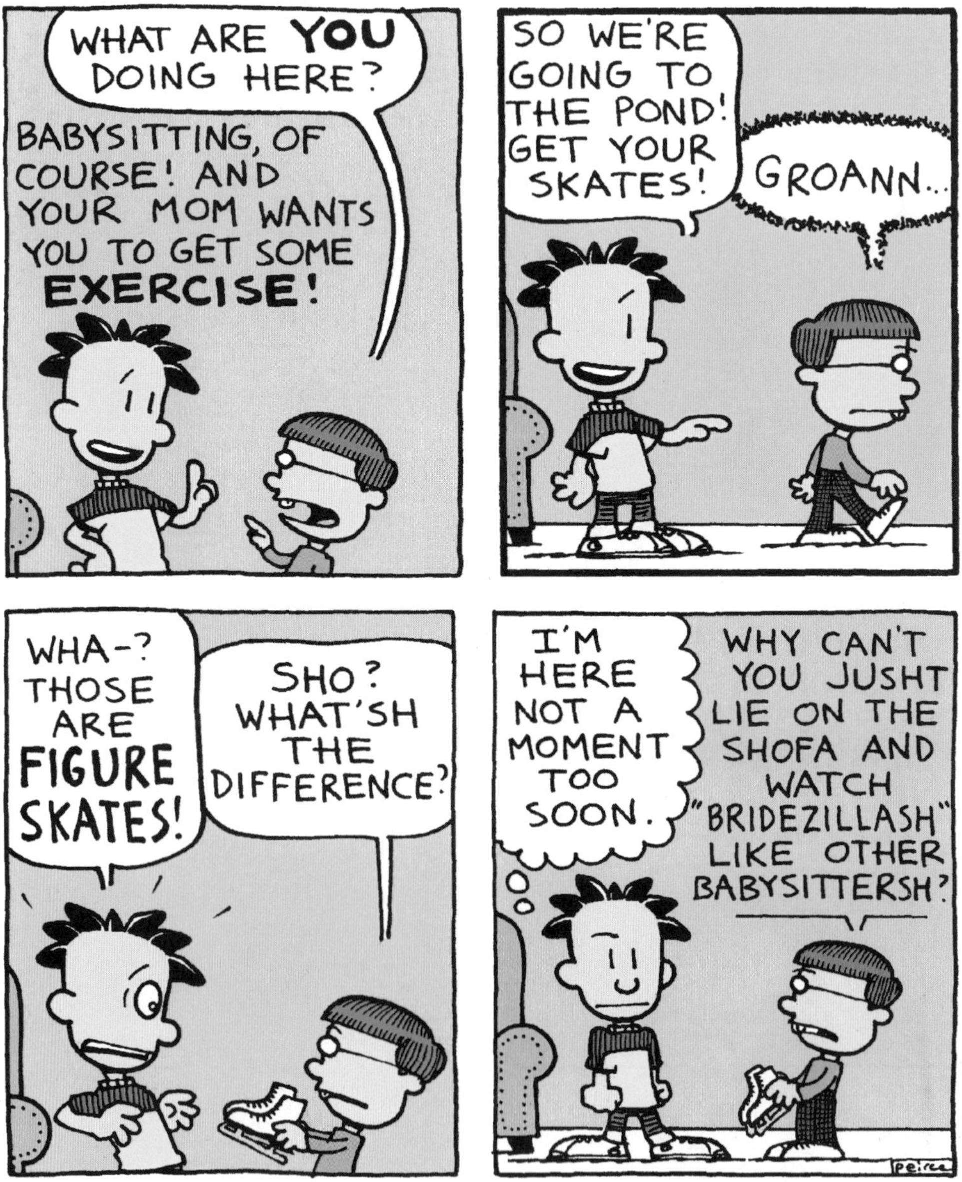
WHAT ARE YOU DOING HERE?
BABYSITTING, OF COURSE! AND YOUR MOM WANTS YOU TO GET SOME EXERCISE!
SO WE'RE GOING TO THE POND! GET YOUR SKATES!
GROANN...
WHA-? THOSE ARE FIGURE SKATES!
SHO? WHAT'SH THE DIFFERENCE?
I'M HERE NOT A MOMENT TOO SOON.
WHY CAN'T YOU JUSHT LIE ON THE SHOFA AND WATCH "BRIDEZILLASH" LIKE OTHER BABYSITTERSH?
peirce

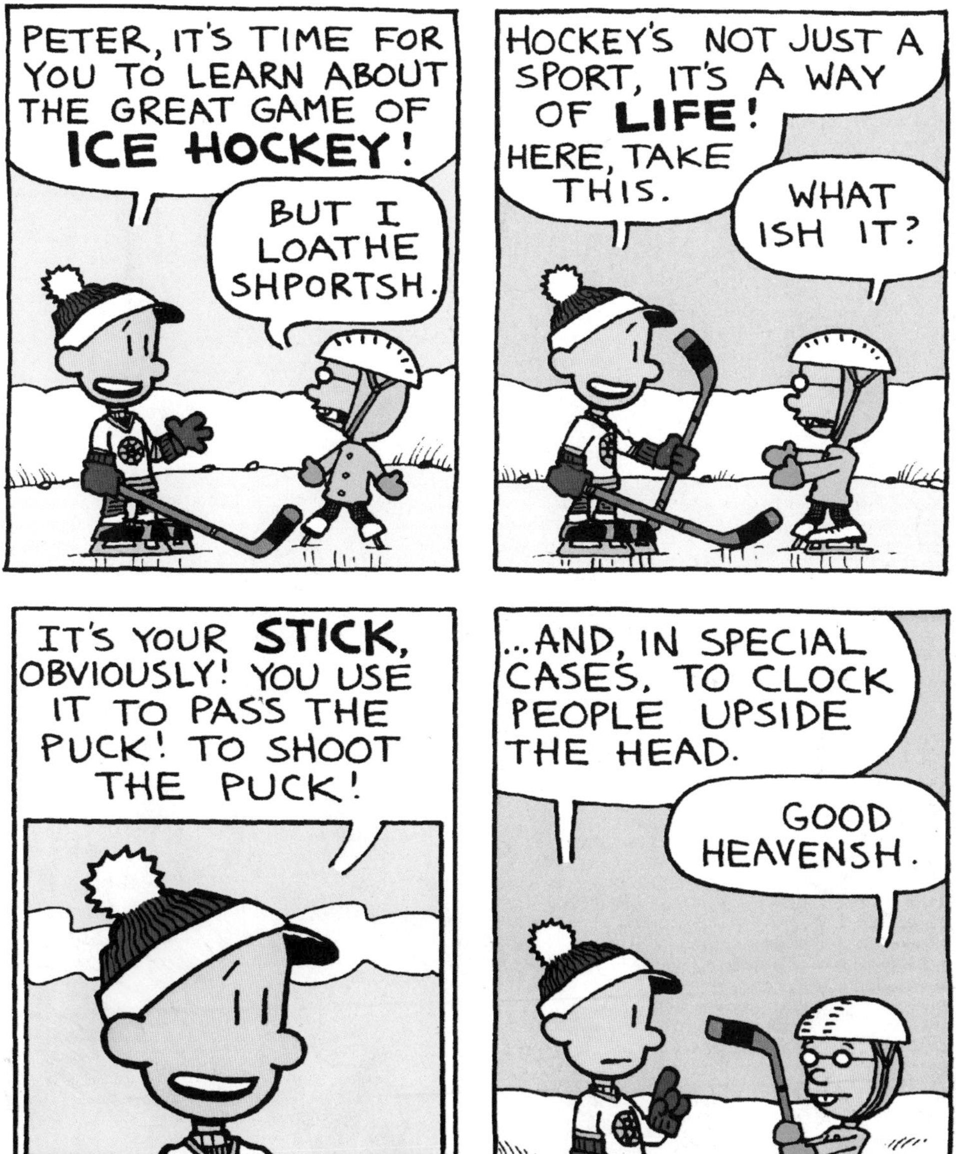

PETER, IT'S TIME FOR YOU TO LEARN ABOUT THE GREAT GAME OF **ICE HOCKEY**!
BUT I LOATHE SHPORTSH.
HOCKEY'S NOT JUST A SPORT, IT'S A WAY OF **LIFE**! HERE, TAKE THIS.
WHAT ISH IT?
IT'S YOUR **STICK**, OBVIOUSLY! YOU USE IT TO PASS THE PUCK! TO SHOOT THE PUCK!
...AND, IN SPECIAL CASES, TO CLOCK PEOPLE UPSIDE THE HEAD.
GOOD HEAVENSH.

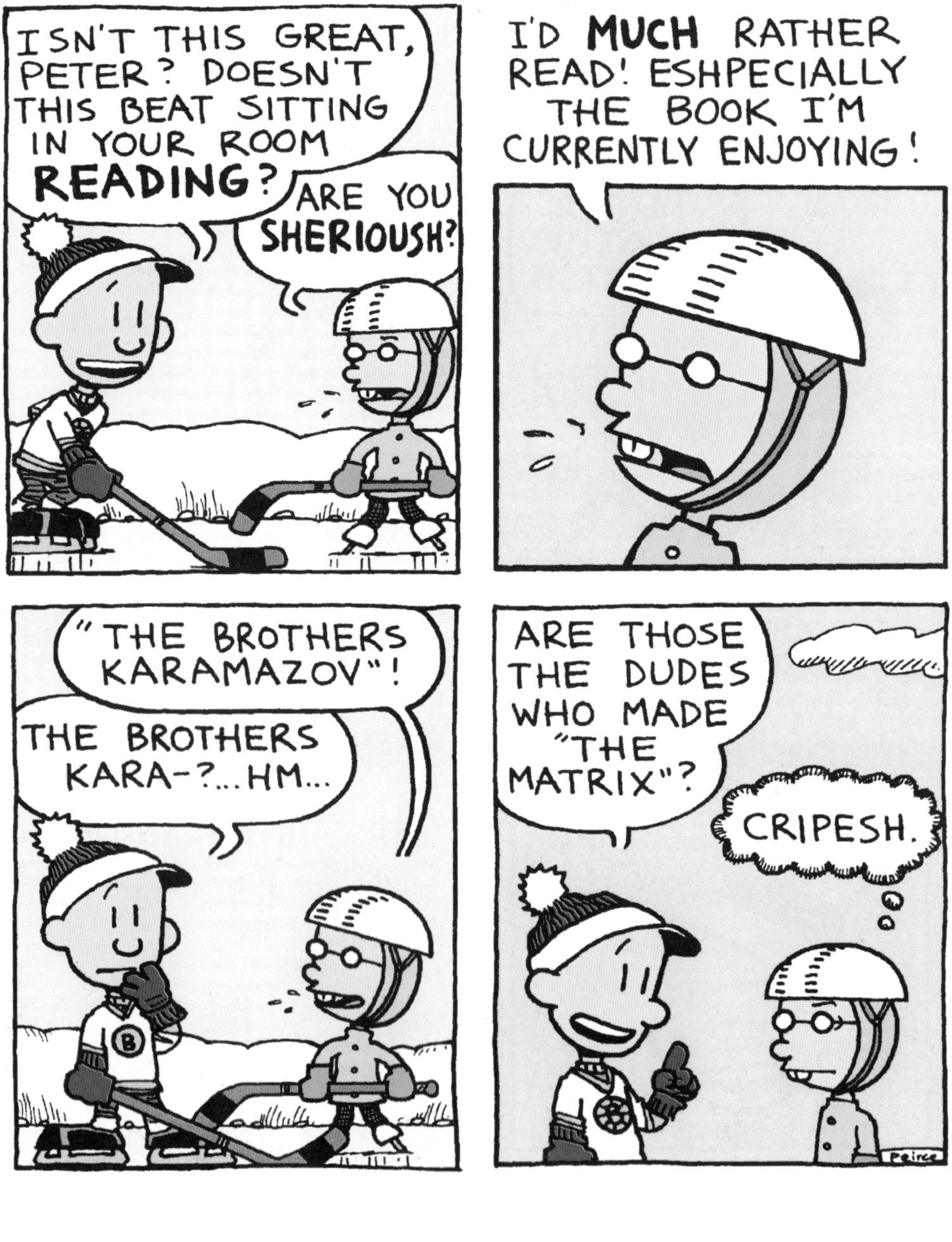

ISN'T THIS GREAT, PETER? DOESN'T THIS BEAT SITTING IN YOUR ROOM **READING**?
ARE YOU **SHERIOUSH?**
I'D **MUCH** RATHER READ! ESHPECIALLY THE BOOK I'M CURRENTLY ENJOYING!
"THE BROTHERS KARAMAZOV"!
THE BROTHERS KARA-?... HM...
ARE THOSE THE DUDES WHO MADE "THE MATRIX"?
CRIPESH.
Peirce

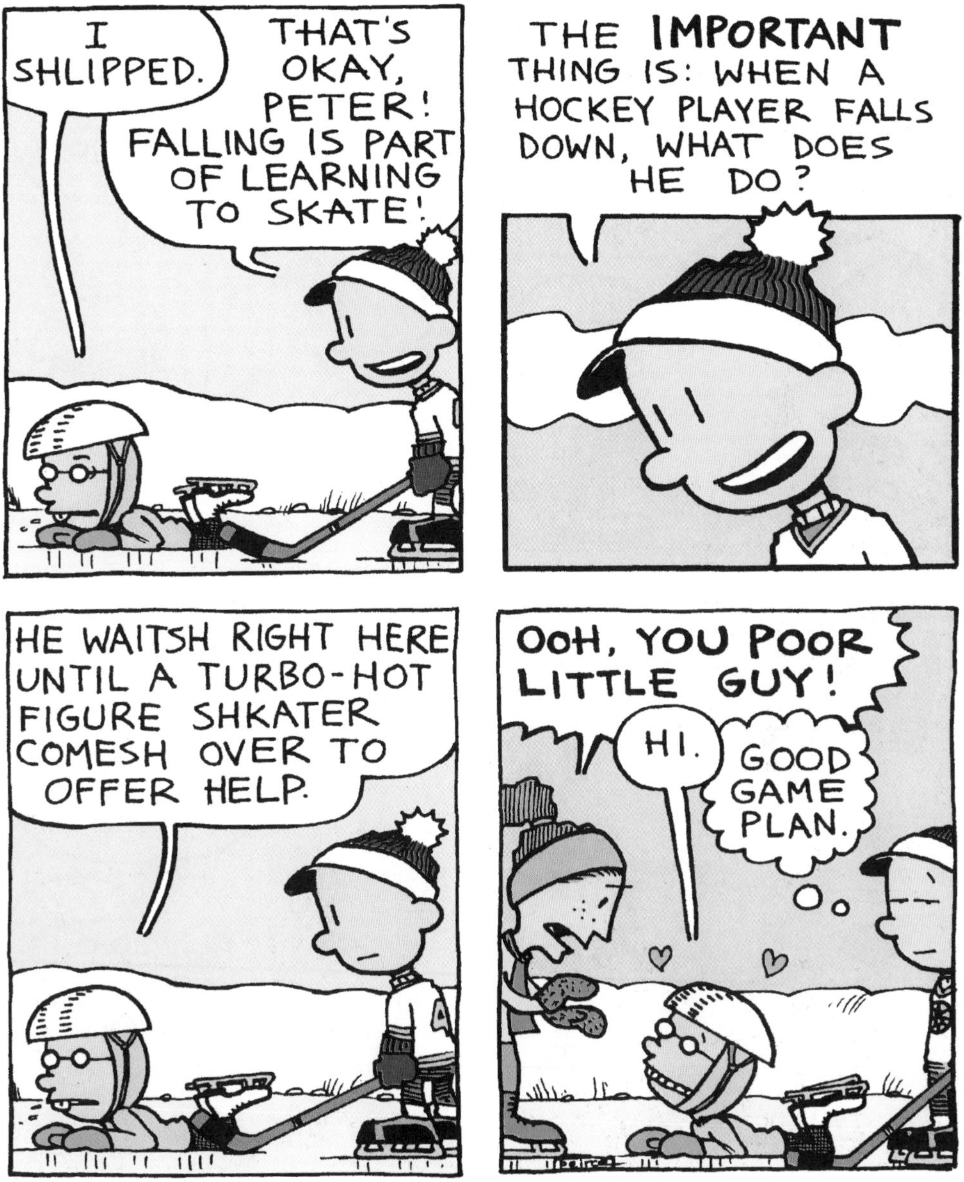
I SHLIPPED.
THAT'S OKAY, PETER! FALLING IS PART OF LEARNING TO SKATE!
THE **IMPORTANT** THING IS: WHEN A HOCKEY PLAYER FALLS DOWN, WHAT DOES HE DO?
HE WAITSH RIGHT HERE UNTIL A TURBO-HOT FIGURE SHKATER COMESH OVER TO OFFER HELP.
OOH, YOU POOR LITTLE GUY!
HI.
GOOD GAME PLAN.

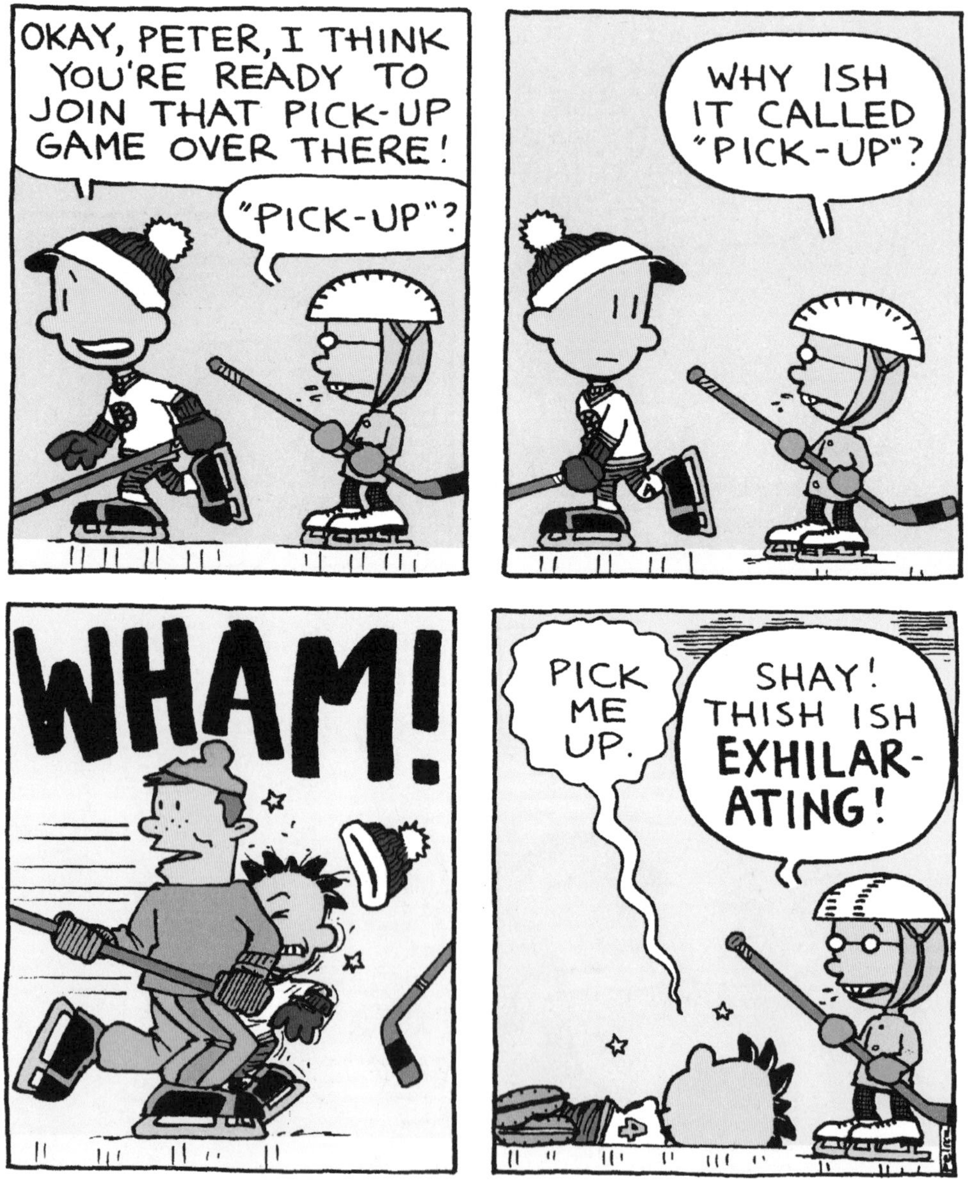
OKAY, PETER, I THINK YOU'RE READY TO JOIN THAT PICK-UP GAME OVER THERE!
"PICK-UP"?
WHY ISH IT CALLED "PICK-UP"?
WHAM!
PICK ME UP.
SHAY! THISH ISH EXHILAR-ATING!

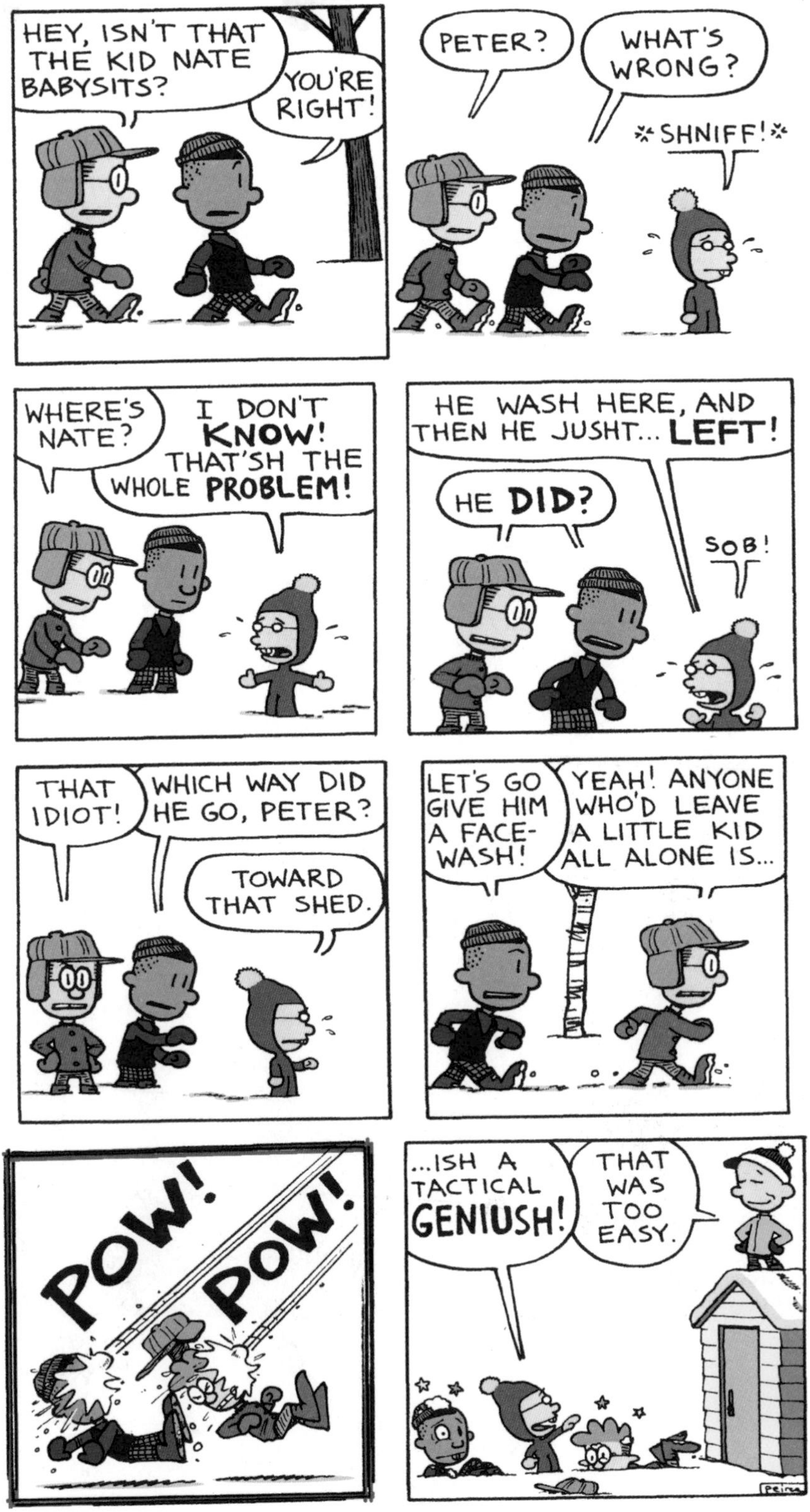
HEY, ISN'T THAT THE KID NATE BABYSITS?
YOU'RE RIGHT!
PETER?
WHAT'S WRONG?
SHNIFF!
WHERE'S NATE?
I DON'T KNOW! THAT'SH THE WHOLE PROBLEM!
HE WASH HERE, AND THEN HE JUSHT... LEFT!
HE DID?
SOB!
THAT IDIOT!
WHICH WAY DID HE GO, PETER?
TOWARD THAT SHED.
LET'S GO GIVE HIM A FACE-WASH!
YEAH! ANYONE WHO'D LEAVE A LITTLE KID ALL ALONE IS...
POW!
POW!
...ISH A TACTICAL GENIUSH!
THAT WAS TOO EASY.
peirce

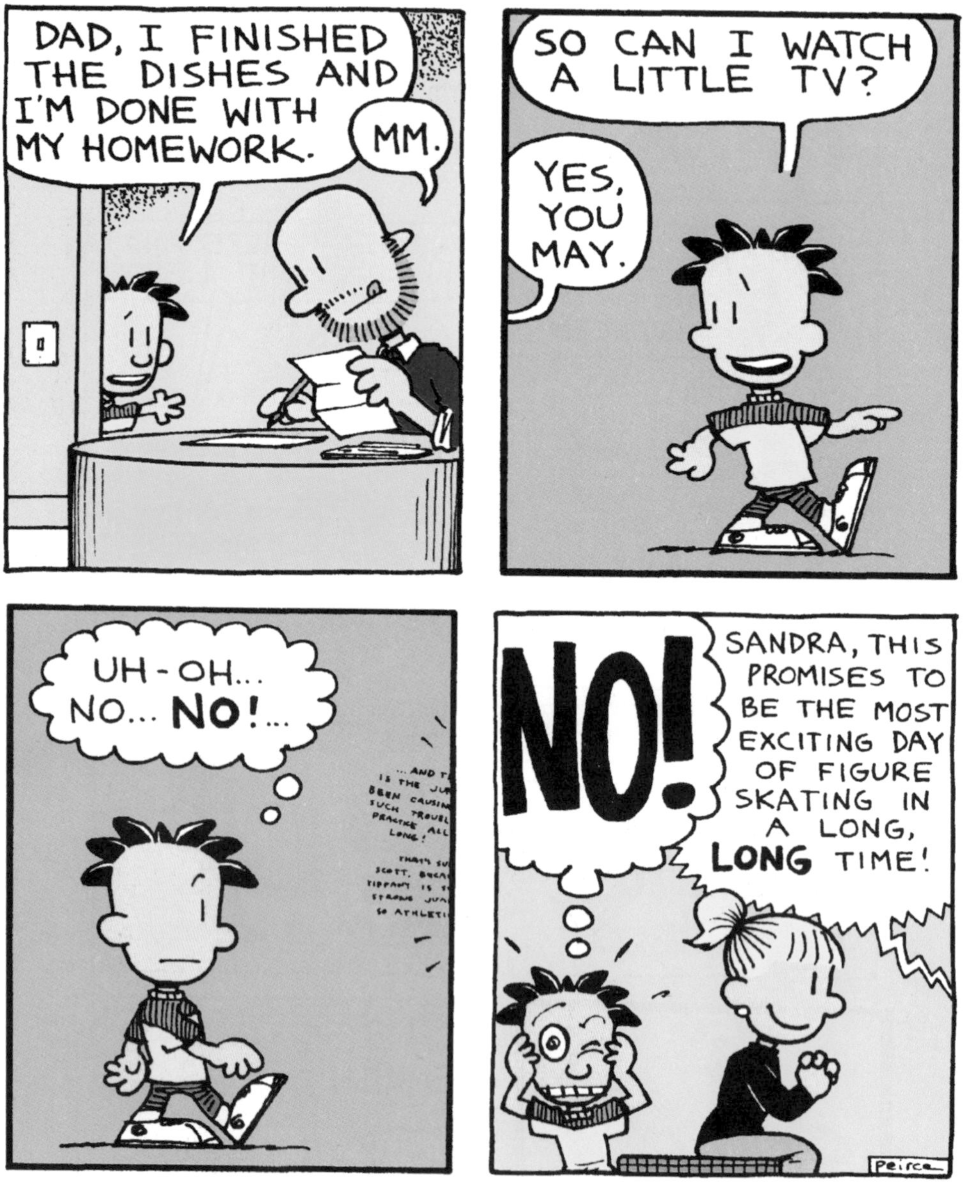
DAD, I FINISHED THE DISHES AND I'M DONE WITH MY HOMEWORK.
MM.
SO CAN I WATCH A LITTLE TV?
YES, YOU MAY.
UH-OH... NO... **NO**!...
NO!
SANDRA, THIS PROMISES TO BE THE MOST EXCITING DAY OF FIGURE SKATING IN A LONG, **LONG** TIME!
Peirce

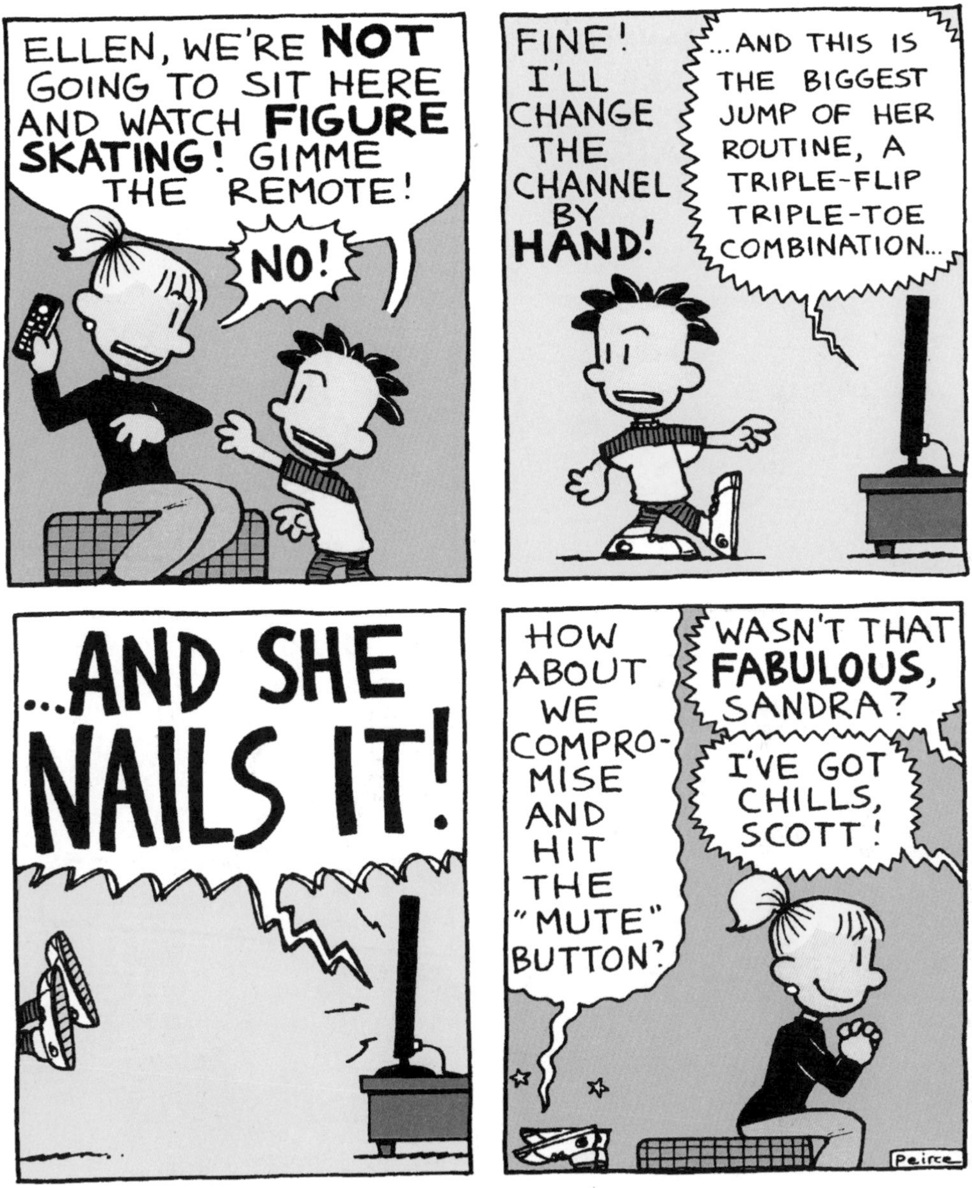
ELLEN, WE'RE **NOT** GOING TO SIT HERE AND WATCH **FIGURE SKATING**! GIMME THE REMOTE!
NO!
FINE! I'LL CHANGE THE CHANNEL BY **HAND**!
...AND THIS IS THE BIGGEST JUMP OF HER ROUTINE, A TRIPLE-FLIP TRIPLE-TOE COMBINATION...
...AND SHE NAILS IT!
HOW ABOUT WE COMPROMISE AND HIT THE "MUTE" BUTTON?
WASN'T THAT **FABULOUS**, SANDRA?
I'VE GOT CHILLS, SCOTT!
Peirce

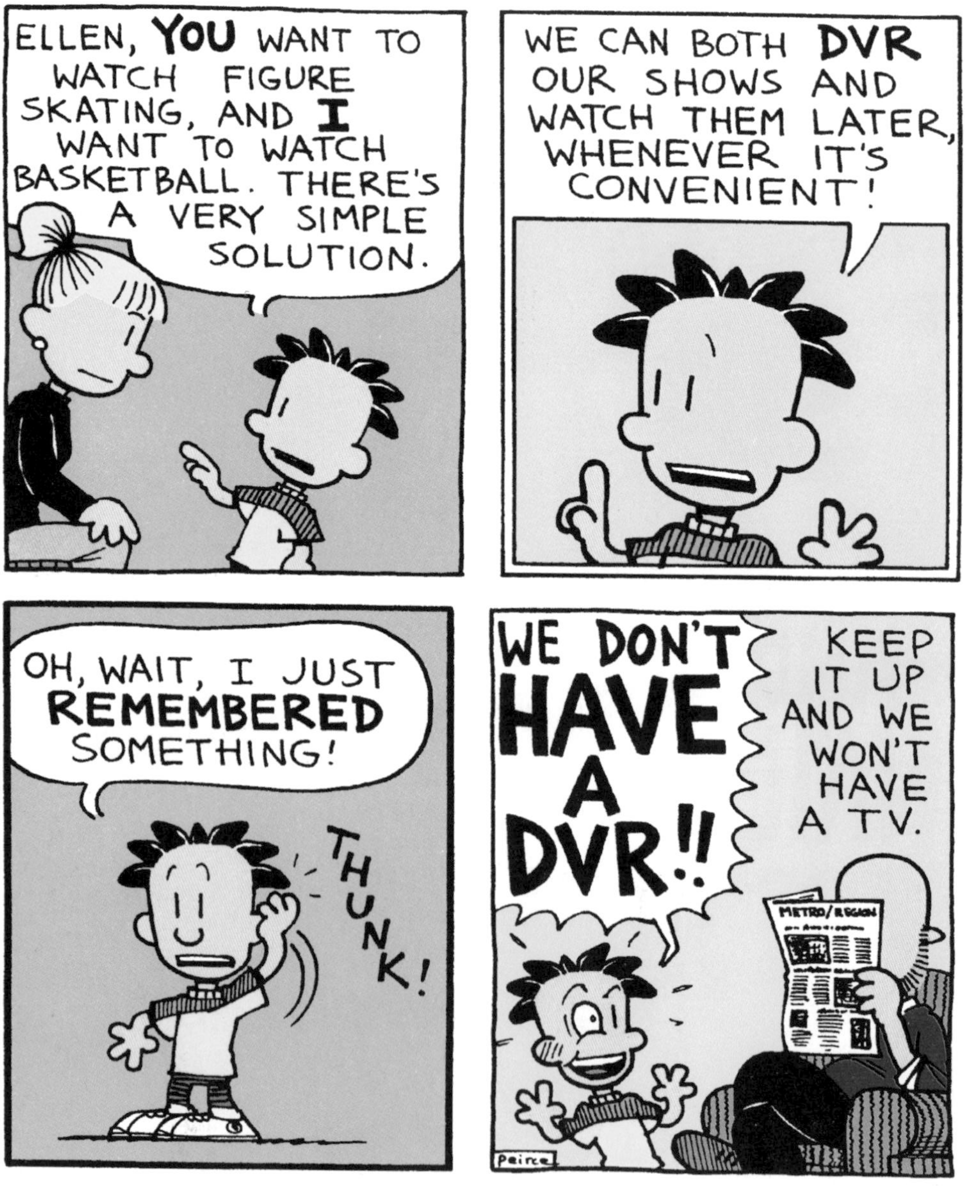
ELLEN, **YOU** WANT TO WATCH FIGURE SKATING, AND **I** WANT TO WATCH BASKETBALL. THERE'S A VERY SIMPLE SOLUTION.
WE CAN BOTH **DVR** OUR SHOWS AND WATCH THEM LATER, WHENEVER IT'S CONVENIENT!
OH, WAIT, I JUST **REMEMBERED** SOMETHING!
THUNK!
WE DON'T HAVE A DVR!!
KEEP IT UP AND WE WON'T HAVE A TV.
METRO/REGION
Peirce

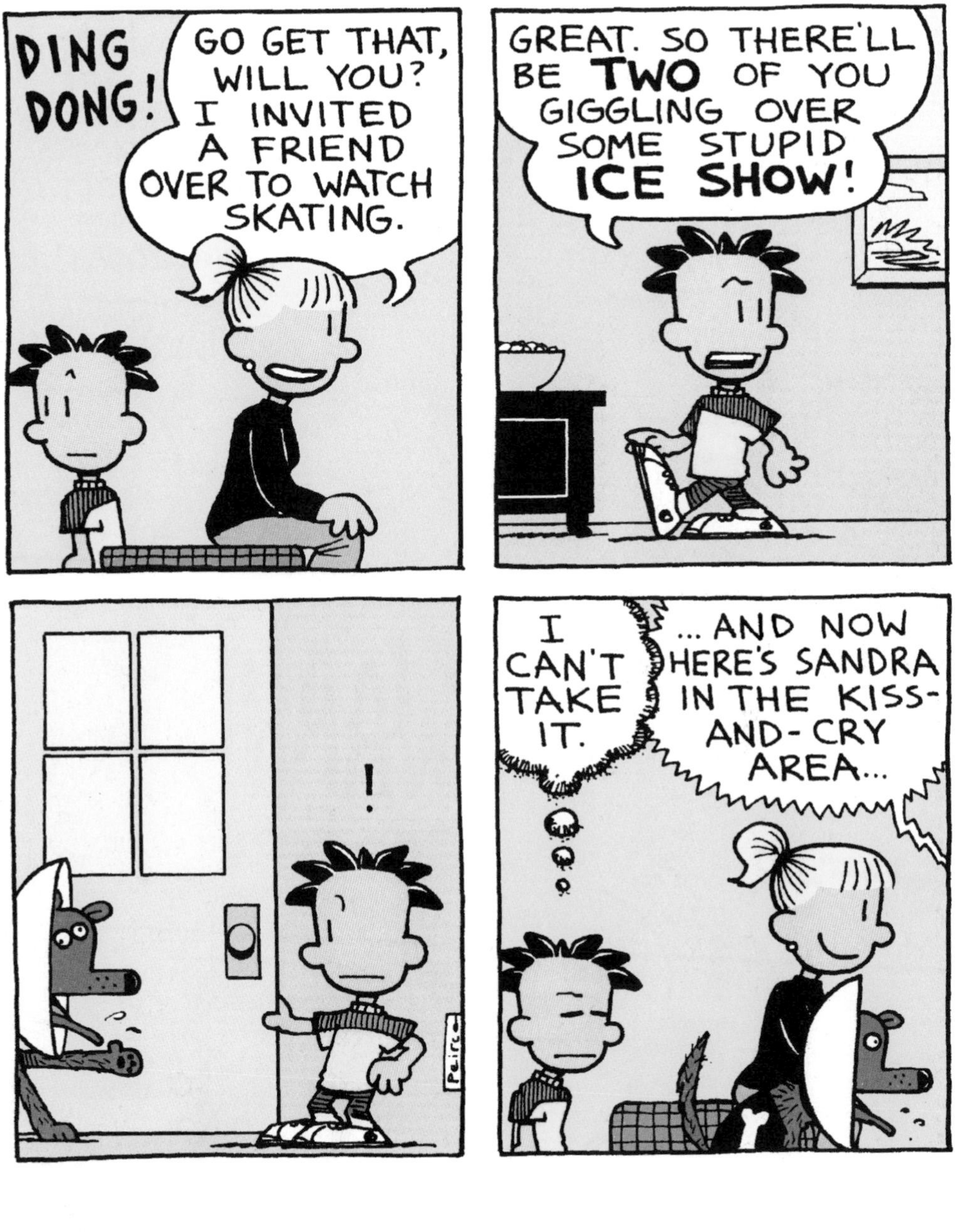
DING DONG!
GO GET THAT, WILL YOU? I INVITED A FRIEND OVER TO WATCH SKATING.
GREAT. SO THERE'LL BE **TWO** OF YOU GIGGLING OVER SOME STUPID **ICE SHOW**!
!
I CAN'T TAKE IT.
... AND NOW HERE'S SANDRA IN THE KISS-AND-CRY AREA...
PEIRCE

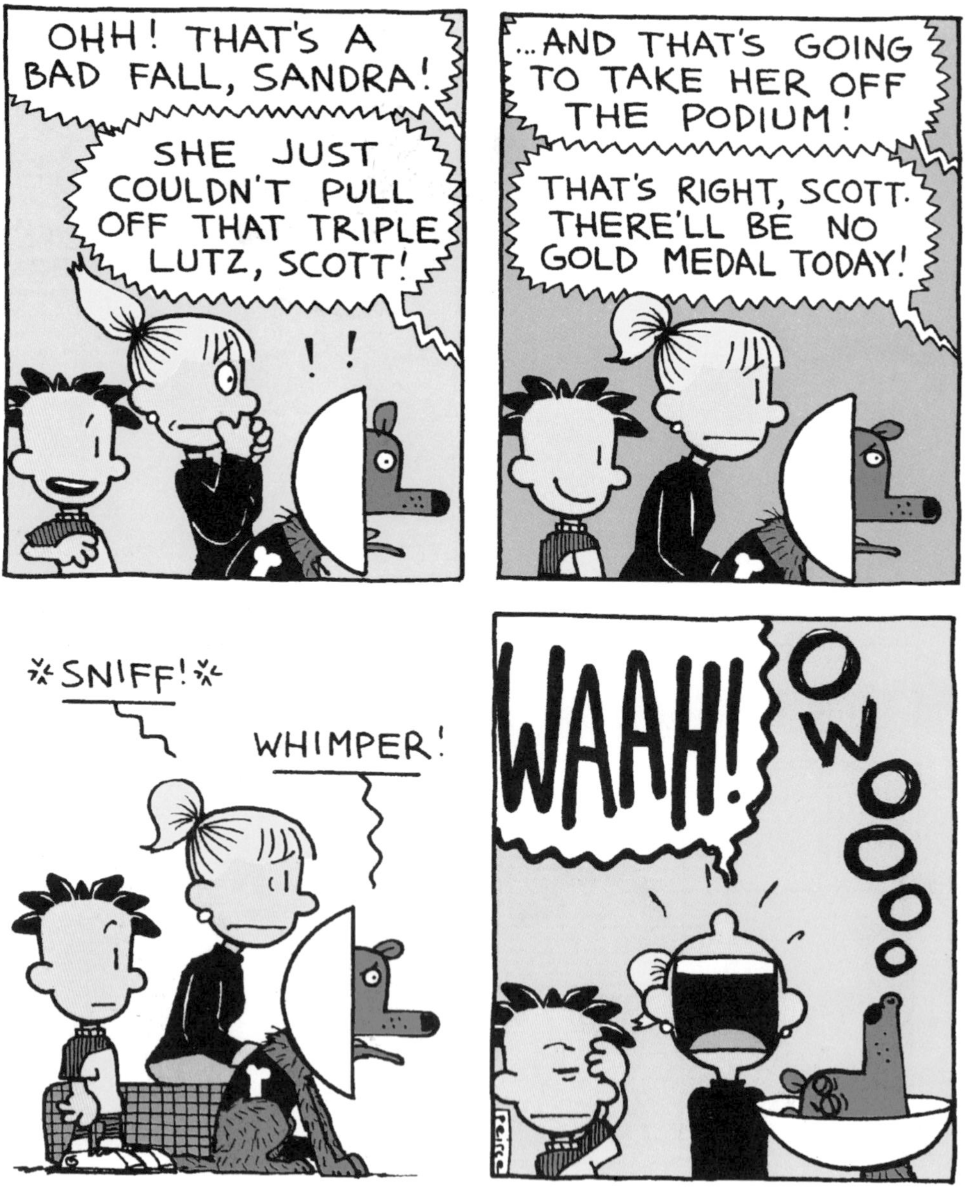
OHH! THAT'S A BAD FALL, SANDRA!
SHE JUST COULDN'T PULL OFF THAT TRIPLE LUTZ, SCOTT!
! !
...AND THAT'S GOING TO TAKE HER OFF THE PODIUM!
THAT'S RIGHT, SCOTT. THERE'LL BE NO GOLD MEDAL TODAY!
SNIFF!
WHIMPER!
WAAH!
OWOOOOO

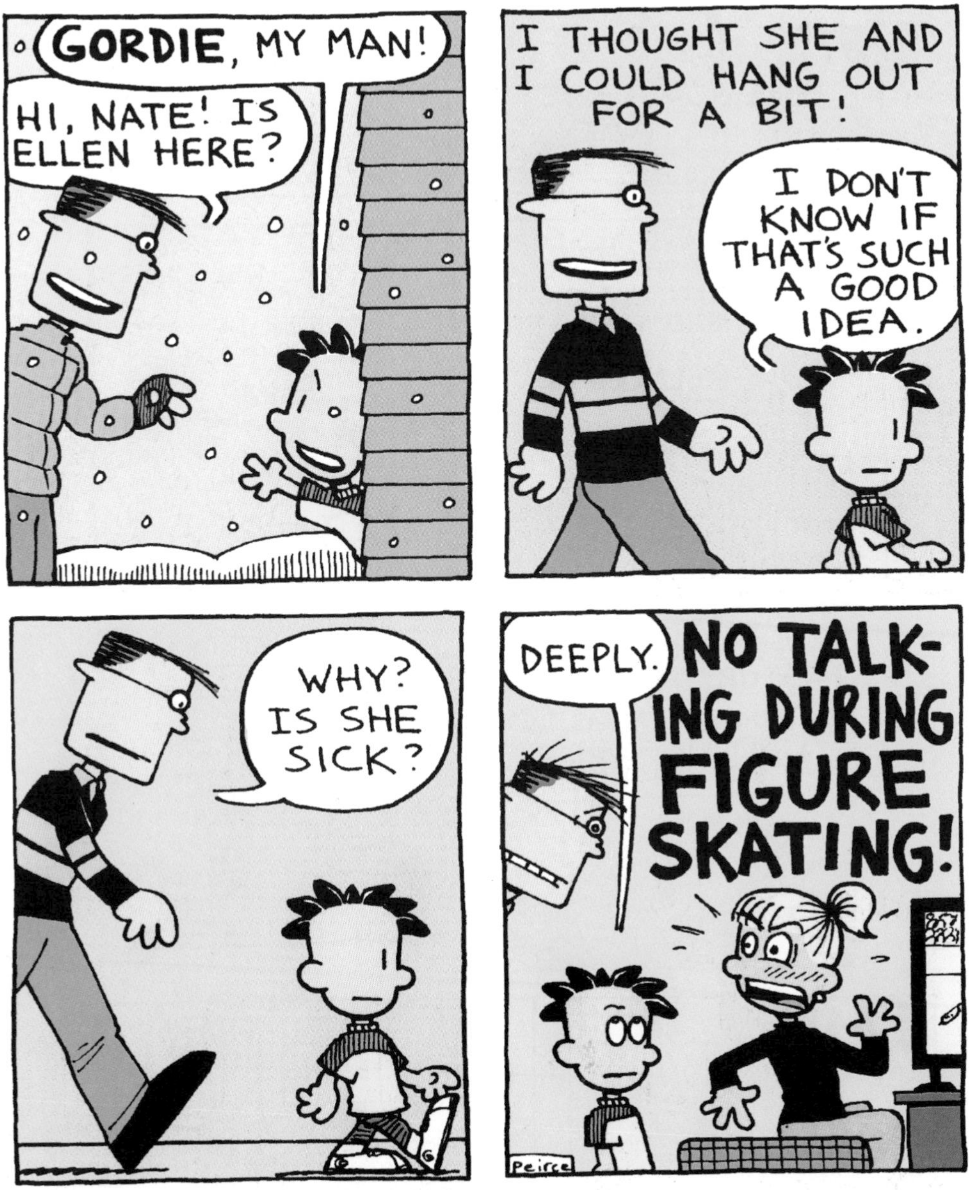
GORDIE, MY MAN!
HI, NATE! IS ELLEN HERE?
I THOUGHT SHE AND I COULD HANG OUT FOR A BIT!
I DON'T KNOW IF THAT'S SUCH A GOOD IDEA.
WHY? IS SHE SICK?
DEEPLY.
NO TALKING DURING FIGURE SKATING!
Peirce

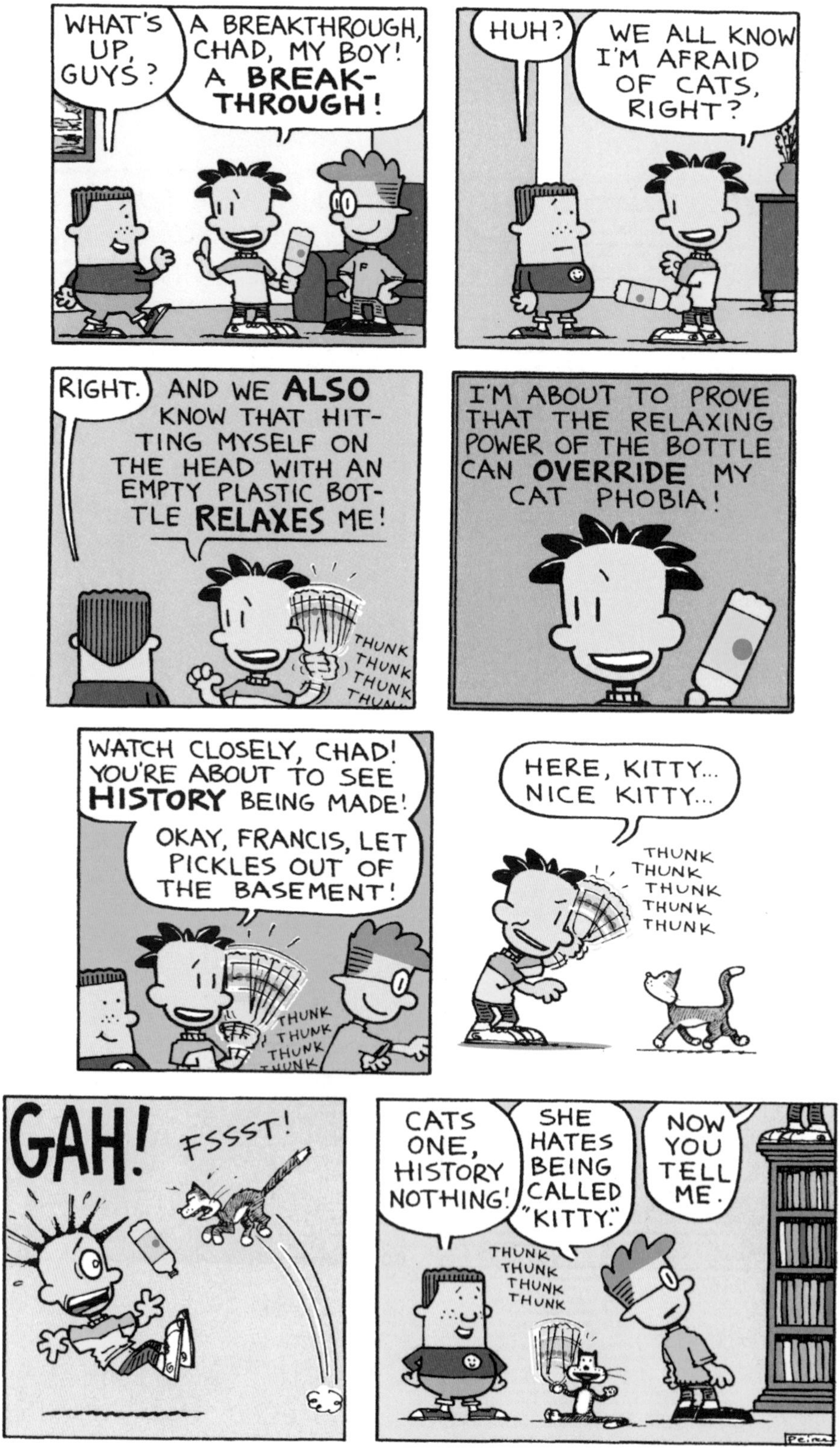
WHAT'S UP, GUYS?
A BREAKTHROUGH, CHAD, MY BOY! A **BREAK-THROUGH**!
HUH?
WE ALL KNOW I'M AFRAID OF CATS, RIGHT?
RIGHT.
AND WE **ALSO** KNOW THAT HITTING MYSELF ON THE HEAD WITH AN EMPTY PLASTIC BOTTLE **RELAXES** ME!
THUNK THUNK THUNK
I'M ABOUT TO PROVE THAT THE RELAXING POWER OF THE BOTTLE CAN **OVERRIDE** MY CAT PHOBIA!
WATCH CLOSELY, CHAD! YOU'RE ABOUT TO SEE **HISTORY** BEING MADE!
OKAY, FRANCIS, LET PICKLES OUT OF THE BASEMENT!
THUNK THUNK THUNK
HERE, KITTY... NICE KITTY...
THUNK THUNK THUNK THUNK THUNK
GAH!
FSSST!
CATS ONE, HISTORY NOTHING!
SHE HATES BEING CALLED "KITTY."
NOW YOU TELL ME.
THUNK THUNK THUNK THUNK

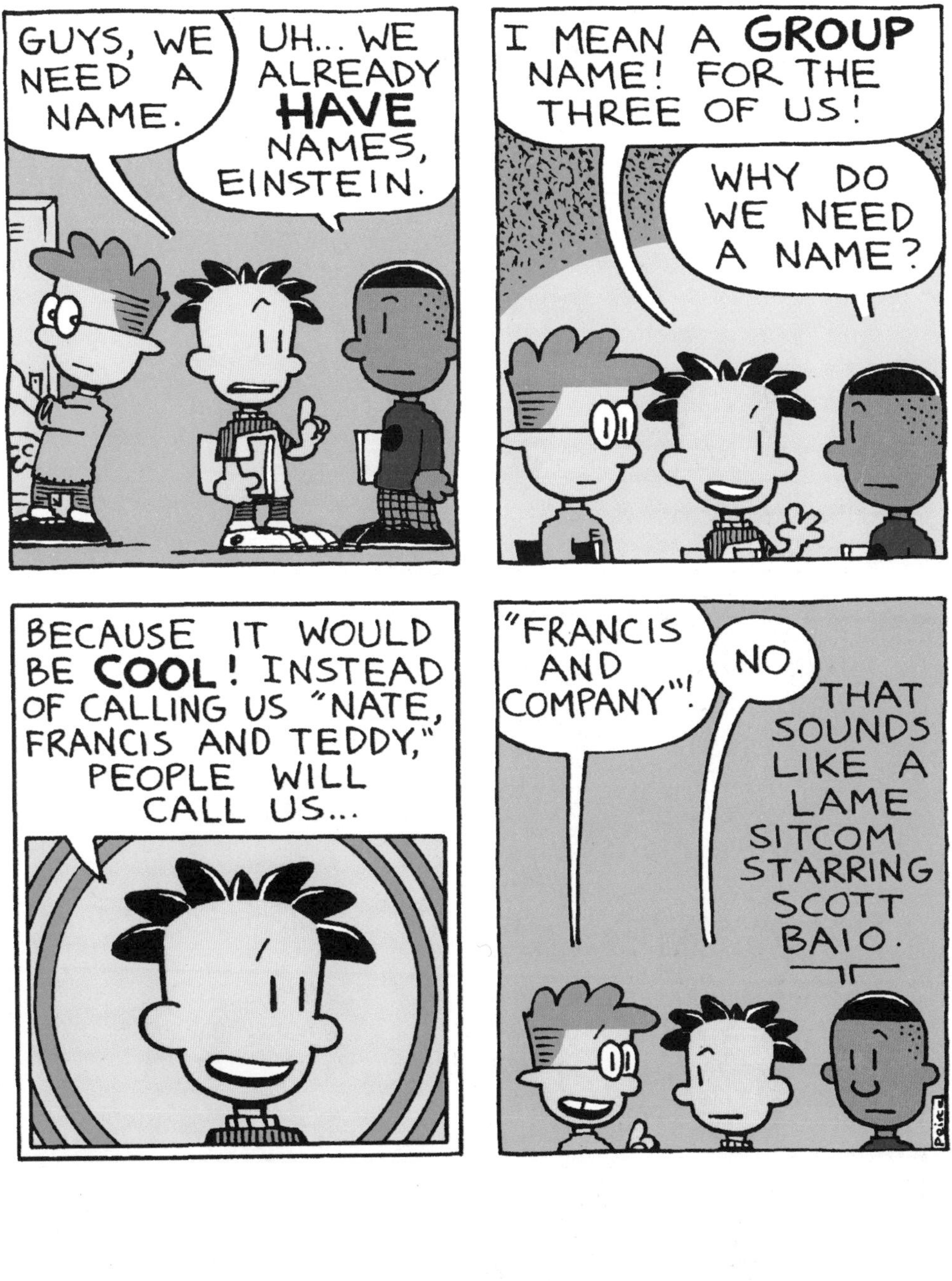
GUYS, WE NEED A NAME.
UH... WE ALREADY **HAVE** NAMES, EINSTEIN.
I MEAN A **GROUP** NAME! FOR THE THREE OF US!
WHY DO WE NEED A NAME?
BECAUSE IT WOULD BE **COOL**! INSTEAD OF CALLING US "NATE, FRANCIS AND TEDDY," PEOPLE WILL CALL US...
"FRANCIS AND COMPANY"!
NO.
THAT SOUNDS LIKE A LAME SITCOM STARRING SCOTT BAIO.

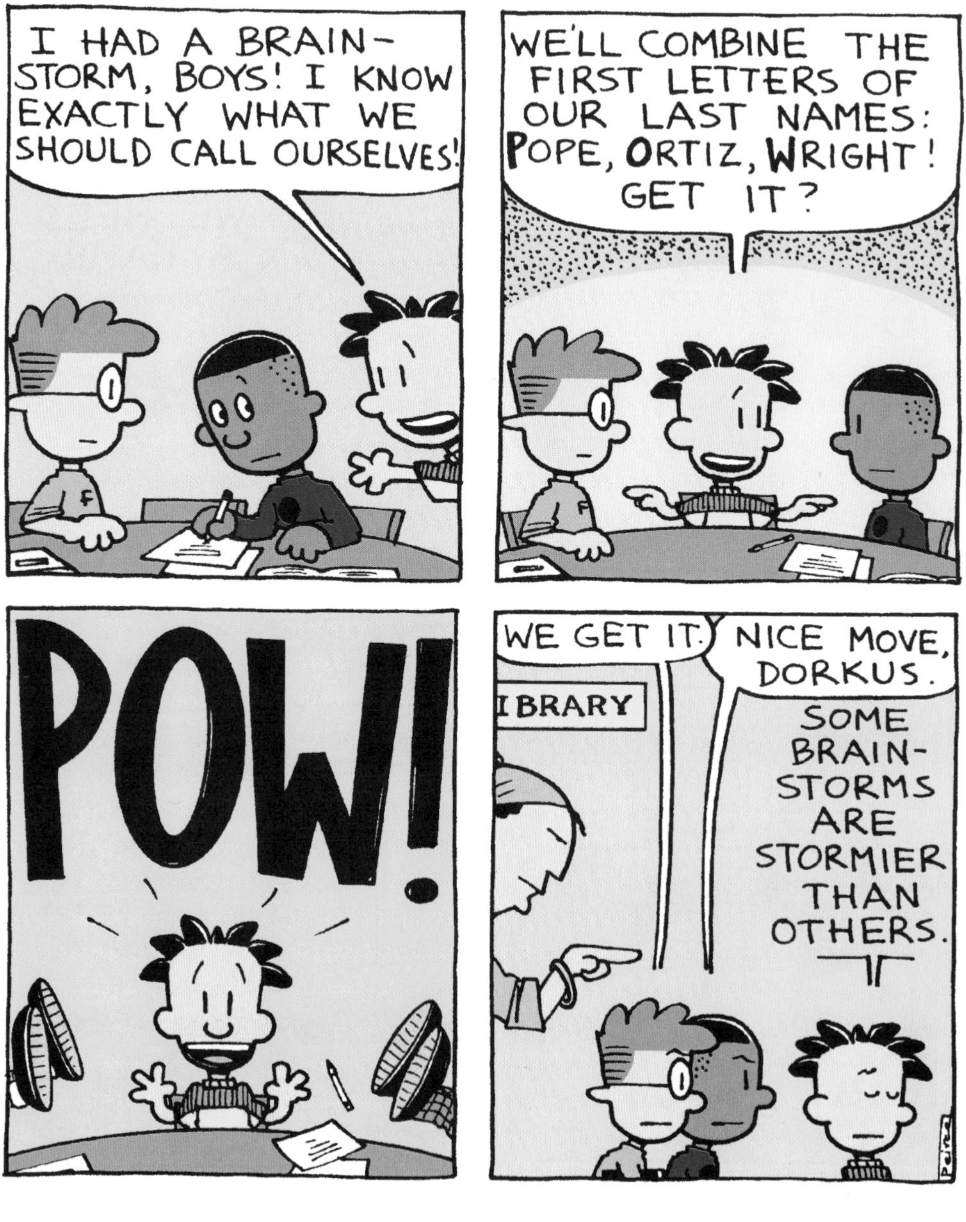
I HAD A BRAIN-STORM, BOYS! I KNOW EXACTLY WHAT WE SHOULD CALL OURSELVES!
WE'LL COMBINE THE FIRST LETTERS OF OUR LAST NAMES: POPE, ORTIZ, WRIGHT! GET IT?
POW!
WE GET IT.
NICE MOVE, DORKUS.
IBRARY
SOME BRAIN-STORMS ARE STORMIER THAN OTHERS.
Peirce

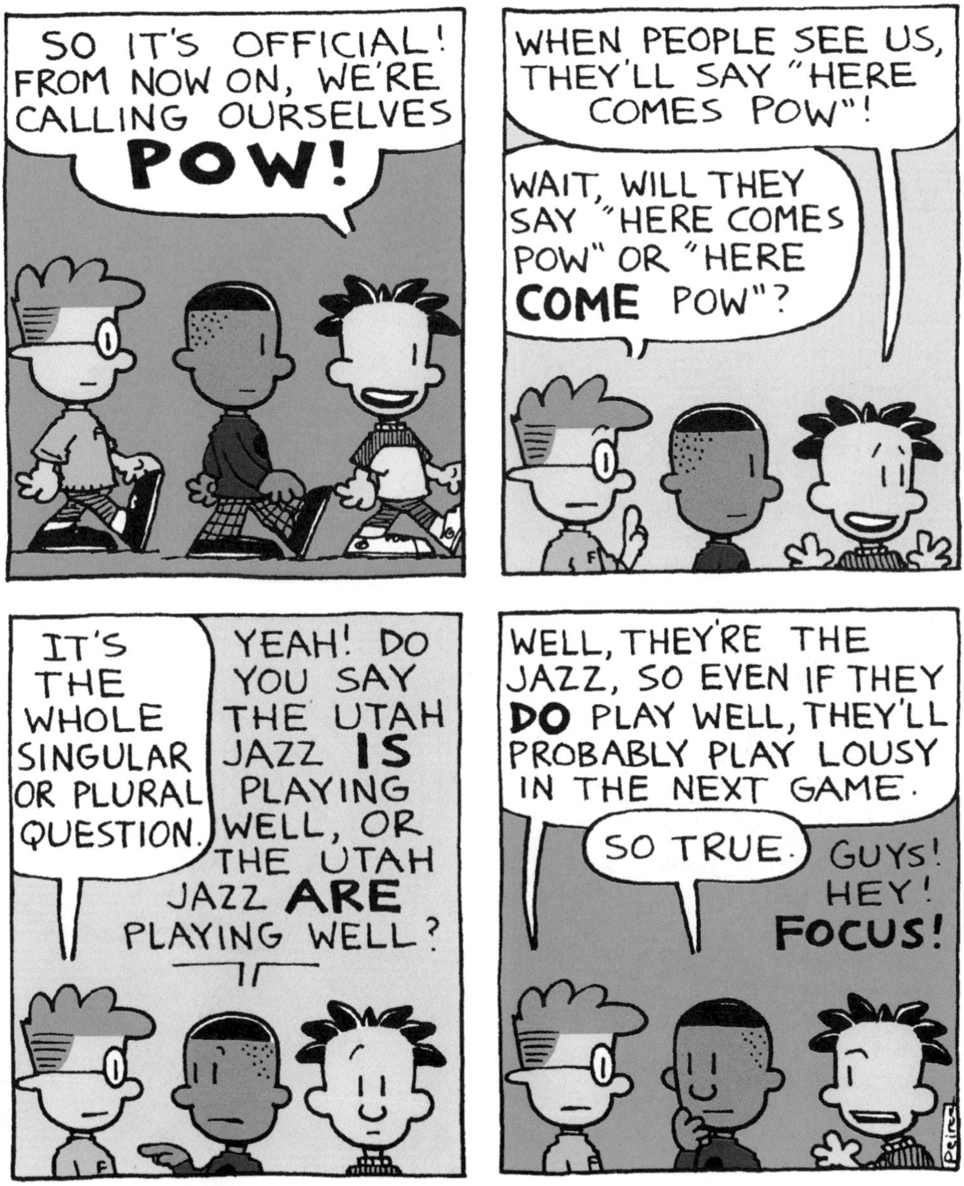
SO IT'S OFFICIAL! FROM NOW ON, WE'RE CALLING OURSELVES **POW!**
WHEN PEOPLE SEE US, THEY'LL SAY "HERE COMES POW"!
WAIT, WILL THEY SAY "HERE COMES POW" OR "HERE **COME** POW"?
IT'S THE WHOLE SINGULAR OR PLURAL QUESTION.
YEAH! DO YOU SAY THE UTAH JAZZ **IS** PLAYING WELL, OR THE UTAH JAZZ **ARE** PLAYING WELL?
WELL, THEY'RE THE JAZZ, SO EVEN IF THEY **DO** PLAY WELL, THEY'LL PROBABLY PLAY LOUSY IN THE NEXT GAME.
SO TRUE.
GUYS! HEY! **FOCUS!**
Peirce

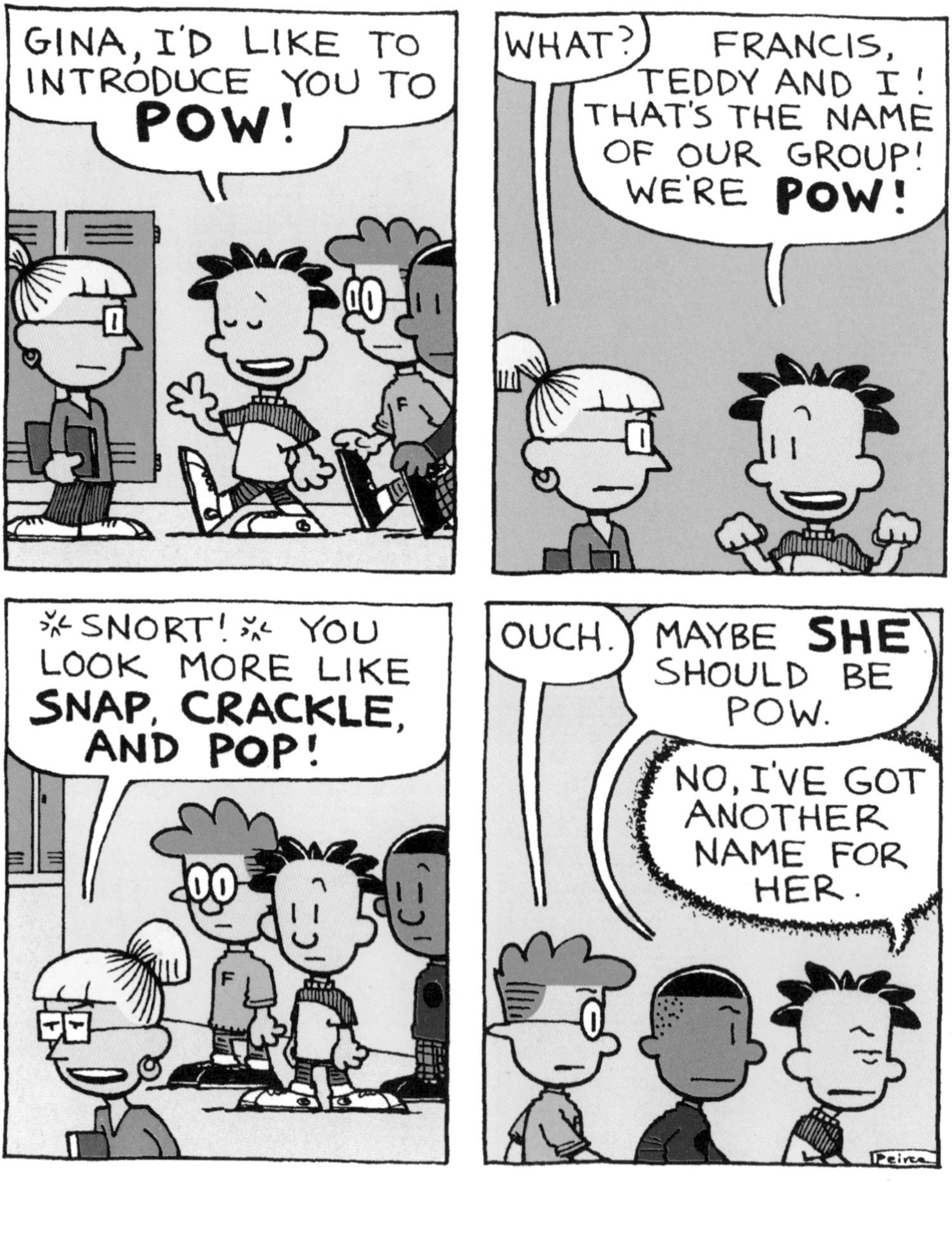
GINA, I'D LIKE TO INTRODUCE YOU TO **POW**!
WHAT?
FRANCIS, TEDDY AND I! THAT'S THE NAME OF OUR GROUP! WE'RE **POW**!
SNORT! YOU LOOK MORE LIKE **SNAP, CRACKLE, AND POP**!
OUCH.
MAYBE **SHE** SHOULD BE POW.
NO, I'VE GOT ANOTHER NAME FOR HER.
Peirce

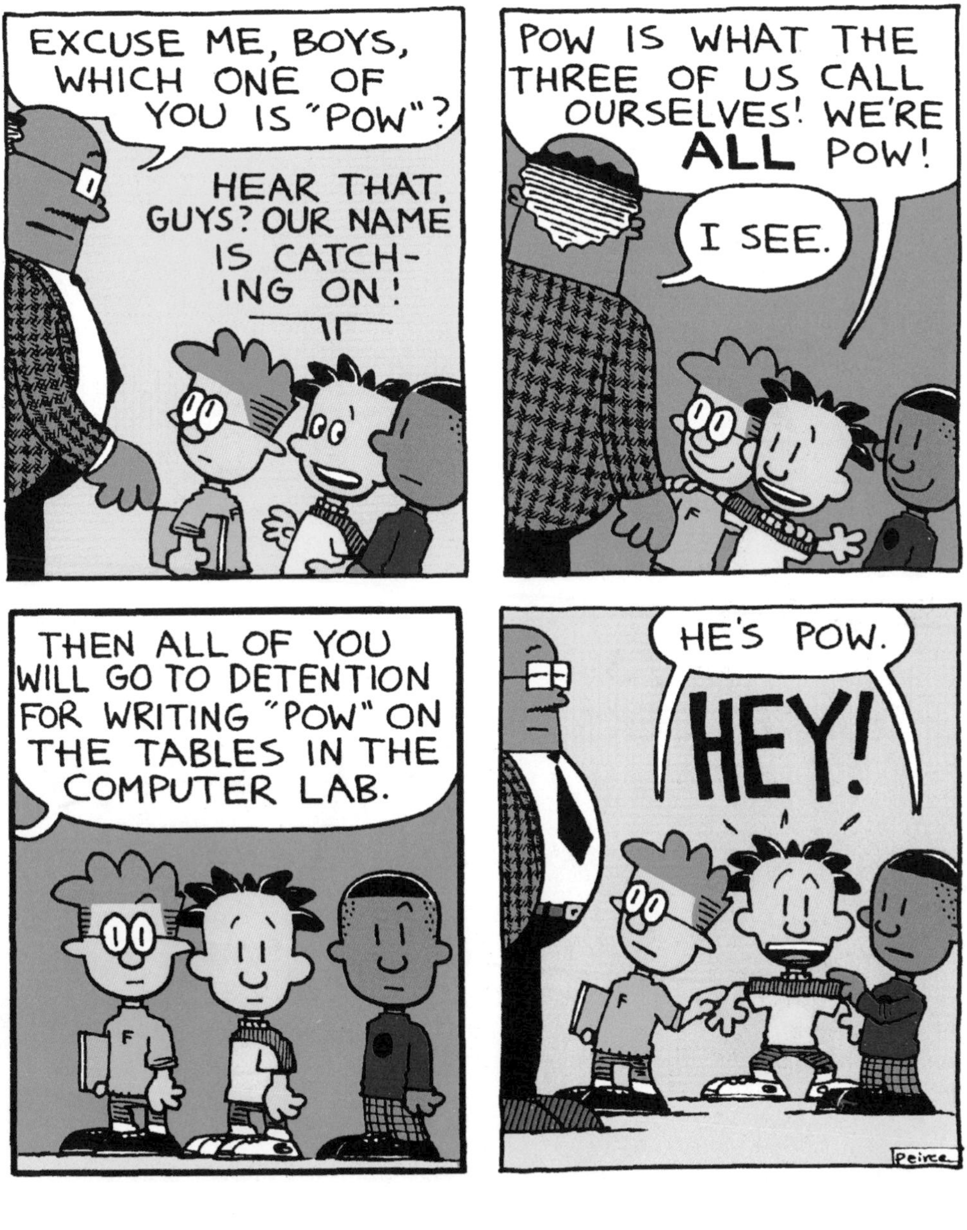
EXCUSE ME, BOYS, WHICH ONE OF YOU IS "POW"?
HEAR THAT, GUYS? OUR NAME IS CATCHING ON!
POW IS WHAT THE THREE OF US CALL OURSELVES! WE'RE ALL POW!
I SEE.
THEN ALL OF YOU WILL GO TO DETENTION FOR WRITING "POW" ON THE TABLES IN THE COMPUTER LAB.
HE'S POW.
HEY!
Peirce

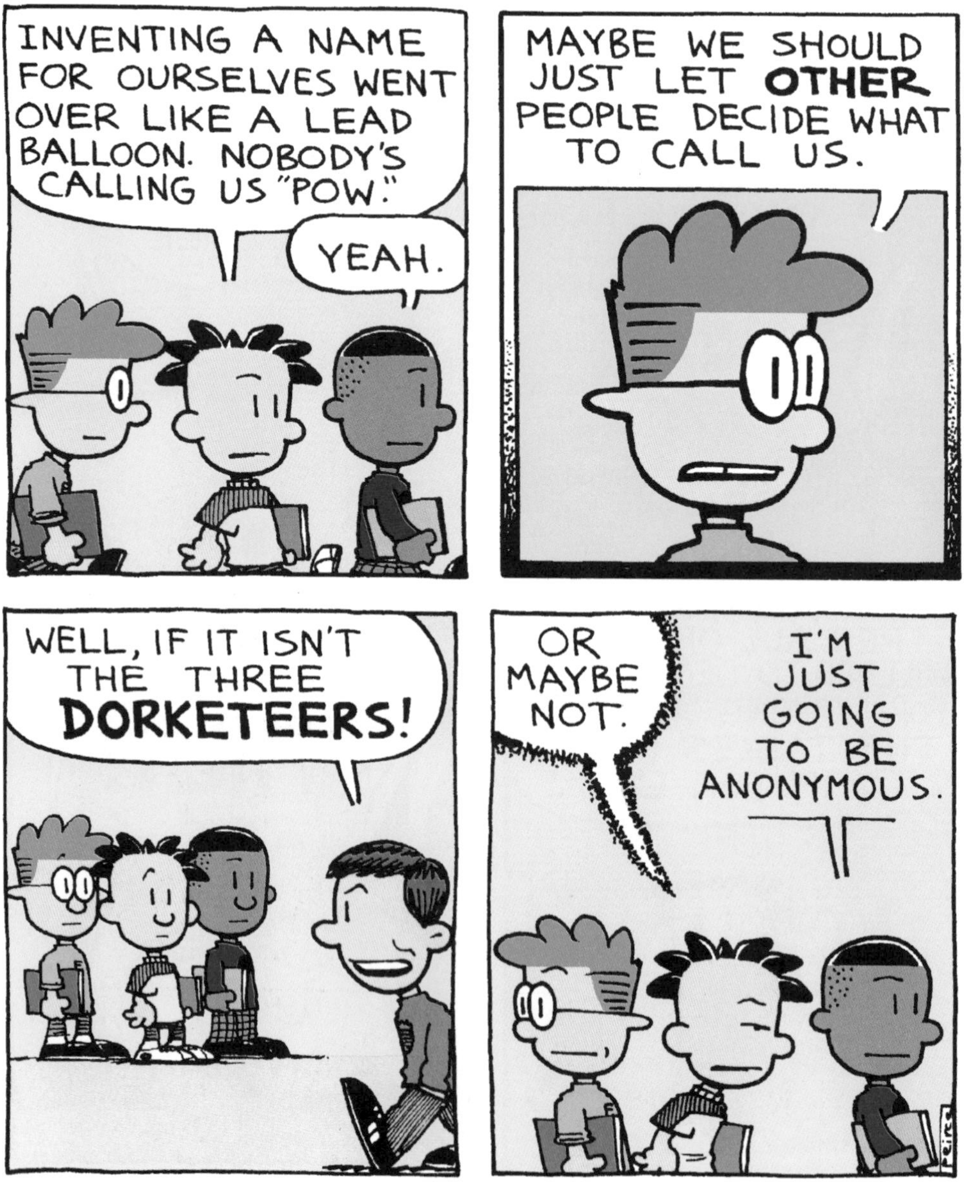
INVENTING A NAME FOR OURSELVES WENT OVER LIKE A LEAD BALLOON. NOBODY'S CALLING US "POW."
YEAH.
MAYBE WE SHOULD JUST LET **OTHER** PEOPLE DECIDE WHAT TO CALL US.
WELL, IF IT ISN'T THE THREE **DORKETEERS!**
OR MAYBE NOT.
I'M JUST GOING TO BE ANONYMOUS.

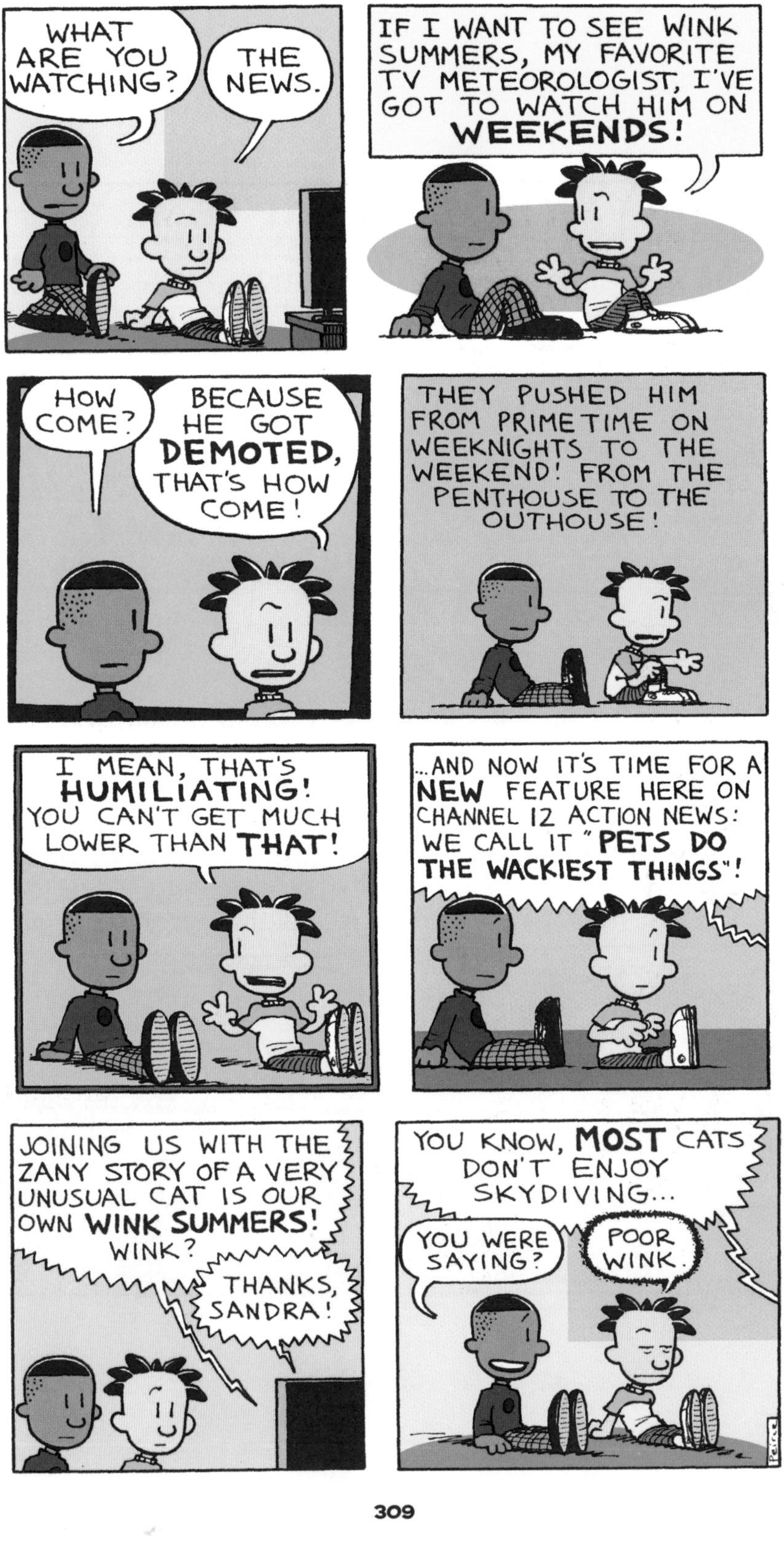
WHAT ARE YOU WATCHING?
THE NEWS.
IF I WANT TO SEE WINK SUMMERS, MY FAVORITE TV METEOROLOGIST, I'VE GOT TO WATCH HIM ON WEEKENDS!
HOW COME?
BECAUSE HE GOT DEMOTED, THAT'S HOW COME!
THEY PUSHED HIM FROM PRIMETIME ON WEEKNIGHTS TO THE WEEKEND! FROM THE PENTHOUSE TO THE OUTHOUSE!
I MEAN, THAT'S HUMILIATING! YOU CAN'T GET MUCH LOWER THAN THAT!
...AND NOW IT'S TIME FOR A NEW FEATURE HERE ON CHANNEL 12 ACTION NEWS: WE CALL IT "PETS DO THE WACKIEST THINGS"!
JOINING US WITH THE ZANY STORY OF A VERY UNUSUAL CAT IS OUR OWN WINK SUMMERS! WINK?
THANKS, SANDRA!
YOU KNOW, MOST CATS DON'T ENJOY SKYDIVING...
YOU WERE SAYING?
POOR WINK.
PEIRCE

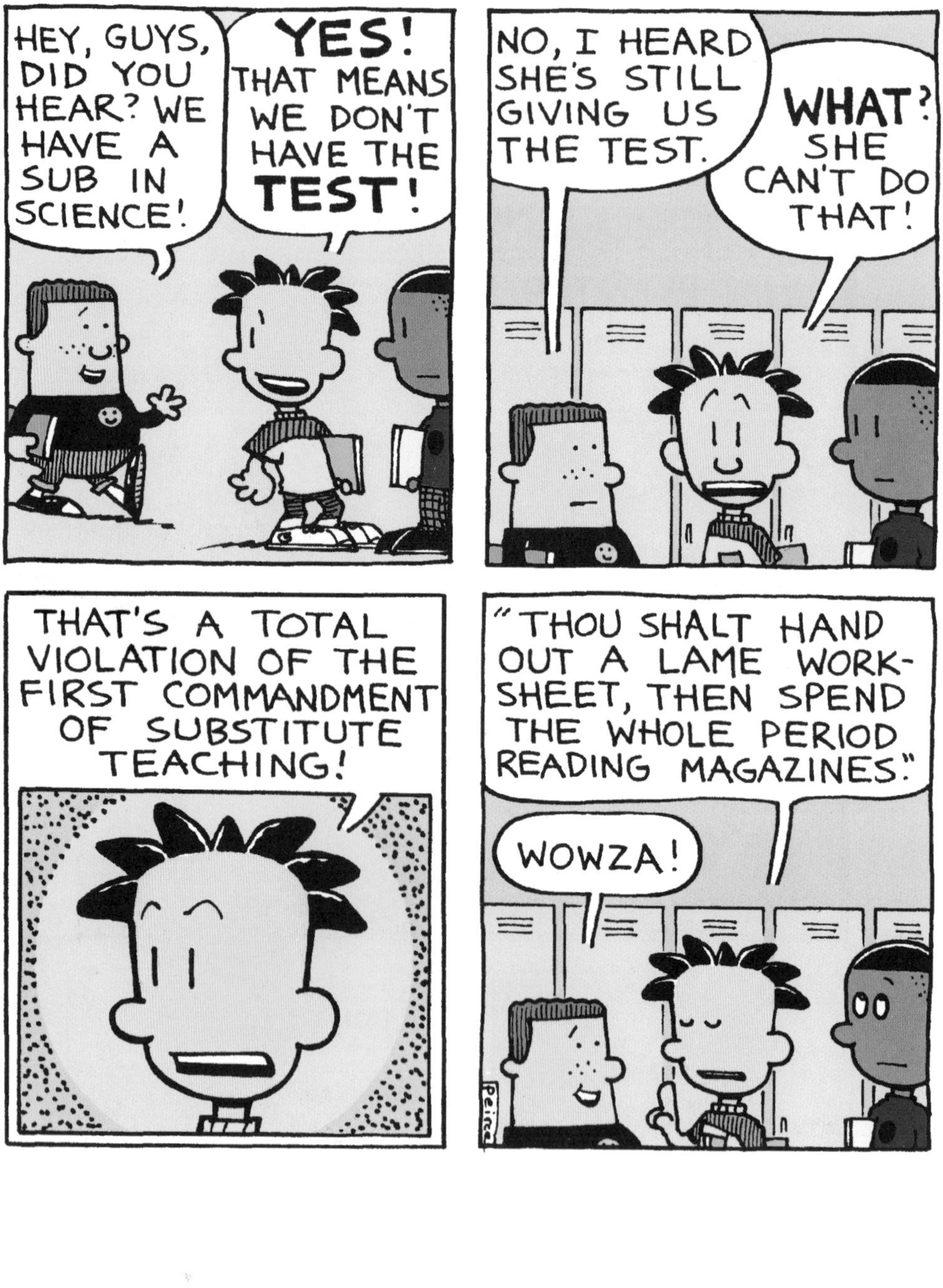
HEY, GUYS, DID YOU HEAR? WE HAVE A SUB IN SCIENCE!
YES! THAT MEANS WE DON'T HAVE THE TEST!
NO, I HEARD SHE'S STILL GIVING US THE TEST.
WHAT? SHE CAN'T DO THAT!
THAT'S A TOTAL VIOLATION OF THE FIRST COMMANDMENT OF SUBSTITUTE TEACHING!
"THOU SHALT HAND OUT A LAME WORK-SHEET, THEN SPEND THE WHOLE PERIOD READING MAGAZINES."
WOWZA!
Peirce

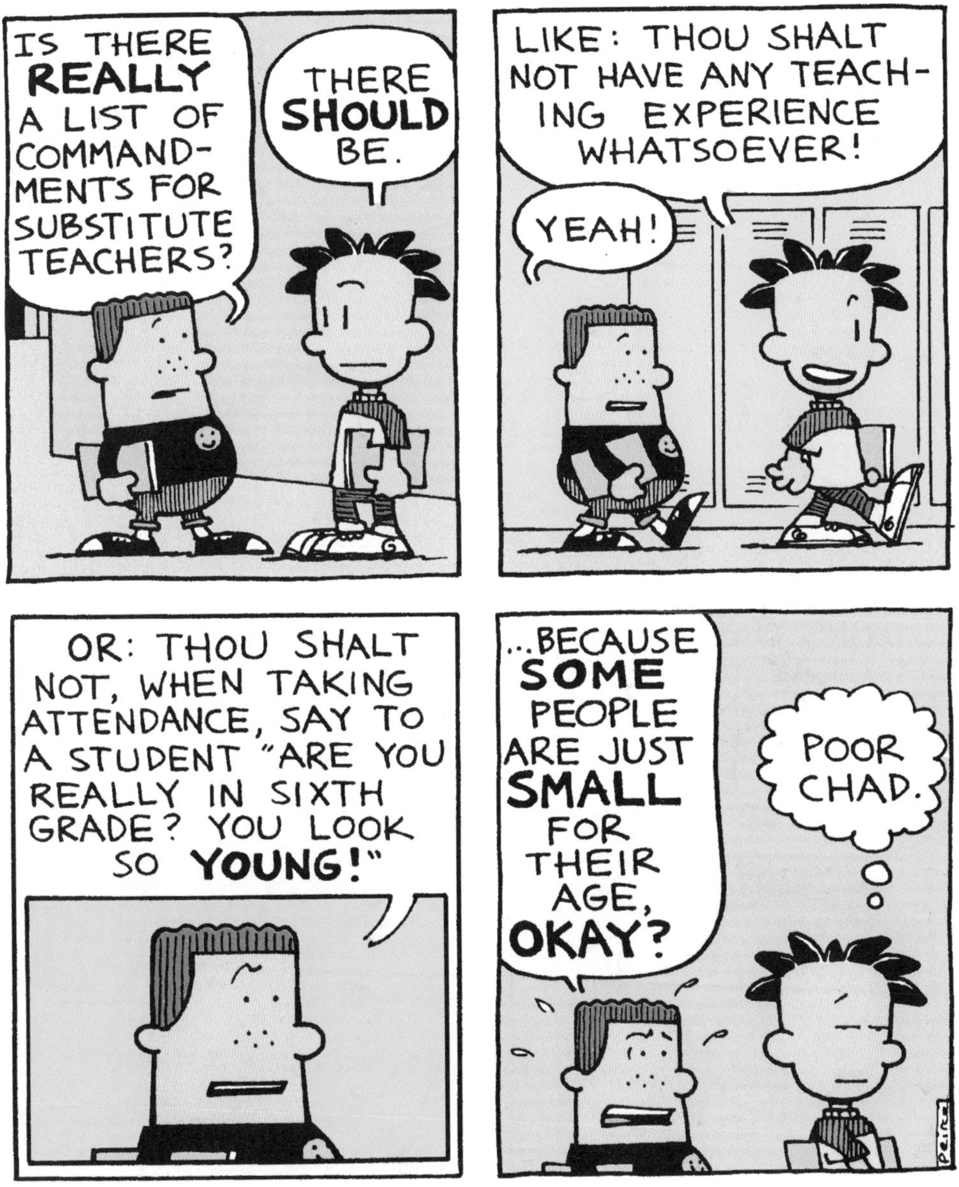
IS THERE **REALLY** A LIST OF COMMANDMENTS FOR SUBSTITUTE TEACHERS?
THERE **SHOULD** BE.
LIKE: THOU SHALT NOT HAVE ANY TEACHING EXPERIENCE WHATSOEVER!
YEAH!
OR: THOU SHALT NOT, WHEN TAKING ATTENDANCE, SAY TO A STUDENT "ARE YOU REALLY IN SIXTH GRADE? YOU LOOK SO **YOUNG!**"
...BECAUSE **SOME** PEOPLE ARE JUST **SMALL** FOR THEIR AGE, **OKAY?**
POOR CHAD.
PEIRCE

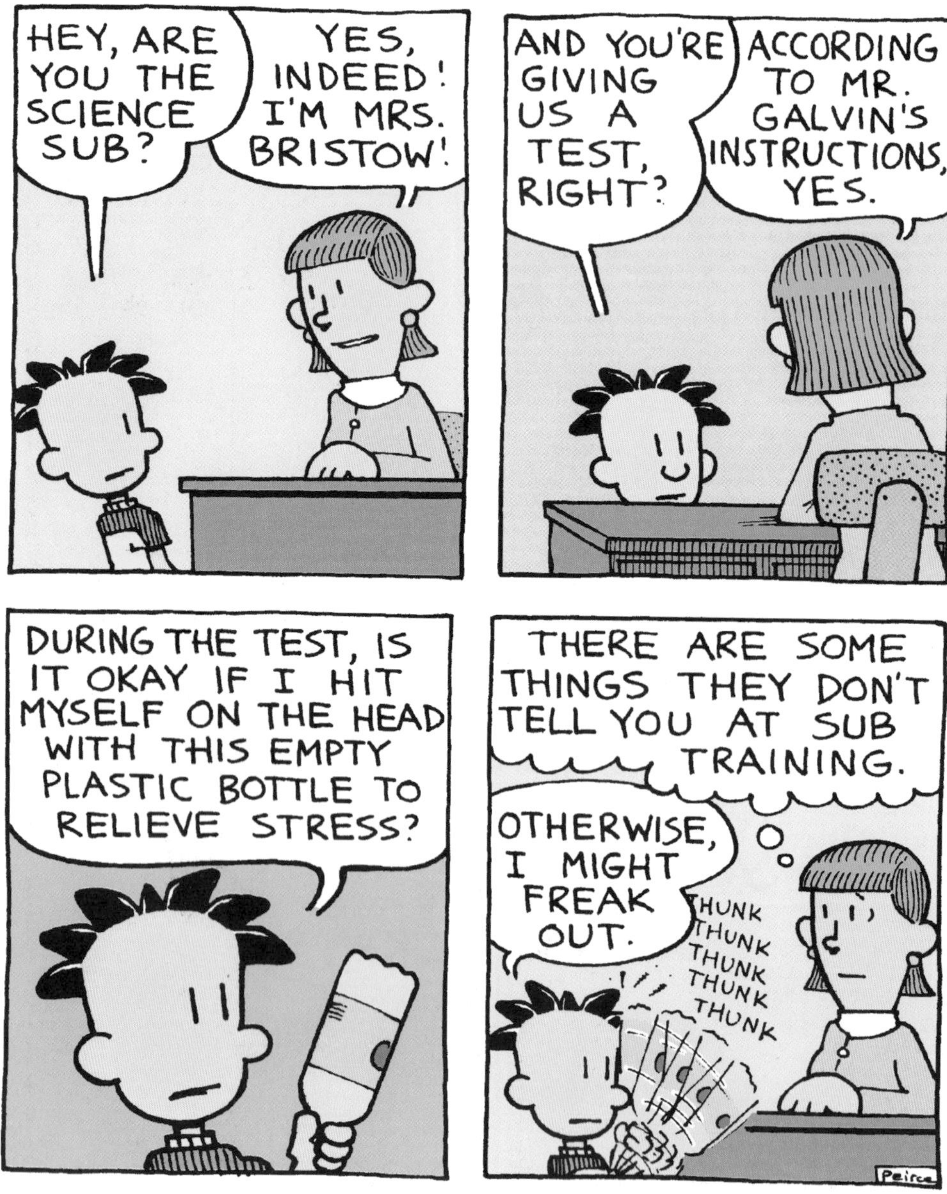
HEY, ARE YOU THE SCIENCE SUB?
YES, INDEED! I'M MRS. BRISTOW!
AND YOU'RE GIVING US A TEST, RIGHT?
ACCORDING TO MR. GALVIN'S INSTRUCTIONS, YES.
DURING THE TEST, IS IT OKAY IF I HIT MYSELF ON THE HEAD WITH THIS EMPTY PLASTIC BOTTLE TO RELIEVE STRESS?
THERE ARE SOME THINGS THEY DON'T TELL YOU AT SUB TRAINING.
OTHERWISE, I MIGHT FREAK OUT.
THUNK
THUNK
THUNK
THUNK
THUNK
Peirce

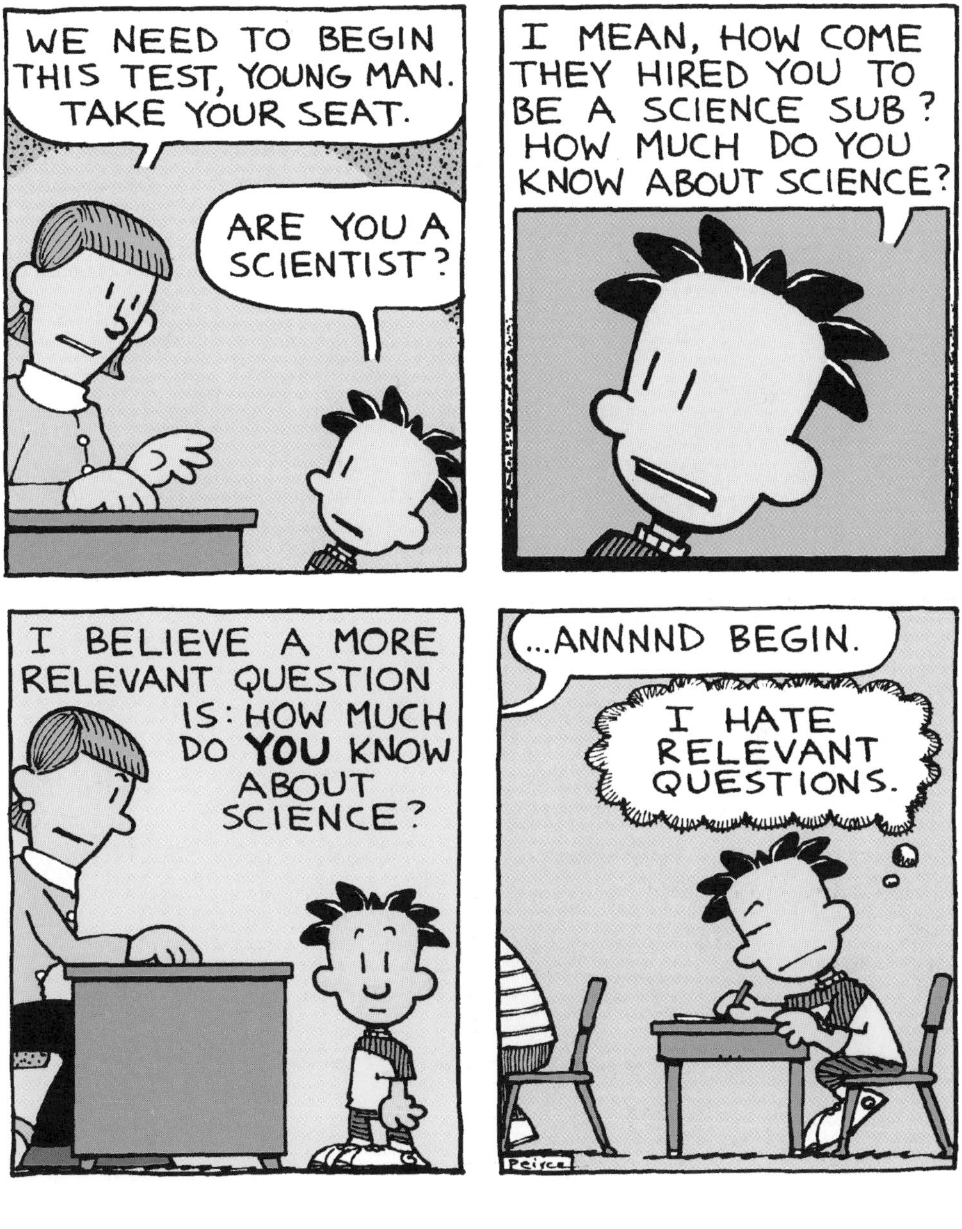
WE NEED TO BEGIN THIS TEST, YOUNG MAN. TAKE YOUR SEAT.
ARE YOU A SCIENTIST?
I MEAN, HOW COME THEY HIRED YOU TO BE A SCIENCE SUB? HOW MUCH DO YOU KNOW ABOUT SCIENCE?
I BELIEVE A MORE RELEVANT QUESTION IS: HOW MUCH DO **YOU** KNOW ABOUT SCIENCE?
...ANNNND BEGIN.
I HATE RELEVANT QUESTIONS.
PEIRCE

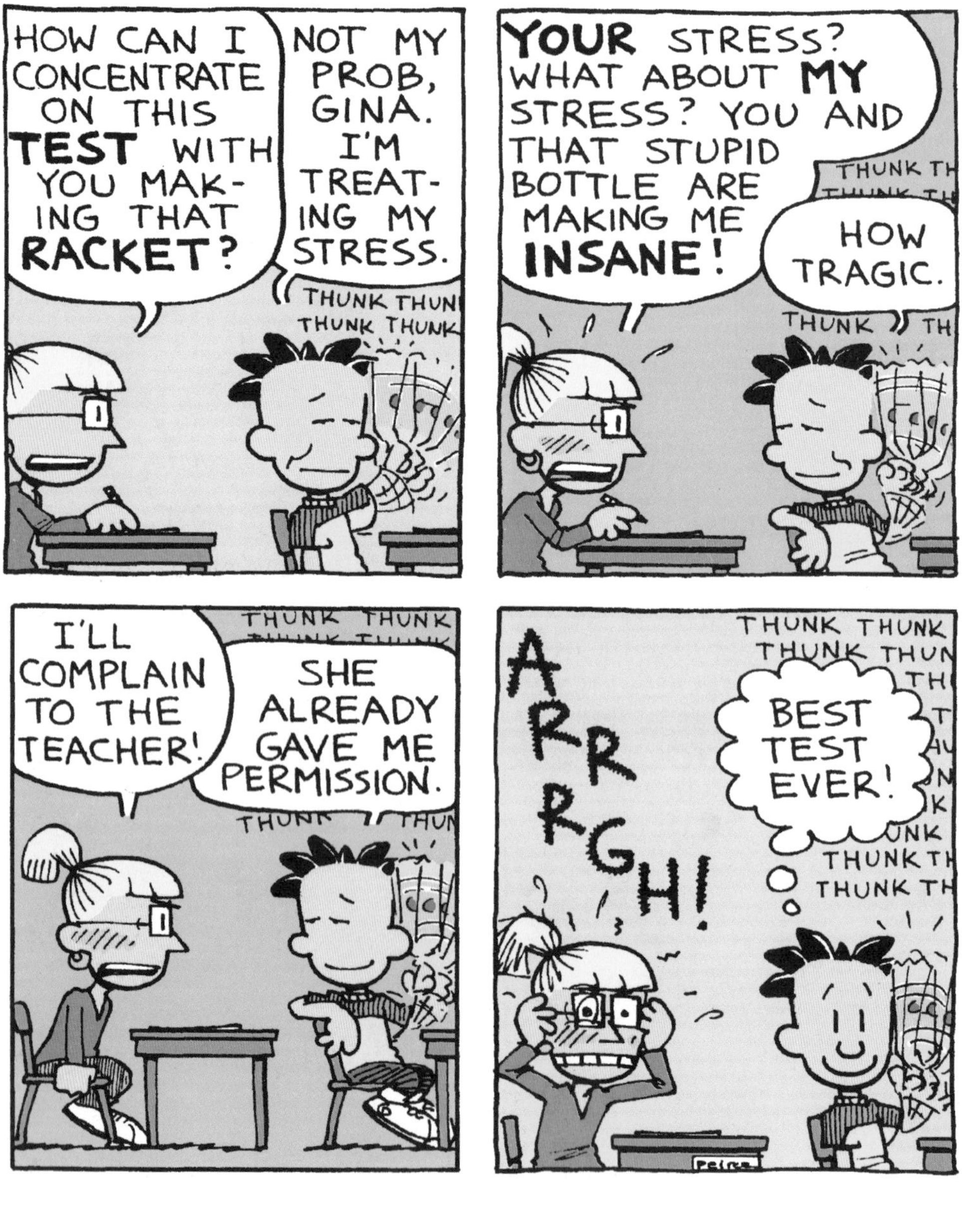
HOW CAN I CONCENTRATE ON THIS **TEST** WITH YOU MAKING THAT **RACKET**?
NOT MY PROB, GINA. I'M TREATING MY STRESS.
THUNK THUNK THUNK THUNK
YOUR STRESS? WHAT ABOUT **MY** STRESS? YOU AND THAT STUPID BOTTLE ARE MAKING ME **INSANE**!
HOW TRAGIC.
THUNK
I'LL COMPLAIN TO THE TEACHER!
SHE ALREADY GAVE ME PERMISSION.
THUNK THUNK
ARRRGH!
BEST TEST EVER!
THUNK THUNK
THUNK
THUNK
PEIRCE

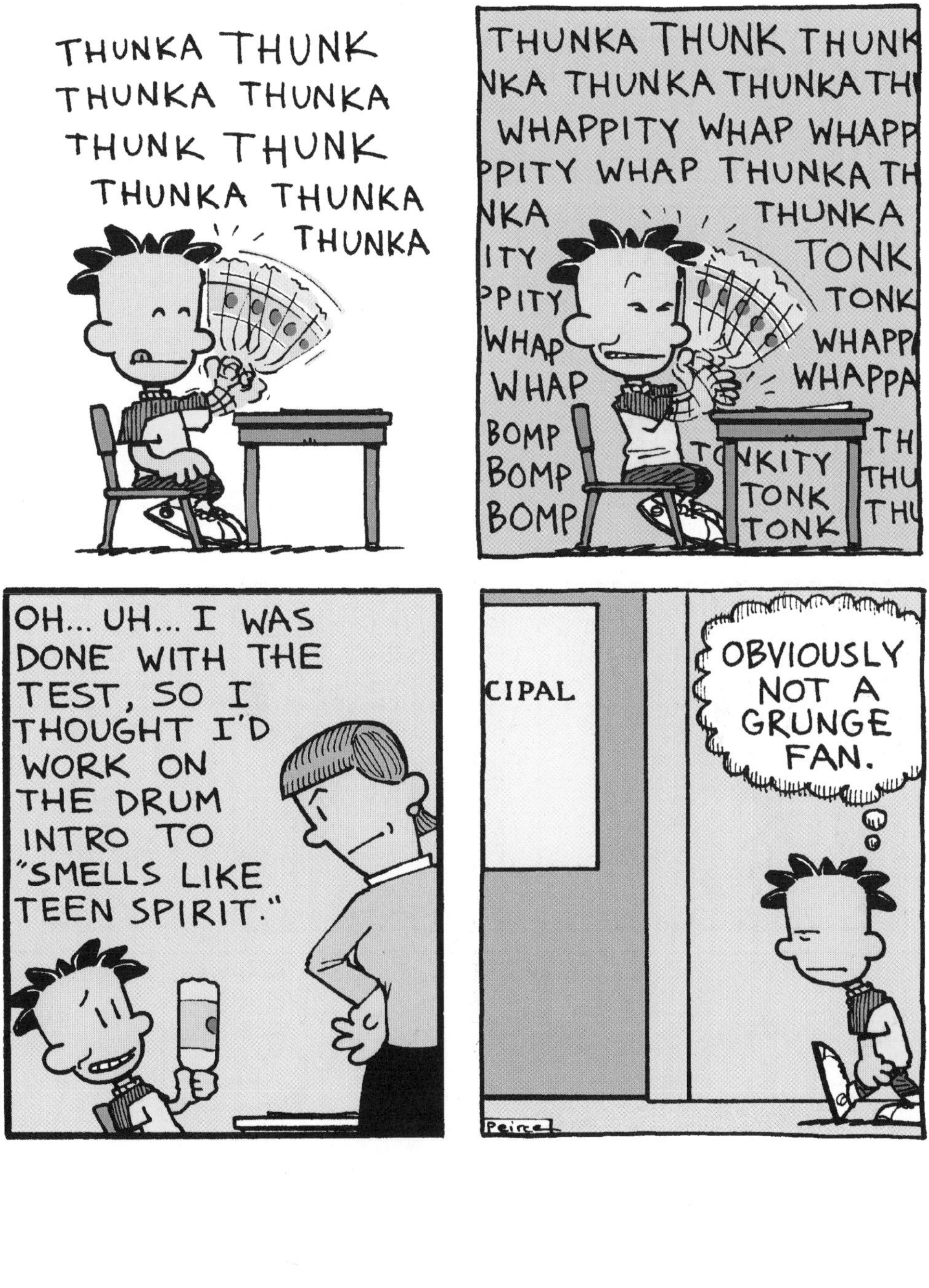
THUNKA THUNK
THUNKA THUNKA
THUNK THUNK
THUNKA THUNKA
THUNKA
THUNKA THUNK THUNK
NKA THUNKA THUNKA TH
WHAPPITY WHAP WHAPP
PPITY WHAP THUNKA TH
NKA THUNKA
ITY TONK
PPITY TONK
WHAP WHAPP
WHAP WHAPPA
BOMP BOMP BOMP
TONKITY TONK TONK
TH THU THU
OH... UH... I WAS DONE WITH THE TEST, SO I THOUGHT I'D WORK ON THE DRUM INTRO TO "SMELLS LIKE TEEN SPIRIT."
CIPAL
OBVIOUSLY NOT A GRUNGE FAN.
Peirce

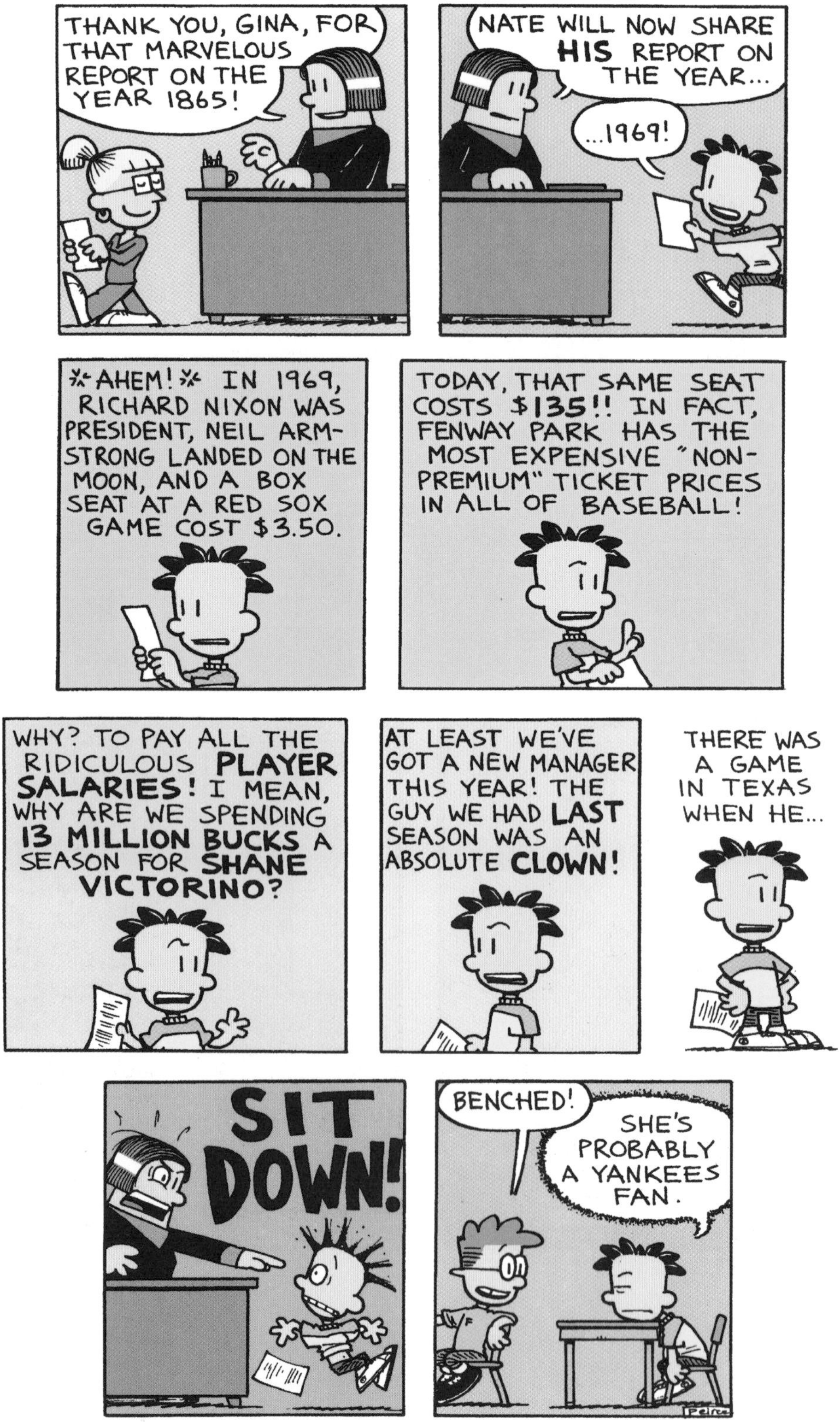
THANK YOU, GINA, FOR THAT MARVELOUS REPORT ON THE YEAR 1865!
NATE WILL NOW SHARE HIS REPORT ON THE YEAR...
...1969!
AHEM! IN 1969, RICHARD NIXON WAS PRESIDENT, NEIL ARMSTRONG LANDED ON THE MOON, AND A BOX SEAT AT A RED SOX GAME COST $3.50.
TODAY, THAT SAME SEAT COSTS $135!! IN FACT, FENWAY PARK HAS THE MOST EXPENSIVE "NON-PREMIUM" TICKET PRICES IN ALL OF BASEBALL!
WHY? TO PAY ALL THE RIDICULOUS PLAYER SALARIES! I MEAN, WHY ARE WE SPENDING 13 MILLION BUCKS A SEASON FOR SHANE VICTORINO?
AT LEAST WE'VE GOT A NEW MANAGER THIS YEAR! THE GUY WE HAD LAST SEASON WAS AN ABSOLUTE CLOWN!
THERE WAS A GAME IN TEXAS WHEN HE...
SIT DOWN!
BENCHED!
SHE'S PROBABLY A YANKEES FAN.
Peirce

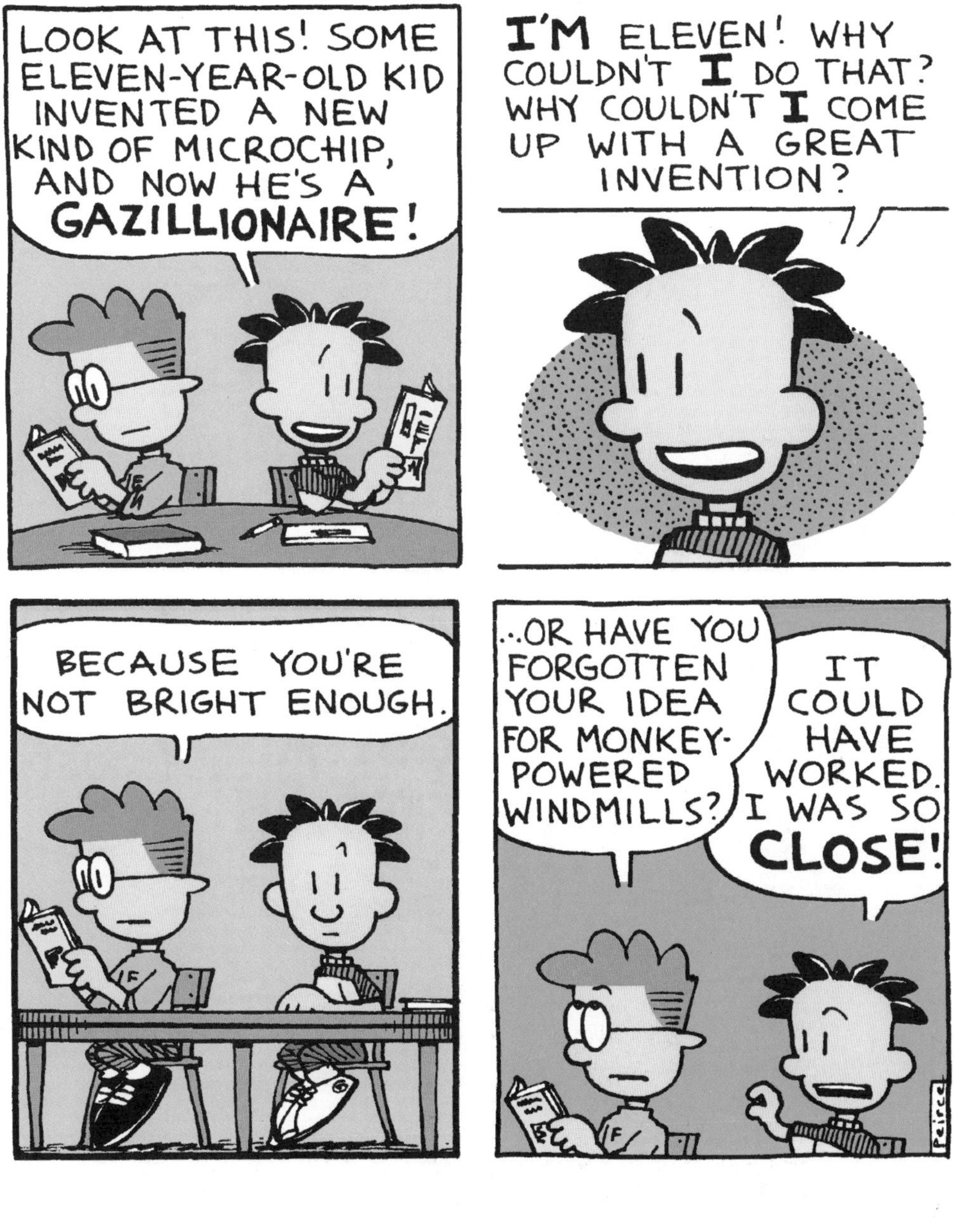
LOOK AT THIS! SOME ELEVEN-YEAR-OLD KID INVENTED A NEW KIND OF MICROCHIP, AND NOW HE'S A GAZILLIONAIRE!
I'M ELEVEN! WHY COULDN'T I DO THAT? WHY COULDN'T I COME UP WITH A GREAT INVENTION?
BECAUSE YOU'RE NOT BRIGHT ENOUGH.
...OR HAVE YOU FORGOTTEN YOUR IDEA FOR MONKEY-POWERED WINDMILLS?
IT COULD HAVE WORKED. I WAS SO CLOSE!
Peirce

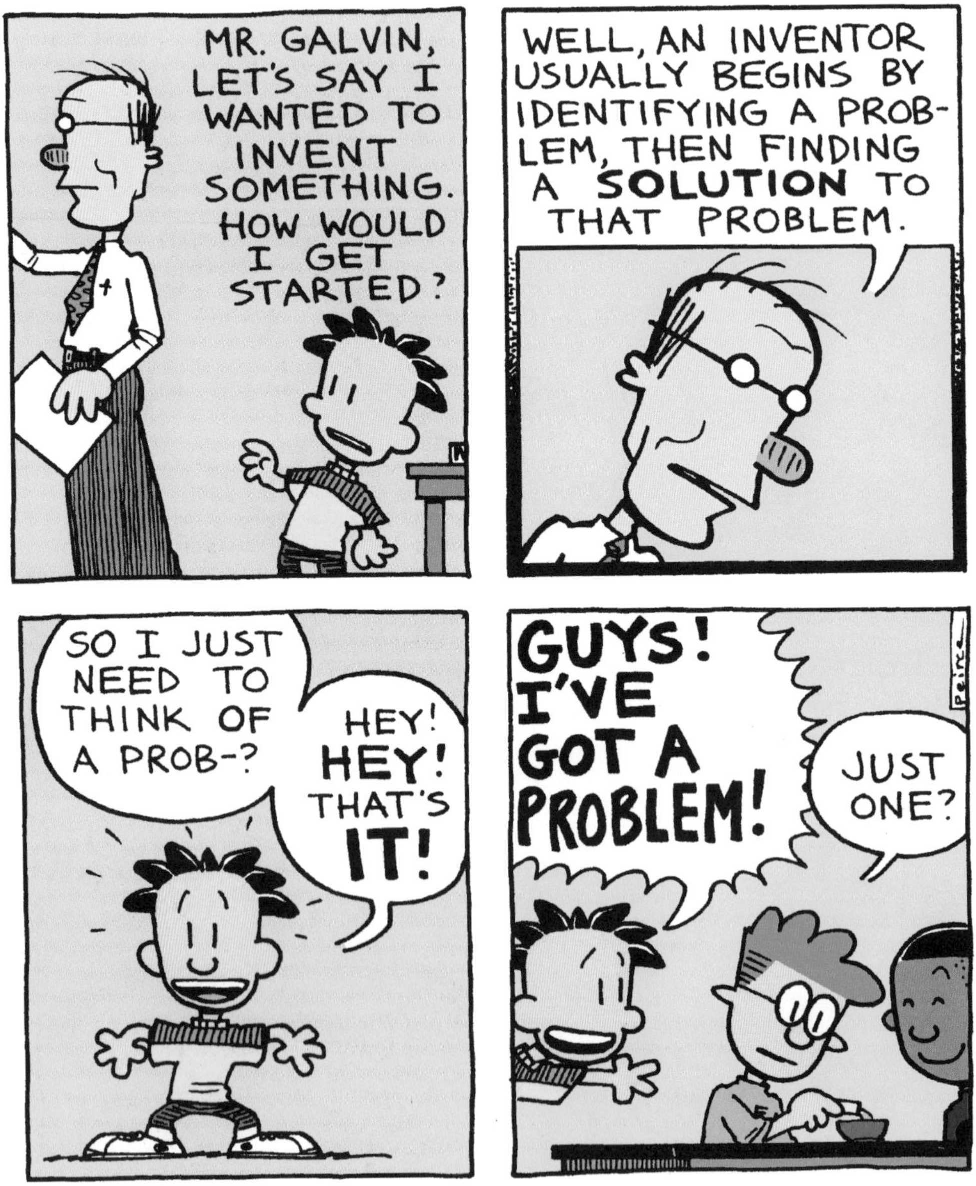
MR. GALVIN, LET'S SAY I WANTED TO INVENT SOMETHING. HOW WOULD I GET STARTED?
WELL, AN INVENTOR USUALLY BEGINS BY IDENTIFYING A PROB-LEM, THEN FINDING A SOLUTION TO THAT PROBLEM.
SO I JUST NEED TO THINK OF A PROB-?
HEY! HEY! THAT'S IT!
GUYS! I'VE GOT A PROBLEM!
JUST ONE?

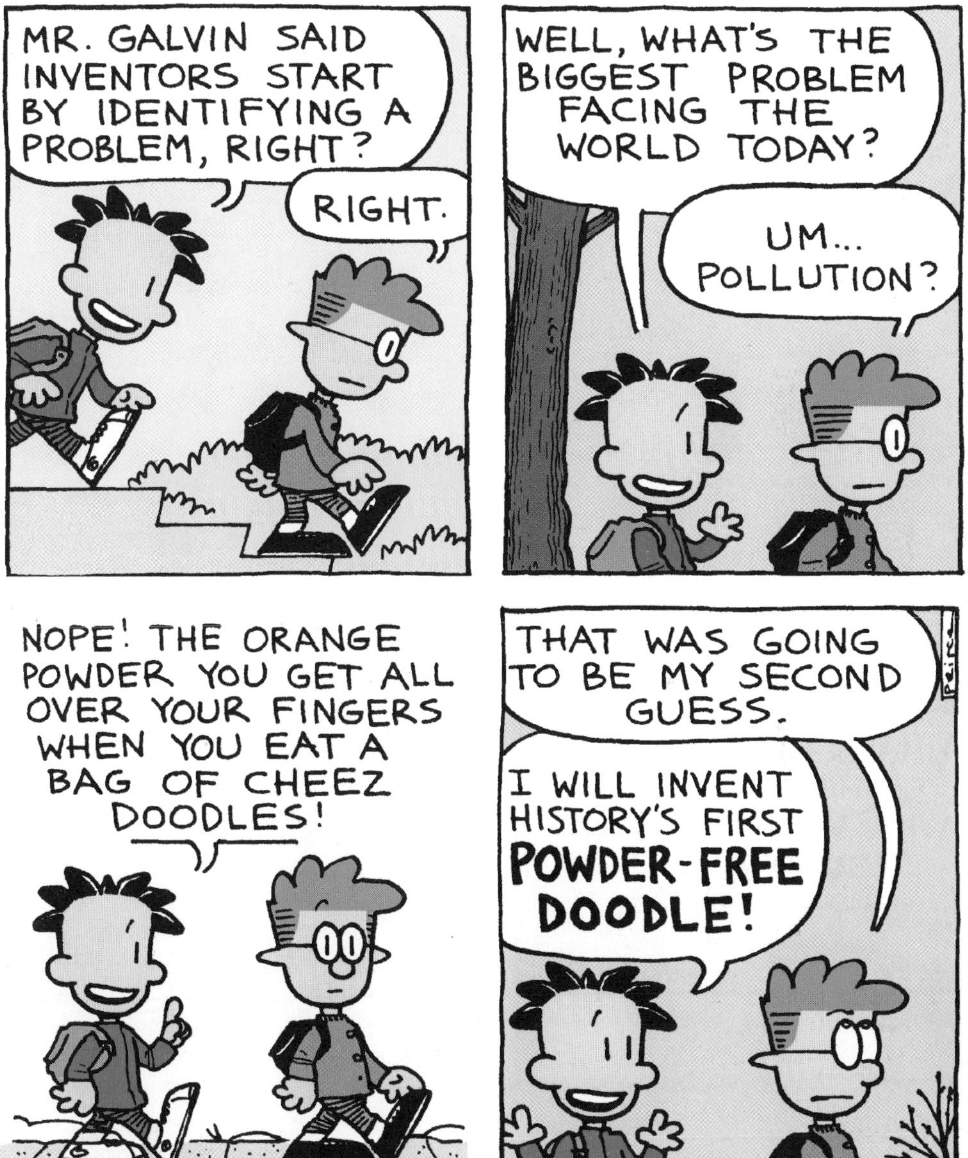
MR. GALVIN SAID INVENTORS START BY IDENTIFYING A PROBLEM, RIGHT?
RIGHT.
WELL, WHAT'S THE BIGGEST PROBLEM FACING THE WORLD TODAY?
UM... POLLUTION?
NOPE! THE ORANGE POWDER YOU GET ALL OVER YOUR FINGERS WHEN YOU EAT A BAG OF CHEEZ DOODLES!
THAT WAS GOING TO BE MY SECOND GUESS.
I WILL INVENT HISTORY'S FIRST POWDER-FREE DOODLE!

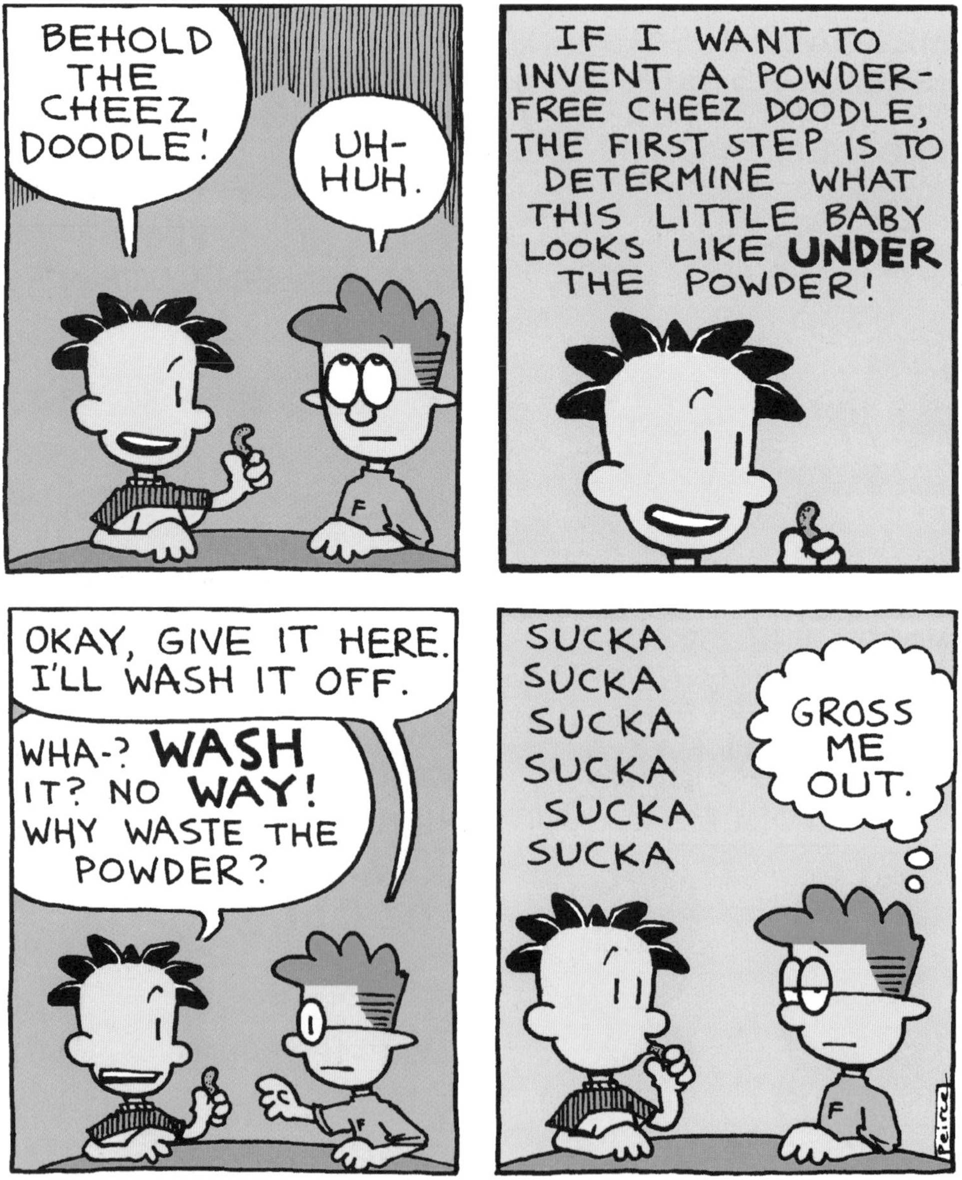
BEHOLD THE CHEEZ DOODLE!
UH-HUH.
IF I WANT TO INVENT A POWDER-FREE CHEEZ DOODLE, THE FIRST STEP IS TO DETERMINE WHAT THIS LITTLE BABY LOOKS LIKE **UNDER** THE POWDER!
OKAY, GIVE IT HERE. I'LL WASH IT OFF.
WHA-? **WASH** IT? NO **WAY**! WHY WASTE THE POWDER?
SUCKA SUCKA SUCKA SUCKA SUCKA SUCKA
GROSS ME OUT.
Peirce

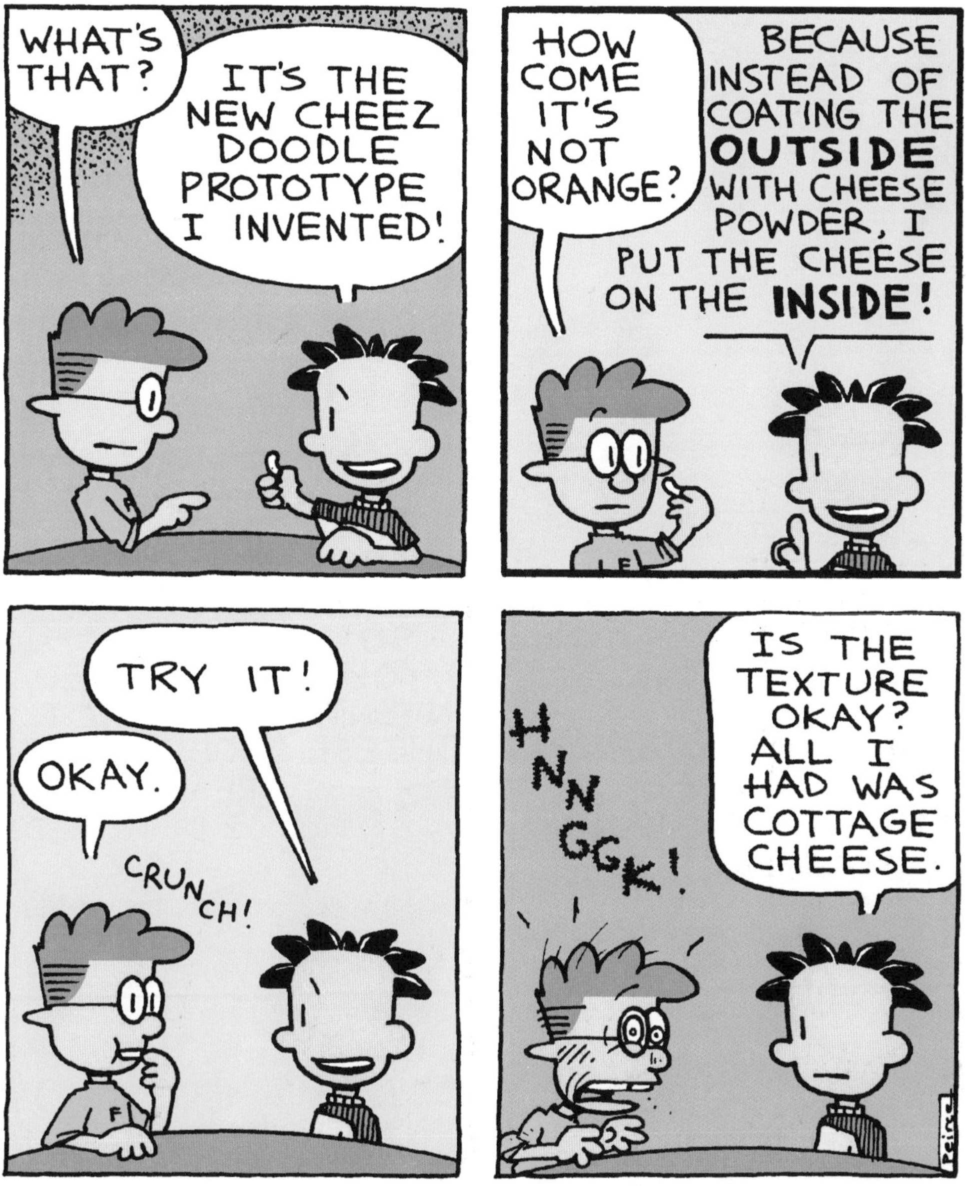
WHAT'S THAT?
IT'S THE NEW CHEEZ DOODLE PROTOTYPE I INVENTED!
HOW COME IT'S NOT ORANGE?
BECAUSE INSTEAD OF COATING THE OUTSIDE WITH CHEESE POWDER, I PUT THE CHEESE ON THE INSIDE!
TRY IT!
OKAY.
CRUNCH!
HNNGGK!
IS THE TEXTURE OKAY? ALL I HAD WAS COTTAGE CHEESE.
Peirce

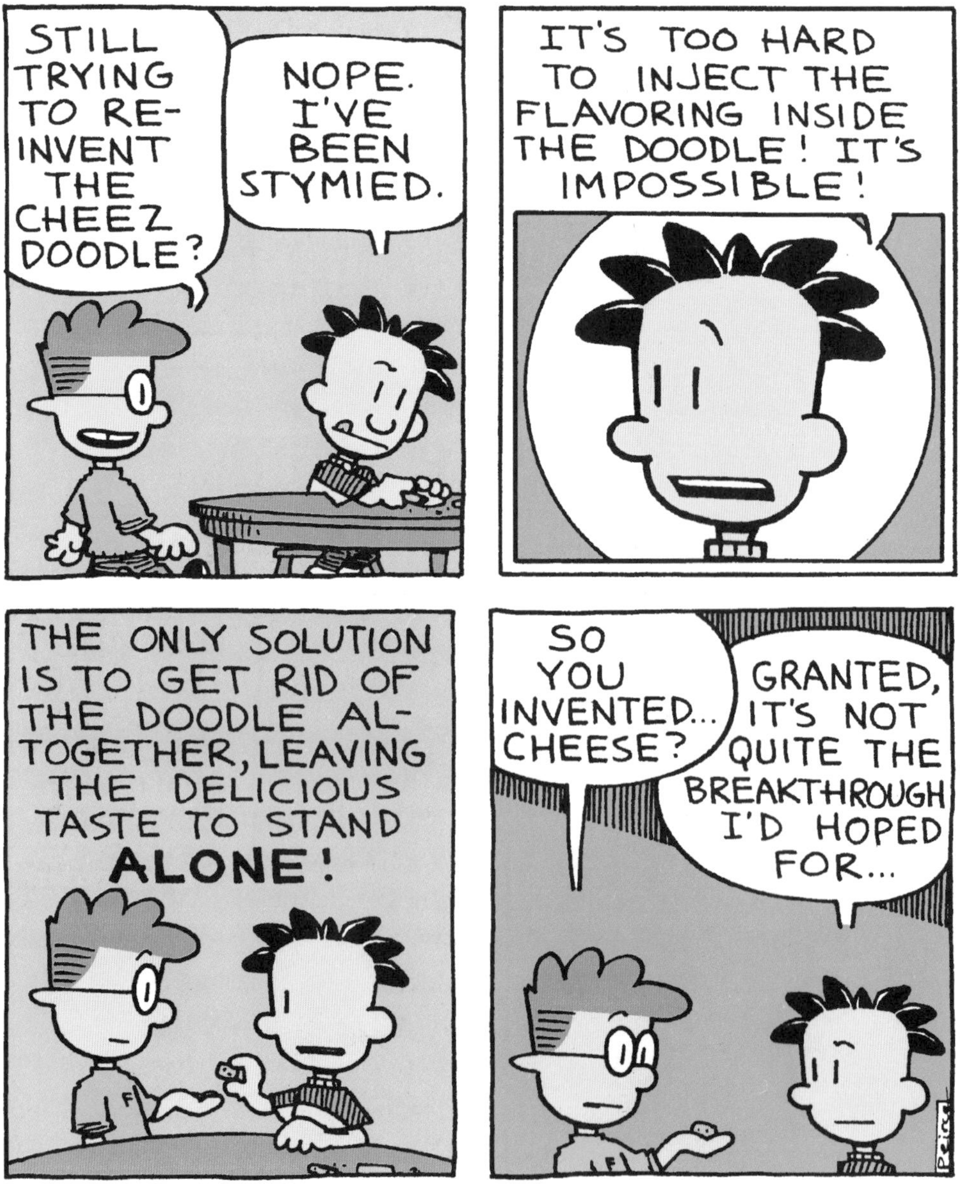
STILL TRYING TO RE-INVENT THE CHEEZ DOODLE?
NOPE. I'VE BEEN STYMIED.
IT'S TOO HARD TO INJECT THE FLAVORING INSIDE THE DOODLE! IT'S IMPOSSIBLE!
THE ONLY SOLUTION IS TO GET RID OF THE DOODLE AL-TOGETHER, LEAVING THE DELICIOUS TASTE TO STAND **ALONE**!
SO YOU INVENTED... CHEESE?
GRANTED, IT'S NOT QUITE THE BREAKTHROUGH I'D HOPED FOR...
Peirce

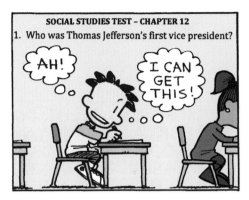

SOCIAL STUDIES TEST – CHAPTER 12
1. Who was Thomas Jefferson's first vice president?

AH!

I CAN GET THIS!

THOMAS JEFFERSON REMINDS ME OF JEFFERSON AIRPLANE! WHAT WAS ONE OF THEIR BIGGEST HITS? "WHITE RABBIT!"

WHO'S THE WORLD'S MOST FAMOUS RABBIT? BUGS BUNNY! WHAT DOES BUGS BUNNY EAT? CARROTS!

WHAT COLOR ARE CARROTS? ORANGE! WHAT RHYMES WITH ORANGE? NOTHING!

WHAT'S THE NUMERICAL EQUIVALENT OF NOTHING? ZERO! WHEN THE TEMPERATURE'S ZERO, HOW'S THE WEATHER? COLD!

WHEN THE WEATHER'S COLD, WHAT DO PEOPLE SAY? BRRR! WHAT'S ANOTHER WAY TO SPELL IT? BURR!

JEFFERSON'S FIRST VICE PRESIDENT WAS AARON BURR!

2. When was surrende

TIME'S UP, PEOPLE! HAND 'EM IN!

IT MAY BE TIME FOR A NEW SYSTEM.

WHAT DID YOU PUT FOR QUESTION 10?

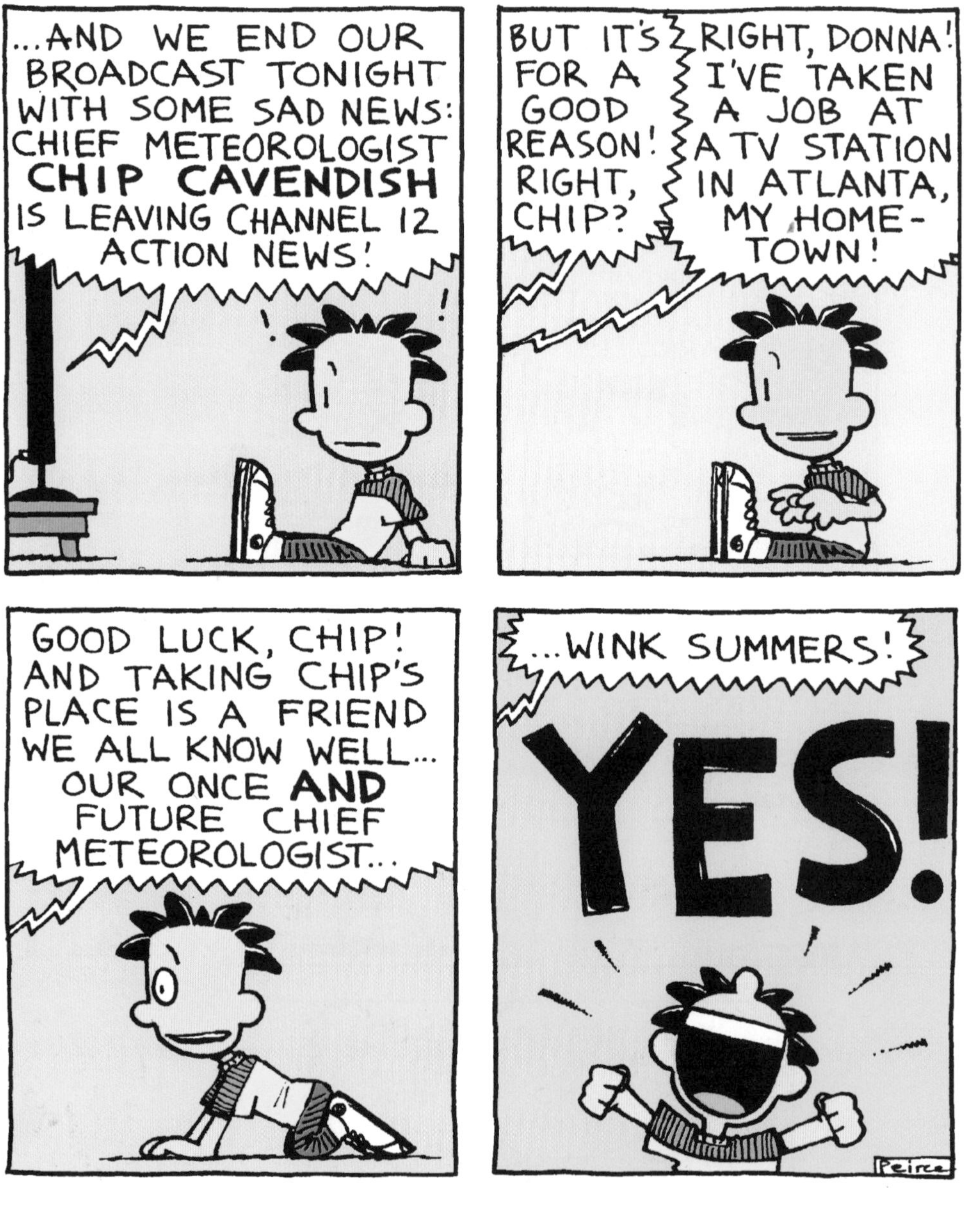
...AND WE END OUR BROADCAST TONIGHT WITH SOME SAD NEWS: CHIEF METEOROLOGIST CHIP CAVENDISH IS LEAVING CHANNEL 12 ACTION NEWS!
!
!
BUT IT'S FOR A GOOD REASON! RIGHT, CHIP?
RIGHT, DONNA! I'VE TAKEN A JOB AT A TV STATION IN ATLANTA, MY HOME-TOWN!
GOOD LUCK, CHIP! AND TAKING CHIP'S PLACE IS A FRIEND WE ALL KNOW WELL... OUR ONCE AND FUTURE CHIEF METEOROLOGIST...
...WINK SUMMERS!
YES!
Peirce

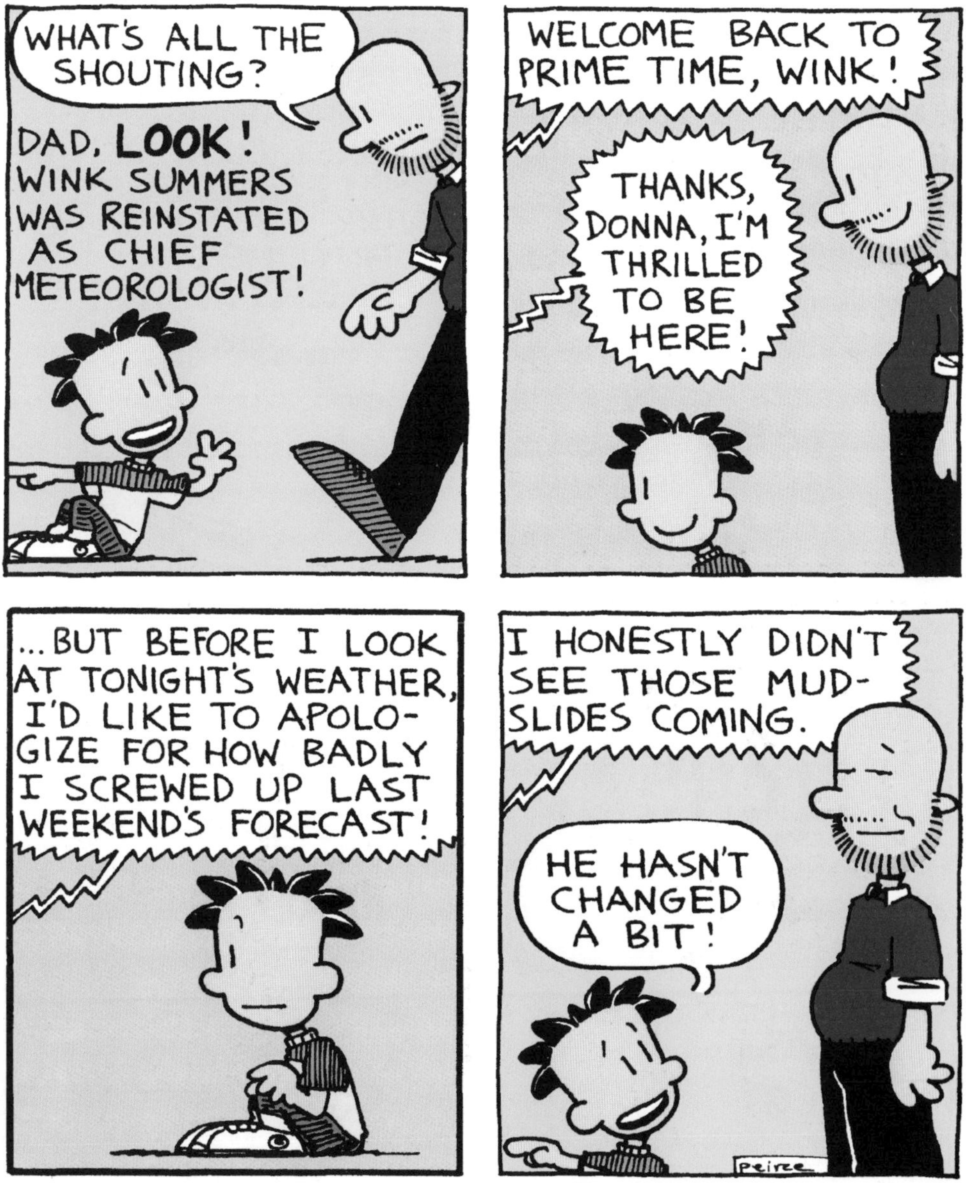
WHAT'S ALL THE SHOUTING?
DAD, **LOOK**! WINK SUMMERS WAS REINSTATED AS CHIEF METEOROLOGIST!
WELCOME BACK TO PRIME TIME, WINK!
THANKS, DONNA, I'M THRILLED TO BE HERE!
...BUT BEFORE I LOOK AT TONIGHT'S WEATHER, I'D LIKE TO APOLOGIZE FOR HOW BADLY I SCREWED UP LAST WEEKEND'S FORECAST!
I HONESTLY DIDN'T SEE THOSE MUDSLIDES COMING.
HE HASN'T CHANGED A BIT!
peirce

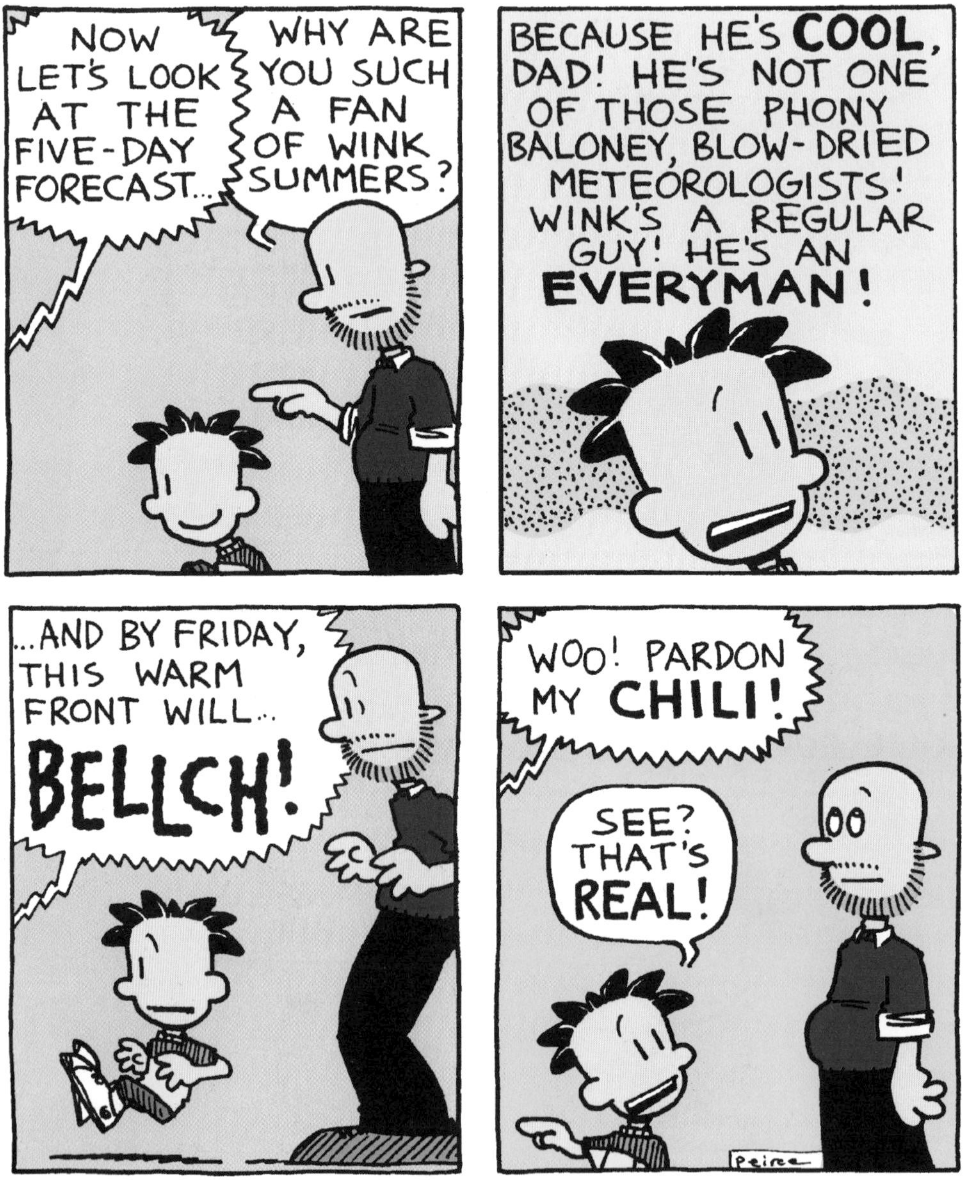
NOW LET'S LOOK AT THE FIVE-DAY FORECAST...
WHY ARE YOU SUCH A FAN OF WINK SUMMERS?
BECAUSE HE'S **COOL**, DAD! HE'S NOT ONE OF THOSE PHONY BALONEY, BLOW-DRIED METEOROLOGISTS! WINK'S A REGULAR GUY! HE'S AN **EVERYMAN**!
...AND BY FRIDAY, THIS WARM FRONT WILL... BELLCH!
WOO! PARDON MY **CHILI**!
SEE? THAT'S **REAL**!
Peirce

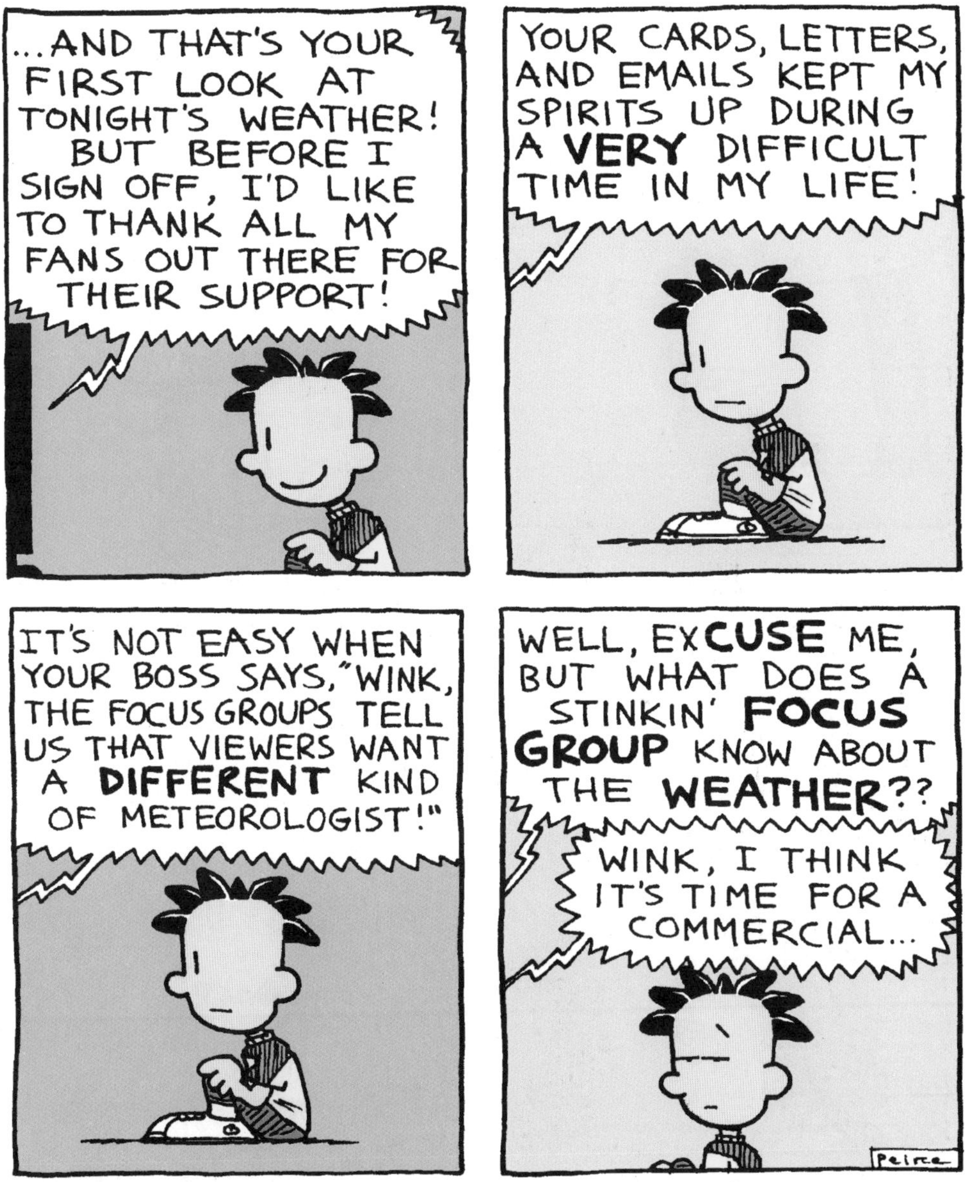
...AND THAT'S YOUR FIRST LOOK AT TONIGHT'S WEATHER! BUT BEFORE I SIGN OFF, I'D LIKE TO THANK ALL MY FANS OUT THERE FOR THEIR SUPPORT!
YOUR CARDS, LETTERS, AND EMAILS KEPT MY SPIRITS UP DURING A **VERY** DIFFICULT TIME IN MY LIFE!
IT'S NOT EASY WHEN YOUR BOSS SAYS, "WINK, THE FOCUS GROUPS TELL US THAT VIEWERS WANT A **DIFFERENT** KIND OF METEOROLOGIST!"
WELL, EX**CUSE** ME, BUT WHAT DOES A STINKIN' **FOCUS GROUP** KNOW ABOUT THE **WEATHER**??
WINK, I THINK IT'S TIME FOR A COMMERCIAL...
Peirce

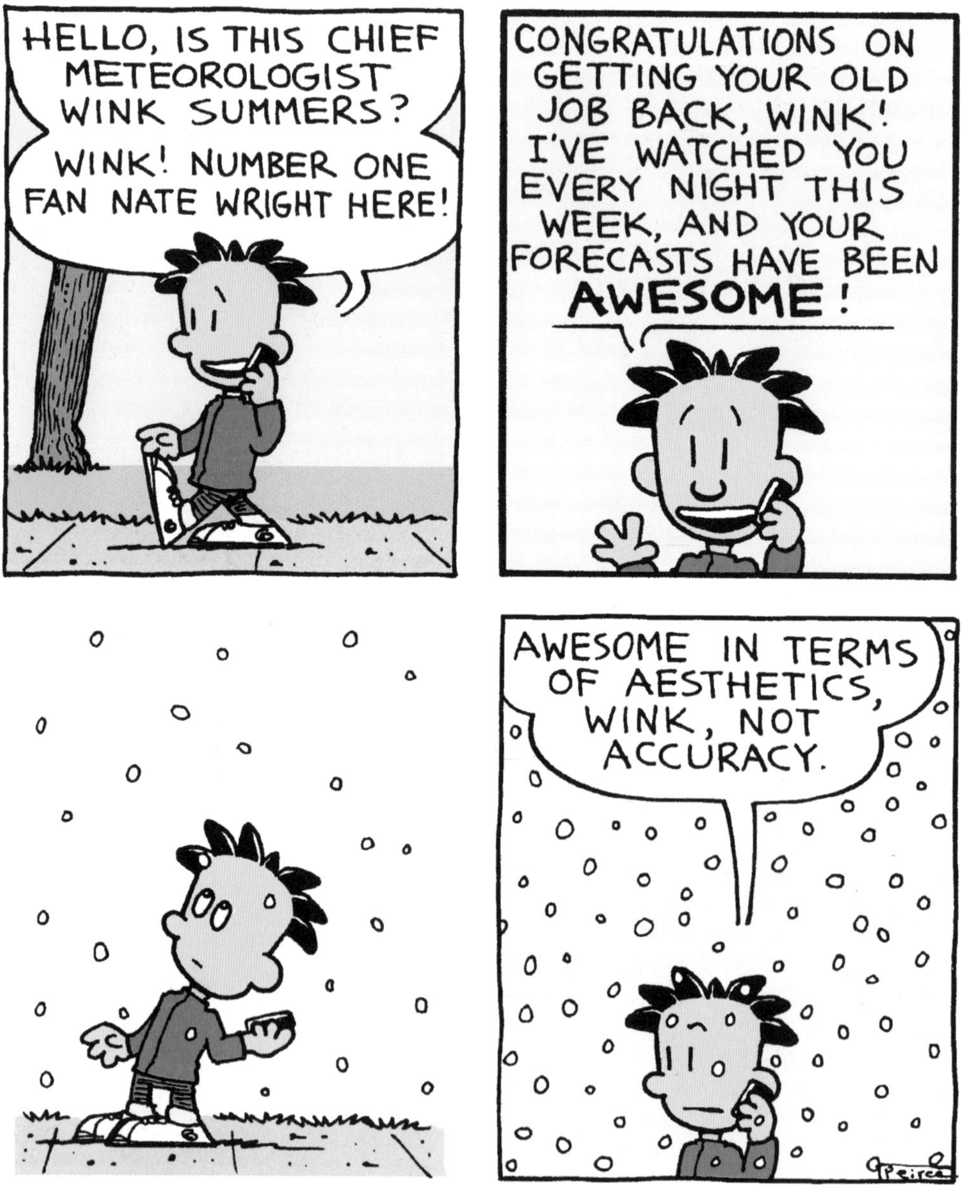
HELLO, IS THIS CHIEF METEOROLOGIST WINK SUMMERS?
WINK! NUMBER ONE FAN NATE WRIGHT HERE!
CONGRATULATIONS ON GETTING YOUR OLD JOB BACK, WINK! I'VE WATCHED YOU EVERY NIGHT THIS WEEK, AND YOUR FORECASTS HAVE BEEN **AWESOME**!
AWESOME IN TERMS OF AESTHETICS, WINK, NOT ACCURACY.
Peirce

SAY, WINK, NOW THAT YOUR PROFESSIONAL LIFE IS BACK ON TRACK, MAYBE YOU CAN GET YOUR **PERSONAL** LIFE ROLLING AGAIN!

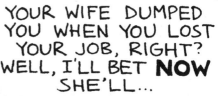

YOUR WIFE DUMPED YOU WHEN YOU LOST YOUR JOB, RIGHT? WELL, I'LL BET **NOW** SHE'LL...

WHAT? SHE DID **WHAT**? AL**READY**? TO **WHO**?

SHE MARRIED THE **SPORTS** ANCHOR?

THE JOCKS ALWAYS GET THE GIRLS.

Peirce

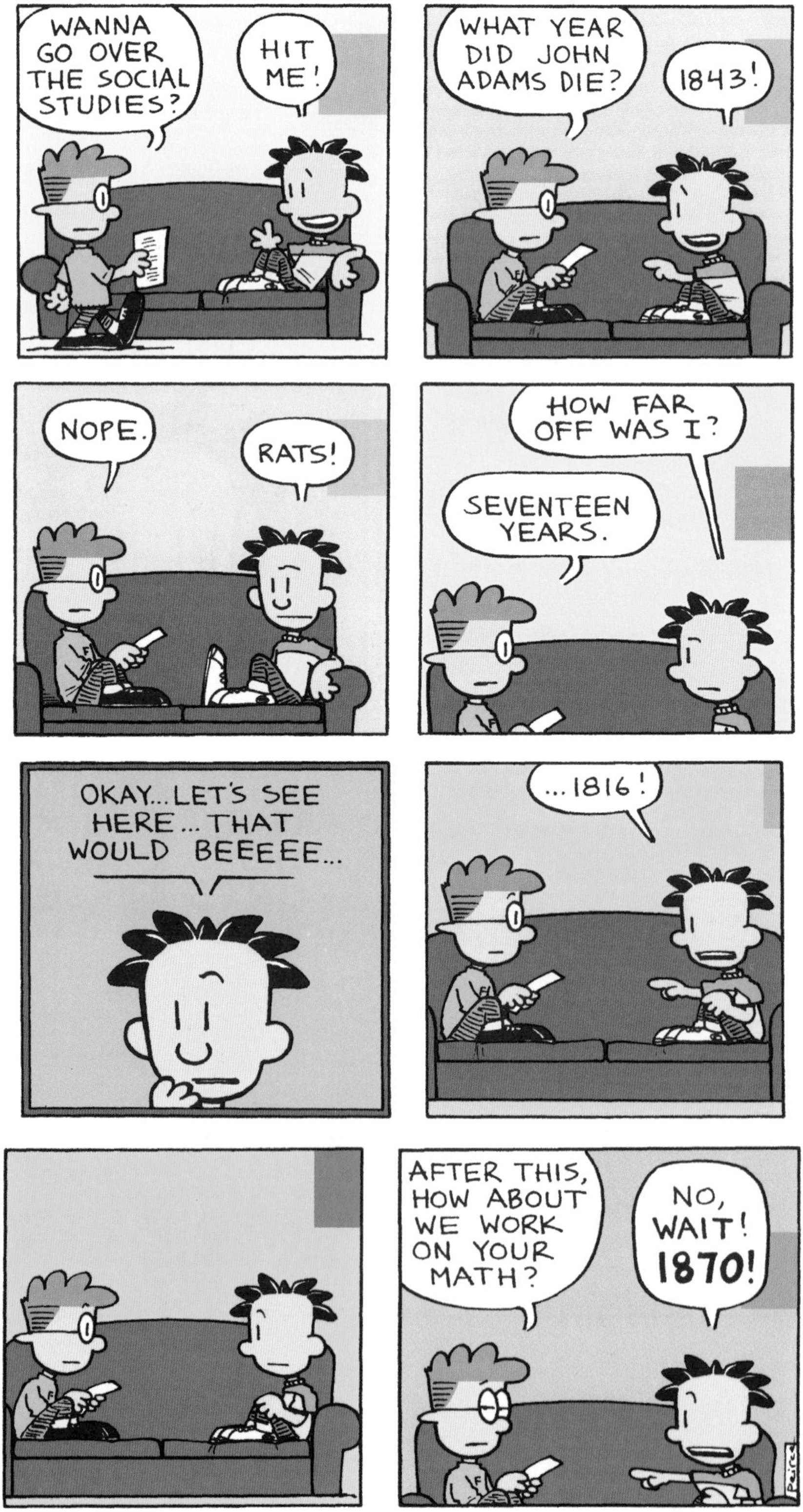
WANNA GO OVER THE SOCIAL STUDIES?
HIT ME!
WHAT YEAR DID JOHN ADAMS DIE?
1843!
NOPE.
RATS!
HOW FAR OFF WAS I?
SEVENTEEN YEARS.
OKAY... LET'S SEE HERE... THAT WOULD BEEEEE...
...1816!
AFTER THIS, HOW ABOUT WE WORK ON YOUR MATH?
NO, WAIT! 1870!

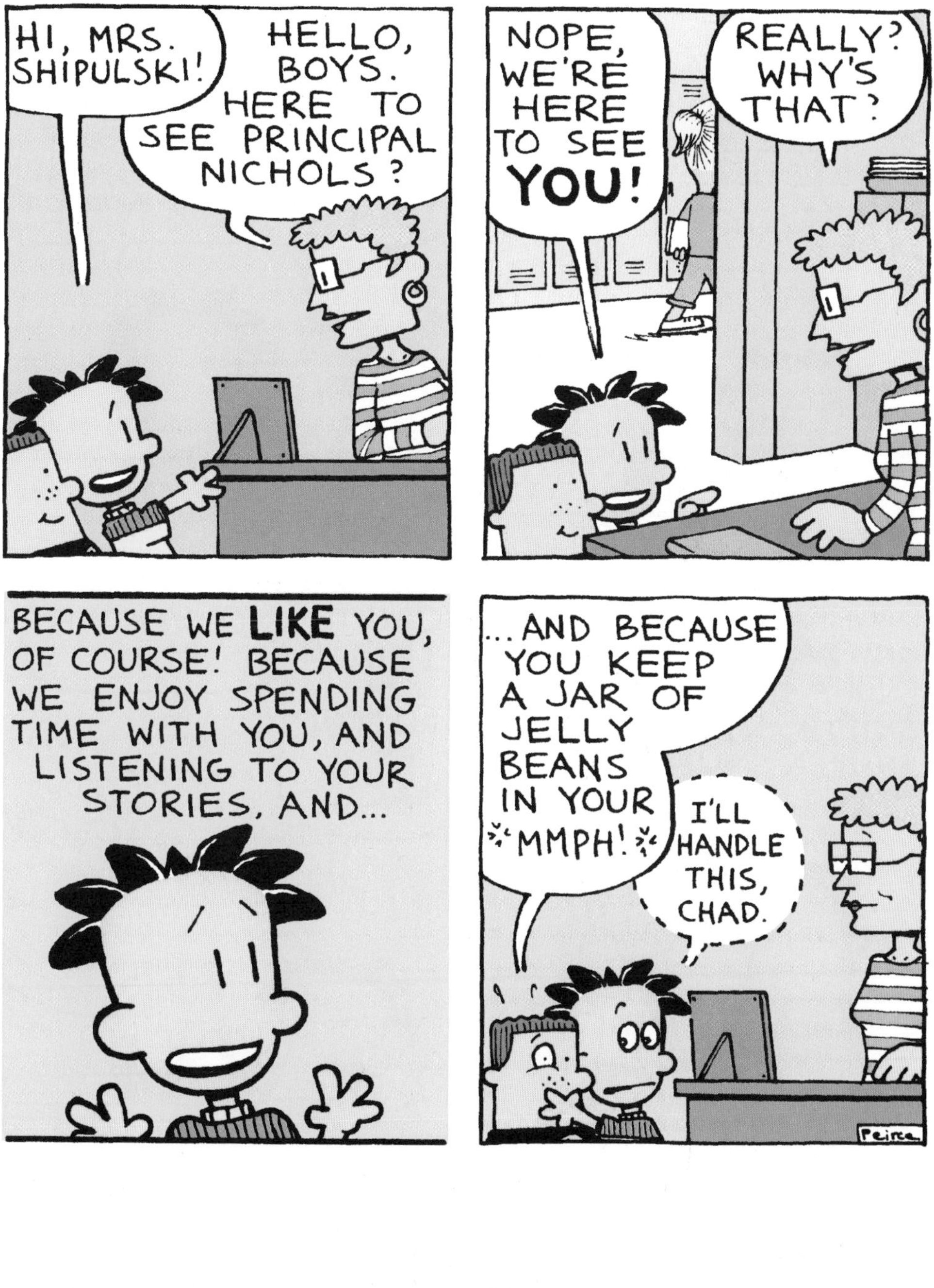
HI, MRS. SHIPULSKI!
HELLO, BOYS. HERE TO SEE PRINCIPAL NICHOLS?
NOPE, WE'RE HERE TO SEE YOU!
REALLY? WHY'S THAT?
BECAUSE WE LIKE YOU, OF COURSE! BECAUSE WE ENJOY SPENDING TIME WITH YOU, AND LISTENING TO YOUR STORIES, AND...
...AND BECAUSE YOU KEEP A JAR OF JELLY BEANS IN YOUR MMPH!
I'LL HANDLE THIS, CHAD.
Peirce

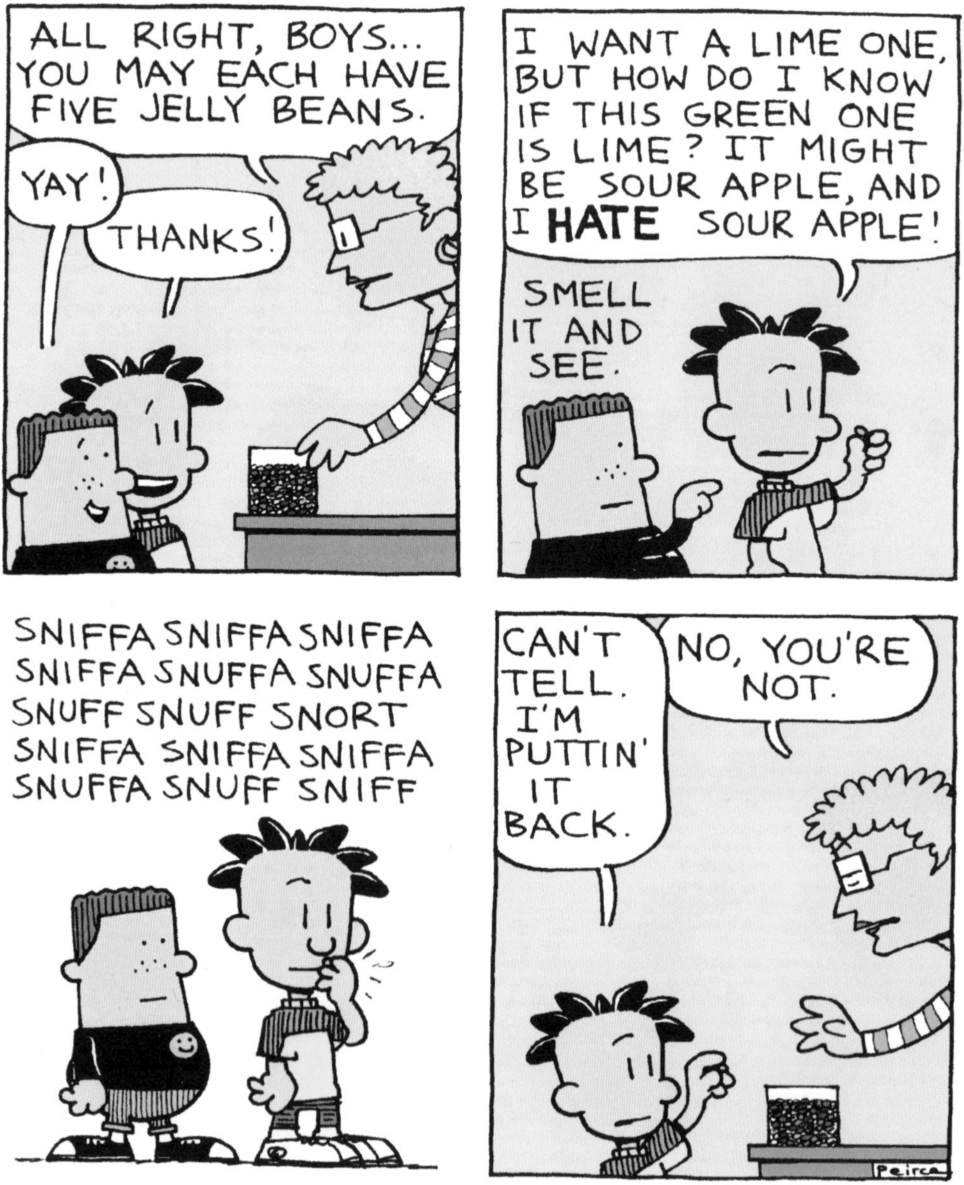
ALL RIGHT, BOYS... YOU MAY EACH HAVE FIVE JELLY BEANS.
YAY!
THANKS!
I WANT A LIME ONE, BUT HOW DO I KNOW IF THIS GREEN ONE IS LIME? IT MIGHT BE SOUR APPLE, AND I **HATE** SOUR APPLE!
SMELL IT AND SEE.
SNIFFA SNIFFA SNIFFA SNIFFA SNUFFA SNUFFA SNUFF SNUFF SNORT SNIFFA SNIFFA SNIFFA SNUFFA SNUFF SNIFF
CAN'T TELL. I'M PUTTIN' IT BACK.
NO, YOU'RE NOT.
Peirce

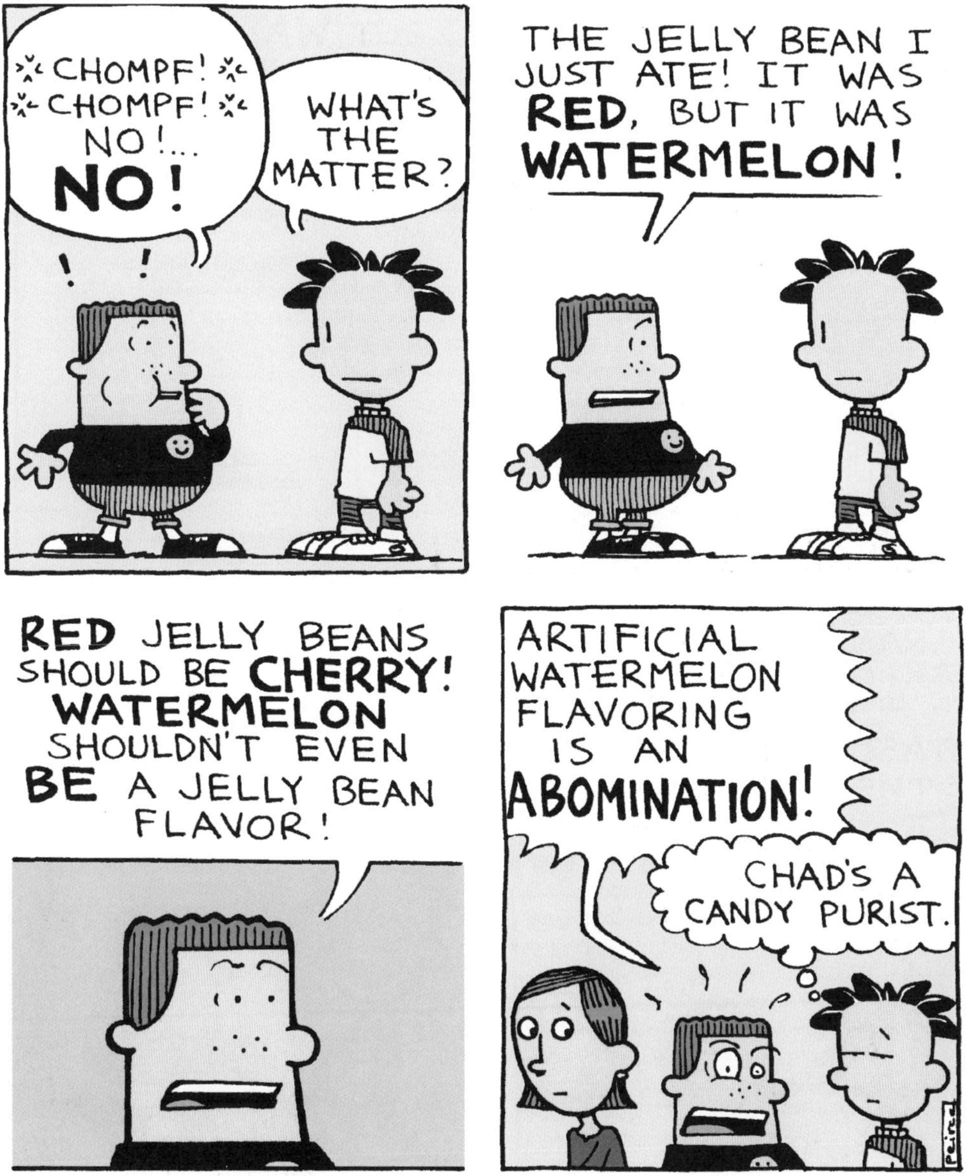
CHOMPF! CHOMPF! NO!... NO!
WHAT'S THE MATTER?
! !
THE JELLY BEAN I JUST ATE! IT WAS RED, BUT IT WAS WATERMELON!
RED JELLY BEANS SHOULD BE CHERRY! WATERMELON SHOULDN'T EVEN BE A JELLY BEAN FLAVOR!
ARTIFICIAL WATERMELON FLAVORING IS AN ABOMINATION!
CHAD'S A CANDY PURIST.
PEIRCE

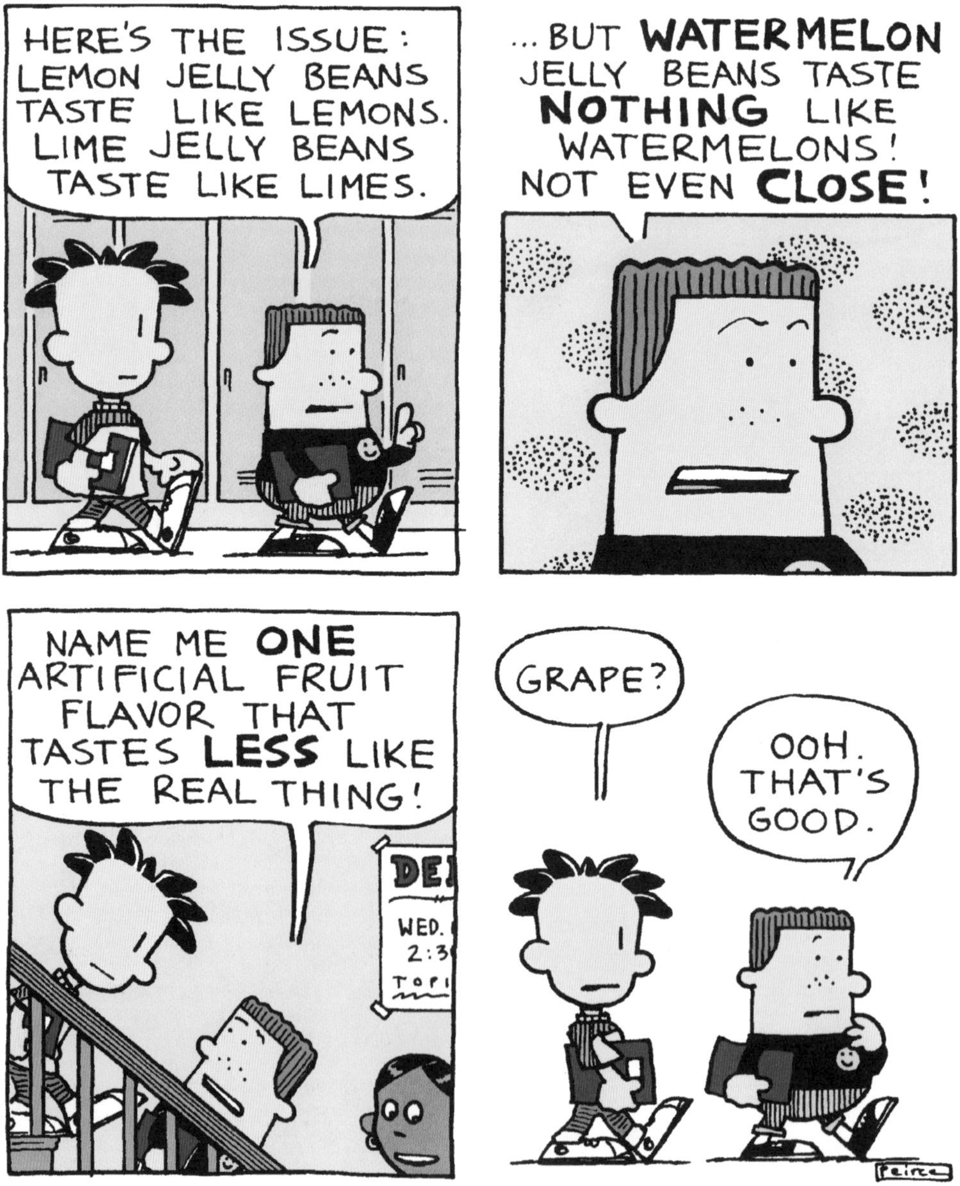
HERE'S THE ISSUE: LEMON JELLY BEANS TASTE LIKE LEMONS. LIME JELLY BEANS TASTE LIKE LIMES.
...BUT WATERMELON JELLY BEANS TASTE NOTHING LIKE WATERMELONS! NOT EVEN CLOSE!
NAME ME ONE ARTIFICIAL FRUIT FLAVOR THAT TASTES LESS LIKE THE REAL THING!
GRAPE?
OOH. THAT'S GOOD.
Peirce

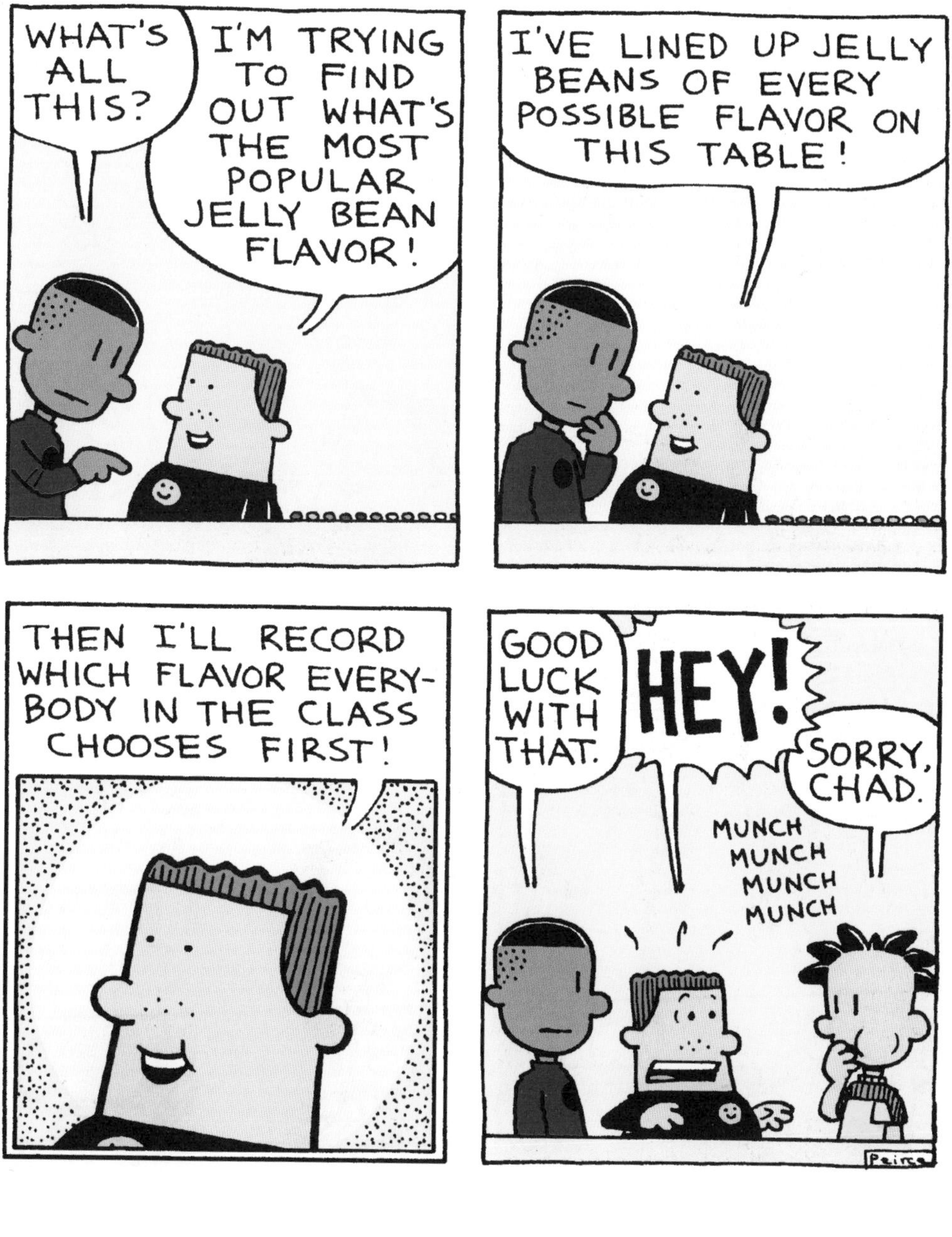
WHAT'S ALL THIS?
I'M TRYING TO FIND OUT WHAT'S THE MOST POPULAR JELLY BEAN FLAVOR!
I'VE LINED UP JELLY BEANS OF EVERY POSSIBLE FLAVOR ON THIS TABLE!
THEN I'LL RECORD WHICH FLAVOR EVERYBODY IN THE CLASS CHOOSES FIRST!
GOOD LUCK WITH THAT.
MUNCH MUNCH MUNCH MUNCH
HEY!
SORRY, CHAD.

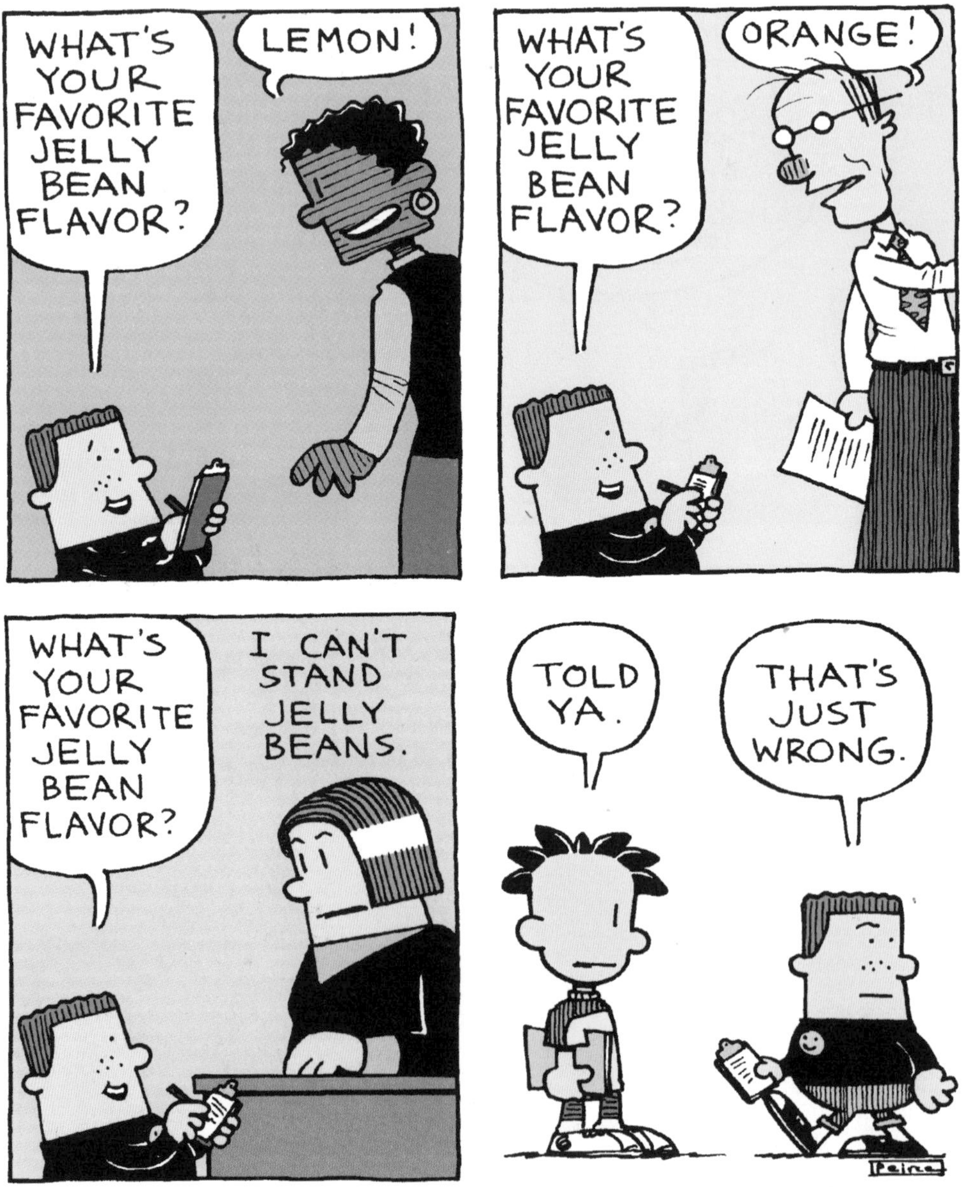
WHAT'S YOUR FAVORITE JELLY BEAN FLAVOR?
LEMON!
WHAT'S YOUR FAVORITE JELLY BEAN FLAVOR?
ORANGE!
WHAT'S YOUR FAVORITE JELLY BEAN FLAVOR?
I CAN'T STAND JELLY BEANS.
TOLD YA.
THAT'S JUST WRONG.
Peirce

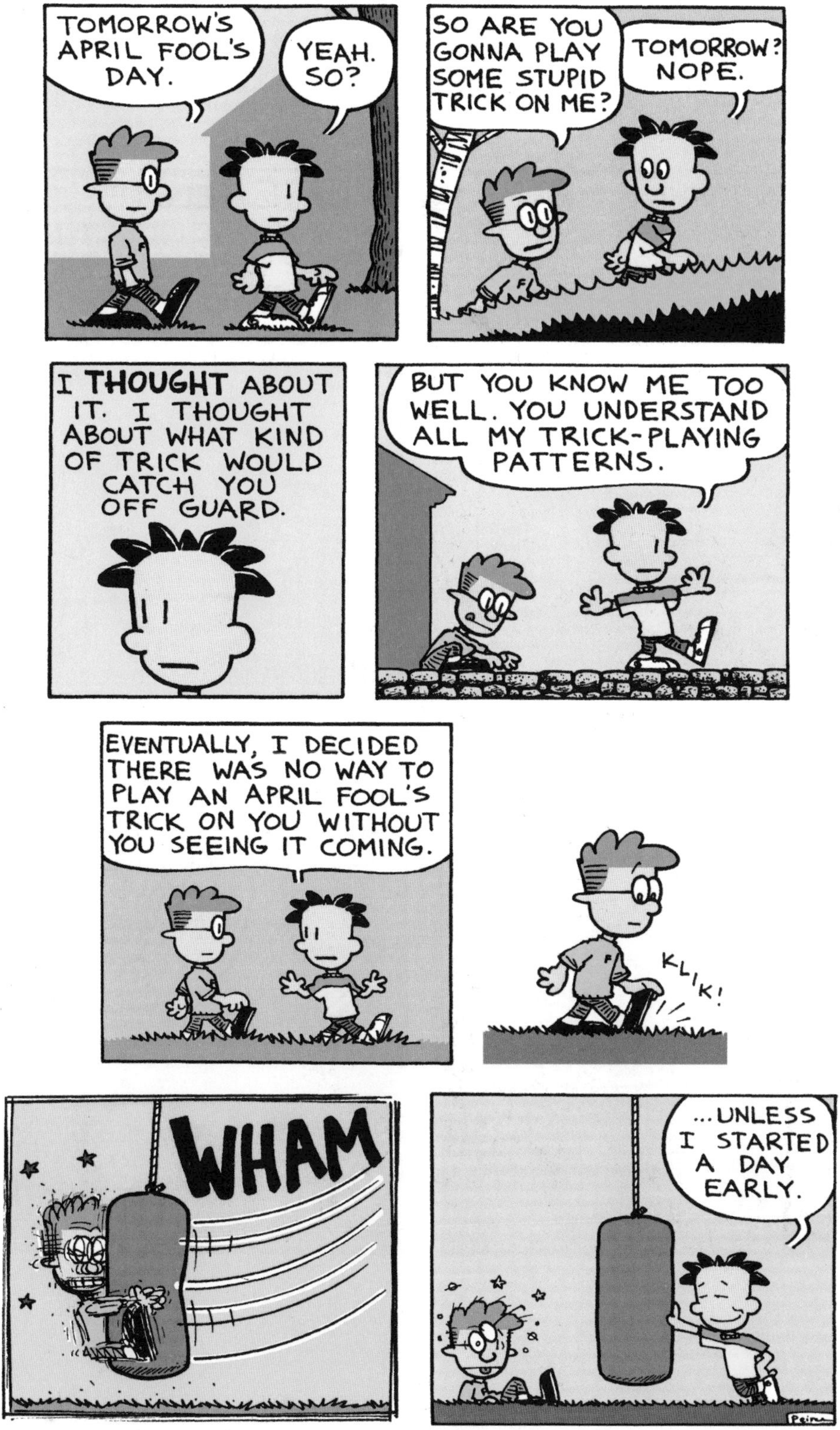
TOMORROW'S APRIL FOOL'S DAY.
YEAH. SO?
SO ARE YOU GONNA PLAY SOME STUPID TRICK ON ME?
TOMORROW? NOPE.
I THOUGHT ABOUT IT. I THOUGHT ABOUT WHAT KIND OF TRICK WOULD CATCH YOU OFF GUARD.
BUT YOU KNOW ME TOO WELL. YOU UNDERSTAND ALL MY TRICK-PLAYING PATTERNS.
EVENTUALLY, I DECIDED THERE WAS NO WAY TO PLAY AN APRIL FOOL'S TRICK ON YOU WITHOUT YOU SEEING IT COMING.
KLIK!
WHAM
...UNLESS I STARTED A DAY EARLY.

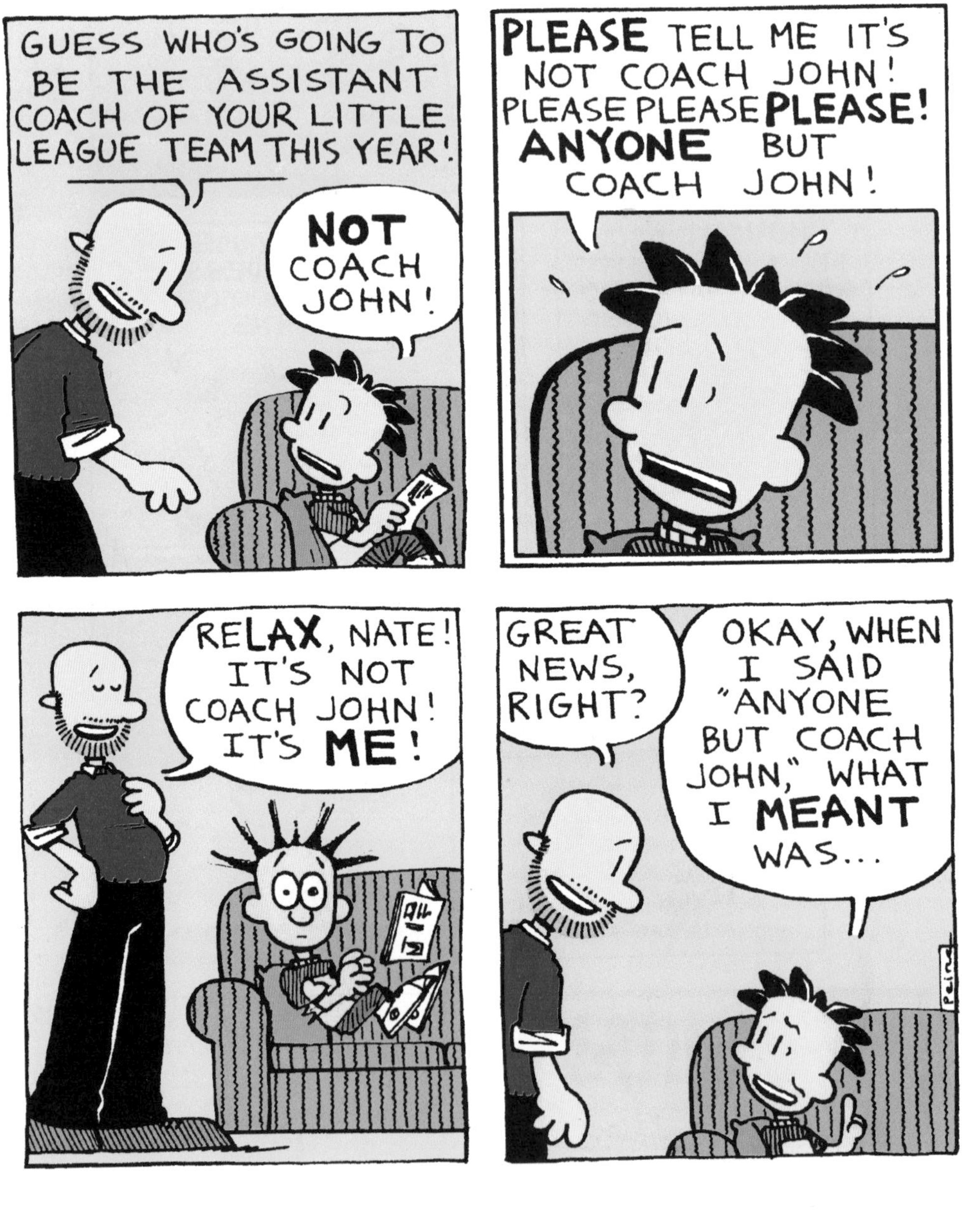
GUESS WHO'S GOING TO BE THE ASSISTANT COACH OF YOUR LITTLE LEAGUE TEAM THIS YEAR!
NOT COACH JOHN!
PLEASE TELL ME IT'S NOT COACH JOHN! PLEASE PLEASE PLEASE! ANYONE BUT COACH JOHN!
RELAX, NATE! IT'S NOT COACH JOHN! IT'S ME!
GREAT NEWS, RIGHT?
OKAY, WHEN I SAID "ANYONE BUT COACH JOHN," WHAT I MEANT WAS...
Peirce

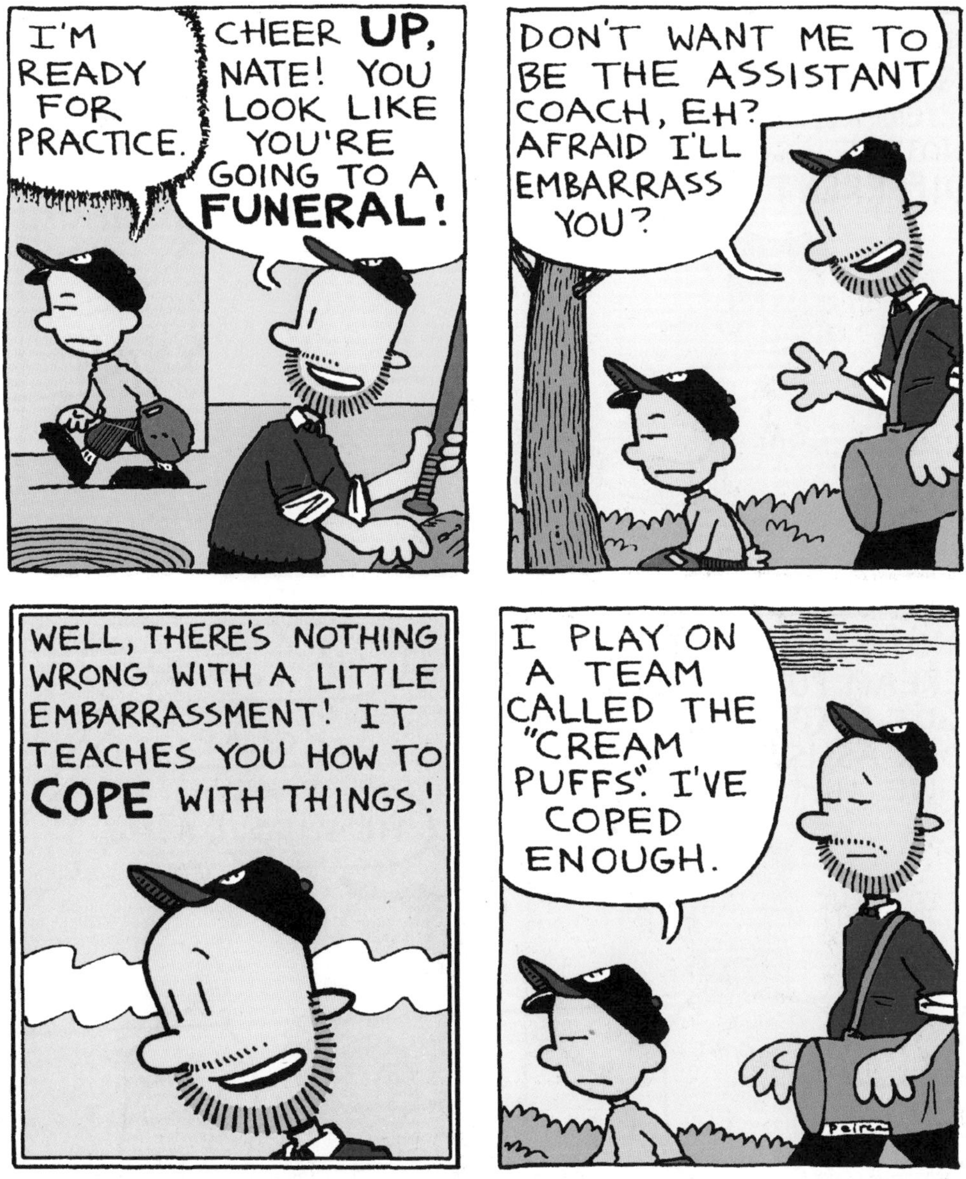
I'M READY FOR PRACTICE.
CHEER UP, NATE! YOU LOOK LIKE YOU'RE GOING TO A FUNERAL!
DON'T WANT ME TO BE THE ASSISTANT COACH, EH? AFRAID I'LL EMBARRASS YOU?
WELL, THERE'S NOTHING WRONG WITH A LITTLE EMBARRASSMENT! IT TEACHES YOU HOW TO COPE WITH THINGS!
I PLAY ON A TEAM CALLED THE "CREAM PUFFS." I'VE COPED ENOUGH.
Peirce

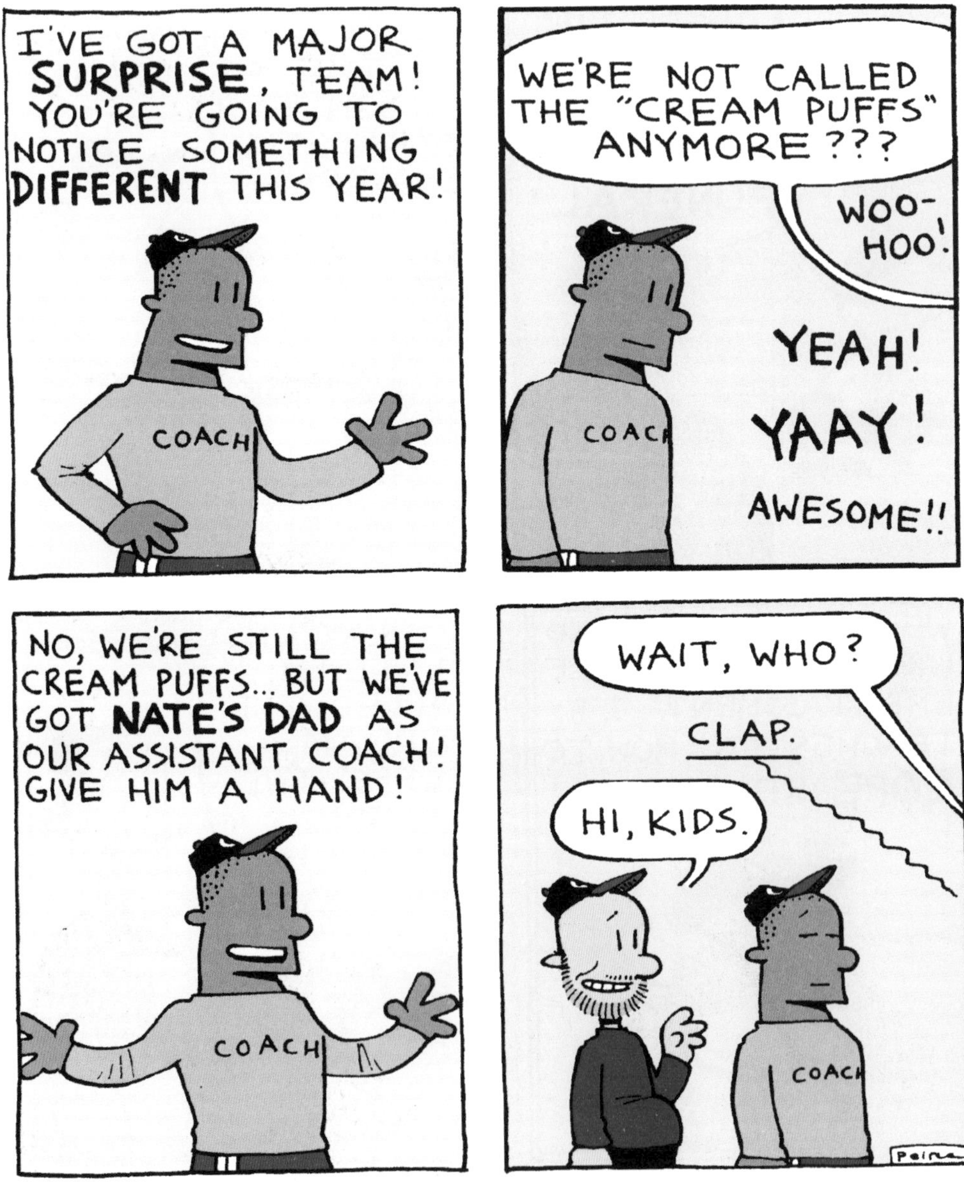
I'VE GOT A MAJOR **SURPRISE**, TEAM! YOU'RE GOING TO NOTICE SOMETHING **DIFFERENT** THIS YEAR!
COACH
WE'RE NOT CALLED THE "CREAM PUFFS" ANYMORE???
WOO-HOO!
YEAH!
YAAY!
AWESOME!!
COACH
NO, WE'RE STILL THE CREAM PUFFS... BUT WE'VE GOT **NATE'S DAD** AS OUR ASSISTANT COACH! GIVE HIM A HAND!
COACH
WAIT, WHO?
CLAP.
HI, KIDS.
COACH

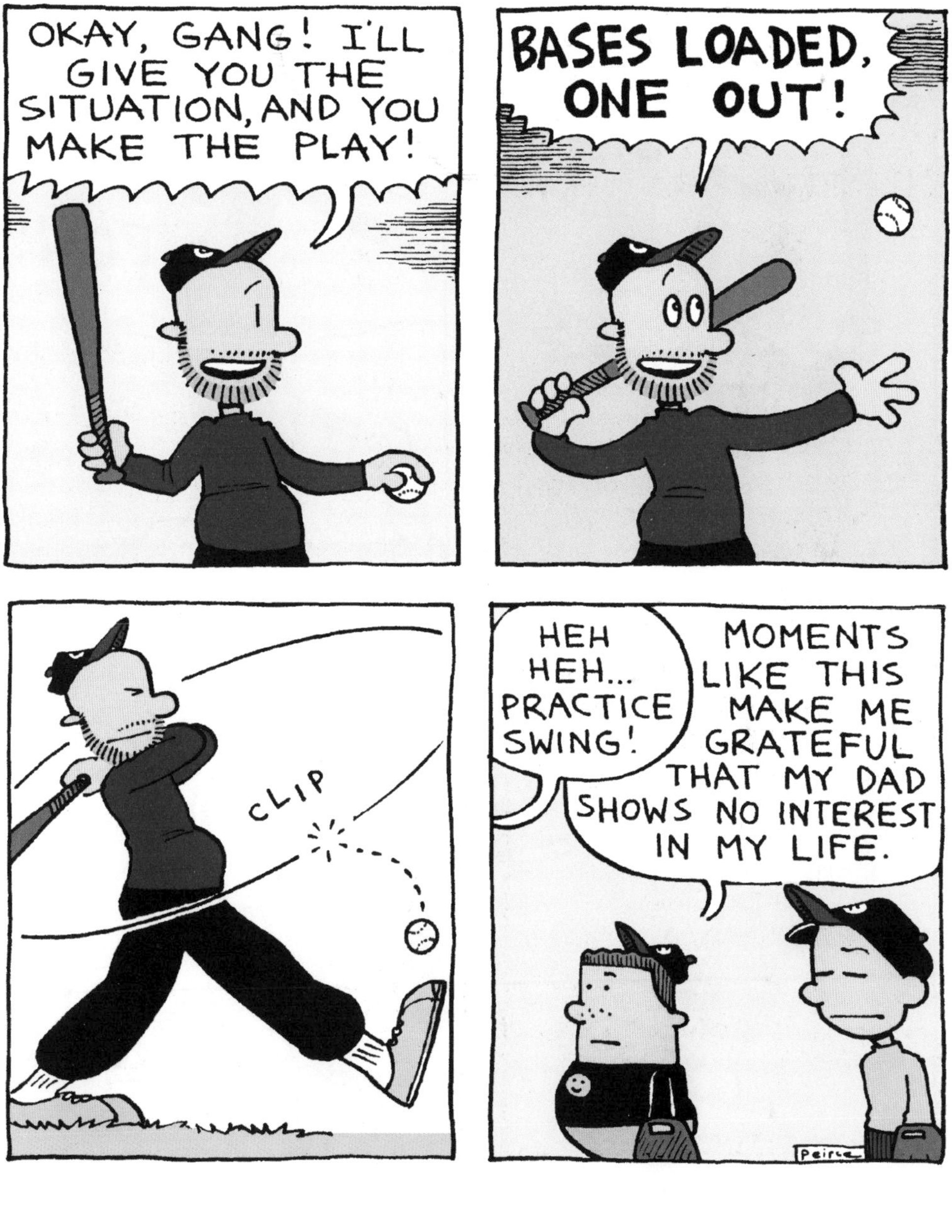
OKAY, GANG! I'LL GIVE YOU THE SITUATION, AND YOU MAKE THE PLAY!
BASES LOADED, ONE OUT!
CLIP
HEH HEH... PRACTICE SWING!
MOMENTS LIKE THIS MAKE ME GRATEFUL THAT MY DAD SHOWS NO INTEREST IN MY LIFE.
Peirce

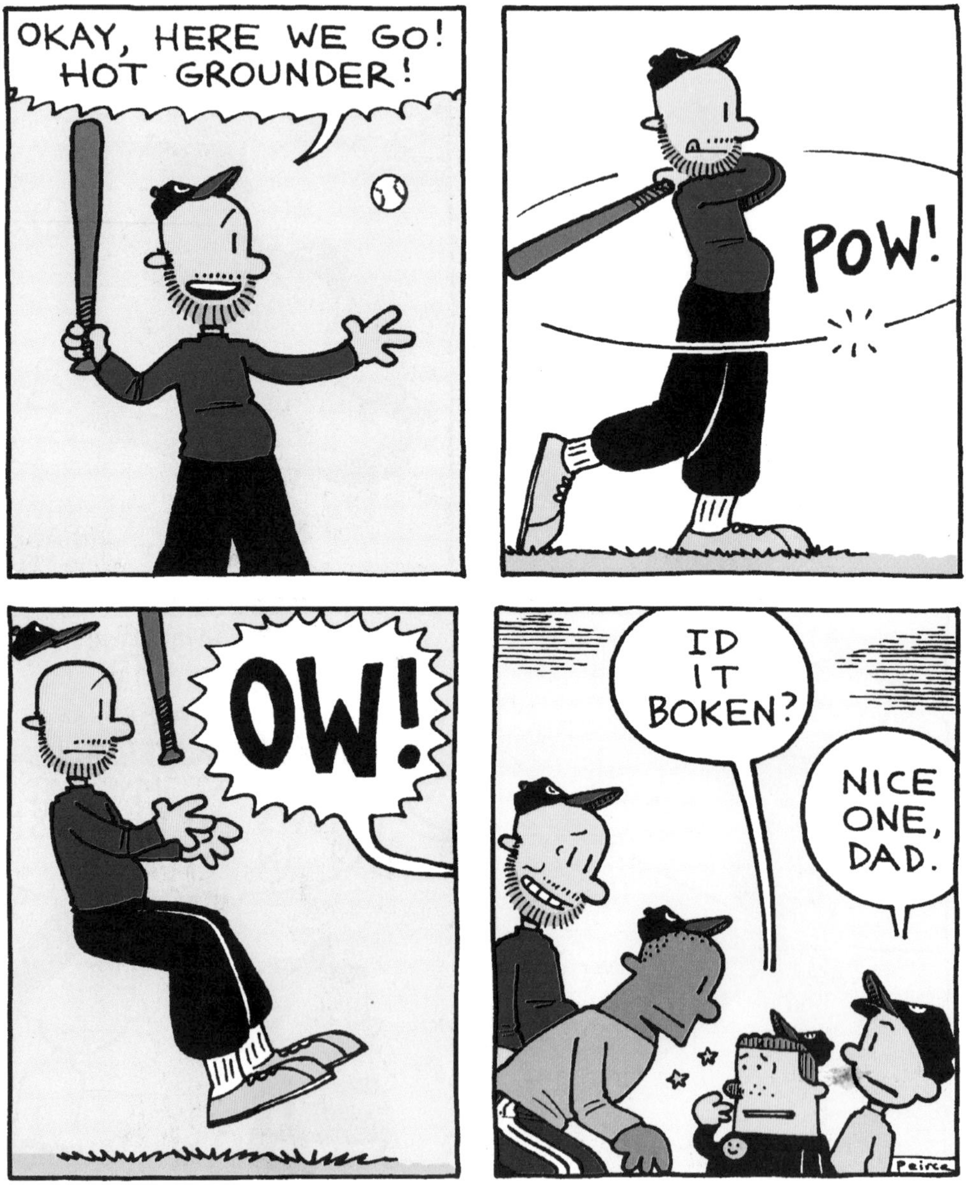
OKAY, HERE WE GO! HOT GROUNDER!
POW!
OW!
ID IT BOKEN?
NICE ONE, DAD.
Peirce

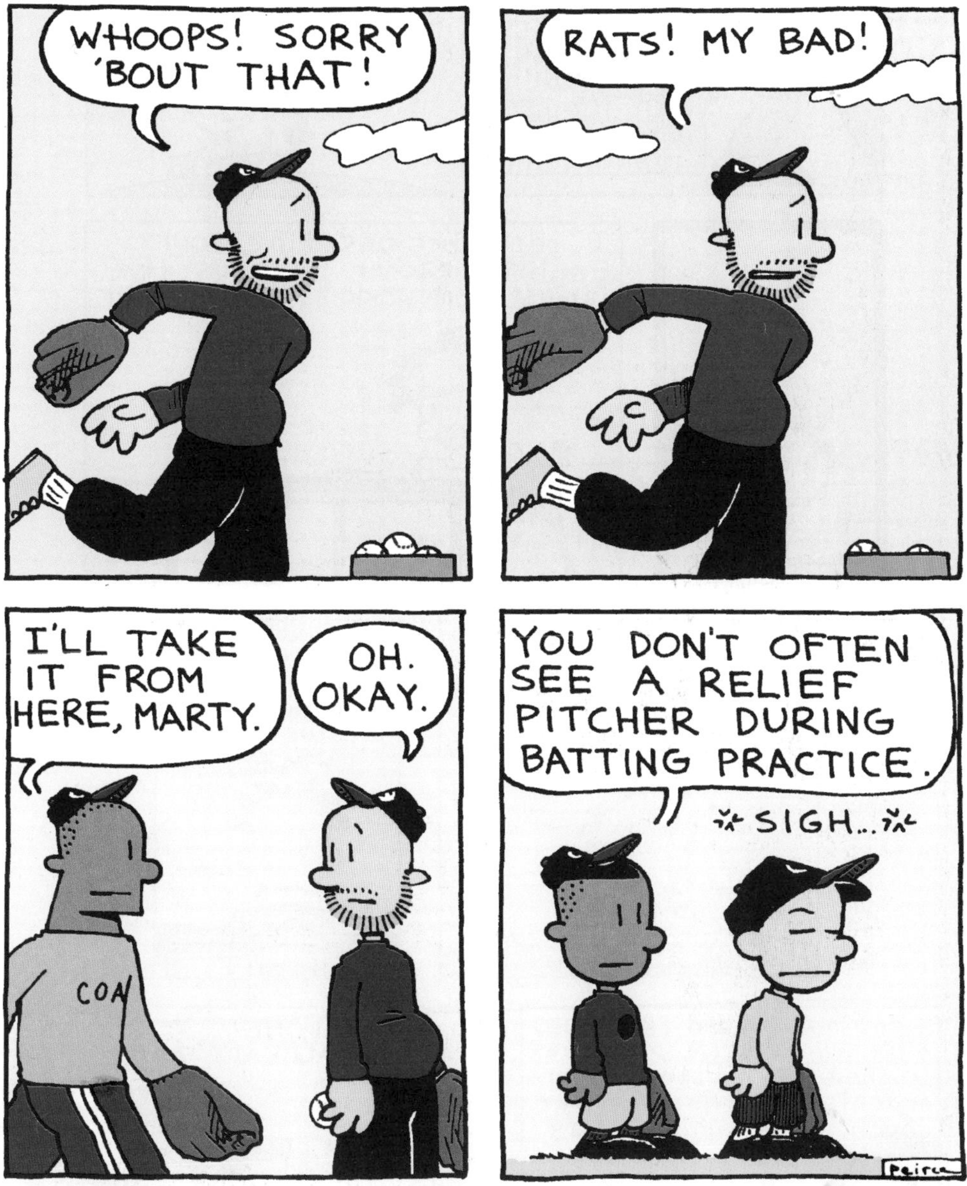
WHOOPS! SORRY 'BOUT THAT!
RATS! MY BAD!
I'LL TAKE IT FROM HERE, MARTY.
OH. OKAY.
COA
YOU DON'T OFTEN SEE A RELIEF PITCHER DURING BATTING PRACTICE.
SIGH...
Peirce

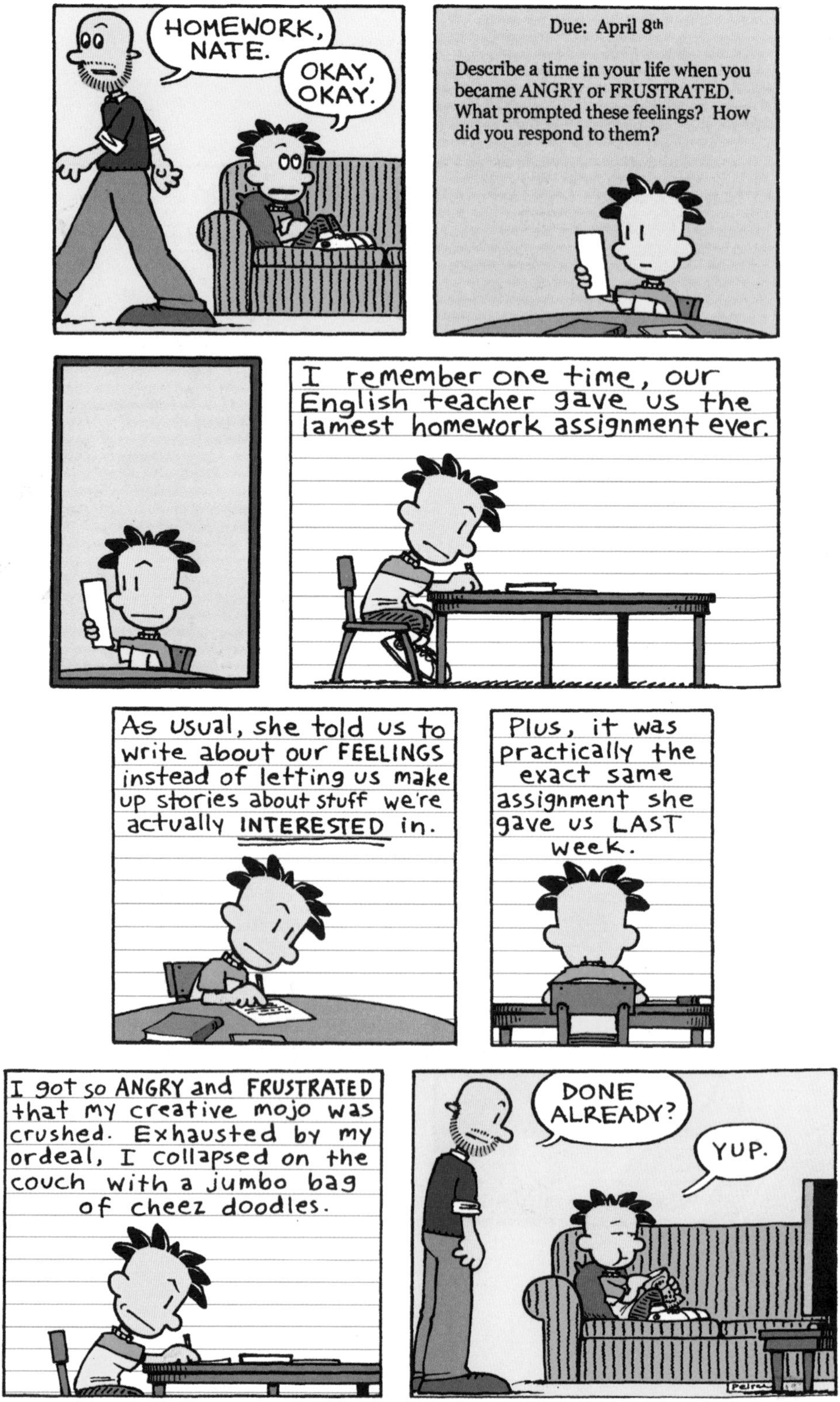
HOMEWORK, NATE.
OKAY, OKAY.
Due: April 8th
Describe a time in your life when you became ANGRY or FRUSTRATED. What prompted these feelings? How did you respond to them?
I remember one time, our English teacher gave us the lamest homework assignment ever.
As usual, she told us to write about our FEELINGS instead of letting us make up stories about stuff we're actually INTERESTED in.
Plus, it was practically the exact same assignment she gave us LAST week.
I got so ANGRY and FRUSTRATED that my creative mojo was crushed. Exhausted by my ordeal, I collapsed on the couch with a jumbo bag of cheez doodles.
DONE ALREADY?
YUP.

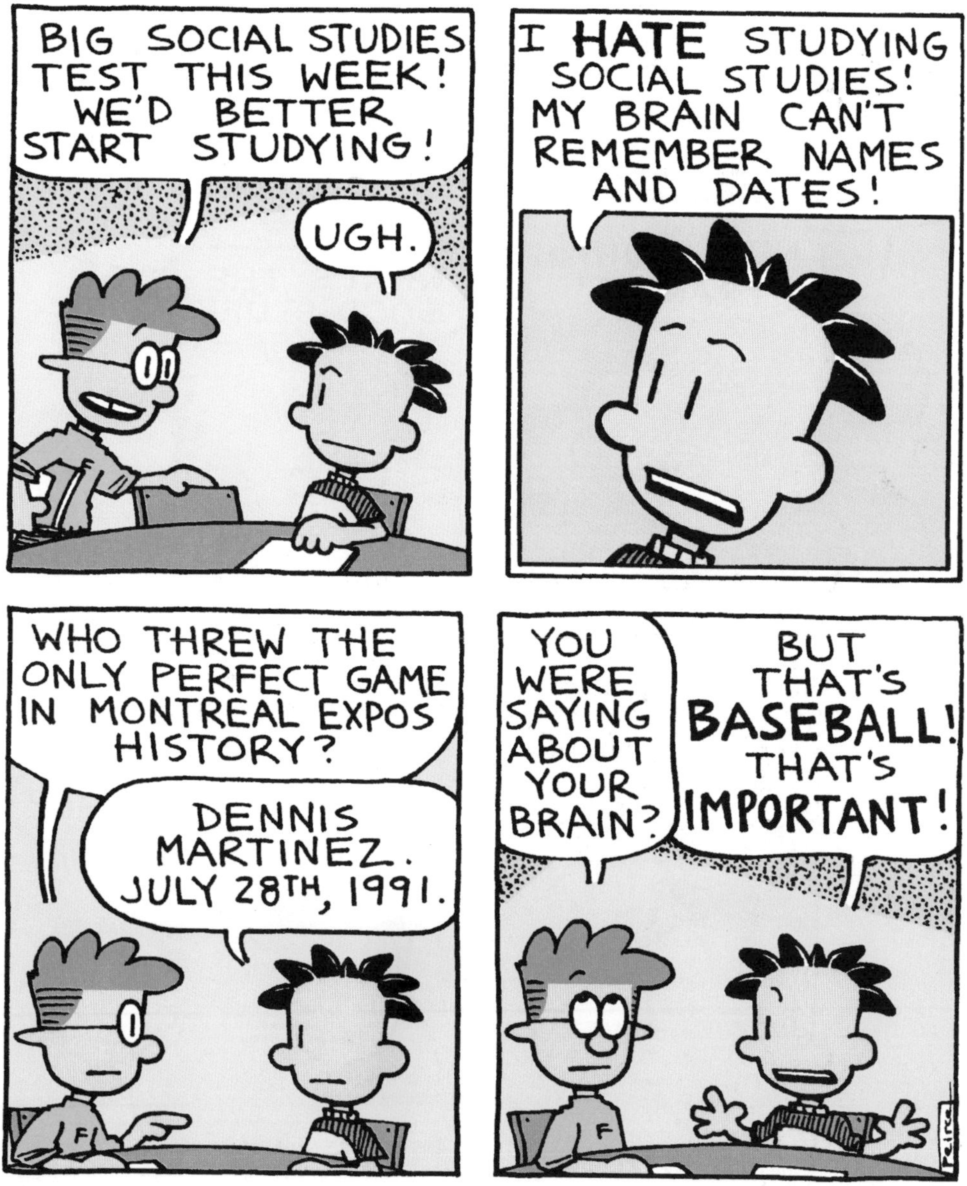
BIG SOCIAL STUDIES TEST THIS WEEK! WE'D BETTER START STUDYING!
UGH.
I HATE STUDYING SOCIAL STUDIES! MY BRAIN CAN'T REMEMBER NAMES AND DATES!
WHO THREW THE ONLY PERFECT GAME IN MONTREAL EXPOS HISTORY?
DENNIS MARTINEZ. JULY 28TH, 1991.
YOU WERE SAYING ABOUT YOUR BRAIN?
BUT THAT'S BASEBALL! THAT'S IMPORTANT!
Peirce

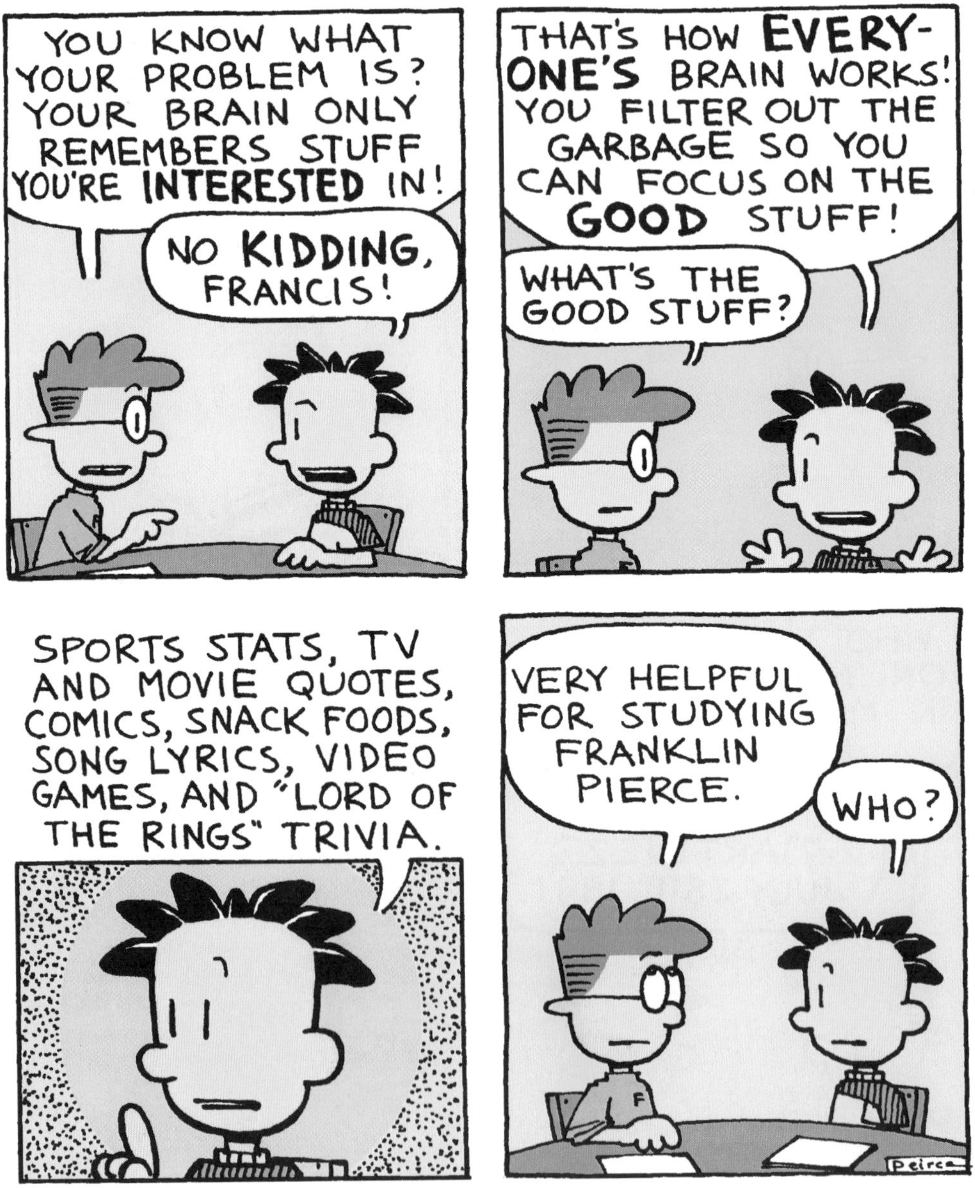
YOU KNOW WHAT YOUR PROBLEM IS? YOUR BRAIN ONLY REMEMBERS STUFF YOU'RE **INTERESTED** IN!
NO **KIDDING**, FRANCIS!
THAT'S HOW **EVERY-ONE'S** BRAIN WORKS! YOU FILTER OUT THE GARBAGE SO YOU CAN FOCUS ON THE **GOOD** STUFF!
WHAT'S THE GOOD STUFF?
SPORTS STATS, TV AND MOVIE QUOTES, COMICS, SNACK FOODS, SONG LYRICS, VIDEO GAMES, AND "LORD OF THE RINGS" TRIVIA.
VERY HELPFUL FOR STUDYING FRANKLIN PIERCE.
WHO?
Peirce

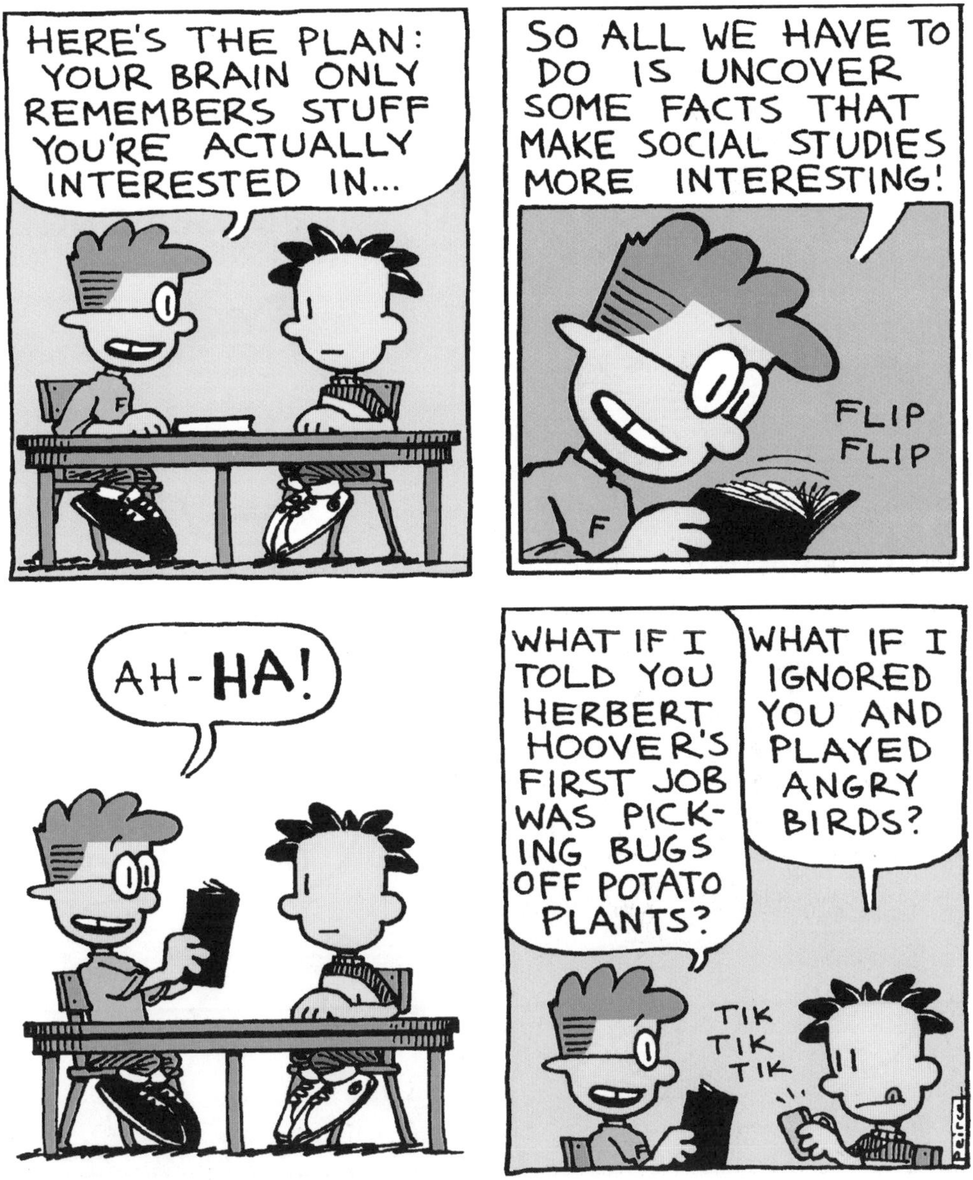
HERE'S THE PLAN: YOUR BRAIN ONLY REMEMBERS STUFF YOU'RE ACTUALLY INTERESTED IN...
SO ALL WE HAVE TO DO IS UNCOVER SOME FACTS THAT MAKE SOCIAL STUDIES MORE INTERESTING!
FLIP FLIP
AH-HA!
WHAT IF I TOLD YOU HERBERT HOOVER'S FIRST JOB WAS PICK-ING BUGS OFF POTATO PLANTS?
WHAT IF I IGNORED YOU AND PLAYED ANGRY BIRDS?
TIK TIK TIK
Peirce

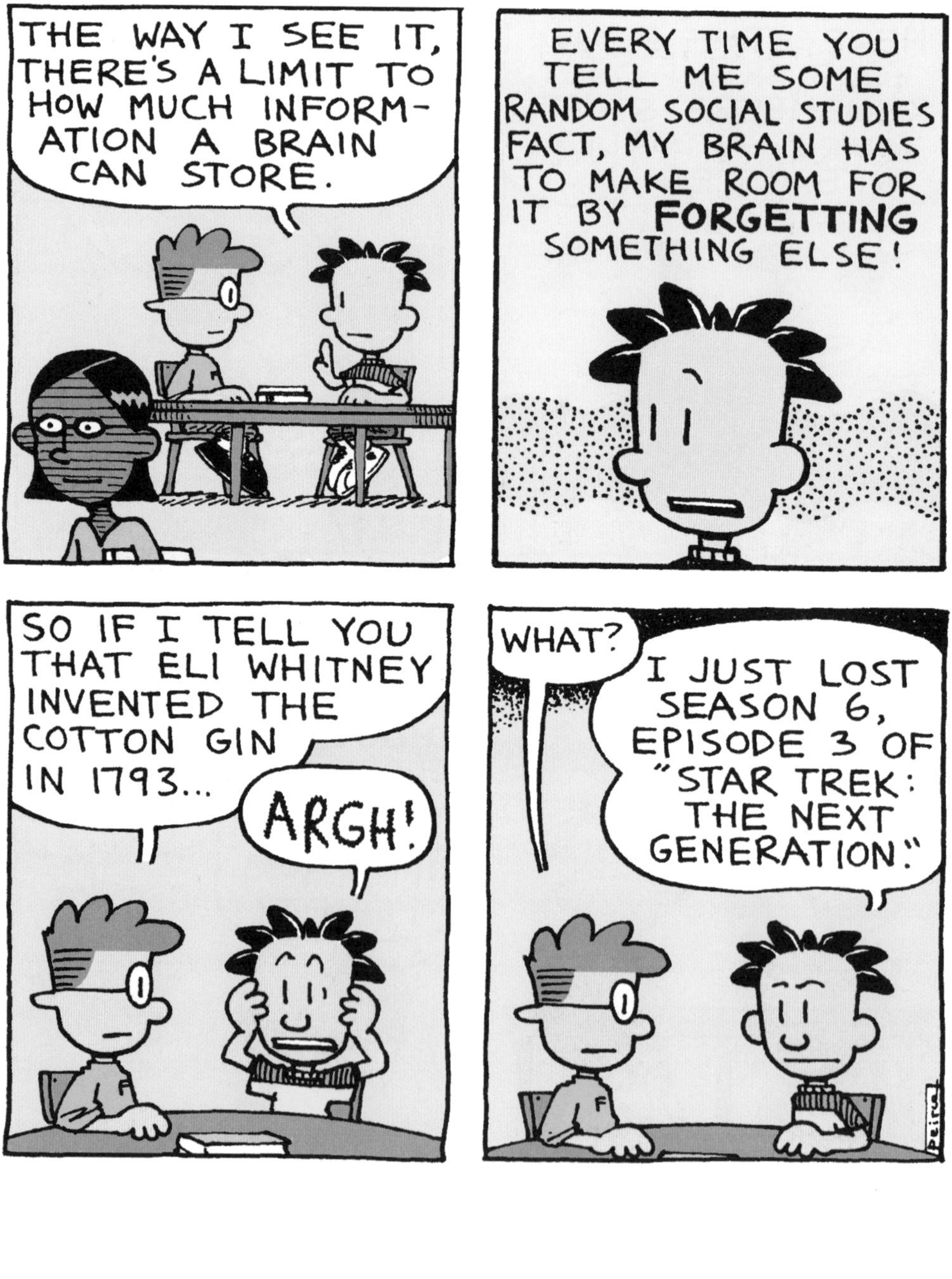
THE WAY I SEE IT, THERE'S A LIMIT TO HOW MUCH INFORMATION A BRAIN CAN STORE.
EVERY TIME YOU TELL ME SOME RANDOM SOCIAL STUDIES FACT, MY BRAIN HAS TO MAKE ROOM FOR IT BY FORGETTING SOMETHING ELSE!
SO IF I TELL YOU THAT ELI WHITNEY INVENTED THE COTTON GIN IN 1793...
ARGH!
WHAT?
I JUST LOST SEASON 6, EPISODE 3 OF "STAR TREK: THE NEXT GENERATION."
PEIRCE

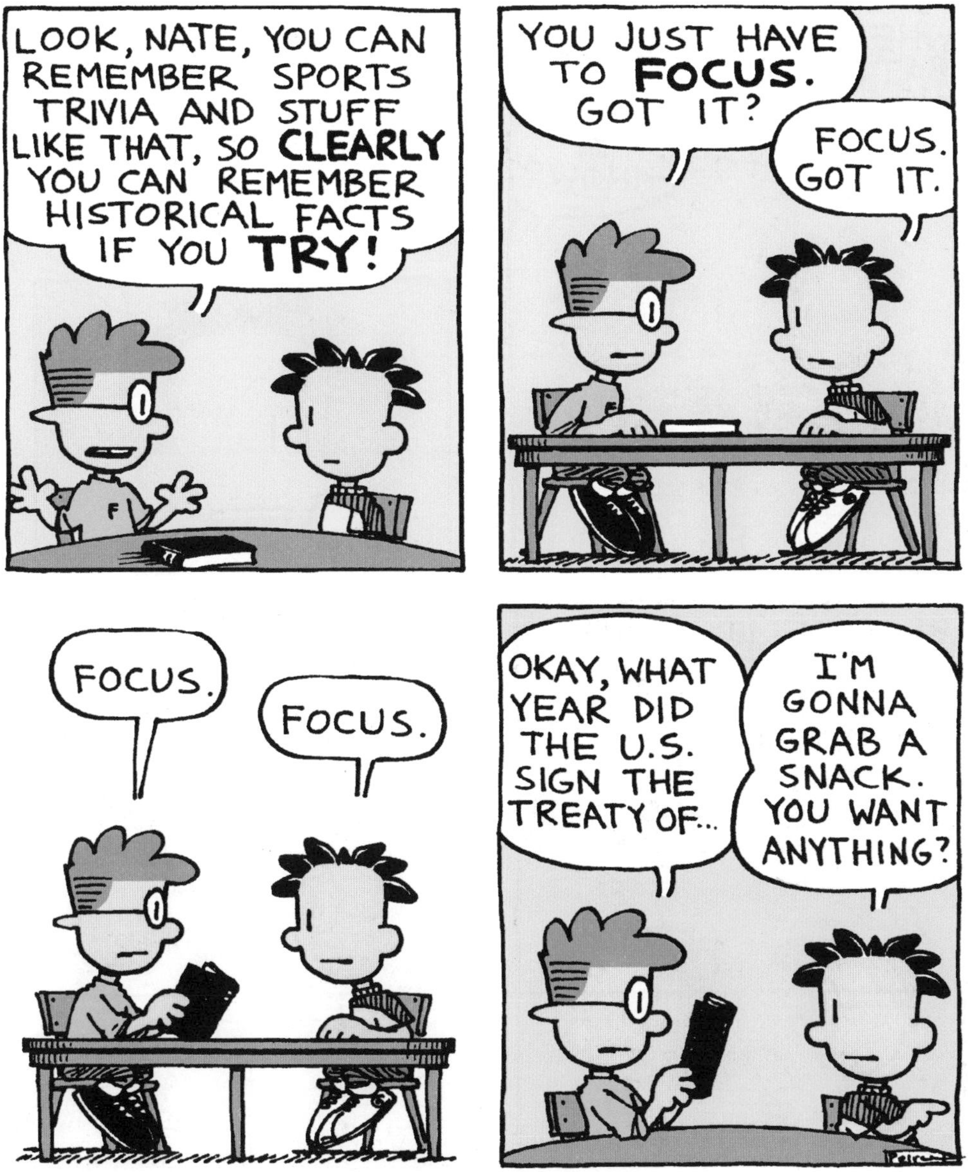
LOOK, NATE, YOU CAN REMEMBER SPORTS TRIVIA AND STUFF LIKE THAT, SO **CLEARLY** YOU CAN REMEMBER HISTORICAL FACTS IF YOU **TRY**!
YOU JUST HAVE TO **FOCUS**. GOT IT?
FOCUS. GOT IT.
FOCUS.
FOCUS.
OKAY, WHAT YEAR DID THE U.S. SIGN THE TREATY OF...
I'M GONNA GRAB A SNACK. YOU WANT ANYTHING?

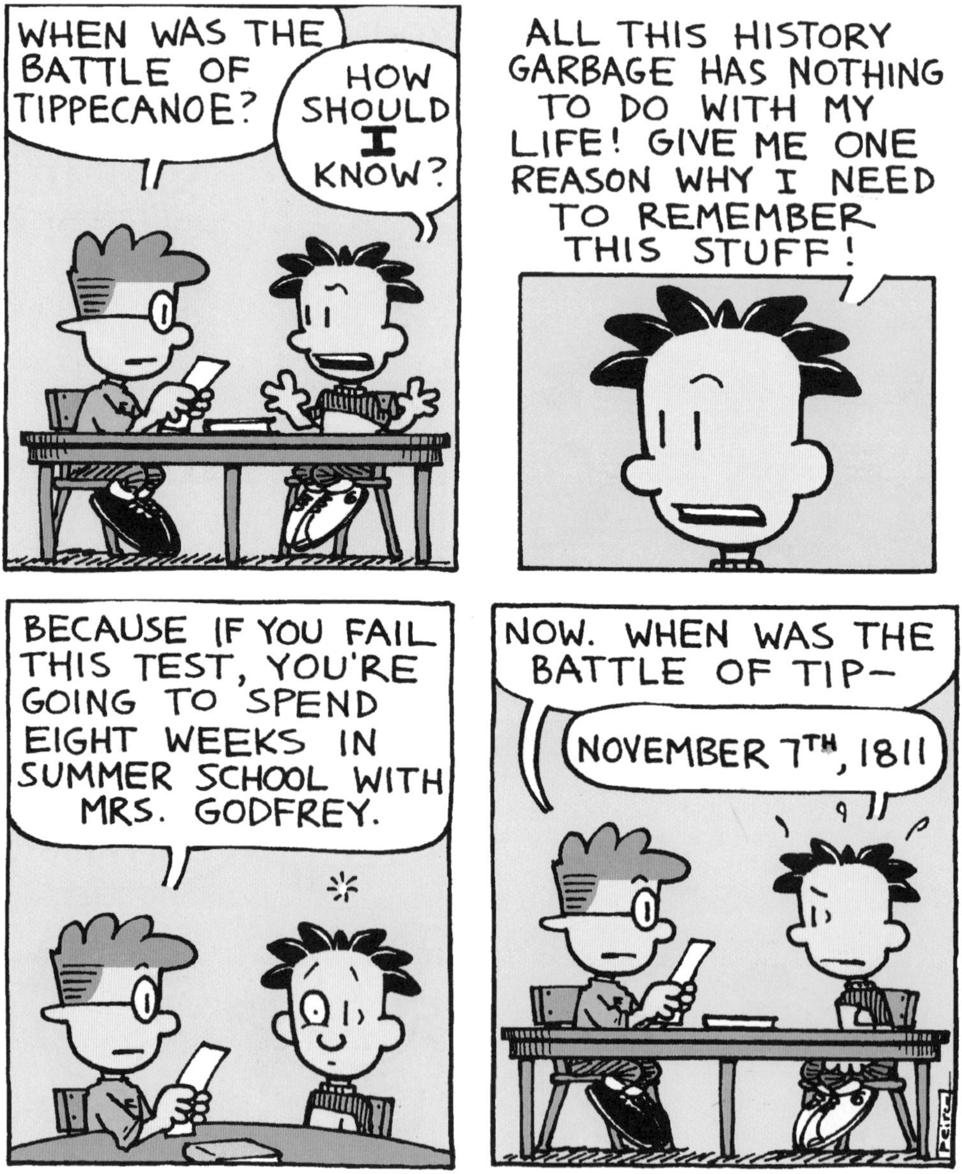
WHEN WAS THE BATTLE OF TIPPECANOE?
HOW SHOULD I KNOW?
ALL THIS HISTORY GARBAGE HAS NOTHING TO DO WITH MY LIFE! GIVE ME ONE REASON WHY I NEED TO REMEMBER THIS STUFF!
BECAUSE IF YOU FAIL THIS TEST, YOU'RE GOING TO SPEND EIGHT WEEKS IN SUMMER SCHOOL WITH MRS. GODFREY.
NOW. WHEN WAS THE BATTLE OF TIP—
NOVEMBER 7TH, 1811

Look for these books!

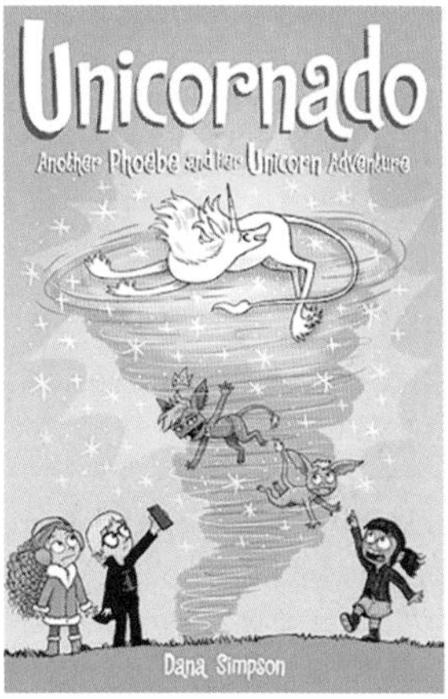
Unicornado
Another Phoebe and her Unicorn Adventure
Dana Simpson

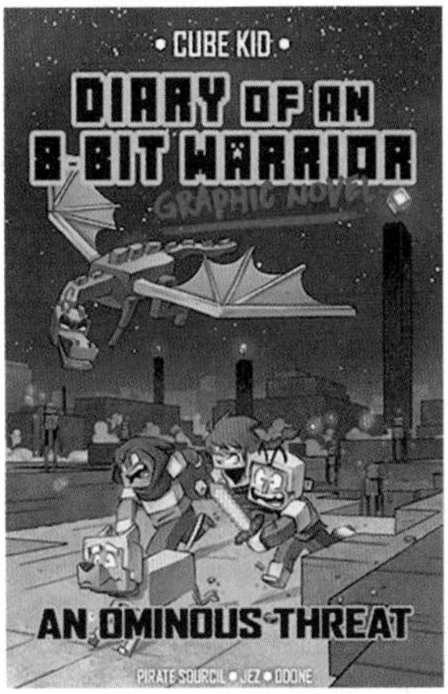
CUBE KID
DIARY OF AN 8-BIT WARRIOR
GRAPHIC NOVEL
AN OMINOUS THREAT
PIRATE SOURCIL • JEZ • ODONE

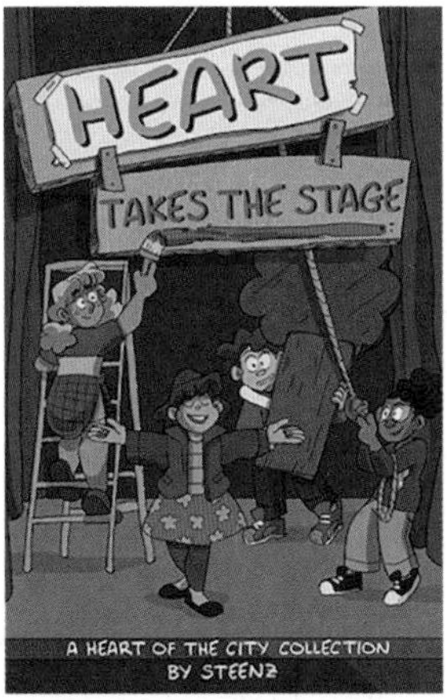
HEART
TAKES THE STAGE
A HEART OF THE CITY COLLECTION
BY STEENZ

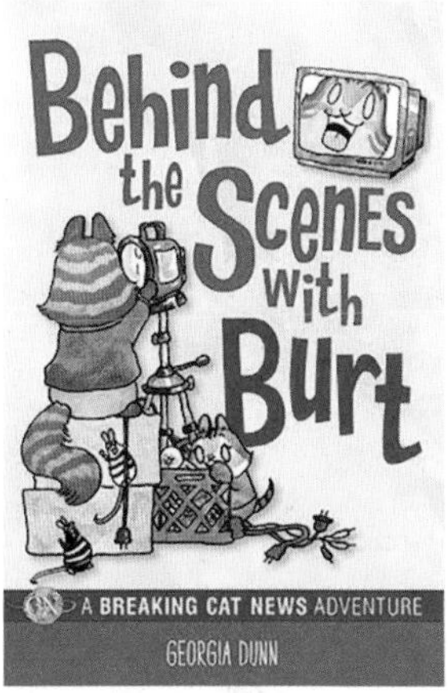
Behind the Scenes with Burt
A BREAKING CAT NEWS ADVENTURE
GEORGIA DUNN

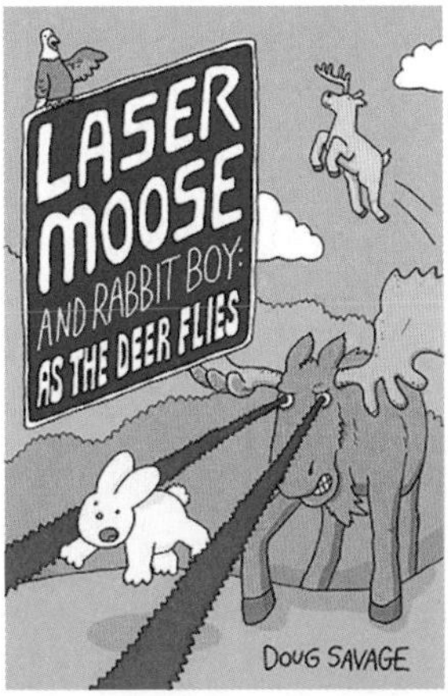
LASER MOOSE
AND RABBIT BOY:
AS THE DEER FLIES
DOUG SAVAGE

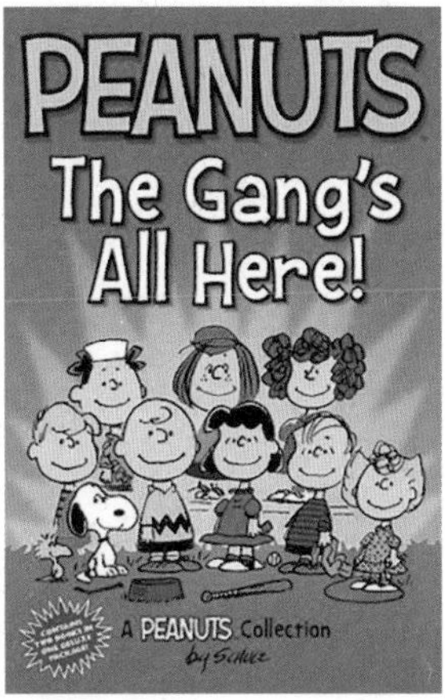
PEANUTS
The Gang's All Here!
A PEANUTS Collection
by Schulz

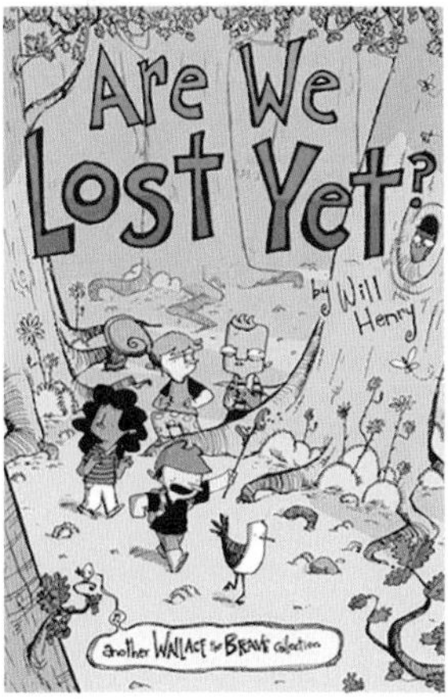
Are We Lost Yet?
by Will Henry
another WALLACE the BRAVE collection

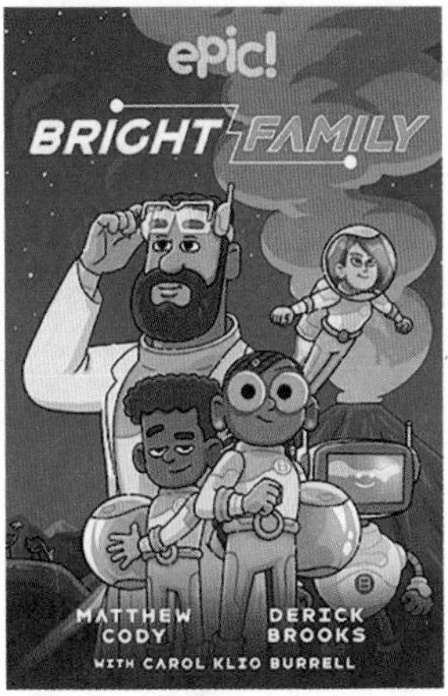
epic!
BRIGHT FAMILY
MATTHEW CODY
DERICK BROOKS
WITH CAROL KLIO BURRELL

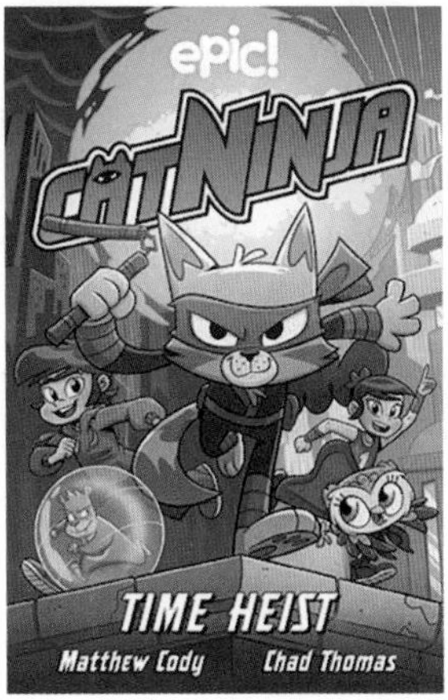
epic!
CAT NINJA
TIME HEIST
Matthew Cody
Chad Thomas

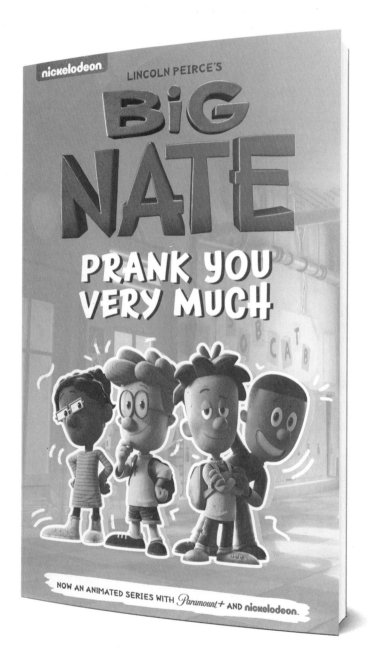